Violet Dawn

By Kristy Nicolle

Queens of Fantasy Saga
The Aetherial Embrace- Book 8

First published by Kristy Nicolle, United Kingdom, June 2021

QUEENS OF FANTASY EDITION (1st EDITION)

Published June 2021 by Kristy Nicolle

Edited By- Jaimie Cordall

Adult Paranormal/Fantasy Romance

ISBN: 978-1-911395-22-5

www.kristynicolle.com

HIGH LORDS & LADIES CHARACTER GUIDE

FAE

FAE OF NIGHT- KINDRED OF APOLLO
HIGH LADY HYPNOS
HIGH LORD MORPHEUS
HIGH LADY KODIAK NGUYEN
HIGH LORD ALISTAIR SOL
FAE OF LIGHT- KINDRED OF APHRODITE
HIGH LORD PHINEAS BECKETT (FALL)
HIGH LORD QUINN ARLET (SPRING)
HIGH LADY NEVE EIRWEN (WINTER)
HIGH LADY EMBER CYRUS (SUMMER)

DRACONIANS

DRACONIAN- KINDRED OF HECATE
HIGH LADY GENEVIEVE THOMAS
HIGH LORD LUCIEN DELAURENT
DRACONIANS- KINDRED OF NEMESIS
HIGH LADY ANASTASIA DRAGOS
HIGH LORD GAGE LEE

EQUINIANS

ARESIAN EQUINIANS- KINDRED OF ARES

High Lord/Chieftain Asher Oswald

High Lord/Chieftain Landon John Archard

ARTEMISIAN EQUINIANS- KINDRED OF ARTEMIS

High Lady Aliandara Montgomery

High Lady Evangeline Senft

SEPHILIM AND NEPHILIM

SEPHILIM- KINDRED OF ZEUS

High Lord Aro Black

High Lord Caleb Abara

NEPHILIM- KINDRED OF HERA

High Lady Storm Shaw (Deceased)

High Lady Harmony Baker (Deceased)

For Leanna Rae Herr
Warrior doesn't even begin to describe you.

above my heels, and has three-quarter-length sleeves, which are heavily stitched with lotus flowers and vines.

I examine the hemlines in closer detail as I tug a brush through my tangled hair and yank it up into a high ponytail with a hair clip I find enclosed with my outfit. I don't have any makeup, so I simply douse my face in the cold water poured from a brass jug and into a matching basin at the far end of the room, washing away the remnants of last night's tears.

I appear from behind the curtain, drawing it back with a quick and decisive motion that startles Diane, who is leaning against the hall's opposing wall, waiting. She straightens like she has been burned, and I feel immediately uncomfortable.

I'm not used to people being so on edge around me, and I'm not liking it either.

"Please, no need to stand on ceremony," I beg, and she smiles a little.

"They said you weren't like other High Ladies," she admonishes, flushing as she begins to lead me down the hallway and toward wherever I'll be dining. "Oh, and that looks really nice on you, by the way. I was wondering if the coat would be too much, but you make it work— I know that Nephilim skin isn't used to this kind of sun exposure, I didn't want you getting your shoulders burned—" She's motherly as she looks me up and down with a caring yet critical eye, our steps falling into time upon the worn mishmash of rugs.

"I love it. You really made this?" I ask, ignoring the comment about me being abnormal for a High Born as I examine the cuff around my left elbow.

She nods, flushing with pleasure at the compliment.

"How do you do such intricate embroidery?" I ask her. She shrugs, her abdominal muscles tightening in a ripple beneath the hem of her shirt as she inhales.

"I don't remember; I just get started with a rough idea, and then when I look up, it's done. It surprises even me!" She gives a small laugh, and I feel the weight of my guilt about last night lessen as my heart stops aching momentarily. Her good mood is oddly infectious.

The two of us fall into a comfortable silence as we pass a myriad of rainbow-hued glass panels, trickling water features, and jewel-toned silks scattering every room.

I let myself settle into my skin as the morning heat slowly builds like background static, the villa sprawling on endlessly until, with sudden abruptness, Diane says, "Ah, here we are."

I don't know why I'm expecting a closed door, but there isn't one. Instead, we turn a corner and find ourselves on an airy veranda.

The view from here is stunning with the ground-level platform of sandstone bricks surrounded by Grecian columns. They're thick with climbing vines and desert flowers, framing the view which overlooks the decadent gardens preceding the Oasis with elegant subtlety. The enormous pool of water is an odd green shade this morning as it captures the blue sun's cold light.

"Ah, High Lady Freemont! There you are! I thought you'd gotten lost," Evangeline calls out, and I feel relieved at the sight of her.

Diane dismisses herself silently from my side, and I stride across the weave of sandstone bricks before pulling out a chair and seating myself across from the two women.

"I'm so glad you're alright—" I sigh, and Evangeline shrugs slightly, looking amused.

"Oh, don't worry about it. It was nothing if not a little excitement to pep up an otherwise boring evening if you ask me—" She smiles kindly over piled golden platters of scrambled eggs and fresh fruit. Thick toasted slices of bread are arranged with artistic flourish near where Aliandara is eating ravenously with glinting gold cutlery.

"Please, eat, Kairi." She beckons me to join her, and I take a sip of the orange juice held in a gold-rimmed champagne flute in front of me before surveying the breakfast offering.

"So, you are okay?" I ask Evangeline, reaching for the toasted bread and then helping myself to eggs and grapefruit.

"I really am, though I couldn't say the same for some of the Nephilim," she admonishes, and I feel my heart falter in its beat. A lump forms in my throat, which I try to swallow but cannot.

"Was it— how many died?" I ask, losing all appetite.

Aliandara gives Evangeline an irritated glance.

"The number matters not, Kairi. They cannot be saved now," she says it with what I assume is kindness coming from her, but her words still sting. "Eat," she demands, eyeing my breakfast as her dark hair glistens with the sunrise.

"I'm not feeling that hungry—" I whisper, sitting back into the plush dining chair upholstered in indigo silk. I notice absently that it matches the lapis lazuli core of the table as I rest my fingers on the coolness of its metallic edge.

"Kairi, do you have any idea how much tax I have to pay to get fresh Nirvana fruit out here? Eat your damn breakfast. Besides, you are going to need it for what I have planned for you today. I won't have you fainting like some pale and fragile princess from a fairy tale, thank you very much." Aliandara's tone takes me by surprise and my head snaps up.

"What are you talking about?" I ask her, reluctantly taking a thick piece of toast between two fingers.

"Well, if the Nephilim will not teach you to defend yourself, then I will. I cannot have Aro Black threatening you while you stand there like a fucking goldfish now, can I?" She cocks an eyebrow, and Evangeline spits with surprise, resulting in orange juice dribbling down her chin. She dabs frantically with a napkin, blinking fast as her cheeks flush.

"Attractive—" Aliandara rolls her eyes, and Evangeline raises both eyebrows incredulously in return.

"I could say the same for you with profanity like that, my lady." Her tone is dripping in sarcasm, and the two share an intensely comical yet irritated glare.

I watch them, glad the scrutiny is off me for a second while I take a bite of my toast.

I expect it to taste like ash as most food seems to when I am riddled with guilt, but it's delicious. I realise suddenly that I have not eaten in well over a day.

If I were a mortal, I'd be in a coma.

"I wanted to say— to say I'm sorry about last night. I shouldn't have just stood there. It was stupid." I'm stuttering as I pick up a fork and tuck into steaming and fluffy scrambled eggs.

"Kairi, do not waste my time apologising for what has happened. If I were interested in that, I would also be apologising to you for the way I stood by as Aro killed you without mercy. I could apologise for so many things, but that does very little, don't you think?" she asks with seriousness, taking a sip of her juice and pointedly staring at me with wise silver eyes.

"You— you think you need to apologise to me?" I ask her, floored.

"Well, Lucien DeLaurent certainly thinks so. But I have to wonder— I have to wonder where that young lady I saw went. Did she die that night? What happened to that fearless, plucky little mortal with a tendency to stare far too much and get herself into trouble?" she asks.

I suddenly feel transparent.

"I— I don't know what you mean," I reply and watch Evangeline shift in her seat, studying my face closely.

"Oh, I think you know exactly what I mean, Kairi. Do you even know who you are, anymore?" she demands, and I feel a shudder run up my spine. I bite down on my bottom lip hard, and Aliandara nods knowingly. Then I attempt to open my mouth after a long pause, but she raises an elegant hand, tattoos shimmering.

"No need to say a word, Kairi. I have my answer."

The silence that follows is deafening, the two women going back to eating with elegant yet complete reverence for the food before them.

I return to eating myself, pushing eggs around my plate and hearing Hera's voice once more.

Never forget who you are.

Swallowing hard, I find my voice once more, knowing that I am done eating as my stomach starts to churn again.

"You're going to teach me to defend myself?" I ask, further relieved as they turn to me as if they have suddenly remembered I'm there.

Evangeline takes in my expression and then looks to her lover with a wide toothy smile, her face alight with excitement.

Aliandara gives me a wicked and slightly terrifying wink.

"For starters—"

THE POSSESED

LUCIEN

IT FEELS ODD APPROACHING Genevieve's suite from inside the Astrid Keep instead of taking my usual route via her balcony.

I straighten my cravat, nervousness rooted deep in the pit of my stomach. One of her guards gives me the side-eye from within the shadowy depths of his dark steel helmet, which I promptly ignore.

Taking a deep breath, I knock three times and wait.

The silence following the sound of my knuckles on mahogany seems to last an eternity, until suddenly, the wait is over.

"Enter," she calls, and so I do, stepping into a room that had once seemed so familiar but that I haven't dared enter for over two months.

The jade walls encase me as I pass the threshold, leaving it behind as I step fully into the malachite hue of the suite. The guard who had side-eyed me closes the door behind me with an ominous, too-soft click.

Genevieve stands, perfectly straight before a smouldering and recently extinguished hearth. The ashes in the grate stir as her wings spread wide.

I'm no fool and know she's more than fully aware of how intimidating she looks. Wearing a high-collared jade dress coat, ivory leather dragon-riding trousers, and knee-high black boots with weathered silver buckles, her white hair is pulled high atop her head, her emerald eyes sharp as knives as they dissect me.

She's got a sword visibly strapped to her outer thigh, her hands neatly folded before her, pale fingers steepled.

I don't flinch as she refuses to blink, staring at me as though she is wishing I might combust by her will alone.

I feel fortunate as I swallow that she does not possess such a power.

"Lord DeLaurent." My name is a curse that is exalted from her lips as more of a hiss than a word. She doesn't move forward, remaining statuesque in front of the fireplace and staring at me like I'm a piece of shit.

Not that I blame her.

"Lady Thomas." I give a small bow, my freshly brushed tresses falling in a silky curtain of pale blond across my shoulder in a show of subservience.

We pause then, the echo of her anguished screams haunting a space between us that had once felt like a comfortable armchair one might sink deeply into with a hot cup of tea.

Now it feels like jagged glass.

"Where is she, Lord DeLaurent?" Genevieve breaks the silence, each of her words carefully formed upon the plump pallor of her elegant lips. They remain pressed into a thin line as I cock an eyebrow, eyes narrowing.

"Who, my Lady?" I ask, addressing her with the title of a superior, despite the fact we are of the same standing.

I know she has the power here, the power to wound me in a way equivalent to only a fraction of how I have hurt her. Nonetheless, I'm cautious, my emotions close to the surface like hot rabid blood after my late-night excursions.

I feel more vulnerable than I'd ever admit to her.

"You know damn well who, Lord DeLaurent! That Nephilim who you sacrificed my beloved Algoric to save," she hisses, her index finger and thumb rubbing together in a quick and repetitive motion I've seen only a few times.

It's how she manages her rage. How she stops herself from snapping necks and plunging blades through hearts.

I wonder, in a moment of morbid curiosity, what she's pondering doing to my sorry ass.

"I don't know where she is. Last I heard she was being made a High Lady. We agreed not to see one another after that. She's supposed to find a husband now— the next King. It's over." I say it, knowing full well I'm lying but unable to admit that I've just come from bedding her.

Genevieve doesn't need to know; after all, what's done is done. Not only that, but as far as I'm aware, nothing has changed despite last night.

It really is over.

The thought is crushing, but I also know it's true.

"Do you think I'm stupid, Lucien?" she sighs, running a hand back through her scarlet roots. I straighten, breathing in deeply as I take a step forward.

"No, but I am wondering why you might think I know where she is—" I ask, choosing my words cautiously and pulling my face into a look of alarm.

"That's none of your business," Genevieve snaps.

I narrow my eyes, playing the game like the pro I have trained to become over the past two centuries.

I know why Kairi came here, but I want to know how Genevieve found out and why she has her nose in the business of the Sephilim.

It worries me, the thought of what she might be planning in her grief after shutting herself off from both me and her people.

"I'm serious, Gen. If she's in danger—" I warn her, my tone less cordial as it takes on a feral edge rising from deep in the back of my throat.

"It's High Lady Thomas to you. And why should I tell you? After all, the last time you went to her aid, I lost the most precious thing in the world to me, not that you care," she spits.

Suddenly, I see it.

Behind her vehemence, and the cruelty of her expression, it flickers. The weakness of her loss, the gaping void that I'd left her to fill. I have made decisions that cost her dearly, and to prevent further loss of life, I discarded her pain in making a choice that was best for everyone. Does she think I did so lightly? That I don't care that I've hurt her?

Doesn't she know how haunted I am by what I did, despite the fact I could never in good conscience take it back?

"That's what you think? You think I don't care?" I demand, stunned as I realise how deeply the wound had cut.

"No, Lord DeLaurent. I know you don't care. If you did, then you would have proved so with your actions." She suddenly turns, staring into the mirror hanging above the hearth, maintaining eye contact suddenly unbearable.

I watch her hands unfold, worrying through the fabric of her coat. She looks at me indirectly from the looking glass, the fire in her eyes growing dim as the embers at her feet.

"Lady Thomas, I know what I cost you. I know. I promise you that I know. I knew even in making the decision. I wasn't ignorant of the consequences of my actions," I admit, lowering my gaze.

"So that's supposed to make me feel better, that you knew you were taking from me?" she asks.

"No. It's not supposed to make you feel better. I don't want you to feel better. If you did, it would mean that you didn't love Algoric as much as I know you did," I explain, and she purses her lips, jaw tensing as her fist balls at her side.

"You don't know anything," she bites back with venom, swallowing hard and crossing her arms across her breast, back still to me.

"I know I stole the only true love you've ever known. I know that I took that from you. You don't think I lie awake at night, thinking about everything I did wrong? About how I betrayed you so entirely? Do you think I don't hate myself for making the choice I did? It was impossible."

I feel my rage building now, like icebergs splitting through a once calm sea, sharp and senseless.

Does she think me so heartless that I would make such a heinous choice without real thought, without real struggle?

She turns then, exhaling a sigh. She looks tired, exhausted despite her immortal beauty.

"You really had no idea that Lord Black captured the Solis Castra last night?" she asks, still stiff as a statue.

I feign surprise and anguish, feeling low for doing so but knowing that revealing my rendezvous with Kairi is only going to cause her more pain.

I will become a liar if it means I hurt her no more. I can hardly hold more disdain for myself than I already do over this whole situation.

"No. I did not," I reply, keeping my face stoic.

"And what, you don't care? You aren't going to run out of here to her aid like some disgustingly pathetic white knight?" Genevieve chastises me, and I shake my head.

"She's no longer a mortal, and she no longer needs my protection. She will manage." I feel almost cruel saying the words as I fight my overwhelming desire to spew the truth that I do wish to save her.

"Shut up—" Genevieve hisses suddenly, and I cock my head.

"Excuse me?" I ask, cautious.

Slowly, I take a half step toward her, like I'm approaching a caged snow leopard.

"Nothing," she retorts, her face becoming feral for a moment before retaining its ghostly composure.

Is that what Gage was talking about?

I had dismissed him as being worrisome, but now I wonder if he was right to be concerned.

"Genevieve—" I begin again, my voice low in warning.

"Lucien, stop acting like you give a fucking damn. It's pathetic," she snaps again, and I throw back my head in an uncontrolled laugh.

It's ridiculous, and probably going to get me killed, but I can't help it.

"Genevieve, don't be so ridiculous. I do give a damn. You are my best friend. You always will be because, even if you do not like me, you still love me, and I still love you. We are cut from the same cloth, remember?" I implore her, and she rounds the chaise longue, her eyes alive with fury-stoked flame once more.

"No! You don't get to speak of such things, Lucien. You broke us. What we had— is broken!" she cries, getting closer to me than I ever thought she would again.

"So, let me fix it—" I whisper to her as she squares up to me, gazing intently into the full fury of her eyes.

"You can't fix this, Lucien. You can't bring Algoric back," she replies, her hands trembling and forming fists once more. Her pale wings quiver as she stands before me, regal yet undeniably shattered.

"No, but I can make sure you don't push love out of your life forever, Genevieve. I won't let you be alone, not ever. You should know that. I thought you did." I take her hands in mine, feeling the burn of her skin melting my flesh like wax.

I don't flinch though, drawing on my cryomancy and focusing on counteracting the heat of her.

"Lucien— How can I forgive you? How can I possibly ever—" She sounds unsure then, for the first time since the conversation began.

"You don't have to forgive me. But you do have to realise that I'm not your enemy. I'm not the one who made this situation happen— not really. I reacted as best as I could. It just wasn't good enough. I failed you. I know I did. I don't want forgiveness, but I need you to have peace." I hear the hiss of her skin being rapidly cooled by my icy magic, and her eyes grow wide. I pull her knuckles to my lips, placing a cool kiss upon them.

"I'm sorry, Gen." I feel my eyes prickle with tears at the familiar scent of her. "I never wanted to hurt you. I am so, so sorry. Please believe me. My heart is broken, too, because in losing Algoric, I lost a part of you," I admit, looking back up to her face.

What I find there isn't what I expect. When I'm fully expecting her to slap me, or perhaps draw her sword and impale me just for the hell of it, she's silently sobbing. Her chest rises and falls like tectonic plates that cannot contain the immensity of her emotion, enormous globules of steaming salt water falling in sizzling trails down her face.

Her tears scald me as I refuse to let go of her hands.

"I don't— I don't want to be alone, Lucien. I'm so alone," she whispers, and I feel my heart break at how someone so seemingly composed and strong can be so fragile on the inside.

I pull her into my arms then, feeling her stiffen slightly before relinquishing and crying on my shoulder.

I've known this woman for almost two centuries, and this is the first time she's ever cried on me.

To be honest, I didn't know if she was capable of this kind of vulnerability, which I understood because I felt the same, once.

It's as if Kairi has given me the confidence to bare it all, and that surrender has transferred to Genevieve as well.

I stand steadfast against her spindled form, pressing my lips to the blazing curve of her scalp.

"I'm here, Genevieve. You're not alone anymore—" I vow to her, stroking her hair with a soothing cool palm. She screws up her eyes, long eyelashes fluttering wildly as she fights more tears.

"You're not going to run off with her, not going to leave?" she sniffles, pulling back and looking up at me with red eyes.

It's a foolish promise to make, and I'm certainly no seer, but I know that I owe her at least my best effort. She is not Kairi, but I love her too, and I don't want her to hurt anymore, especially not because of me.

"No, Genevieve. It's over— it's really over."

I feel my own eyes fill with tears at the truth of my words, an onslaught of memories from last night filling me with dread as Kairi's wanton gaze reflects from the tumultuous surface of my consciousness.

I shake my head, dispersing the image and squeezing Genevieve with no intention of letting go, imagining for a moment she's no Draconian, but a Nephilim with caramel locks instead.

I clutch her, and she grips onto the shoulder blades so nobly framed by my wingspan, drained as she slumps against me, crying silently into my lapel.

We stand, entwined in our grief, as I make my vow, meaning every word.

"You'll never be alone, Gen. I promise. I'm not going anywhere."

ARO

I'm standing on my balcony, hunched over the exquisite railing and staring out over the falls, bored, when the sound of a throat being cleared nervously sounds behind me.

"Yes?" I demand, hopeful that the messenger has come to end the monotony of the Solis Castra. I had never felt this way before I had spent my days roaming the Blazen Plains, but now I find that the comfort of it all, the opulence and quiet toil, cannot compare to the constant adrenaline buzz of the Equinians' way of life. I've been here only a week, but I know from the past seven days alone that I have changed.

This world is too orderly, too mundane for my new taste for violence.

"I have come to inform you that Chief Landon is approaching with the first delivery from the outer villages, my Lord." Dawn's meekness causes me to turn, if for no other reason than to relish the discomfort of her posture.

My eyes fall on her sullen face which, while extraordinarily beautiful as always, cannot hide the disdain and fear that lies right behind her eyes. I have watched it grow over the past week, an interesting thing to observe at least.

"Thank you, Dawn. I will head to meet them immediately. Please ensure to secure the balcony before you leave."

I take several modest paces toward her, placing my hand on her linen-covered shoulder.

"I don't know what I'd do without you, darling Dawn. Always taking care of me—" I am rewarded by the shudder rippling down her spine which is, as always, perfectly straight within the confines of her gown's basic corsetry.

I smile at her before moving into the suite beyond, but she doesn't return the expression, bestowing upon me a giddying sense of power.

I pull on the lapels of the fine coat which encases my broad shoulders to straighten it, the onyx velvet still overly confining where I've become used to baring my chest muscles.

Running my hand down the fabric, I exit the room, striding along the corridor and taking the stairs this time.

Listening, I hear the whispers of guards who haven't yet heard my soft footfall, the fluttering of skirts around fast-moving nervous ankles, and the tinkle of crystal chandeliers stirring in the Soleus breeze.

Of all the sharpened senses that the dragon's power had suddenly gifted me, the hearing is the most disconcerting of them all. I am glad I can tune into it at will because if I chose, I could hear the pulse of someone's carotid artery at the opposite end of the room.

Until you have the choice, you cannot realise that there are certain things you don't want to hear.

I had tuned into Kairi's heartbeat, the pathetic muscle fluttering like a bird trapped in a cage as I had gotten closer and closer to her wispy breathing.

I wonder, not for the first time and most certainly not for the last, if she realises how much easier her life would be if she simply crowned me King. I am not unreasonable, and I'm sure if the two of us were given time we could get back to where we once were.

If I'm honest, I miss her innocent gaze looking up at me, the softness of her skin, and the scent of her that never fails in calming my otherwise indomitable rage.

The guards I could hear whispering spot my shadow and straighten as I approach. Smirking, I can't help but quip as loudly as possible, "No, it doesn't happen to every man— at least not to me anyway." I see the colour drain from one of the Guard's faces and his eyes widen. The friend in which he was confiding looks at me with a cocked eyebrow.

"I have rather excellent hearing. You might want to remember that in future before dragging your impotence into the walls of my castle," I bite, increasing my speed and gliding past them, a sharp chill overcoming my stare.

As I walk down the corridor they're supposed to be diligently guarding, I hear their armour creak as they turn back. "Eyes forward gentlemen, or I'll assume you don't need them," I call back, listening for their sharp inhale and smiling as it reaches me.

Descending through to the lower levels of the Solis Castra, a smile continues to play on my lips at the memory of their startled expressions.

I do so love it when people underestimate me.

Soon I am descending the narrow confines of the spiral staircase that descends through one of the rooms, hidden from the grandeur of any public eye, used for storage and event preparation.

Down within the redundant catacombs, the familiar sound of copper cookware clattering on marble surfaces and hot iron rings becomes a cacophony of busyness in my head.

I tune my hearing down, closing my eyes momentarily and allowing myself the grace to adjust as I hit the crystal floors. The roar of the Oblivion Falls just beyond the walls is unavoidable, the low eaves of the ceiling causing the immensity of its audible fingerprint to magnify to a rumble heard even above the calls and clatter of the busy kitchens.

As I make my way across the small cleared entrance space, I feel eyes rise and fall on my figure.

Then, something I am not expecting happens.

The kitchen falls into silence, the only sound a plate smashing somewhere as it falls from the fingers of some careless Nephilim of low birth. The sound of shattering china pierces the air, but I refuse to flinch, simply continuing in my journey toward the entryway of the underground tunnels.

However, as I round a granite countertop holding crystal bowls full of apples, I cannot help but pause to take one. Selecting the reddest, I see her then, Alicia the head cook, a woman who had once given me such sass and attitude about my last-minute requirement of her services.

Taking several steps over to her, I sink my teeth into the flesh of the apple, its juices tart as they stream over my tongue in sour rivulets. Swallowing hard, I square up to the woman, looking down my nose at her.

I cock my head and feel her shudder as she curtseys a little too late for my liking. Straightening, she swallows, pushing a strand of her dark hair behind one ear where it's come loose from her topknot.

"Lord Black, what a surprise." Her voice is sweeter than the sugar which surrounds us in enormous burlap sacks, though hers is utterly laced with a subtle poison that she's hoping I won't notice.

"This tastes like shit. I suggest you get rid of the rest of the batch. If I catch you serving these to me or any of my guests, I'll have your throat slit." I press the apple into her palm, sweeping past her with a disgusted glance.

I hear her exhale as I pass before she barks. "Well, you heard the High Lord, back to work, and throw those apples out!" Suddenly the room erupts into chaos, louder than it had been before.

Reaching the wooden door leading down into the entryway tunnels, I glance back over the curve of my wing, finding several Nephilim eyes staring at me and wide with fear.

I smile, glad to see things are finally changing. People are finally taking me seriously, are finally realising that I have the power to make their lives miserable.

Taking the steps two at a time with a jaunty rhythm, I descend into the deepest depths of the Solis Castra, this part of the building lit only by old-fashioned flickering sconces which adorn its cobblestone foundations.

I can hear the sound of hoofbeats, the low utterances of men who seem rather irritated, and the intermittent tinkle of falling crystal shards as I hit the dust-covered stone of the unkept floor with a spring in my step and head toward the gargantuan mouth of the main tunnel.

Then, as he appears within the glow of the nearest flickering sconce, I hear the Chief's voice ring out from the shadows.

It appears I've arrived right on time.

"Keep moving, men! We don't have all day!" he barks, and I find myself looking up at him straddling Rogue, the height making him no less intimidating as his broad shadow falls over me.

"Chief, how did it go?" I ask, watching as he swings a leg over Rogue's spine and dismounts with ease. Her coat blazes as the oil slick of its sheen captures the reflections of dancing flames.

"Well, I can't say it was the most entertaining work I've ever super-vised. As I said, I am no miner, and neither are my men—" he grumbles in complaint, scratching his jaw with dirty fingernails bitten right down to the quick.

"And If I had needed a miner, I surely wouldn't have asked you. The crystal is on the surface of Soleus, no mining required," I retort bitterly, watching as the procession of men pushing carts full of amethyst emerge looking downtrodden.

"You made them walk all this here? Why on earth—" I begin, but he cuts me off.

146

"You said I could utilise the people of Sparrowdale and Hawkwood. I don't see why my horses should tire themselves hauling what they can," he snorts, a little like a stud himself as I cock an eyebrow.

"So, this is why it's taken you so long? It's been a week," I sound pissed because I am.

I've been endlessly bored waiting for this delivery, with little else to do but read and torture the household staff, which while fun, is hardly productive enough to warrant the effort. If it hadn't been so entertaining I probably wouldn't have bothered.

"Actually no, for someone who claims themselves as destined to be the next King of Aetheria, we had a surprisingly enormous amount of resistance to your orders. There was rioting, my men got a lot of sport out of it for sure, but I'm not entirely certain these people want you as their King. Did that ever occur to you, Lord Black?" he asks, resting his hand on the hilt of the curvaceous dagger sheathed at his thigh. I glance down at the blade and straighten as my jaw tenses.

"I'm not all that worried about the people if I'm honest." I shrug, and he laughs as a weary-looking Sephilim, who I believe is a metal-worker that I've employed privately before, trudges past with another wheelbarrow of crystal.

"I'm beginning to think this alliance was a very bad idea on my part if that's the case. You cannot simply rule people who hate you, Lord Black. You don't have that kind of power, I don't have that kind of power either, and the people know it. They may be less powerful than you, but they are greater in number, which you seem to have forgotten."

His dark eyes glower in the flickering sconce light, the air of the tunnel musty and full of aether-rich dust. Rogue shifts from one hoof to the other in the dimness of it all, impatient as her rider glares at me impetuously.

"So you suppose I don't have the power? Really?" I scowl at the Equinian, the shimmering of his metallic tattoos making him visible even as he moves in and out of the darkness, pacing.

"I suppose you're a lot of talk and not a lot of action. You claim to have this grand plan, but so far my men have done the work in securing the Solis Castra for you, and my men were the ones having to beat your citizens into submission. You might understand why I'm sceptical of your influence—"

"That would probably be because I don't have influence, I have mastery. I have dominion." I hiss, balling my fists at his lack of faith in my power and letting my wings spread wide in a gesture of dominance.

I had thought branding him had been enough to prove myself, but apparently, he needs a further demonstration.

"What you have is acid reflux from eating a dictionary. Pretty words don't fool me, Lord Black. It's time to put your money where your mouth is. I'm done playing—" His threat is empty to me, like a balloon that exists only due to the volume of nothingness within its flimsy skin.

"Very well then, Chief. If it is a display of my utter power you wish, then so shall it be. Besides, I have just the man for the task. He's been due his just desserts for centuries. And I, for one, will be happy to serve it to him."

THE METAMORPHOSIS

KAIRI

I INHALE, PULLING BACK the arrow shaft so that the nock latches onto the bowstring. My grip is tight on the ornate brass of the bow as I make sure my lips are in line with the arrow rest. Peering beyond it, I focus on the target at the other end of the paddock.

"Just relax, Kairi. You're a natural," Evangeline promises.

I let the tension fall away from my shoulders.

Having held my breath as long as I can manage, I check my aim one last time and release the bowstring, exhaling heavily as the arrow flies through the air. The fletching of three feathers becomes a whirl of grey and chocolate, blurring visibly for only a moment before the vibrational ping of the arrowhead piercing its target can be heard.

I blink, lowering the bow, which feels far too at home in my hand for it to be mere coincidence.

The air stirs around me, sticky and dry as the immense cobalt orb of the sun grows ever closer to the horizon beyond the glassless windows of the stables. It will be night soon, and I can't help but feel impatient for its arrival, if for no other reason than the reprieve from the heat. Jarringly, I'm also nervous as the twilight approaches, for I know my training with Aliandara will resume. The thought alone makes my muscles ache.

"Perfect!" Evangeline claps slowly, cocking her head as she observes the arrow penetrating the bullseye of the target. "I haven't seen such skill since Rohana first started shooting. Are you sure you're not an Equinian?" Her eyes narrow and I feel the tips of my Fae ears burn slightly. A Unicorn in a nearby stall snickers, flicking its lustrous tail and pulling its ears back before it begins munching diligently on more hay.

I shrug, stretching my neck from left to right, dispersing an archery-related kink.

"Definitely not," I smile, though I can't deny that I had taken to archery with such ease it's as though I've been reunited with an old skill, rather than learning one entirely new.

I wonder then if Storm could shoot, and if this is yet something else of myself that actually belongs to her.

The thought makes me wilt, my shoulders sagging as my wings follow suit.

"Well, I'm glad that I got the chance to help you discover the skill anyway. The Nephilim— they don't put much stock in weapons training— from what I've heard anyway."

Evangeline looks uncomfortable as she walks over to the target and pulls the arrow free, fingering the brass tip gently as a thoughtful notion passes ghostly across her face.

I wonder what she's thinking, if she's feeling pity for me, or if she's guilty for turning me so against the nature of my fellow Kindred. Either way, I'll never know, and maybe that's for the best.

"I think it's crazy too. Given what is happening. The Nephilim— they seem so pliant," I admit, speaking my thoughts brazenly as her baggy lilac harem pants billow in a sudden yet slight breeze. The gold of her tattoos shimmers as she turns back to face me, handing back the arrow so I can put it away.

"Aetheria, it's not as beautiful underneath the surface, is it?" she comments, and I give her a kind smile, bending down to place the arrow back with its fellows in the brass and leather quiver beside my slippered feet.

"Things rarely are, I suppose. I mean, I fell for Aro, for his face and his charm, and look at what lies underneath it all. I don't think Aetheria itself is bad, I just think that the people with power over it are corrupt. I want to believe it could be the fantasy I originally thought—"

My words taper off as my thoughts turn to Lucien. Of how he and I shared the same vision. Aetheria as a place of refuge, of sanctuary, rather than conflict and prejudice.

The Goddesses had told me they wanted unity among the Kindred as well during my Kindred vision, but I'm not fooled into thinking that unity is sought for peace. It is sought instead for the sole purpose of forging a more ferocious army against whatever threats might try to infiltrate The Higher Plains.

I wonder as I stand there, looking at Evangeline and her mastectomy scars that she had chosen to keep, if she feels as used as I do.

"Do you ever feel manipulated? By the Gods and Goddesses?" I ask. She gives an odd half-smile, pushing one of her dark curls behind her ear.

"I used to, but if it weren't for the conflict, for the pain, I wonder if we would ever see true light. After all, you cannot have light without shadow, and you cannot choose good if you've never seen evil. I guess I see it as a process, distilling each individual down to their essential core—" she elaborates, and I nod slowly, realising that I'm not the only one with strong opinions about the concept.

It makes me feel comforted, knowing I'm not just confused and frustrated because I'm young.

I place a hand on her shoulder, smiling.

"Thanks for teaching me how to shoot, you've been very patient" I compliment. High Lady Senft blushes, the sparkling pools of her eyes metallic in the dusk.

"Patient? Not likely, you picked this up very easily, Kairi." She laughs, and I find myself blushing this time.

"Well, you say that, but I don't think the stable door over there would agree with you. Nor the Unicorn inside—" I eye the puncture wound where my first arrow had flown off course by a full two metres, frowning.

"They're used to it. It's why we have the archers train in here, so that they are acclimated to arrows flying everywhere. It's no good having a fleet of great archers if the steeds they're riding on get scared every time the bowstring gets released," she explains, her gaze becoming intense.

"What was it like, the war between the two Equinian races?" I ask her, seizing the moment to gain some further information about the history of Eclipsia.

"I don't know to tell you the truth, I am a rather recent addition compared to most of the Equinians, especially Aliandara. I like to tease her by calling her a cougar, which you can imagine goes completely over her head—" she chuckles to herself, flipping her raven curls over one shoulder. I smile, feeling the ache of long hot days fully in my shoulders.

"She's a very complex woman—" I observe.

Evangeline smirks, her eyebrows quirking as her cheeks rise into flush apple rounds.

"Tell me about it. Oh, look whose ears are burning—"

At the mention of ears, I reach up instinctively to make sure my hair is still covering my own.

Turning to follow Evangeline's gaze, I find Aliandara approaching us through the sliding wooden door of the sweeping semi-circular stables.

I recall first seeing them with the moon-eyed High Lady when she brought me here, and how I was awed by the number of Alicorns and Unicorns that they hold. The enormous structure, filled with the potent aroma of cut hay and manure, houses around two thousand identical and well-equipped stalls, as well as multiple livery cupboards and archery training sites. Aliandara had also informed me, quite proudly, that the building spreads in a sweeping wooden curve of sturdy architecture around the entire circumference of the southern side of the city, in as much shade as the stout oriental skyline can provide.

"And what, if my ears were burning, might they be overhearing?" Aliandara smiles with feline wickedness that entirely becomes her, fabric pluming around her as if she is a male peacock in heat, jerking her chin skyward.

Approaching with majestic strides, her silver irises are dulled by the low-hanging wooden beams of the stables that cast thick and intermittent darkness over her, like a curtain being drawn and opened, over and over.

"Oh nothing, we were just talking about what a benevolent ruler you are. You know, the usual." Evangeline feigns innocence as Aliandara rolls her eyes.

"Nice to know you're still an awful liar—" she shoots back, turning to me as her features return to their usual stony indifference.

"Are you ready?" she enquires, eyes hooded.

Truth be told, Aliandara looks tired, fatigued even, and I know how she feels.

"If I say no can I go back to bed?" I ask her and she smirks.

"Not likely, Lady Freemont. Nice try though. Come on."

She turns from me, and as she does, I follow her, taking a moment to examine what she is wearing as we leave Evangeline to take care of my bow and quiver.

Her gown, which's slit high up both of her thighs to allow for free movement, is made from black cotton twisted around her body in numerous panels and cables stitched together with rosy golden thread. She has a lot of skin on show, her tattoos peeking through the design provocatively. I catch a few of the images inked on her skin, a winged Unicorn, a desert rose, arrows crossed like a compass— and try not to stare too long, remembering how much she disdains my curiosity.

Exiting the stables through the sliding doors, we are blanketed in the cool twilight, the contrast of caramel-dusted skin and dark fabric making Aliandara appear more tanned than usual. I watch the thick braids of her dark hair cascading down her spine in a blackish-blue serpentine trail, slipping effortlessly between hues as she moves.

"Come on," she urges me to hurry as her long legs work quickly, her calves slipping out of the slits in her skirt and revealing that she is wearing no shoes. Her bare feet are tattooed as well, even on the soles which I glimpse briefly as I scurry, following on her heels.

She leads me to the usual paddock where we practice hand-to-hand, a simple gated patch of sandstone that's dusted with glistening sand and surrounded by modest Arabian-style fence panels. She opens the gate, letting it swing back for me to catch as she passes into the training area without so much as a pause.

Following her and closing the gate behind me, I find myself recalling the first time I had stepped into these closed quarters with her only a week ago.

I was terrified.

I've never been in a fight in my life, not really. And certainly not one where I stood a chance. Consequently, it's been seven days of gruelling drills, bruised limbs, and aching muscles that never seem to stop complaining.

My mind is filled with overtures of Aliandara saying "No!", or "Again!", or "Not like that!"

When I think about what my tutor has explained repeatedly, I don't move in a way that's fitting for a warrior. I move like a figure skater and one who has been hypermobile her entire life to boot. Typically, I am weak in areas that I should not be due to increased flexibility and strong in areas that are of no use. It's making tussling with the High Lady of Artemis both painful and frustrating. I can't remember a night since my arrival when I haven't collapsed into bed feeling like I've gone ten rounds with a grizzly bear.

I wish I could quit, could simply continue to run, but as Aliandara reminds me, I have tried flight to no avail. Fighting is the only option I have left.

If I do not learn to defend myself, Lord Aro Black will capture me and torture me until I agree to crown him King, and then he will set his sights on the innocent people of Aetheria who oppose his rule.

We have not even gotten to aerial combat yet, seeing as how I'm still struggling to grasp even hand-to-hand, and so I can say I'm thoroughly grateful that I don't also have sore wings at least.

As Aliandara turns to me, I find myself wishing that I could learn to fight in a single three-minute montage set to inspirational music. Like, where are those training drills with football stadium steps I remember seeing so many clips of?

As it is, the only sounds that accompany our training are Aliandara's disdain and my grunts of effort. Not very inspirational at all to be honest.

"Ready yourself," Aliandara warns me, stepping back and balling her fists in an offensive stance. Her skirt flutters around her legs, the muscles of her thighs sheening with definition and elegant gold filigree.

I brace myself in turn, my wings rigid as I tuck them in tight. I would not let Aliandara braid my hair, much to her irritation, but she had said that I should at least keep my wings from being used against me by my opponent when on the ground.

Because that is what my life has become, oddly.

Where before I felt trapped by my body, I am now learning how to make myself into a weapon, and how to avoid being made a weapon for the use of others.

I didn't know it would be this hard, but then again, being the victim, being weak, and being used, wasn't easy either.

Resigned to my fate, Aliandara pounces forward through the arid space between us and spins on the ball of her bare foot. She twists, her high kick landing just beside my shoulder. It is a purposeful overturn, probably for my benefit, so I block her with my forearm, pushing her so she over-rotates and ends up with her back facing me. I take a small leap forward, bringing the inside of my forearm so it is throttling her. I can feel her pulse beneath the crook of my elbow, but not for long as she throws her head back with savage accuracy and hits me square in the nose.

I grunt, stunned.

My eyes stream with the pain as I stumble back a few paces, and she takes the second I'm disoriented to throw me over her shoulder.

Using her height advantage and more muscular body to lift me from the ground, she proceeds to use my chokehold against me.

I crash down into the paddock floor, the gritty golden sand embedding itself in my bare lower back just below the hem of my cropped shirt.

Looking up at Aliandara, I simply gape.

She snarls and steps back, shaking her head and scowling.

I get to my feet, the back of my head pounding in time with my throbbing nose. I feel a trickle of blood run down into my mouth, the iron of it fizzy on my tongue as I spit into the sand.

"Give me a minute," I breathe heavily, bending over and trying to reclaim my calm determination which seems to have all but evaporated.

"You don't have a minute, Kairi. If I were Aro Black you'd be dead right now." Aliandara taunts me with a wicked glint in her eye and a fact I know only too well is true.

I hate her at this moment, her cocky stance causing my blood to boil. My chest aches, but as expected she does not give me a chance to recover, darting forward and moving to strike me in the diaphragm with an open palm. I block her, gasping as I dart out of the way, my wings flaring out to help me balance.

I feel drained as I counter two more quick blows from the Equinian High Lady who seems to be nothing short of possessed as she continues to rain down in her assault.

She's moving too fast, so much so that I can't even process what's happening. Suddenly I find myself falling backwards again, my legs swept from beneath me as she dips and kicks my ankles out in one deft rotation.

My lungs burn as my spine hits the stone beneath me hard, knocking the wind from me once again, causing me to sputter.

Aliandara leaps upward with one powerful beat of her quicksilver wings, bringing down her whole weight upon my chest.

I lie there, pinned beneath her, frozen.

"Fight back! For the love of Artemis!" she hisses in my face, getting up close so I can smell the sweat slicking her forehead.

Her hair falls around her, eyes wildly feral as her jaw tenses.

She's frustrated.

Welcome to the club.

She steps back from me, not offering to help me to my feet.

155

I continue to lie on the ground, staring into the endlessness of the Aetherial sky as my heartbeat thuds loudly in my ears.

"Get up!" she hisses, but I feel suddenly paralysed.

What's the point in getting back up if I'm only going to be knocked right back down again?

"*Get up!*" Aliandara roars, her voice taking on an undeniable leonine quality. I flinch at her outburst, then sigh as I pull myself tenderly to my feet.

The world tilts as I right myself, my chest aching and my limbs jelly. Shimmying, I clear my feathers of sand.

"What the hell is wrong with you? Where is the girl, the mortal, who stood before Lord Aro Black and chose to die rather than back down? Where is the woman who leapt from the balcony of the Solis Castra rather than be caged?" she demands from between gritted teeth.

I feel myself getting angry.

"I'm not Storm. I never have been! If that is who you're hoping to find by beating me half senseless then you might as well quit now. I'm not her. I'll never be her. She was—" I feel my voice fading, as I realise that if I speak aloud what Storm was, I will be admitting to myself exactly what I am not.

A ruler.

A fighter.

Fearless.

"I don't want Storm. I want High Lady Kairi Freemont. You act like you're helpless, but you're not, you're only afraid. Don't wait to be hit, strike!" Aliandara retorts, colour flushing her cheeks as her eyes flash sharp with cold light.

I watch her step back, preparing to launch at me again, but I beat her to it, using my wings to propel me forward in a spinning kick. She grins, her lips drawing back into a wily grimace as she catches me by the ankle, raising her eyebrows in challenge.

Using my wings to gain extra airtime, I bring my other leg up, slamming it into her abdomen and pushing her back. I tumble to the floor, but this time I'm prepared and roll out of the feint without pause.

I ball my fists, turning to find her regaining her balance.

Then, as I grit my teeth, something changes.

The air, which had before been dry and still, feels electric in a way that is amplified from anything I've experienced conducting.

I feel the vibrating electric charge as an energy that calls to me, an alluring pulse only I can hear.

Aliandara wastes no time, darting to leap toward me, but before she can I've instinctively reached out, my body harnessing the energy in the air and funnelling it without conscious thought into a bolt of electricity that shoots from my fingertips and catches her in the jaw.

She crumples into a heap on the ground, and as I stare at her I feel the charge continuing to build. It gives no sign of stopping.

It ripples through my muscles, making them contract and heating my blood.

I ascend without effort, hovering as the sky overhead clouds over in fast motion and blankets everything in shadow. The wind picks up, ruffling my hair from its low ponytail, which is coming loose.

Then, as a roll of thunder swathes the skies in teeming darkness, rain begins to fall hard upon the earth.

My body relaxes, going limp, and I slowly return to the floor, my fingers sparking with remnant charge.

The rain comes down so hard it bounces off the sandstone underfoot, and I watch as Aliandara raises her face to the sky, closing her eyes and letting it drench her skin.

You'd think she's never seen rain before.

The water dampens my hair, and I feel the tips of my Fae ears beginning to protrude from beneath the drapery of my ponytail.

Aliandara stares at me then, opening her eyes as rain streaks her face in glittering rivulets.

"How?" she asks, her voice guttural in its surprise. "How did you do this?"

"I didn't do anything, it's just a bit of rain," I insist, but she shakes her head.

"You know I've lived a long time, and one thing I've never seen is rain in Eclipsia. Not ever. Not in over half a century. This is you, Kairi. You did this."

Ignoring her shock, I offer her a hand and she takes it. Tensing, I feel the last of the current discharge from my arm and into her. Her eyes lock on me amidst the downpour, hair sodden and eyes shining like moons among the grey downpour.

"Your ears— they're—" Fat droplets of rain pour off her nose and cling to her eyelashes like diamonds.

"We should talk—" I reply, chest rising and falling heavily.

The tempest of the clouds swirling above continues to teem.

The rain continues to pour as Aliandara and I strip off our sodden clothes in her private baths. Well, I say private, but what I really mean is they belong to her. The room is little more than a domed marquee propped up on four Grecian columns that are thickly swaddled with desert flowers and vines.

The air is fragrant and dense with essential oils, the pitter-pat of rain slamming against the roof of the baths the only other sound that can be heard as damp fabric falls from long limbs and puddles on the tiles with a slap.

Aliandara walks past me, nude, her languidly long legs of silken, tanned skin glimmering so intensely it makes my eyes hurt.

She descends into the dark teal of the waters filling the bath which sprawls the entire length of the room, the steaming water sourced from a myriad of veins built into the floor, the same as those I had observed in the courtyard.

I see the phases of the moon adorning her spine in a poker-straight line, shimmering white gold in the light of nearby flickering gas lamps that tremble with the sudden wind.

Shivering a little, which I honestly find a little odd considering I've spent most of my time in Sapphire City praying for a stiff breeze, I follow her, careful not to slip on the emerald and magenta tiles adorning the walls and bottom of the sunken pool.

The water is warm, and I assume heated by underground vents similar to those I'd learned of in Drakos Vale. It caresses my skin, and as I submerge myself fully, any remnant of lightning dissolves as my skin is blanketed in silence and heat.

Aliandara swivels as she reaches the side of the pool opposing me, resting her long muscular arms along the edge of the tilework and spreading her wings so they rest beneath her.

I wade deeper into the pool, pulling my hair from its elastic and submerging myself with closed eyes for a second, letting the water soak my hair.

As I resurface, I catch the High Lady watching me with an unreadable expression, but turn from her, settling on the opposite side of the pool and resting my wings against the cool tiles as I let my shoulders unravel with the heat.

"So, all is not as it would appear. What are you Kairi Freemont?" Aliandara demands cooly, eyes narrowing.

I shrug, tension melting by the second.

"I don't know what you mean, I'm just a girl swept up in circumstances she doesn't understand," I feel the answer is honest, but Aliandara only laughs, making it clear she doesn't agree.

The crystal teal of the water trembles between us nervously as we stare at one another, the truth of my rebirth laid bare among the rising pungent steam.

"You have ears— like one of them," Aliandara accuses me. I don't react with outrage or defensiveness. I simply state the truth, willing my heartbeat to remain calm.

"I don't know why. I do not know anything. All I know is I woke up like this after Aro murdered me," I explain.

Her eyebrows rise on her creaseless forehead, eyes gazing past me and into the downpour that is still striking the ground beyond the bounds of the canopy roof like bullets.

"You realise, elemental affinity, such as control of the weather— it's also a Fae trait," she ponders her own words, saying it as fact but appearing not entirely present as her eyes mist over.

"Aro has control over electricity, all the Sephilim and Nephilim do. It's how we conduct," I remind her, trying to make less of what happened.

"This is not the same. The rain, the sky— I have never seen such power and believe me I would not admit that to you lightly, Kairi." She thinks carefully, pausing before choosing her next words and exhaling heavily.

"Aren't you angry? Seeing your potential? Aren't you furious that you were born into such a subservient race? I'd be tempted to recognise you as Equinian if it weren't for how placid you have become, how hopeless. Evangeline informs me that you are gifted in archery as well," she adds.

"I'd hardly say that" I retort, rolling my eyes and giving a slight snort.

"I don't care what you'd say, you know nothing of your power. And I cannot help but wonder, if you are genuinely so modest, with such low self-esteem, or if this is some game. Are you acting stupid on purpose?"

She doesn't look at me as the accusation leaves her lips, examining her elegantly long fingers. Water drips from each of her lacquered nails as it catches the flickering lamplight and turns molten.

"You think I enjoy getting a beat down? I wouldn't act this pathetic on purpose, trust me," I shoot back. She cocks a brow, lips pursed with frustration.

"Then why, when you seem to be capable and strong, do you shy from your power?" Aliandara asks repeatedly.

It's the same question I've heard from her a million times in the past week.

This time though, I realise I have an answer.

"Because I honestly don't feel powerful. In fact, I feel absolutely no different than I did as a mortal. I have this new body, but I'm still that girl inside. I'm still terrified. I'm still the girl who fell for Aro Black, the girl he manipulated and murdered so easily. I thought— I don't know—"

I slick my hair back against my skull, pushing the water from my forehead. "I thought I'd change. Be wiser, not feel so afraid. My body is immortal, but my soul— it's just the same as it was before," I explain, taking a deep breath.

"Everyone wants me to be Storm, to be this mythical figure of hope who will deliver Aetheria into some better future— but I'm not her. I'm just me. Hera made a mistake." I speak my fears aloud and Aliandara gives me what I can only describe as my first glimpse of her empathetic side.

"I see," is all she says, letting silence fall like a veil.

We sit there for a few moments, listening to the rain.

My anxiety grows as we float across from one another, wondering if she is realising what I have known all along.

I'm not cut out for this.

I'm not what Aetheria needs.

I'm too weak, too human.

Aliandara, though, doesn't say anything, we simply stare at one another.

"What are you thinking?" I ask her, unable to bear the silence any longer as my anxiety crests, drenching me in its cold blanket of doubt.

I let my legs extend before me in the water, slowly undulating as I drop my gaze to my feet.

"I was thinking that while I'm the best person to teach you how to fight, I'm not the right person to teach you to trust in yourself. Your self-esteem is scarily low, and I feel like that's far more urgent than teaching you to throw a spinning back kick." Aliandara answers my question without pause or any sign of doubt in her voice. She's clearly decided that where my identity crisis is concerned, she can't help me.

"So— what are you suggesting?" I push her for more information.

She smiles, a little wistful, her eyes milky as though she is not seeing me at all.

"I believe this is a job for the most confident person I know, Kairi," she sighs, moving to get out of the baths with a sudden jerk, as though she's snapped out of a trance.

I follow her with a soft gaze, curious as ever as the scent of essential oils plume where she has disturbed the water.

"And that is?" I enquire.

Looking back over a bare shoulder, she gives a lopsided and oddly girlish sly smile.

"I would have thought you'd know exactly who I was referring to by now. After all, he was drunk at your Ascension ball."

I stand in my room, finally dry as the storm continues to rage outside my glassless window. I look back over one shoulder at the four-poster bed longingly, wishing that I had the luxury of taking the night off, of simply falling into the soft hold of the mattress and surrendering to unconsciousness.

However, Aliandara seems to think my mental health and lack of self-confidence is an urgent political matter, so I am once more standing before the mirror, dressed in a freshly ironed pair of harem pants and a crop top that ombres from the lightest of mint green into an electric baby blue. I have my hair pulled back into a high ponytail for the first time in what seems like forever, and with the middle eastern outfit and the pointed ears, I'm beginning to think I look like a Genie. That is, if it were not for the enormous, feathered wings, still damp from the baths, against my spine.

I examine my ears a moment longer, frowning, and unsure if I like them or not. I had not been free to examine them in the dormitories at the academy for fear of being caught, so I have been taking my sweet time assessing their pointed tips.

I know the real reason I'm fixating, and it's because I'm putting off leaving. I hate self-examination. The thought of having some centuries-old Fae looking at my personal issues seems so utterly ridiculous that I'm beginning to feel pathetic.

After all, what kind of sad case gets blessed by a Goddess and walks around feeling unworthy, feeling weak and useless, in an immortal body with all the potential that mine has to offer?

Someone ungrateful and self-absorbed that's who, and it wouldn't surprise me if Morpheus came to the same conclusion.

Still, Aliandara won't stand for me playing possum the next time I'm confronted by an enemy, so my options now are to face my fear or her scorn.

Personally, I'll take my fear. I mean, she is rather terrifying.

Closing my eyes, I focus on the air currents around me that are more chill than usual. I become aware of my feet on the ornate rugs smattering the floor, and take a deep breath, tasting the citrus of electric potential on my tongue.

I picture it then, from that night, Aramis's lush forests and rich aubergine sky. I can almost smell the tropical flowers before I've even conducted.

Then, as I teleport, the act leaving only the echo of a whip breaking the sound barrier, I feel the moistness of Aramis soil beneath my feet, and I am there, back in the clearing where Lucien and I had danced among the Fae.

It takes me a few moments to get acclimated to the muggy heat after the relentless aridity of Eclipsia, but once I accept the thick blanket of fragrant floral air pressing in on my skin from all angles, I find myself gawping.

I had known Nirvana was incredible as a mortal, but now I'm seeing it fresh, and it's like this is the first time. My angel eyes bring out every vivid petal, every twisting bloated vine, and glimmering jewelled insect against the velvet of the night sky overhead.

It isn't raining here, so the bioluminescent plant life remains shadowy as a mass of emerald foliage, and yet the vivacity of the flowers and fruits still doesn't fail to take my breath away.

I'm fixated on an enormous purple hibiscus with gold pistils when my attention is drawn down from what I'm seeing into a visceral place inside my gut.

It starts weak, a subtle throb, like the ache from an old injury, but shortly it is overwhelming me in a way I don't know how to describe.

It's as if someone has an enormous set of speakers plugged into the soles of my feet and has turned the bass way up so that my femurs are rocked with seismic tremors.

It ripples up my body, humming, throbbing, pulsating, as I pull my foot up from the mossy lushness of the floor beneath, trying to see if I'm standing on anything that could explain the sensation.

I find nothing, and so prick my pointed Fae ears, listening into the surrounding jungle to find the source.

Again, there is nothing.

Nothing visible, nothing audible, and yet the sensation of an enormous heartbeat rocks through me from the earth below, like I have been jacked into an electrical circuit against my consent.

Something stirs in the bushes to the left of me, and I spin, tensing instinctively.

I guess Aliandara's training is teaching me something at least.

Though, what I see I'm not prepared for, no amount of physical preparation could have readied me.

A leopard, glowing, emerges from the shadows of the clearing, its fur like nothing I've ever seen. Where usually the coat of the enormous cat would be gold and black, this leopard is neon green and cyan, its entire lithe silhouette coated in a peacock feather design.

It creeps closer, extending a saucer-sized paw out from the undergrowth. Then, from beside it, another animal materialises, this time a glowing lilac stag, also walking toward me.

I hear a titter, like the sound of rice hitting the inside of a copper saucepan, and find several Sprites emerging from the darkness as well. Each of the silhouettes becomes unmistakable as they emerge from the trees, glowing wildly like festive lights. The Sprites dance across the moss of the floor, fluttering to and fro with elegant leaps and mischievous pirouettes, leading a procession of other glowing animals behind them.

A silver fox, glowing ghostly, appears beside a glimmering golden meerkat— bounding forward without pause.

I know this fox; Neve had called it Winters Rage.

There had been another if I recall, but I cannot find it among the cluster of phantasmic animals as a magenta and violet tiger appears, followed by a pure white spider monkey that looks like an agile phantom as it swoops down from the canopy overhead.

I examine them as they come to me, the vibrations in the soles of my feet no longer intrusive but in tune with my pulse like I've been calibrated to the earth beneath.

I reach out to touch the leopard that stalks closer, and it nudges my hand with a cautious and whiskered maw as several Sprites clamber up my arms with featherlight steps and nestle on my shoulders. Two of the tiny child souls reborn introduce themselves, a girl called Skye and a boy who declares himself River.

They both have dark hair and boast brightly coloured Dragonfly wings that pop against the pure white of their miniature outfits. River looks mischievous as he uses my left arm like a bannister rail, sliding down it as the slightest breeze ruffles his untamed hair. Skye, however, is content to remain on my shoulder, looking down at the mystical gathering of odd neon animals.

She points excitedly, and I find that she's looking at a smokey lilac and white lemur, its striped tail curled into a neat spiral as it watches me with wide and unblinking eyes that shimmer like moons.

I hear another rustle, and turn, expecting to find the glow of more of Aramis's animals come to say hello.

Instead, though, I do not find an animal at all.

Morpheus stands, hip cocked, with his feathered viridian hair braided off his face, his cheekbones seeming hollow as he treads carefully forward. I find the feather of his dreamcatcher earring sparkling, catching the light radiating from where I'm standing, surrounded in the middle of the clearing.

He gives me a curious stare, his eyes flitting between my face, the myriad of creatures, and the pointed tips of my ears.

He doesn't smile, nor does he laugh as I expect, instead he merely says, "Well, isn't that interesting—"

IN SEARCH OF LOST TIME

KAIRI

"HELLO MORPHEUS," I SAY with a sweet smile, raising a hand so that Skye, the tiny Sprite resting on my shoulder, can be safely placed back on the ground.

Her tiny feet tickle my palm as I bend, and she dashes off. I watch her dance over to the spider monkey who is scavenging the floor for fallen fruit as I straighten, compensating differently due to the weight of my wings.

"I'd say funny seeing you here, but the world seems to have been short of humour as of late," Morpheus ponders, the waxy surface of leaves around him reflecting the glow of neon animals onto his pale skin.

"Can't say I disagree with you there. What are these— animals?" I ask him, gesturing around as I take several steps out of the grove's epi-centre where the creatures are clustered. His brows, artfully plucked as they are, pinch together, his forehead crumpling as he appears to be trying to think far too hard.

I have the sudden urge to tell him not to hurt himself, but think better of it and bite my tongue.

"The spirits of Nirvana, and Sprites that have decided to join you for the mere mischief of it I believe— though, I have no idea why you should be able to summon them."

He cocks his head, examining me so the dreamcatcher hanging from his earlobe swings wildly among his feathered locks. His eyes land on my pointed ears once again, and I shrug.

"I didn't summon them, I just arrived here and they started crawling out of the jungle toward me," I deny his claim, though I recognise as soon as the words fall out of my mouth just how ignorant I sound.

"These creatures, these spirits, are a mystery to us, Kairi. God knows we are no scientists, but the one thing I can tell you is that they do not simply appear as they will. It's Nirvana's reaction to being connected with a source of power similar to its own. That's why only Fae High Lords and Ladies of Light have the ability to do it," he informs me, and I blush, finally reaching him.

My steps slow across the vine-strewn ground as I reach the edge of the clearing, the shadows of the luscious plant life casting me fast in shadow.

Turning back, I find the source of the darkness caused by the distinct and sudden absence of the spirits I was surrounded by only moments ago. The only creatures that remain are the two Sprites, River and Skye, who I catch disappearing back into the undergrowth out of the corner of my eye.

Turning back to Morpheus, I find him examining me more closely, and I stare him directly in the eye.

"Aliandara sent me here, to find you. So, I'm lucky you stumbled across me," I admit, feeling the clammy Nirvana air sticking to my skin.

"Aliandara— as in High Lady Montgomery, sent you to me? Of her own free will? Well, if I didn't think times were desperate before then I do now—" he chortles, his eyes refusing to stay trained on my face. "I was just out for my late-night walk. I like the peace you see, helps me construct my poetry," he admits, unblinking even still.

"You won't find any other Fae traits, it's just the ears," I say abruptly, getting sick of being ogled at. This, I cannot deny, is ironic considering how I usually tend to be the one staring. Aliandara might have been right when she said it was rude—

"Well, having seen you with those spirits I would say that's blatantly untrue." Morpheus' face is deadpan, his voice having lost its melodic undertone.

I don't know how to reply as the truth of his words crashes into me mercilessly. If I had come for subtleties or pussyfooting, I should have known better.

Morpheus has never been anything other than direct.

In fact, I'm not sure he knows how to be.

"Come on, let's go back up to my villa, it's muggy as all hell out here." Morpheus parts the vines at his spine with a graceful hand, pirouetting on the ball of one foot, and gestures for me to go first.

"Brains before beauty—" he quips, smirking as I step past him, my high ponytail swinging between my shoulder blades.

We tread carefully through the maze of the jungle undergrowth, wary of becoming tangled in the haphazard vines which look quite like snakes in the half-light.

It's funny, how my Nephilim eyesight makes the jungle appear even more beautiful than it had before, when as a mortal the mere fact I couldn't see well had spiked fear in my gut and led me to flee.

It occurs to me as we find the path that fleeing seems to be what I'm good at, what I'm used to, and the one time I had tried to stand up and fight I had lost my life in only a fraction of a second.

It's no wonder I'm so content to flee when standing and fighting last time ended so well.

"So, the ears, when did they appear?" Morpheus inquires, falling in step at my side.

I purse my lips, exhaling heavily.

"When I awoke from my Kindred vision as a Nephilim. They were just there— Lucien told me not to tell anyone and I agreed that it was better kept secret. I've been hiding them with my hair," I reply, seeing the edge of the jungle approaching as a crescent moon of gold becomes visible, a speck at the end of the long jade tunnel.

"Ah, so that explains why you had that awful hair-do at your ascension ball, got it." He comments so slyly and with such an innocent tone it takes me a moment to realise that he's insulting me.

"Hey! I'm amazed you remember the ball at all with the amount you were drinking!" I retort, recalling him tottering between different social circles with a staggering gait.

"And what makes you think that I was drunk?" he asks with a smirk. "I find it adorable you think someone as old as I am could be intoxicated by the poultry amounts of liquor those flutes hold, it's extremely sweet of you. I am quite touched by your naivety, it reminds me of when I was— well, no I don't think I've ever been that naïve."

I open my mouth to retort, to say something about the vast amounts of liquor I was certain I had seen him pouring down his throat, but something suddenly seems off.

He had seemed to know exactly what he was saying when he threatened Aro.

"You were faking it—" I say, gasping slightly as my mouth pops open. He giggles like a little boy, giving me a jagged Cheshire smile, ears twitching merrily beneath his mane.

"You'd be amazed what people will say when they think the person standing behind them will be too drunk to remember it, I've learned some quite interesting little titbits that way," he admits.

"Cunning," I retort, wondering how many secrets he holds within his well-groomed head.

"Indeed. Well, I must make up for my lack of biceps in this world. Wielding words and a paintbrush isn't too effective against the likes of Aro Black, as you can imagine," he sighs, and I feel his pain. "So, why are you here exactly?" he probes, our steps scuffling as the dirt of the path turns to the familiar moonstone gravel of his villa's driveaway.

The trees rescind, becoming stout succulents with thick leaves that tickle my ankles instead.

"Aliandara says I'm having an identity crisis—" I roll my eyes.

"Well, I'm hardly surprised. A Nephilim with the body parts of a Fae—"

I shake my head at the assumption.

"It's not that, it's Storm. Everyone wants me to be her, and despite the fact we look so similar, that my soul once belonged to her, I'm not. I'm no trailblazer— I am not brave like that," I sigh, and Morpheus' face turns hard and stony.

"I'm not sure why Aliandara would think I could help with that," he asks, brow furrowing.

"She thinks because you took Storm's memories that you can help me know myself. Also, you are extremely confident—" He smirks at that. "I guess— I guess if I knew more about her, I could see how we're different, see what I'm not and how to fix it—" I admit, biting down hard on my bottom lip.

Morpheus frowns, looking thoughtful as the space behind his irises clouds slightly.

"I returned her memories to you, Kairi. I'm not sure what else you think I can do—" He looks hopeless for a second, as though disappointing me is affecting him deeply.

I wonder why he should seem so emotional over the situation of someone he barely knows.

"I know you did, but I can't seem to focus on any one moment, any one memory of hers. I had some clarity before I was changed, but now it all just blurs together— it's overwhelming," I admit.

Morpheus narrows his eyes and examines me for a second, his eyes flitting between my face and my ears once again.

"Perhaps— Perhaps there is something I can do— Or rather something you can do," he suggests, causing my stomach to knot.

"What is it?" I push him, curious as a cobalt firefly dithers in the warm air.

"Come up to the house, I'll meet you there—" I go to open my mouth, to ask what he's talking about, but before I can he dissolves in a flamboyant puff of teal smoke.

I should have known.

Morpheus is never what he seems.

I continue my journey up the cliffside toward the modern-style villa that looks over Aramis.

When I reach the top of the incline, not even out of breath thanks to my immortal lungs, Aramis sprawls before me, as though some giant has scattered bejewelled trinkets and thingamabobs amongst the enormous blades of grass of his front lawn.

Somehow these trinkets have come together to create a microcosm for the meagre creatures at his feet.

The city shimmers dully, like uncut precious stones beneath the golden moonlight, but I don't have time to stop and take it in. After all, The High Lord Fae of Night is waiting.

I continue through the zen-style greenery which is sparsely and precisely placed just so between scatterings of dove grey slate and ivory stone slabs, finding myself outside the revolving glass of Morpheus' circular front door.

I let myself in, leaning against the pane and stepping into the open air of the villa's giant main room. The infinity pool which runs up to, and then beyond the enormous panoramic window glistens cerulean as my bare feet patter upon the floor.

I stare around me, searching for any sign of Morpheus as I spin in a circle. Finally, when I come a full three hundred and sixty degrees, so I'm once more facing the excessively ornate mural of Apollo reaching out from a cloud to Morpheus, I find the man himself.

He is standing, arms draped lazily and with feminine elegance I cannot help but envy over the balcony railing of the landing on the upper floor.

"Well don't just stand there, spit spot!" He turns in a whirl of violet tones and overly expressive motion, leaving me to climb the spiral staircase after him.

My ponytail bobs against the bare flesh between my wings, as my soles navigate the curvature of the stairs.

As I ascend, I take a second to glance back into the main space, realising with surprise that I'm relieved to be back here.

I smile faintly, catching the expression as it flits over my lips with a ballerina's featherlight grace and gentle temper, remembering I am here with a definite goal in mind and increasing my pace.

I reach the top of the staircase and hurry, finding a door at the end of the passageway to be propped open. I head for it, unable to resist glancing at the door to the suite where I'd stayed before on the way.

I will never forget opening my door to find Lucien wearing velvet leggings.

My eyes crease at the corners, my cheeks flushing as I remember examining his bulge and losing my own feeling of self-consciousness. Now I'm immortal, I can see why the Kindred of this world wear such revealing outfits. After all, most of their bodies are on the divine side of the flawless spectrum, and nobody I've ever met seems the least bit self-conscious.

When I reach the open doorway at the end of the art-peppered hallway, I'm surprised. I had thought I'd find Morpheus' bed chambers, but instead, it appears as though I'm standing on the edge of some kind of meditation studio.

The entire room is walled either in glass or mirrors, the ceiling strung with artfully draped lengths of silk. The air smells of incense, and the teak of the floorboards is scattered with large velvet pillows in matching shades.

"Pull up a pillow, Kairi." He returns to a viridian cushion with silver tassels in the middle of the room. It is embroidered with a platinum dreamcatcher, which disappears beneath him as he crosses his legs and gets comfortable.

Grabbing an aubergine pillow of my own, I toss it lightly onto the floor beside his.

Then, I watch as he moves it so the cushion is opposing him instead.

"Sit," he gestures with a gentleness I am not used to from him. Usually, his exuberance is enough to bring a smile to even the grumpiest of faces— except of course maybe Aliandara's, but as I sit before him, crossing my legs and suddenly enveloped in surrounding silence, I find him entirely serene.

"Now, I'm going to try to teach you something, but I don't want you to be surprised if you can't manage it. By all reasonable assumptions, you shouldn't be able to even attempt this, but given your little display of Fae-ness back there I think it might be worth trying, alright?" he explains, brushing his vivid mane back with long and casual fingers. I see his dream-catcher-less ear is studded with silver rings, about seven in total.

"What are you talking about?" I ask, confused and a little scared.

"I'm going to try and teach you to dream walk. I think that way we should be able to visit individual memories from your past life," he explains.

My eyes widen.

"You think I could do that?" I ask him, incredulous.

He shrugs.

"As I said, I have no idea. But it's worth a shot, yes?" he adds, and I nod. "Very well, straighten your spine, lay your palms open on your knees, and close your eyes," he instructs.

I frown.

"So, we're going to meditate?" I query, having expected there to be some kind of potion or amulet involved.

"Exactly, Kairi. Meditation for mortals is a way they may reach out into the space between dimensions and float, to gain the peace of separating the soul from the body. Mortals come here in dreams, that is true, but they cannot cross into the Nether of their own free will without severing that connection permanently. The Gods and Goddesses, the Titans, and Fae however can maintain the tether between body and soul in a way that mortals cannot. The only mortals that can cross by choice are rare, oh and the dead of course— but that is another story. In fact, I knew a Medium once, a remarkable human being—" he gets a starry look in his eyes and then shakes his head as I lean in, intrigued. "That is beside the point—" he scolds himself, "We must stay focused. Come now, close your eyes." I straighten once more, my weight settling heavily into the plush feather down of the cushion as I close my eyes.

I let my palms fall open.

"Now Kairi, I want you to focus on your breathing, and I want you to centre yourself at the third eye. Right between your brows," he instructs.

I do so, feeling a little bit silly, but continuing regardless.

After a few minutes of what Morpheus goes on to call belly breathing, I exhale in a childish raspberry.

"Is it supposed to take this long?" I ask him, and he chuckles.

"It's only been a few minutes. Return to the position please and focus," he scolds me, but I can hear the amusement in his tone.

I breathe in, the muggy Nirvana air rich with jasmine oil filling my lungs. I let the darkness swallow my anxiety and focus on the point between my brows.

A kind of lightness comes over me, as though who I am and what I am are coming apart and one is drifting ever so slightly from the other as if it's been caught in a gentle ocean current. I can feel gravity pulling on my soul, kind of like I am in a centrifuge, and yet I'm free.

I open my eyes and find myself looking into Morpheus's amused face.

"Well, I'll be. A dreamwalking Nephilim—" He whistles and claps me on the shoulder with his non-corporeal palm. I feel the impact and wonder how that can be, grinning wide.

He prances around me, pointing his toes like a dancer and turning a wildly daring pirouette amongst the surrounding clouds, his laugh tinny like coins hitting a corrugated roof.

I take a moment to glance around me, finding endless grey mist on all sides, even underfoot. The ambivalence of it shouldn't surprise me, but it does.

"I expected something more— I don't know, magical." I shrug and he rolls his eyes.

"You young Kindred are so unimpressed and impatient. This place is pure magic Kairi, but you must harness it. The explorer moulds the dimension to their will. That is why everyone's Kindred vision is different. You see, in essence, what you want to see," he explains, and I blink slowly, thinking about the implications of this.

"So, when I saw Hera, Aphrodite, Hecate, and Nemesis— that was because I wanted to?" I ask him, the mist tickling my ankles in a lukewarm caress.

"So that's what Hypnos meant when she said your Kindred vision was unusual—" he muses, placing a finger on his chin and examining me carefully.

I see a thought, or perhaps it is better described as a suspicion, flit across his face, but it is gone before I can ask him what he's thinking.

"We should get moving. I don't know how long you'll be able to keep this up being new at it and all— I've been practising this skill and the astral projection associated with it for centuries, which is what it takes to maintain any lasting control."

I nod, not wanting to waste time with a reply. I came here for answers of a different kind, and I intend to find them before my time runs out.

"So, where to?" I ask, peering in all directions.

"Weren't you listening? That's up to you, my dear. It is your past life you wish to visit, so you must conjure it from the raw star stuff of the Nether."

I don't know what he means, but as Storm's oddly familiar yet strange face flits through my subconscious, a wooden door with heavy steel hinges materialises from tendrils of grey smoke. They coil, so-lidifying before my eyes, and I exhale.

Magic.

Stepping forward, I take a deep breath and reach out for the steel of the iron doorknob, its damp surface chilling my fingertips.

"Ready?" Morpheus demands, and I turn back to him with an ex-pression bordering on tragic.

"No," I reply, and turn the door handle, letting myself into the past.

I don't know how I know it's 1829. Or that I'm in London, and yet I feel as though denying this fact would be like denying the truth of oxygen, or gravity.

As my feet fall ghostly upon chill wooden floorboards and my ears are greeted by the crackle and pop of a stifling hearth, I just know. I know exactly where I am, and when I am. I just don't know why.

The sound of footsteps on creaky wooden stairs signals that the answer may be fast approaching as Morpheus steps into the room behind me, closing the magical door and sealing us in the past.

The room is simple, a wooden table, several wooden chairs with legs that are mismatched in size, the odd ember or spark rising from the hearth and out into the cold clutches of the house.

Looking at the low beams of the ceiling, at the ragged nature of tea towels hung from the back of one of the chairs crowding the table, it is clear to me why fires were so common in London, and yet— It's 1829. And I know that Briar wasn't poor by any standard from what I've seen in past memories.

So, what gives?

The final creak on the staircase implores me to get out of my head and watch, as a man with a monocle which he is cleaning with his splodged handkerchief enters the dim confines of the front room. Behind him, a woman with a tear-stained face follows. But it isn't Briar.

Her face could be recognised as similar in an odd half-light I suppose, but I know immediately it isn't her. The woman's red eyes are too far apart, her running nose too wide and her jaw too soft with a thin layer of chub.

"Mrs. Patterson. I am sorry. There is nothing left to be done," the man apologises, though I can tell his pain is masked by a layer of cold indifference, the kind that is practised.

"Doctor, I thought— I thought that maybe there was something you could do. I can't lose him, not my Robin. He's— he's my baby."

She's trying to hold herself together, worrying the edges of her tatty apron with fraught fingers, bottom lip trembling.

"He is too small, his lungs too far gone, Mrs Patterson. I am sorry. I truly am. But I must warn you, that you are running too high a risk in caring for the boy. You have four other children to think of. They would suffer worse in the workhouse, as orphans, if you understand my meaning—" He coughs, covering his mouth with his handkerchief so he doesn't have to decide what to do with his expression.

"You're saying I should just leave him to die alone? I am his mother!" she wails, suddenly furious as she stamps her worn leather boot upon the floorboard beneath her fraying hemline.

I glimpse around the room, trying to work out what the thin film of black dust is, finally realising that it is the soot from the fireplace. I do not suppose by the looks of things they have money for a sweep.

I still wonder though, what this has to do with Briar— what this has to do with me.

"Good day, Mrs. Patterson. I have other patients. I'm sure you understand I'm a very busy man." The doctor turns his back on the weeping mother, and I want to smack him.

How can he just leave her like this?

Mrs Patterson stands stone still, sniffling and holding back yet more sobs in the smoky air of the family room as the doctor crosses it in four stout steps. Then he disappears out into the London smog curling thick beyond.

As the wooden door slams shut in its frame, the woman falls to pieces, slumping to the floor and looking up to the sky.

"Why Lord— Why my little Robin?" she asks.

I look at Morpheus who is standing beside me, seemingly unmoved by the spectacle, cocking an eyebrow in question.

He shrugs.

"I don't know. Your party, I'm just tagging along—"

I turn away from him again, just in time for the door to burst wide open, letting in more stagnant air from the street outside.

In the doorframe, I find her at last.

Miss Briar Shaw.

174

She's carrying a wicker basket on one arm, her coat and bonnet wrapped tight around her body to protect her from the wind tunnels of London's winding cobbled streets and underpasses.

"Elena?" Her voice— my voice, but with a stiff English accent that drips with the marks of proper etiquette lost to my west coast easiness, calls into the dimness of the house.

"Elena!" she repeats, seeing the woman on the floor in a puddle of soot-stained skirts. Quickly, she turns to close the door behind her.

She rushes across the floorboards, each one emitting a creak as she does so, her dress coat of jade green felt sticking fast to the curves of her shoulders.

She looks down at the crying woman, who I assume to be the professed Elena, as she squats.

"I just saw the doctor out in the street, he told me. Elena, I'm so sorry—" Briar breathes, wrapping her in a hug.

"Do you think— do you think this— this is me being punished?" Elena wails, and Briar's brow creases beneath the tight curls of her fringe.

"Come on, let's get you up—" She helps Elena to her feet and then walks with her until she collapses onto one of the mismatched chairs. The chair groans under her weight, a sure sign of its disrepair.

"I think I'm being punished—" Elena continues, salty tears rolling down her flushed apple-round cheeks.

"Punished for what, Elena? What could anyone possibly punish you for, my darling sister?" Briar asks, placing a gloved hand over Elena's trembling fingers. Their eyes meet across the wooden table, and I continue to watch, feeling oddly uncomfortable, as if I am intruding.

"For disappointing Father. For marrying for love, for breaking off my engagement—" she sniffles, and Briar's eyes widen.

"Then I should be punished too. My engagement was also broken off. I too must be a great disappointment to father," she admits, smiling slightly.

"It's not the same, sister, and you know it. Your betrothed was tragically killed in battle. I ran away with the baker's boy. And look at where it's gotten me— look at what I've done to poor Robin."

Her shoulders roll forward as the grief in her chest begins to rise toward overflowing again.

"This is not your fault, sister; it could never be your fault. You love him more than anyone. I know that, and so does God. I promise you." Briar squeezes her sister's hands.

"And that's why what the doctor is suggesting is so ridiculous. He wants me to leave him. Wants me to abandon him! Says that I may get sick too staying with him. I mean, we've been keeping him upstairs, keeping contact minimal where we can, Briar." Briar nods, drawing the strings of her bonnet from beneath her chin and placing it on the table. "I can't leave him. How can I let him die alone? What kind of mother does that?" she asks, her anger and sorrow fighting for dominance beneath the watery lakes of her light blue eyes.

Briar pauses a moment, her own eyes filling with tears.

"Elena, I know you are a good mother, the best. So, I ask you, what kind of mother leaves three other children orphaned in this world— This cruel world?"

Elena's crying stops for a moment, strangled in her throat.

"Do you agree with him? You think I should abandon my little boy to die?" She sounds as though she's just swallowed the flames from the hearth and is ready to blow them into Briar's face. Ready to burn the world for the injustice of it all.

"He won't be alone, Elena." She holds fast to the hand that Elena is trying to pull away.

"Don't try to give me some holier than thou verse from that damn book!" she hisses, rising to her feet in fury.

Briar stands as well, though she is perfectly calm, her face a porcelain mask of propriety and strength.

"He will not be alone, Elena, because I will tend to him. I will be with him when he passes. Even if it means I too become deathly ill," Briar announces, and I watch her sister's rage extinguish. Her fists uncurl at her sides, fingers wistful and robbed of purpose.

"No, Briar. No. You cannot do that. I won't allow it." She covers her mouth with her limp fingers, eyes filling with yet more tears.

I watch on, my heart racing.

"I cannot let him die alone, and I cannot let my nephews and nieces lose their mother. I have no one, sissy. Please, if I am to die, I want it to matter. This way, it will mean something," Briar says earnestly.

"Briar—" Elena whispers, the sound only just escaping between her fingers.

"Please, I ask you this favour," Briar smiles slightly, her eyelashes wet still with unshed tears.

"Are you not afraid? You act as if you're asking me to allow you to take him for a stroll around the local park—" Elena chokes on her words, placing her hand over her heart.

I wonder if hers is beating as hard as mine, or harder.

"I— I am terrified, sister. But that does not mean I am doing the wrong thing. If anything, fear means I've thought this through, means I'm fully aware of the consequences." She exhales, and I notice her hands shaking.

It reminds me of my own hands, of the way I tremble, the way my breath catches when I am afraid.

Briar continues, "I am afraid, so afraid, of what lies beyond— and yet, I am afraid of watching your family fall apart more. I suppose I've been lying awake at night in my spinster's bed, thinking that life is merely choosing which fears must be overcome for the right of things. Pain and fear are unavoidable, so then I must ask— what is worth such pain? I think, as always, love is the answer," she finishes, and I feel my own eyes filling with tears, my heart slowly breaking.

Elena looks at Briar, speechless, before throwing herself into her sister's arms. I hear her whispering a muffled and devastated 'Thank You' into Briar's shoulder as tears escape her eyes as well.

I had said it, spoken words so similar only eight weeks before.

Have I forgotten so easily?

Real freedom is choosing what to suffer for.

Had I lost my chronic pain, and thought that the lesson no longer applied? Had I thought I was done, that my pain was gone, so my suffering was over for the rest of my immortal life?

Foolish. I have been so foolish.

I have been chosen for a reason, for my fortitude, and for my strength. I might not be Briar, but whatever our souls are made of, I see now that they are more the same than I had realised.

I would have made the sacrifice she is proposing, I am that person, even now. I had watched her story before and seen a stranger, but I find myself now looking at a past echo of who I fundamentally am now.

That is why I have spent the last eight weeks convincing myself that my duty to Aetheria is paramount.

If anything, the moment I am witnessing truly solidifies it.

This is why I was chosen because I am the kind of person with the heart that makes the tough choices, not the easy ones.

I turn to Morpheus as the two sisters hug, feeling empowered at the sight of someone I recognise, and not the stranger I had expected.

"I've seen enough," I inform him, and his eyebrows rise in surprise.

The memory dissolves around us like smoke at the slightest of whims, curling and twisting into plumes of colour and scent long since lost.

GENEVIEVE

The sunlight hits the frost-laden branches of the blurring pines with sharp indifference, rebounding and blinding me as I glance out the side of Lucien's sleigh, a beautiful yew bow clutched in my bare fist.

My knuckles are white, my fingertips flushed pink with the cold, eyes hawk-like as they scan the surrounding forest for any glimpse of the prize we so hungrily give chase.

Lucien is on the reins, his pale hair blown back from his angular jaw with the speed of our endless forward motion, his dark-scaled wings blending in with his attire. He looks regal in a black leather tunic made thick with furs that bunch around his throat, the many buckles, which fasten the garment around his muscular torso, catching the too-bright light and flashing wildly as I gaze upon the tension in his upper bicep.

The dogs are silent but for a cacophony of heavy panting and the crackle of paws compacting snow, the air clear and fragrant as it wakes my mind more fully than it has been in weeks.

I continue to watch for signs of the animal we are trailing, a rare white doe that has been eluding us now for miles.

I wonder if it's hypocritical that I should warrant the death of an animal just for my amusement, but then I am suddenly reminded that keeping the doe population in check isn't quite the same as slaughtering a dragon in cold blood.

The sleigh continues to race over the snow, dogs toiling endlessly beneath the cloudless aquamarine of the sky.

And yet, I am still uneasy.

I look to Lucien, who catches me staring at him. His eyes are kind in their cerulean intensity as he returns my interest with a fleeting

178

glance, his expression softening from steel to silk and back again as he turns his eyes once more to the road.

He straightens, and then his attention is drawn from me entirely as the heart-shaped snowy rump of the doe comes back into view.

I feel my heart wilt, though whether it is for the fate of the creature or the fact that my spell over Lucien seems to have broken, I can't quite tell.

The dogs, picking up the intensifying scent of venison, run harder without command, and my braided hair is whipped back from my face as we slide around a copse of trees, trying to head the doe off as she takes refuge within its pearly white cover, exhausted.

It is hardly surprising, considering that we've been chasing her for almost five miles, or so I'd estimate.

Lucien gives a silent pull back on the reins, and the sleigh slows to a gradual halt.

Hopping down from the cushioned bench, I give a hand signal, indicating he should take the left side of the copse while I make sure the creature doesn't turn back the way we've come.

I draw the yew sheath of an arrow between my fingers from the ornate quiver at my spine, loading it into my bow so I am ready to shoot on the fly.

Sometimes when hunting, if the tree cover is thick enough, I have been able to get an aerial advantage by stalking my prey from the skies.

This clump, however, isn't luxuriously thick, but instead sparser than usual. Mindfully, I tread with ghostly steps across the white blanket of snow, peering in through the meandering branches of trees dripping with icicles that hang like jagged teeth.

As I quietly pace around the circumference of the area, I find her. The doe.

Nestled among the cover of ivory foliage, ears pricked, her odd blue eyes spread wide as saucers beneath enviably dark lashes.

I've seen those eyes before— that mortal look of terror, but I think of it not as I draw back my arrow so my knuckles graze my cheek, take a steady inhale, and then release.

The arrow pierces the air, flying between several branches without brushing a single one. Then, faster than I can blink, the arrow has reached its target, striking the doe through the eye.

I hear the creature collapse, its laboured breathing from the chase dissolving entirely as a hint of rust hits my flaring nostrils.

179

Moving to claim my prize, I am stopped suddenly by something, another pair of eyes on me.

Lucien peers at me through a gap that runs the length of the copse, his expression strange and dreamlike.

I cannot help but smile, proud of my kill as warm blood rushes to my cheeks.

After a moment, Lucien disappears, and just as quickly I hear his tread approaching.

"That was a breathtaking shot, Gen," he compliments me, a little breathless as he closes the distance between us.

I flex my wings, straightening and feeling the quiver, cold and metallic, pinched between them.

"Why, thank you." I smile, smug as I brush a loose lock of snowy hair behind my ear.

"I mean it. You're just incredible."

Lucien comes close all of a sudden, closer than he ever has before. I find myself panicking.

He's taller than me, but only by an inch or so, and as our eyes meet, I see something there I've never noticed.

Appreciation, not only for me as a fighter, as a High Lady, but for me as a woman.

My heart races, and I wonder momentarily if this is how the doe must have felt, being chased.

"Lucien what are you—" I whisper, my voice caught in my throat.

I'm suddenly paralyzed on the spot, feet welded to the snow.

"Just, be quiet. I want to— I want to try something—" he implores me.

Removing his gloves, he shoves them in his pockets, placing one hand on my lower back, and the other on my jawline.

He doesn't say anything more but instead acts with more gentleness than I've ever known.

His lips meet mine, and it's like I melt into his body entirely. I have never been truly kissed before, not like this.

I've been pawed at and hungrily devoured, but I have never before felt such enveloping coolness, felt so safe.

I return his kiss with soft but eager lips, the taste of him quelling a burning in my chest I hadn't realized was there.

We stand among the snow, the landscape around us pure white, inhaling one another as our arms intertwine tightly. I anchor myself to him in this way, letting my warm fingertips run in elegant swirls across the smooth marble of his skin as his tongue explores the inside of my mouth.

I groan a little, wanting more than anything to stay standing on this spot, exposed but also more secure than I've ever felt, desire pooling in an entirely foreign manner in my stomach like molten rock.

The kiss ends, and we stand, staring at one another, before both breaking out into wide toothy grins as our hearts collectively flutter like caged dragons having been at last set free into the night.

The blue, heaven-eyed doe who had so enraptured Lucien at first lies dead among the trees, forgotten.

I'm woken from my dream by the familiar, yet newly light knock of Lucien's fist on the wood of my suite's double doors.

He seems to know that I'm not quite ready for him to come barging in using the balcony any time he feels like it as he has done so many times before.

I'm lying on the chaise longue where I'd fallen asleep, the white-lipped python curled over my shoulders like an invisible shall. The serpent slithers, curling around my wrist.

If I couldn't feel his scaly flesh against mine, I wouldn't even know he was there.

I hear the door click open after a long silence falls, despite the fact I haven't yet answered. Lucien and I have become closer, perhaps more so than we were before, and as he walks across the threshold, I feel my heart still fluttering from my dream.

"Hey, did I wake you?" he looks worried, treading carefully toward me as if the floor is scattered with eggshells.

"No," I lie, pulling myself up so I'm sitting upright against the back of the chaise longue, my jade green nightgown twisted tightly around my legs.

"Oh good, I know it's late. I just wanted to check in and make sure you were doing alright," he admonishes, brushing his long platinum locks behind his ear. I look him up and down, finding him to be wearing riding boots and trousers.

"Did Ebonara get to stretch her wings?" I ask him and he nods, eyes turning glassy with pity. It irks me, that look, and I know he must be thinking about Algoric.

"Yes, it was a surprisingly nice night despite the poor visibility," Lucien's voice is clipped as he drops to the floor and strips off his overcoat, revealing only a flimsy linen button-up beneath.

He loosens the collar as he leans back against the edge of the chaise longue, crossing his legs. I catch a glimpse of his tattooed chest beneath the garment and glance away so my attention is on the flickering hearth instead.

The sudden chill of his icy palm on the top of my right hand sends a small tremble running rampant up my spine.

Turning back, I find him gazing up at me from the floor, as if I were the moon.

"How are you, really?" he asks, imploring me with those deep blue eyes. I sigh, feeling my blood heat in a way that is uncomfortable even to me.

"I— I am lonely, Lucien. I am tired of the four walls of this chamber, and yet, I do not think I can face the outside world and the open skies without my Algoric. I'm sick with it," I admit.

Lucien nods, face marred with concern.

"Why didn't you say? I can accompany you. You know it's no bother—" He looks at me as if I'm stupid, and a slight venom climbs acidly into the base of my throat.

"I thought you'd be too busy worrying about Kairi," I say coldly, my face turning heavy and stony, so much so that I could not smile even if I wanted to.

I feel the snake around my wrist tighten, a comfort as its scaled flesh and mine press flush together.

"I am not worried for Kairi, Genevieve. She is safe, she is with the Equinians," Lucien reveals.

I scowl.

He said he was done, that he wasn't trying to protect her anymore.

"I thought you said she could look after herself," I snap.

The serpent slithers, invisible, onto the floor and makes its way toward the fireplace now, soaking in the heat as it listens in.

Folding my arms across my chest, I glare at Lucien, halfway between despair and rage.

He shakes his head, turning to face me entirely.

"She can, I just happened to hear from High Lord Gage that she had made it safely to Sapphire City. It's simply gossip I suppose that he felt I would want to know, that's why he brought it up. After all, not much else exciting has happened in the last week, things have been rather quiet, with you hiding away up here—" he admonishes, squeezing my hand and looking at me with an expression of complete peace.

I exhale heavily, the chasm in my chest that has been left by the dragon bond I had shared with Algoric screaming to be filled.

Even with him here in the form of a snake, it's not the same.

"Will you— will you take me out then, Lucien?" I request, and I wonder if he can sense that something about us is different now too.

Is he noticing the sweet yet rough undercurrent in our touches, the painful intensity of the way our eyes meet?

He smiles at me, caressing my knuckles with the pad of his thumb and I feel myself melt, the need to be shoulder to shoulder with him intensifying as his rich wintergreen aroma turns my mind foggy.

Spinning, I lower myself onto the floor so I'm sitting beside him with my back against the furniture and legs sprawled out in front of me, letting my head fall so it's lying on his shoulder.

He grips my fingers tightly, surely, and kisses me gently on the crown of my head.

"I'll take you into the town, and we shall go to a local tavern. I'll reserve one of the private rooms upstairs at The Drake's Heart and we can have dinner, and then a sleigh ride so you can look at the stars. How does that sound?" he asks me, lips still pressed against my scalp.

I smile, letting my lashes flutter as my lids droop.

We sit, side by side, perfect mirrors of one another, and I let myself wallow, reminiscing on my dream and the truth of what it has revealed.

"Perfect, Lucien," I whisper in return. "Just perfect."

13

PARADISE LOST

KAIRI

I LEAN AGAINST THE enormous pane of glass that spans the entire back wall of Morpheus' private studio, gazing out over the foliage that twitches lightly in the breeze outside. I stare into my reflection, still unused to the enormous wings at my spine, but that isn't what irks me. Now, as I gaze into the lilac eyes reflected at me, I see Storm more than ever.

The sun is rising slowly into the sky, a wonder to me as I realise that time moves differently when you're dream walking. I can't help but question how long I'd been sitting, my body here but nobody at home within my mind. It's curious, but the thought makes me feel oddly sick.

Hearing Morpheus stir at my spine, I look back to him getting to his feet from where he has remained, cross-legged, upon his cushion. He stretches as our eyes meet, gangly limbs seemingly endless as he folds them up over his head and then allows his left forearm to dangle loosely at his back where his wings flutter, iridescent in the bright glow of the spotlighting.

"So, did that help you? Did you see what you needed to?" he probes, stepping over the cushion where I had sat and taking large strides toward the window. My nose wrinkles as his pungent scent swims through the warm air between us.

"I— I think so. Is that really how she died? She sacrificed herself for her sister— so her nephew wouldn't have to die alone?" I query, astonished. I already know the answer but want to see him nod anyway.

"I believe so— yes," he replies, placing his hands deep into his skin-tight pants pockets.

"I see," I whisper, my voice becoming strained as I think back to the looks on the two women's faces, to how desperate they had been.

"I don't. I don't understand why the past, Storm's past, matters to you so? You're not her, that much is clear even to me—" Morpheus adds, and I feel my breathing become slightly shallow. The fact that he sees through me so easily is unnerving.

"Aliandara says, and I think she's right, that I froze up at my ascension ball in front of Lord Black because I don't want to accept the power I have now. That I'm trying so hard to be myself, and not Storm, that I'm displaying some kind of victim mentality in order to define myself as separate. I guess I thought Storm and I were different because her heroism came only after she was made immortal. The memory I just saw proves me wrong on that count and any other. Storm was a normal mortal just like me. She was not gifted her bravery, she chose it." I reply, thinking through the process by which my life has so radically changed in the last three months.

I have been abducted, tricked, undone, remade, and given a whole other past I couldn't have even imagined. Is it any wonder I'm so utterly confused about how to take my power back when everything that has happened to me has felt so beyond my control?

The only choice I did make, the choice to flee with Lucien and then stand up before Aro, got me, and by extension Algoric, good and killed for our trouble.

"So— Why did you freeze?" I ask Morpheus, eyes sharpening as they focus on his face. His brows rise.

"I beg your pardon?" he asks, tilting his head in affront.

"Well, you didn't freeze like I did, but you didn't fight either. The Fae never fight, from what they've been teaching me at the academy anyway. Forever pacifists?" I enquire, feeling my throat tighten as Morpheus' features become pointed, his lips pursing like he's just eaten something sour.

"Fighting is stupid," he shrugs as though he's a young boy being queried about being bullied at school.

"It might be, but you don't seem powerless to me. You have skills, and you're smart. You could easily go toe to toe with Lord Black. All of the Fae could, now I think about it—" I say, looking at him with a sincere half-smile. He doesn't return it.

"I won't be flattered into war, High Lady Freemont. I have never been a fighter. I am an artist," he reminds me, and I blink slowly.

"Even if it means your people become slaves to the Sephilim again?" I ask.

He laughs at me like I'm a naïve child, irritating me.

"You act like servitude is the worst thing in the world. If it were, do you believe the Nephilim would be so placid?" He brings my race into the discussion and it gets me thinking.

Why don't they fight?

"So, what are you saying?" I demand, placing a fingertip on the windowpane and trying not to look him in the eye, instead focusing on the mist cast by my close breathing.

"I'm saying that not everything broken needs to be fixed. Sometimes in life, you take what you're given, and you make the best of it. I thought you would understand that having been in such ill health during your mortal life."

This angers me, my fingers dropping to my side and clenching into a fist.

"I resent that. I fought for every moment I felt any kind of joy, any kind of real living when I was in such chronic pain, Morpheus. If I had simply let things be, I would have ended up suicidal, or worse, and left all those who I loved behind to grieve just so I could be free. Sometimes fighting isn't swords and arrows, sometimes it's taking your next breath, and then the one after that— sometimes it's doing what's best for everyone, and not only yourself."

He opens his mouth to retort, to say something no doubt witty and cynical, but before he can his attention is drawn elsewhere.

I follow his enraptured gaze, straightening as I push off the window and make a half-turn, coming to find Hypnos and another Fae I have never met standing in the doorway.

"Hypnos, My Sweet, how was the dress fitting?" Morpheus purrs, flitting across the floor soundlessly as he closes the distance between him and his lover. She blushes, her pale skin growing only slightly rosy beneath the billowing plumes of her white, cloud-like hair.

The Fae behind her steps forward, interrupting the couples' tender yet silent exchange as Morpheus reaches for Hypnos' ring-studded fingers.

"Not yet over." The Fae woman looks irritated, and as I take several steps over toward the gathering, I take in her appearance. Her features are Asian, with a kind of porcelain quality that is only exaggerated by the powder blue tresses of her hair that fall from a relaxed updo and in front of her pointed ears.

She's wearing the most incredible Kimono I've ever seen, the entire piece of silk coming alive with pastel foliage that's so detailed it could be real and rooted in the flesh of her body beneath. Her hair is decorated with several bejewelled combs, the pinks and blues of teardrop topaz glimmering as they catch the light. The stones, I also notice, match the hues of her wings, those of a Dragonfly, that shimmer, paper-thin, from beneath two slits that vanish discreetly beneath a bundled knot of fabric I believe is called an Obi against her spine.

The beautifully dressed Fae gives me a curious glance, prompting Morpheus to make introductions.

"Ah yes, Kairi, this is High Lady Kodiak Nguyen, designer extraordinaire. And Kodiak, this is the latest edition to the Nephilim aristocratic ranks. High Lady Kairi Freemont." His elegant fingers move quickly as he gestures to both of us in turn with an open palm.

Kodiak smiles stiffly, her eyes an unnerving blue.

"Ah yes, so it was your ascension ball that ended in bloodshed?" she enquires, tilting her chin up and brushing one of her sweeping bangs aside.

"You weren't there?" I ask, unsurprised as I figured if she was I'd remember. Then again, that night was such an overwhelming blur I wouldn't be surprised if I'd missed her or forgotten meeting her entirely.

I pray for the sake of not offending her that she didn't attend. Also, it would be nice to know there was at least one High Born Kindred who hadn't watched me gape like a fish at Aro Black.

"No, I dislike formal events very much, especially political ones. I'd rather be sketching or working with Alistair in the studio getting ready for the coming seasonal shows—" she admits, and I notice as she smooths her hair again that her fingers are entwined with thin silver wire that coils and whirls around her digits almost organically. I watch them, transfixed, before returning to the moment.

Nodding, I give a small smile, relieved I had not made a huge faux pas by forgetting her.

"So that's why you're here, you're designing something for Hypnos?" I enquire, and she nods only once but with undeniable enthusiasm before her mouth contorts into a kind of grimace.

"Well, I'm supposed to be, but we were rather rudely interrupted," she looks irritated, her wings twitching and throwing beams from the spotlighting in random directions.

"What, by whom? It's rather late— or should I say early now, for visitors," Morpheus looks alarmed as his thumb rubs the back of Hypnos' alabaster wrist.

"Come, they're here to see you," Hypnos says softly, turning on her foot so the robe that clings to her flares slightly at its silken hem.

She walks briskly from the room, leading the three of us down the long corridor towards the landing, which hovers above the far end of the open-plan living area.

As we reach the top of the spiral staircase, I look beyond the teal waters of the sunken infinity pool below, finding two figures I don't expect talking amongst themselves by its edge.

"Ember, Neve— whatever brings you here at this hour?" Morpheus calls with jovial volume over the twirling bannister as he bypasses Hypnos and begins taking the steps two at a time.

The High Ladies look at us, their eyes widening when they land on my silhouette as I finally reach the bottom of the staircase.

"What is she doing here?" I hear Neve hiss, never one for subtlety.

I take a moment to drink them in and find both women in long billowing skirts and matching corsets, one of tangerine and one of mint hue. Their wings are extended, erect, and beauteous in the clean light that pours in through the enormous windows, pooling over their delicate edges and catching among the thin veins of the appendages in crystal clear reflective rivulets.

Neve crosses her pale arms over the jewel-studded boning of her mint corset, cocking an eyebrow at me expectantly.

"Well?" she snaps, and Ember rolls her eyes.

"Easy Neve, we're here on an urgent matter. Besides, perhaps she might help us out by conducting us back to Lumeria?" Ember suggests, her golden lacquered nails creeping back over her shorn dark head as her plump lips form a generous smile.

It doesn't reach her eyes.

She's anxious, and I can't help but wonder why.

Neve exhales heavily, her breath misting as though it's a cold Arctic morning in December rather than the humidity of early morning Aramis.

"Fine, you're right. We do not have time. Morpheus, you need to come with us," she barks, the final word coming out as a feral hiss that shakes a dark curled lock lying frigid on her shoulder.

I watch her bare feet fidgeting beneath the partially translucent gossamer of her skirt, eyes darting between my face and the High Fae Lord, an odd anxiety blooming in my stomach.

Whatever is rattling someone as ferocious as Neve can't be good.

"I'll just be getting back to my fitting then," Hypnos nods at Ember and Neve before she and Kodiak depart.

I look after them, wondering why they aren't more curious to know what's brought the two women here in the first place.

Still, they're older than me. Much older. And one of them was a Goddess.

Perhaps this is but a bore to them by now. Perhaps such drama seems unimportant when your life has spanned across thousands of devastating wars and even more heartbreaking sorrows.

"You need to come with us right now, to Lumeria." Ember's eyes are fiery and luminous as she speaks with an utter and blazing conviction. Her tall willowy silhouette is glowing from the bright orange of her gown, but despite her bright and cheerful attire, her face looks like she may rip out someone's throat with her teeth.

My gut begins to churn, disliking the look of anxiety on a woman I have always known to be so confident and self-assured.

Morpheus turns to me, sensing the urgency of the pair.

His eyes darken as they meet mine.

"Give a Fae a ride?" he asks, ruffling his viridian mane. I smile awkwardly, feeling odd that now I have a skill these incredible creatures do not. Maintaining the mask of my smile and trying to cover the fear that is growing inside me, I shiver in my crop top as Neve takes a step closer.

I hold out both my hands and Ember, Neve, and Morpheus clumsily place their own hands upon mine, each trying to get as much contact as possible. Neve's hands are the most identifiable of the three by far, each of her fingers ice-cold and pale against the warm pinkness of my own.

I've never conducted three other people before, and it's probably the most any Nephilim or Sephilim can manage. Nerves flutter alive in my belly, and my palms turn slick and jittery as I taste the air for electric currents I might harness and utilise for my own means, closing my eyes and taking a deep breath.

"Well hurry up—" Neve's impatient growl is shattered by lightning splitting the air around us, cracking open space and time, and peeling it back so we might jump right through.

In the time it takes to blink, we are no longer surrounded by the humidity of Aramis, but the incredible fragrant gardens of Lumeria instead.

I hear the change, as the song of nature transforms from the teeming and plucky lusciousness of the jungles to the quaint early morning birdsong and buzzing bees of Lumeria's thick forest. The air is ripe with floral perfume, and I feel the lightest of breezes tickle my face as I take a moment to simply be.

I open my eyes, realising I must look a little odd as the hands which had clung so tightly to my palms fall away.

The scent of wisteria climbs around me in lush vines as I inhale, but then cough slightly as an odd undertone to the scent lodges in my throat and causes bile to quickly rise into my gullet.

I glance around me, eyes widening as I feel my instincts prick, like prey that has suddenly sensed a predator in the long grasses.

Then as I look, and I mean really look at Lumeria, I suddenly realise that something is well and truly very, very wrong.

LUCIEN

I return home in the crisp skies of pre-dawn, my wings grateful for the cool air that chills each vein that runs as a tiny, bloody river throughout their span. After hours on the floor of Genevieve's suite, it's nice to stretch them.

The sight of the house I had toiled to build with my own two hands is, as always, a comfort. I cannot help but dream of the confines of my bed, as cold as it may be without Kairi, and the oblivion of sleep.

After so many years of feeling a distance between myself and others that I could not explain nor breach, emotions have been unleashed, running both wild and close to the surface of my usually reserved façade.

I swoop low, righting my body several feet before the deep treads of my boots meet with compacted snow, the powder which is usually a stark white having become an odd periwinkle grey glisten in the half-light.

I don't shiver, but I recoil in a flinch as the mist of my breath comes into contact with my sharp cheekbones. Striding forward toward the porch, I feel well and truly bone-weary.

Removing my leather gloves from both hands I reach for the chill steel of the door handle, twisting it and letting myself in.

When I cross the threshold and am engulfed in the familiar scent of timber and the remnants of what has been far too many cups of late-night tea, I realise with a skip of my heart that I am not alone.

"Hey," Kairi says shyly from beneath her thick rows of eyelashes. She looks up through them from where she's perched on the second step of the staircase.

The door remains open at my spine as I stand on the threshold, frozen, wondering if I'm dreaming.

"What— what are you doing here?" I demand, my brain sputtering for the right words.

The very sight of her has disarmed me entirely, and I'm sure I must look like an utter idiot as I allow a blast of wintry air into what was an otherwise snug hallway.

Kairi shivers, and I notice she is wearing something I don't recognise, something which shows a lot of skin and allows me to watch as goosebumps rise on her arm and along her collarbone. Reactively, and almost automatically, closing the front door as quickly as I can manage behind me, I seal us and the remaining heat inside.

As I turn back to face her, I find that she has silently risen from the staircase and is right in front of me, the smell of lavender and something earthy, reminding me of the stables behind the house where I was born, coming over me in a wave.

I look down at her, her eyes brimming not with the joy I expect or the love I desire, but instead with a deep melancholy.

I cock my head, bringing my chill fingertips to her cheek as I search her for the source of her pain. She wraps her arms around my neck and pushes herself flush to me right there on the doormat.

I embrace her, inhaling deeply and letting the warmth of her body seep in through my clothes. I take a half step back, moving in to kiss her gently with all the tenderness I can muster.

The world dissolves, and all that exists is the taste of her and the way she makes my heart frantic and rabid within the cage of my ribs.

Too soon though, she shakes her head, breaking the kiss.

The moment is lost forever to time.

"Have you been waiting here long?" I say dumbly, my mind still reeling with the closeness I had feared may be gone forever upon our last parting.

"Not long, maybe twenty minutes. Where were you?" Her tone is a little accusatory and I cock a brow, amused. She realises how she sounds and quickly adds, "Not that it's any of my business, I just—" she stutters, flushing as she takes yet another step back, the space between us widening further like a cruel grin.

"It's fine, I was with Genevieve. We've managed to work through some things since you and I last uh— saw each other." I give a small smile, though it's at the memory of exactly how much I'd seen of Kairi last time we'd been this close, rather than my mended friendship.

She flushes, and I see the tips of her Fae ears turn red too, both of them exposed.

She catches me staring.

"I'm glad you and Genevieve are fixing things; I know how much— she means to you." Kairi's pause makes me wonder how exactly she perceives our relationship.

A small furrow forms between my eyebrows and I try to read her as she stands awkwardly before me.

"Why are you here, Kairi?" I cut to the chase, wanting to keep the worlds in which I am Genevieve's best friend, and Kairi's part-time lover entirely separate. The two women are not exactly the best of friends or even the worst of enemies. They just seem to sort of avoid one another with a mutual distrust that I suppose I cannot help but understand.

"Oh Lucien, I came here from Lumeria. You need to come with me, it's— well, it's better if I just show you." Her eyes are sparkling as she begins to wring her fingers, and it looks like she might cry.

I find her beautiful at this moment, enchanted by the depth of her feeling and the luxurious size of her heart.

She is more human than I've ever been, and I think that perhaps it's the thing I love most about her.

"Lumeria? What are you doing in Lumeria? I thought you were in Sapphire City with the Equinians?" I ask, stripping my jacket from my increasingly tense shoulders and over my wings before flinging it with casual finesse into the air so it catches over the balustrade. I uncuff my shirt, loosening the sleeves and rolling them up before shrugging a little to further loosen the collar as I undo yet another button. One of my tattoos peeks from beneath the thin white linen, and I find Kairi's eyes pinned on it as she distractedly chews on her bottom lip.

"Kairi?" I ask her, pushing a silken lock of hair behind my ear and frowning down at her, confused.

"It's a long story, and I'll tell you I promise, but we need to go," she implores me, grabbing my hand and locking our fingers together.

My stomach flips, but I can't tell if it's nerves from being so close to her or anxiety about what it is she's so desperate to show me.

Either way, I know I won't be in the dark much longer as her current tears my world in two.

When the blinding lightning has receded, and the crack of it has become but an echo in my mind, I find myself somewhere I had doubted I would see again this side of the century.

Lumeria, with its thick perfume of mixed blooms and warm calm air, surrounds me, my hand still locked with Kairi's.

It takes me a few moments to orient myself, but once I do it takes me exactly three short breaths to realise that something is wrong.

The scent of the place has irrevocably changed, and rather than being the gentle lulling musk that I have always known, it has warped into something putrid and sweet with rot.

My nose wrinkles and Kairi looks at me, watching my reaction as I suppress a gag.

It's then, as I'm gazing at her, that something alarming catches my attention. The sight is not startling because it is new, but because it is utterly uncanny in its familiar wrongness.

We are standing in the Rainbow Grove, except the name no longer rings true. The circle of Hawthorn trees are— dying. If they aren't dead already. And where once multicoloured veins of pure light magic had climbed through the bark like eager fingers, now there is only darkness. The blackened veins weep mouldy ichor profusely, the white-ish bark of the trees stained and flaking as their branches wilt like they've lost all hope of ever reaching the sun.

I turn, the silence of the woods suddenly eerie as though I've entered a place where me and Kairi are the only living creatures for miles.

"What—"

I go to take a step as I ask my question, but my foot catches in a slimy root and I stumble, losing both my balance and the end of my sentence as the rotting tendril comes loose without a fight.

I try to kick it off me, its roots exploding up out of the earth like a dead worm and thudding with a moist splash as it lands, lifeless viscera of the earth's rotting corpse.

I stare at it; at the way it leaks dark fluid into what had once been fertile soil but now feels like a swamp beneath my heels. The smell grows more intense, and bile climbs up my throat, latching onto my gullet like it has claws.

"What the hell is this?" I manage to blurt out at last, my outrage clear as I spin on the spot, looking to the shrivelled, brittle mesh of what had once been a healthy canopy overhead.

"We were hoping you could tell us," Kairi says, blinking slowly and covering her nose with the back of her hand.

"We?" I ask, looking for anyone else hiding in the fetid damp shadow surrounding us.

I find no one and turn back to her.

She takes nimble steps over the hardest pieces of earth, her slippers already muddy beyond saving. Her wings flutter, helping her balance as she picks her way towards the edge of the trees. I follow, glad to turn my back on the death that has infected the grove so completely.

How has this happened? I ask myself, brow furrowing deeper with each step.

Kairi holds out a hand to me as I reach her side, guiding me toward what counts for a path in these woods, but is barely more than a time-worn trail of flattened grass.

As we make our way through the trees and pass by more patches of rot, we also start to find healthier-looking forest as well. I crane my neck, and Kairi observes me closely as I find tulips, hydrangeas, and St. Anne's Lace coming into bloom more and more frequently as we weave back to the main settlement.

"It gets worse the further out you go, but it's been spreading quickly, according to Phineas," Kairi explains and I glance at her as we pick up pace near the edge of the city.

"They've been measuring it, for how long? How did they first discover it?" I ask her and she shrugs.

"That's the thing, this started about two or three days ago. Things just started dying, all at once, and nobody knows why. That's why they sent me to get you. They said you'd helped them with something like this before?" She looks to me like I might be able to fix it, and I feel resentment bloom in my chest, wondering how this has somehow fallen to me.

I cannot help but wonder if the Fae would come to the aid of the Draconians if a similar situation arose in Drakos Vale but looking into Kairi's concerned eyes quells my bitterness so I abandon my train of thought.

"I helped them with a case of wicked bad lichen before. This— I've never seen anything like it. I wouldn't even know where to start. Have they thought about torching it? Like doing a kind of reset in the parts of the forest that have succumbed?" I ask her and she sighs, shaking her head.

"That's the thing, Lucien. It's not just the forest— the plants, and the trees it's—" Her eyes fill with tears and her bottom lip trembles.

She doesn't finish the sentence, instead grabbing my hand in hers and pulling me after her.

It takes me a few minutes to realise where we're headed once we reach the main stretch of Lumeria's sprawling network of pathways.

The enormous trees loom overhead, the rising sun reaching dappled fingers of weak light through the canopy and tinting the world around us lime as it hits the lush healthy grasses on either side of the path. I hear the stream that comes to a bend a little way further into the sprawling city of treehouses and flowering meadows, but Kairi tugs me off the main path before we get that far, pulling me through the entryway to the tree that is inhabited by both the High Lord Fae of Light.

She doesn't falter as she leads me up the spiralling staircase, still strung with yards of pinecones and acorns just as it had been when we'd been here previously. Before I know it, I'm standing in the same entryway where I'd struggled to ask Quinn for sanctuary as he had fussed over lemon wedges or something.

With a sense of Deja Vu, my boots creak on the floorboards, but this time something is different.

I put my finger on it as my eyes travel the length of the twisting branch which forms the base of the decorative table central to the entryway.

The vase atop it is full of flowers, but they are wilting, dying as petals fall from the stem one by one like slow tears.

"Come on, he's through here—" Kairi is being unusually coy about what I'm to find as I follow her, and it's not until she treads confidently past the hanging chairs where I'd bargained for her life that I realise why.

195

She pulls a veil of thin vines, with tiny flowers budding every few inches, aside allowing me to pass beneath the doorframe and step into Quinn and Phineas' bedchamber.

The room is dim, and an enormous four-poster bed is lush with vines that twine between each of the posts, forming a natural and fragrant canopy of flowers of every hue you can imagine.

Staring at the bed, and then up at the glowing jars filled with luminescent algae, which are the only reason any of this is visible, my eyes are fast drawn to where a sudden wheezing begins to emanate.

The tempest of the ailment rises like a wave, and soon I find Quinn to be the source as it grows into a full-blown coughing attack. Phineas is at his side, holding his hand and Morpheus is opposite him, watching with a concerned glance.

I look at the canopy of flowers once again, noting the edges of silken petals beginning to curl.

Quinn himself is paler than I've ever seen him, his hair ratty and limp, teeth chattering, and limbs stiller than I could have ever imagined on the self-professed 'King of Spring'.

"Quinn— what happened?" Quinn's quivering lips part to reply, but Phineas shakes his head, pushing him back down onto the velvet pillows supporting him as another fit of coughing overtakes him.

"No, you rest. I'll talk. Lucien, Kairi. Come outside. Morpheus, you'll stay?" he asks with enormous dark eyes and Morpheus nods, puckering his lips.

"I wonder if it might be wise if I make one of Hypnos' home remedies. The ingredients are close at hand here in the forest and it would help him get some sleep—" he says, running a long finger down the sharp edge of his stubble-less jawline.

"That would be very kind. I'll be right back and then you should go and retrieve what you need," Phineas thanks him, swapping places with the High Fae of Night so that Quinn might be tended as closely as possible.

Phineas rounds the far bedpost, fingers tracing its curve absently as Kairi and I retreat into the living room.

As he emerges into the full light of the sitting area with its panoramic glassless window, I see that Quinn is not the only one who looks rather the worse for wear. Phineas' usually vibrant head of hair seems dull somehow, his eyes sunken into his milky flesh which has turned bruised around the eye sockets. His lips are pale and cracked, and his shoulders slouch, rejecting any of his usual majesty.

"Thank you for coming, Lucien, I didn't know who else to call. I can't help but think of that time you helped us with the lichen problem and well—" He places a hand on the back of his neck, eyes dropping to the floor under the weight of his fear. I cut him off before he can display any more grief, scared he thinks I have answers I don't.

"That wasn't this, Phineas. I've never seen anything like this before— it's not organic— this isn't biological— it's magical and you know it," I profess and Phineas goes weak in the knees, stepping back and slumping into the hanging armchair behind him. He places his head in his hands, sighing deeply.

"I know, I just— I had to do something; I've never seen him ill like this— hell I've never seen him ill, period. Kindred don't get sick, you know that," Phineas admits and I glance at Kairi who looks more concerned than Phineas and Morpheus combined.

I love the way she cares, and yet I wish she wasn't looking to me to be the saviour. I don't like letting people down, and even more than that, I don't like letting her down.

"I can consult some of the books in the library at the Academy, or perhaps some in my study— but I don't know. This seems like Fae territory to me—" I admit and Phineas sighs, standing once more and placing a heavy hand on my shoulder.

"I thank you for it. I don't know why I thought you would have the answer, it was probably foolish of me. I just, I love him, Lucien. I can't just sit by idly and do nothing," he explains, and I think then on how I would feel if it were Kairi. If it were me watching her die a slow and agonising death.

I had watched her die once, quickly and without suffering, and I had not liked that one bit.

"I will do my best to find anything I can among the archives I have access to, I'm sorry you're going through this. Quinn is strong though, Phineas. He will fight this, and you must stay with him through it all," I add solemnly, thinking of the woman standing beside me, the woman I would die to protect. I feel guilty I'm suddenly so relieved it's Quinn and not her wilting in bed beyond the floral veil.

"I should return to him, so Morpheus might go and make a tincture to help him get some rest—" Phineas dismisses himself with a small, sad smile and an unenthusiastic nod before he heads back through the curtain of flowers and into the bedchamber to be with his lover.

Morpheus exits shortly after, giving me and Kairi a sly sideward glance as we stand, huddled together in the middle of the enormous treehouse, out of place and options.

"You really think you can find something in Draconian books?" Kairi asks, sounding hopeful.

"I don't know, but it's the only thing I can do, so I'll do it," I vow. She pulls her body close to mine in one swift movement, clinging on tightly.

I get a face full of her feathers as she whispers, "Thank you, thank you for saying you'll help."

"Anything for you," I whisper back, embracing her in turn and finding myself not wanting to let go.

"I have to get back to Eclipsia, it's early. I have training—" She breaks the embrace and looks at me, delivering a blow with the hard set of her features.

"But— I barely got to talk to you. I want to find out what you've been doing— about why you came here. We need to talk more about this as well—" I stutter, trying pathetically to think of reasons that might make her stay a little longer.

"Lucien—" Kairi breathes, dropping her gaze. "Lucien, I'm sorry."

"Sorry, whatever for?" I demand, confused as she drops with a thud into the hanging chair I had once sat in across from Quinn. The chair swings slightly, her wings bristling the edges of the wicker cage holding her weight.

"What I did, what— what I took. I'm sorry. I should never have, not knowing—" She's red in the face and suddenly I feel sick.

She is apologising for our night together.

"Kairi. Please shut up." I retort, keeping my face neutral.

"Lucien, it wasn't fair. I showed you something you can't have," she confesses like she's guilty of some hideous crime.

"I said shut up, Kairi. I knew what I was getting into. I would do it again, a thousand times over. In fact, knowing that I might not have you for long makes me want you all the more. So just— shut up, please." I'm angry, enraged that she's treating me like some pathetic lovesick schoolboy. I can handle the pain, and I will suffer whether I enjoy her in the meantime or not. I might as well, given that it's far too fucking late and I'm balls-deep in love with her anyway.

"Did you actually just tell me to shut up?" she giggles, her shame melting as she rises from the chair with sluggish limbs.

I cross my arms over my chest, wings flaring as I tense my pectorals.

"Yes. And I'd do it again. For example, I'd do it when you no doubt try to decline my invitation to our first official date tomorrow night." The words have left my lips before I've even thought through what they mean.

I look at her, at her beautiful face, then at her beautiful body.

Merde.

"But I—" she begins, but I lunge for her, pressing my lips to hers and shutting her up the best way I know how.

The kiss melts us both, her tense body yielding to mine as our fingers become gentle yet inquisitive. Mine bury into her hair, and I end up stroking her cheek as I give her a stern look, our foreheads close enough to touch.

"You can pick me up at eight," she breathes.

14

THE DEATH OF THE HEART

ARO

THE DAY HAS PASSED too slowly, my anticipation for the arrival of sunset building moment by moment.

True, I could have just slaughtered Caleb and been done with it, but where is the theatricality in that?

Stepping out beneath the long awning leading to the front entrance of the Solis Castra, I pause to appreciate the landscape I've chosen, the setting that I've orchestrated so perfectly.

The sky is blanched with yellows, lilacs, and the faintest tint of bloody red around the edges of scudding clouds, an artist's palette of colour that will forever equate to this night as it is set into memory like stone, or perhaps even legend-like steel.

I am dressed in a black shirt, jet velvet breeches, and an onyx cravat that's clutched at my throat by a star-shaped ruby the size of a baby's fist. It is the brooch I bring out for my most anticipated occasions, as I find that the red facets bring out the glisten in freshly shed blood with a kind of exquisite effortlessness that should not be ignored. I let the pads of my fingers rub incessantly across the ridges of my palms, the weight of the amethyst sword on my hip causing the leather belt around my waist to sag considerably.

The gardens pass on either side in a whirl of glistening teardrops that reflect jewel tones onto the white marble of the columns supporting the awning, a beautiful sight, but one I don't have time to contemplate.

I'm a few moments late, of course, because what kind of king doesn't take full advantage of his right to keep people waiting?

Reaching the end of the awning, I let my wings stretch from my sides in a feathery yawn, the golden tinge of my otherwise onyx feathers turning bloody in the oddly warm light of the setting cobalt sun.

The crowd awaits down the sprawling steps, ringing the edge of the courtyard that usually receives carriages and incoming cavalcade from the guests invited to large local events. The amethyst willows that line the sterling silver quatrefoil panels of the gate stir, but only slightly, bringing a tinkling into the air that merges with the audible static rising from the falls to the east.

Eyes rise to my statuesque face as I take in the crowd, a mixture of important Nephilim and the majority of the Sephilim military. Encapsulating them as though they are concerned they may try to flee, Chief Landon John's men sit mounted on their winged horses with bored, brutish faces.

I take the steps at a leisurely pace beneath my freshly soled shoes, the crowd less than rattled by my arrival, irritating me immensely.

Soon though, that will all change. Soon, the disrespect will be but a memory.

The sound of clattering manacles rings true above the cacophony of everything else, but it is a few moments before the clanking of crystal and metal chains reaches the crowd. They stare up over my wingspan as I hit the courtyard, watching as Chief Landon John brings High Lord Caleb Abara down the stairs. His thick bottom lip is split like a ripe fig, weeping globules of blood down his chin. I have no doubt that he fought the Equinians with everything he had, which is in my mind undoubtedly sad.

I see the garb he had worn to Kairi's ascension ball crumpled upon his slumped form as he limps down the stairs, a tall and burly Equinian on either side of him, his biceps crushed in their grasp. The manacles I had heard long before anyone else do not sparkle, dull compared to the surrounding amethyst. I wonder if that's because it is sapping Caleb's power, or because the stone is just a particularly dull tone.

I step aside, folding my hands at the base of my spine as I draw them behind me, the lowest feathers of my wings tickling the edges of my thumbs. Caleb is shoved down the last three steps, his wings bound at his spine with steel wire that cuts against the bone. It's something I haven't seen used in my time among the Sephilim, but that didn't stop me from wanting to see exactly how much damage it could inflict when I stumbled upon it in Midas' vault yesterday morning.

Tripping, the High Lord falls to his knees, the aether-dusted marble of the courtyard ripping clean through his breeches on contact. His wings strain against the binding wire and I smile discreetly as an agony-laced grunt spills from his lips.

Several of the Nephilim gasp, adding greater dramatic tension to the air as Chief Landon dismisses the two men who have escorted the prisoner from his cell. I spot Silver among them, her tempestuous eyes sly as they dart from one High Born to the next. She chews on her bottom lip, wringing her delicate skirt in her hands, her breathing noticeably shallow by the quick motion of her corseted bosom.

"You're all gathered here to witness the public execution of High Lord Caleb Abara. Who is guilty of High Treason against the future King of Aetheria," I wait for someone to object to my claim, but the consequent silence speaks for itself.

Smiling, I continue, taking a step toward Caleb's slumped silhouette, still hunched over his knees protruding bloody through his breeches, his wings tied in such a way that he looks quite ready for the spit.

"I am extremely pleased to inform you all, that this execution is not to be like those that have gone before it. This is not only the public actualisation of a death sentence but a display of my power. I have been sitting on some information for some time, and I feel you will all find it quite illuminating indeed. If you had any doubt that I am to be your future King, I ask you to watch the events about to unfold, and reconsider those doubts carefully." I take a deep breath in, stepping forward and pacing close to Caleb. I notice him quivering and maintain proximity not only as it casts him in my physical shadow, but also to show that I do not fear him, nor do I think he stands any chance of attempting to escape.

I watch the Equinian soldiers among the crowd lilt as their steeds shuffle from foot to foot. They appear, even still, unimpressed.

Balling my fist at my side and allowing my knuckles to brush the pommel of the sword, I continue.

"For you see, I have discovered the secret Midas was so close to before he met his untimely end. I have discovered a way for us to take control back from the Gods and Goddesses who gave us this life. A way for us to redistribute the power they've given us in a manner more fitting to those who deserve it in the eyes of us— mere Kindred immortals." I smile wider still, stretching my fingers as I turn to face Caleb and, more importantly, Chief Landon.

"Bring forward the sword!" I command Leo, who stands beside another guard, awaiting my orders at the top of the shallow staircase.

The redheaded warrior nods, disappearing a moment before sweeping down the stairs in a stylish yet understated glide, his russet brown wings outstretched and soft looking in the dying sunlight as they slice through the air.

Effortlessly stepping out of the manoeuvre, I allow myself to appreciate his little performance as several of the Nephilim in the crowd bat their eyelids in a way so predictable it might as well be an evolutionary response.

The esteemed Captain, whose fiery locks and violet eyes become matte-like velvet as he looks up into my shadow, hands me the sheathed weapon, bowing slightly as he presents it.

I take the weapon in one hand, not two, at ease with the power it represents as well as the considerable weight.

Dismissed as I turn, I feel Leo depart from my spine with the stirring of the wind and the subtle sound of rustling feathers.

"Chief Landon John, step forward," I gesture to him with my free hand, watching as a surprised look comes over his face. I glance back at the crowd, giving them a wide and toothy grin, which a few, though not many, return with enthusiasm.

The Chief wasn't expecting me to ask him to participate, which is exactly what I wanted.

I don't want this to look staged.

"I would like to thank you for your loyalty to the crown, Chief Landon. I wish you to take this sword and deliver the killing blow to our prisoner." I say it, a stony façade falling over my face to hide my excitement.

I have debated this moment over and over, first thinking to take Caleb's power for myself. However, I realised that I need the loyalty of my military more, especially the Equinians. In sharing my new method of obtaining more power than a single Kindred could ever conceive of having, I hope it proves my loyalty to the pegasi riding brutes. Hopefully to the end of finally earning their undying respect and willingness to fight for my cause.

The Chief's thick blond braids have been freshly woven against his skull, so tight that I can see the pale skin of his scalp as he turns to examine the sword, lifting its weight from my palm and unsheathing the blade. As he does so, his muscles tense, indigo veins rising and becoming barely visible beneath the surface of his endlessly swirling tattoos.

The crowd gives a welcome inhale as the amethyst of the sword's blade hits the dying light of the cobalt sun, and I find myself admiring the handiwork of the blacksmiths I had chosen for the task.

They have done well.

"It is a thing of beauty, Lord Black," Landon compliments me, and I nod, satisfied.

"And she is not only for show, Chief. If you would please do me the honour—" I gesture to Caleb, who looks up at me, his eyes wide and empty as he shakes his head.

"Any last words?" I ask the treasonous bastard, smug as I pucker my lips.

"You will never be King, Aro. Never." He spits blood onto the pavement beneath him and I laugh, my shoulders shaking overdramatically beneath the expertly tailored seams of my morning coat.

"I'll take that under advisement," I retort, taking a moment to commit the image of him completely at my mercy to memory.

Then, satisfied with the utter hopeless resignation on his face, I look promptly to Landon.

"Kill him!" I issue the order, and the Equinian High Born wastes no time. Spreading his legs into a strong and balanced stance, he whips the enormous blade back behind him, readying to swing it as though it was made of featherlight silk.

I watch him carefully as he lets out an Equinian war cry, bringing the blade down within seconds and severing Caleb's head from his body in a single, merciless sweep.

The head rolls toward me, landing at my feet as the eyes, still open, gape up at me, his mouth still moving slightly in its dying prayer to Zeus.

The once majestic seeming Sephilim is reduced in my mind to little more than the wet fish he truly was inside.

In fact, it's a rather pitiful end for one of Zeus' chosen, even Caleb. Then again, perhaps he should have chosen where to place his loyalty more carefully.

That choice should have been given over to leaders with my conviction long ago, but then, I suppose you can't tell a God that. It would be too much for his pride to take.

I hear a groan from behind me, my eyes tearing themselves from Caleb and toward the Chief. His muscles are tense to bursting, veins popping and metallic ink shimmering as lightning sparks from his

PROLOGUE

KAIRI

I STAND AMONGST THE lavender, staring up at the emotional toil of the stormy sky.

The clouds pulsate like a beating heart, the surface tension of each gunmetal grey plume threatening to burst and shed its salted tears down over the thirsty summer soil of Hickory Oaks.

The cotton of my violet nightgown flutters around my bare ankles, the soles of my feet pricked by grass dry with the season and gold like the sun. My irises narrow to violet discs spinning around the orbit of my dark pupils as I take in the sky, endless and incomparable to anything man-made, utterly sublime.

As I draw in a deep breath, it strikes, vibrating up through my soles and rocking the core marrow of my bones. The thunderous rumble causes the surrounding field of lavender to tremble, undulating like a violet wave as a stiff breeze picks up, and goose pimples rise to attention along the length of my bare arms.

My hair is swept back from my face, my fear piquing as I reach up instinctually to hide the new Fae points of my ears, only to find them smooth and round, undeniably mortal.

Turning back, I find the familiar silhouette of my wings has vanished, leaving only an uninterrupted view of the fiery horizon behind me where the sooty outlines of galloping horses speed in onyx hues, untamed and unstoppable.

I reach for my shoulder blade, feeling the smooth skin beneath my fingertips, and shudder— The sky is looming overhead in increasingly insidious shades of charcoal mapped through with sharp obsidian edges.

A crack splits the air like a whip hitting solid ice in the valleys of Drakos Vale, startling me, the blinding light causing my heart to stutter in my chest.

1

Aro.

My mouth goes arid, and I waste no more time, turning on the ball of my foot despite the burn of dry grass beneath, taking flight in the only way I know how.

The lavender rushes past me, the once soft-looking blooms slashing against the bare skin of my legs and feet. The air tastes like electricity, the tang of citrus and iron tangible upon my tongue. It doesn't seem enough as I make my way through the seemingly endless field of purple, the farmhouse an empty beacon of shadow against the horizon.

The crack of lightning reaches me again, cleaving the world in two, making my heart rumble like the thunder that I know will soon follow, and my feet race faster and faster as underbrush skins the soles of my feet bloody.

I can see it.

See him.

His black eyes, those monstrously beauteous jet wings outstretched and ready to soar overhead, circling.

His lips twisted cruelly, his soul blacker than I had ever expected.

My spine aches where once he had cut her wings from her silken skin, from where he had assumed to make her his and his alone.

He had tried to cage me too, and yet— I continue to evade him.

Running, sprinting, panting, I fix my eyes on the farmhouse, the only shelter in view. But as I run harder, breathe deeper, I realise I'm getting no closer.

The field of lavender grows like a single moment that's been pulled out through a wrangle, wrung of every ounce of fear as it stretches endlessly in every direction.

The world illuminates and dims again with another lightning strike, and I realise that I cannot escape.

Stopping, my breath coming as ragged phantasmal wisps that flit from my lips and disappear into the dark of the sky overhead, I dare to look back.

Then I stop, my racing heart stalling abruptly as I inhale and hold the breath captive, eyes widening.

I straighten, then turn fully to face my pursuer.

"There is no escape from me," she says, her voice an English echo of what mine has become, her face a pristine mirror image of my own.

Storm.

I stand before her, seeing her wings outstretched on either side, glorious and glistening with aether. Her pearlescent gown is embroidered with fiery irises, decadent jewellery adorning her neck, wrists and lobes. The light catches within the dangling stone facets, blinding me completely.

As I shield my eyes, lightning forks behind her, and thunder strums the air hard and deep like the strings of a bass.

"I don't— I don't understand," I pant, straightening and trying to swallow my fear.

Above, the cloud ruptures, sunlight and rain showering down upon what had only moments before been shrouded in ominous shadow.

Her lustrous hair catches the beams, setting it alight in an otherworldly explosion of pure gold, a halo forming around her silhouette.

I stare up at her, trembling, as rain begins to patter upon the thirsty earth.

It leaves her untouched but hits my skin in large chill plops, causing me to shudder.

"What do you want from me?" I ask, feeling as meek as I sound.

She doesn't smile, her lilac pupils locking with my own and creating a momentary connection so intense I feel it in my soul. The breeze builds around her, ruffling her feathers, and yet the rain still evades her as I begin to feel the damp seeping into my bones.

"I want you to remember who you are," she says simply, echoing Hera's only too recent words back at me.

I wilt then, and as the heavens tip over with cold water, I stand frozen amongst the droplets and lavender.

With each raindrop upon my skin, I feel myself evaporate a little more.

Eventually, as I am slowly soaked through, I become but the ghost of a memory, and fade.

A SENTIMENTAL EDUCATION

KAIRI

I AWAKEN TANGLED IN hot sheets, my heart racing and heavy within my chest.

It had been a dream, but my body has yet to get the message. Even though I had turned and once again found Storm, found me staring into my eyes, I had thought it was him. The thought of him alone is enough to terrify me so completely I wonder how I had ever become infatuated with even the notion of him, to begin with.

Shame blankets me as I lie, breathing heavily among dishevelled pillows, long hair strewn out across the mattress in matted disarray.

I take a moment to centre, to compose myself as all good Nephilim should, focusing on the peachy mid-morning sunlight falling in through the stained-glass windows that rise high above the boundaries of gossamer netting set by the four-poster bed.

Aether sparkles as it dances in the sunbeams like fallen stars of the dawn, and suddenly something occurs to me.

Mid-morning.

I'm late, on today of all days!

I pull myself up so I am sitting, shedding the warm silk sheets like the cocoon of a butterfly, my plush feathery wings spreading on either side and stretching wide.

If you'd told me even a few months ago that I'd be waking up without throbbing joints and aching bones, I'd have laughed in your face while secretly dying inside at the unthinkable possibility of escape from Ehlers Danlos Syndrome. Now though, my freedom is reality— or fantasy rather.

My whole life is a fantasy now.

And yet, it isn't like I expected it to be.

As if the realities of our dreams ever are.

Maybe that's why, despite my lack of need for sleep, the desire has never been stronger to let go and simply float into oblivion.

I have been spending the time I must studying, the time I have left waiting for Lucien's intermittent visits, and the time in between dreaming, hoping for a glimpse into a world where neither I nor the Draconian High Lord of Hecate must sneak and lie simply to stand side by side, our fingers intertwined.

The image is vivid in my memory, the way his last touch had lingered like melting snow upon the tips of my fingers, each motion of his skin on mine as unique as the crystalline icy flakes themselves.

The pinkness of the surrounding alcove, which is draped off from the main common area of the dormitory, is stifling as I wipe my hand against the warmth of my brow, the poreless skin of my new face still foreign to me as the flawless silk of it meets with my fingertips.

I run my perfectly rounded nails through my hair, feeling them snag upon far too many caramel tangles.

I sigh.

I'm late, and I have a dead cat on my head.

Typical!

Swinging my legs over the side of the bed, I take a moment to watch the amethyst anklet above my right foot swivel. Then I hurry around the bulbous room, my wings brushing against the silk of the drapes and the flimsy gossamer of my bed curtains.

I had been blown away when I had first seen this room, first let my eyes take in its exquisite detail and incomparable grandiosity. Now though, I'd rather be in a cardboard box if I could only be there with him because I've learned the hard way that home can be no physical place.

As I approach the vanity beside the balcony door, which still stands ajar from my late-night excursion, I almost trip over my own feet, which decide to tangle themselves among the silken sheath of my white nightgown.

Jesus, Kairi. Graceful. Real angelic. I hiss at myself, stopping my fall by catching myself against one of the bedposts and giving a harsh exhale.

The breath causes several locks of my hair to unstick from my forehead, flying loosely like golden threads that had not so long ago been straw.

6

I scramble with a haphazard balance over the drapes pooled on the floor, hoisting the nightgown up to my calves as my wings ache with a sudden light breeze brought in from the cracked French doors. They itch to fly, to surf rising currents and dive from the tops of clouds made solid, but instead, I'm due in History class.

Slumping onto the vanity's plush velvet stool, I grab a rose quartz hairbrush, the weight of it once immense but now feather-like to my new Kindred muscles. Yanking it through my hair, I pull tresses into orderly and uniform curls that fall far past my shoulders and down to my waist in a torrent of rich toffee hue.

My pointed Fae-like ears poke from beneath the mess of my hair, and I sigh as I stare at them with a slight hatred, my disdain for having to constantly hide them growing by the day.

The pain of the brush yanking against my hair this way would once have reduced me to a watery-eyed, shaky mess, but it's something entirely more overwhelming that makes me feel like crying this morning. I am left now to recall the night before in flashes as I force myself through the numerous steps of my new morning routine.

I knew it would be hard, but I didn't realise quite how much.

Lucien and I, dancing slowly upon a cloud, not talking as we both knew what was coming. My head rested against the heavy yet reliable beat of his heart, I was spending every ounce of energy I had, refusing to recall dancing with Aro similarly on that night which seems both aeons ago and merely yesterday, trying not to mar our final moments alone together.

"Are you sure you want to do this, Kairi?" he inquired, tilting my chin to his and forcing me to stare into the deep blue of his eyes. His face was almost desperate, the chiselled structure of his skull only magnifying the intensity of his sadness.

"No. But I know I don't want more people to die," I replied.

Last night, had felt more like a goodbye than any other time I had parted from Lucien; it had felt like a betrayal too, but in betraying him, I'm saving Aetheria.

That is why I was put here, why I was reborn an angel.

My heart is broken, my insides numb at the image of Lucien's destroyed expression, the razor-sharp edges of his cheekbones becoming seemingly indestructible beneath the moonlight as he clenched his jaw and balled his fists, watching me leave.

We both knew it was a risk, that it was against the rules, that it was in no way going to end well, and yet something about the sentimentalist which thrives within us both had been unable to let go.

I have cried my tears, and though I can still feel his desperate longing upon my lips from the last kiss we had reluctantly pulled to a close, I have also spoken my last selfish truth.

I am afraid.

Afraid of failing the people of Aetheria, afraid that by running away with him I will start a war that will get him, his beloved dragon, and his people killed.

Most of all though, I'm scared that without all the obstacles, without all the rules, the cons, and the circumstances which have once again pulled us apart, I might have something real.

I don't want to believe that. I can't. Not after what had happened last time. Not after Aro.

Regardless, I will never know what could have been, and maybe that's a saving grace. Maybe that's not only fate but the Goddess protecting me and my heart from further wreckage.

And so, tonight, I will make good on my promise to that Goddess.

I will stay quiet as they make me a High Lady and bite my tongue as the Aristocrats of Soleus attempt to find me a husband who most definitely isn't Lucien DeLaurent.

The ritual of getting dressed as a Nephilim, to say the very least, isn't a simple one.

With hefty wings to compensate for and the fact I'm also layered up like a Russian doll in corsets, petticoats, and stockings, it begins to feel more like a long-drawn-out punishment than a basic daily routine.

It's been an adjustment, and I'm grateful that the corsets I've been wearing per the Finishing School's uniform policy are at least front lacing.

I'm aware that soon, as a High Lady, I'll be given a handmaid to lace my corsets for me, but for now, I'm enjoying my meagre independence.

I pull the topmost layer of the white gown embroidered with silver feathers over my head, and as the slight puddle train pools on the crystal of the floor, I press the fabric down over my corset. Then, wrangling my wings out of the slits in the back of the garment, still unpractised and clumsy, I sigh with impatience. I've been doing this for months, and yet despite the fact I'm late, I still cannot find an easy way to don the dresses without at least a little struggle from my new feathered appendages.

Finally dressed, I slip my stockinged feet into silk slippers and yank back the velvet drapery dividing my part of the dormitory from the others.

Eve and Delphine are nowhere to be seen, unsurprising as I'm supposed to be with them in class.

They didn't wake me, not that I expected them to.

The three of us exist in a kind of dance whereby we orbit one another but never make true and meaningful contact. I had been lucky last night that they had been out at some extra etiquette classes I hadn't been invited to attend, I suppose because a High Lady has far more freedom. It has made sneaking out easier, that's for sure, and I'm grateful they seem to have these extra classes regularly enough that I can make a date with Lucien and be sure I'll be able to take my leave without being interrogated.

Striding across the dormitory floor at a swift pace, I grab one of the history textbooks off the coffee table in the centre of the clover-shaped chamber and hurry beneath the high arch of the double doors.

As I walk the corridors, the scent of violets and lily of the valley makes me nauseously nostalgic for memories I'd much rather forget. Trying to ignore its floral snare, I focus on a few stray girls with free periods hanging around an ivory piano and gossiping, their wings adding grace to their silhouettes that I cannot see in my own.

Approaching with increased haste and growing tension in my shoulders, my feet whisper beneath the heavy silk of my skirt, and the group of immortal young women falls into silence, leaving many purple eyes boring into me in a way that's the farthest thing from subtle you can imagine.

I suppose I shouldn't be surprised that I feel a distance between myself and my fellow s.

They know I'm different, that I'm destined to become a High Lady, and that I'm Heirbound, no less, so one day I will be their Queen. They also know that I had run away with a Draconian and had faced off with Lord Black as a mortal.

It's true, they know these things.

But they don't know me.

If they did, they'd also know the rumours about me— the embellishments that have been made surrounding my reason for fleeing to Drakos Vale— are nothing more than fabrications.

It doesn't make my life here very easy, being the odd one out, the one with secrets and more responsibility than I ever signed up for.

I definitely don't feel like a High Lady - or even almost a High Lady.

In fact, I feel further from that now than I had as a mortal.

I turn several sharp corners that lead into more winding corridors, wondering suddenly why I feel so out of place.

Storm, me in another life, had lived here and flourished within these walls.

So why not me?

I woke in a new body with wings and the ability to soar, and yet my soul remains grounded like chains bind it inexplicably to the mortal earth.

My internal monologue, which is becoming more melancholic since my time here in the school began, is interrupted as I realise I'm facing the door of my classroom. On either side of the dark wood hang portraits of Sephilim fighting other Kindred, some Equinian, some Draconian. The colours are bright and the faces of each soldier divine in their righteousness. Something within me sours as I raise a fist to the door and knock, tearing my gaze from the lying canvases.

There is no escaping the past here or, at least, the past they want you to see.

"Come in." The Spanish accent turns the call fluid and beautiful as it dances through the air.

My heart pounds as I bite the bullet and lean forward, pushing the door open. It creaks loudly, of course, drawing a full spectrum of curious eyes.

Trinity is propped against an elaborately carved marble desk at the head of the small class of just ten students, ankles crossed, a book splayed open in her palm.

Black hair glinting, her head turns to me and she merely cocks an eyebrow, giving me no grace as the silence of my lateness echoes around me like shameful thunder.

"Sorry I'm late," I apologise, not realizing how breathless I am after my hurried journey here. My corset presses into my chest as I swallow hard and close the door behind me, then weave through a sea of unimpressed faces to sit at my desk. It's right in the back of the octagonal tower room, a stark contrast to the way I'd always planted myself front and centre at college.

Trinity doesn't give me the benefit of acknowledging my presence but merely picks up where she was before my interruption.

As she reads aloud, sunlight falls in voluptuous columns through the thin crystal slats of the tower roof, its apex home to an enormous crystal that catches the sunlight in its prismed droplets and flings rainbows in all directions. I glance casually over my shoulder at Delphine's book, which is laid on the next desk over before its owner, catching the page number and flipping quickly through my copy of the second-hand text.

When the pages fall flat, revealing their contents fully, I am surprised to see a face I recognise.

High Lady Genevieve Thomas.

In the watercolour illustration, no doubt drawn by a Fae hand, she is powerful and strong, more monster than woman, her alabaster scales jumping from the page as if they've been cut individually by a diamond-tipped drill. In the image, she's wearing a snowy white ensemble of scaly armoured panels and leather, straddling the enormous white dragon that had been her companion for over half a century.

Algoric.

Her agonised screams at his slaughter echo through my head, and the only thing I can do to make them stop is to take a deep breath and focus hard on what Trinity is saying, as I swallow down the bitter-tasting memory.

"Can anyone tell me what caused the Sephilim and Draconian conflict in the 17th Century M.C.?" She uses the acronym for Mortal Calendar, as none of us can be exactly sure of the years passed since Aetheria was first inhabited. The records aren't brilliant, which never made sense to me before I was a Kindred myself.

I do not know why, but something about being Immortal seems to make the accumulation of days and years less important and single moments more memorable, like scarce diamonds in an infinitely large field of soot.

I see Delphine raise her hand from the desk next to me, her nose tilting upward slightly as her auburn hair falls in restrained curls over one shoulder.

"Yes, it was the Draconians' refusal to help in protecting Aetheria from harm—" she says, voice weak and high pitched as her hands tangle within the satin of her skirt, rustling.

She sounds like a mouse, a misinformed mouse.

I grit my teeth, feeling my face flush at the notion that Midas' bid to subdue the Draconians was anything but an ignoble ploy to weaponize the beautiful creatures.

Trinity nods, but before she can continue, her eyes glide over me for a moment. I could swear she is trying to work out what it is I'm thinking, but before I could meet her gaze, a small cough comes from a girl I don't know in the front row.

She's petite, with dark hair and sharp white-lilac eyes that seem to pick apart whatever they land upon, hungry for flaws. Her back is poker straight within the confines of her white corset as she inhales to speak.

What is her name? Is it Rebecca? I wonder, having met so many new people recently, it's a wonder I retain any of their names.

"Yes, Raina?" Trinity asks, eyes sweeping from my form as though they'd never lingered there at all.

"Is it true that the Dragons could rip a man in two? That they're faster even than Kensari? Were you there? I've heard that you were, that you fought one yourself—" Raina explodes with this information as if she's been waiting for this exact moment to unbottle her store of long-accumulated rumours and idle gossip, most of which is passed from the women who work keeping the school's many corridors polished and pristine.

I knew the staff here were gossiping, but I didn't realise that gossip extended to politics.

Trinity looks at Raina straight in the eye then, and the words leave her lips.

"Yes, it is true," is all she says, and as the last syllable falls silent, I am on my feet, the elaborate baroque legs of my desk scraping upon the quartz of the floor. A sea of heads turn to find me, chest rising and falling far heavier and faster than it should.

"Liar." I breathe, watching Trinity's eyebrows rise in faux surprise.

"Sit down, Kairi," she says calmly, her dark pupils dilating as they challenge me with intensity.

"Not until you tell the truth. Dragons—" I begin, and her eyes flash a warning. I don't care though, and my wings begin to vibrate with rage against my spine.

If I'm going to be married off to some random Sephilim for the sake of Aetheria, I at least want people to know the truth of why I'm doing it.

I continue, "Dragons are kind and gentle creatures; they would never hurt someone intentionally. The fact is that Midas—" I begin, but Raina cuts me off.

"You expect us to believe that? Just because you're all hot and bothered for some scaly High Lord who has probably never looked at you twice doesn't mean you can go around telling people Dragons are like damn puppies. We might not be Heirbound, Kairi, but we're not stupid." Her outburst surprises both me and Trinity, who I expected to be the one to challenge me. Both our gazes twitch sideways to Raina, who is glaring at me like I'm a piece of dog shit on the bottom of her precious silken slipper. Her wings betray the adrenaline coursing through her, the feathers outlining the limbs vibrating ever so slightly in the jasmine-scented air.

Trinity sighs.

"Girls, enough. Raina, you would do well to remember that Kairi will one day be your Queen. I wouldn't piss her off," she speaks frankly, the language surprising both of us as Raina's ferocious gaze softens slightly, though more with fear than actual respect.

As I'm getting ready to respond, a soft chiming sounds, lyrical and beauteous as it wafts effortlessly through the thick tension building inside the room.

"Alright ladies, that's all for today. I want you to continue reading the chapter on the Sephilim/Draconian Conflict and ready yourselves for an oral test next seminar." She snaps the book shut in her palms, the harsh motion expelling a few glittering particles of Aether into the sunlight pouring onto the white marble of her desk. The gold embellishments shine as she rounds the surface, calling back to me over my shoulder as I gather my book to leave not ten minutes after I arrived.

"Kairi, I want to talk to you," she says gently, but it isn't gentle enough to stop Raina from flipping her hair back over one shoulder and shooting daggers at me while sticking out her tongue.

I sigh, rolling my eyes.

I walk between the rows of desks, mine still out of line with its fellows from where I had stood so abruptly, my wings tucking in tightly to avoid disturbing any others. I stand before Trinity, waiting in silence as the last girl leaves the room and closes the door behind her with an indiscreet bang.

"That was very stupid," Trinity states, not looking at me as she sits down in the chair behind the desk.

I don't know how to reply, watching without a word as she slumps back into the chair with a sigh.

"I disagree," I reply as she stares at me, her beautifully statuesque features stone beneath the golden shimmer of her skin.

"You would. You're young and reckless. You cannot simply—" she begins, but I cut her off again, raising my eyebrows this time.

"What? Tell the truth? Stop you demonizing the Draconians? Oh, how terrible, for me to be wanting all the Kindred to get along. I must say, I think you should reconsider anointing me High Lady. I'm such a very bad apple. Yes. So very evil." I ooze sarcasm, tired after the turmoil of saying goodbye to Lucien, followed by my less-than-relaxing night terror.

"You're young. That means you don't see the big picture here."

I open my mouth to protest, wanting to remind her that this isn't my first time around the cosmic merry-go-round, that I've been here before.

Before I can though, she's on her feet again, slamming her hands on the desk and letting her fingers claw. Her crimson-tipped wings flare out behind her, and I take a small step back as she pins me with her eyes.

"You don't understand the role you're playing here. Your people, The Nephilim, need to have confidence in you," she implores me, "You need their loyalty, or your crown is as good as a tin can. How can they trust you if you are telling them everything they and their fellows have ever believed is a lie when you undermine their elders and their teachers? How can their loyalty lie with you if they don't know where your loyalties lie? This isn't a game, Stor—" She begins to call me by the name of who I once was, or still am, or maybe never will be again.

I don't even know.

My heart plummets, tension leaving my body.

"Kairi— I didn't mean to. It just slipped out," she apologises quickly, her wings drawing back into her as she straightens and takes her weight from the desk.

I force my posture straight and nod.

"It's fine. Not the first time." I shake my head, letting the mistake roll off me and swallowing my hurt before continuing with as much poise as I can muster.

"I see what you are saying. But I can't lie either, Trinity. I refuse. I won't pretend like they're monsters. He saved my life," I remind her, wondering how dead I would be right now if it had been up to The Nephilim to protect me.

"You underestimate us, Kairi. If Lucien DeLaurent hadn't appeared like a shining white knight, you wouldn't have been left to die, let me assure you of that." She sounds sure, but it seems like a smokescreen to me. Big words to make me curtsey and bow my head like a good girl.

The Sephilim were wrapped around Aro's finger, so I know that they would not have stopped his plan. It makes me curious as to who she supposes my mystical saviour would have been.

I bite my tongue, supposing she assumes The Nephilim would have risen to the occasion. It is then I desperately want to ask how exactly needlepoint would have saved me against the likes of Lord Black and his enormous black-winged Lion, Ariah. Instead, though, I swallow the hatred I feel toward the female fragility here. Images of the sickly-sweet flowers, the frilly doilies, and the fine lace pools insipid in my stomach as I recall its incessant snowy purity. It sits there, burning like vitriol a moment before dissipating amid the fire that had forged me as more warrior than Lady.

I simply shrug, not sure what to say, wondering why they had accelerated my education in the name of anointing me High Lady as quickly as possible if what she's saying is true. They said they needed someone for The Nephilim to look to after what happened, they told me that it was of utmost importance I take to my new role as quickly as possible to provide stability.

Trinity is examining me thoughtfully, trying to work out what I'm thinking as she interrupts my wondering.

"I know it is not easy. But once you are anointed a High Lady, once you have been initiated into Nephilim society fully, you will see. You will understand why keeping the trust of your people and taking the advice of your counsel is so important." She gives me an uneasy crimson smile, and I can't help but sigh, struggling to stay angry at her for too long.

After all, she might be the closest thing I have to a friend around here.

I haven't seen Vail in weeks, not since she was last here running some kind of errand, and the other Nephilim I knew before I was re-born are out in the world of Soleus with the other integrated Kindred.

"Speaking of High Born, in particular a Draconian High Lord, is there anything I need to know before we go forward with preparing you for the ceremony today?" The mention of Lucien, of the ceremony waiting for me beyond this moment like a vicious buzzsaw designed to hack off my wings, causes me to shift uneasily on the balls of my feet, my pointed Fae ears burning beneath the elaborate drapery of my hair.

I gaze at her tanned face, at the deep purple hue of her eyes and her voluptuous lips, wondering if she doesn't see right through the lie I'm about to tell before I've even begun.

"No. I don't even know why Raina would bring him up. I haven't seen him since that day— when I was killed by Lord Black."

Uttering his name feels like speaking a curse aloud.

"People can be cruel, Kairi. I know better than anyone. Did I ever tell you how I became a Nephilim?" she asks, changing the subject.

I exhale slightly, shaking my head.

It's not exactly something you just ask.

After all, everyone here has a death story, and most of them are as tragic as they come. I expect a woman like Trinity to be no different. After all, the hardest steel is forged in the hottest fires. Hera had taught me that.

"I was drugged and raped by one of the men in my village as a young woman. Nobody believed I'd been drugged, even though I told them as much. The rapist denied my claims, denied it all, of course. Said it was consensual. Upon examination, it was proved that my virtue had been stolen. So, I stood amongst them and explained how if I hadn't been drugged, I would have killed the man. I would have died rather than let him steal my worth." Her eyes are cloudy as she recalls the tale, and I feel my corset pinch in a little tighter at the thought of such a strong woman being overpowered so easily.

"So, what happened? He went free?" I enquire, and she smiles a little, eyes twinkling as she strolls around the side of the desk, leaning against it with one hip as she continues.

"No. I told them if they didn't believe me that they should let me prove my ability to defend myself by letting me duel the man who had assaulted me. They all laughed, of course, because what could a woman possibly have to gain by challenging a fully grown man, except humiliation? I think it was almost a sick joke to them when they agreed that if I could beat him, they'd put him away."

She smirks.

"You beat him, didn't you?" I ask, feeling my cheeks flush with a warm pleasure.

16

"Of course. I was trained by my father in our outhouse at the back of our allotment whenever he came home from overseas. None of them knew that, of course. They also didn't know that my father knew to teach me to fight like a woman, not like a man. I knew how to use my opponent's weight against him in a way most men never even have to consider."

She flips her hair back over one shoulder, a smug expression of utter satisfaction resting over her refined features. I gaze at her, at the way she's so put together after having suffered something like that.

It gives me hope.

"So, if you won— how did you end up here?" I enquire.

She shrugs.

"Ah well, the men who vowed to put him in prison laughed their promise off as a joke. That night, he crept into my room through the window and slit my throat. Fear not though, I did not go quietly." She smiles again at that, though this time, the expression is far more vicious.

"Anyway, enough of this long-forgotten drama. We have more important things to think about. You become a High Lady today, and I do believe that I'm supposed to be accompanying you to the Temple to prepare. That was the agreement, wasn't it?" she enquires, placing her hands on her hips and straightening as she heads over to the door, looking at me over one shoulder. Her eyes dance, excited. It's probably how I should feel.

Instead, all I feel is dread.

They never said duty would be easy, but I didn't know it would cut this deep. I didn't know it would feel like I'm losing myself to who I was over a hundred and fifty years ago.

She beckons me to the threshold of the room, and as I abide her call, I feel myself slowly approaching a second threshold too.

Step by step, I walk with her, away from who I have always known myself to be and towards the stranger I once was.

2

BLEAK HOUSE

LUCIEN

I DON'T FEEL THE snow as it pelts my face, allowing my wings to billow like leathery parachutes from my spine as I bank left and then right. I glide, disinterested, through the coverage of clouds thicker than a winter blanket over the jagged teeth that rim the borders of Drakos Vale.

I'm numb to it all, everything except the heavy leaden lump of flesh in my chest that had soared so readily on the journey to Soleus and now weighs three times as much for one reason and one reason only.

Kairi.

I had known getting involved with her was against the rules; I knew it would end in pain, in heartbreak— at best. Maybe death at the worst. And yet I couldn't stay away, not knowing she was so close, not knowing she felt the same way.

After everything we've suffered, I thought I'd been through the worst thing I could go through, watching her die in the rain that day before The Temple of Zeus at Aro's casual hand.

I hadn't expected there could be something worse than her death, but the notion of another man making her his wife is enough to dwarf the event of her passing into a mere inkblot on my internal landscape.

I had trusted she would come back to me; trusted Hera would bless her. After all, I have never met someone so enchanting. How could Hera not choose her once again?

But this, this is different. Once she's married to another, to a Sephilim, she'll be lost to me forever.

And yet, she'll still be within reach—

The idea sends a shudder through me, and I cannot help but acknowledge the pain as I sweep across the stormy skies that hover low in an endless opaque shadow. It makes my entire body harden, wishing I could become a statue so none of this emotional baggage could touch me.

From the sky, I see the twinkling lights of Vega City, the early hours of the morning yet to breach the farthest side of the western mountain peaks, near Gemina Two. The icy veins of the river that run close to the settlement don't glimmer as they will beneath the weak sun in only a few hours. Instead, they lie pale, matte, and bleak as I begin my descent.

I could go home, I probably should go home, and yet the idea is repulsive to me as I consider walking around the enormous lodge without her. I had once loved solitude, loved being alone with my thoughts, and now I can't stand it.

Instead, I settle for an early morning stroll around the still sleepy streets of the city, the embroidered suit I had worn for my final meeting with Kairi still clean-cut and crisp, though my lapel is damp with her tears and the scent of lavender.

Touching down upon the ground, my wings flare out behind me forming dragonesque shadows on the snowy ground, and I feel myself exhale a breath I had not realised I was keeping trapped inside.

With the expulsion of it, I sag, brushing my long blonde hair from where it clings to one of my sharp cheekbones and chewing on the inside of my bottom lip, fighting the urge to simply stand here and wallow.

Instead of letting the melancholia settle over me like a damp and chill fog, I go for my second most used coping technique when it comes to an uncontrollable situation.

Fury.

I ball my fists, feeling ice crystals forming upon the love line that crisscrosses my left palm, the shards cutting into my skin with a delicious pain that keeps me anchored to now and unable to dwell on the empty future that lies unspooled at my feet like tawdry grey twine.

I take a step from where I have landed atop a sloping cobbled path that winds around the toothy mountains and spirals down into the clustered thatched roofs and wooden-beamed eaves of the city's shopping district, pushing onward with long and angry strides towards the town.

I kick stones absentmindedly, palms still curled closed as my heart becomes no less heavy in my chest but picks up pace, hammering against the inside of my ribcage like it's pummelling a punchbag from the inside out.

Then I realise it's not only the situation I'm angry at; it's Kairi.

I'm angry that she had declined to run away with me the second she learned she would marry a Sephilim and crown him King of Aetheria.

We had fought so hard to keep the crown out of Aro's hands, but how do we know that whoever she chooses will be any better?

I shake my head, dislodging several snowflakes that have landed in my hair and refuse to melt against the glacial skin of my scalp, knowing I'm not being fair. Shoving my hands into my pockets as I increase my pace, I grind my teeth, admitting what I don't want to.

She'll choose well.

I know she will.

That's what makes it even more unbearable.

She had lost her mortal life to stop the crown from being used to dictate this dimension. She wouldn't give all that up now to someone unworthy.

And yet, she still felt obligated to the Nephilim, to the Sephilim— to the whole aristocracy. She still believes that it's her identity, her destiny to suffer for the greater good.

She had explained she would not pick me because she could not be selfish. Could not choose her happiness over the happiness of everyone else.

Since hearing these words, the sentiment has been slowly driving me insane, chilling my blood substantially at the mere whisper of the memory.

My boots click against the frost-slick cobbles, the sound empty and cold.

I hear my own words echo in the back of my mind yet again as the scent of thick gravy and roasting meat fills my nostrils, freshly baked bread also among the concoction as the cooks and bakers of Vega City begin their day.

"Run away with me, Kairi." I had pleaded, sounding far more pathetic and more desperate than I had intended.

What has she made me?

A blunt sword where once I had been a sharp killing blade?

Or perhaps a slow-melting glacier perishing under the weight of its inability to stop the inevitable—

The sun is coming up, the claws of its weak stark sunbeams latching onto the horizon and streaking what had been a blanket of navy, silver, and grey. I let it coat me in a sombre half-light as I recall the look on her face.

Not only apprehension there, but terror.

Fear— of committing to me entirely.

Looking back on this now I wonder if I've overestimated our connection, if I'm only dreaming when I think she could stand at my side.

After all, no woman I've ever truly desired has ever wanted me, so why would she be any different?

Genevieve had always teased me about having high standards when it came to women, but the truth is I've always been scared. Scared of loving someone at long last and having my heart shattered.

I hadn't known this before Storm, before Kairi— I hadn't known I was so afraid of really being seen— being appraised and judged.

I feel deeply and with a passion that I find myself unable to quell. That makes me too vulnerable, the fact I have to live with the rejection for eternity seemingly too awful to risk even a glimpse of the devastation.

I stare in through leaded windowpanes, the dark diamond patterns interrupting my pale reflection. I'm fragmented in the image, and it mirrors how I feel inside. Half of me terrified to hold on to the way I feel about Kairi, the other half of me terrified to let go.

I'm stuck, and as I pass a Draconian jeweller, I'm caught staring at engagement rings that sit within the confines of leather boxes lined in plush velvet.

Would I ask for her hand?

For forever?

After so little time?

Yes, my consciousness screams.

"Don't be so ridiculous," I mutter under my breath as I turn my back on the window and continue walking through the city's central district.

Passing by several closed carts, which usually sell roasting chestnuts or fresh coffee, I come next to the main courtyard, the statue of Hecate and Nemesis glinting and crowned with fresh frost.

Even this place is tainted, the capital city of my home continent contaminated with the faded memory of lavender in the air and light blue eyes wide with wonder at every detail I'd long since failed to notice.

I round the corner of the statue, looking up into Hecate's face, the stoniness of it fitting how I feel exactly.

"Why did you do this? Why do I love her? She's not mine to love," I say aloud, my bitter tone echoing out into the cold morning air and startling me as several ash-white doves with silver beaks scatter. The truth hurts more than I want to admit.

I had risked it all for her, had betrayed someone I've loved deeply as a friend for more than one hundred and fifty years.

Genevieve and I haven't spoken, not since Algoric's death.

Not that I haven't tried.

I turn from the statue, casting my shadow upon the Goddess that had given me immortal life, knowing I will find no answers here.

I can't stop Kairi from marrying a Sephilim, not if it is what she intends to do. Not if she feels it is her duty and destiny.

But— I can fix things with Genevieve. Or at least I can try anyway.

I just hope that, after two months of constantly trying to apologise and being turned away by High Lord Gage, she'll let me in.

The Astrid Keep lies nestled within the silhouette of Gemina One, its peak made glorious and ominous as the sun casts its light onto the slate inclines, setting the white tip alight.

I dive between layers of cloud, finding guards posted seemingly randomly throughout the airspace, though I know they're anything but. Alone, and to an individual, they seem random, but from an aerial vantage far higher than mine, you'll find them crisscrossed in a pentagram, surrounding the Keep's summit.

Their armour emits a dull silver glow as the dawn drenches their dragonsfire-forged steel helmets, each scale pronouncing itself against the rest. The soldiers are stationed without dragons, unsurprising but also foolish in my opinion. The rest of Aetheria knows that the long-forgotten creatures still exist, that they did, in fact, not go extinct. Not utilising them only makes us more vulnerable than is necessary, and though nobody has seen sight nor sound of Lord Aro Black, that doesn't mean he's not out there, plotting his revenge and lying in wait.

Yet Genevieve will not risk losing another dragon, not after Algoric.

It had been my fault.

I dragged both her and the dragons into the political mess of Kairi's escape from Soleus and the clutches of Lord Black. I had saved her, but it had a steep price, and it had never occurred to me that the price wouldn't be mine to pay.

Genevieve and I have always been close, and now I'm left feeling as though I'm not only heartbroken by Kairi's future engagement but also like I'm missing a left arm with Genevieve's too-noticeable absence.

I made a point of saving Kairi, and in saving her, yet another point became abundantly clear.

I would put my personal quests before my people, before the greater good, and before Drakos Vale.

Maybe I had not been the one to plunge an amethyst sword into Algoric's skull, but I might as well have been.

The sound of his dying cries still haunts whatever dreams I manage to find these days, the memory of watching such a powerful creature perish causing a detestable shiver to run up my spine in an unstoppable cycle of disgust and disbelief.

I descend, relishing the distraction of more physical discomfort as the wind tears into me on my left side, causing me to compensate by diving toward the balcony at a different angle than I'm used to.

I approach too fast, hair whipped back from my face, ears popping uncomfortably, and instead of landing on top of the railing I'm aiming for, I slam into it with my chest.

"Graceful. I can see what the angel sees in you." High Lord Gage's voice drips with sarcasm, but I ignore it, wrapping my fingers tightly around the delicate filigree of the railing and breathlessly hauling myself up and over.

I collapse onto the floor, snow slurry pouring off my wings and onto the stone where it joins a slick lake of chill melted flakes. I look up to find the long-legged High Lord Gage Lee smirking at me and flashing several of his metal teeth. He's resting in a steel chair with his feet propped on a small matching table, his wing covering the book in his palm and protecting it from the snow. His dark hair though is speckled with the stuff, his face glacial as he reads me without subtlety.

"Well, aren't you just radiating joy and happiness today, Lord De-Laurent." Gage's tone irks me as I exhale heavily, pulling myself to my feet.

My ass is wet from the floor, causing an uncomfortable damp patch to spread down each of my legs.

Gage had been my student, and not long ago he had idolised me. Now he's lost all respect, finding me deplorable for my betrayal of Genevieve in her vengeance.

He doesn't understand why I did it, why I didn't order a retaliation attack, but why should he? He's young, and I still barely understand how I had made such a decision even eight weeks on.

"Good morning, Lord Lee." I use his proper title, knowing that I should afford him respect even if I don't receive it in return. I bow my head, my white hair falling in damp and bedraggled tresses across my face as I brush down my thighs and tuck my wings behind me.

"If you're here to see her, I can tell you that you're shit out of luck," Gage states, looking up almost unwillingly from the page he's reading.

"Look, I know that I screwed up. I just want to apologise," I say, my words coming out breathlessly. I've rehearsed this scene a hundred times in my head when I lie awake at night, restless.

I didn't quite account for flying into the balcony first though.

In my dreams, I'm far more composed.

"Lucien. She is done. Done. As in, she would rather talk to a Sephilim than to you. I'm not letting you in to see her, and not because I'm trying to be an asshole. I have opinions about your actions, but I do not hate your guts. Genevieve, on the other hand, well, I'm an empath, so I suggest you listen to me before I end up having to clean your entrails off the malachite." He looks deeply into my eyes, and I feel him poking around in my mind, scanning my response as I weigh up how to react.

I chew the inside of my cheek, sighing.

"Fine, I'll go. But this isn't over," I retort, stiffening as I make the vow, and Gage gives me a tired glance. I square my shoulders, defiant, but he just sighs.

"It is, Lucien. Let go."

This comes, not as a command, but as a plea.

Feeling untethered, as though I have no real home to return to any longer, I spread my wings and allow them to pump, harnessing the wintery air and rising once more into the dull morning sky. It seems endless and lonely as I pass by statuesque and unfeeling soldiers who had once respected me and who I thought I was.

It turns out home isn't a place at all, and the two women I had thought I could always find comfort with are falling away from me like dead stars, collapsing in on themselves and leaving only dark silence behind.

GENEVIEVE

I lie beneath the surface of the tepid bathwater like a viper lying in wait, eyes closed as I taste the air of the bathroom around me. As I float weightlessly, my mind wanders to a place where the universe is fair, and where the cavernous and gaping hole in my chest can be filled by molten hate alone. I run my fingers over the tips of my wings that are folded beneath me in the enormous egg-shaped tub, wishing I was touching Algoric's beautiful face instead.

In my mind though, the image of his wise and gentle gaze has been replaced by one of him lifeless, rivulets of silver blood gushing from the wound in his skull and pooling upon the rain-slick cobbles before The Temple of Zeus.

I am not okay.

And so, I sink deeper into my fantasy of vengeance.

I'm standing atop the peak of Gemina One, air flying in whirling icy blades around my form, snow whipping through my hair and melting on contact, sizzling against my scalp. My green eyes flash in the golden moonlight as they land on his bastard silhouette, the form of him dark as sin against the thick blanket of cloud that surrounds us.

It's just him and me.

His rigid, unfeeling cold against my scalding rage.

The snow beneath my bare feet evaporates in a sibilant hiss, and he turns, those blackened pools of deep indigo sparking maliciously like flint hitting steel.

I waste no time, leaping forward into the storm that divides us and spreading my talons wide, engorging my shadow as it falls across Lord Black's face.

He shuts his eyes against the vicious bite of the cold, his armour a blackened version of the jaundiced gold of the other Sephilim, as though everything he touches he taints.

I wrap a gloved hand around the hilt, pulling my ruby-handled sword from the sheath strapped across my back. Water droplets settle on the broad width of the weapon and trickle down in slow, reflective torrents.

He launches himself upward as well, drawing the amethyst sword he had used to kill Algoric. His lips spread wide in a feline grin, locks wild around him as his dark wings sprawl out into the night and aid him in rising fast through the clouds.

I don't give him a chance to escape, heart pounding as adrenaline courses through me like an uncontrolled blaze, blood simmering gently just beneath the skin.

Rising fast and behind the cover of cloud, I look down on him like a bird of prey ready to dive.

As he reaches a height ten feet below me, I freefall the distance between us, clinging on to my sword and clenching my teeth as a visceral growl escapes the back of my throat.

Our blades clash as he raises his sword a moment too late, the weight of my attack forcing him off balance. He falls through the sky in an uncontrolled spiral of inky locks and steel feathers.

The clang of the two swords meeting in mid-air echoes off the clouds like thunder as I dive, pulling my wings in tight behind me to speed my descent, a dart racing toward the continent I have sworn to protect.

I glimpse him again quickly as he tumbles in and out of an aether-thick cloud, his silhouette leaving momentary punctures clean through them as he tries to catch himself, wings flailing.

Taking a deep breath of air pungent with wintergreen and the fading sickly sweetness of lilacs, I speed up my pursuit, my enormous wings relishing the thrill of diving at such high speed.

I've missed riding Algoric, missed feeling the untouchable speed of his enormous wingspan.

Lord Aro Black is the reason why, and now he must pay.

I gain on him, sword drawn back in one arm, other outstretched in a claw as I grab him by the tip of his wing, halting his descent and yanking him up by the feathered appendage without mercy.

His face goes slack as he sees me drawing the sword, but suddenly, it isn't enough.

Death by a blade this long isn't nearly personal enough, isn't nearly painful enough.

I let us fall then, like a stone through water, watching the jaws of Drakos Vale rise to swallow us as we hit the ground with an enormous thud.

Snow rises and disperses in a large circumference around the point where my feet touched the ground with immense force, a shockwave of biting cold.

Aro lies there, sprawled on the floor beneath my merciless gaze, the wing I had grabbed seemingly broken or at least sprained. His eyes go hollow as I drop the sword in my palm, letting it fall to the ground with a clunk.

He goes to raise his weapon with futile determination as I kick it aside with my free foot, kneeling atop him and pinning him to the earth. He could conduct, and I know it, but something about his gaze says he'd rather try and beat me through sheer physical prowess alone.

I don't give him the chance, grabbing an athame hooked through my belt and stabbing him straight through the eye socket.

He cries out, his agony a sick thrill.

I feel the back of the orifice and halt, pulling back and relishing the jellied massacre that comes along with it.

I shove the blade between his lips then, pressing down on his chest with all my weight and slipping his own dismembered eyeball in between his lips.

Choke on it. On your perverted view of a world trapped in your orbit and yours alone, I think as steam begins to rise around us from where I've come into contact with the snow.

He whimpers, causing me to smile as I whip back the blade, cutting the side of his mouth gaping wide and then slashing his carotid clean through in a single vicious swipe.

I watch as the blood pours, mixing with sizzling snow, and at last, I feel myself released.

Slumping onto my heels atop his still-warm corpse, I let my head hang back and scream to the sky.

"Genevieve!?" I hear Lord Gage's voice echo out as I reach the climax of my fantasy, my hand firmly planted between my legs, right at the tender apex of my thighs.

The door flies open, breaking the magic of my fury.

My eyes snap open, and as I am about to question what the hell he's doing interrupting my private bath, I see why he's standing there— looking at me with wide eyes.

The entire bathtub is foaming, the water at boiling point as it jumps out of the tub and splashes loudly onto the floor. The resulting puddle has spread from the tub and sprawls across the entire bathroom and under the door.

I guess that's how Gage knew to burst in.

I have done this before, but never unintentionally.

I mean, who wouldn't utilise my powers to keep the bath a little warm during such miserable winters?

I place my hands on both sides of the tub, inhaling the smell of jasmine oil, which lingers, slightly burnt, in the air.

Hoisting myself up, I take another deep breath, letting my wings surface from beneath the waterline and trying to calm myself as I lean back into their familiar leathery hold.

My skin is probably the closest to a tan I'll ever get, and I watch as the energy surging through the water slowly dies down, the bubbles ceasing as the temperature falls, and the contents of the bath fall still, steam rising slowly and in tendrils that caress my flush face.

"Are you alright?" Gage asks me, looking extremely concerned. I almost want to laugh.

I mean, it's not as if the heat can hurt me; I am too resilient for that now.

"Don't you knock?" I growl, frustrated and immodest as I get up out of the water and step out, stark nude.

Gage blushes, grabbing me a towel from the rail beside him and handing it to me whilst turning his head, averting his eyes.

As I reach out to take the jade cotton in my fingers, they brush his and he gasps, flinching away at the scalding flesh. The towel drops between us, but I snatch it out of the air before it can fall, trying very hard to quell the fire in my blood.

"There was— there was water coming from under the door—" he stutters as I wrap the towel haphazardly around me, hoping that my damp skin will cool before it dries. Whenever I dry myself and I'm angry, the fabric turns crispy and sharp like tiny thorns.

"And why were you sneaking around in my room? I thought you were keeping guard on the balcony?" I snap at him again, running my long nails back against my scalp where my white hair is plastered to my skull, dripping rivulets down the sensuous arch of my spine.

"Yeah, about that. Lord DeLaurent made an appearance. Again." He gives me a look that confuses me as I feel him probing around in my subconscious for an emotional response.

In reply to this, I let my anger flare slightly once more, marching clean past the High Lord through the swill on the floor and into my bedchamber with a defiant tilt to my chin.

He knows my feelings about Lucien. That is why I had asked him to sit on my balcony in the sleet.

"Have you considered hearing him out?" Gage asks, swinging around on the ball of his foot and following me into the room as I plop down on the side of the bed, the tips of my alabaster scales catching the sheets beneath me. I stare at the bathwater as it slowly laps at the edge of my bedside rug, soaking it through.

"You already know what I'm going to say— so why do you insist on continuing to prattle on? Merde." I cuss him under my breath as he puckers his full lips, contemplating whether to pry further. I shoot him a warning glare as I reach for the bottle of cooling peppermint moisturiser, unscrewing the citrine crystal lid before tipping it up in my palm.

The lotion comes out in a thick dollop, and my head snaps up, eyes piercing the High Lord, who is watching me closely.

"What are you still doing here?" I bite at him, and he scowls, stiffening inside his suit. Slowly, I begin applying moisturiser to my upper arms, a daily and much-needed ritual due to the immense heat just below the surface.

"It's just that—" he begins again, but something else catches my ears, making his twaddle entirely irrelevant.

Gen— The voice is familiar, and my heart stops in my chest, suddenly stone cold.

"Get out!" I bark at Gage, shoving him aside as I rise quickly to my feet and let the towel drop to the floor. Gage emits a sigh and rubs his forehead before following orders and leaving the room.

A gust of wind blows into the suite as he returns to the balcony, chilling me. My skin heats in retaliation, the remaining bath water evaporating into the air before cooling as condensation and clinging to the malachite walls and floor.

I stand, trying to hear over the gale, and then it reaches me again, riding the tail of the breeze.

Genevieve.

It echoes around my skull like a heavy and intoxicating mist, and I chase it, trying to cling onto it as though it's my last breath.

I sweep the room, throwing open a gilded silver chest at the foot of my bed and pulling out a sheer silk robe in crimson. I slip it over my shoulders, the skin on the back of my neck rising in a ripple of nostalgia. I glance at the dragon brand on the inside of my wrist as I dress with haste, surer that the voice belongs to Algoric than I want to admit. After all, it's been two months. I have not been that long without talking to him in almost 500 years.

Genevieve—

It is him. I'm sure of it now.

I burst out of my suite and into the chill of the corridor beyond, ignoring the guards surrounding my door, who look shocked at my sudden appearance.

My hot soles slap against the crystal of the floor as I descend the spiralling corridors through the Astrid Keep, overwhelmed with the scents of Drakos Vale that I have missed, having rarely left my room lately.

The abandoned cold of the throne room isn't lost on me once I reach it, my blood pounding around my body like a call to war.

Gen—

It's there again, like a wisp of smoke too fast for me to catch.

I need to find the spark, the source of the blaze.

Running across the throne room floor, the place has been unused for eight weeks except for access to the lower levels, and I find dust upon the ivory throne at the head of the chamber. The vaulted ceilings loom overhead as the sconces that line the walls remain unlit and shrouded in veils of gossamer cobwebs.

I let my fingernails, filed into sharper points than I've ever donned before, bite into the flesh of my palm, feeling the blood spill with a small sigh that escapes my lips and clouds as it hits the cool air in front of my face.

I hold out my palm over the hematite seal in the floor, Hera's crest stamped clearly into the metal, before stepping onto it without pause.

The seal grinds against the surrounding stone as it descends into the cavernous catacombs beneath the throne room, and my heart refuses to still as it beats like a prisoner against the inside of my ribs.

I leap from the makeshift elevator before it even halts, my bare feet causing small puffs of dust to rise from the floor. This minute detail alone takes me back too readily, reminding me of how the snow had billowed out from me in my murderous fantasy. The scent of furnaces, smouldering coal, molten metals, and perspiration hits me as I hear the blacksmiths beginning their day.

I fly past them as they raise their heads, sensing my presence as the thin robe I have shrouded myself with clings to my long, skeletal limbs.

I haven't been eating in my grief, and I wonder momentarily if I look weaker in their eyes.

The thought fills me with dread, but then a soothing response comes from within.

Genevieve—

My name. Only ever my name. Repeatedly beckoning me like the homey hearth I had so longed for in mortal life but had found only within the chest of a dragon.

The walls and ferociously lit clawed sconces pass me in a blur as I ruthlessly pursue the sounds dancing within the emptiness Algoric had left behind. I hold my breath as I turn the corner into where he had once taken up residence, trapped by the cruelty of those too prejudiced to understand that even a dragon could be gentle.

Before the full chamber comes into view— I close my eyes, saying a silent prayer to Hecate as my heart practically turns to stone.

Nothing.

Only an empty cavern and some long cold steel chains lying in the centre of the room.

My heart shatters all over again, the sharp pieces of its once fractal whole tearing at my soul and leaving my essence with edges more jagged than any serrated blade.

I take a few steps forward and wait— willing the voice to return.

Nothing.

Turning on the spot, I find myself staring at the shackles as I rotate a full circle, the emptiness and silence of the cavern ominous and gutting.

The sight of the steel bindings, not just of their emptiness but of their mere existence, opens up a void inside me, the shadows of my grief growing long as the flame of my momentary hope turns weak and sputters out.

I fall into the darkness.

Collapsing to my knees, letting my head hang back, I scream to the stars I cannot see.

There is no release here.

Not for me.

3

WAITING

<u>ARO</u>

BENEATH THE BLISTERING HEAT of the enormous cobalt sun, sand drips from the hooves of Rogue, the Chief's pegasus, like glitter.

Sweat flows in the carved definition between my pectorals, a ravine of salt swan-necking around my pounding heart.

"Ready to go again?" he asks, grinning at me with dark eyes that catch the light of the early morning and seem to devour it whole.

I sigh, feeling the unbearable heat sapping at my energy reserves despite donning only my armoured chausses and wings for protection against the curved blade swinging easily from Chief Landon John's hand.

Phillippe, the newest pegasus to join this Equinian tribe, shifts moodily beneath me, apparently as uncomfortable as I am atop the sweeping golden dune.

I'm not the biggest fan of horses, but when the Chief had informed me that his latest risen Kindred, the clan's cook Holden, had a steed that supposedly couldn't and wouldn't be tamed, I couldn't say no to the challenge.

The amethyst sword lies heavy against my thigh as I straddle Phillipe's spine, but it's not the weapon I'm using for this particular fight.

Still, I refuse to let it out of my sight.

There is no relief here from either the heat or prying eyes, and after my run-in with High Lord Lucien DeLaurent, I had vowed I would grow stronger, that I would not only rely on the power I have absorbed from the murdered dragon but that I would learn as much as I could from the Equinians while I remain in hiding from the rest of Aetheria.

"One minute—" I breathe as the winged black stallion rears beneath me, outstretching his fantastical feathered appendages and beating them hard.

What the hell is with this pegasus?

The glossy coat of the animal gleams gold momentarily as it reflects the glint of the sun bouncing from the sand beneath. Landon laughs as his own steed stands stone still, a magnificent and obedient specimen of which he has complete control.

"Do you control your women this well?" He arches an eyebrow, his long braided blonde hair blowing slightly in the merest whisper of a breeze.

I grit my teeth.

"As a matter of fact, I find women to be easier to tame than any horse," I say, eyes glinting as Storm— or Kairi's face swirls into being within the dark void of my consciousness.

"Ah, that'll be why you're out here hiding then, will it?" Landon asks, chuckling as he throws his head back.

Rogue shifts uncomfortably beneath him, causing Phillippe to begin his agitated dance atop the sand once more.

I glare at him as he falls silent, letting go of Rogue's mane, which he holds onto with bare-knuckled authority whenever he rides. Aresian Equinians don't use saddles. Or bridles. In fact, they would laugh at the thought.

"Look, Aro. If you're finding women easier to break than horses, you're courting the wrong women." He gives me a sly smile and I wonder what he's thinking as he adjusts his posture, squaring his shoulders so the brassy tattoos of Ares catch the new sunlight and are set ablaze against the bland tan of his bulging biceps. The only gear on his torso is two leather straps securing his weapons to his spine while his legs are covered in baggy scraps of hide from kills he's made himself.

Out here in the desert, if you can't make a successful kill, you walk naked beneath the sun. If you can't beat one of your own when challenged in hand to hand, your head is shorn as well.

"What the hell would you know about women?" I ask him, cocking an eyebrow with surprise now. Equinian men live a solitary existence out in the deserted lands of The Blazen Plains, their only contact with their female counterparts being when they are permitted to stop at the Sapphire of Eclipsia for their monthly water tithe.

34

"I know I wouldn't be hiding from one. Especially not a Nephilim. Do you know they are making her High Lady tonight? I heard around the camp that Aliandara is preparing to leave for the big shindig at the Solis Castra." He drops this information like a bomb, and I feel my temper begin to flare, the dragonsfire that lies only slightly beneath the surface rearing its head.

Suddenly, a whinny cuts through the thick haze of the desert air laden with the scent of molten gold and sage, and I find myself thrown to the sand below.

Phillippe gallops off across the shifting sands merely seconds before lifting off into the cloudless lilac of the sky overhead. His silhouette becomes but a speck of darkness too quickly.

I hear Landon's laugh again, the tinniness of it rattling against the bones of my skull and making me ball my fists as I whip the wicked pair of sickles from my back and take up a fighting stance.

The white marble of the handles takes the heat that is ebbing off me in waves. I guess my smouldering skin had been what had startled Phillippe in the first place.

"Did you hear what I said?" Landon asks as I struggle for better purchase on the ever-moving dune beneath my feet.

"Yes, I heard!" I growl, wondering if he hasn't gotten the hint that I have absolutely no desire to talk about the bitch that stopped me from claiming the throne.

"It's just you never ask about her. The girl. It's almost as if you're trying to forget all about your little ploy for the crown." Landon dismounts Rogue, who watches both of us with quivering nostrils and anxious eyes as the Chieftain pulls his other sickle from his spine.

My eyes flash dangerously as we begin to circle one another, and I start to recall all that I had lost because of one woman.

She doesn't know what's good for her. Doesn't understand her own weak mind or the heart that wanders endlessly searching for what is right before her. But I will change all that, for I know what she needs, has always needed.

I spit into the sand as I continue to sidestep the outlying edges of the space that we have wordlessly declared our arena.

"I haven't forgotten," I mutter in a low growl, realising that my time with The Equinians, the way it is beginning to draw out longer than even I had expected, is getting noticed. It is making me look weak to them, not that I care.

An elephant in heat is weak in the eyes of an Equinian.

35

I had wanted to get stronger, to master my new powers, but as I circle with the chief of this far western tribe, I wonder if I'm not waiting for a sign as well.

Hercules had come and told me I had opened my eyes to what Zeus wanted the Sephilim to see all along, but I have seen nothing of him since, and I hadn't wanted to know whether Kairi had returned to Nephilim form either. I had wanted to stew and rage, to let myself marinate in my own hatred until I could come back to the game so strong that failure was no risk at all.

Have I grown stronger?

Landon becomes bored of my circular dance, lurching forward toward me and using his sickles to try to disarm me in a quick and well-practised lunge. His enormous golden wings spread wide and glisten as he compensates for the lithe forward motion, eyes feral behind the charcoal spread across his forehead and down his nose. A symbol of his authority.

I retreat, my wings helping me balance as I find myself on lower ground, teetering on the edge of a steep sloping dune. Landon takes no time in launching another attack, this time sweeping the exquisitely sharp curve of his sickle in a high arc aimed at slicing into the side of my throat. I duck, the sudden downward momentum stealing my tenuous balance and causing me to topple over backwards.

The momentum of my fall picks up quickly as I become a floundering tornado of outwardly flung golden sand and hacking coughs, my lungs fighting the onslaught of the fine metallic grain. I grimace, letting my eyes squeeze shut and cursing silently. I should have known better than to trust the sands of this place, for they are ever-shifting and as unreliable as a modern woman's temperament.

I come to a halt at the bottom of the dune, speckled with gold and panting heavily, my weapons lost somewhere up the slope. I stare up into the sky, at the leaden ball of immense cobalt fire that blasts my skin with relentless heat. A dot appears then and I wonder if I'm seeing things. That is until it begins eclipsing the orb slowly as it grows larger.

Landon John wastes no time as he dives through the air, pinning me beneath him before I have a chance to roll out of the way, my vision speckled with blue and black solar blots. He draws back his sickle, ready to slash, and in a moment of slight disorientation from the heat and sunlight, I reach out, pushing him back from me with a flat palm upon his abs.

I hear him hiss, recoiling and then standing, silhouetted against the sky, staring down at me with wide eyes.

"So— it is true—" he says, offering me a hand and then thinking twice as he snatches it back.

Breathless, I get to my feet, realising as I glimpse the handprint I've branded him with why he was so reluctant to help me up.

"You really did it, really gained the powers of that beast?" Landon demands as I brush sand from myself, trying to cool my flesh and regain some semblance of composure as I run my scalding fingers back through my shaggy hair. I glance at him as my breath returns fully to my lungs, standing stone still with a sullen expression having fallen like a dark mask over his strong features.

"Yes. It's true," I reply, wondering why I haven't been forthcoming with this information. Maybe it's because I know that if the rumour spreads, as rumours always do, and the wrong people find out I'm not only still alive but more powerful than ever, they'll seek to snuff me out before I've even begun my plan for revenge. Maybe though it's something more, maybe I like the secrecy, the fact that at any moment I might suddenly have the upper hand in a fight, my opponent totally oblivious.

Either way, I've not bragged, not displayed my new potency as I thought I would. Instead, I've been careful and withdrawn around the Equinians in camp, watching them and taking what I can from them without giving anything back in return.

"How?" Landon asks me, sheathing his sickles against his spine.

I watch as the burn on his abdomen begins to fade already, the healing powers of his race second to none due to Eclipsia's extreme proximity to the sun.

"I am not quite ready to reveal that yet. Not until I know I have your full loyalty," I retort, baking slowly under the white-hot sky. We stand dwarfed beneath it, the air dry and stagnant as the conversation becomes suddenly tense.

"Have I not already proven myself? I have allowed you into my clan, revealed to you our sacred lands— I have told no one of your where-abouts." He looks wildly offended as his words drip with disbelief.

"True. But that is no loyalty. You could simply have me killed with the snap of your fingers. I am alone here, and you have an army. What I want is public loyalty. I don't want pity; I want an ally," I announce, walking back to where my sickles had fallen and are now sliding down the side of the dune toward me.

The cool white marble of their handles takes some of the heat from my palms as I pick them up, catching the glint of the sun upon the edge of their blades and almost blinding myself before sheathing them against my spine.

Landon doesn't respond to my request, simply clicking his tongue against the roof of his mouth.

His tattoos shimmer wildly, tumbleweeds and vines wrapping themselves around his forearms. His fists clench as Rogue trots down the dune toward him, her grace upon descent supernatural in its effortlessness.

Not looking back, the chief mounts his steed, fingers entwining with her mane as he kicks his sandals against her gleaming underbelly. She lets out a snicker as she and her rider become one, speaking in a psychic tongue I cannot hear.

The pegasus gallops across the barren flat sands and past me, blowing my hair back from my face before taking off into the clear sky without falter or pause.

I stare after it, wondering if I should take this as a rejection of my proposal or simply part of the Equinian culture whereby silence remains as golden as the sands over which they endlessly ride.

Sweat pools at the base of my neck, dripping down the tanned skin that spans the broad expanse of my shoulders. I feel its hot clutch, rivulets of irritating salt dripping from me as I wish more than anything for a breeze.

I take off at a sprint then, letting my wings bloom outwards, feathers shimmering wildly as I make my own breeze and am shortly thereafter airborne, soaring over an endless sea of metallic sands. They shift visibly beneath me as I soar higher, savouring the air around me as it cools my skin, drying my sweat-soaked brow despite the fact I'm now closer to the sun.

I have not far to fly, and where I could have convected and beat the chief back to his camp, I relish instead the solitude and cool flow of air passing over my skin as I glide upon weak air currents, knowing he will need time to think before announcing an alliance between us.

I wonder if he is blind to what I offer simply because I have no men at my back, ready to die at my command, but he is smarter than that, or so I hope.

After all, I may not have an army, but I have a plan, one that will change the entire distribution of power across Aetheria if it succeeds.

I am at a tipping point, waiting, crouched and ready to launch myself into the process of clawing back what is rightfully mine from the unworthy.

Kairi included.

Soon, I am circling above the camp of Chief Landon John's clan of Equinian warriors.

Tan and dark-skinned figures linger below, some of them with eyes drawn skyward as I distract them from fighting, eating, or pounding metal into new shapes by the molten springs that lay on the very outskirts of the encampment.

The skins that make up tents flutter in the breeze created by my beating wings as I swoop low and land on hot sand near a large fire pit, where Holden is roasting some kind of small rodent. Phillippe is standing at his side, eyeing me with a sparkling intensity that may just be the horse equivalent of a smug grin.

I roll my eyes at him, and though Holden catches the gesture, he says nothing, his entire focus on the roasting joint before him.

The scent makes me hungry, the crackling and drippings of animal fat sizzling upon hot coals looking more appetising than I want to admit.

A few months ago, the crudeness of it would have made me feel sick. But now I see food as more valuable than any jewel, for here it is the scarcest of resources. The Kindred of Ares is lucky they do not truly need it to live but merely enjoy it as an indulgence of sensory pleasure. If it were required for sustenance, I'm sure most of them living out here would be dead.

Perhaps that is what makes them such good warriors, such incredible hunters, the scarcity of meat. Their desperation pushing them to inhuman feats of tracking and endurance over weeks for one meagre kill.

I tread lightly, letting my muscles loosen from the fight with Landon and trying to breathe deep, keeping my temper in check despite the heat. It makes me impatient and irritable, and it also sheds a stark light on why there's so much violence in the camp.

I find Landon beside the makeshift stables, which are truly little more than some ramshackle pieces of driftwood tied into a lean-to and covered with long sharp grasses to protect the horses from the desert night. Rogue laps at some of the water the Chieftain has just decanted from a precious sack kept in a well-guarded cave that's become a makeshift safe.

He hands the sack back to one of the guards, who takes it inside the cave once more in an effort to keep it cool. I hear Rogue's tongue lapping at it, making me salivate with thirst.

Landon walks up to me, then past me, without a word.

I follow him, with little else to do and nowhere else to be. I have all the time in the world, though I'd rather he hurry up. I miss the delicacies of the Solis Castra kitchen, not to mention a working shower.

He stops around twenty metres from the molten springs, watching over them as they simmer.

Ares' Kindred patrol for signs of new life, for these bubbling pools of molten gold, bronze, and silver are where the new Kindred and pegasi will be reborn as immortal.

It's a painful thing, an Aresian rebirth. Being pulled out of a scalding hot mess of metal and hoping you are worthy of surviving the torment.

They're lucky they heal so damn quickly, for if not, they would surely be extinct.

I, for one, have never been more grateful for the fact I was reborn into a nice lukewarm pool within The Temple of Zeus.

"Well?" I hear Landon say, his voice gruff as it hits the arid air.

"Well, what?" I reply, goading him so I might gauge his reaction further.

"What exactly do you consider a public show of loyalty?" he demands, not looking at me but rather crossing his enormous, muscled biceps over his pectorals.

"I do have something in mind—" I admit, folding my arms defensively and letting my wings tuck behind me, narrowing my shadow as it falls on the ground, which has turned rocky underfoot.

"It wouldn't happen to have anything to do with a certain High Lady, would it?" Landon enquires, his eyebrow cocking as he finally turns to stare at me, the thick braids in his hair glowing a bright gold as they're slathered in sunlight.

"Perhaps." I smile, my lips forming a wry line as I exhale with sudden longing.

"My tribe is at your full disposal, Lord Black. But you know, nothing comes for free, and these are Aetheria's most brutal killers I'm offering."

I am thoughtful for a moment, but I don't pause as I hold out my hand to him.

As he turns, the shadow of where I had once burned him can be seen, fading further into invisibility by the second.

"I assure you; your payment will be beyond what you can imagine," I promise him this, not blinking as we gaze at one another with unrivalled intensity.

The Equinian grips my forearm with his hand as I clasp onto his, our masculine fingers digging into each other in a long-awaited and bloodthirsty vow.

LUCIEN

The skies are no closer to mid-morning as I hover over the jagged teeth of Drakos Vale's rugged jawline, and my heartbeat is mercilessly heavy even still.

I had gone to see Ebonara, wondering if she might be up for an exhilarating early morning flight, but she was curled up asleep, twitching as though she was having some kind of terrible nightmare.

It wouldn't surprise me. After all, she watched one of her own brutally murdered in the only too recent past, and I've felt the depth of her grief for Algoric through our bond deeply.

My stomach twists into tighter knots as my mind circles the events with Lord Black and Kairi endlessly, my body mimicking the endless repetitive loop of my thoughts as I circle aimlessly through the thick layers of cloud and sleet.

I don't know why, but I find myself descending without conscious thought, plummeting toward a familiarly tall natural structure silhouetted against the low-hanging sun, which, as usual, seems too far away to be of any real use.

My boots touch down on crisp snow, the crunch of their rubber soles soothing to my ears as I walk through the familiar chill. I make my way up the last of the incline and toward the barely visible entrance to Gemina Two, the twin of the mountain housing The Astrid Keep from which I've just come.

Guards stand either side of the door, looking frigid in their oxidised reptilian armour as their breaths fog in front of their faces. Upon seeing me appear out of the sleet's static haze, they both bow slightly out of respect for my position, though the respect no longer reaches their eyes. I've noticed this increasingly, ever since I declined to go to war over the capture and death of Algoric.

I don't reply to the two men vocally, my words caught like wet newspaper beneath my Adam's apple, merely nodding to both of them as they pull open the enormous double doors that lead into the observatory. I wonder what I want to say to them as I pass, my people, those who have vowed to die under my order. Do I want to apologise for being so weak? For saving Kairi?

No. Because if I could go back, I wouldn't do anything differently.

I step upon the moonstone of the entrance hall, banging the snow from the treads of my boots and letting my wings shake cold droplets of icy runoff onto the floor. My suit jacket is damp, and as the warmth from within the stone walls begins to seep into me quickly, I remove it, loosening the cravat at my throat and slinging it over my forearm without care for creasing the fine silk. The scent of jasmine hits me as I clear the entranceway and the space around me opens up into the foyer, the water-repellent dome overhead shrouding me in a pale periwinkle sheen.

Tucking my hair behind one ear, I wonder what I'm doing here.

As I stand, looking up at the thick blankets of clouds that let intermittent and weak columns of light pool upon the circular crystal floor, I hear a door open, followed by voices.

"Concerning, yes?" I hear Anastasia's soft tone when the door at the end of a singular corridor, beside the archway that leads to the spiralling staircase, opens with a sudden jerk.

Someone I have not seen in years steps out of the room I've never even noticed before. Urania, the muse of Astronomy making herself known to me as she steps into the light of the windows that line the walls, leaded from apex to sill.

Her silver hair glistens with a dull lustre, the waves of it falling to just below her jawline in a sharp-cut bob. She glimpses me as she steps past her host, turning back to Anastasia.

"Indeed. We will continue this discussion another time, High Lady Dragos. It seems you have a visitor. Bit early, isn't it?" she comments. Giving Anastasia a poignant and knowing look, she jerks her angular chin toward me, her dark skin a stark contrast to her silver hair and the matching velvet of her off-the-shoulder gown.

Her cape sweeps behind her as she walks directly toward me, stars and nebulae peppering the fabric in glitter flowing from beneath her Fae wings that shimmer in an opulent mix of iridescent and pearlescent hues. Stones encrust her face like a mask, her silver eyes gazing deep into me as if I'm seeing doubles of the fullest moon you can imagine.

"Lord DeLaurent," she says without a smile or kindness reaching her eyes, merely brushing past me like a beauteous and wintry gale.

I stare back after her as she moves to exit the mountainside observatory, turning slowly once more to find Anastasia beneath the arch separating the corridor from the glass-ceilinged dome in which I'm currently standing, legs aching, heart cold in my chest.

She looks at me, her attire not at all what I'm used to seeing her wear.

She's wearing a floor-length navy silk robe with glittering cuffs and collar, cinched at the waist with a diamond-encrusted slip of fabric. Her wings are tucked neatly behind her, bare feet poking from beneath her nightclothes.

"I'm assuming I didn't wake you?" I ask her, wondering what on earth she's doing entertaining a muse at this time of the morning.

"Actually, I was just about to retire for the day. I've been on a nocturnal schedule for a few weeks now. Most of my work, you can imagine, is done in the hours of the night or early morning," she explains, turning and beckoning for me to follow her.

I have never been in her suite before and always wondered where in the complex she keeps residence. It had never occurred to me that it would be at this altitude and not down in the bowels of the place with the starlight pools where Draconian Kindred are reborn.

I stop on the cusp of her threshold, and she turns back, raising her eyebrows as her pale blue eyes look wearily at me.

"Well, don't just stand there like a statue, Lord DeLaurent. You're letting the heat out," she snaps, causing me to give her an apologetic look before stepping hastily inside and shutting the heavy wooden door behind me.

I turn to look at her abode, unsurprised at the grandeur but still unable to stop myself from taking it all in.

The scent of jasmine is more pungent here, the vaulted ceiling painted navy and sporting an enormous mural of the constellations in silver, diamonds encrusting the locations of each one of their constituent stars. Silver gilds the walls, curling in vines of blossoming stars and blooming nebulae that scatter across the canvas of the space.

The sound of trickling water meets my ears, and as I take several steps past a glass table, the surface of which is balanced upon the golden horns of a ram statue, I find the source within her bedchamber.

At her altar, which sits beneath the glass canopy that forms an outcrop from the natural rock foundations of the inner room, a small statue of Nemesis stands, holding an urn and pouring what looks to be silver liquid starlight into a bowl that is modelled on the Earth. I also spy several jars full of different incense, herbs, and crystals, as well as a deck of Tarot cards with silver edges, all surrounding the central icon.

The altar is beautiful, but by far, the centrepiece of the room is the fireplace where she stops, taking a silver poker and stoking the azure blaze as she turns back to face me.

"Why are you here?" she asks, getting right to the point.

Placing the fire poker, sporting a dragon coiled around the length of it, back into its holster beside the silver hearth, she strides over to a low velvet couch. Here a steaming teapot of dark ceramic spotted with golden stars stands, steaming upon a coffee table propped on the spine of a golden bull.

"I— I don't know. I just— couldn't go home," I admit, and she nods, looking tired.

Behind her, the balcony door stands ever so slightly ajar, the enormous expanse of the moonstone balcony sporting only a simple pewter stool and old-fashioned telescope from which she observes the stars.

I wonder what she has been looking at.

"I'm not surprised. The cosmos is in chaos," she sighs heavily, taking one hand to her forehead where her dark brows pinch together and setting the other atop the teapot before her. "Tea?" she asks me, and I respond without pause.

"Goddess, that would be amazing," I say, walking around her four-poster bed, raised on a shallow moonstone plinth that separates the cosy living area and the small sub-chamber from which I've come.

Depositing my jacket on the armrest, I sink into a high wing-backed armchair upholstered in glittering pearly velvet and studded through with metal buttons sporting tiny dragons. Sighing, I finally allow myself to slump after the night's constant motion. My wings tuck in behind me, creating a rigidity that annoyingly prevents full comfort.

"You look as I feel currently reading the unrest among the stars," Anastasia sighs, mirroring me and pouring the tea into one of the clean matching cups of fine dark china. The tea smells like peppermint, reminding me of the forests that lie several hundred feet below, and soothing me in a way I'm not quite able to describe. Tucking her raven locks behind one ear, she passes me the cup, which I lean forward and take with trembling hands.

"What is wrong with the stars?" I ask her, and she purses her lips, pouring herself more tea and leaning back into the sofa, crossing her legs beneath the sheath of her silken robe.

"I'm not sure. I've never seen anything quite like it, Lord DeLaurent. Constellations are flickering where they shouldn't be, and the more I see, the less I feel I know," she admits, sipping her tea while gazing at me over the gilded rim of her steaming cup.

I take a sip of my tea, blinking as I unwillingly unravel at the calming notes of mint.

"Is it to do with Lord Black, to do with the future of Aetheria?" I ask her, and she chuckles.

"Oh, if only it was something so simple. No, these stars would not bother themselves with a single dimension, Lord DeLaurent. This is something— bigger, far bigger. Something that has been gaining slow momentum for years now. I fear once it reaches a certain point, a point not far over the horizon, it will be too late." She looks ominous, as always, but I feel the hairs on the back of my neck stand on end.

"So, you've heard no further whisperings of Lord Black?" I ask her, the tension growing quickly in me like a weed.

Swallowing, she sighs.

"And so, it comes to light— the reason you are here." She looks a little sad, and yet her mouth pulls itself upward and into a small smirk.

"So that's a no?" I enquire, pushing for a definitive answer.

When it comes to that man, to Kairi, I will take no chances.

"Oh, I didn't say that," she retorts, the corner of her mouth twisting into a bolder half-smile.

I sit upright, spilling tea in my lap at the sudden jerking motion.

"You discovered his whereabouts but didn't tell me?" I demand justification for her silence while tea drips down my already damp pant leg.

"What possible good can you do, getting into an all-out war between Lord Aro Black and the Draconians? You made your choice, a choice to stave off war, and Genevieve paid the price for that. A choice I so happen to agree with, by the way. I won't let her sacrifice be in vain." She puts her cup and saucer down on the table in front of her, the china ringing out in a tinny peel as it hits the glass.

"And what of Kairi? What of the girl who gave her mortality to keep him off the throne?" I demand, putting my cup down on the table harder than I intend. Hot tea washes over the back of my hand, and I jerk back, knocking the cup from the table and onto the floor. It shatters, and Anastasia rolls her eyes.

"Suave," she mutters.

"Look, I'm here, aren't I? For no other reason than the fact that something subconscious brought me here. If you've seen anything about Lord Black's intentions, you've been shown them for a reason. You are a facilitator of fate, Anastasia. It isn't your privilege to decide fate. I thought you had faith. More than anyone," I spit at her, getting to my feet and feeling my blood surging in icy shards through my veins.

If Kairi is in danger, I need to know.

Fuck politics.

"Don't talk to me about faith, Lord DeLaurent. You know nothing of my intentions. You know nothing of the Goddesses or their desires, so do not come in here, bored and restless, and put your heartbreak on me. Do not mistake me for weak just because I cannot melt the skin off your bones. I can do far worse than that, I assure you." She's baring her teeth in a way I've never seen before, in a way that makes her look more demonic than Draconian.

I straighten where I stand, pulling my tea-soaked hand through my damp hair and exhaling.

She's not wrong.

"I— I am sorry about your cup," I exhale, giving her a look. "But it isn't just about Kairi, Anastasia. It's about Aetheria. If not going to war— if my choice results in Algoric's death and Lord Black still claims the throne, it will all have been for nothing. Kairi is marrying someone else. She is going to choose the next Sephilim King of Aetheria, and it will not be Lord Black or, quite obviously, myself. I have already lost her, and nothing will change that, but we must give her time to make this choice; we must protect her right to willingly choose." I am breathless when I finish, wondering if I might not combust on the spot and smash the rest of her tea set for good measure.

Anastasia looks at me, cocking her head and trying to read me for a moment, her lustrous dark mane of hair falling over one shoulder.

"Please, let me give her the chance she died for. The chance Algoric died for."

I watch as she gets to her feet, walking slowly past me and over to her altar, which stands in front of the floor-to-ceiling glass windows that surround either side of the balcony doors.

I watch as she slowly picks the top card from the tarot deck, turning it over in her hands as she lingers near the frosted glass, her body hiding the card's contents from view.

The fabric of her robe swirls around her ankles as she turns back and looks at me over the arching glisten of one of her bejewelled wings a moment. Then, she returns to looking out of the window, sighing loudly.

"I don't know much, but I know that the ball happening tonight to honour Kairi is destined for ruin. Whether that has to do with Lord Black or not, I'm unsure. Either way, death is coming for the Solis Castra, and blood will spill like wine."

By the time she turns back around to gauge my reaction over still steaming peppermint tea, I am already gone.

4

PORTRAIT OF A LADY

KAIRI

THE RUSH OF AIR against my angelic skin is a welcome distraction from the racing thoughts that occupy the airspace between my pointed Fae ears. They remain hidden, even now, beneath the drapery of my hairstyle.

I can't remember ever having loved anything as much as I love flying; not skating or kissing a cute guy for the very first time, not eating chocolate or even reading.

Ever since my first flight, ever since I had taken that leap into the unknown in a body that no longer betrays me, I had shed a physical distrust I hadn't realised I'd been carrying around like lead in my chest.

I have become weightless and each movement, whether it be the reading of air currents and funnels or the mapping of clouds and wayfinding by the stars, comes as naturally as the inevitably deep inhale following such a weighted release of breath.

Flying was easier for me than for my other classmates, which unsurprisingly had not helped with the distance between us, but I couldn't pretend when I was soaring that I wasn't ecstatic for the sake of something as flimsy as a reputation.

That is a lie that I simply can't muster the strength to tell.

The continent of Soleus passes beneath us in a speckled wave of dancing emerald grasses and frothing aether-filled rivers as Trinity and I glide away from The City of The Sephilim towards the horizon. Here, if you peer closely enough and crane your neck a little toward the sun, you can just make out Eclipsia, the home continent of The Equinians, as a speck far off in the vast lilac of the late morning sky.

Our destination is far closer to home though, and as the villages that I will soon be touring pass beneath us in a silence broken only by the wind rushing through my feathers, it comes into view.

The Temple of Hera sits basking in a peachy glow upon a floating island that sprawls as an extension of Soleus on the continent's eastern ridge. The island itself appears to be made of either chalk, limestone, or maybe something more outlandish than I can even imagine.

It seems I still haven't lost my mortal urge to categorise and identify everything, something which Trinity informs me is bad form for a future High Lady.

High Ladies of Hera don't ask questions.

We bank left, beginning our measured descent with grace despite our high speed in the air, skirts fluttering wildly around the ankles of our soft leather flying boots. My hair whips about me in the cool morning air that caresses both my outstretched wings, but Trinity's tight braids hold her tresses tight to her head as we drop a few more feet toward the approaching rose quartz of the temple. She is clearly the older out of the two of us, for I still struggle with the parts of Nephilim life that to her are second nature. Then again, I remind myself that braiding my hair this morning would have left my ears, in all their pointed mystery, exposed to prying eyes.

My wings beat with a frantic kind of grace as my body drops so it is hanging vertically, slowing me so that I skid to a halt upon the top of the pristine white crystals peppering the ground.

Several alabaster peacocks give us haughty looks as our sudden landing causes ripples in the otherwise mirror-esque reflection pool where Swans float idle and majestic as they watch us with silent knowing.

Trinity doesn't break stride as she lands, her practised transition from soaring to striding effortless, as she affirms herself with a satisfied nod. The grey of her teaching attire, speckled red with poppies embroidered around the hem and cuffs, billows out behind her and clings to her in protest of her speed, highlighting the crimson spatter of her wings as they fold in automatically.

I follow her, wondering if we should talk, but thinking of nothing in particular to say because anything and everything that comes to mind feels fake or obvious.

I mean, what is there to say? I, a Nephilim of only eight weeks, am about to become her superior. It feels a little odd, to say the least.

I'm nervous, as I had expected to be on the day of being made a High Lady, but it's something more than that. There's something deep inside of me that isn't sitting right, like a shard of glass long forgotten that continually grates and grinds against the sinew and soft flesh of my gut.

I think again of Lucien, of his face as we had parted ways what feels like a lifetime ago, and my whole body blazes with a heat I try desperately to ignore, hungry for the cool roughness of his skin. Feeling my cheeks redden as I walk with increasing vigour up the shallow crystal steps, I trail Trinity into the cooler shadows of the Temple's main room. As we journey deeper within, I'm glad for the shade, remembering the last time I walked through this enormous entranceway. I had been hand in hand with an ashen-haired Draconian, with what I felt was my whole eternal life spread before me.

I had been naïve, and I realise now just how much, as I'm walking one step at a time towards an entirely different fate.

I'm distracted from lingering thoughts about the kiss we had shared by the reflecting pool when I hear a high-pitched and familiar squeal break the silence heavily blanketing both mine and Trinity's metronomic footfall.

"Oh, my Goddess! I can't believe this day is finally here!" Vail charges forward in an entirely unladylike manner, setting Trinity's expression firmly in stone as she barges right past her and heads straight for me.

Vail flings her arms around me, and I feel a lump form in my throat. I've missed her.

"Look at you!" Vail exclaims, pulling back and holding me at arm's length. The tulle of her sleeves practically vibrates with her excitement as my lips spread somewhat unwillingly into a shy grin.

"Hi," is all I can think to say, my cheeks flushing bright red as Vail examines me, her eyes roaming over my Fledgling School uniform with fondness.

I wonder what her memories of being a Fledgling are like, whether she was popular or whether she felt just as lost as me.

"What are you doing here?" I ask, feeling my voice return in a sudden gush of words that slip loosely off my tongue and into the rosewater-scented air between us.

"I'm here to help you get ready for the ceremony and then the ball," she explains, grasping my hand in hers and squeezing tightly.

Then, another familiar face appears from behind Trinity, whose tall silhouette is watching us as a gentle smile plays on her lips and her arms cross over her corseted bodice.

"And she's not alone."

At the sound of her voice, I sidestep Vail, my heart pounding.

Dawn stands looking meek before me, her pale blue gown underwhelming compared even to mine.

The handmaiden's hair is braided and piled atop her head as it had been the last time I'd seen her. That is when she had tried to save me from Aro, and then he had threatened to beat her for her loyalty.

"Dawn—" Her name echoes off the high ceiling of the temple as I close the space separating us. Then, taking her hands in mine, I look deeply into her eyes. I find brokenness behind her luxuriously lilac irises, her pupils boring into my face with unfaltering sincerity.

"Kairi, I'm so sorry— If I had known, if I had even suspected—" She seems just as lost for words about that night as I feel, and I shake my head.

"Don't you dare apologise. It was not your fault. He had everyone fooled, Dawn." I squeeze her delicate fingers between mine, feeling my heart swell beneath my ribs.

"Now we have all had a few moments to compose ourselves, I suggest we proceed to the parlour. We have a lot to do before the ceremony and even more to do before the carriage arrives to take you to the Solis Castra." Trinity reminds us of why we are here as we turn to face her, not that I had forgotten for even a moment.

The two women, who have come once again to my aid, nod silently, picking up their long skirts and leading the way toward the enormous statue of Hera standing front and centre in the Temple's main room of worship.

The three of them turn right as they reach her sandaled feet, talking over what should be done about my appearance first, wings fluttering behind them.

They are halfway out of the cavernous room and hanging beneath the exit archway when they notice I am not following closely behind.

Trinity turns back, her voice tinny yet sensuous like dark liquid chocolate as she calls, "Kairi, are you coming?"

"Go on without me. I'll be there in a minute—" I mutter, standing before the statue and gazing upward, my head hanging back as I take in the Goddess I'm about to pledge my loyalty to.

The women know better than to argue and so continue walking and talking as their footsteps fade away down the winding quartz corridors.

I take in the voluptuous curves of her body, the boundless and vivacious hunks of stone-made hair in her honour. She has merciful eyes, and yet behind that mercy, there is also a silent demand, a powerful call to action.

I had hoped to know what that action might be by now, hoped that she would come to me, that she would show me the way. But instead, I feel completely abandoned by the Goddess who looms over me, her shadow casting my once hopeful face in darkness.

I'm blessed with an immortal body, but what about my soul?

I still feel human inside, still feel just as fragile and unsure as I had running around Drakos Vale as a fugitive with a broken arm.

I don't want to need Lucien, but the truth is that I've been leaning on our nights together more than he knows.

It scares me how completely I think of him as home, how completely I have fallen for yet another man after what happened with Aro.

I don't want to fear walking out of this temple and trying to find some miracle of sameness in someone else.

I want Lucien DeLaurent. But Aetheria wants me. It wants my heart as a sacrifice for the peace and lives of thousands.

How can I possibly say no to that? How could I turn my back on Aetheria, which is as much of a true love to me as any man ever will be?

No, I cannot abandon duty for selfish reasons.

I have to do this. Have to step forward and finish the work that Storm died to keep in progress.

Even if it means that I am destined for a loveless eternal marriage, for the confines of a cold hard throne and lukewarm Soleus summer nights instead of the comfy rustic charm of snow-capped peaks.

I have been chosen by Hera, blessed.

Or so they say—

Staring up into the eyes of the Goddess who gave me wings, I say a silent and humbled thanks before turning away and heading towards my future with my head held high and fingers tightly furled.

The Temple of Hera is no small place with maybe fifty rooms in total having been skillfully woven into the maze of its enormous quartz architecture. I'm currently sitting in one of the preparation parlours usually used for brides before they stand before Hera when taking their marriage vows.

I'm not here for that purpose, but with the speed everything seems to be moving, it terrifies me to think that I could be here under that guise soon.

Dawn and Vail stare with irises in different shades of purple, examining every inch of me.

I feel amazing, my skin having been soaked in fine oils during a bath that lasted well over an hour before being buffed and smoothed by their expert hands. I glow slightly, aether having been applied gently and sparingly to the spaces beneath my collarbone and just above the swell of my cheeks.

I'm barefaced besides this, no make-up, only fragrant floral potions having been dabbed attentively onto my skin while my waist-length hair was being made silken like liquid caramel and threaded with tiny pink roses, each lock brushed until it sheens. My hair falls over my shoulders and down my back, and ever since they began working on it, I have been feeling an increasing tension between the two women. It can only mean one thing.

They've noticed my ears.

"You look perfect," Vail admonishes.

"You two don't have to act all weird. I know you've noticed my ears. Please— I'd appreciate it if you wouldn't mention this to anyone." I give them a slightly desperate look, rubbing the pad of my thumb atop the now glossy sheen of my manicured nails.

"Of course, I would never—" Dawn stutters, flushing slightly.

Vail, however, is less flushed and more curious as she steps forward, brushing my hair behind the pointed tip of my ear with gentle fingers.

"Did I do this?" she enquires, and then I see the fear behind her inquisitiveness. "I mean, I brought you back— I— did I do the ritual wrong?" Her eyes threaten to fill with tears.

I shake my head, my glossy mane undulating around my face as my skin catches milky light dripping down from the pearlescent light fixture.

"No, it wasn't you. I don't know what it means either, but I do know that it wasn't you. Lucien told me to keep it quiet— the last time we saw each other. I thought that was sensible." I swallow the lie easily despite the fact I feel a great amount of affection for both the women standing in front of me. However, I know I've made the right choice when the floor-length mirrors set into the crystal walls expose the tension in their bodies at the mention of his name.

"Well, we can most certainly help you hide this. Many hairstyles that were quite popular in the late 1800s would do the trick," Dawn adds thoughtfully, and as the words leave her mouth, I wonder if they'll make me look more like Storm than I already do.

I swallow the notion like a bitter pill, sitting back down on the pouffe of cream crushed velvet behind me with a sigh.

I'm wearing a simple white gown of partially translucent material, and I stare at the outline of my nakedness beneath as I wring my fingers in my lap, my wings impatient and restless at my spine. The gown is embroidered with silver peacocks' feathers, spectacularly blooming lilies, and pomegranates dripping with spilt seeds.

The moment passes, the silence of our thoughtfulness broken as Trinity enters from the long corridor outside.

In her palms, she holds a box made of pale wood veined through with pearlescent lustre. It dons the hefty metal decoration of an ornamental lotus on the lid. Looking between us, she hastily steps across the room before placing the box down on the vanity where I have just spent the last hour or so being preened.

Vail and Dawn remain silent, scrutinising every motion she makes with the supernatural grace and fluidity only ever achieved by Hera's blessed.

Opening the box, she lifts something from within it, turning to me and giving a small smile as I glance nervously at the object in her hands.

A diadem made from delicate argent vines that hold not leaves but feathers as they intertwine, clutching clusters of amethyst and rose quartz like ripe fruit.

She hands the piece to Dawn, who goes about setting it upon my head, burying the band deep into the volume of my hair. It's heavy, for such a delicate piece, but comfortable.

The three women step back, appraising me a moment before Trinity gives a nod of satisfaction and rummages into the grey folds of her skirt, searching her pockets for something.

When she pulls it out and it is exposed to the light, I smile.

This I have been looking forward to.

"Give me your ankle," she asks without gentleness, but I'm already pulling up the thin veil of my gown from around my ankles so she can access the anklet of amethyst around the top of my foot.

It's customary for all fledgling women to be cuffed during their time at the school, to be tethered to the grounds and unable to use their power to conduct while they are in training. The schoolmistresses had told us it was to prevent us from getting lost somewhere or stuck in another dimension, but I knew better.

I knew because I noticed that they did not require them to be worn by the current Sephilim class who had come to the school for a few formal dance lessons.

We haven't even been allowed to stray from the airspace around the school, and whenever we needed Sephilim present for our classes, they had come to us. I'm in a body with limitless potential, and yet somehow, it's been made into a cage yet again by the rules of Soleus society.

The anklet pops off as Trinity turns the key in the tiny silver lock holding the two halves of the piece together. I roll my bare ankle, glad to be free of the extra weight.

Trinity sighs, her usual Spanish flare peppering each syllable.

"There, now you are ready."

The ceremony is neither particularly grandiose nor crowded. Instead, it is private, so private it is to be for my eyes alone.

The only sound I can hear as I enter the most sacred chamber of worship in the entire temple is the harpist that's playing somewhere close by being piped in through the vents in the ceiling. Then, as the doors are sealed behind me, I'm left with only my thoughts.

My bare soles on the crystal are cool, my wings feeling heavy upon my shoulder blades as I bask in the baby pink warmth of the sunlight dripping in and bathing the rosy quartz of the walls.

The stone floor sinks into an enormous pool of water central to a space adorned with lilies and roses in a variety of pink and white shades. The air is pungent and warm, the steam from the hot water rising in lazy tendrils like crooked fingers beckoning the onlooker to submerge themselves.

I stare through the slight fog, right into the golden eyes of Hera.

The statue of her isn't half as big as the one in the main temple. No, this one is more intimate. Humbled despite her gleaming metallic curves, she's on eye-level with me as I gaze softly into her face across the sacred bath, searching for answers and swallowing hard.

Nostrils flaring, I take a gentle step deeper into the room, the mugginess of it clinging immediately to my skin and infusing every inch of me with the scent of floral blooms.

I've been walked loosely through this ceremony a hundred times by Trinity, but now I'm finally here, I'm afraid.

Not afraid of what might happen but afraid that, in fact, nothing might.

Silence from the Goddess in my time of need has never seemed as sinister as it does with me standing here, exposed by the flimsy gauze of my floor-length ceremonial gown, flowers in my hair, and heart beating raucously in my chest.

It's a wordless ceremony, and Trinity could only give me so much information. After all, the High Ladies that should have been around to offer me guidance, to tell me what to expect spiritually, are long since dead.

I wish now, despite the fact I've been pushing her away, that I had better access to Storm's memories. Maybe they could tell me something, bring some comfort.

I realise I've been standing frozen to the spot for too long, that I need to move forward, but I'm paralysed entirely by my anxiety.

I sigh, rubbing my sweaty fingertips on the inside of my palms as I take a few steps over to the edge of the steaming water, trying to relax.

The edge of the pool slopes downward, gradually levelling out halfway across the room.

Closing my eyes, I whisper a quick plea into the lonely darkness of my subconscious.

Please, Hera, give me a sign.

Exhaling heavily, I begin my descent into the water, the heat and strong perfume of it cloaking me like a blanket. My dress becomes weightless, floating around me as I place one foot in front of the other, descending the ramp with slow precision. My wings drag behind me, slicing through the surface, tips vibrating with my unsteady breathing, and I find myself actively trying to calm myself as I'm swallowed up to my chin.

As I reach the centre of the pool, I gaze at the statue a final time before I submerge myself completely.

The thud of my blood in my veins and my heart in my chest are the only sounds that follow me beneath the surface.

I wait, submerged, floating free as my wings keep me under. My gown swirls around me in pale gossamer spirals, my hair flowing out from my face, a nimbus of caramel silk.

I wait, knowing I don't need to breathe but having to fight the urge to resurface out of habit.

A moment passes in silence, then another, the diadem growing heavier by the second as it digs its claws deeper into my skull.

Blinking, I peer through the rich teal waters and plead for anything I might take as guidance, twisting and turning, desperate for some vision.

I hang there in the water for longer than I know is necessary, waiting, but find nothing.

Eventually, I surrender to the obvious, surfacing and beginning along the path to the exit ramp at the far end of the room.

I stagger from the waters, spattered with sodden petals, dripping, my gown clinging to every curve of my silhouette. My hair is pressed back against my skull, the efforts of Dawn and Vail lost to the ritual, and to whom I had been before, emerging on the other side, exposed, and finally a High Lady.

I present myself before the statue, falling to my knees, wings sagging around my spine with the weight of their waterlogged feathers, skin flush from the heat.

Clenching my damp hands together, I bow my head, kneeling before the Goddess that has chosen me for duties I am yet to understand, waiting even still for an answer.

I sit down there so long my knees begin to throb, my body shivering as the water on my flesh cools and causes it to rise in goose pimples around my tired limbs.

It's not physical exhaustion, no— this is something else.

It's a feeling of abandonment, growing larger as each second passes with nothing but silence and the empty efforts of a harpist in the other room.

The ceremony is supposed to be the place where Hera and her High Ladies intersect for the first and only time. Where they merge and converse before the Nephilim is set free upon Aetheria to carry her message to the masses.

I wonder then if maybe I'm not supposed to be a High Lady at all, whether there's been some mistake. Glancing at the Heirbound mark on my wrist, I momentarily hate the deviation of it from any that had gone before, a swirling silver crown hanging above the three-tentacled star, as though I need reminding of what is at stake.

I tremble, feathers shaking, breath rattling inside my ribs, squeezing my eyes shut and hoping for something, anything to happen. Every whisper in the air causes my Fae ears to prick, even the slight breeze calling the hairs on the back of my neck to attention.

I'm still waiting for a sign when the chamber is unsealed and I, High Lady Kairi Freemont, am called to return to the parlour.

Vail waits for me outside the door as I emerge, dripping onto the crystal of the floor. Looking at me, she inspects every inch of my trembling body down to my erect nipples, now protruding grossly through the completely transparent gown.

"How was it?" she enquires, but I can only shrug, gutted through and through.

She wraps me in a large white towel, my hair a sopping mess of flower petals and ratty tangles.

The diadem, though, stays exactly where Dawn had placed it, immovable against my skull.

The journey back to the parlour is a blur, and my entire body trembles as I feel disconnected from the world around me. Vail's hand serves as the only tether to Aetheria, and as I re-enter the parlour, the curious eyes of Dawn scan my face for answers.

Vail shakes her head, and my teeth continue chattering as the two women crowd me. Despite their closeness, sudden loneliness grows weedlike within my chest, threatening to choke my ability to connect.

Why would Hera turn her back on me now?

I wonder then if I've done something wrong by carrying on with Lucien during my time at the school, but even the thought of yet another person disapproving of our relationship whilst knowing nothing about it makes me furious.

The fury warms me enough for me to be able to let go of the chasmic abandonment and overwhelm I'm feeling and focus on what's going on in the here and now.

If Hera wanted me to choose the next King of Aetheria, then she got what she wanted, Lucien or no Lucien. I'm doing what she wants, getting dressed up as an ornament for the perusal of suitors. It's supposed to be my choice, my right to select the next King, and yet the mere concept has never felt more like a farce.

As I muse on this, a flurry of activity stirs around me, though the tugging of brushes through my locks and stripping of my tired body eludes me entirely as I'm lost in the injustice of the entire situation.

The process of beautification, of cleansing me of my imperfections and making me desirable for someone else's benefit begins again, this time more rigorously than before.

My hair is washed in a basin full of warm water laced with essential oils, my chill skin towelled dry and then gently powdered. The gown I'm to wear I haven't seen until now, as the only part of the process I had been involved in was having my measurements taken. Caleb, the only Sephilim High Lord remaining in Soleus, had designed it, and as such, I'm nervous.

I don't know Caleb very well, only that he was too weak to stand up to Aro before it was too late. My respect for the man isn't great, but I am hopeful he will have chosen something at least not hideous in which I am to be introduced to the Aristocracy.

It was in a single meeting I had with him, when said measurements were taken, that I was informed my ascension ball was to be different from those that had gone before. Caleb said I needed to show the withstanding strength of the Sephilim and Nephilim alliance despite Lord Black's too-recent treachery, and so, not only had Hera and Zeus' most highly regarded Kindred been invited but the High Lords and high-ranking officers of the Equinians and Fae as well.

It hadn't surprised me that the Draconians had been excluded from the guest list, and if I'm honest, the decision flooded me with relief.

The last thing I want is to be meeting potential husbands while the man who unwittingly stole my heart stands by and watches through devastated eyes.

Swallowing this painful thought, I allow Vail to lead me to the very back of the parlour where a dressing area is curtained off from the rest of the room.

Dawn draws back the cream silken curtain, revealing the gown, in all its glory, hanging from the swirling silver body of an intricate dress form.

The skirt is enormous, the edges of its voluminous sprawl pressing against the walls of the cubicle in lilac duchess satin. The bodice narrows into a tiny waist that I'm shocked will fit me, and the entire garment is encased within an intricate and stiff-looking cage of shimmering alabaster embroidery. Vines sporting the shimmering outline of peacock and eagle feathers, pomegranates, lilies, and lotus flowers give rise to the tiny silhouettes of cuckoo birds. I track it with wide eyes, noting the thickly embroidered veil coming away from the gown at the top of the corseted bodice, taking on a life of its own as it forms two delicate sleeves that drape flat just below the shoulder.

I swallow hard, blinking, wondering how much the gown must weigh.

"Ready?" Dawn asks, stepping past the wide skirt carefully as she moves to begin unlacing the back.

I nod, unable to give her a vocal response because, in all honesty, I feel like I've never been less ready for anything in my life.

After another hour of wrangling me into the enormous dress, my feet are wedged into silver heels, and my throat is clutched by a thick platinum choker dripping with pear-shaped amethysts. The diadem, its claws digging deep, is repositioned amongst my newly styled hair which is up off my neck in a sophisticated low knot that leaves only a chosen few curled ringlets to fall over my left shoulder. My face has been heavily painted, so much so that I feel even less recognisable than the first time Dawn had remade my features as a mortal.

The gown restricts my breathing, the cage of the enormous skirt pinching the soft skin of my hips as I ensure my ears are fully covered by my new hairstyle.

The final touch is added once I'm done adjusting my tresses, a pair of white satin elbow-length gloves, as is tradition. I wonder why I must be gloved though as nobody at this ball is wondering if I'm really the Heirbound or not. They all know I've been marked as the future Queen.

"My Lady, shall we proceed to the carriage? You know where we're going, just outside of Sparrowdale—" Vail suggests, bowing respectfully with a soft smile that just touches her violet eyes.

I swallow, nodding again, still lost for words. I've seen the artist's rendition of where the procession will begin a hundred times, but this will be the first time I've conducted by myself without a watching teacher.

I'm nervous.

Licking my bottom lip and tasting the grape of the shimmering gloss adorning it, I nod, tensing my jaw and balling my fists as I take a deep breath.

I close my eyes, feeling for the electricity in the air, the currents of static, which are invisible to most but that I can tune into as a low-level rhythmic hum.

As I focus on the image of a meandering river bend being embraced by a low and quaint stone bridge, that same static trails over my bare collarbone and up the side of my face.

The sound of a whip cracks, cleaving my world in two as my wings spread instinctively wide and the parlour dissolves around me.

I am carried miles down to the floating continent below.

When I open my eyes, I find the babbling stream, hit by the slowly fading light of the late afternoon sun, has been made real before me. I feel my feet firmly beneath me on crushed quartz, my gloved hand suddenly nudged by something. I look down, finding Catticus' muzzle buried deep in the palm of my silken glove.

I want to bend, to nuzzle into the familiar scent of his fur, which still retains the lavender musk of hot summer Tennessee nights, but the dress makes this difficult. I haven't seen him in so long though and can't help but wonder where he's been. Kensari weren't allowed at the school, not surprising considering fledglings rarely if ever formed a bond with one so early on in their development.

Catticus settles for a scratch between the ears, which elicits a deep and rumbling purr, and my eyes are drawn to the carriage which will be taking me to the Solis Castra. It's open-topped, sort of. The bottom of it is gleaming white and draped in hundreds of crystal lilies that have been wrapped and draped upon every crevice and curve of the vehicle with emerald ribbon. The selenite of the flowers continues up into a glassless cage that covers the top of the carriage like an elaborate small aviary on wheels.

I step forward, tasting the now-familiar zest of lightning as Vail, Trinity, and Dawn conduct in behind me.

"Wow, I haven't seen this in—" Vail looks thoughtful, but Trinity answers for her.

"Around a century and a half. I had to pull it right out of deep storage and have the entire thing cleaned," she exclaims, looking at them with worried eyes.

I know why they're worried, but I try not to let it bother me.

It's because Nephilim High Ladies seem to have oddly short lifespans for immortals, none of which is accidental, I'm sure. Catticus nudges my palm, his blue eyes glittering as his jowls spread in a kind smile.

I'm with you, my Lady, he whispers in my ear with a telepathic rumble, giving me comfort I don't expect.

I step forward with him at my side, approaching the carriage, which is linked to two pure white does, their throats encased in rose quartz collars extending to full-body harnesses and reins.

The carriage driver, who sees me approaching, pulls the door open with a gilded handle and draws down a small ladder, bowing his head in respect. Then, as I pause to let the enormous, winged lion ascend into the carriage before me, I watch his eyes widen, and one of his blonde eyebrows cock.

"You can't seriously be considering taking your Kensari with you in the carriage for the procession?" Trinity voices her discomfort with the arrangement as I look back over the edge of one of my wings, blinking slowly.

"I'm not allowed to take him?" I ask, turning so my skirt flares. I hear Catticus making his way into the shining carriage, the entire thing creaking atop its delicate spoked wheels beneath his compact yet muscular body.

"Well— there's no rule, but—" she begins to reply, her eyebrows knitting sternly together. At her confirmation that I'm not breaking any official rules, I shrug, turning from her wordlessly and clambering into the vehicle after my leonine companion.

My skirt fills most of the empty space between the two benches set at the front and back of the carriage's plush interior, and Catticus sprawls out on the bench at the front, his back to the driver's seat.

As the driver resettles himself on the slats of the bench and brings the reins into his palms, he looks back over one greyish wing, eyeing the Kensari with a half-amused, half-concerned glance.

"All ready, my Lady?" he calls back as I'm arranging myself so I will be able to see out of both sides of the carriage.

I look back to Dawn, Vail, and Trinity a moment, who are all standing with their hands clasped firmly in front of them, watching me with both anxiety and pride.

Vail gives me a reassuring smile, barely noticeable to the others, and I feel myself straighten in my seat.

"Yes, onward driver." I issue the decree in a voice that sounds nothing like me, full of authority and entitlement. I've been told we have a tight schedule and that no stops will be permitted. The thought of this alone makes me feel exhausted.

Seconds later, we are pulling forward, the white, heart-shaped rears of the doe swaying from side to side as the driver urges them onward. Their fur shimmers with aether as we pass over the very first bridge of our journey, a tour of all five Soleus villages, which will take several hours to complete.

First up is Sparrowdale, the village most unmarried Nephilim are assigned to.

We approach quickly, though I've been warned to remember that the journey between each of the villages is long even by carriage, and so settle into my seat with passive resignation.

Catticus eyes me, and I wonder where he's been.

Long time no see. I try to reach him telepathically for the first time, my words ringing out sharp as crystal in the psychic space between us.

The carriage rolls to the left, and he gives a forlorn smile, whiskers twitching.

Indeed. I never was one for education.

I laugh, feeling the feline sass coming off him as the world of Aetheria ambles past us at a consistent rhythmic speed.

Indoctrination, more like— I retort. A low rumble echoes in the cavernous depths of the lion's throat, a laugh if I ever did hear one.

I'm sure I don't know what you mean.

He gives me a sly wink, licking one of his enormous paws as the first village rises on both sides from where before there was only flatland. Sparrowdale isn't linear or logically laid out as I have come to expect from mortal cities but, instead, sprawls out in random directions like a crack. The paths, an assortment of clear quartz shards and rounded rose quartz pebbles twist and turn madly like vines. I try to follow each one to its termination point to little avail.

The main road is wider than those that shoot off to an array of small Nephilim-run stores, but the town is still cramped. Within only a few streets, I find a food market that is an explosion of Fae imported fruit and homegrown vegetables, residences, spas, and of course vineyards and farmland worked by some of the lowest ranking among them.

Normally, the town would be bustling, but today, the place is silent. However, it couldn't be further from empty. The streets are lined, packed to breaking point with solemn faces waiting to see me pass.

The procession then suddenly becomes something that I do not expect, and that is too much for me to bear.

In the silence, of both Hera and those who are now my people, I look into the wide eyes of bystanders, and my heart enters freefall. The expressions worn are collectively ashen, and I wonder if they've been threatened into attending this.

Is this normal— The silence? I ask Catticus, who turns his enormous mane to me as it ripples in a sweet breeze that tickles the side of my neck.

The carriage continues to plod forward.

What do you think? Catticus asks, his azure-teal eyes hooding slowly.

Why are they so quiet? Fear? I counter impatiently.

Do you think the Nephilim who sided with the Draconians against Lord Black would get a warm welcome? I'm surprised you're this naïve— even if you are technically new here. The comment irks me, and so I do something impulsive as all hell.

"Driver! Stop the carriage!" I blurt, causing the man behind Catticus to startle out of his dazed driving routine.

"I'm not permitted to stop, my Lady. We have a tight schedule to keep!" he calls back over one shoulder, shaking his head as if I'm crazy.

I purse my lips, eyeing the glimmering and trembling cage of selenite surrounding me. The air moves easily enough between the columns, and yet I seem to be trapped inside.

No more of this.

I close my eyes, balling my gloved fist and conducting from the seat where I'm sitting. Catticus roars in alarm as the lightning cleaves the air and causes the metal of the encaged carriage to shudder, but I'm too busy falling onto the street a hundred yards behind to flinch.

I had not thought to stand before I conducted, and so I'm left to tumble backwards in my beautifully intricate ascension gown onto the ground.

The crowd suddenly goes, if possible, more silent than they were before— and time freezes. The moment hangs in the air as my skirt blooms around me like a flower and I'm left sitting in the middle of the road, a single lock of hair coming untethered from my updo and falling across my face.

I hear the carriage stop suddenly with a jerk, hooves skidding atop quartz further down the road.

I watch, waiting for the driver to conduct back and scold me, but before he can a woman is standing in front of me, offering a shy and freckled hand.

Her skin is beautiful, just as all Nephilim skin is, and yet the inside of her palm is a tad rougher. I can immediately tell she's not shy of a hard day's work.

"My Lady." She bows her head, keeping her hand outstretched.

I reach out with my gloved palm and take it, allowing her to help set me on my feet. Readjusting my diadem, she stares at me in amazement, almost as though she's shocked herself by coming to my aid.

"What's your name?" I enquire, giving her a shy smile as I regain my composure.

"M-M-Melissa," she offers, visibly shaking and refusing to meet my gaze.

"Well, Melissa, come with me." I take her hand, storming down the street.

The rest of the crowd watches us with a collective and sharp inhale as I re-approach the carriage. When I meet up with it, a disgruntled driver gives me an irritated glare from beneath the brim of his cream leather cap, but I ignore him.

Reaching up, I gingerly untie the closest Selenite lily from the back of the vehicle, letting the emerald ribbon it is tied with come loose in my fingers. I turn to her, pulling her wrist to me and tying the flower around it like a corsage, this time curtseying to her instead.

"Thank you so much." I let gratitude radiate from my face, hearing the crowd begin to mutter at her back. She stares at the crystal flower on her wrist, not responding to me as her lips quiver.

"What do you do here?" I ask her gently, leaning forward and picking up her chin with my silken fingers. I meet her eyes and smile, letting her know we are the same, and that she has my respect just for being here. She unfreezes suddenly, her caramel-tipped ivory feathers fluttering with excitement.

"I sell vegetables," she blushes, and I grin wider.

"Ooh, what kind?"

"My Lady, we don't have time—" The driver is now at my side and reaches out to lay his fingers on my arm.

I spin.

"We will make time," I hiss.

Spinning back, I see the crowd begin to inch closer, step by step, coming to me as I strike up a conversation with Melissa about squash and lettuce. Then, I loop my arm through hers, the gargantuan skirts of my gown pushing against the flimsy linen of her own.

Turning toward the crowd, I beckon them forward, feeling more confident and surer of myself than I've felt since sneaking out of the Academy to follow my heart back to Lucien.

I glide atop my heels with confidence, passing the carriage and putting distance between the driver who has now been rendered useless.

Catticus gives me a toothy roar as I pass, and I grin back at him.

Then, I address them, not as a High Lady, not as Storm but as Kairi Freemont. My voice is a melody of wonder and curiosity as it spills from me, my intuition guiding me to exactly the right words.

"So, will you kind people show me Sparrowdale? I want to see how you live."

5

THE HOUSE OF MIRTH

KAIRI

I SPEND AN EQUAL amount of time in each of the five villages between where the procession begins and ends. After Sparrowdale, we move onto Hawkwood, where I am shown many armouries, libraries, and am even treated to a display of the newly graduated Sephilim in flight as they soar over the sturdy howlite and turquoise tiled roofs of their homes.

After the Sephilim wave me a hearty and genuine goodbye, I proceed through the final three villages of increasing luxury, which house high-ranking Sephilim and Nephilim couples.

Swanworth is the first, and as the carriage driver gets increasingly agitated at my constant stopping and starting, I have Catticus dismount the carriage and stand by my side. Then, looking around at the nervous faces of working-class couples that stand, clinging to one another, I ask the driver to inform the Solis Castra that I fully intend on being fashionably late. With Catticus keeping pace with my billowing skirts, I walk up to the masses and introduce myself with a low curtsey and an outstretched hand.

When the initial caution has worn from the poreless faces of the men and women of Swanworth, they show me the way they construct intricately detailed boats to carry cargo up and down the river, providing timber and metal to the surrounding villages and then receiving them for future distribution in turn. Swanworth is quaint, but there is no mistaking the fact that it is the largest of the villages as I had been taught before even stepping foot here from books.

Once my tour and talks with the people are finished, I conduct without breaking stride, getting the hang of the skill more easily than I had expected and landing with perfect grace within the walls of

Dovedon, where soldiers and their wives are housed. After my tour here, I continue on to Eaglecrest where the High Lords, Captains, and other high-ranking military officers or aristocrats are housed. Their wives bustle and preen within the towering splendour of amethyst townhouses sporting golden roofs, many of which have turrets and vast balconies crammed with delicate place settings perfect for taking afternoon tea.

The towns of Eaglecrest, and Dovedon to some extent, are more modernised, with a high street sporting different boutiques as well as theatres, music halls, museums, and even several grander halls where smaller balls can be held when not intended to reach the heights of the Solis Castra. It is also here where the courts of Soleus reside, bringing justice to those who have crimes committed against them. It surprises me that, after living a life on earth, even the blessed feel the need to commit illegalities.

Through the shaking of hands and the smile I keep plastered on my face, I sweat beneath the lowering sun, fully expecting a humid night ahead.

Progressing from the lowest classes of Nephilim and Sephilim, right up to the town of Eaglecrest where the upper classes roam on the very outskirts of The City of The Sephilim, I watch the joy diminish at my breaking protocol. Where the Nephilim and Sephilim in the first two villages I'd met, and even the couples in Swanworth, were very accommodating, I begin to see eye-rolling and unsubtle whispers as I brush elbows with aristocrats and military leaders. In fact, the residents of Eaglecrest look practically insulted at my having abandoned my carriage to actually speak with them and ask about their way of life.

I spend as little time as possible within the plush and ridiculously high walls of their fair town, finding the architecture over the top even by Aetherial standards as I send Catticus ahead of me to give Caleb fair warning in case the carriage driver has yet to arrive.

Finally, after several too-tight handshakes and awkward bows, I conduct from the judgemental gazes. When the blinding glare of the lightning dies, I'm relieved to be standing, finally, upon the front steps of the Solis Castra in front of the entryway awning.

Chaos erupts around me as the final dying rays of sunlight flutter into wisps on the horizon, and I'm rushed at by several guards, Trinity, and Lord Abara.

"Are you alright?"

"Whatever happened?"

"Why are you so late?"

The questions hit me in a peppering of mixed curiosity and irritation. I raise my eyebrows, surprised anyone cares that I'm late.

After all, it's barely twilight.

Ignoring the guard's first question, I turn to Lord Abara, who is standing in a gleaming and pristinely pressed morning coat and breeches of black and silver velvet.

"I decided to stop and speak with the people," I admonish simply, finding the High Lord's eyebrows rising in surprise. He swallows, the enormous selenite clasp that keeps his cravat pinched tightly around his dark Adam's apple bobbing.

"The people?" Trinity interjects before Lord Abara can reply, and I nod as he turns now to stare at her instead.

"Yes. I thought seeing as I am to be their High Lady, I should know them. How else will I know how best to serve them?" I ask.

She looks flabbergasted.

"But— that's— that's— not how it's done." She blows a rogue hair from her eyes in frustration, her chest rising and falling heavily in a white gown dripping with garnets. The bloody stones also stud a collar that's tight around her throat, making her look as though she's had her windpipe slit.

"Well, maybe it should be," I suggest without apology, feeling bold.

After all, *why should I apologise?*

Aren't I a High Lady now?

Aren't I the one who they're putting all this responsibility on?

Why charge me with such immense pressure and then diminish my judgement simultaneously?

"I'm here now. Shall we begin?" I prompt the High Lord, who bites his plump bottom lip a moment, running a hand back over his shorn head before nodding with several rapid blinks.

"Yes, why— yes—" he stutters, pulling out a handkerchief from his inner pocket and wiping his forehead with it. I brush past him, leaving a wafting trail of essential oils in my wake and not waiting for anyone else to clear my path as I breeze beneath the vast length of the awning. Fiery roses of ruby glint in the dying sunlight, winking blazing scarlet at me as I pass.

I look back over my shoulder, my wing flaring as Catticus leaps up and over one of the bushes of sapphire hydrangeas lining the entrance, padding diligently to my side and letting the top of his head lie just beneath my gloved fingertips as his luscious wings fold in to cocoon his spine.

"Are you coming?" I call back, acknowledging the two soldiers who fall in on either side of me, escorting me into the building.

Within the Solis Castra, it's cooler, a fact I'm grateful for as my heels ring out heavy and hard against the amethyst. I can hear the party, the guests waiting on my arrival because I was supposed to be here over two hours ago, but I cannot bring myself to be sorry.

I had seen Soleus, really seen it. Not in a book, or from afar, but walked its streets and talked with its people. If the cost is to be a little late, I'll happily pay it.

We wind through the corridors, to one of four ballrooms held in the castle, and my heart beats faster as we pass through the smallest on our journey, the room I had danced in with Lord Black.

His face, even in memory, shakes my newfound confidence. The hairs on my arms and the back of my neck stand on end, remembering how I had let him plummet backwards off the side of the building with me in his arms.

My stomach contorts itself into a knot, and my pace becomes less sure as we ascend three flights of stairs before finally reaching the ballroom that's both the largest and farthest away from the entrance, with a set of twelve-foot-tall glass doors leading out to the gardens overlooking the falls.

"Seeing as how you're late, we have adjusted tonight's programme. You will be introduced and then begin dancing with the suitors we have selected for you immediately," Trinity says, catching up with me, her cheeks rosy and flustered.

"Selected? Aren't I supposed to choose the suitors?" I cock an eyebrow as we stop before the enormous oak and gold doors of the octagonal ballroom.

"Well, of course— but you cannot simply meet every Sephilim in Soleus, Kairi. You must have somewhere to start," Trinity looks at me as though I'm a naïve puppy and she is a wizened old woman. Though I suppose in reality she is, she just has way better skin.

"Are you ready? I don't wish to keep our guests waiting any longer." Caleb makes a point of acknowledging once again that I am late, so I square my shoulders, take a deep breath and nod, not giving him the courtesy of a vocal response.

Caleb then repeats the same gesture to both the guards flanking me, who unstick themselves from my sides with immediacy and slip inside the gargantuan doors. I hear a sliver of the conversation from within the room escape before immediately falling silent.

My heart pounds.

Swallowing hard, I hear them announce my new title.

"Presenting to you, for the very first time, High Lady Kairi Freemont." As the words fall into nothingness, the doors are pulled forward, and I step with them into the glistening light that falls from eight long crystal chandeliers. Collectively, they create the illusion of the entire room being presided over by a shimmering two-dimensional sun, the symbol of The Aetherial Court.

I see the faces of the guests, the rustling of feathers stilling as I am hit by the force of the magnified light. I pace gingerly then into the centre of the ballroom, the floor of which is solid amethyst and covered with a weave of glittering gold vines. The feathers in place of their leaves match my dress perfectly, leading me to realise just how orchestrated each and every detail has been.

I look at the crowd, turning on the spot and acknowledging them as I search for familiar faces. Aliandara stands out to me in a beautiful navy gown and a bolero made entirely of citrines, and I see Leo beside Vail a little further around, though they're both pushed toward the back of the crowd which has cleared the centre of the room for my arrival. I feel my heart pound as I search for his face, for Lord Black.

I know that Caleb had told me the security had been tightened around the Solis Castra for the event, and yet, still I'm expecting to find him among the crowd, leering at me.

I, however, don't find his empty eyes, meeting instead the unimpressed gazes of various Equinian Chieftains, and finally, Morpheus and Hypnos, who give me sly smiles. I curtsey low, unsure of how to move the proceedings forward as they scrutinise my gown. As I rise again, I'm extraordinarily glad that Catticus remains at my side, the security of his toothy grin giving me the strength to stand straight once more with my head held high.

Standing expectantly, the room slowly lowers its collective heads and bows in return.

Then, the crowd rises and disperses.

I find myself suddenly descended upon by familiar faces.

"My, my, don't you scrub up well Lady Freemont," Aliandara makes the sly comment as she saunters forward, her dark lacquered nails clicking rhythmically against the stem of her champagne flute.

"How very kind of you to say, Lady Montgomery." I smile at her with tight lips and then turn to the woman whose hand is clenched in her free palm.

"I'd like to introduce my lover, High Lady Evangeline Senft," she pulls the woman forward for my attention, the light cream of her gown floating ethereally around her body and rose gold wings. I notice that the gown twists around her torso with elegant precision, and the closer I look, the more apparent it becomes that where once Evangeline had a pair of breasts, a golden design that twists into running horses, lunar phases, and arrows now runs wild across her chest instead.

"It is rude to stare, Lady Freemont. I'd have thought you'd have learned that now. How long have you been immortal? Eight weeks, is it? You're just as wide-eyed and transfixed as you were when I met you last," she makes the comment and I can't help but smile more genuinely this time. Lucien was always saying that about me, always teasing me about my intense fascination and wonderment with the world around me.

"I do apologise. I have just never seen such beautiful designs wrapped around the upper torso like this, it's stunning." I speak with more confidence than I'd dared the last time we met.

Evangeline's eyes shimmer and grow wide, the chocolate irises deep and warm.

"Stare away, Lady Freemont. I'm proud of them, a fact that Aliandara knows well. If I wasn't, I would never have begged Artemis to let me keep the scars from my surgery," she's encouraging, and Aliandara purses her lips, face falling sour.

"Surgery?" I enquire further, interested as I turn so that I'm facing Evangeline with my entire body.

"Yes, breast cancer," she states proudly, her lithe form hardening slightly beneath the fluid silk of her gown as she puffs out her chest with pride.

I beam at her, ignoring Aliandara's bored expression as she takes a sip of whatever fizzy concoction it is she's drinking.

"That's freaking badass," I reply, watching Aliandara almost spit out her drink with relish.

Evangeline laughs, delighted.

"Hey— hey— Storm!" The name of my predecessor fully and loudly slips from Morpheus' lips as he makes a direct surge for me through the crowd, pulling Hypnos behind him. He's also got a glass in hand,

and I wonder exactly how many he's had to drink as he teeters slightly on the balls of his spritely feet.

Donning an electric blue suit that's lined with pops of pearlescent embroidery forming peacock feathers, no doubt a thoughtful tribute to Hera, I see Hypnos slap his arm with the least muster I can imagine.

Her eyes remain dreamy as always beneath the cloud of her wispy blonde hair.

However, before the Fae couple can reach me, A soft hand on my shoulder causes me to turn away. Caleb stands, a young man with hazelnut-coloured curly locks at his side.

"High Lady Freemont meet Corporal Danby, a promising candidate for future Officer status in our military. I thought I'd best find you a partner; the dancing is about to begin." I give a casual smile to the Corporal, whose muscular physique is slathered in a pristine, tight-cut white suit jacket and silver breeches. His throat is clutched by a teal satin cravat, the symbol of The Aetherial Court highlighted by shadows deeply stamped into a pewter seal at its core. His wings are huge, perhaps the biggest I have seen excluding Leo and Aro, and each steely feather is tipped brassy beneath the dangling chandeliers.

"The band is set up outside, and I thought it would be nice to take your first dance out in the gardens. Come." High Lord Abara doesn't waste time, and as Corporal Danby gives me a shy smile from beneath generous lashes, his cheeks flush deep red.

His obvious discomfort puts me surprisingly at ease as we pass through the parting crowd and then the enormous open double doors, emerging into the fast-dying twilight.

Here, at the end of the sprawling outdoor patio, musicians stand beneath an elegant silver bandstand topped with panels of stained glass. The band of Nephilim are ready to begin playing as their wings tuck narrowly behind them, allowing yet another musician, Vail, to join them from within the bustle of the other guests. She smiles at me and picks up her alabaster violin from its stand before tucking it adeptly under her chin, but I do not return her gesture.

I'm entirely overwhelmed.

The surrounding willow trees drip with emeralds and have been adorned with strings of lit amethyst, the fountains further out from us setting a delicate ambience as I see Kensari playing in the clouds far off near the horizon that dips below the curve of the crescent-shaped falls. I realise then that at some point Catticus has vanished yet again.

The feline is more elusive than smoke, and his absence fills me with yet more anxiety.

My attention is drawn back to people flocking out of the inner ballroom and surrounding the extended dance floor; eyes hot on my spine as their lips cease.

Corporal Danby turns to me, his spine poker straight, taking my gloved hand in his and leading me gently to the centre of the dance-floor.

I've been taught the steps so many times and danced them with so many Sephilim in class I should have them branded into my brain, but as the music begins to rise to fill the sweet summer night air, my mind goes blank.

The Corporal's deep indigo gaze reaches mine, and his tan skin darkens in the shadow of his wings as they flare out on either side of him and he bows deeply. I curtsey in return, feeling my heartbeat accelerate at the realisation I cannot for the life of me remember the beginning of the waltz I'm about to perform.

As he pulls me close to him, trapping me within the cage of his arms, the scent of violets reaches me.

I go rigid in his embrace.

Suddenly, the music hits the first notes that I should know how to waltz to, the notes indicating I must step forward. I go to move, foot rising off the floor, but the Corporal whispers quickly in my ear.

"Wait."

Instinctively, I place my foot back on the floor beneath my skirts, and then after another count of eight beats has passed, the Sephilim who has just saved me from social mortification begins to lead with grace and humility.

He was right. I had been so panicked I had almost started one count too soon.

"Oh, my goodness, thank you—"

"You may call me Ambrose, Lady Freemont," he whispers in my ear as we begin to dance together beneath the newborn stars.

The bejewelled and heavily painted crowd watches on, scrutinising my every move with this stranger.

"Ambrose, thank you." I look up into his dark eyes, my wings stretching out at the appropriate time in the music, trying to ignore the incessant discomfort of being watched.

"It was nothing, Lady Freemont." He blushes, and I smile gratefully.

"Kairi, please call me Kairi," I say, tilting my chin as he begins to step forward rhythmically.

"Can't have a beautiful woman like you embarrassed," he compliments me, and I find myself suddenly laughing. It's a deep and throaty sound that originates from somewhere far down in my stomach.

He looks surprised, and I shake my head.

"I'm sorry, it's just, I still am not used to the blatant flirtation of men from different periods than I. Men today are far more sly," I admonish. His arm coils tighter around my waist, and at his proximity, butterflies rise in my gut just as fast as a tide of severe guilt.

"Well, if I'm going to be honest, you should also know that I arrived late to the ball. You see I was enraptured by a High Lady actually making time for her people." He twirls me out and then pulls me back close, a calculated move but still exhilarating as my skirt billows, providing a cool breeze upon my stifled ankles.

The compliment should make me want to soar, the chiselled jaw and wide curious eyes of the man dancing with me any woman's dream—but there's something that just doesn't fit right.

There's no sarcasm, no real appreciation here. Merely flattery and smoke blowing.

"Thank you, that's very kind," I admonish, hardening slightly as the dance becomes faster.

Under the scrutiny of Aetheria's aristocracy, we dance, Ambrose clearly enjoying every second of our time together as he tries to sweetly ask me about my interests. He tries, he really does, and as the waltz passes on ever slower, I feel myself floating above my body and looking down on the entire event, receiving only a detached aerial view.

Unfortunately, despite my lofty view only one of us is on cloud nine, and it isn't me.

LUCIEN

I watch her in the arms of another, her face radiant as she laughs. Crouching on a cloud and sheltered from aerial detection by the cover of Ebonara's camouflaged wing, I feel my temper prickle like someone has shoved a sea urchin where my heart used to be.

Her eyes, lilac and wide, glisten beneath the scattering of cold and distant stars, but my attention is only briefly pulled from the man with whom she is dancing, the diameter of her skirt not large enough to keep him from pressing flush against her tiny torso. He has a head of caramel locks, thick and shimmering like the brass tips of the feathers that adorn his generous wingspan. They match, the two of them, like two halves of an obvious whole.

I have never felt so wrong, felt so completely erroneous in my mere existence, and so I am taken back, watching, to the last time I felt so very ugly, so very monstrous. The memory is crystal clear, though it probably shouldn't be. After all, this all happened more than two hundred years ago.

My family history is one of inane human vices and victimhood that was chosen rather than fate. When I look back on my forefathers, on the men who had carried the title DeLaurent, I find the majority of them to be a blatant explanation as to why I have never been worthy of my own desires.

My great-grandfather, Louie, was a rich and talented man and one of the best jewellers in all of Paris. Upon learning of the conception of their first long-awaited son, he and his wife moved for a quieter life in the countryside.

My grandfather, Lucien, grew up among the idyllic French countryside surrounding St Lucien, for which he was so named, running barefoot along dusty country paths edging vast fields of crops and spending his childhood in the shadow of the town's church, La Courneuve, curia noa.

Louie knew that the most valuable thing he could do for his son was to take him on as an apprentice when he came of age, and so Lucien was trained too in the art of fine metals and lapidary. When he was just seventeen years old, Lucien told his father that he was tired of country living, that he desired a greater pace of life, and that he wished to move to Paris to make his fortune just as his father had before him. Louie, proud of his son, gave him a large portion of the family estate so that he might purchase premises and materials to start his own venture. He had seen how hard-working Lucien was, seen how his son may be just as talented as, if not more so, and so sent him away with all possible faith in his abilities and future success.

Upon moving to Paris however, Lucien was taken in by the allure of city living. By the loose women who walked on street corners and potent liquor and drugs found in opium dens and bars.

To cut a long story short, Lucien never did start that venture but, instead, drank, gambled, and whored until he was in such debt he couldn't bear the thought of returning home. His vision of success had faltered in the face of physical desire and a hunger for excitement he had never imagined in the quiet countryside of his youth. He cowered from my great grandfather until one day, he received a letter informing him that his father had died from a disease of the lung, with his mother following in shock only two days later.

He, their only son, had inherited the family fortune, including their house in Saint Lucien. At this time, Lucien was living on the streets and was so indebted to so many crooked people he never had a chance to put the money his father ashamedly sent him, for fear of him dying in squalor, toward a better life. As soon as those francs landed in his hand, they were soon taken by another.

With the family fortune, Lucien paid off his debts and returned to Saint Lucien after twenty years of debauchery, penniless, with the house in St Lucien his only asset. Everything that his father had worked for had come to ruin because of his darker appetites, and as he returned to the small village where he had been born, he felt shame even stepping through the familiar front door.

The house was rundown, the wooden eaves full of rot, and the floorboards splintered and uneven underfoot. Furniture once lovingly cared for had become brittle in the harsh winters as a lack of coal in the fireplace had led the house to become cold, damp, and unwelcoming.

My grandfather, to his credit, broke at the sight of what had once been the home of a loving and wealthy family and so walked to the church in the middle of the night amid the cold, dry air of winter, and sat amongst the deserted wooden pews that he had not frequented in over two decades, looking for an answer.

He found her then, the daughter of a local carpenter who had recently killed her first hen at the age of only sixteen, begging for forgiveness in the darkening church lit by only a few dying candles.

Her name was Melody, and soon after meeting, the two of them fell in love. Her father, the carpenter, helped to teach Lucien everything he knew so that he could undo the damage to the family home that had come about because of his recklessness. Then, upon completion of the house repairs, he made my grandmother an honest woman, and the two were married.

My father, John DeLaurent, was born to the couple and named for my grandmother's father, to whom my grandfather owed both his sobriety and the good fortune of a wife and child.

That was how my father became a carpenter and how, after the frivolous actions of only one of my ancestors, the wealth that my family had accumulated was simply fritted away like sand off a dune.

I was born in 1799, and my father, John, was never frivolous about anything. We lived with my grandparents in that very house until they died, and then we made it our own. I was named for my grandfather, obviously, and it is a fact that has always irked me.

I grew up knowing wood, knowing the scent of it and how it whorled and warped over time, how it could become damp and rotten in the wrong conditions. I was taught to respect it and, above all else, to respect the little money that carpentry brought in. It wasn't as much as I would have made had we been a family of jewellers, not even close, for the skill wasn't nearly as rare, but it was enough. I often wondered why my grandfather had never bothered to teach my father this skill, but he claims he did not want to offend his father-in-law. I, however, think it was because the drink and drugs had melted away the knowledge as if he had put a blow torch to it.

I, myself, became a carpenter, and it wasn't long before the first time I found the woman I felt I had been searching for in the pews of the very church where my grandfather had first sighted my grandmother.

In my mind, the foolish romantic that I was, it was serendipity, and as weeks, and then months passed with me attending church more diligently than I ever had in my life, I finally worked up the courage to speak to the preacher's daughter, Miss Lucille Toussant. She had blonde hair that shimmered like straw woven into gold and pale blue eyes that reminded me of the sky on a perfectly clear day. She wore the finest gowns I'd ever seen and carried with her a lace fan from which she would allow herself to flirtatiously peek from time to time.

I was a fool, but I was also hopelessly besotted, and so I approached her with an open heart.

Roturier.

That was what she called me as she spat on me, in the courtyard of the church one Sunday after Mass, before informing me that her father was hoping to become Archbishop. She continued to mention I should consider checking my status as a mere carpenter's son before approaching other women out of respect. Apparently, the fact that I was merely standing before her was damaging her reputation and making her feel unclean.

This moment more than any other in my young life changed me dramatically. It made me hungry for power I had never before desired despite the warnings of my heritage about the consequences of chasing unhindered lusts.

It broke something in me that day, as though I had suddenly realised I was inside a cultured cage I couldn't see, touch, or taste.

That was the first time I had ever felt hideous, felt unworthy, felt less, and despite my immortality, it seems I am still yet to shed the identity of a poor carpenter's son, spat on by the preacher's daughter.

I feel the wind stir around me as Kairi begins to dance on with another man, and then another, and suddenly I cannot bear to watch any longer.

Anastasia had said that blood would be spilt, but perhaps I had it all wrong and the blood that was to be spilt was mine after I tackled some unlucky suitor to the ground and had Ebonara disembowel him in front of the entire aristocracy?

That would not be good for Draconian political relations.

With this thought lodged firmly at the front of my mind and the realisation that the woman I had risked it all for will soon, well and truly, belong fully and legally to someone who can match her grace and beauty step for step, I turn my back on the festivities and beckon Ebonara to follow me into the darkening velvet sky of the night.

KAIRI

The night is progressing with all the speed of an icicle melting in Drakos Vale, the bright lights of the chandelier beginning to grate on my nerves as I plaster on yet another wide smile, more than fully aware of several hungry male gazes resting on the nape of my neck.

"So how are you liking it, dear girl?" Quinn asks me, the brown locks of his thick mane braided haphazardly and peppered with lilies in honour of Hera. The High Born Fae of Light and I stand, teetering on the edge of the dancefloor of the inner ballroom as couples of all races spin and twirl.

"It is more than I ever imagined for myself, that is for sure," I reply, wondering if he is prying for a more profound answer.

Can he see my disappointment, my longing to be somewhere else?

Neve turns her dark head of hair from whatever it is she's been glaring at, the ice crystals that weave amongst her crown of braids glistening with the same sharp blue pallor as her irises.

"And where is the Draconian I almost froze solid?" she asks, baring her teeth with a slight smile. Phineas and Ember both exchange uncomfortable glances, their outfits just so happening to match in gold silk, though I doubt they planned it that way.

Ember has a beautiful circlet adorning her head and resting just above the points of her dark fae ears, and I stare at them, unable to help myself as I remember those same ears tucked beneath my updo. My eyes flit to Phineas' ears, who is mimicking a fashion I once saw Morpheus wearing, a golden and autumnal-looking leaf dangling from a brass chain hooked through one of his earlobes.

I swallow, the tension becoming obvious between our small gathering when suddenly a warm palm comes to rest on my shoulder.

My stomach drops, and I suddenly wonder what's worse; explaining why Lucien isn't here to High Born Fae of Light or turning to face yet another Sephilim suitor.

My choices, quite frankly, suck.

"May I steal you away for a dance?" A familiar voice gives quick relief like ice to a burn as I turn and find myself staring into Leo's eyes.

"You may—" I admonish, offering him a gloved hand as I turn.

"I must be off, thank you for coming." I give the Fae High Born the pleasantries I was trained to, grateful for the out in answering Neve's question. Then I feel guilty.

Surely, I owe them more honesty than simple avoidance?

They helped me survive when I was running for my life, scared and alone with only Lucien, a Draconian, for protection. Now I'm stuck in a shimmering web of politics and words not fit for public conversation. The thought of it makes me feel like I can't breathe.

"Shall we?" Leo suggests, squeezing my gloved fingers tightly and marching me into the centre of the space, the current song conveniently dying down so another might rise in its place.

He forms the traditional Sephilim cage with his arms, allowing his wings to stand erect as I take my place and bring my wings to attention as well. The medals of honour on his chest shimmer a cold silver against the pristine white of his tunic, the uniform donning his lengthy body different from the other Sephilim soldiers I've been dancing with. I suspect this is a matter of rank rather than choice.

The waltz, one in a long line of similar dances slightly too pompous for my taste, begins. The masses of people begin in their synchronised and refined movement seamlessly, Leo and I now among them.

"Might I inquire as to why you asked me to dance?" I bat my lashes, glancing sideways toward the bandstand where I have no doubt Vail is still pulling her bow across violin strings with finesse and poise. "We both know there's someone else here you'd much rather waltz with."

"I was saving you from having to answer the High Lady Fae of Winter's question, my Lady." Leo, always polite, renders me silent as I realise he was eavesdropping.

"Thank you," I whisper, pushing myself closer to him as he drops his own voice in turn, our proximity to the surrounding couples ebbing and flowing like a dangerous tide as we talk of things not meant for ballrooms but war rooms instead. Though, with the absolute purpose of this event, I'm beginning to wonder if they can not be one and the same.

"You should be careful, people are listening and waiting for you to declare your alliance, my Lady. Why do you think you're being courted only hours after ascension?" He turns a sharp ninety degrees, and I follow as the music rises in a dramatic flourish of violins and cello, my skirt and wings flaring out behind me.

"I assumed it was because the other Nephilim know only too well the average lifespan of one of their High Borns," I admonish grimly. He cocks his head, eyebrows rising. It's clear he hadn't thought of it like that.

"Perhaps, or maybe you sneaking around with a certain High Lord of Hecate hasn't been as discreet as you imagine. Perhaps they're afraid you're going to make the next King someone with a Dragon instead of a Kensari—" he whispers, and suddenly my heart is pounding in my chest.

I'd thought about it, choosing Lucien, but the very notion of it seemed so dangerous that I am never able to dwell on it for more than a moment, a moment that can only be described as one of weakness.

"And why would I do that? What Sephilim or Nephilim is going to answer to a Draconian? There'd be wars breaking out all over Aetheria in the name of my betrayal, and I'd have my throat slit in my sleep. Not only that, but Lucien would be dead in a week if he was lucky—"

I remind myself of the warning I'd been given by Caleb during the meeting proceeding my dress fitting, the way he'd informed me that all the other Kindred except Draconians would be attending my ascension ball.

Then, I falter in my step in a way barely noticeable to anyone except my partner.

"You knew?" I ask him, suddenly realising what he's saying. He gives me a half-smile as if he's thinking how incredibly naïve I am but cannot say anything due to my status.

I suppose I should get used to such tongue-biting.

"You are the Heirbound, Lady Freemont. Did you really expect Lord Abara to leave you unwatched, even within the high walls of The Academy?" His eyes soften as mine blaze with irritation. "For what it's worth, I kept your secret— Nobody else knows. I just wanted to warn you that –"

He's cut off as his head jerks to one side, a sudden fork of lightning tearing apart the fabric of the air like tissue paper. A blur of gold clatters to the floor like discarded dinnerware, and then another. Blood is exhaled in a mist of spittle as several bodies splay amongst the dancers, the wind knocked entirely from them as they gasp for breath.

The music dies, the crowd immediately silenced as the soldiers writhe on the floor, their wings bleeding profusely as feathers float loose in the wake of their falls.

"Lady Freemont— run—" The soldier closest to me gasps, reaching out to me with his bloodstained gauntlet.

I feel the colour in my face drain, but have no time to act as the mind-numbing shatter of glass breaking hits the air like a razor blade.

The window opposite me explodes, showering me with jagged rain as a whinny rides the night air that flows in from outside, thick with the scent of lilacs.

I brace myself, knowing what's coming before I've even sighted him. Fear roots me to the spot, my heart thumping frantically against the boning of my corseted bodice.

6

AN UNTAMED STATE

ARO

MY WORDS RING OUT like a sword grinding on bone as a sea of shocked faces stare up at me. The dark pegasus, Pestilence (or Pest for short), breathes heavily between my thighs as the steel shoes adorning his hooves crush glass into splinters. Luckily for me, the Chief had seen my need for a more reliable mount before we began the skyride to Soleus, and so he continues to stand obediently. I draw a steel broadsword from my bare spine, eyes flashing with delight as the crowd takes several desperate steps backwards. I leave my amethyst blade sheathed heavily against my hip.

"Well? My invitation— lost in the mail or simply not sent at all?" I look now to Caleb, whose darkening gaze flits between the steely rage of my face and the tumultuous battle still raging in the sky behind me.

He doesn't reply, the silence between us growing long like a late afternoon shadow, so I turn my attention to someone more interesting.

Kairi stands with her bosom rising and falling in desperately heavy and fast breaths as her wide Nephilim eyes take me in.

She's stunning, as I expected, and yet I know the transformation has made her immortal at a level only skin-deep. She is still the meek mortal I courted and captured only too easily, and she still has no idea what is good for her. I decide not to grace her with my acknowledgement, letting my eyes glide to the man by her side instead.

Leo, the one Sephilim I had expected to find on the cloudscape, fighting in the battle outside, stands tensely on her right, his hands hanging empty but tense at the hem of his formal tunic.

"Captain Bond, perhaps you can explain to me why I, as a High Lord, was not invited to such an auspicious occasion as this?" I cock my eyebrow, looking down on him and feeling my palm tense around the hilt of my sword until my knuckles pale.

Leo's eyes narrow quickly as he steps forward toward Pestilence, who tosses his dark mane with an aggressive snort.

"We all thought you were dead, My Lord." He bows his head, giving me relief as his wings spread wide behind him. The span of him blocks Kairi from my view momentarily, drawing my full focus.

At last, some respect.

The clatter of more hooves rings out suddenly, the Chief bringing Rogue to a grating halt as her full bulk and immense speed hits the fine amethyst of the floor. She skids to a standstill, the Equinian Chief is breathing heavily like a labouring cow, irritating me immensely.

"My Lord, we have taken the surrounding skies with as much ease as predicted. Our second squad should be arriving any moment— Ah, I hear them coming now, in fact."

Honing my hearing and making use of my incredible sensory enhancements, I make out what it is he's referring to as the gallop of horse hooves on crystal ring out in a rhythmic pitter-pat, growing louder by the second as the Equinian soldiers race through the Solis Castra's winding corridors.

It's almost been too easy, as though they really were sure I was dead. Could that possibly be true?

Well, more fool them.

Dismounting Pestilence, I hear the thunderous pounding of approaching hooves reaches its zenith just as the second squad of soldiers comes bursting in through the enormous double doors to my left.

Holding my sword tightly, I walk over to the flailing bodies of soldiers cut down, the ones who had tried to convect here before it was too late, who had tried to warn the newest High Lady.

I kneel on the chest of one of them as the gruff voices of Equinians herding the cowering crowd can be heard. The barking of orders is quickly followed by the rustling of duchess satin and velvet breeches against feathers.

The compliance pleases me immensely. Not that it should be surprising. I had instructed the soldiers to take hostage the most vulnerable, the women. One move from anyone else, and they'll be responsible for the spill of innocent blood. Not only that, but I know Nephilim. They're too weak to risk causing anyone else harm trying to save their own skins by conducting out.

"As you can see quite clearly, Ladies and Gentlemen, I am not dead." Swinging my arm back, I plunge the sword straight through the eye socket of the flailing and injured soldier that is being slowly crushed, pulling the blade out with a yank that results in a shower of blood spatter peppering the crowd in front of me.

Leo flinches as his tunic is speckled crimson, and I cock my head. Kairi takes a single step back, her face drained of colour.

"This is what a dead Sephilim looks like; take note, Captain." I give Leo a frosty gaze that masks the ferocious fire just beneath.

Then, standing, I let the tip of my sword hang close to the floor where fresh blood pools beside the heel of my leather boot.

I don't take my eyes off Kairi as I step over the body of the man I've just killed, licking my bottom lip thirstily and squaring my shoulders before walking slowly over to Lord Abara.

The soldiers around him tense, but before they can act, I hold up a single finger, a signal to the waiting Equinians I have at my command. I hear the commotion behind me, hear the desperate cries of Nephilim ladies as Chief Landon's Equinians take them hostage, pressing freshly forged blades to their delicate perfumed throats.

Gasps emit from some of the less seasoned Sephilim, but I know they won't move. Just as I had intended, I find the fear in their eyes that their selfish actions to escape might cause the death of the innocent-faced maidens I have taken hostage. It is perfect.

The air is electric, despite the fact nobody is conducting anywhere, and Caleb stares at me with wide eyes.

"Well, Lord Abara. What's it to be? Your surrender or the death of innocents? To be clear, I have more soldiers on the way, the Solis Castra surrounded and the guards either dead or unconscious. Make your choice."

I glance sideways at Kairi as she takes another step back into the crowd, and smile, her fear satisfying me a great deal.

After all, it was she, a mortal, who had stood up and humiliated me, exposed me before the Aristocrats of Aetheria. Now, I will show them what a mistake they made in letting the Draconian Lord DeLaurent ever raise a hand to me.

I wait a moment, watching him carefully and feeling the room collectively inhale.

"Aro, why are you doing this?" The voice is not one I expect, but it causes me to turn away.

Pivoting reluctantly from Caleb and toward the centre of the room, Landon takes the Sephilim in one of his dish-sized hands, shoving him to his knees. Then, he summons two burly warriors standing idly by the door to hold him as well.

I find the High Lord Fae of Night at the source of the pathetic question hanging in the air, and smile.

"Ah, Morpheus. A little unusual seeing a Fae High Lord at such an occasion, especially when not even I was invited."

I peek back over my shoulder at Caleb with a face full of hatred and spit at him. He glowers up at me, furious as he struggles fruitlessly against the enormous men who have his biceps in their unforgiving fists.

He could conduct, but he knows that would cost him precious Nephilim lives. The man values his reputation, I'll give him that, but too much, to the point where it becomes a weapon one might use to render him useless.

"Cuff him." I reach into the pocket of my chausses, pulling out a pair of amethyst-lined steel shackles and throwing them to Landon with a half-hearted smirk.

I turn back to Morpheus.

"What is it you want? Why are you doing this? If you're going to murder Kindred before my eyes, I at least want a reason. I want to know why." Morpheus sounds less sure than I have ever heard him as he steps forward, his nimble gait a whisper upon the floor.

As he gets closer to me, the guards tighten their holds around the throats of desperate maidens, eliciting a torrent of synchronised and pitiful whimpers.

"Why? That isn't obvious? This could have all been avoided if Zeus and Hera's plan for myself and Storm could have come to completion. As it is, the girl—" I look back at Kairi and continue to stare her down. "Knows nothing of what is good for her, or of duty. She is a High Lady, but her interest is solely her own. I cannot fathom how Hera could have been so very stupid. She is putting Aetheria at risk of being overrun by the Draconians. I will not stand for it. Not after everything I have sacrificed to keep the crown from falling into the wrong hands."

Kairi wilts, and so I step back and make a half-turn, spreading my wings wide and watching as my sudden proximity drenches her in darkness, snuffing out any light in her eyes as they fall from me.

She flinches at my sudden motion.

I come within touching distance as I re-sheath my bloody steel sword, reaching out to touch her cheek.

She trembles as the back of my bloodstained hand meets with her delicate blush.

"Look at me, or I'll have everyone in this room slaughtered—" I whisper, giving her a light slap across the face as she keeps her eyes planted firmly on the floor.

Reluctantly, her eyes snap up, but where I expect to see a sudden rage, to see new fire, there is none. Her spirit has seemingly faltered in the gale of what has passed, and the fact she seems so very malleable as she quakes and swallows hard at my very presence makes me smile wide like a Kensari that's just spotted its next kill.

"I gave you the opportunity to do this willingly, the easy way, Kairi. Don't act like the victim here. You chose this, don't forget." My whisper turns into a hiss as I wait for her to respond, but where I had expected to find defiance, there is only silence.

"Enough, Lord Black," Morpheus snaps, causing my eyebrows to rise quickly in surprise.

"No. Never enough, Morpheus. The time for waiting has long since expired."

I take several steps toward the luminous mess of his viridian mane, smiling as the scent of liquor reaches me, his irises cloudy.

"Ah, but of course, you are inebriated. I should have known better than to expect you to have suddenly grown a backbone. You Fae are all the same—" I snarl, eyes lingering on the Fae of Light who are watching me with glazed expressions. High Lady Neve Einven restrains one of her infamous snarls as her counterpart, High Lady Ember Cyrus wraps dark, ring-clad fingers around her ghostly pale wrist.

Quinn and Phineas stare at me, and I wait for retaliation, not expecting it but goading them nonetheless.

"As I thought." I glower, turning my eyes back to Kairi.

She takes a step back as I advance once more, a lion cornering a helpless, wide-eyed lamb. At her retreat, I feel my mouth flood with saliva, jaws aching to stretch wide and close vice-like around her pretty throat. My wings pull back as I straighten my shoulders and tilt my chin upward so I might look down my nose at her, but before I can get within three feet of the hem of her overly wide skirt, a soldier so inconsequential I've never even noticed him steps between us, a naïve mask of defiance barely veiling his fear.

He stinks of it.

"Leave her alone." The man with caramel curls and deep indigo eyes challenges me, his hand resting on the hilt of the sword at his hip as the crowd becomes even more silent than before. They collectively inhale and stay that way, teetering on the edge of a moment that might turn out to be lethal or triumphant.

I want to laugh, knowing the only blades accompanying the formal Sephilim uniform are far more ornamental than vicious.

And yet, here he stands.

Curious.

Most curious indeed.

I see the echelons on his uniform, identifying him as a lowly Corporal, his boyish looks not even approaching anything like that of a man.

"I will never leave her alone, boy. She isn't a woman; she's Hera's Heirbound, and just as with the crown only she can bestow, I will not rest until she belongs to me." I say this plainly, without the real volume the statement probably deserves. Its desperate weakness makes it eerie like the ghost of a prophecy I am destined to fulfil. The hooves of pegasi shuffling at my spine signal the Equinian soldiers becoming restless, waiting impatiently for my command.

They want me to order them to cut him down, but it is not their strength he is challenging.

My sword sings as I remove it from my bare spine once more, skin rippling as the half-dried blood of my last victim clings on, defiant.

He meets my first swing, parrying me with a move so obvious as to be almost laughable. Then, as he moves to make a half turn and land on a blow across my spine, he anticipates my step forward too late. I lunge forward in half the anticipated time, catching him mid-spin. I hear the surprise in his gasp at my unnatural speed.

Placing my forearm tight across his throat in a chokehold, I feel the frantic rustle of his feathers as I run the length of my blade across his throat, tracing a precise and deep gauge atop the edge of my forearm. I hold Kairi's gaze as I murder him within feet of her, wanting her to know that it was in her power to stop his grisly fate. Then, as fresh arterial spray flings off the blade, I break away to observe it coating Leo and Caleb, who stand stone still, watching on my right as the source of the bleed opens fully in a gaping scarlet waterfall over my arm.

The Sephilim Corporal dies pitifully in my arms as a few stupid Nephilim gasp from behind Equinian blades held at their throats, and I feel the grip of my power over the room tightening.

Kairi stands, trembling as I shove his lifeless body toward her, face first. She watches, unmoving, a deer in headlights, and I wonder why she doesn't try to fight back, try to use her powers to retaliate in some way. Then, I realise that it's because my power has her petrified, traumatised even.

A warmth pools in my stomach at the way I affect her even now, at the way I can undo her with a single slash of my sword, with a single glance in her direction.

The Corporal face-plants the crystal dancefloor, spattering her ascension gown and tinting both her and the whole night crimson forever in the memories of those who might have loved her.

KAIRI

I'm misted in scarlet as Ambrose's body hits the floor, his head disconnecting from his spine and rolling sideways so his shocked expression stares up at me, blank.

Guilt washes over me, drenching my insides cold.

I'm frozen in place, my heart pounding, mouth dry, the skin on my cheek burning as though it's been burned by an icy flame from where Aro laid his fingertips upon my skin.

I should move, conduct, flee. Everything in my body is tense and ready for me to run, and yet I'm so stiff I'm practically a statue rooted to the spot. The High Lord's salacious and self-satisfied gaze runs up and down my silhouette, causing goosebumps to rise on my blood-flecked arms and chest. Where once my silken gloves had been immaculate, they're now stained with blood as well, my hands trembling within their confines as I try and fail to clench a fist at the injustice of it all.

The eyes of the room are resting upon me, expectant. Even Leo, a military Captain, and the Equinian Chief whose men are holding

Nephilim at sword point are transfixed like I'm the lynchpin holding this entire tragedy together at its core.

Except I can't rise to catalyse anything. The mere sight of Aro brings back how a single flick of his wrist had taken my mortality, of how his galaxy-esque irises had bewitched and ensnared me so completely.

I can't even claim it was against my will because it wasn't.

I had walked to him willingly, without fear, and with a smitten smile on my face. I had let him touch me, and the mere thought of it makes me sick.

I wasn't to know, but I still can't stop the effect he has over me, can't stop the petrification and re-living the violence, the heartbreak, and the self-doubt he had brought to light.

He had shown me I was irrevocably weak, that I was foolish, naïve, and not prepared for the truth of this world. He had made me a victim, and I know he'll do it again.

I shrink from the light, able only to manage a half-step backwards as the powerlessness of the situation dawns on me.

People are going to die, and I cannot move to stop it. I can't even move to surrender to him.

The room is silent except for heavy breathing and flesh rising and falling beneath the nip of razor-sharp sword edges.

"This is who you have been hiding from?" The Equinian Chief on the back of a black pegasus throws his head back and chuckles in a raucous eruption of deep sound, the tattoos of brassy gold on his chest and biceps rippling with amusement.

Aro turns, looking back at him with disdain, mouth opening to say something, to defend his honour, before clamping his jaws shut and thinking better of it.

I almost want to laugh at the thought of him running from me.

I know only too well it wasn't me at all, but the Aristocrats with real power that he was fleeing from. Morpheus, Aliandara, Neve, Asher, Caleb, Lucien— they're his real adversaries, the ones with armies and command of the elements, dragons, or unicorns.

If it had only been me and me alone standing in his way, he would have the crown already.

Desperately, I find myself wishing for Lucien to crash through one of the windows, to come to my aid, to save me.

That, more than Aro, is what truly terrifies me.

Gritting my teeth, I watch as Aliandara steps out from among the crowd, her chin tilted upwards, a dagger I hadn't seen her with earlier clutched in her fingers. Her dark hair shimmers with the stark light from the chandeliers, eyes steel as she steps firmly between myself and my worst nightmare.

"It seems I have underestimated you, Lord Black. And it seems I have overestimated you, Chief Landon," she bites out, kicking Ambrose's head aside and widening into a defensive stance before me. Her navy gown is noticeably torn up one side of the skirt, a leather holster peeking out from where the fabric closes again around her upper thigh.

"Ah, Lady Montgomery. What an incredibly predictable surprise," Landon sneers, his lips puckering sideways. I watch as the High Lady of Artemis tenses entirely, taking another step back toward me and presenting as though she may charge Lord Black.

I watch him tense in turn, adjusting his grip on the thick pommel of his broadsword. Aliandara takes another step back, lithe like a panther, and this time, my eyes are drawn to where her free hand is stretching out behind her, beckoning me with a lifeline.

"This has gone far enough, Lord Black. You're out of your mind if you think I'm letting you anywhere near this young lady," Aliandara snarls, twizzling the dagger between her fingers.

Her free hand, outstretched behind her, clenches and releases desperately.

Then it occurs to me what she's doing.

She's distracting him.

I don't trust Aliandara, but I will trust any advice that doesn't come from within me at this point. Swallowing, I keep my eyes on Aro, not letting myself appear distracted or suddenly relieved.

Slipping off one of my gloves as he begins to retort, self-involved in his own ego, I discreetly slip my palm into hers, and in a flash of lightning, we're gone, leaving what I'm sure will be an utter massacre in our wake.

We land in a whirl of silk skirts, elegant limbs, and an upchucking of golden sands, rolling down a slight incline as my first conduction with a passenger comes to a clumsy conclusion.

"Well, it took you long enough! I thought I was going to have to witticism Lord Black to death!" Aliandara spits, finding purchase on the sand much easier than I.

I watch as she throws her shoes off into the darkness of the desert night with obvious frustration. I open my mouth to reply, but she merely shakes her hair free of sand, gesturing to my feet as she gets to hers.

"Take those monstrosities off. We have people to save and places to be." Her torn skirt flies around her as a gust of sudden chill wind in the otherwise humid night of what I hope is Eclipsia.

She stares down at me, her hair flying out from her face, moon-like eyes round and demanding in the dark. Her golden tattoos shimmer dully under the jaundice of the rising lunar orb which seems bigger than I can ever remember seeing it. "Well, what are you waiting for? I was hoping we'd reappear in Sapphire City, but I see now I should be glad we didn't reappear atop Oblivion Falls." I gape at her, still splayed on my ass in the sand, as she rolls her eyes.

"Well! Get up!" she barks, jolting me out of the trance her appearance has cast over me.

Pulling off my heels and hurling them with the little enthusiasm I can muster, I slowly and clumsily get to my feet, brushing heavy sand from the deep pleats of my skirt.

The High Lady of Artemis places a hand to her brow, shielding her eyes from the glare of the moon as she brings an index finger and thumb to her lips, silver wings bristling at her spine.

Without pausing, she lets out a single sharp whistle, which is soon swallowed by the thick surrounding darkness of the desert.

"What the hell were you trying to do back there?" she turns on me without waiting to see what will become of the sound she made, and I find myself flushing furiously beneath her scrutiny.

"I wasn't trying to do anything—" I stutter, the chill of the air around me causing my blood-spattered skin to rise in goosebumps as I tear off the glove I am still wearing.

"I should say so. I have never seen anything so incredibly feeble! You just— stood there." She is outraged as she flings both her hands up into the air, shaking her head so the black of her hair catches the moonlight and tinges blue. I open my mouth to protest, to tell her she's wrong, but I can't.

She isn't wrong. I had, in fact, just stood there while Aro threatened everyone in the room and killed someone who had dared defend me in cold blood.

"I'm sorry— I—" My throat is dry, the words barely able to make it past my lips.

"Don't apologise. Don't ever apologise— but also— don't just stand there." She looks at me with a withering and disgusted half-glance before, luckily for me, something catches her attention.

From the jet of the night, a whinny breaks the tension building between the Equinian High Lady and me. I breathe out, relieved as a black alicorn with cobalt highlights in its coat swoops down from above, landing seamlessly atop the sands beside us at a gentle canter.

Lady Aliandara reaches out to the creature, its eyes silver and glowing just like her own. She strokes its nose and then runs her hand along the onyx-swirling horn that's protruding from between its brows.

"Well, thank the Goddess Stabbatha is more proactive than you. Come on, we don't have all night!" She leaps gracefully onto the silken spine of her steed, and I smile at the name. She ignores my amusement though, merely grabbing onto the wild mane of the alicorn and kicking her heels into its belly.

"Follow closely behind please, you can do that, can't you princess?" Flipping her hair back over one shoulder, she gives me a look of utter disdain.

I feel myself wilt further.

"Yes," I reply simply, spreading my wings. I'm grateful for the distraction of impending flight as she makes an encouraging whistle with pursed lips. Then, Stabbatha rears a little before lurching forward. I follow, letting my wings pump as I leave the heels that had caused me to totter all night behind me, leaping into flight off the edge of the dune.

As we ascend, Aliandara wastes no time, her face and tattoos gleaming with the promise of bloodshed.

"Faster, Stabbatha" she commands the alicorn with a gentle sternness, turning to me before she continues.

"We have no time to lose. The woman I love is trapped with that lunatic, and I know just the warriors to return her to me. Come along, Kairi— we need to get to Sapphire City. It's going to be a long night."

7

ONE THOUSAND AND ONE NIGHTS

KAIRI

STABBATHA TREADS THE SKY as if it were little more than deep blue velvet smattered with stars beneath her hooves, and the journey passes without much idle chat between me and Aliandara.

Eclipsia sweeps beneath us in an endless unfolding of golden dunes that, when looked at from this height, give the impression of a tumultuous metallic ocean undulating in slow motion beneath the enormous golden moon.

We come into view of what Aliandara calls Sapphire City shortly after I'm beginning to wonder if I might not be being led around in circles for the sameness of the scenery.

As the city becomes suddenly more than a speck in the distance, I discover that the cyclical sprawl of it is the only thing visible for endless miles on every side. The urban spattering of jewel tones centres around an enormous Oasis, gleaming like a radiant sapphire among the dull, moon-bathed jaundice of the surrounding desert.

As we near the glittering gaslit streets, I find the structure more uniform than anything I've seen in Nirvana, Soleus, or Drakos Vale. The layout of the buildings, which lie noticeably low to the ground, appears to be constructed in a pattern like a simplistic maze you might receive on the back of a children's menu.

I follow Aliandara's lead as she tightens her grip on the mane of her dark-horned steed, its enormous, feathered wings drawing back to slow its momentum, readying to land. I pull back my wingspan, letting my body drop with gradual momentum through the air, which grows increasingly warm as my shadow grows larger and more defined upon the sand.

We touch down amongst the most formally arranged and logistically managed gardens I've ever seen, sprawling from the water's edge.

Aliandara brings Stabbatha to a trot and then a halt, patting her neck fondly before dismounting without pause. Her pale thigh becomes luminous from within the darkness of her navy gown as she strides forward without pause.

I stand, gaping, amongst the overwhelmingly intense scent of desert flowers, cacti, succulents, and palm trees with fanned leaves that fill every available nook and cranny of their artificial beds in neat rows. Gas lamps dangle on erected golden poles every few feet, flames flickering tantalizingly against the slightest arid breeze.

"Let us not stand here like morons, Kairi. Follow me," Aliandara snaps, looking back over the swirling tattoos that decorate her tan shoulder to flash me a look of impatient disdain as she flips her windswept hair from where it blankets her collarbone.

I jump, taking quick steps toward her as she beckons Stabbatha silently and the mount trots obediently in her wake, horseshoes clipping the quartz and turquoise pebbles that soothe my feet with cool facets.

Trailing her, the air shifts in its aroma toward one of burning coals, roasting meat, and spices.

My nostrils flare.

Meandering through the mosaic design of the gardens, we finally reach an enormous statue of a warrior riding a bucking unicorn. I assume her, bow in hand, to be Artemis.

The statue is huge as is almost every monument I've seen to the Gods and Goddesses, but before I can get lost in the details of her seemingly fluid armour, a familiar face catches my attention.

"Rohana, summon the guard. There's a situation at the Solis Castra. I want our people retrieved. High Lady Evangeline is inside as well as several of our high-ranking huntresses." The blonde Equinian stares at me, her golden wingtips vibrating as her eyes dart from my face to the skies overhead and then to Aliandara.

"It is as we feared," Rohana acknowledges, and Aliandara nods with a grave expression.

"Get our people out," is all she musters in reply, her tone clipped like an errant thorn.

Rohana, taking in my appearance with a final sad glance, nods firmly before taking off from standing. I watch as her nimble form disappears into the sky overhead and she begins her flight toward the outskirts of the city.

"You thought this might happen?" I ask, feeling meek as my brow creases and my eyebrows dip together. Aliandara sighs, turning to me.

"Let's get inside. We can talk there. It's late." She sounds defeated, bone-tired, and that more than anything is terrifying.

We exit the gardens that are blocked off from the beginning of the city streets by shards of blue topaz that protrude from the ground in jagged spikes. The gardens may be as beautiful as any I'd seen in The City of the Sephilim, but as we move deeper into the city, I realise how incomparable the two locations really are.

The streets are lined with sandstone sidewalks, barely better kept than the roads with chips and cracks spidering through almost every stone slab. Miniature dunes of sand slope from the facades of each and every building, the tiny piles a small homage to their bigger surrounding siblings.

Equinian women are active here at the epicentre of the city, and I find them wearing crop tops and billowing harem pants in jewel-toned silks accompanied by worn slippers. Not one of them is without braided locks or weapons on their person. The tattoos that mark their skin range from blocky and Aztec-looking to Baroque swirls and fleur de lis, dancing across their tanned or black skin in metallic hues spanning from brightest gold to the colour of ionized steel.

There is one undeniable departure from The City of The Sephilim, and that is the laughter and the atmosphere. Despite being hardened by their training and the extreme weather conditions, the female population here can be heard singing, giggling, and chatting merrily in a cacophony that fills the air like a low and relieving hum.

Even at this late hour, the city is alive.

"It's very busy—" I comment as Aliandara turns a sharp and calculated corner; she nods as she stares up into Stabbatha's glimmering irises.

"Yes, it is. Most markets in town run during the night. It is simply too hot to shop during the day." It's the first comment she's made that doesn't make it sound like she utterly hates me, so I take it, not replying as I note woven rope bags full of produce and bundles of fine fabrics clutched in various palms.

It makes me wonder if they farm here, if they can support themselves.

I'd heard Morpheus saying about Equinians hunting illegally on Nirvana soil, but I had figured it was because they were bloodthirsty for sport. Seeing the reality of a city surrounded only by sand and hot air, I begin to wonder if it's hunger rather than entertainment that drives them to trespass.

It is true Kindred don't need to eat to survive, but the urge and the pleasure never go away.

We cannot have come far from the centre of the city when Aliandara seems to pick up her pace, leading me directly toward a villa at the end of an extremely long and dusty road. Sand blows around my ankles, lodging itself between my toes and tickling the tops of my feet as I trail behind, eyes wide and fixed on the Arabian-looking architecture that rises on the horizon.

Eventually, we reach an enormous metal archway that rises into a high spike-topped gate on both of its curving sides. It is inlaid with Lapis Lazuli, and two female guards stand alert on either side. They straighten considerably as we near them, the gas lamps dangling above their heads from twisted steel vines illuminating our tired faces.

"Lady Aliandara, what on earth—" exclaims the dark-haired woman on the left. She's stocky and not overly tall, but her face is hard and her body laden with thick slabs of muscle that are decorated by tattoos twisting into Celtic knots and silver clovers.

Both guards are dressed in flowing immodest panels of gold and bronze, the designs both functional and aesthetically feminine. I envy their protective gear as I look down at the blood-spattered gown hindering every ounce of free movement I still possess.

"Jessica. Take Stabbatha to the stables, and then return here and watch for trouble." The High Lady gestures to her steed and Jessica nods stiffly before leading the mount away.

Aliandara does not say goodbye, at least not that I can hear, and I watch as her quicksilver feathers visibly relax as soon as the other guard allows us through the gate.

Slipping inside, I can see the land that the open plan Villa is sitting on is waterside and ringed with tall palm trees that stir rhythmically with bristling fanned leaves. The metallic sand continues to rub underfoot, and where I had expected a towering and intimidating structure as Aliandara's residence, I find something entirely demure.

There are no windows, only glassless voids into which the sparse desert breeze of the Blazen Plains can reach through and tantalize at will. The sandstone walls have bronze in place of mortar with intricate carvings engraved into the brickwork, accompanied by the occasional jewel glittering like the stars reflected in the still Oasis waters to the west.

The scents of Adenium and, interestingly enough, the plant named California Poppy in the mortal world, seep through the air like an oil, coating my skin. I breathe it in along with the vast night sky overhead, relishing the feeling of stretching my wings in the wide-open space.

Aliandara doesn't pause as she treads up a mosaic path tiled from jagged coloured quartz shards worn smooth, eventually reaching the entrance of the building. I follow, watching as she draws a heavily jewelled velvet curtain aside from a doorway holding no actual door.

Ventilation is clearly important, and I find myself hanging on to each stirring of the too-still air like a starving man clings to a stale morsel of bread.

I can't even imagine how hot it gets during the day.

Aliandara lets the curtain fall behind us as I pass over the threshold, her eyes scanning my body. We head through a narrow yet shaded corridor, the ground beneath my feet strewn with finely embroidered rugs. Window sills giving glimpses into darkened rooms pass us by, through which creeping and thirsty vines fall like the tangled locks of a long-lost princess.

The place is surprisingly low on security personnel, especially given the way walls suddenly fall away in place of columns and the low ceilings will spontaneously cease and open fully to the sky. It reminds me of a Sultan's palace out of *One Thousand and One Nights*, being plusher and more open-plan than where I had expected Aliandara, a fierce warrior and seeming hardass, would rest her head at night.

The trickling of water meets my ears as we pass a central circular courtyard, a fountain topped by a statue of Artemis holding a cup that is overflowing with water mesmerising me.

The water from the fountain flows in small yet organised streams that cut through the floor like veins, meeting as they flow further away from the side of the villa that faces the oasis.

I watch, fascinated.

"The waters keep my personal baths filled; it is a luxury I suggest you take advantage of before you sleep." The Equinian High Lady notices me watching and speaks into the silence.

I nod, feeling suddenly ashamed of my dishevelled appearance.

I had just stood there.

I can't get over it.

The girl who had died willingly to stand up to a man with aeons more life experience, and innumerably more power than she, had frozen in the face of that very same man.

What has Aro done to me?

What have I let him do to me?

Aliandara exits the courtyard, remaining silent as she leads me past luxurious mosaic murals and a wall-less sitting room peppered with plush cushions and satin couches in crimson, aubergine and emerald. Vases and antiques fill every nook and cranny of the walls, which have divots punched into them for displaying just such valuables.

"Here is your room. I will send Di to take your measurements. She is my personal seamstress and seeing as how you cannot wear that gown any longer, I will see to getting you several sets of climate-suitable clothing. You should expect to sleep naked as most of us do here. I will have no guard placed outside your room, so fear not being disturbed." She gives me a sly look as she says this, her eyes glistening.

"You just want me to sit here, to do nothing, while people die?" I ask her, stuttering.

"As opposed to what you did back there at the Solis Castra? My warriors will take care of it. You need only rest. Besides, you're what he wants, and I didn't just risk my neck to simply hand you back to him, helpless as a newborn."

I want to feel offended by her harsh tone and condescending stare, but I cannot. All I feel is guilty and a sense that what she is saying is far truer than I want to admit to myself.

"Aliandara— I—" I want to thank her or redeem myself, but she interrupts me.

"We all have our trauma, Kairi. The key is to remember that it does not define us. Goodnight."

She waves me through the thick emerald curtain, its velvet partitioning the sleeping chamber from the rest of this wing of the house, and shortly after, I hear her dampened footsteps fading upon the oriental carpets.

The rugs continue to sprawl into the luscious chamber she has assigned me, the walls peppered in bottle green mosaics and drapery that blows with a slight breeze. The bed, central to it all and surrounded by solid gold furnishing, is a four-poster dressed in cold white cotton sheets and stacked with aubergine and emerald satin pillows.

It looks inviting, but the wind that stirs through the room reminds me that I am once more alone with my thoughts.

His eyes flash through my memory, causing my blood to chill and my muscles to tense as I remember how helpless he had made me feel.

I will have no guard posted outside your room.

The words and the wicked glint in Aliandara's eye echo from memory, banishing Aro's darkness momentarily.

I need only a moment to realise what she'd implied; that she's letting me know that I'm free. That I am shackled no longer but that I take flight at my own risk.

I don't even consider what could go wrong as I close my eyes and conduct to a far less sultry climate in a bolt of world-shattering lightning.

The scent of wintergreen drenches my skin, and I feel myself relax, exhaling as far as my corset will allow.

I'm standing on the porch of Lucien's house, the cold of the swirling snowflakes around me a cleansing burn upon my bare shoulders.

I inhale then exhale again, feeling it in my bones.

Home.

I hear the front door open behind me and turn, my blood-spattered lilac skirt blooming out around my ankles as Lucien peers out into the darkness of the night.

"Kairi?" he sounds wide awake, despite the fact he's shirtless and wearing cotton pyjama pants that hang a good inch above the ankles that sit at the bottom of his exorbitantly long legs.

"Lucien—" I breathe his name like a magic spell and feel myself stepping with bare soles across the cold wooden decking of the porch that separates us.

I fall into his arms, hating myself as I crumble into a sobbing mess and he clutches me to the chill, tattooed flesh of his broad chest.

Tears fall for my lost courage, for Ambrose, for the innocent people I had left behind as Aliandara and I fled from the Solis Castra. I thought my rebirth had meant an end to the running, but here I am again, shivering and terrified in the arms of the Draconian who can't help but save me.

Who I can't help but run to—

"Shhh— Shhh—." Lucien strokes my hair, stepping back and pulling me across the threshold into the warmth of the high-ceilinged entrance hall.

I take it in through tear-filled eyes, half wanting to smile and half wanting to scream at the fact I'm back here again.

Lucien pushes me back from his embrace, looking deeply into my face as his dark sapphire irises glisten with concern.

"Kairi— what are you doing here?" He looks at my gown, at the dishevelled way my once pristine hair sticks to my forehead, at the way I'm freckled with blood. He immediately rushes forward to examine me.

"Are you hurt?" he enquires urgently, but all I can do is shake my head. The fact that I had gotten an innocent Sephilim Corporal killed becomes a thought too painful to speak.

Wordlessly, he watches me tremble only a moment before he pulls me off my feet and carries me and my enormous skirt up the thick wooden staircase. He kicks open his bedroom door as we cross the landing, ducking as he manoeuvres me through the doorframe and sits me down on the edge of what I assume is his bed.

"Stay here, I'll be close—" he vows, turning and tucking his leathery wingspan in neatly. His tattoos ripple in the moonlight coming from overhead as he turns back with a worried glance, and it's all that I can do to turn my head slightly, locating the source of the glow.

He has an enormous skylight over the bed which, if I wasn't so shaken, I would be admiring.

I'm numb as I sit there, bare feet dangling just above the wooden floorboards, the scent of him permeating me and slowly calming me with each passing moment.

I don't know how long I sit here, simply focusing on my next breath, but by the time I come back to myself, letting my fingers brush through the silk of his sheets, he steps from a lit doorway opposite, steam billowing behind him.

He walks across the room in quick and definite strides, holding out a hand and taking my palm in his. Guiding me with gentle sureness, he leads me into what turns out to be a vast ensuite.

Central to it all, a deep, copper, egg-shaped tub billowing steam stands on metal feet atop glittering navy tiles, the walls of the room a warm mahogany panelling that hugs vast frosted windows.

"Let me help you with that—" Lucien doesn't pause to look me in the eyes, for which I'm grateful, turning me slowly on the spot and unlacing the back of my gown so I can take it off myself.

He removes the diadem from where it continues to bite into my skull with vicious teeth, setting it down on a copper vanity. Then, when I'm standing, barely dressed in a gown that's beginning to peel away from me, he looks at me, lips pressed into a neat line.

"I'll just let you—" He turns to leave, and I make my first sudden movement in I don't know how long.

"Don't—" I whisper, giving him a wide-eyed look as the thought of him disappearing, even into the next room, fills me with dread.

"Kairi it's— not appropriate—" he stutters, the steam seeming suddenly warmer as it turns our vision hazy.

"I'm asking, Lucien." I swallow his name like a tonic, the taste of it as comforting as freshly baked bread but sharp enough to keep me alive until my next breath. "Don't leave me alone— Please."

He purses his lips, exhaling in a jagged staccato as if he's physically pained.

"Alright," he coughs, and I turn from him then, letting the gown I've been holding to my chest fall and pool in an enormous messy pile of sparkle and blood around my ankles. I step out of my thong and hear him undressing behind me as I pull a few glittering pins out of my hair, allowing it to fall down my back in long waves between my wings.

Lucien steps around me, naked now except for his stunning tattoos, long blonde hair tied back into a sleep-mussed braid, wings hanging malleable by his sides. He climbs into the tub, his wingspan lining the high-reaching arch of the rim farthest from the faucet and cocooning his spine. His talons lose their sheen, becoming matte with warm condensation.

He extends a dripping hand out to me over the edge of the tub, blinking demurely as his eyes sweep over my breasts and naked thighs. Swallowing, I take his hand, stepping over the rim and into the hot water.

I lower myself so I'm sitting between his legs, the hardness I feel at my spine as I lean back conveniently hidden beneath a veil of bubbles that smell heavily of jasmine.

I don't say anything, leaning back into his chest and letting the steaming water caress my muscles as he runs his nose along the back of my neck and buries it into my hair. Working his way up around my ear, he finally comes to rest his lips on the crown of my head, and we simply sit for a while, holding one another amid the rising steam. I feel his heartbeat heavy against my back, his manhood throbbing along with his pulse as he wraps me tighter and tighter in his arms.

"Kairi, what happened?" he asks me after he feels my muscles unravel against his torso. He runs a finger along the edge of my shoulder, causing my stomach to flood with a steady thrilling hum.

"Lord Black, he came— he had an army. He killed Ambrose—" I whisper, my voice barely audible as his cheek presses into the pointed shell of my ear, arms entwining themselves tighter around my torso like protective vines.

"Who is Ambrose?" he asks next, and the question makes me feel physically nauseous. The idea of ever being in anyone's arms but his— it's not the way things are meant to be.

"One of the suitors," I reply simply as he picks up a sponge from seemingly nowhere, wetting it and beginning to scrub my forearms clean of red.

"It's alright. I was there. I saw you—" he breathes his admission as a sigh in my ear, and I feel my heart shatter.

"You were there? But— Did you see what happened?" I'm wondering, if he was there, why he hadn't stepped in, why he hadn't acted...

Then again, I remind myself, I lost my right to expect that of him when choosing to dance with prospective husbands.

"I was, but when I saw you dancing with him— I left." Lucien clears his throat of obvious discomfort, scrubbing at my skin harder to distract himself.

"You— you left?" I ask, on the verge of tears yet again.

"You looked beautiful," is all he says, his voice rough against my ear.

"I'm sorry—" I apologise, but he only laughs.

"No, I'm sorry. It's not fair to you that I was watching. This bath is too hot for me—"

He pushes my body away from his chest, removing himself from the tub in a dripping mass of bubbles on flesh and long steaming limbs scented with the night-blooming flower. His skin is flushed red, quite different from his usual pallor, but even so, I know the heat is only an excuse.

"Lucien, wait—" I twist, watching as he moves toward a towel ring clutched between a dragon's glistening silver jaws. Pulling down an enormous navy towel, he wraps himself in it, looking back over his shoulder at me with steely eyes.

"No. It's alright, Kairi. Please, relax in the bath. You need it." His face crumples as he turns, and then I'm alone in the hard metal tub, cold among the bubbles.

I sit in the bath for another ten minutes, resting my sore feet on the warm copper of the faucets and looking down at my angelic physique. Lucien had wanted me, and I, him, yet something is bothering him, and I don't understand why.

My feathered wings cradle my back, damp and heavy at my spine as I take a deep breath and decide that enough is enough.

Using the rim of the tub, I get to my feet, dripping suds and water onto the tiles underfoot as I step out.

Walking over to the towel rings, I pull myself a towel from beside the one that's been left empty, wrapping it around my breasts and pulling it under my wings, scraping wet hair over one shoulder so it's off my back. I let the feathers flutter, shedding water and weight as bubbles spatter the floor.

I pad back through to the bedroom, leaving my gown and accessories peppered across his bathroom floor.

"Lucien?" I call, but the volume is unnecessary.

He's sitting, still wrapped in his towel, on the edge of his circular mattress, head hanging so his braid is draped over his left shoulder, shrouded in moonlight falling uninterrupted through the skylight. In the pureness of the light, I see the darkness of him made definite in the jagged outline of his wings and the slashes of his archaic tattoos. I find him entirely beautiful.

I make my way across the room to him, boldly taking my water softened fingertips and running them along the line of his jaw.

He visibly shudders as I pull his gaze up to mine.

"Lucien, what is it?" I ask, not forcefully but with as much earnestness as I can muster. I'm shaking a little, maybe from shock, or maybe from the fact that this night seems never-ending in its surprises.

"I'm a fool, Kairi. Even after all this time—" His jaw tenses and his lips go slack. I stare deeply into his eyes, narrowing my own.

"If you're a fool, then I'm— well I don't even know what I am. How can you say that, Lucien? You saved my life. Are you saying that was a mistake?" I feel my fears surfacing, but he shakes his head.

"Never. It could never have been a mistake. My mistake was thinking I could ever be deserving of someone like you— you are so— you're so pure. Just look at you, for Hecate's sake!" He's on his feet now, gesturing to my damp wings, cupping my cheek with an open palm and clutching my forearm with a tight fist.

I bear it, the pain of his too-tight grasp, refusing to look away.

For the first time that night, I find my voice.

"Lucien, it's not about deserving. I want to be with you. Don't you know that?" I ask him, scared now as my heartbeat accelerates.

Have I been so unclear? Does he mistake my longing to keep my people safe for a desire to be rid of him?

"Kairi, you don't understand. I saw you dancing with him— and you know— I thought you would be better off! I should just let you go, this— whatever the hell this is— it's not good for you." I feel my eyes water at his words, anger and sadness hitting me like a wrecking ball. "You deserve more. You deserve to love someone who can adore you in front of the world, someone who you can stand beside and be proud of." He tears his hands from my skin and walks toward the end of the bed, gazing up at the stars with stiff shoulders. Cold silence rolls off him in place of the steam we had so recently basked in.

I feel my heart break a little, not at how he sees me but at how he sees himself and the void he perceives between us. There has never been a void in my eyes, not really. Even as a mortal, when he was some immortal winged mystery, I've only seen him as sanctuary and then as home.

I tread around the curve of the bed frame, stepping in front of him and staring at him with wide, watering eyes as I kneel. He doesn't meet my gaze for a moment, imploring the sky for guidance. However, as I reach up and slide my fingers along the razor edge of his jawbone and up into his hair, he glances down at me. In his eyes, there is pain, and there is self-loathing.

Reaching up to him, I let my towel drop around my ankles and push my naked body to his, taking his tongue in my mouth and kissing him deeply. The scent of peppermint and wintergreen fogs my thoughts as a guttural and pained groan emits from his throat.

When the kiss ends, I firmly say, "Never let me go."

He looks at me with wide eyes, blinking, but before he has time to talk himself out of it, I kiss him again, deeper this time, as I push him back onto the bed so I'm straddling his towelled waist. I let myself moan as I run my fingers down the curves of his enormous biceps.

He shudders, then grips my forearms, stopping me.

"Kairi— I can't. I— Kairi—" I begin to kiss him again, and he's breathless as my nipples harden and push into his pectorals.

Blinking hard, he tightens his grip, stopping me.

"I haven't— I've never—" he's stuttering now, a blush spreading across his sharp cheeks, his eyes anxious and scared.

"Never?" I ask him, surprised.

After all, he's got to be two hundred years old—

"I never, I never found the right— it was never— Oh Goddess, I'm fucking this up, aren't I?" He's trembling, his chest rising and falling like a cresting wave as I feel the heat between us settle.

"And you keep saying I'm the pure one here?" I whisper to him, biting my bottom lip and giving him a sly smile from beneath my eyelashes.

"I didn't want— I wanted it to mean something," he admits, coughing slightly with embarrassment.

My heart flutters at the antiquity of the statement, but I understand. I go to get off of him, to find something more sensible to put on and cuddle up with him in his bed when he grabs my wrist and pulls me back into his arms. I look down at him through the drapery of my damp tangles as he places a hand on my cheek and another around my lower waist.

"This. Kairi. It means everything," he says shyly, unwrapping the towel from around his waist willingly and pulling my flesh to his body. I'm immediately consumed with an icy desire that spreads across my skin in a blizzard of intensity, cooling the fear that's been engulfing me for days.

I guide him, pushing him so he is sitting up straight against the headboard and letting my wings flare out, casting his pallor in shadow and eclipsing the moon.

I dip, lowering my head so I'm kissing him as I explore his body with my hands, gently at first as I venture down the mounds of his pectorals and then the V cut of his lower abdominals.

When I reach his manhood, it is engorged and scalding to touch. I wrap my fingers around it, gently massaging him as he pulsates within my grasp. His eyes roll back in his head as he slumps against the headboard, a growl escaping his clenched teeth.

I can tell he's sensitive, as I expected, and don't waste any time as I widen my stance and lower myself onto him. He stretches me deliciously, his eyes widening as he kisses me ravenously with half-stifled moans escaping him. He struggles for breath against my lips in his surrender to his own pleasure.

I smile at him as I trail my lips down his neck, rising and falling on the length of him as it throbs and hardens further inside me.

"Fuck— oh fuck!" he exclaims, placing his hands on my hips. I let him control my pace, let him take one of my nipples in his mouth as I ride him, my wings beating wildly behind me as he runs his hands up and down my back. I feel my orgasm building as his touch sends my nervous system into overload and throw my head back so I'm staring up at the stars. I slow a moment, giving him time to catch his breath, not wanting things to be over so soon.

He kisses my throat and adores every inch of my breasts slowly, panting slightly as I rock gently and with delicious friction against the length of him.

I tease, hearing him stifling his moans as he grips my back with desperate fingers and inhales the scent of me like I'm a drug.

Finally, when he can stand it no more, he pulls me flush to him, kissing me and bracing his legs against the inside of my thighs. I feel myself reaching climax as he swells, his fingertips stimulating me with cool traces across my behind.

"Kairi— oh Goddess— Kairi, I'm so close—" he urges me on, and I purposefully tighten my muscles as I let out a strangled cry, his hips grinding into me so hard I think I might pass out as I peak as well. His fingers dig into my ass cheeks, and I let out an instinctual animal cry into the night, riding my pleasure and his as he empties himself inside me.

We both go limp, but we can't stop kissing, not even for a moment. His hands won't stop exploring my body, and as I lift myself off of him, he pushes me backwards, climbing atop me with hungry lips and starving fingers, one course not nearly enough to sate.

Wrapping my legs around his waist, I feel him hardening once more as his lips greedily trace my earlobe. I pull him close to me, the coolness of his skin bliss on my burning flesh. As I'm kissing his shoulder, he surprises me by entering me, fully hard once more.

I stare up at the moon as he whispers breathlessly into my ear.

"You are everything."

8

DEAD SOULS

ARO

I STARE AT MYSELF in the mirror on the front door of my wardrobe, straightening the dark indigo velvet of my collar and peering down my nose as I appraise the completed look.

Aether shimmers in the air in high concentrations, landing in my tousled and freshly washed locks, glimmering. The amethyst sword, which has still not left my sight, hangs innocuously against the outer curve of my right thigh, sheathed and waiting for its next meal.

I'm grateful to be out of the armoured chausses and even more grateful for the fact I have my beloved four-poster back. Sleeping on the desert floor certainly does not suit me. In fact, I doubt it truly suits anyone.

"What would you like me to do with these?" Dawn asks, causing me to cock an eyebrow as I peer back over the dark feathers of my right wing. I had forgotten she was there, both a side effect of my self-adoration and her slight tread.

She's holding up my chausses, having picked them up from the floor where I'd shed them like a sticky second skin, her face impassive and calm as ever.

"Burn them," I say, turning away without acknowledging her any further. After all, I don't have time to make small talk with Nephilim handmaidens; I have business to attend.

Pivoting on the heel of my soft black leather boot, I sweep through the room like a storm. Dawn's light locks and periwinkle-tipped feathers ruffle, and the golden buckles of my shoes catch the light as I move to leave. She rushes to beat me there, opening the double doors before I can reach out to touch the gilded handles and bowing low with respect. Her meekness makes me smile, but the expression doesn't reach my eyes, just as weaker emotions seem to no longer touch my soul.

The scent of lilacs blooms up off the velvet of my lapels at the full spread of my wings, the tails of my morning coat flying upward as I take flight over the balcony railing just beyond the exit of my suite. I could take the stairs, but the impression wouldn't be half as dramatic or intimidating.

I plunge, falling into the central hall of the Solis Castra, past a blur of stained glass, ombre purple hues, and sparkling aether dancing leisurely through the florally fragrant air.

My boots impact the crystal floor with a muted thud, and I find myself surrounded by Equinian soldiers, tending their steeds idly without turning their attention to my sudden landing. This irks me. After what just happened here, they should fear my presence alone.

However, I pass through them like a shadow unperturbed, gliding up a set of shallow stairs and quickly navigating the tall and narrow corridors that lead toward the site of what had too quickly turned from a night of merriment into an unnecessary massacre.

The double doors of the ballroom, where Kairi had cowered before fleeing, stand open with several Nephilim servants mopping the floor clean. Rivers of blood now carve it into ugly amethyst fragments where once it had been a beautiful macrocosmic mural of golden filigree.

I shake my head, finding Chief Landon standing far across the octagonal chamber on the balcony beside an antsy Rogue, refusing to watch as Sephilim and Nephilim remove the last of the bodies.

It didn't have to be this way.

She should have bent to my demands, but instead, she ran.

With Aliandara no less.

That could be problematic.

I sigh, careful to avoid the bloody puddles and staining my new shoes as I pick my way rapidly toward the Chieftain's bulky silhouette.

"Funny, all this blood, and yet, the Fae and Nephilim managed to escape while you got distracted by Rohana and her horse-riding whores. Didn't you tell me you had the most brutal warriors in Aetheria?" I mutter, clicking my tongue against my teeth in dissatisfaction.

Chief Landon John twists back from where he's gazing beyond the horizon, the dawn not far off, my voice reaching him and causing his posture to stiffen instinctively.

His hand pauses as he strokes the rump of his onyx pegasus, but he does not turn to fully face me, merely returning to stare into the endless sea of clouded sky beyond Soleus.

"You didn't mention that Aliandara would send a force of her own. You know better than anyone that most of my men have personal grievances with the women she dares call warriors. I can't be expected to maintain control when it comes to our mortal enemies. Neither would I want to—" he admonishes, not seeming sorry in the slightest. Raising his chiselled chin in defiance, his jaw twitches beneath a blanket of thick stubble.

"The Fae High Lords and Ladies fled. I was hoping to bargain with them on my terms— now I have been robbed of that opportunity due to your negligence," I spit at him, and he smirks.

"What might *you* possibly want to negotiate with *them*, Lord Black? The Fae are good for two things, killing slowly— and, well, I suppose they make good liquor," he admits, the corner of his lips turning upward.

I roll my eyes.

"How generous of you to acknowledge that fact. I'm sure Morpheus will be flattered by such a glowing review." I pause a moment, exasperated by the Chief's lack of urgency. "It might interest you to know that, despite their placidity, the Fae have the largest populace of any Kindred race. Interesting, don't you think?" I enquire, and he laughs, his head thrown back, tattoos trembling as his braided locks shimmer cold in the pre-dawn light.

"Why should it matter when ten Fae don't equal one of my Equinians in strength, intellect, or power?"

His arrogance amazes even me, and that is saying something.

"Regardless, I'm concerned given things with Aliandara and the turn they've taken. I did not expect her dissent so early. Not only that, but if I am correct, you didn't manage to maintain your hold on any of her people or subdue any of the soldiers she sent to retrieve them—"

My comment is meant to humble him, but unsurprisingly, he only angers, balling his fists at his sides and grinding his teeth behind the cracked veil of his lips.

"Lady Evangeline was rescued as my guards were focused on containing the Fae High Lady, Neve— she froze three of them solid, you might have noticed, " he gives the excuse, and I give him an unimpressed side glance.

"But she still escaped— correct?" I pour my salty attitude into his wounded pride and watch him recoil.

"Correct," is all he says this time.

No excuses, only his failure laid bare before us both. The silence between us is thick enough to bite and chew.

"I see. Well, then I would say that you and your men are not adequate for my needs," I begin, and he turns to face me now, tensing as veins rise close to the surface of his biceps, their dark rivers contrasting against the linework of his radically metallic tattoos.

I gaze up at him, unafraid as my palm lingers over the pommel of the amethyst sword strapped to my hip beneath the finely embroidered hem of my jacket.

I wonder suddenly what Ares' power tastes like—

"Which leads me to my next question. What are our chances of recruiting some of the other clansmen?" I pull my hands behind me, feeling the crushed velvet and tips of my feathers brush my strong fingers.

Landon's face turns several shades of angry before his eyes narrow.

"What exactly are you implying?" he queries, suspicious.

Rogue senses the tension, exhaling a heavy breath and fluttering the mighty wings that lay flat and definite as sheening onyx stone against her flank. Her tail flicks, aggravating the aether surrounding us into swirling tornadoes before they dissipate lazily amidst the humidity.

"I'm implying that we find you more warriors." I don't blink or falter in my reply, and he smiles.

"You want me to poach warriors from under other Chieftains? How— despicable."

His face becomes a thoughtful mask as aether settles in the masculine lines of his face, and he glances at Rogue.

"Is it poaching if they leave willingly? Besides, if you are divided, you are far weaker than you need be. It's idiotic, having so many clans merely because Aresian Equinians can't get along in large groups. All it shows is that you lack disciplined leaders."

I shrug to myself, letting the taunt hang between us like a severed horse head.

"You want me to leave and head back to Eclipsia? One might think you're trying to get rid of me, Aro. Then again, I can't imagine you'd be as naïve as that. You should know by now that Equinians would die before answering directly to a Sephilim," he adds, and I titter with fake amusement, wondering why he thinks I need what he defines as warriors and I define as a divided and brutish rabble.

"No. As if I'd try anything so crude."

He gives me an affronted look, and I exhale heavily before continuing, "I want you to send some of your men to Eclipsia, for you are far too obvious as a recruiter. I also want you to accompany men to the riverbanks of Soleus, to the flower fields. I need all the amethyst harvested they lay eyes on. No exception." I don't give him the courtesy of facing him as I issue the order.

Then I hear him snort, sounding more like a horse than a man.

"You're talking about warriors, not miners, Aro. My men aren't field hands, and their steeds aren't cart horses. I won't have them degraded as such." His voice is sharp, defiance dripping from every syllable.

I shrug, examining my nails with faux interest. It's the first time they've been clean in well over two months.

"I care not if you want to acquire the peoples of Sparrowdale or Hawkwood to handle the labour. I'm not fussy about who, but it must be amethyst, all of it, and I need it quickly. You're also to keep this as quiet as possible," I explain, pursing my lips as I fall once more into calculated silence.

"Very well, let's get to it then—" Landon grabs a fistful of Rogue's mane and moves to turn her away from the glow of daybreak.

"Of course, you will leave your best men here to protect the Solis Castra until I can ascertain my level of influence over the aerial fleet," I add, not looking back at him.

He doesn't reply to that, but I assume he's heard me as I note the slightest pause in his otherwise metronomic tread.

He leaves me on the balcony, alone, presumably heading back inside to begin barking guttural orders at men who are standing pathetically idle despite the fact there is so much still to be done to secure the throne.

A few minutes pass, and I contemplate the days to come, the steps that must be taken, and the sacrifices made. Then, I hear a familiar footfall approaching from behind and make a half-turn, coming face to face with exactly who I expect.

"Captain," I acknowledge him, and he bows deeply, his red hair chill yet fiery, blazing in the blue sunlight. I notice his white formal tunic is spattered even still with the blood of the Corporal I had beheaded entirely for Kairi's benefit.

"My Lord, I am relieved you have returned at last. Things have been— difficult since you left," he admits, chewing his bottom lip in the most unattractive manner imaginable. His wings quiver as he straightens fully, and I look him directly in the eyes.

"You did not search for me," is all I can say. He shrugs with a spine like a steel rod.

"I was not allowed, my Lord. Lord Abara had all military forces redirected to defence against potential attack by the Draconians. The stand-off at the Temple of Zeus changed many things. People are scared of the Dragons as is to be expected," he informs me, keeping eye contact effortlessly.

I stroke my jaw with my index finger a moment, breathing in the fragrant mist rising off the Oblivion Falls. They sprawl out in a fog-slathered crescent toward the horizon, frothing madly.

"And how am I to know what you say is true? What proof do I have of your allegiance?" I demand in a cold tone.

My muscles tighten and heat with the slightest hint of Dragonfire beneath my clothes.

"My allegiance? The proof stands just over there. You see her, the blonde?" Leo points out the girl I know to be Vail, who is helping clean shattered glass from the floor of the ballroom. Her enormous bloodstained skirts plume around her slender waist.

"Vail?" I ask him, looking down my nose at her from a distance. She is pretty and demure, but I've heard her speak, and the southern drawl gives me endless violent urges.

She is, though, I recall, an excellent violinist, and her role as an unexpected advisor during my initial courtship of Kairi cannot be forgotten.

"Yes, my Lord. I wish to marry her. But due to my job, I won't do that in a war-torn country. We need unity. One king, and a king with a vision at that, for true peace. I believe you are that man," Leo explains, nodding with certainty as respect glimmers, a steady sun in the centre of his dark irises.

I return the gesture, feeling my doubts slowly dissolve. I can tell he cares for Vail by the way he had rushed to her side as I burst in through the window, but I can also tell that he is tense even now. I wonder though if it's not me but the hungry way several of the Equinian soldiers are staring at the woman he wishes to claim for himself.

"Very well, you clearly care for her. I also know you are one of the most level-headed and sensible Sephilim I have ever known, and

I know that we understand one another. We are going to need to prepare ourselves for all eventualities," I inform him, and he nods, eyes hardening.

"And what of The Heirbound? We will need to ascertain her location and extract her so she can serve her purpose. The quicker we have someone on the throne, the better," he expresses with a passion I've missed, and I nod. He practically read my mind.

"Exactly, I have an idea where she is, but I can't see any point in trying to infiltrate Sapphire City. Aliandara wouldn't stand for it, and it would cause more losses than it's worth. No, I intend to wait Kairi out. She will break, eventually coming to me, and I am nothing if not patient," I explain. "If she does not come, I am sure she can be persuaded— After all, you know her. How many bodies do you think she will allow to pile up before she succumbs to guilt and surrenders to her fate? Her heart, Leo, her tender heart— that is what will undo her. It is what will make me King. Ironic given her hate for me— don't you think?" I smile to myself, a warmth of certainty spreading through my chest. Silence befalls me again, and I stand, wondering if Leo will offer his thoughts.

Leo looks thoughtful but remains tight-lipped, his wings widening in a formal stretch as the sun begins to peak timidly over the horizon in beams of brightest cobalt. Then he turns from me, giving a slight bow once again, and moves to return to helping Vail pick up shattered glass.

I watch the two of them, the tenderness of how he kneels beside her, and I smile.

A man in love is a man with something to lose. Just as a woman with soul, with conscience, and morality, is a woman who can be played like a fool.

GENEVIEVE

I lie, sprawled along the chaise longue, my pale milky legs peeking from beneath the emerald satin of my nightgown, staring into the flickering tongues of the hearth's meagre blaze.

The orange light is captured by the whiskey in my glass, setting the amber liquid ablaze and dancing in my palm as I take another slow sip, eyelids fluttering.

I have missed you, Gen. Algoric's voice swims lazy circles in my head, and I smile, relief flooding me as the voice at last returns.

I had remained on the floor of Algoric's old chamber far too long, and my bones are chill from the stone, the heat on my skin extinguished entirely by grief.

"And I have missed you—" I say aloud, my voice soft and unfamiliar to me. The last two months have been a flurry of hissing and biting remarks at servants or High Lord Gage Lee. I can't remember the last time I spoke out of delight instead of fury.

Continuing to eye the flames, I let my head loll back onto the arched pillow of the upholstery, a peach glow cast intermittent on my pale skin.

You're in so much pain— The voice comments, and I shrug, distracted immediately by a knock at the doors.

Ignore it. We should be alone a while—

"What?" I bellow, agitation rising fast in my chest as I take another sip of whiskey. My eyes linger over the rim of the cut crystal tumbler as the door is sheepishly pushed open.

From outside, a figure I don't expect steps into my domain, his face and white tunic spattered crimson with someone's blood.

"High Lady Thomas." Captain Bond sounds breathless, his hair slightly damp and dark, eyes frantic as he steps further into the room.

His red locks catch the firelight, becoming vibrant as I wonder what the hell it is he's doing here.

This is against the rules.

It's a trap— Algoric mutters, and I blink several times, watching the Captain as he fidgets on the spot.

"You shouldn't be here. This is beyond rude and quite against our agreement if you recall. How do I know you're not—" I begin, but the boy dares to interrupt me.

"Trust me, I wouldn't have conducted myself into a courtyard full of armed Draconian guards alone if it wasn't important," he snaps, eyes hard as flint.

The disrespect, Algoric snaps, causing me to sit bolt upright.

I toy with the idea of scalding him for his disobedience, but my curiosity gets the better of me.

"Well then, you've interrupted my contemplation. Let it not be for no good reason." I down the rest of my drink, stretching my wings and getting to my feet, depositing the empty tumbler atop the writing desk near the door with its fellows. There had once been four of the beautiful crystal glasses, but only three remain after I had shattered one because of Lucien DeLaurent what feels like a lifetime ago.

Captain Bond straightens, his dark chocolate feathers unruffled. He hadn't flown here but rather conducted directly from Soleus.

Risky indeed.

"Lord Black, he has seized back the Solis Castra by force. He murdered many of the Nephilim guests at Lady Freemont's ascension ball," he explains, running a hand back through his hair.

I feel my eyes hood with heavy lids.

Even the thought of Aro Black makes me both irrationally angry and inexplicably tired.

"I see. And how did he accomplish that? I assume he wasn't alone?" I raise a single eyebrow, turning and leaning back against the diagonal tilt of the ornate mahogany as I fold my arms across my silk-slathered breasts.

"Captain Landon John of the Aresian Equinians. His clan have allied themselves with Lord Black, they came out of nowhere and held guests hostage." He continues his report, dead in the face. I narrow my eyes.

"You're playing a dangerous game, Captain. Sneaking away at such a time." He doesn't respond to this, casting his eyes to the flames in the fireplace so they don't have to rest on my face. "What happened next?" I ask with an exhale. It is clear he's not here for small talk, not that if I desired such a thing I'd go to a Sephilim for my fill.

"Kairi fled, conducted out of the hall with High Lady Montgomery. After that, it was not long before Aliandara sent a unit of her own to retrieve her people too. The Fae fought their way out, but many died. None of the High Born Lords or Ladies perished, at least... but still. It was an unnecessary massacre." He looks sad, but I remain untouched by the story. All massacres are unnecessary in my experience, but his kind are the last people I'd expect to hear that from. Perhaps he really is different from the rest.

Then, something occurs to me, something that causes my ever-fiery blood to run chill.

"And where is she now, the girl who has caused so much pain to me and mine?" I ask him, glowering. My fingertips twitch with the urge to ball into fists.

"I couldn't possibly say with any certainty, but my guess would be somewhere well-guarded. If Aliandara has had anything to do with it," Leo comments, his voice hesitant as I sense his fondness for the Heirbound.

I wonder what exactly it is about that girl which causes men to become such utterly pathetic creatures.

"Hmm. Interesting—" I run a long shaking finger along the curve of my ear, pushing my alabaster locks back over my shoulder.

Leo stands, waiting for me to finish my sentence, but his very presence sets my teeth on edge, the supposed innocence on his face nothing but an obvious façade.

"Well, is that all?" I ask him with blunt impatience. It cuts him, and I want to laugh. I had never realised our little arrangement was sentimental to him.

Since when do the Sephilim have hearts?

They don't. It's a trick, Gen, Algoric says, mirroring my thoughts back at me in a hissing Draconian tongue I have missed.

"No. That's the update." He straightens, staring forward without emotion, sweeping it beneath his mask with practised skill.

"Get out then," I say, turning from him and walking over to the balcony doors. Ripping open the gossamer drapes, I yank them open.

I see the flash of his conduction momentarily light the grid of glass windows stark white before I am plunged back into the shadow abated by the hearth alone.

"Gage, get in here," I call out of the cracked door into the clear, post-blizzard, pre-dawn air.

I hear a book slam shut and then an umbrella shutting as I turn from the door and return to pacing the floors of my bedchamber, restless with anxiety.

"Yes?" Gage asks, his hair defiantly spiky against the damp. One of his metal teeth flashes as he talks, and I place my hand on my chin, stroking gently and thinking.

"I have a job for you," I admit, feeling stupid and weak for what I'm about to say. I have pushed against this for the last eight weeks, but now I must know about the location of Kairi Freemont if I am to protect my people.

"I need you to go and get High Lord DeLaurent. Tell him I want to speak with him immediately," I bite out, watching Gage's eyes widen. His white and aqua-scaled wings shimmer slightly, contrasting against the dark jade of the .

Don't do this, Gen. He is not worth extinguishing your rage. He killed me— he killed us. Algoric's sibilant tone echoes throughout my head, and I flinch, the betrayal of my pride, of my cause, stinging deeply.

Gage looks at me, suddenly concerned.

"Are you alright Lady Thomas?" he enquires, taking a step forward and reaching out. I flinch backwards, narrowing my eyes as I realise he's probably trying to pry inside my head with his infernal empathic tendencies.

Tensing, I vow I won't let him know about Algoric. At least, not yet. He must remain mine for longer before I am ready to relinquish him to the world once more.

It's been so long since I felt connected to him, since we had any conversation through the bond. It feels too tenuous to share. Or perhaps I'm only afraid I'm going mad.

"Very well, I will leave at once." Gage straightens, his spine suddenly stiff as his wings stretch, obviously itching for a good early morning flight. I bet he misses riding Aqua as well, I know the longing for Dragon flight more than he can imagine.

"Thank you, Gage," I say, realising how much my grief has taken a toll on those who surround me.

High Lord Lee never asked for personal guard duty, and yet it had fallen on him regardless. I am lucky he seems not to care for my rage and violence, though, I can guess why. He tolerates it because he understands where it comes from.

He's felt it.

As he turns back to flash me his metal teeth yet again, I see just how much. His eyes, ringed dark, appear bloodshot, and his mouth is crowded by creases from pursing in worry. I feel it in the relief he feels and how his shoulders drop considerably. It is like I've just lifted an immense weight from him with only my gratitude.

"My pleasure, Lady Thomas." He turns then, heading back out to the balcony to begin his journey to find Lucien.

He should be grateful you haven't murdered him yet— Algoric adds, silently reading the slightest warmth that begins to bloom around my heart.

"You're angry—" I speak aloud, glancing from one end of the room to the other for the source of his voice yet again.

As are you, Gen. As you should be. I was murdered. He reminds me of this jagged fact, and I feel guilt for letting my grief rescind, tears threatening to fill my eyes.

"I know. And I have missed you more than you can imagine. Please— show yourself to me— I beg of you." I plead like the broken girl I had once been in the attic above her father's Parisian Whorehouse.

I am not as I was. I am afraid if you see me— I am afraid your desire for avenging my death will falter. I am afraid your relief in my mere existence will overshadow the enormity of what has been stolen from me. Algoric admits, sounding more like his old self as his voice softens with anxiety.

"I will avenge you, my Love. How could I not? You are and always will be my world," I vow, and I hear nothing but silence as I wait. Standing in the centre of the room, I turn with painful slowness as if he will suddenly appear out of thin air.

"I just— I need to see you. I need to be by your side again—" I beg, staring up at the ceiling as if the voice is omnipresent.

Gen, please understand. I must not only have vengeance but a promise the same fate will not befall the other Dragons. Are you willing to make that sacrifice?

I nod without hesitation, without knowing what I'm agreeing to because I don't care. Whatever the price, I will pay it.

Very well, I'm in the .

He whispers this to me as if it is a secret so precious that speaking it too loudly, even psychically, would cause the illusion to shatter.

I don't wait, tearing the door of my suite open and charging down the hall, my feet slapping against the crystal floors as the guards stationed outside my rooms look at one another in confusion. They do not follow me, lucky for them as I would have no qualms in screaming at them to back off despite my hurry.

I know, for this, I must be alone.

I let my wings tuck into my body as tightly as possible, making me more aerodynamic and allowing me to reach the height of my sprint as I finally burst through the huge doors leading from the throne room.

I expect to find a Dragon, to see his enormous mint green eyes staring down at me, his scaled jaws twisted into the smile I love so much.

But there's nothing.

Come to the throne, my Love. Algoric beckons and I slow my step, heart thudding a frantic and tragic lament in my chest as I pace toward its ivory spines. I realise then it's been far too long since I sat upon it.

"Where are you??" I call, passing over the hematite seal of Hecate and biting my bottom lip so hard I draw blood.

Come closer—

At least I know I'm not dreaming.

Ascending the shallow steps leading to the platform on which the throne sits, I hear my heartbeat in my ears, my wings trembling and hands shaking.

I'm standing before the throne, staring around wildly for anything, for anyone, for the other half of who I am— heart caught like a lump of scalding coal in my throat.

Then, it happens. The air just above the seat of the throne ripples, a camouflage being drawn back, and I come eye-to-eye with an enormous White Lipped Python.

I don't have to wonder if it's Algoric. I know it is because he has his mint-green eyes. I watch as the scales on his long body undulate through white, the spectrum of the rainbow, and then black before starting the cycle again.

He's huge, coiled in my seat, slithering as he rises in a tall column of scale-coloured vertebrae.

Staring into my eyes, his tongue flicks out across his reptilian lips, and my eyes fill with tears as he says quietly, and with utter sincerity,

And so, my love, we meet again.

123

9

THE SUN ALSO RISES

LUCIEN

I FEEL HER STIR; the feather-soft down of her wings tickling my chest. My nose is pressed into the nape of her neck, lips delicately caressing the top of her spine even in sleep. My right wing is thrown over her, shielding her from the dawn pouring in where once starlight had veiled us instead.

I inhale her, pressing my body closer into her back, the aroma of jasmine bath oil mingling with the natural lavender haze that wafts from her milky skin. She is so warm, something I usually detest, but I cannot help but bask in it now, her heartbeat more comforting to me than any other sound I can recall.

I feel her move again, trying to get up, but I tighten my hold around her further still, kissing her shoulder with featherlight adoration.

"Stay—" I whisper, still half blanketed in a gloriously deep sleep, the likes of which are new to me. I do not wish to give it up easily.

I feel her wings close around her as she rolls over in the cage of my arms and open my eyes a crack. My lips spread wide into a smile against my consent.

"Good morning, *mon ange*—" I rub the tip of my nose against hers, kissing her tenderly and letting my fingers roam between the feathery masses of her wings. She trembles, closing her eyes slowly so I can see each of her eyelashes quivering.

"Good morning," she replies as the kiss ends, the taste of her leaving my mind swimming in a sea of ecstasy.

I pull her close to me, and for a moment, I think she will give up the fight, but then she sighs.

I hate that sigh more than I've ever hated anything, my fingers reluctantly stopping their tender exploration of her flawlessly curvaceous silhouette.

"Lucien, I have to go—" she says in a half moan as if the thought physically pains her.

I wonder if it does, if she feels the utter dread that is clutching me at the thought of ever leaving the bed's weightless cocoon.

"Shhh—" I silence her with more kisses, caressing her breast. She exhales a tiny moan, and I feel myself harden against the apex of her thighs, still damp from all the previous ways I've loved her.

"I can't, please— don't make this more difficult than it has to be. I can't be here. This is the first place Aro will look for me." She brings her hand to my cheek, looking into my eyes with the lilac oceans of her own.

I see her fear, see her longing to stay.

And so, I let her go. Aro's name severing the tightly woven spell last night had cast over both of us like a razor-sharp blade.

We untangle, and I feel myself wilt as her weight lifts from within my arms.

I lie on my side, sheets draped over my waist as she rises and stretches, her outline tantalising as it is bathed in the new day that catches the tips of her feathers and adorns them in a prismed glow.

She turns back to look over one shoulder, giving me a half-sleepy, half-flirtatious glance, a smile curving her lips.

She is radiant.

"You know— for someone without any experience, I feel like I've just gone ten rounds with an actual dragon— a dragon that was very horny—" she baits me, and I roll my eyes.

"Oh stop, I'm aware I have a lot to learn, Kairi. I'm very much looking forward to further instruction from you— I promise to be a good student. I'll study really hard—" I cock an eyebrow and she throws her head back in a full-out throaty laugh that melts my gut into a puddle of molten chocolate.

"I'm serious, Lucien. I have been with other men; surely you must have guessed that— but you are insatiable. I've never had such a— mutually beneficial sexual encounter," she admits, and I reach out, gripping her fingers and bringing them to my lips.

"I aim to please, my Lady," I purr, wondering if I can perhaps salvage things and lure her back to bed if I smoulder hard enough.

She kneels back on the mattress and kisses me deeply, pulling back as I reach for her.

"Nice try—" She smirks, hopping backwards and then moving about the bedroom, looking for something to wear.

I remember the gown she had arrived in, blood-spattered, which is still lying in a discarded puddle on my bathroom floor.

"Kairi—" I want to vocalise what I'm feeling, to thank her for last night, but the words seem inadequate as they lodge in my throat.

"Yes?" She looks back at me, still nude, her hair mussed from my pawing and clawing.

"There are pyjamas in the dresser— borrow a pair of those." I wave a loose hand at her, observing her lithe and angelic form as she slowly dresses in my clothes, sliding her beautiful wings through the slits in the garment's material.

The pyjamas are too big for her, and I smile at the memory of her wearing them when I first rescued her.

Once she is fully dressed and has fully buttoned my shirt, she straightens and then pauses.

Our eyes lock.

Then, I find the words for her.

"Last night, it was the best night of my life. Thank you." I prop my head in my palm, lazily sprawled upon the mattress as she scans my outline with her entranced yet melancholy gaze.

"Lucien, you don't have to thank me for that. I wanted to. I wasn't doing you a favour, you know." She's adorable as she blushes, chewing on her bottom lip.

I envy her that.

"Do you really have to go?" I ask, worrying I'm coming across as needy. She grins at me, eyes glinting.

"You really would go again, wouldn't you? After what— how many times, like, eight?"

She's trying to lighten the mood; and I wonder if she realises I will keep her here forever, just watch her sleep if she allows it.

"Yes, my Lady. As I said, I aim to please—" I repeat in a low growl.

She shakes her head, curls tossing around her flushed face as she laughs to herself again.

I hang onto the sound like it might be my last breath.

"Overachiever—" She bites down harder on that bottom lip, and I increase my smoulder level to just below scorching.

Not bad for a cryomancer.

Inhaling deeply, I watch her resolve harden into steel.

"I have to go. I'm not safe here— and neither will you be if I stay. I'm sorry, Lucien." She looks panicked, and I wonder what's suddenly occurred to her.

"I can take care of myself, you know—" I mutter, feeling dejected.

"I know, but if anything happened to you because of me, I couldn't stand it." She's deadly serious, blinking in hurried bursts of fluttering lashes.

I wonder then if she is holding back tears.

Reaching out a hand, she comes forward, dropping to her knees by the edge of the bed.

I kiss her forehead.

"Damn it, Lucien, I don't want to need you," she whispers, a single tear falling down her silken cheek.

"And I don't want to need you— Love's a bitch, ain't it?" I cock my head, gazing into her elegance full force. She shrugs.

"No matter what happens, Lucien. I do love you. Something in me always has—" she confesses, and I feel my heart squeeze, terrified.

After everything, I realise that nothing has changed.

She still can't be mine; she still has a duty to Aetheria.

Last night was— a glimpse into a life I'll never have.

"I'll never love anyone else. Not after you— after this." I vow, and she shakes her head.

"Don't say that, please. I want you to be happy—" I open my mouth to respond, but she stands now, stepping back.

"I really do have to go. I'm sorry—" I sense fear in her that wasn't there only moments before and wonder how things have gone from playful to distraught in only a matter of moments and a few choice words.

Then, a blinding flash cleaves the past and future in two, creating a clear divide between last night and this morning. Between becoming a part of something incredible together and being torn apart once again by circumstances we both detest and cannot change.

Then, she is gone, and I'm left alone with my raging desire and the fading scent of lavender upon my skin.

I lie flat on my back, staring up through the skylight at a cold rising sun as it floods my bedroom with a stark chill, making her absence all the more obvious.

I close my eyes, my eyelids thin veils of flesh against the onslaught of sunlight but enough to allow me to fall into the past. Into reliving the night that has cracked open my world and flooded it in her sparkling starlight.

I replay it like an addict, savouring each moment of the night which will forever be as elusive as smoke through my fingers now it's over.

The feel of her mouth on mine.

The taste of her soft flesh pressed against my hard muscles.

Her wide eyes looking up at me as she took me in hand, as I closed my lips around the pucker of her nipple.

Those groans and the way they echo out of her, her pleasured cry becoming an angel song in the darkness of my lonely mind.

Her silken fingertips caressing parts of me I didn't know could feel so alive.

My skin still hums with it, with her adoration and care.

Suddenly, a knock at the front door downstairs destroys my pathetic and torturous reverie.

I bolt upright, grateful for the sudden distraction as I shed the sheets that smell of me and her, of what we had made together beneath the stars.

I pad across the floor, nude, pulling open my armoire and selecting a pair of pyjama pants identical to the ones Kairi had taken.

I yank them on, leaving my chest bare and tattoos exposed as the person knocking on my front door begins rapping once again.

"I'm coming, I'm coming—" I mutter under my breath, suddenly drawn back into a horrifically intense memory of last night.

I blink hard, shaking my head and trying to shed the moment as I feel my manhood beginning to stir again.

You're insatiable— Her words replace the memory on repeat as a breathy echo, and I wonder if what happened between us was normal.

Is it always that intense? That difficult to stop?

It makes me suddenly wonder how regular couples manage to get anything done at all.

I mean, who could be bothered getting dressed and attending bullshit political meetings when they could be doing that instead?

I dash across the landing, my feet slamming down on the stairs as I take them two at a time and with careless speed, noting a broad male silhouette with pale wings coming into fuzzy view through the frosted stained glass of the front door.

As I meet with the rug that spans the length of my hall, I know then who it is I'll come to face before I even pull open the door.

The freezing air of post-dawn Drakos Vale floods over me, extinguishing the embers she had left behind as I palm the door handle and greet Gage with utter confusion.

He merely stares across the threshold of the house I had built with my own two hands before he was even a speck in Nemesis' eye, his young face noticeably worried with deep lines that sprawl like ancient valleys across his otherwise young expression.

"Lord Lee?" I query, finding his eyes tumultuous as a chocolate storm.

"Lord DeLaurent." The formal address makes me bristle, wondering what on earth could cause him to seek me out.

For the past eight weeks, it's been me chasing him all over the Astrid Keep, trying to get access to Genevieve and failing dismally.

"You've been summoned by High Lady Thomas," he announces without feeling, his words slow and thoughtful despite their ambivalence.

My eyebrows rise high on my forehead as I run my fingers through my platinum bedhead, my heart losing its featherlight glow and becoming heavy as molten rock within my chest.

"Is this a joke? Aren't you the one who told me less than twenty-four hours ago that she was fully ready to disembowel me if I tried to see her?" I demand, crossing my arms over my chest.

"No, Lucien. This is no joke— I'm— I'm worried about her. There's something that's not quite right." Gage swallows hard, his silver cravat bulging atop his Adam's apple as he shoves his hands deep into his pockets.

"And you want me to fix it?" I almost laugh, feeling as though he's trying to exploit me somehow after months of opposing me at every turn.

"No, I'm here under her wishes. She wants to see you. It's just that I wanted to mention before I came here, I sensed something in her psyche, something not quite right," he admits. I only shrug.

"She's been through a lot, Lord Lee. Maybe you should just give her the benefit of the doubt right now. She's clearly unstable, not to mention grieving, which I'm hoping I can help with."

I feel suddenly superior, sensing his youth as he stands before me, stuttering and shifting his weight uncomfortably.

"You don't understand, Lucien. It's as if she's— I don't know how to explain it." He pulls his hands from his pockets and holds them up in an exasperated shrug.

I let my lips pucker a moment, my mind a tornado of worry for Genevieve mixed with the fading memories of last night.

"Well, if she's asking for me, then she has good reason. I'll just get dressed, and then we can be on our way," I sigh.

Gage goes to move across the threshold and into the halls.

I'm worried immediately that he'll sense something off, that he'll realise Kairi was just here.

My instincts recoil at the idea.

"You, uh, wait out here. I'll be two minutes," I say, slamming the door in his face before he can protest.

I rush back up the stairs, my wings itching for flight to dissipate my unspent sexual energy, wondering what on earth has given Genevieve a change of heart.

It's funny because I had thought both the women in my life were self-destructing, collapsing under the weight of their own power.

It seems I had forgotten that just as the sun sets and relinquishes the world to darkness, it will always find a way to rise again.

KAIRI

I stand for a moment, tears running down my face as I rematerialize in the middle of my villa suite. I had left here what feels like both forever ago and only seconds ago as a mess.

I return as something not much better.

I take in the opulence surrounding me, the jewels studding the walls, the fine cotton of the bedspread, the high ceiling and the careful mosaic design that is sprawled across the walls. It is beautiful, and I feel like I don't belong here.

I think of him and longing fills me as a selfish desire I wish to shy away from desperately.

It would never be enough time with him. Especially not after last night. Not after what we had done— what we had experienced together.

Why had I done that? Put us both through such ecstasy, knowing full well that I was going to have to sever the connection again come morning?

It had been more painful than I had expected, just as the sex had been like nothing I'd ever experienced. It was incredible.

I feel unsteady on my feet at the emotional polarisation of the last twelve hours. My skin hums with the ghost of his undeniably skilful yet virgin touch, the tiny hairs on my arms rising in the slight stirring of the arid morning air. Feeling both sated and full of desire, the soreness of my hard-worked limbs becomes apparent as I make my way over to the bed, letting myself slump down on the mattress.

I lie back, gazing up at the mosaic work adorning the ceiling, trying not to let my heart crack in two at my determination that what happened last night can never happen again. I cannot do that to him. Not if I am to marry another, to choose the next King of Aetheria.

I have to be strong.

To top it off, he had never been with a woman before, and that shocked me.

Now, I wonder if I should have been the woman to open his eyes to something so addictive, so new. The fact I'd taken his virginity like that makes me feel dirty inside, makes me feel ashamed of putting my desperation above his innocence.

I wouldn't blame him if he hated me right now. After all, I can't deny I've been beyond selfish. I had let myself run to him, been weak in seeking out the sanctuary of his embrace and the sureness of his gaze without thought for how hard it would be for him to let go yet again.

I am weak, and I am hurting him because of it.

Everyone I touch, everything I lay my eyes on seems to become a target for pain, for death. And yet I had needed him so badly last night. Despite everything inside of me screaming that I shouldn't be so pathetic and willing to cause him more pain. I had knowingly gone to him and put him in yet another precarious position, not just emotionally but politically as well.

Guilt rises in my gut, making me feel nauseous as I taste the remnants of peppermint on my bottom lip from our last kiss. I throw one of my outstretched wings that spreads across the mattress over my face, shielding my shameful blush from the sunlight pouring in through the window.

Someone clears her throat, and I startle, wondering why nobody had knocked before entering. As I sit up, I remember that the villa has no doors, only curtains.

Standing just beyond the arched entryway is a petite blonde woman with silver tattoos climbing her neck. They disappear beneath the choppy cut of her jaw-length bob, and her milky blue eyes are wide with nervousness as she takes me in.

"High Lady Freemont, my name is Diane. I've brought you some clothes, and then I've been asked to escort you to breakfast—" she explains in a sweet voice. She does not blink, her posture tense within baby blue harem pants and a matching crop top that is embroidered heavily with dancing equine silhouettes. The silver tattoos on her neck creep down over her toned midriff on the left side, and as I stand up in my less-than-elegant pyjamas, she catches me staring. Her wings are delicate in an eggshell blue and greyish hue, each feather swallowing the morning sunlight with its matte elegance.

"Is this your first time in Sapphire City?" she asks with prim reserve. Taking several light steps toward the four-poster bed in silk slippers, she places a magenta bundle of linen atop the sandalwood chest at the footboard.

"Uh, yes, I haven't been blessed long," I inform her, feeling ridiculously underdressed as I take a few steps forward and lean against one of the bedposts.

"Well, I hope you'll enjoy your time here. It's a very special place. Now, I will leave you to dress, but I'll be just outside if you need anything. Then, when you're ready, I'll show you to breakfast."

I thank her with a brief smile and a quick nod as she turns on the heel of her slipper and exits beyond the emerald velvet of the curtained archway.

I glance out of one of the windows, finding the sun still low and wondering what time it is.

Regardless, Aliandara is eating early, so I guess I am also.

It takes me around twenty-five minutes to dress in the heavily embroidered magenta and orange ombre harem pants and crop top. I haven't been provided with a bra or underwear, so I'm assuming the Equinians go commando, which somehow makes an odd kind of sense.

I have, however, been provided with an overcoat that covers my shoulders and rises in a high collar. It is floor length, stopping just fingers. Shocked, he releases the bloody sword as though it's burned him.

I watch the Sephilim power flow into him as forks of electrical charge, watch him throw his head back as it settles in his blood and beat his enormous wings, casting lightning down from the sky as the man who he had moments murdered ago had so preferred to avoid.

The power I witness truly has been wasted on Caleb, on his sensibilities and self-righteous morality.

Lightning strikes the place where I have just been standing, cracking the courtyard stones in two.

Turning back to the crowd, I give a smile, their wide and fearful eyes bringing me more satisfaction than I had realised was possible.

"And so, Ladies and Gentlemen, I present to you, the future of Aetheria—"

KAIRI

I'm brushing out the tangles of my long hair after a particularly short but brutal training session with Aliandara when I sense a presence stirring at the curtain of my bedchamber.

Twisting, I find Aliandara leaning casually against the archway, watching me with narrow eyes.

"Hi," I say, turning my attention back to the looking glass where I'm preparing for my date with Lucien.

"Hello. I just came to inform you that I won't be dining with you this evening. I have too many preparations to make for the tithe ceremony tomorrow night," she sighs like a physical weight is bearing down on her slender shoulders.

I cock an eyebrow, puckering my lips.

"What's the ritual for again?" I enquire, wanting to talk about anything besides the obvious fact that I'm about to leave for Drakos Vale.

"It's a monthly custom that allows the Aresian Equinians and their pegasi access to the city and the oasis for a single night. Artemis' power is highest at the full moon, so we feel most protected at this time. It was a condition that was proposed and integrated after we won the war," she explains and I nod slowly, a curl snagging on the comb I'm wielding with impatient fingers.

"I see. So, the Aresian Equinians come only for the waters?" I ask, my tone dripping with obvious innuendo.

She gives a sly smile.

"Not only for the waters. Some of them wish for— company as well I suppose," she adds.

"I can imagine their lifestyle— it must be quite lonely—" I admonish and she shrugs, as though the notion of empathy has never occurred to her.

A warm desert breeze stirs through the room, bristling through the blueish-black thicket of her braided locks.

"I suppose it must. Though, I suppose all of us are a little lonely in one way or another." Her statement strikes me as odd when I think about the obvious and tight-woven bond she holds with Evangeline but say nothing as I realise the comment is directed at me.

"I suppose it was a little pointless of me to come here and inform you I won't be dining with you. You aren't dining here tonight anyway, are you?" She hits on my true intent with spectacular and unabashed accuracy, and I shift on the three-legged stool, ringed with tassels, I'm sitting on.

"You know, you can never be together. Not really." Her words pierce me, more in the fact that she thinks I'm not fully aware of this fact than in the brutality of their truth.

I stop my rhythmic combing and tilt my head toward her, eyes wide, imploring an explanation.

"He can never be King, Kairi. It will cause Aetheria to break apart at the seams," she says plainly.

I narrow my eyes, wondering then.

"As opposed to what Lord Black is doing, which is unifying everyone in a utopian sweep of kindness and generosity?" I state with a blank expression embedded with sarcasm. She blinks slowly, visibly chewing on her bottom lip.

She appears vulnerable then, more like a mortal woman than I've ever seen her look.

"You think that Lucien DeLaurent is the next King of Aetheria?" she demands, an incredulous venom impregnating every syllable.

"I didn't say that. But I don't think that my Sephilim choice is exactly ideal either, do you?" I snap. She sighs again, something wistful

206

in the way she brings a hand to run the length of the velvet curtain beside her.

"I suppose you have a point."

She doesn't meet my gaze.

"I know nothing can come from this, but— I love him, Aliandara. And as long as this conflict rages between myself and the crown, I will take comfort and love where I can find it. I'm tired of being scared, and the only time I don't feel that way is when I'm with him." It's more of a speech than I intend to make, but it feels right as the words hit the warm aromatic air.

"And your emotional desires— that is more important than giving the people of Aetheria some kind of stability?" she asks.

I shrug again, misery blooming like poison ivy in my heart and leaving a stinging burn in its wake.

"I never asked for this, you know," I sigh.

"None of us did, but we all have the responsibility to one another, regardless—" She turns and looks back over her shoulder as I set the comb down atop the gleaming gold surface of the vanity.

"Make sure you're within city walls by the time the moon rises tomorrow. I need to ensure you're safe and hidden away before the clans arrive," she issues the order without feeling, and I wonder if she thinks me stupid, or irresponsible, or selfish, or perhaps even all of the above.

Maybe I am.

The curtain stirs in her wake as she leaves me alone with my guilt, with my shame, and so I stand, assessing myself in the looking glass a final time.

Minimal make-up, provided kindly by Diane, and an outfit that I am sure is utterly unsuitable for Drakos Vale weather. It's the warmest crop top and harem pants I own, tailored in a thick jade velvet, but my bare midriff still tenses at the thought of the snow and frost that awaits.

There's a cold hopelessness in my eyes as I stare into my reflection, my Fae ears pointing obviously from beneath the half-up-do that knots my hair and leaves a torrent of angel curls falling over my left shoulder.

It might be selfish, but I won't give up time with Lucien until I have to. I've never felt this way about anyone before, and if I don't heed both of our desires while I still can then I know I'll spend eternity regretting it.

With a final nod to my reflection, I shove down the emotions which threaten to ruin what promises to be a wonderful evening.

Then, reaching into the air for that electric connection, and in a flash that leaves only billowing drapes behind, I'm gone.

I materialize on the upper landing of Lucien's home, anticipation pooling heavy and electric in my gut as the lightning that had brought me here dissipates into the warm air.

Across from where I'm standing, I find the door that leads to the adjacent room open. Walking several paces across the wooden floorboards, my heart is a gentle pitter-pat against my ribs, calmer than it has been in days. I feel the tension leave my shoulders as I cross the threshold of what had been my room when I was mortal, finding a garment bag hanging on the front of the wardrobe.

The message is clear, a piece of thick parchment with the words 'Wear Me,' scrawled in sloping dark ink.

"I'm here to dress you my Lady, and Kaiden is outside with the sleigh," Aska's brisk tones ruffle my soft curls as they reach me and she stands, her pale wings causing the air to churn. I flinch as I turn, finding her concealed and statuesque just behind the door.

"Oh, I see— very well." I feel a little of the tension return as the fact I'm not alone suddenly hits me.

This place though, I cannot deny it feels like Lucien, from the warm yet cool wood of the carved balustrades to the carefully laid and polished floorboards that smell of wintergreen and peppermint.

Finding someone else here is jarring.

"Come, the night approaches." Aksa is dressed in a plain linen skirt that rustles around the heavy tread of her boots. Her blonde hair is piled up in braids, and she wastes no time in shooting me an appraising if not slightly judgemental glance before taking the garment bag in hand and pulling the zipper down.

Slipping out the garment, I feel my eyes widen and my mouth fall slack.

"You made this?" I ask her and she nods, her smug face catching the pure white light caught in hundreds of crystals encasing the A-line gown. It has a sweetheart neckline, which is made complete by net sleeves that glisten like fresh frost.

"I did. Though, not quickly. The beading alone took me about three weeks." She purses her lips, eyes slightly scornful as she exhales a heavy and irritated breath.

Ignoring her, I reach out to touch the silver fabric dripping with jewels.

It's the most perfect dress I've ever seen. Incredible, yet entirely understated, and exactly what I would have chosen for myself.

"You designed this?" I ask her again, and she shrugs.

"I helped; Lord DeLaurent did the majority of it though. After you turned, he was always waiting for your next meeting, so he was sketching a lot. I guess he was better at designing gowns than he thought, considering he usually works with wood and steel. I don't think he ever thought you'd actually wear it, but he said I could sell it off if not."

"Thank you, for putting in all this work," I breathe, pulling back my fingers from where they're placed, gentle on the silk of the bodice.

"I was well compensated, I assure you—" is the only way she can think to reply, and I wonder if she hates me.

"I know you don't like me, I'm sorry if I've offended you," I say, exhaling with regret. The velvet of my jade harem pants rubs against my thighs as Aska considers me a moment and I straighten, tensing defiantly beneath her scrutiny.

"You do not offend me, it is the way in which you make the High Lord lose his focus, on his people, on Drakos Vale and its best interests. Still, I am only a seamstress. It isn't my place," she continues, dropping her gaze. I sigh, my breath coming in tense wisps as I suck air in through my teeth.

"Still, I apologise. I never wanted to cause problems for anyone," I assure her, pushing a loose lock back behind one of my ears.

"I suppose it is not your fault." She gives me something like a grimace that might have been a smile if it had reached her eyes.

I accept it, nodding and appraising the dress a few moments more.

"Undress and I'll help you get into this gown. There's a cloak as well, and shoes." She allows me a glimpse of the cloak, which lies pressed against the back of the garment bag. Pure white velvet embroidered with the phases of the moon in silver and periwinkle blue peeks out flirtatiously. I look closer, finding lilac feathers intertwining with the lunar orbs, soft like new sunlight as they curl around the waxing and waning phases.

I stare in wonder at Lucien's outpouring of emotional energy. He had designed this dress for me, with only me in mind. The thought makes me flush warm as I begin to strip, unable to wait to slip into its glistening frosted clutch as though it were his.

Once I am dressed, the gown mostly concealed by the gloriously white cloak with a fur-lined hood and inner pockets to keep my hands warm, Aska escorts me downstairs. The flat glittering ballet slippers murmur in a low rustle on each stair as the heavily jewelled top layer of my skirt swishes with a kind of majestic foreboding that might make anyone who was waiting for me in the hall look up with wide eyes.

Nobody is waiting though, and I wonder as Aska leads me back out of the house, exactly where she is taking me.

Beyond the porch I find Kaiden standing propped against the sleigh, his midnight blue wings a shadow against the dying twilight. Spectral Mountain dogs are restless, scrapping amongst themselves. As I appear atop the porch steps though, Kaiden lets out a harsh whistle and they cease, sitting with ears pricked forward as he rises to his full height, pulling his lapels straight.

Kaiden smiles at me, his thick dark hair and large brown eyes a warm contrast against the surrounding white. His breath fogs as he takes several steps forward, capturing my hand in his leather-gloved palm and leading me across the packed snow. My feet chill through the bottom of my slippers as he helps me up into the body of the sleigh.

Turning back, Aska gives me the tiniest smile from the porch where she is standing beside a rocking chair, before lowering her head in a courteous bow.

"Thank you, for helping me. You are an incredible seamstress," I call, complimenting her. She blushes at that, and her smile widens if only a little.

Kaiden climbs into the sleigh beside me, and as Aska returns to the house, I presume to clean up after me, I feel glad at having melted her icy disposition.

"Where to?" I ask Kaiden as he takes the reins in hand. He looks at me with rosy cheeks.

"Ah, I'm under stern orders to keep that in strictest confidence, my Lady. Congratulations on your title, by the way."

He lets out a high-pitched whistle, pulling hard on the reins, and I wonder if it's anything to be congratulated on.

The dogs, frantic with energy beneath the low-hanging orb of a newly waning moon, do not waste any time. They take off at full speed, the sleigh jerking forward across the fresh skin of powder that blankets layers of impacted snow beneath, making a right turn so that we are pulled toward the frozen lake where Lucien and I had skated what seems like several centuries ago.

The wind bites into my skin as the night continues to fall like a glittering star-studded veil over the pale face of the continent, and I pull my hood up over my head, shoving my hands deep into my inner pockets. My gown glitters as I sit in peaceful silence with Kaiden, who has never failed to make me feel comfortable, watching the alabaster trunks of yew, fir, pine and beech trees fly past us as we hit the outskirts of the initial stretch of forest. The dogs pant loudly with a kind of brutal rhythm, the sleigh gliding across the snow as though it were air.

After a while, I recognise the icy blue vein of the river on my right and the climbing mountain range approaching on the left. Turning to the driver, my brow creases.

"Are we going to the Astrid Keep?" I ask, and he shakes his head, his grin spreading mischievously.

"There's no point in guessing, Lady Freemont. I can guarantee you that you have never heard of where we are headed—" He seems smug, and I give him a curious look, my wings stinging as the feathers catch the fast-moving icy breeze like razor blades. Feathers ruffling, I realise then that it's been a good while since I had a proper flight. The tips of my wings itch for it as I glance up at the endlessly beckoning sky, but stay seated, crossing my ankles beneath the heavy layers of my skirt.

The journey invigorates me, despite my longing for flight and free-fall among the aether thick clouds scudding scantily among the rising mountain peaks rising on either side. I am sorry when the sleigh finally pulls to a halt.

"I thought you said we weren't heading to the Astrid Keep?" I ask, glancing at the familiar doors that are carved into the base of the nearby mountain.

Kaiden rolls his eyes as he adjusts his wings, tucking them in close against the broad back of his dark trench coat.

"Lucien said you were impatient. Come on." He extends a hand to me, dropping the reins and helping me to my feet from the padded bench.

I follow him, staying silent as he leads my cautious velveteen steps across the snow, a group of footmen moving past us in a flurry to attend to the sleigh and dogs left behind.

We reach the enormous wooden doors and sweep beneath their arched apex. My feet cool further but do not dampen as my slippers move from snow to chill stone, glad for the luxuriously warm cloak as I pull it closer around my shoulders.

"Yep, this looks like the Astrid Keep to me—" I sigh dramatically, giving Kaiden a cheeky grin as I shake several stray flakes from my wings and pull my hood back from my face.

"You modern Kindred, I'll be interested to see how your patience improves after one hundred years," Kaiden sighs, not breaking stride as he walks over the left-hand wall. It's covered by an ornate tapestry with some kind of Latin doctrine stitched into it but Kaiden discards this as he sweeps the heavy weave away and pushes an otherwise unextraordinary stone deeper into the wall than its fellows.

The guards, standing in their dark steel armour, peek out from within the gaping dragon mouths of their helmets, giving us an uncomfortable side-eye.

I wonder what they must make of it all as the panel of the wall swings back, tapestry and all, with the grind of stone upon stone.

"After you," Kaiden steps aside, smirking at my wide eyes as I tread over the newly created threshold.

There is a small hallway lying ahead of me, lit with flickering sconces of ornate steel design. Too quickly though, the passageway descends into a tightly curling spiral staircase that corkscrews down into the earth.

Kaiden pushes past me, barely possible within the narrow confines of the secret space, leading me towards the staircase without looking back. My footsteps are soft as my soles finally warm and I find myself reaching out from within the cocoon of my cloak to put a steadying hand on the wall as we take to the narrow and uneven staircase. My stomach is alive with butterflies, excitement causing my blood to run hot in my veins.

It becomes increasingly evident as we move down the spiral staircase that it is archaic in build and I can guarantee if I was mortal, I'd have broken an ankle. Luckily for me, my wings help me balance, and shortly I have descended what feels like a hundred stairs, my calves burning in a way that makes me feel content and in control of what had once caged me.

"This way."

Kaiden doesn't stop as the passageway opens around us past the heavy oaken door leading to and from the staircase. Beyond, the ceilings soar upward, testifying to exactly how far beneath the snow-slathered ground we have come.

"What is this place?" I enquire, finding the floors gradually smoothing the further down the hallway I travel. It reminds me a little of a cathedral at night, with candles and sconces everywhere to keep out the dark of the earth pressing in on all sides.

"Not for me to say, my Lady." He looks back over the curve of his retracted wing, his eyes glittering with devious pleasure as he catches me stopping to take in the details of the hallway.

"Come, we don't want to be late," he presses me, stopping only a moment before I nod, flushing, and scurry after him.

He takes me through several antechambers of octagonal design laden with heavy furniture and rich jewel-tone velvets that are draped as décor in their own right.

Finally, after having seen not another soul for the entire journey here, we arrive at an immodest set of double doors.

"In you go. Here I leave you—" Kaiden says, pushing open the door and stepping back so I might step through.

"Thank you for escorting me." I give him a warm smile and he returns it without hesitation.

"It was my pleasure to escort such a beautiful woman," he replies, bowing. It makes me slightly uncomfortable, yet another part of being a High Lady I'm not used to.

I turn from him, my stomach fluttering with excitement at the prospect of being alone with Lucien and far enough from the surface that nothing and no one might bother us.

Some people might feel trapped by the thick stone so buried in the earth, but not me.

I feel safe.

Stepping into the room, I gape as I spin towards its centre.

The ceiling is raw stone and geodes half split open and polished to perfection. Every type of crystal you can imagine shimmers overhead like a rainbow spectrum of stars made malleable.

The room is simple, not to detract from the natural magnificence of its uneven, jewel-encrusted walls and ceiling, the floor a black marble that reflects the crystals overhead as they flicker in the candlelight.

I find my attention drifting to where a table for two is set, plates covered by cloches with a simple pair of candelabra lighting the air around it gentle and intimate.

"Told you her jaw would drop," I hear Lucien's amused tone and my head snaps around, back to the doorway where he and Kaiden are standing, watching me like a pair of naughty schoolboys.

"Fair enough. I forgot how damn impressed the new Kindred are with just about everything— I owe you a drink," Kaiden mutters begrudgingly as he saunters off beyond the doorway and out of sight. Lucien laughs, the sound beautiful as it echoes off the surrounding walls.

Then, we are alone, the two of us standing only metres apart, staring.

Lucien is wearing a white shirt and dark trousers that rise high on his waist, the collar on the shirt open so I can peek at the tattoos I have so recently spent no small amount of time tracing with my tongue. His hair is lying in soft silken waves around his face, framing the sculptor's architecture of his skull as his eyes come alive with the orange of the flickering candlelight inside the room.

He steps across the threshold, and I dash to meet him, throwing my arms around his shoulders. He lifts me, hands swooping beneath my cloak to hold me under my arms, spinning me a full three hundred and sixty degrees before he lowers me into a more intimate embrace.

"Well, hello there—" he murmurs into my hair, inhaling me.

I smile, the scent of wintergreen and peppermint washing over me like a drug.

"This— everything— the room, the dress, the room— where are we?" I ask him, stumbling over my words as my cheeks blaze beneath his adoring gaze.

"We are in one of the ceremony rooms in the Academy of Arcane Arts. You are the first Nephilim ever to set foot within its walls," he informs me, and I feel the weight of what he's saying.

"But—" I begin, and he smirks, cutting off my concerns before I've even made them known.

"I trust you, and that should be enough for anyone," he insists.

"But— High Lady Thomas—" I counter and he shakes his head.

"No, no talk of politics, or war. Only us, just for tonight. I think we deserve it. Besides, I am famished. I spent my entire day in the library looking for ways to help Quinn."

He leads me with a delicate hand toward the table, the black linens in perfect contrast to the silver tableware. My reflection, warped in one of the cloches, stares back at me, beautifully alien as he takes the cloak from my shoulders.

"That dress, it's even more perfect than I had envisioned. I must send flowers to Aska, snowdrops perhaps—" he muses, placing the cloak over the back of my chair and taking his own seat across from me.

I baulk, my mind comparing this night with one I would be rather wise to forget but know I never will.

Where Lucien's idea of a date is intimate, with a tiny table and faint candlelight, Aro would have had me at the end of a metres-long dining table, all for the sake of impressing my mortal eyes.

"This is incredible—" I breathe, and gaze up at the ceiling in ever-increasing awe, my heart stuttering as I take it all in with greedy eyes.

"Yes, you are Kairi—" he whispers, and I shoot him a shy gaze.

"Want some more cheese with those crackers?" I ask him with a high-pitched chuckle. He rolls his eyes.

"Indulge me, please. I have never been allowed to woo a woman before," he insists, straightening in his seat.

I draw mine closer to the table, eager to find out what is beneath the cloche. My stomach rumbles as I pick up a starched napkin and spread it over my skirt. The colours match almost exactly, and I wonder momentarily if Lucien had thought of even this detail when he planned the evening.

"Go ahead, let's start."

He gestures to the plate in front of me, so I lift the cover. A cloud of steam billows from beneath, coating my cheeks in a warm fragrant haze.

"What is this?" I demand, my mouth flooding with saliva.

"Lamb chops with a cognac Dijon cream sauce," he informs me, removing his cloche and taking the silverware beside his plate in hand. I have no doubt it is made of actual sterling as he twirls an intricately moulded fork in his fingers. It catches the candlelight, dazzling me.

"Did you choose this?" I ask, picking up my cutlery.

He frowns.

"Yes. Why, is there something wrong?" He looks instantly troubled, and I shake my head, finding his attentiveness sweet if not a little strange compared to mortal men I have dated.

"I just wanted to know if this was a favourite of yours, it smells amazing," I assure him, letting my knife sink into one of the lamb chops and watching it fall apart like butter beneath the blade.

"Oh. Well yes, actually. It's a French dish as you probably guessed. My mother used to make it for special occasions."

I stop, the mention of his mother enough to keep air between my lips and the dripping piece of tender lamb.

"What?" he asks, looking alarmed again.

"Lucien, relax. I just— I've never heard you talk about your family before. In fact, now that I think about it, I know very little about you at all—" I place the meat into my mouth, letting a small grunt of pleasure escape as the flavours ravish my tongue.

"You know me better than anyone," he retorts, and I feel a wave of sadness roll over me.

How he has lived so many years, single and untouched, I'll never know.

But then, perhaps now is the perfect time to find out.

"Wine?" he asks me, and I nod enthusiastically.

He pours from a bottle that's been placed in a silver bucket between us and uncorked before my arrival.

The red liquid splashes into the pewter-rimmed goblet before me as he pours generously and I stare into it, wondering.

"I want to know, you know— about your life," I add. He looks at me, an eyebrow cocked in question.

"What about it, exactly?"

Mirroring his words from the night we had first made love, I look deeply into his eyes across the table.

"Everything, Lucien. Tell me everything—"

The meal passes in both a blur and what feels like a hundred years as Lucien talks and I listen attentively, my heart becoming strangled at some points of his tale and fully broken at others. If the girl who had destroyed his self-esteem so entirely was still alive, I have no doubt I'd punch her right in her bitch mouth.

As the thought occurs to me, I wonder if I am in fact High Lady material.

Our plates both entirely cleared, I lean back into my seat, taking a moment to appreciate the clusters of emerald, ruby, and sapphire embedded into the ceiling and flickering with warm tones. The candles between Lucien and I are now but stubs of their former selves, coated in rivulets of wax that's long since dripped and dried.

Finishing my glass of wine, I watch as he goes to pour me another.

"No, I have had enough. I am not French remember—" I smirk and he rolls his eyes.

"We're not all alcoholics you know!" he defends himself and I shake my head.

"It was my impression you were breastfed on Merlot, especially given the number of times wine makes an appearance in some of your stories!" I laugh at him, my cheeks flushing warm from his company, and of course, the wine, of which I am on my third glass and teetering dangerously, apparently, on the edge of a fourth.

"You know the first time I ever saw you I was a little drunk," I say, smirking. He cocks an eyebrow.

"I know. You were wavering on the spot as if you were looking for escape routes. If I couldn't smell poison, I would have assumed Lord Black had already drugged you—" he smirks right back at me.

I scowl.

"I was not looking for an escape!" I stutter, and he throws his head back in a deep belly laugh.

"Ah no, that came much later— I had to do the heroic thing and break you out of a tower first," he snorts, and I find myself unable to stop laughing.

"It's all a bit ridiculous really, isn't it?" I say it aloud and suddenly it really is, all, very ridiculous.

The beautiful man across from me sighs out deeply, nodding.

"Indeed, Kairi Freemont. Indeed."

"You know, I don't think Aska likes me very much— she says I distract you from your people, from your job keeping them safe," I reveal, my heart falling with a suddenness that catches me off guard.

"Aska should learn to keep her opinions to herself," Lucien grumbles, and I look up at him through quaking lashes.

"Should she though? What happened— with Algoric. Lucien, I—" I begin, but he holds up a hand.

"Kairi, I don't want to talk about this, not now, not tonight," he is dismissive, but I carry on anyway.

"But I do. I do want to talk about it. I'm beginning to feel like blowing it all to hell. Just for the sake of being yours. The other night— what I did, what we did. It would be so easy for me to let it burn, to let it all burn and let you keep me safe in your little cabin by the lake. I love you so much—" I confess. He looks stricken.

"You couldn't live with yourself," he reminds me, reaching out with a gentle hand.

Covering my fingers with his, I feel the cool chill of him and my throat tightens, the longing of being so close to him almost unbearable.

"I don't want to live without you either, Lucien. I— I have never felt like this about anyone before. It's not just love, it's—" I begin, but he raises my fingers to his lips, getting up from the table and coming closer to me. I rise from my chair, trembling slightly as he wraps his muscular forearm around my waist.

"Unbearable." He lowers his head, finishing my sentence and leaning his forehead against mine. Breathing deeply and rhythmically in time, our bodies press flush against one another.

"In all my life— I've never felt so at home with anyone." I bite down hard on my bottom lip, but he brings a hand to my chin and tilts it upward, kissing me.

"And in all my life, I have never loved another. I thought there was something wrong with me, and thank goodness for that. Knowing that you were to be mine, I would never have wanted to fall for another, *mi amore*. I know now why I have waited so long, know that I was waiting for you. And I'd do it again—" he breathes against my cheek crushing me to him. I feel my eyes well with tears, the desire for resolution, for an answer, so intense I feel as if I might die if I have to wait a second longer to know what will become of us.

"Lucien, what are we going to do?" I ask, shaking in his arms. He swallows hard, his Adam's apple bobbing.

"We are going skating Kairi, and then I am taking you to bed. I want to make love to you, deeply— Each time might be the last— and while that breaks me, it also makes me love you all the harder while I can," he confesses, his voice now a whisper against the shell of my ear.

I wrap my arms around him tighter, swallowing.

It wasn't the answer I wanted, I wanted him to say that we could simply throw caution to the wind, that we could run away together, or stay here and never return to the surface. I wanted him to condone every selfish urge that has taunted me ever since we met.

But he's too good for that, too noble, and it's one of the reasons I will always love him.

It is also the reason that we can never be together, not really. Because we know deep down that responsibility to our people, to Aetheria, is something neither of us could survive walking away from.

And so I let him lead me from the room to the lake where we will dance upon the ice and in the sky above, and then to his bed, where we will make love for what could be the last time.

Then, as inevitable as a returning dark tide, the violet dawn will cleave us apart once more.

15

THE SOUND AND THE FURY

GENEVIEVE

I PERCH ON THE cloud overhead, concealed but able to see the lovestruck couple twirling beneath me. My fists are balled, shaking with humiliation and rage as I sit in one of my best gowns, livid and seething.

So, this is why he didn't show up? Not some great emergency, Gen. Her. Algoric whispers this in my ear, my body hissing as slow-falling snowflakes settle in my lashes and sizzle on the crown of my head.

How dare he? How dare he lure me out of doors only to stand me up for some Nephilim harlot! I retort, gritting my teeth and baring them in a feral snarl. Algoric hisses his dissent, slithering around my forearm as he journeys beneath my hair to snake around my neck, my only comfort the constant motion of his scales sliding against my skin.

He is a man, what did you expect? Algoric retorts, his serpentine lips close to my earlobe now. I turn my head, nuzzling him slightly, my heart breaking beneath the shards of rage and fury that cut me deeper with every breath. What Lucien and I had was beautiful, but it seems more fragile than I had realised. Now I am left with only jagged edges, glinting in the undying blaze of my fury.

No. It is not his manhood that made this decision. It is worse. It is his— heart. I swallow uncomfortably at the notion of his affection for the girl, watching with narrow eyes as the two of them laugh and swirl intimately together upon the glassy surface of the lake.

It is the very same lake that had almost killed me not three months ago, but it seems as though Lucien has forgotten that entirely.

The girl, her wings spread out behind her, is a flurry of diamond-en-crusted silk and duchess satin, her skirts sparkling as though she were a star in her own right. Lucien certainly looks at her as though she were one.

He has never looked at me like that, and while I have been deluding myself like a fool imagining he has feelings greater than he knows, seeing the real thing on his face shatters that notion so completely I feel as though I am the stupidest woman alive.

The two of them fly together, clutching one another, her twining her arms around his shoulders like a delicate flower and he clasping his around her waist with steely protective force. Their lips come together passionately, and bile rises in my throat. Her cheeks, the flushed rosy porcelain of a virginal maiden from a fairytale, are soft as he brushes snow from her face, tilting his head and melting entirely beneath the perfect lilac of her gaze. I cannot look away, and yet I feel myself breaking apart at the sight of his happiness.

Nausea rises further within me, and I feel my throat constrict like my heart is lodged right there in my windpipe.

Turning to launch myself into the sky, I debate wholly whether or not I should spread my wings and soar away, or simply plunge like a stone, shattering the ice beneath and ruining their evening in all its dreamlike perfection.

Who knows, maybe I would get lucky and she'd drown.

Lucien certainly deserves it. His latest betrayal stinging perhaps worse than the first with the audacity of its freshness.

Wait— Algoric implores me, journeying down the length of my left arm in an ever-writhing coil around my wrist, squeezing in condolence.

I see what he sees then, the two of them touching back down to earth and walking, hand in hand, over to the porch to remove their skates.

I take the opportunity to reposition myself, flitting like a pale shadow across the backdrop of the night and landing, whisper-soft, upon the roof of Lucien's ridiculous lake-side house.

Sweeping away new snowfall, I crouch adjacent to the skylight I know hangs over his bedroom.

I don't want to wait, to watch in the shadows, and yet a part of me, the inherently self-destructive part, needs to know. I need to see for myself how involved these two have become in all its blatantly grotesque glory, to learn what it is Kairi has that I do not.

Gen, are you sure? Algoric's uncertain tone wavers around the inside of my skull like a weak breeze, but I hush him with a flick of my wrist.

Despite my dismissal, I cannot deny I am grateful for his caring. At least someone does.

It doesn't take long for the happy couple to enter the bedchamber, her cheeks still flush from the cold and growing only rosier as he takes a white cloak from her shoulders and proceeds to unbutton the gown she is wearing with careful fingers.

My eyes widen as he falls to his knees upon the small train of her skirt, kissing her spine as he pulls the decadent fabric apart, adoring her even still as though she were a present.

I don't want to believe it, don't want to consider that after all this time Lucien has given himself to this girl of all people. That he is no longer untouched as he has been for so long.

The knowledge of this is part of what made me feel safe, made me feel like our relationship was genuine and that he didn't want to use me as so many men have done before. His virginity was almost like insurance.

Now though, the illusion that he does not harbour such desires is shattered as well. He pulls the gown off her body like it were a second glittering skin and lies her pink wanton flesh down slowly on his bed. I watch as he kisses her breasts and nipples, her neck, her stomach, and then have to pull away from the ledge as he reaches the apex of her thighs. The last thing I can bear to watch is Kairi's eyes widening with the pleasure and surprise of his exploration.

Bile rises in my throat once again as I snatch myself away from the skylight, hearing a groan I will remember for the rest of my days echo out into the night.

Genevieve— Algoric's summon is lost in a blizzard of other sounds, none of which are welcome, as I leap, feral, from the roof.

I land with a thud in a pit of snow that turns to chill water beneath my feet, leaving me sinking in a scalding puddle that's frothing at the surface.

My heart is racing, my temperature rising, and so I dash to the edge of the closest treeline, only just making it as I feel vomit climbing into the back of my throat.

I wretch, my hand charring the bark of a nearby tree black as I bend double, the thick trunk of an off-white fir the only thing keeping me standing.

I am sick, violently, my eyes streaming boiling tears as my face, nose, and mouth burn like I've swallowed dragonsfire.

Panting, I finally manage to stop the dry heaving as it wracks through me one last time. Algoric's voice reaches me through the din of panic as my heart races faster than I had thought possible, every thump a lament to the furiously fast wingbeats of the dragon I had lost.

Oh, Genevieve. Let's go home— His sympathetic tone turns my blind heartbreak and the panic of having truly lost Lucien into a full-blown rage.

How could he have done this? Continued to choose this girl over every-thing he has already stolen from me, and for all the risk he has already brought to his people?

I am disgusted, my veins running hot and heavy under my skin like rivers of molten lead.

Wiping my mouth on the sleeve of my best gown, the gown I had chosen to wear to dinner with the man I had thought was my best friend, I spread my wings. Rising into the night, a silent scream remains trapped in my throat as I slice into the sky overhead and angrily slash the clouds asunder.

When I arrive at the suite I had left only an hour and a half ago, after more than two hours of not so patiently waiting for Lucien to arrive, I find it is occupied.

I spy him from the balcony as I land, robbing me of the private reprieve I had been praying to Hecate for all the way here.

"And what on earth are you doing here?" I snap, yanking the glass doors of the balcony open and stepping inside. A gale follows me like an icy fist as it punches its way through the heat of the room, stirring the drapes of my four-poster bed.

Leo turns to me, having expected me to enter through the double doors flanked by guards. His eyes fall on my face and I find him pale.

"Are you alright, Lady Thomas?" he enquires, his freckled nose scrunching up as he takes in the scent of me.

I feel suddenly embarrassed at the state of me, at seeming so un-done. I probably still have tears dried on my cheeks, and my hair has become nought more than an ashen tangle as I had flown, furiously and without discipline in my hurry to get back here.

I take a deep breath through my nose, letting my nostrils flare and trying to calm myself. Algoric is tight around my left wrist like a security blanket only I can see. His eyes are closed and I wonder if he had fallen asleep on the way here, lulled by the sensation of flight in which he can no longer partake.

"I am fine. You did not answer my question. Why are you here? This is the second time you have simply shown up without the courtesy of arranging a meeting first. This was not our agreement," I bite, walking hastily across the room and pouring myself a drink into a cut-glass tumbler with shaking hands. I hadn't eaten, expecting to be filled by the chefs of the Drake's Heart Inn in Vega City with Lucien, so as the liquor slips down my sore throat I feel it begin to loosen my tension immediately, pooling in my belly with exaggerated effect.

I don't offer the Sephilim a drink, merely turning to stare at him with eyes that demand an explanation over the rim of my glass as I take yet another sip.

"It's urgent. I don't have long before they realise I'm missing. I had to come— I had to tell you, what I've just seen— it changes everything."

He's panting almost, not with strain but with the actual weight of his words. I blink slowly, my heartbeat beginning to quicken.

"What is it?" I ask softly, for the first time seeing the man behind the feathered wings and the blessings of a God I despise.

"Genevieve— we have a huge problem. Aro, he had Chief Landon John kill Lord Caleb Abara tonight, publicly." He enunciates clearly for increased impact as I walk past him. Then, sitting on the chaise longue before the fireplace, I clutch my glass between tense fingers and cross my legs beneath the jade velvet of my skirts.

Looking up at Leo, I give him my unbiased attention for once.

He exhales, and I cut in with obvious impatience before he can continue.

"Is that all?" I demand, disappointed.

He shakes his head, eyes wide.

"Lady Thomas— Lord Black, he has discovered a way to steal the power of those he slays— and he is teaching others. He is harvesting the amethyst of Soleus and forming weapons— I believe he has your dragon's power running through him. I have been trying to work out for days how it could be possible— but upon seeing Landon John absorb the powers of the High Lord he had just decapitated with an amethyst sword— I—" He stops, out of breath, the chocolate brown tips of his feathers vibrating with the trembling weight of his anxiety. He takes a few paces across the room and then back again, watching me intently as I turn over this new information in my mind.

Downing the entire contents of my glass, I suddenly realise with a shudder what exactly he is saying.

"He doesn't need the dragons anymore— to have their power. Doesn't need the Draconian's cooperation—" I say aloud and Leo nods, looking at me with a grim expression.

"Indeed. And if he needs only to kill them to steal their power, for himself or his army— then we are in big trouble," he admits, and I look for a moment at my wrist. At the place where Algoric— or what is left of the majestic beast that he was, is curled around my wrist, snoozing peacefully.

"This is not only a problem for the Draconians, Lady Thomas. If he weaponizes this new magic— this ability to kill and absorb power— well, he could potentially become so imbued with magic he would be unstoppable. Taking the crown, well— he would not need it. He could simply declare himself King. Nobody would oppose him with so much power stolen."

"You are correct," I say, trying to keep my expression neutral. Yet beneath, my mind races. The images of the fire, death, and the blood spatter of wars long since ended fall over me like ice water.

I blink with slow thoughts, remembering that perhaps the only reason the Draconians and their dragons had survived the war was Midas' insistence that the dragons were not killed. He had wanted their power, and he could only do that if they were still breathing and had the Draconian riders to tame them.

Now though— Lord Black might slaughter every last one and gain everything which they had been gifted by Hecate and Nemesis.

I shudder, my mind whirring with the endlessness of the night.

Seeing Lucien and Kairi together— like that had begun to unravel me, but now I feel as if I have been completely ripped open and exposed.

"Thank you for telling me this. I know it is not easy for you to come here. I would also understand under the current circumstances if you decide to align your interests with Lord Black—" I look into the faceted cut glass of the tumbler between my fingers, my mouth dry as my pulse ebbs heavily against my skull.

"Never. I will never align myself with him, Lady Thomas. I could not live with myself for a moment, let alone forever." The answer is what I would expect from a soldier; honourable, righteous— predictable.

Boring.

I nod, brow furrowing as I stare back into the firelight of the hearth, existing now only as dying embers.

"Thank you, Leo. You have given me a great deal to think about," I say, my voice lilting as my mind wanders far from the present.

"I will arrange our next meeting as we agreed, I am sorry for the intrusion." His goodness, his courtesy and his respect takes me by surprise, softening the edges of my rage and fear if but a little.

It is enough.

I turn back to him. "May the Goddesses protect you, Captain—"

It is the first time I have ever offered this kind of divine blessing to a Sephilim, and as I sit there and look back into the fireplace, listening to his departing footsteps, I cannot help but wonder if it will be the last.

Indeed, Leo has given me much to think about. For I am the only High Born of Hecate who seems to care what becomes of our people.

So now, I must ask myself— what will the cost of survival be in the new world that fast approaches, and more importantly, am I willing to pay it?

If you'd have asked me yesterday, or a month ago, I'd have told you that I would stand and fight until I had no more breath in my body and every bone of me was shattered.

Algoric whispers as though in a dream, catching my last thought and giving me a small reptilian smile, his eyes still closed.

Oh, how suddenly things do change.

LUCIEN

I wake gently with the dawn, the down of her feathers tickling my face. Opening my eyes, I find her lying across from me, serene in sleep. I watch her for a few moments in the weak rays of the new sun that pour down upon the bed, thinking of everything I want to say to her.

I want to tell her that she's the most beautiful creature I've ever seen. That last night, and the one we had spent together previously, have been the best of my very long life. I want to tell her never to leave, to let the world go to hell, so long as she's in my arms while it happens.

Neither of us could let that happen though, not with any good conscience, and perhaps that is what makes us two halves of the same whole.

Sighing, I shift so I'm propped on my forearms, crawling over her naked and sleeping form, inhaling her as I go.

I let my wings spread from my spine, tremoring with the pleasure I feel coming off my body like a low hum as my cock meets with the curve of her behind.

She stirs, and I wake her slowly, kissing the tender skin between her wings before running my hands up the sides of her curvaceous silhouette and nibbling on the bottom of her earlobe. She hums, ecstasy the entire wavelength of the sound as I push her inner thighs slowly apart, reaching around to cup the full weight of her silky breast in my palm and pinching her nipple between my fingers as I find myself sliding into her with ease.

She's still slick from the antics of the previous night, and the tight clutch of her body makes me elicit a stark, raw moan as my first sound of the day. She shudders, tilting her backside up to meet me, making the first thrust as deep as possible. I lay my head in the pillow-soft hold of her wing, letting the feathers tickle my face and ground me as I grind into her with deliberate slowness.

She squirms beneath my caress, pressed into the mattress on her front by my weight, crying out into the pillow as I take my leisurely time, smiling into the musk of her.

I feel myself ebb and flow as I grind, a tide building to exquisite climax within the woman I love, wanting to fill her so completely that all memory of any other is erased. Like the sea, I wish to turn the churned sand of her darkest moments smooth and pristine by touch alone.

"Kairi—" I whisper in her ear, picking up my pace and letting my finger run circles around the outside of her nipple. The action seems to send her unexpectedly over the edge as I lay my tongue against her neck, her wings shuddering against my chest as she clenches around my pulsating shaft.

The heat, the wetness of her, and her unstifled moan beneath my hands most of all send me over the edge as I grit my teeth, my abs and thighs tensing as the orgasm hits me like a tsunami, blowing me away.

I empty myself, clutching onto her so hard I fear she might break as I hiss into the warm silken locks of her hair, thrusting wildly, my wings shuddering as I ride the climax to its sweet conclusion.

Panting, I collapse atop her spine, closing my eyes and letting the moment hang, precious. I kiss her shoulder blade, cleaving from her as I run my index finger along her bare back in swirls and gliding lines, breathing her in deeper still.

She rolls over beneath me, and I rise to kiss her, holding her close, her eyes hooded heavily with tired lids.

She curls up into the side of my warm body, my heart still pounding within my ribcage.

"Mmm. Can I go back to sleep now?" she grins, looking up at me sleepily.

Her still erect nipples press into me, soft as rosebuds near to blooming.

"Of course you can, I just thought you should wake up the right way—"

"Hmm, feel free to wake me up anytime—" She smiles softly to herself, her lilac eyes sparkling even as they remain cloudy and full of sleep.

I brush a stray lock from her face as she lays her cheek against my pectoral, breathing quickly from where I'd put her body through its paces. She grins into me as she lays a kiss on the place above my heart, nuzzling back into the sheets and dozing once more. I return the gesture, planting a kiss on the crown of her head, closing my eyes and memorising the weight of her body as it presses into me and our breathing synchronises.

I run my rough fingertips down the length of her arm, coaxing her back into sleep, if not for the fact that I'm sure she's exhausted then for the pure joy of being able to watch her restful within my arms.

I stay like this a while, pressing her against me and savouring the seconds we have left together.

After all, who knows what today may bring?

I don't know what it is that wakes me with the force of an Equinian slap, but when I find myself opening my eyes again, Kairi is on the opposite side of the bed, balled up and breathing deeply, lost to dreams.

It takes me a few seconds to put my finger on exactly what it is that has roused me so suddenly, and then I realise.

It's the intense heat of the bed, the way the sheets are clinging to me and making me just slightly too warm in a way that isn't at all comfortable.

The heat brings with it the realisation that I've been waiting for.

Genevieve.

"Merde!" I exclaim, scrambling to my feet. I slap my hand over my mouth, afraid to wake the angel in my bed, but Kairi doesn't stir, still lost to this world as I had been only moments ago.

Rushing across the room with all the stealth I can muster, my aching body manages to shove itself into some black slacks and a fresh t-shirt, wings getting caught in the cotton as I haphazardly pull the thing over my head while balanced on one leg.

Shit! Shit! Shit!

I stood Genevieve up.

I actually— oh my Goddess I can't believe I did this.

Stupid bastard!

I curse my lovesick heart, giving Kairi a glance over one shoulder as I hesitate to leave. I could wake her, but a part of me hopes if I don't then she'll somehow sleep the day away and be here when I return.

Decision made, I stumble with a racing heart out of my bedroom, clattering down the stairs without even grabbing a coat from the bannister. I don't even bother with shoes, wrenching open the door to find a figure there I hadn't even registered through the frosted glass.

Anastasia looks up at me, an eyebrow cocked in disapproval.

"Whatever it is, Lady Dragos, I have to go—" I throw the words at her, clicking the door shut behind me without pause.

"Oh, I know! You went and screwed up royally. I just thought you'd feel better having someone here to make sure Kairi knew where you'd gone— and also to you know, protect her in case Lord Black comes looking—" She is wearing a dove grey cloak, the gown beneath it a stark snowy white, her dark hair tied up against her skull in an elaborate braid. Among it all, her eyes are nothing if not condescending.

I should be irritated with her, but I'm not, I'm only immensely annoyed at my carelessness.

I hadn't even thought about leaving Kairi sleeping and totally unprotected—

"Shit. Yes, okay, thank you. I have to go— there's tea and coffee in the kitchen—" I shout back over my shoulder.

"Lucien, don't you want to put on some shoes?" she calls back, and I shake my head, my bare feet already meeting with the morning's fresh skin of snow. It doesn't hurt, and I know for all my shortcomings I won't at least get frostbite. The snow bites wet and hard against the soles of my feet as I stumble into the most haphazard take-off I've ever attempted.

I leave Anastasia watching from the doorstep behind me, my wings stretching out into the oddly clear air as I rise. The lake where I had been skating only hours ago shrinks into the distance as I beat my wings as hard as I can muster, climbing too slowly in height.

My heart is frantic, as I chastise myself the entire way there, not seeing the luscious white forests or being able to appreciate the carnivorous-looking mountain range.

No, all I can do is think about how I have utterly failed my best friend when she needs me the very most.

Thank goodness she doesn't know I was with Kairi last night, or else I fear she might do something reckless—

I had been so ready to be with Kairi again— the plans I'd made had slipped my mind, the fact I was amazed Kairi had even agreed to a date completely overriding my memory of the promise I had made to Genevieve.

The guilt eats at me, shredding my insides with claws and teeth that snag on my heartstrings and viscera, gutting me in a way that's torturously slow as I soar as fast I can towards the Astrid Keep.

When I finally arrive, I see that her balcony doors are open and breathe a sigh of relief.

Maybe she is not angry, maybe she was not up for the outing either—

Hope clutches at me desperately as I descend my familiar trajectory, letting my leathery wingspan billow out behind me. Slowing, I fall through the pine-scented air sharp with a cold I barely notice, mind racing with a hundred what-ifs.

My bare feet touch down on the light dusting of frost that blankets her balcony, my heart in my throat as I step in through the open glass doors and past the phantasmal gossamer curtains dance on the early breeze.

"Good morning, Lucien," Genevieve's voice is steady, not angry. I search for her, finding her sharpening a dagger I had given her for the winter solstice a few years back with flint in front of the fireplace.

"Genevieve— I'm so sorry. I didn't even— I don't even have an excuse. I completely forgot about our arrangement!" I burst.

She shrugs, nonchalant.

She doesn't even look at me.

"Can you forgive me?" I ask, almost pleading, but she still doesn't look at me, getting to her feet and sheathing the dagger in her thigh holster.

That's when I notice.

She's wearing travelling garb. White leather pants and an armoured corset beneath a fur-lined leather waistcoat of the same hue and fabric. The attire is studded through with rubies, making the bloody stain at the roots of her hair all the more obvious.

"What did you spend your evening doing— Was it at least important?" she asks me, ambivalent as she paces over to a chest that lies at the end of her bed.

"No— I was reading in the library at the Academy. I suppose the time just got away from me!" I confess, heart skittering as the lie passes my lips.

"Get out," she barks, still not turning to face me.

"But— I don't understand—" I begin, and she shakes her head.

"Oh please, how stupid do you think I am? I saw you fucking the Nephilim harlot, Lucien. I know why you left me sitting here for hours— waiting."

She spins, her words flying through the air like knives as her green eyes blaze malicious.

"Genevieve I—" I begin but she laughs.

"Get out of my sight, Lucien. We are done here. I thought you were my friend, but you're just a liar with his brain in his manhood," she spits, and I recoil slightly.

"Genevieve that's not fair—" I straighten, feeling my defences rise.

"I don't care if it's fair or not. I am no longer your concern, and neither are the people of Drakos Vale. I have seen where your loyalties lie, and I am tired of waiting for you to fuck-off with your little angel-slut and abandon us for good. It ends now. You are nothing to me, and nothing to the Goddess you promised to serve. You are a disgrace and even looking at you makes me sick!" I open my mouth to retort, my eyebrows incredulously high on my forehead as my heart slams itself into my ribcage, breaking parts of itself free of the whole and leaving them to perish.

She does not pause to gauge my reaction though, she simply buckles a bag of white leather over her shoulders and under her wings, pulling her braids from beneath it with a quick and powerful flick of her wrist.

"Wait—where are you going?" I ask her, concern punching through the wall of guilt that's been stopping me from speaking.

"Like you care. Don't you dare try to follow me either. The next time you get in my way, I won't have any qualms about cutting your pretty little head off. I hope that Nephilim bitch is there to watch!" She bares her teeth, hissing like an animal.

"Genevieve, please. You're my best friend—" I say, the sentence coming out with less force than I imagine. I sound weak, even to myself.

"No, Lucien. I'm your last resort. Now get out of my way," she snarls, wings spreading so her talons slash dangerously close to my face.

"Genevieve please, just— at least tell me where you're going." I can't come up with adequate words fast enough, and as I'm standing there blocking her exit she shoves me sideways, her scalding hands leaving bubbling flesh behind.

I wince, recoiling with a single and measured step back, but I don't let the expression of my pain travel any further, steeling myself to remain assertive.

"I'm going to do what I should have done a long time ago, and what you will never do, Lucien. I'm going to save my people by putting my personal life aside."

She moves to the edge of the balcony and I watch as she pauses, wondering if she'll reconsider, if I can reach her even after everything or if I have lost her forever.

Her wings spread even wider as she prepares to take off, answering my question, but before she does anything else she glances back, face sullen.

"Don't come after me. If you do, it'll be the last time," she whispers. It might sound almost sad if she weren't so utterly terrifying.

She moves suddenly; my hair blows back from my face as she launches herself into the early morning sky from a running start. I stand paralysed as I stare skyward, silently wishing for a familiar flash of emerald.

Genevieve disappears into the darkness of fast-gathering storm clouds, never once looking back.

16

THE FLOWERS OF EVIL

<u>ARO</u>

THE NEPHILIM I REQUESTED is not pleasing me as I thought she would. I can tell she's not moaning out of pleasure, but fear, and while usually, I'd find that a turn-on, today I find myself glancing at the picture of me slaying a dragon on the far wall. The thought of myself murdering a mighty dragon is seemingly more exciting than some winged has-been virgin.

I continue to thrust deeply, taking her from behind like a prize stallion would mount his mare, but my mind is elsewhere.

She's bent over on all fours, nude, her breast jiggling every time my crotch collides with the bare moistness of her.

Sighing, I tense myself, ready for this to be over.

I let my fingers dig deep into the skin of her backside, hearing her stifle a higher-pitched cry than she's been attempting before as I fill her entirely, willing the climax on as though it's little more than doing the dishes. Just another chore to be completed.

Usually, helpless maidens fill me with lust at the thought of dominating their innocent quaking bodies, but today— today something is off.

I grip into her so hard my knuckles turn white as I swell with climax, a hot burst of fluid filling her as I ejaculate, shuddering. She cries out, this time more in pain than in any kind of pleasure, and it's not until I fall back onto my haunches, trousers a puddle around my knees, that I see why.

I've branded her, leaving two handprints on her buttocks, the flesh that had once been smooth and creamy now bubbling like spent candle wax.

My eyes deaden, the orgasm fading as quickly as it came, leaving me even more bored than I had been before I ordered the Nephilim be brought up here in just a robe.

Sighing, I pucker my lips, licking the bottom one. It's slightly dry from where I've been panting with the effort of getting myself off as though I were alone.

"You may go—" I say, lolling onto my side with an exhausted sigh.

The Nephilim scrambles up off the rumpled cotton sheets, glancing at herself in the mirror hanging on the front of my wardrobe as she robes herself, wings fluttering wildly and struggling to protrude through the back of the garment.

I hear her gasp, seeing the marks I've left on her, and then a small sob creeps from her lips, stifled as she covers her mouth and dashes from the room.

She leaves the door open in her distress, and I roll my eyes for what feels like the hundredth time today.

Fucking women.

Giving a low growl which stems from deep frustration despite the fact I should be calm and content, I yank my pants up around my waist, zipping and buttoning the fly before striding over to the door and slamming it shut.

I exhale, finding myself alone once more. For a moment I consider taking a long bath and furiously masturbating while thinking about Silver.

My hands are sticky with melted flesh, so I go to the bathroom, washing them in the amethyst basin and watching as the pink film swirls down the drain in a bloody foam.

I breathe in deeply, wallowing in the calm of my heartbeat, the itch in my wings and my knuckles.

Why hadn't it been enough to satiate— even for a little while?

I would have taken Kairi in a heartbeat and ridden her bloody— so then perhaps what I'm attracted to isn't the meek quivering maiden after all—

The half-baked notion deflates as a knock sounds at the door.

The thought of some update, some change, invigorates me. Since Caleb's execution, things around here have been achingly dull.

I button my shirt, tucking it into my pants hastily with only partially dry hands before exiting the bathroom, shutting the door behind me, and walking over to one of the armchairs in front of the cold fireplace.

"Enter—" I call, using my most authoritative tone and trying to seem calm, though I am more curious than I should be about who it is that has come knocking. I sit, crossing my legs leisurely and taking up a casual stance, disinterest crawling habitually over my face.

After all, there are only so many virgins you can deflower before you start getting bored, and only so many books that can keep my high intellect entertained before impatience inevitably begins to creep in.

There's a pause, and then the door opens. I hear a scuffle beyond it, so push myself to stand again.

When the couple step into the room at last, one far more willing than the other, my lips spread into a feline smile.

I haven't been so surprised or excited since killing Kairi Freemont.

"Lord Black, my men found this— thing in our airspace as they were exercising the pegasi this morning—" Chief Landon announces, shoving High Lady Thomas forward and into the room. He relinquishes the curve of his sickle from where it's been softly kissing her throat.

She trips over her own feet, hands bound behind her, falling to knees which are covered in skin-tight white leather. She stares up at me with wildly angry eyes, her nostrils flaring like she might actually breathe fire.

I cock my head slightly, fascinated.

What the actual dickens— I take tentative steps forward as she scrambles back to her feet, shaking her luscious white hair wildly like a snow leopard.

"And what, are you doing here?" I ask, voice more purr than threat. She baulks at my voice, her teeth gritting and jaw tensing visibly. Her taloned wings flare, and I cock an eyebrow, endlessly amused by her obvious discomfort.

"And why would I tell you that, you son of a bitch—" she snaps back, her pallid skin not even slightly flushed at my presence. I watch as her eyes dart from my face to the painting on the wall behind me, the flash of her too recent past delicious as I fight a smile.

She struggles against the thick rope bindings holding her fast, and I laugh to myself, shaking my head at her fruitless exertion.

"Don't you laugh at me, you have no idea what I'm capable of—" the High Lady snarls, and this time I throw my head back, laughing in a loud cackle that bounces abruptly from the crystal walls and fills the room.

"Getting caught apparently— don't they teach you stealth with those monstrous things?" I gesture to her wings, and she bares her teeth.

"I am going to kill you, Lord Black— and I'm going to enjoy it—" she declares, green eyes wild with a rage I've never found anywhere else.

Landon watches us with intensity, judging me on how I handle this wildcard. I see his fingers twitch as she takes a short half-step toward me, and I know he's tasting the air, trying to pick up a current to use.

He's getting better at managing his powers, though he's still electrocuted three servants this week by accident. I dread to think what he'll do with the abilities on the battlefield with even an ounce of learned control.

I look between the two of them, the judgemental Chieftain and the compromised High Lady, straightening before drawing in a deep and unhindered breath.

I take a small step forward then, closing the gap between myself and the Draconian bitch who refuses to heel, bringing a scalding finger to her cheek. As it makes contact with her skin, she inhales despite herself, shock visible in her eyes as she realises that the magic of the dragon she had so loved now runs hot through my veins.

"And yet, every time we meet, you are bound, and I am in control. Isn't that interesting?" I ask, watching as she shudders with rage. My finger lingers on the sharp architecture of her face, an ache blossoming in my gut as I observe how a mere touch can so infuriate her.

"You *think* you're in control, Lord Black. And that arrogance makes you vulnerable." She tilts her chin up in defiance and I feel something stirring, turning raucous in my gut as my top lip curls in disgust.

It might be hatred, or perhaps even a desire to see her utterly under my power once and for all, but a small thrill dances through my body, leaping across synapses and pirouetting down my spine as a delicious heat suddenly blooms in my stomach from the seed of what had only just been discomfort.

My eyes narrow, pupils darting between the Draconian and Equinian, each watching my reaction as intently as the other.

"Do you want me to announce another execution, Lord Black?" Landon asks, shifting his enormous bulk within the billowing leather of his well-worn chausses. I watch as his hand fidgets upon the handle of his preferred scythe before he sheaths it, fingers then leaping quickly to linger over the amethyst sword I have gifted him instead.

237

He's anxious to kill again, and I have no doubt he thinks a High Lady of Hecate will make a delicious addition to his newfound power.

I, however, won't be giving her to him. If anyone will have her power, it will be me.

And yet—

Inner turmoil tugs me in opposite directions until, with a final grasp of Lady Thomas's chin between my sharp yet short nails, I push her away from me with a heartless shove.

"Hold her in the dungeons. Under guard at all times— and make sure that you get a set of Kyanite manacles on her," I bark.

The Chief looks surprised, his pectorals sagging.

"But—" he begins as I turn away, causing me to snap my head back over my shoulder.

"I'm sorry Chief, did I stutter? Take the Draconian bitch to the dungeons before I have you thrown in right along with her! I have to think about what to do with her, and I don't want that decision to be rash. She might be useful in the coming days—"

I don't want to explain myself, but the incredulity on the Chief's face leaves me feeling as though he's too stupid to realise the true value of what we have here.

"Very well, Lord Black. Come on you—" he grunts at her, grabbing her forearm. She resists, and I watch her face slacken and contort as he sends an electric current ricocheting through her nervous system in punishment. He glares at me, cocking an unruly and challenging brow.

"Got a problem with how I'm treating the prisoner, my Lord?" his voice drips with icy cold sarcasm and I consider striking him as he hikes the unconscious High Lady up over one shoulder. She beats hard with tiny, hard fists against the vast feathered panels of his wings.

Then, as I watch her unruly and inefficient retaliation to his man-handling, I wonder if he's trying to bait me. Cooling my heels, I keep my posture stiff and my head held high as I reply.

"No, of course not. I don't want her dead, what you choose to do to entertain yourself between now and when I decide her fate is entirely up to you. So long as she's alive when I come to my decision," I lie through my teeth, an odd feeling creeping up the back of my throat and burning my tongue as he stalks out of the room with thunderous tread, slamming the door behind him.

I stand in the middle of the room, looking down at the floor, at where High Lady Thomas had fallen.

Her voice, insipid with bitterness, with rage— echoes inside my skull.

I am going to kill you, Lord Black— and I'm going to enjoy it—

The audacity, to come to my kingdom alone as if she'd been invited as a guest, only to be furious she had been captured tickles me, and I find myself smiling at her stupidity. She's supposed to be my elder by many years, but she doesn't seem to be too bright despite it.

And so now, I am left with a conundrum.

What to do with the bitch?

The thought of her on her knees echoes around in my skull like a bird's shrill cry, my heart beginning to race as I recall the feral glint in her emerald eyes.

Perhaps then, I will take that bath after all—

GENEVIEVE

If I hadn't believed Leo's claims about Aro's new method for stealing the power of other Kindred, I do after Chief Landon John conducts us, very badly I might add, down into the stark brightness of what I assume to be the Solis Castra dungeons. My gut churns with motion sickness, my limbs frozen in place by the electric current transferred into me via the rough grip he has on my upper arm. I wonder momentarily, stumbling over my own spasmodic limbs, if he had intended to render me almost unable to walk or if the consequence was accidental.

As he hauls me, grunting and cussing, along behind him, I assume not. Algoric tightens his scaled clutch around my forearm, invisible to all who cannot feel the cold rush of his blood pressing against the scalding riptide beneath my skin.

The dungeons are clean, something I had not expected, with each of the barred amethyst caves containing shimmering piles of golden hay and a simple wooden bucket for relieving oneself.

The dark violet stone spits light out of its own accord from all angles; ceiling, floor, and walls as I have seen it do in smaller chunks before as lanterns. This time though, the overwhelming brightness of such an enormous light source hurts my eyes, causing me to wince as my pupils dilate into dark saucers within my aching skull.

I'm dragged across the smooth amethyst floor, the soles of my white leather boots sliding on the flawless facet and preventing me from maintaining any kind of traction, muscles twitching and elastic beneath my pale leather pants.

My legs burn a little as the sparks from the Equinians' stolen power reduce to embers, burning the ends of my synapses and leaving me with numbness in my toes. My nose fills with the scent of lilacs, the aroma so strong I feel nauseous as Chief Landon pulls something from his makeshift leather pants and holds it up for examination. A jangle of metal on metal can be heard, so I glance up, tearing my gaze from my feet as I struggle to put one in front of the other.

Odd-shaped and archaic-looking golden keys hang on a large metal ring beneath the scrutiny of the Chieftain's dumb gaze. They glitter, jaundiced and jagged at the tip in the too-bright light of the stark corridor.

After a few moments of me trailing him with hands still bound behind my back, the Chief stops outside the cell farthest from the entrance of the dungeon, a single corridor stretching back with reflective walls so the passage seems to go on forever. The light bleaches my skin as I catch my ragged reflection in the floor beneath my uncoordinated gait. Beside me, the Chief becomes a sickly yellowish colour, the tattoos which wrap around the back of his generous biceps fading as the contrasting darkness of his skin is diminished.

He unlocks a barred amethyst gate, carved from a single crystal slab, and yanks it open, the hinges unexpectedly soundless.

Stepping back, he grunts, jerking his head toward the open doorway and glaring at me in place of direction. Stepping forward, I breathe deeply, trying to ignore the vile perfume of lilacs as it soaks into my skin, the fading pine-fresh mountain air of Drakos Vale long behind me.

His meat-slab hands grab my wrists as I pass, the sickly-sweet aroma of sweat and blood long since dried creeping over my shoulder as it rides the fetid current of his breath.

"Wait. I have someone coming with your binds— Can't have you melting anything now can we?" His tone is snide, the heat of his lips caressing the side of my face and causing me to tense against my better judgement.

Suppressing a shudder, I stand, acutely aware of my pulse beneath the rough skin of his hands as they clamp down on my bones. For a moment I find myself wishing I was made of marble.

I know what he's thinking; that he's pondering how easy it would be to snap bones so thin. That in itself is a folly though because if he knew Draconians, knew anything about our inadvertent strength, he would know not to underestimate me on looks alone. I might be small, but I'm also wily, and with strength proportional to men double my size.

A Goddess who had been raped and manhandled by another would never allow her Kindred to be so unprepared.

The silence ticks past slowly until, finally, footsteps approach. The Chief chastises whoever it is that's brought the binds, and as I turn, expecting to see some meek Equinian youngling, I am met by a familiar gaze.

Wherever I go. There you are— I muse, looking away before Leo can catch me staring with surprise disguised as disdain.

I let the men free my wrists of rope, stretching my arms out in front of me for the crystal manacles to save my shoulders. Keeping my head high, my spine straight, and with wings tucked in tightly, they bind me.

Because I let them.

The talons atop the peak of each phalanx glisten menacingly, but I seem to be the only one paying them any attention.

Bound, I step across the threshold and duck, bending so I can fit beneath the low crystal ceiling of the cave-like cell. My wings fold against my spine as tightly as they can and I sit, uncomfortable, watching the two men lock the cell door.

The Chief gives me a final lingering look of disgust, but Leo pauses, staring into my sullen face and trying to read me.

"Coming, Captain?" I hear the Equinian call back to the Sephilim, who jumps as the Chieftain's voice echoes, bouncing loudly between the walls in a cacophony of jarring consonance.

"Of course," he replies, turning on the spot and walking away from me without another word.

I prop myself against the jagged crystal shards of amethysts that stud the back wall of the cell, hands weighed down in my lap by the kyanite binds.

Algoric stirs, having stayed stone still and invisible the entire time I'd been in company. His tongue flickers out, dragon-esque and comforting as it nips the side of my elbow.

I sit there, watching him closely as his scales undulate in and out of existence, my eyes beginning to burn beneath the brightness of the incessant glowing walls.

It is then that I realise the reason for the lighting. These cells were designed to be as uncomfortable as possible. The floor is both jagged and sharp so you cannot rest upon it and every inch of the space is illuminated so there is nowhere to hide or find respite in the dark.

My head begins to throb; sharpened Kindred senses never having seemed more of a curse.

My body aches too as I lay down, letting the cool of the stone floor bite my cheek. I've been up all night, my mind racing and heart pounding with both rage and heartbreak, and I feel around a million years old as I stare out between the bars, exhaustion weighing heavily upon me like a wet blanket. It's like snow, sapping my heat, my fury, and my energy with it.

There is only light, and the scent of lilacs as I close my eyes, unable to escape any of it even behind the pale curtains of my lids.

Sighing, I feel Algoric slither up over my shoulder and up around my neck, the chill caress of his scales the only relaxing sensation I can find to focus on.

Let me help with that—

This is the last thing I hear him say as he wraps himself around my skull, using his body to shield my tired eyes with a serpentine embrace.

The feel of his scales on my eyes, across the bridge of my nose, is cooling, the heat of my body lapped up by his languid silhouette as he wraps my mind up in darkness.

I succumb to the relief, to his love, falling into a vivid sleep.

The sky is full of smoke, the ground a metallic, shimmering, pinkish sludge of churned snow and blood - both dragon and Draconian. I cast my eyes to the sky, where a swarm of feathered wings beat like hundreds of pumping dark hearts, darting between thick sooty clouds and casting blood into the air at metronomic intervals. They are the pulse of death itself, and with each new beat of feathered wings, they bring yet more loss, more screams.

Their heavy crystal weapons clash loudly, the sound cutting through me as I see a violet-scaled dragon fall like a comet, the tail of its meteoric glory a steady stream of silver blood left falling like rain in its wake.

It hits the ground only half a mile away, and I feel the tremor of its demise rise through my feet, and my calves, before it settles and disperses in my hips.

I look down, my hands molten as I find them covered in silver blood-tinged pinkish by the crimson spill of my people. The people I have always sworn to protect.

How I have failed them.

My heart thuds frantically, like a dragon clawing to be set free of its underground prison, tossing loose bone and sinew in the process, and gutting me slowly.

My dark pupils dart from left to right as the quake of the dragon's impact against its homeland disperses through the trees in a shudder of pale leaves and disgruntled birds that take flight, keeping low to the ground in an effort to avoid the fighting.

I stand, frozen to the spot, my blood on fire, my heart becoming slowly encased in icy dread no matter how ferally it struggles.

The world is ablaze, with parts of the forest smouldering from the onslaught of flaming arrows the size of javelins, the sky a sanguine weep overhead despite the cobalt orb of the sun veiled innocently by thick ashen smoke kicked up from the floating continent by the battle.

There are cries of anguish, screams of pain, the whinnying of pegasi reared into a war-hungry frenzy as they leap from cloud to dark cloud, their riders brandishing amethyst and hungry for Hecate's power.

The sounds layer themselves into a physical force, a weapon that launches an unexpected attack on the sureness I had always felt when I resisted the Sephilim's offers of alliance.

It's here, right before my very eyes, pulsing in the air around me like an inescapable and primal drumbeat, each strike of flesh against blade forming a hideous and overpowering melody that sinks into my pores and wraps like poison vines around my soul.

War.

The thing I had so hated Lucien for delaying, the one thing I was sure of for my people.

But now, seeing the Equinians and the Sephilim bearing amethyst swords— absorbing the power of Hecate's blessed as they fall like broken stars— stealing what doesn't belong to them— I realise that I was wrong.

I've always been wrong.

I wanted to fight, to bleed, to slaughter for vengeance and independence, but now I see the truth of the matter is this:

Lord Aro Black has the manpower and the weapons to steal the power of Hecate and Nemesis. The power to kill every last one of the dragons, and their riders without consequence.

The Sephilim no longer require the approval or alliance of anyone. The man who had ended Algoric right before my eyes will become more powerful than all the Kindred races combined, and anyone who stands in his way will end up dead, or worse.

My people, their dragons, are on the edge of extinction, and the hand which will tip us over the edge does not belong to a friend.

I look for Lucien, for a blur of Ebonara's blackish violet scale or a streak of his blond locks amongst the slaughter of the sky.

Unsurprisingly, I find only his absence among the chaos, his betrayal as stark now as the flames that lick at the sky from the tops of charred fir trees. Chastising myself for my foolishness, for the nostalgia of assuming I'd find him fighting alongside me after everything, I make my choice.

A choice I should have made long, long ago.

A choice that will change everything and might, if I'm lucky, save my people.

17

THE POWER AND THE GLORY

<u>KAIRI</u>

THE INTENSE AROMAS OF sandalwood, jasmine, cedar, and thyme drift in through the arched window of Aliandara's Sapphire City villa. It's almost dusk, and I've only just woken from a deep slumber that I hadn't been able to fight after returning from Lucien's bed in the early hours.

Nobody has disturbed me, which I suppose is a good thing, except for the fact that I can't distract from the guilt that is blooming in my heart at how I'd left Lucien without a goodbye.

Waking to find him gone it had seemed like a sign I should spare us both the pain of yet another parting, and yet as I sit curled up in the light cotton of the sheets, the ghost of his caress squeezes my heart uncomfortably. It's like a bond has formed, steel-strong and multi-layered despite our best efforts to avoid such a connection, and it hurts more than I ever imagined it might, slicing through the soft flesh of my heart. We seem to have forged a chain with the heat of our lustful bodies that will stretch distance but not slacken. The pull of him is always there, a visceral magnetism lodged in my chest.

A deep breath escapes me as I teeter on the edge of last night's memory pool, only too tempted to take a deep dive and drown myself in the sensations which, though so new, have also come to feel like home. Before I can though, a small tap on the sandstone arch leading out of the room steals my attention.

"Yes?" I call, slipping out from under the sheets and running my hands down the front of my simple linen pyjamas. They're midnight blue, with silver thread around the hemlines and collar, loose-fitting and easy to move in, keeping me cool despite the fact I've slept well through the hottest part of the Eclipsian day. I wasn't comfortable sleeping naked, not without the safety blanket of Lucien's precious skin.

Evangeline slips through the curtain, parting it with a gentle hand, her dark eyes and wildly curly dark hair glistening fiery beneath the lit sconces. Her face is bathed lilac by the dusky light falling in through the window, accompanied by sounds of the approaching Lunar Tithe ceremony as she smiles.

"I thought I'd sit in with you for the rest of the evening, is that alright? I figured you'd be staying in as well—" she asks, and I see that she's bought a crocheted bag of craft supplies as well as a three-legged stool I'd expect to find next to an archaic spinning wheel.

"Of course, this is your home after all! But, if I might ask, why aren't you out there for the tithe ceremony? I would have thought you'd be required to attend, being a High Lady," I enquire, leaning to slump back on the side of the mattress and letting my fingers caress the intricate bedpost.

"I have my reasons." She's guarded suddenly, so I go to change the subject, moving so I'm fully supported by the bed and crossing my legs in front of me. Before I can speak again though, there's a sudden loud purring in the air.

I look to the curtain once more, only to find Catticus struggling to get through its heavy velvet folds, paws protruding beneath the fall of it with agitated steps. A laugh precedes his entrance as Jess, the guard I had met my first night here, helps the enormous Kensari enter my suite.

"I found this one roaming the property, I figured considering we are keeping your identity quiet a giant winged lion might give the game away a little," she explains, her face glowing and her strong shoulders glimmering with steely Celtic knots.

She's clearly anticipating a night full of fun, much like all the other Equinian ladies of the city, her makeup freshly applied, nails lacquered a jade green, and her dark honeyed locks pulled up tightly into a high ponytail. Her outfit consists of fine bottle-green silk that's embroidered with silver knots that match those on her skin, the harem pants and crop top keeping her cool while casually highlighting her incredible abdominal muscles and the definition in her back.

"You look beautiful, Jess," Evangeline compliments her and the guardswoman blushes.

"Well, you know—" she shrugs, clearly embarrassed by the attention as she goes to turn on her heel and leave.

"Say hello to your father for me, won't you?" Evangeline calls after her, causing Jess to stop in her tracks just inches away from the curtain. As she pauses, the material continues to flutter in the cool night breeze dancing in circles through the window.

"Of course, thanks, Angie." She gives a polite and yet obviously cheeky wave and then is gone, leaving Catticus and me alone with Evangeline.

"Angie?" I look at her quizzically, cocking my head and running a hand absently through my sleep-matted curls.

"Yes, my mortal name. Seems a little too informal for this world, don't you think?" She places the stool she brought with her down onto the floor, proceeding to perch on it elegantly as her lilac skirt sways around her ankles. Her craft bag, set down on the floor, becomes the full focus of her attention as I respond.

"So, you and Jess are friends?" I ask and she nods, pulling something metallic from her bag and placing it in her lap before crossing her slippered feet with prim elegance. You wouldn't know from her poise just how deadly she can be with a bow.

"Oh yes, she's my personal security. My best friend," she says, and suddenly I feel lonely, not only for Lucien but for the incredible women I'd left behind in Soleus. Vail and Dawn— Trinity, even though they are so different from me, have been a desperately needed comfort that I now notice is chillingly absent, like someone has ripped a warm blanket from my shoulders.

"That's awesome," I reply, watching as Catticus leaps up with feline agility onto the bed. He sprawls his languid body across the entire width of the mattress, setting his head in my lap. It is heavy, his thick white mane tickling the soles of my feet.

I've been worried. He snorts, sounding irritated. I rub him between the ears, digging my nails into his warm scalp.

I'm sorry. Everything has been a little— I search for the word, but as I pause in thought, he interrupts me.

Did I say you could stop with the head rubs?

My lips twitch into a small smile as I continue to massage the enormous cat's skull with both hands, his incredibly soft paw pads stretching and recoiling in delighted shudders. A low purr elicits from his chest, the rumble of it rattling through my pelvis.

"What an incredible animal— Does he have a name?" Evangeline asks, bringing out two knitting needles and casting on with her metallic-looking yarn. The click of them soothes my mind as I continue to finger the thick fur of Catticus' mane.

"Catticus— Well, that's what I named the tabby he was when we originally met." I shrug as an amused half-smile graces her face; her eyes cast downward on her knitting.

"Catticus Finch by any chance, To Kill A Mockingbird?" she asks, and I nod, feeling myself light up at her acknowledgement of the inspiration for my cat's namesake.

"You've read it?" I ask and she smiles widely as her finger loops around the inside of the metallic yarn she is manipulating.

"I have indeed. I died in 1982, so it was written twenty-two years before even my death," she acknowledges.

I nod at the new information, realising that she might be the youngest Kindred I've met so far.

My actual name is Agamemnon. Not that you asked— Catticus says with feline disdain, his voice half slurred at the relaxed state of his body as it echoes around the inside of my skull. I laugh, shaking my head.

"What?" Evangeline asks, looking up suddenly.

"He says that his actual name is Agamemnon—" I giggle and she rolls her eyes.

"Well, that's just a mouthful," she directs the comment at the lazing lion, and he sits upright just long enough to let out a small growl from between his enormous jaws, before collapsing back against me.

Evangeline jumps at the sound, then rolls her eyes again and returns her attention to her work.

"What are you knitting?" I ask, and she puckers her lips, holding up the small piece of work she has so far completed and appraising it with scrutiny.

"Kind of like chainmail underwear, but softer and lighter— It's something I've been trying to develop for a while but It's only just being tested out in the field because I haven't been able to get the yarn to knit tightly enough to be really protective. It's holding up good so far though—" she explains, and I feel my brows rise, impressed by the concept and her skill in its execution.

"Clever— Is that for you know— fighting Ares Kindred?" I broach the topic, curious ever still about the dynamic between the two neighbouring races.

Evangeline looks at me with curiosity as I straighten beneath her stare, tucking my hair behind one of my Fae ears. She doesn't comment, so I assume Aliandara has let her in on that little secret.

"You're not the first one confused as all hell about the dynamic here— It took me a while to understand when I first arrived. There's still parts— still parts that I've come to accept but that break my heart." She stumbles in her answer and I stall in replying for a moment, wondering what it is she means.

"So, the Lunar Tithe ceremony, what is it exactly?" I ask, and she looks up at me for only a second before returning to observing her busy hands with scrutiny. She chews on her bottom lip, seemingly nervous for a reason I can't quite put my finger on.

"Well, it's pretty simple really. The Aresian Equinians bring an offering for Aliandara, and she gives them access to the Oasis for the night. To be honest, it's more of an excuse to get some time in with the opposite sex if you ask me. You've noticed all the tents that have been erected at the edge of the water?" she asks, and I nod, having glimpsed them upon my return this morning.

I look to the window now, where beyond rich silk gazebos are no doubt fluttering in the rich breeze that rises off the water, finding that night has fully fallen and I've barely noticed.

"They're for coupling and smoking various peyote blends. There's dancing, music, food, bathing, most of it nude. That's after Aliandara receives the ceremonial gift offered by Asher and then shoots the flaming arrow and lights the altar to begin the night of course— That is what you can smell, by the way, the incense of the altar. I imagine people are starting to loosen up right about now—" She sounds bored by it all, but I'm fascinated, leaning forward as my fingers continue to trace circles in Catticus' fur.

My eyes drift again to the black velvet of the night beyond the window, my mind running rampant with all the ways tonight may expose me to the potential allies of Lord Black. I realise also, as a sense of vulnerability dampens my otherwise relaxed spirit, that I'm sitting in a room without any guards or even a door for that matter. Though I suppose I do at least have Catticus/Agamemnon for protection. I place a soft kiss on the top of his head, pressing my cheek to the warmth of his mane as I let out a sigh.

"You look nervous— what's on your mind?" Evangeline doesn't look up from her knitting this time, transfixed by the weave and click of the needles that are balanced between her dextrous and elegant fingers.

"Aliandara said that she's going to try and find out whether Asher had given his allegiance to Lord Black— I'm nervous. I want to hear the words for myself. Oh, to be a fly on the wall—" I muse and she gives me a startled glance as she snaps her eyes from the knitting in her hands to rest on my face, her lips parted as though she's halfway to spilling some deep dark secret.

"You believe Aliandara may miss something, that she may misread his words as genuine when they are not?" she asks. I frown at the desperation in her tone.

"No, I—" I begin to protest, knowing that wasn't at all what I meant. I had only thought that my anxiety would feel a lot more manageable if I was hearing Asher speak for myself.

Evangeline sighs, looking past my face and off into the space behind me for a moment, as though she's trying to glance into the past, or maybe the future.

Then, she rises in a flurry of lilac fabric, turning back and bending to place her knitting on the stool, before whirling back to face me.

"Come with me," she commands, no room in her dark eyes or stiff posture for argument.

I slide off the mattress sideways, my skin cooling as I hit a patch of bare stone between two intersecting rugs with the ball of my foot.

Grabbing my hand between desperate fingers, Evangeline pulls me after her as she exits the room. Placing the index finger of her free hand to her lips, I blink slowly at the gesture, wondering what the hell she's doing.

She rushes down the corridor without stopping once, tugging me away from my room and leaving Catticus behind us. We weave in and out of elegant archways, ducking beneath drapes and flickering gas lamps, the air fetid with smoky incense from the nearby festivities.

Then, we are in a narrow passage I've never seen before, and Evangeline is on her knees before me, her fingers clasping for the edge of the burgundy rug beneath my feet.

I step aside, watching as my heart begins to quicken beneath my chill skin, my breathing the only sound I can hear as it echoes off the surrounding cold walls.

Evangeline yanks up the rug entirely, tossing it aside before she does the same with two others. Then, without pause, she grabs a steel ring affixed to an indent in the floor so deep that if you didn't know it was there the thick oriental carpets would obscure it entirely.

Heaving it upward, she reveals a trapdoor that swings back on groaning hinges, the passage beneath accessible only by a set of chipped and uneven stone steps. They disappear only too quickly into the darkness, a stale air seeping out and filling my nostrils with a thick coat of dust.

"Follow the passage— and tell no one—" Evangeline's voice is a harsh whisper as she reaches out for my hand and pulls me toward the opening in the floor.

"Go! Go!" she hisses, giving me a small shove so I'm forced to make a small and uncalculated leap down into the semi-darkness. My bare feet hit the stone with a thud, the impact reverberating back up through my ankles.

"Evangeline, what—" I turn back to ask, but instead of being met with answers, she closes the trapdoor overhead, encasing me in darkness.

Turning atop the shallow staircase, it takes a moment for my eyes to adjust to the dimness, but I'm immediately aware of the humidity of the air despite its chalky texture on my tongue. My senses prickle, my ears picking up the low yet constant slosh of moving water somewhere nearby. Looking back over my wing and up to the trapdoor, I realise my only real option is to go onward and into the passage.

I take the shallow steps on bare soles, the dust clinging to my clammy feet as I tread as soundlessly as I can. The passageway deepens, and when I reach the bottom of the staircase, my vision has improved enough for me to realise that what I'm standing in are the drainage tunnels for the villa. I creep alongside damp walls, using my fingertips to trace the brickwork and keep close track of the path I'm taking. Fumbling around in the darkness, I teeter on a narrow ledge beside a steady flowing stream presenting only as a teeming surface of silver flashes in the dark.

Then, I hear it.

A low rumble— a laugh.

A man's laugh in fact.

I follow the low hum of conversation, closing my eyes so I can locate the source.

Soon, I see why Evangeline had sent me down into the darkness of the tunnel.

A sharp beam of light suddenly pierces the thick dankness as I turn one of the algae-slick corners, the hems of my pyjama pants slightly damp from where drained water is lapping at the edge of the ledge I'm following. I continue towards that stark piercing light, shadows casting patterns into increasingly defined darkness as I near the origin. It appears to be a grate.

I'm barely tall enough to peek over the bottom ledge, but on tiptoes I can just about clear it to see what's on the other side.

Swaying as the slick stone beneath my toes causes me to struggle for balance, I find myself looking out into a room I've come to be all too familiar with as I wobble.

Aliandara is nude, reclining back against the farthest end of her private baths. My nose is suddenly spattered by a swell of warm water flowing over into the grate and down into the drainage system I'm standing in, and it doesn't take me long to realise why the level of the water is rising.

Aliandara isn't alone.

I watch as a man I think I recognise joins her, also fully nude.

"Ah, Lady Montgomery, you are quite the sight—" The Equinian male lowers himself further into the water, closing the distance between himself and the High Lady with a few kicks of his powerful legs. The feathers of both parties shimmer along with their tattoos, the water beading and hanging from the tips of their wings like diamonds.

"Oh, do shut up, you know exactly where flattery gets you with me, Asher." Aliandara smiles with feline self-love, and I feel my heartbeat quicken. Evangeline knew about this passageway— So does she also know about Aliandara being alone, and not to mention fully naked, with an Equinian Chieftain?

Her words echo out in my memory for a moment.

You're not the first one confused as all hell about the dynamic here— It took me a while to understand when I first arrived. There are still parts— still parts that I've come to accept but that break my heart.

Swallowing, a small realisation bruises the notions I had held about Aliandara.

Evangeline knows only too well what her lover is doing.

As I watch Asher wrap his enormous arm around Aliandara's lithe waist, pulling her close to him and bringing his lips to hers, he bites down hard on her bottom lip, causing her to groan.

I shudder, horrified.

And then something occurs to me—

Is this how Lucien feels at the prospect of me marrying someone else? Is this what he's going through to respect my choice to try and keep the Aetherial Monarchy going?

I feel betrayed for Evangeline at the sight of the seemingly happy couple, so I wonder how much worse it must be for Lucien given how intensely I know he feels for me.

Bile rolls in my stomach, and I hear the two kissing Equinians let out a series of small sighs and groans. Eventually, I steel myself again, daring to peek back into the baths.

Aliandara pulls herself back from Asher's enormous chest, shaking her head like a schoolgirl with a crush, aloof and yet too obviously interested.

"Now Asher, you know the deal by now— how long has this been our little arrangement? Several hundred years I'd reckon—" Aliandara admits, and I feel myself frown.

I thought that the Aresian and Artemisian Equinians hated each other—

Then again, as this proves, I suppose there's a fine line between love and hate.

"Around that, yes—" Asher growls in a low and primal tone.

"And so, you should know by now that it's business before pleasure, dear boy—" She pokes the end of his nose with her wet index finger, cocking an eyebrow with seductive promise.

It almost makes me burst out laughing.

Asher is about as near a boy as I am a narwhal.

"Ah, always business with you woman—" I catch Asher rolling his eyes as Aliandara turns coyly, blocking his view of her perky breasts.

"But of course— you can't think I'm possibly sleeping with you for the pleasure of it alone—" she purrs, and he growls again with narrow eyes, his jaw jutting as the muscle beneath twitches with obvious irritation.

"Do I need to remind you what it feels like to come so hard you can't stand my Lady?" he asks her, voice low in warning.

For a moment I wish I wasn't hiding as I'd quite like to make some serious gagging noises.

"I could ask you the same thing. And if you do want reminding, we have business to attend to first. So, let's get to it." She reaches back over the edge of the bath for something I can't see, breath caught in my throat as she brings a goblet to her lips, drinking deeply and looking at the burly male with provocative eyes.

"So, what is it you want to know?" Asher sighs, leaning back and helping himself to a drink of his own.

"Chief Landon John, he's allied with Lord Black. Do I need to be worried about you as well?" She's so direct it catches me off guard.

Asher simply laughs.

"Not likely, my dear. Lord Black's little pet Equinian has been trying to poach my men—" He swallows another mouthful of whatever alcohol is in the goblet, and Aliandara cocks an eyebrow.

"You don't sound particularly concerned about that—" she comments, kicking her legs in a gentle rhythm beneath her.

"That's the least of my concerns if what my soldiers say is true—" Asher explains.

Aliandara turns to him fully now, listening overtly as her gaze intensifies.

"Which is?" she asks, and he moves to kiss her.

She pulls away, slapping him playfully.

"You're not getting a thing until you tell me whatever it is you're trying to avoid—" she snaps. Her lips twist gently into a smile, but her eyes remain hard as flint.

"If I tell you what they've been saying— let's just say it's a real mood killer." At his confession, my stomach flips and I crane my neck, trying to get as close to the grate as I can so I don't miss anything.

"Well, that's too bad for you then. You either tell me, or I'm leaving." The High Lady lays out his options and he grits his teeth visibly. Leaning back against the wall of the bath fully, his wings droop a little, as though he's surrendering.

"They say that Lord Black has found a way to absorb the powers of other Kindred and magical creatures by killing them," Asher reveals.

My eyes widen.

Aliandara laughs.

"Poppycock. An old wives tale."

"I said the same thing until I asked the Chief for an audience to discuss his blatant breach of Clan etiquette—" Asher admonishes, taking in a deep breath. "And— I was ready to tell him to stop spreading such rumours, until he arrived at our meeting, alone, by conduction," he finishes.

Lady Aliandara stills, and I feel my pulse throb with each passing second.

The heat of the bath fills the tunnel and seems to make the walls close in, the darkness like a blanket used to smother an animal, to calm it before slaughter.

"But that would mean—" I hear Aliandara's voice, but it's far off now like I'm at the bottom of a well.

White stars explode before my eyes.

My heart begins to pound.

My breathing spikes as the humid air refuses to flood my lungs.

I feel my nails dig into my forearms, the sudden pain my only tether to reality as I slump back against the wall of the tunnel, hyperventilating.

My senses sharpen despite my desire to be suddenly and completely unconscious like they might cleave my skull open and cause me to spill brain matter all over the floor.

"It would mean, Aliandara, that we are royally fucking screwed." Asher's voice echoes out in the hazy silence beyond the grate, the water lapping at the edges of the bath like thirsty tongues.

Uttering a prayer to Hera under my breath, I find the panic closing in, my only reaction being to flee, once more, to the only place I can think of that's safe.

GENEVIEVE

"Get up."

The voice of the Equinian Chieftain reaches me as I'm lying on the floor of the crystal cell, my bound arms flung awkwardly across my eyes, where Algoric is still curled, blocking out the relentless light. I feel him retreat, slithering around the back of my neck and down my left shoulder with speed that I don't expect. I move then, dropping my arms to my chest and staring up into the glistening points of the amethyst shards protruding from the low ceiling.

Sitting up, I breathe out slowly, calming my racing heart as the memory of the dreams which had plagued my restless subconscious refuse to rescind into the fog of the past. I can still hear the screams ringing in my ear, the acrid smoke settling in my nostril like a caustic film and causing my throat to burn.

"Come on, I don't have all damn day—" The Chieftain growls, his knuckles rapping on the bars impatiently.

"What, in a rush to torture me?" I sigh, rolling my eyes and getting to my feet with stiff limbs. The manacles around my wrists clatter together as my wings flare, trying to help me balance.

"Fortunately for you, that's not why I'm here," the Chief enlightens me.

I cock a pale eyebrow, surprised.

Standing, my eyes narrow against the harsh light as the Chief moves in a single brisk stride, unlocking the cell door. I straighten as I duck out from beneath the low ceiling, crossing the cell's threshold and coming eye to eye with the same man who had locked me up what could only be hours ago.

How long had I been dreaming?

"Wrists—" he grunts, his jaw ticking as he reaches into his chausses for the key, watching me closely. I tilt my head with a coy smile, holding out the manacles for his inspection.

"So, you threw me in here to what— give me a numb ass?" I query, and he snorts, the weight of the manacles leaving me as he unlocks them.

I retract from him instinctually.

"Not my call, but I hope you at least suffered as much—" His voice is thick with irritation, cheeks warm with blood running close to the surface of the coarse skin beneath his five o'clock shadow.

So, Lord Black is not taking the guidance of his fellow High Born— interesting.

"My ass is none of your fucking concern," I spit at him, bile rising in my throat at the sight of his calloused palms.

"Oh, don't flatter yourself—" Landon rolls his eyes, throwing the Kyanite manacles to the floor with an angry clatter. Without warning, he proceeds to grab my wrist in that enormous hand and conducts us from the dungeon.

The suddenness of the action leaves me with spots on my vision from the lightning tearing the air apart, but after a few seconds of heavy blinking, the room in which we've arrived reveals itself amongst ominous shadows.

A crackling fireplace at my spine leeches the cold of the crystal cell from my bones, and Landon lets go of my wrist before disappearing once more in a flash of lightning.

Before me is an enormous wooden table, the room presenting a high vaulted ceiling and windows sprawling the entire height of the opposing wall. They look out over the crystal gardens of the Solis Castra that

I've only ever seen from a bird's eye view. I note high-backed chairs surrounding the table as I continue my assessment, and my nostrils fill with the scent of meat.

"High Lady Thomas—" Lord Black is positioned, waiting at the far end of the room on my left, where two glass patio doors stand open, a sickly floral breeze floating in and invading the flickering orange light bathing the room.

At the High Lord's side, a black Kensari stands, back to the room as well. Their silhouettes are supposed to be intimidating, man and beast side by side, but I'm not phased. Algoric could have swallowed that stupid winged lion in a single gulp.

I don't reply to Aro's summons, crossing my arms tightly over the pale leather of my corset.

"You will respond when I address you, Genevieve. Especially considering I'm inviting you to dinner. For what you pulled I have every right to have you publicly executed at my hand," he continues, and it is then that I notice the head and foot of the table are set for dining.

Silver cloches cover what I assume are full plates, and finely cut glassware and cutlery glint polished to perfection beneath the vast chandelier overhead.

"You're inviting me to dinner?" I stare at the back of his head, incredulous as he turns, the sunset igniting his silhouette in a nimbus of flame.

"Yes, yes I am." The High Lord Sephilim faces me at last, the black inky feathers of his wingspan dancing with embers of light from the hearth as he takes a step forward.

I take a step back out of habit, but he comes no closer, sitting at the head of the table as his lion companion heels diligently by the side of his chair. He gestures for me to take the seat at the opposite end of the very long table.

It suits me just fine, putting distance between us, and so I obey him— for now.

I pull out the dining chair without breaking the intense gaze I have locked on my dinner companion, seating myself and crossing my legs with a casualness bordering on arrogance.

He lifts the cloche from his plate and implies I should do the same with but a tilt of his head.

Steam billows upward as I oblige him, my mouth watering against my consent as the scent of well-cooked meat fills my nostrils.

I stare at the steak, the mashed potatoes, and the green beans, all of it lavished in a rich dark gravy, eyes narrowing.

"I assumed you like your steak nice and rare— given your— beastly tendencies," Aro says it like it's nothing, but I know he intends to offend me.

He does not.

I pause, putting my finger on the wooden hilt of a provided steak knife, curious as I sit back in my seat, still refusing to eat.

"It's not poisoned you know—" he adds, tucking into his steak with practised elegance. His dark hair falls across his brow as he has the cheek to close his eyes and groan a little in pleasure at his first bite.

I take my chance, grabbing the steak knife from the napkin on which it's been sitting, winking at me before I send it hurling through the air between us.

It doesn't hit him between the eyes, sadly, as he snatches the projectile out of the air before it even gets close, his cutlery clattering to the table and spattering gravy across its polished surface.

I watch as he tightens his grip around the blade, the metal turning molten and running out between his fingers. Letting the wooden hilt go, the shimmering mess of metal and wood splatters on the tabletop beside his discarded fork. Withdrawing his hand, he is calculated as ever as he wipes away the rest of the silver before it has a chance to cool onto his skin.

So, I hadn't been imagining his sudden mastery of skills I have only ever known myself to possess—

Shit.

I watch as he picks up a pretentiously small bell from beside his still steaming plate, ringing it and waiting a few seconds in silence as I stare at him with intense hatred.

A person I can't see pops his head around the side of the door behind me, but I don't turn to look, not wanting to take my attention off the Sephilim who by some sick sort of irony has invited me to dine with him.

"High Lady Thomas requires another steak knife—" he informs the person who I assume is wait staff, and I cock an eyebrow.

"Aren't you worried I'm going to try and kill you again?" I ask him and he smirks.

"Do I seem it?" he counters, retrieving his cutlery before he returns to slicing his steak into delicate strips. I watch him, moments thick in the air between us, the tension only broken by the waiter placing a brand new and equally sharp steak knife beside my plate before retreating on soft heels.

"As I said, it's not poisoned. Eat." This time it's not a request, but an order.

Who the hell does he think he is?

"I am well aware it's not poisoned Lord Black, I'd have thought you'd remember that Draconians can smell poison. In fact, wasn't that a point of contention for you rather recently?" I ask, eyes glinting as I take the cutlery in hand. Though this time I move to eat.

I start with the vegetables, placing a single green bean between my teeth and snapping it in half. Juices and seasoned butter run across my tongue and I find myself cursing the resources available to this evil bastard.

Then again, if the world were fair, I'd be sitting at the head of the table, and he at the foot with a steak knife jutting out of his forehead.

"So, what exactly is it I'm doing here?" I demand without meekness, keeping my eyes fixed this time on my plate as I spoon potatoes into my mouth. Algoric curls from where he was wrapped around my wrist to lie coiled in my lap, tongue tasting the air with silent relish.

"I could ask you the same question—" Aro blinks back at me as I raise my head in response, his dark eyes bottomless and without humour.

"You captured me, remember?" I retort. He laughs to himself, picking up the goblet in front of him and taking a sip of what I assume is wine.

I'm tempted to take a hit from my glass, but then I'd rather keep a clear head, no matter how tempting it is to drink in the barbed discomfort of his presence.

"And you were flying, alone, in Sephilim airspace. You can't tell me you weren't looking to get caught, Lady Thomas. Even I'm not that naïve, though I'm sure I must seem young to you." He takes another bite of his steak, chewing with exaggerated vigour. The diamonds studding his lapels glint orange, the candles on the table between us casting his sunken cheeks into deep hollows as he leans forward, silently imploring me to respond.

"And why, Lord Black, would I have any inclination to even be in the same room as you? You murdered my dragon," I hiss, hacking at my steak with angry slashes.

"Ah, but that's just it. I'm wondering if you've come to realise that I may very well not be done with murdering dragons. You've heard of my newfound powers from others no doubt, and now you've seen them for yourself." He gestures to the mess of cooling metal which had only a short while ago been my steak knife.

Putting a chunk of steak into my mouth and letting watered-down blood mix with the gravy in the back of my throat, I consider outright denying his claim.

Instead, though, I deflect.

"Your newfound powers are as unimpressive as your taste in meat cuts—" I spit at him as I finish swallowing. This time he laughs properly from beneath the cumberbund that's tightly binding his abdomen.

"Oh, do save your vitriol, Genevieve. I dare say if we are to work together, you'll be needing it."

I sit back, letting my cutlery clatter to the plate before me in defiance.

"You've gone mad. I would never work with you. You're a lunatic," I hiss, my heart pounding against my consent. I wonder why it's rebelling so, wishing that the reality of the situation before me was anything but the truth.

"We're all lunatics here, Genevieve. The pawns of Gods and Goddesses who could not give a shit if we live or die so long as we keep their little kingdom safe. The question isn't who is or is not crazy, the question is which madman has the most power. And I know you've figured that one out for yourself, or you wouldn't be here—"

He is cocky as he takes another sip from the depths of his overly decadent goblet, my hands twitching as the will to throttle him clutches at me and refuses to surrender.

"Fuck you— you don't know anything about me, or why I'm here—" I bite back, and Aro shakes his head, mouth curving into a smirk that causes my blood to boil. My hands ball into fists, and Algoric climbs my left arm, unspooling from where he's been teeming in my lap and wrapping tightly around my wrist once more.

"Alright then, if that's the way it's going to be." Aro rises to his feet, taking a napkin I had not seen him unfold from his lap. I watch as he dabs at his pale face, scrunching up the fine linen into a ball and leaving it atop his half-uneaten meal.

He takes the length of the table in several long strides, leaving his winged lion curled in a furry puddle, snoozing beside the far-left leg of the table.

I rise to meet him, anticipating violence.

260

Kicking my chair back, it topples and Aro raises a hand. Stepping back, I ready myself to fight, but before I can block, he's gripped me by the wrist and the room has dissolved in an ear-shattering crack.

Stomach churning, I find myself standing not in the Solis Castra dining hall, but instead back in my suite.

"What the hell do you think you're doing?" I snatch my wrist from him, glaring as I protect the other where Algoric is curled tight.

The warmth of the dining room hearth vanishes as the late evening bite of Drakos Vale flows in through the open balcony doors. Glancing from left to right with a more frantic gaze than I intend, I am grateful to find us alone.

"I'm returning you to where you belong. I won't have you pretending you just so happened to turn up in Soleus. I won't have an ally in denial or pretending she's been forced into working for me. You want to be on the winning side of this thing, whatever it turns into? You come to me and you get down on those pale knees. You pledge your allegiance to me, willingly, and publicly. You ask my mercy for the people you know full well I'll slaughter at the very first opportunity I have. There's no room for pride here, Genevieve. You're either my subservient or you're on my list of Kindred to end in short measure. There is no in-between." Aro's eyes glint like obsidian within his angular skull and I feel sick as I realise he's smug at my fight, amused by my self-respect.

I want to tear out his windpipe with my teeth, but I suddenly notice the sword at his hip as his hand flutters toward it with apparent absentmindedness, though I'm sure the action is intentional.

I stand there, frozen, remembering him astride Algoric, that same sword drawn and ready to plunge deep into the dragon's brain. The serpent on my wrist tightens in warning, and I let out the breath I've been holding. He senses the loss of fight in my form as my shoulders slump, wings drooping on my spine.

"Any questions?" he demands, and I think on this for a moment, trying to show him that his control isn't as definitive as he believes it to be.

"Yes. One." I lick my bottom lip, "Why so intent on making Kairi Freemont your Queen? I know she is the Heirbound, but with the power you claim to possess, the matter of who possesses a piece of metal should not count for anything. In fact, I think that your choice to pursue her makes you look like Hera's bitch."

He looks like he has been visibly slapped as my words reach him and his entire face tightens, wings perking up as his shoulders stiffen and his eyes narrow.

"A graceless savage such as yourself couldn't possibly understand," he snaps, his fingers balling into a fist.

I smile, satisfied.

"When you're ready to kneel before me you know where to find me. But know this: I won't give you this chance again. You have twenty-four hours, and after that time window has passed, I'll assume you have decided where your loyalties lie, and that it isn't with the real power in Aetheria."

His face becomes a mask of hard indifference, and I bite down hard on my tongue to keep me from screaming at him like a Banshee.

The sheer arrogance of him echoes throughout the room as he gives a small spin on the spot, wings flaring and causing his shadow to grow, drenching me in its darkness.

"I await your return with relish—" he grins, and then with a small chuckle, like that of a demented schoolboy, he's gone.

18

RABBIT AT REST

LUCIEN

I'M STARING INTO THE depths of my third cup of tea when lightning disturbs the previously still atmosphere of my kitchen. The copper pans hanging overhead flash, blinding me in a momentary blaze that is there and gone in the blink of an eye. My heart flips, wondering if I'm going to be dealing with Kairi or the enemy, slipping from the stool at the kitchen's centre island and tensing as I clench my fists, defensive.

Kairi appears across from me, her too-fast breaths and tear-stained face overtaking all the free space in my mind. My heart slows noticeably but takes on a lead-like weight that taxes me.

Her breath is coming in wheezing shudders that wrack her small frame, her eyes wide and terrified as she places a trembling palm to her collarbone like she might try and pull out her own windpipe just so she can take a decent breath.

I round the kitchen island, the soles of my bare feet silent as I close the distance between us like a vice, clutching her to me.

I feel her panic as though it were my own, her body wracked visibly by anxious spasms in my arms.

"Shh—" I place a kiss on the crown of her head before stepping back. "Kairi. Look at me. Look at me—" I beg, her lashes thick with unshed tears and shaking with fear. She squeezes them shut, the tears loosening from her lashes and trickling down her cheeks as glittering pearls, her breath continuing to come as a panicked half-pant half-wheeze.

"Kairi! LOOK AT ME." I shake her slightly, her eyes jerking open and boring into mine. "Deep breath," I order her, using the most authority I can muster despite the fact her fear is also causing my instincts to flare with panic. "And hold—" I continue, and she does as I ask, her lilac eyes glistening as the heavy rhythm of her breath stops abruptly. I count to four in my head.

"And exhale—" I implore, and she does as I have asked yet again, her breath warm as it escapes from between her lips and caresses my cheeks.

Her shoulders slump then, and I take her into my arms once again, feeling her heart hammering in a decelerating rhythm against my chest. I clutch her as she melts against me, the energy draining out of her like ice water as quivering feathers tickle the back of my hands. Her wings press into my forearms with increasing weight as they go slowly limp against her spine. The heat of her body seeps into me with gradual abandon as we stand for a few minutes, the only sound her slowing breaths.

"Would you like a cup of tea?" I ask her in a whisper, not loosening my hold even slightly.

She does not reply in words, simply nodding slowly as her breath hitches, catching in her throat. She sniffs, bringing a hand to her cheek to wipe away the drying saltwater as she takes a small and willing step back.

"I'm sorry— I shouldn't have— I just—" She looks like she's about to start panicking again, so I reach out, taking her fingers in mine and squeezing her palm.

"Hush. Please do not apologise for coming here. Not ever," I implore her and her angelic features soften atop the horrified contortion stirring beneath the surface. "Sit, I will get you a blanket and make you some tea. We will talk when you're ready, there is no rush *mon ange*—" The endearment rolls from me in my native tongue, as though it has been waiting for her to make itself known for over one hundred and fifty years.

She blinks slowly, looking up at me and sniffling again, bewildered as a doe caught in a trap as she glances around the room.

"Sit—" I repeat, guiding her to a stool and waiting until she is seated before walking from the kitchen and into the sitting room opposite. I grab an extremely thick knit cream blanket from the chocolate-coloured sectional sofa, tossing it over my forearm and returning to her with haste.

I place the thick woollen weave over her shoulders, wrapping her in it as though this blanket can protect her from the whole of Aetheria. I place a kiss on her cheek from behind, letting her lean back into me for a moment. I feel her heartbeat even now, fierce in her chest, even though it has slowed considerably.

"I'll make you some tea," I inform her of my intention again, setting another kiss upon her head and then stepping back. Walking over to the steeping teapot on the hob, I reach up to retrieve a teacup and saucer from the top shelf. It's copper rimmed and fine, one of my better pieces of flatware, and the elegance of it reminds me of the recipient as I fill it to the brim.

I carry it, hands steady, over to the island, placing it in front of Kairi and then taking a seat on the stool next to her and returning to my own cup.

We sit in comfortable silence for a few minutes, and I reach out, taking her left hand, which is protruding from the thick blanket wrapped tight around her shoulders.

Running my fingertips across the back of her knuckles, I hear her swallow more tea before putting the teacup back in its equally fine saucer and looking at me.

"I'm sorry—" she begins again, biting her bottom lip in shame. I shake my head.

"Don't you dare apologise," I reply stiffly, holding my breath in a kind of self-imposed punishment and feeling my features turn icy.

"It's not fair of me to keep turning up here like this, Lucien— it's just—" She begins to cry again, and I shake my head as I squeeze her warm fingers in mine.

"It's just you feel safe here. I understand that, Kairi. Trust me, after all you've been through, I know." I exhale heavily, drowning the final dregs of my tea and giving her a compassionate glance.

Even crying, she is more beautiful than anyone I could have ever imagined would be mine. Except for the fact she is not mine, she belongs to the Aetherial monarchy and their barbaric traditions— and I won't be the one to tell her to choose otherwise. It's a choice she has to make on her own, and right now I strongly suspect that she doesn't recognise her strength and the fact that she could simply walk away.

I couldn't blame her, but I know others would.

"How do you bear it?" she asks me, sniffing hard and letting go of my hand so she can pull the heavy blanket tighter around her.

Moonlight falls upon our backs, casting our silhouettes side by side upon the island surface. I look into her tear-stained face with a questioning glance.

"Bear what?" I ask, moving to brush her hair from her shoulder so I can observe her more closely.

"The thought of me with someone else?" she blurts, turning to me so our eyes lock, anchoring one another with the intensity of the gaze.

"I don't, Kairi— When I saw you dancing with that Sephilim, it felt like I was being gutted," I admit, remembering the feeling of unworthiness, of helplessness I had felt as I watched her that night.

She shuffles on the stool, looking uncomfortable.

"What is this about?" I enquire with a kind of impatient concern now, wondering what exactly has caused her to arrive here in such a state.

"I saw Aliandara and Asher— I saw them together in the baths at her villa. I was trying to eavesdrop to hear what Asher had to say about Aro. She's in a relationship with Evangeline and sleeping with Asher— and Evangeline knows. It's just— it made me consider being in your shoes—" she admits, flushing deep red like a small child who has been caught stealing sugar cookies right before dinner.

"You had a panic attack because you saw Aliandara cheating on her partner with Asher? Kairi, that isn't the same as what's happening between you and I—" Momentarily, I condemn her as overreacting. She swallows hard, shaking her head.

"That's not why I had a panic attack, but it's why I want to apologise to you. Running to you is so easy, Lucien. It's what my instincts tell me to do every time I get scared— and yet, I put myself in your shoes, and I realise now that what I'm doing is hurting you. I'm sorry because it's selfish—" she explains, and I throw my head back and laugh a little.

"Merde, Kairi. I would be more hurt if you didn't run here every time you were scared. Don't you know how much that means to me? That after everything the Sephilim and Nephilim have probably told you about the Draconians, that you still return to me as a place of safety? I should be thanking you for the compliment, not inducing an apology or the guilt that comes with it," I implore her to release the shame she clearly carries for keeping me in her life, for using me as a crutch, as if she's forcing my hand.

Doesn't she realise I'd willingly volunteer?

I'm nothing short of honoured, even though we might never be together in any real way.

"It's not just that— I mean, that was less than great to discover, obviously— but— Asher, what he had to say about Lord Black. Lucien, I am afraid. I'm more afraid than ever—" She looks like she might cry again, and I narrow my eyes, waiting for her to explain. Instead, she lets out a slight giggle, and then a hiccup-laden sigh.

"Look at me. Some Queen. They want me to choose the next King of Aetheria and at the mere mention of Lord Black I'm sobbing in your kitchen. I'm such a fucking mess—" she swears, and my eyebrows rise on my forehead as she runs a hand back through her hair.

"Kairi, what Lord Black did to you was traumatic as all hell. You died, actually died, standing up to him. I'm not surprised you're afraid," I remind her, and she nods, lips pressing together so hard they blanche to near arctic white.

"That's the thing though, Lucien. I did die. But— a part of me knew that I had a chance at coming back as a Nephilim. A part of me knew it would be an escape from my chronic pain. Not so noble now, am I?" I look at her and frown.

"Kairi, you risked everything. Don't diminish what you gave up. Don't you dare."

"I am so scared, Lucien. Afraid of dying— of losing you— afraid of what will happen if I don't stop Aro, afraid of what will happen if I do— I'm no hero, no High Lady— and certainly no Queen." She blows a loose lock of hair from her eyes, where it has been drawn across her face in a slick tendril when drying her tears.

"And so, what, you thought being immortal would make you fearless?" I ask, biting the inside of my cheek to avoid frowning at the pain riddling her beautiful face.

"I thought— I thought I'd be different, feel different," she admits, flushing as if she's embarrassed. I soften my gaze further, reaching out to touch the soft curve of her cheek.

"I'm glad you're not different," I whisper, leaning forward and giving her a soft kiss on the cheek. "I fell in love with you before the wings, remember?" I remind her, leaning back and thinking of how fragile she had looked in mortal flesh, of how strong the impulse to protect her had been.

It still is, only now I know it's more important to let her find her own power because I have faith in her strength, even if she doesn't. Somehow, she's lost all her confidence, all her fire, and I wonder if it's my fault— if I'm making everything worse. Falling in love with a Draconian wasn't what Hera would have wanted, so perhaps that makes her feel like a failure— makes her hate herself for being deviant and dooming her people.

The thought rattles me as I realise just how much her feelings are creating a divide inside her, a widening chasm she's still straddling—for me.

"I just— with what I heard; I know that I'm not strong enough to fight back. I know that Aro is going to take Aetheria, whether I crown him or not. Maybe— maybe I should just get it over with and stop more people getting killed." She makes what seems like an absurd declaration, surprising me. I turn to her, our knees touching, and stare deeply into her face.

"Kairi, what happened?" I ask, the muscle in my jaw tightening as a knot of concern constricts in my stomach. Kairi takes a deep breath, trying to hide her trembling hands as she finishes the dregs at the bottom of her cup. She fails in her deception, setting it back down onto the saucer with a quivering hand which causes the china to emit a dissonant tinkle.

"Asher said that Aro has found a way to steal the powers of other Kindred by killing them. He gave that Equinian Chief Sephilim powers," she says, and my eyes widen.

My thoughts jump immediately to Genevieve, to her abrupt departure, heart dropping through my body at the implications of the information.

Could this have something to do with it?

No.

I mean, how could she have possibly known about this?

KAIRI

I lay in Lucien's bed, wrapped still in the thick knit blanket he had draped over me as I sipped tea in his kitchen. My head is in his lap, and I'm shivering a little, the goosebumps on my arms refusing to retreat despite the fact I'm layered up.

Now the panic attack has subsided, I'm exhausted, my brain full of a delighted fog which only seems to grow denser as the Draconian High Lord runs his fingers through my hair.

We haven't made love, don't intend to either, and I'm glad of it. Everything is so intense as it races around my mind like a stallion that has been spooked into a frenzy, I don't know if I could handle unravelling beneath Lucien physically right now.

He seems content, his voice a low rumble that soothes me as he reads from the well-worn pages of Storm's not so long-lost copy of Pride and Prejudice.

"There are few people whom I really love, and still fewer of whom I think well. The more I see of the world, the more I am dissatisfied with it; and every day confirms my belief of the inconsistency of all human characters, and of the little dependence that can be placed on the appearance of merit or sense." He reads Austen's words, and I think of how true they are, my heart aching as I recall Evangeline's heartbroken expression when she was closing the trap door on me. She had known what was happening between Aliandara and Asher, that much was clear.

I wonder how she bears it.

Lucien turns the page and pauses, raising his chin and looking at me over the top of the book.

"Are you warm enough?" he asks, and I gently shake my head.

"No, I'm freezing, but honestly I don't think more blankets or even a fire would help. I'm just in shock and my body is all out of sorts. I used to get like this after I had a dislocation—" I muse and Lucien nods, pulling the blanket tighter over my chest.

"Do you want to talk about it?" he asks, and I pucker my lips, feeling as if I am teetering on a knife edge over a howling abyss.

"I'm afraid to. I mean, what can I say? I think it's pretty obvious that this new development means Lord Black is quickly becoming an unbeatable threat—" I frown, letting my eyes flutter closed as Lucien closes the novel and places it onto the richly polished wood of the bedside table. He continues to run his fingers through my hair, causing me to relax further into the feathered wings that lie beneath me despite myself. He gazes at me with sad eyes.

"Don't look at me like that, please. You know what I'm saying is true. If he can absorb the magical gifts of other Kindred, as Asher supposes, once he has amassed a certain amount of power, he will be unstoppable." I return Lucien's stare with a tiring but equal intensity, waiting a moment as his face turns thoughtful and his eyes cloud slightly behind the deep blue of his irises.

He looks up to the skylight, to the smattering of diamond-hard stars that pepper the heavens, thoughtful.

I close my eyes, savouring the darkness and the absence of reality for a moment.

"So perhaps we don't let him get that far—" Lucien muses, and I pull the blanket higher under my chin, fists balling tight into the knit. I don't open my eyes as I try to contain the fleeting heat of my body, sighing dreamily and letting out a yawn.

"And how exactly do you suggest we do that?" I laugh slightly to myself, feeling helpless and isolated, tiny within the comforting confines of my cocoon.

"We unite the Kindred races. He wants to take our power and combine it within himself— but we don't have to do that to have access to all the different kinds of Kindred and their magic—" he speaks this thought aloud, obviously slightly in awe of the notion, and I crack my eyes reluctantly, exhaling heavily and letting the escape of my breath warm my cheeks.

"You're serious?" I say it calmly, but inside I'm exasperated.

"As a Frenchman about good wine—" Lucien retorts. I cock an eyebrow, my eyes opening fully this time as I glance up into his sparkling gaze.

"My, that is serious. It's also insane, by the way—" I try to stifle another yawn, wondering if I can really be so tired after sleeping most of the day. My body isn't what's lagging though, it's my brain after trying to keep up with the speed at which everything is changing.

"What's so insane about it?" he enquires, face genuinely curious.

"Well— for a start, the Equinians and the Fae will never work together. You know that as well as I do. Even if they did put aside their differences, I don't even know that we'd have the numbers—" I am starting to sound as hopeless as I feel.

Taking a deep breath, I burst, "Lucien you're talking about war!"

"I'm fully aware of what I'm talking about." He rests his head back against the headboard with a soft thud, shifting his weight beneath where my head rests in his lap.

"You were the one who didn't want war before— You didn't think that the Draconians could survive it," I remind him and his jaw bulges as he tenses with frustration, searching for the words to express himself.

"If I had done what I was planning to do that night, we wouldn't be here now. You wouldn't be running even still, and Genevieve wouldn't have lost Algoric," he admits, looking guilty.

I release a palm from beneath the blanket to trace his jawline with affection.

"You don't know that. You can't blame yourself for this either, so don't even try it—" I admonish and he laughs, the sound half a strangled guffaw and half an inhale of exasperation.

"You can talk, you're the number one worst person for blaming yourself, Kairi." He strips me bare with his stare, pulling back the curtain of my denial and casting me under the spotlight of his softly spoken truths.

For that, I simultaneously love him and hate him.

He takes my fingers in his and kisses my palm gently, cocking his head and looking into my face as longing and despair roll into a single entity behind his eyes.

"He won't stop killing until he has the throne, and you, Kairi. Even then I'm not sure—" he trails off, and I narrow my eyes.

"You really think we could fight back?" I ask, fear curdling in my stomach like sour milk as I cut him off mid-sentence.

"I don't know, but I know that we're running out of time to decide. Once he reaches a certain level of power, he will be too difficult to take down, and then I fear the rest of the Kindred will fall into line. Even if they don't want to," Lucien muses. I consider this, chewing my lip anxiously as fear drips cold and slow into a torturous and gradually growing puddle of terror in my gut.

"I don't think the Fae and the Equinians will agree to work together," I say flatly, thinking on their starkly different points of view.

"You'd be amazed what enemies will do once they have a common enemy." Lucien looks relentlessly thoughtful even still, and I wonder why.

"What about Genevieve?" I ask him, thinking of the self-appointed dragon queen.

It's obvious the Draconians would be a valuable asset to anyone in a battle, but I wonder if Genevieve would be willing to risk more dragons now the grief of Algoric's loss has fermented into something altogether more permanent misery and less sudden fury. Would she be willing to go after Lord Black even still, or has she grown more cautious than even Lucien?

"I don't think we should get her involved in this until we absolutely have to. She's not exactly stable—" It sounds like he is holding something back, but I don't pry.

Lucien and Genevieve's relationship is something I can't claim to even almost understand.

"The Fae would need an incentive— something so tempting they can't play pacifists any longer—" he continues, beginning to rhythmically stroke through the locks of my hair once more.

"And I suppose we're just swimming in those—" I snort, and his eyes are suddenly angry with disappointment.

"Kairi, what happened to you? Where is that girl who risked it all for the d

dragons? You're so pessimistic now," he demands, and I feel the wind knocked from me.

It was one thing hearing those words from Aliandara, it's another hearing them from Lucien.

"I used to believe that good would always win out, like in stories. I've come to realise recently that is *just* in stories. Real life isn't like that, and Aetheria has a great talent for using its breathtaking surroundings to make you feel falsely secure." I confess to the brokenness of my world view and the impact of my words strikes me harder than I thought it would.

Lucien sighs, his eyes so seemingly heartbroken I can't stand to hold his gaze.

"I suppose I can understand that, but someone has to believe that Aetheria can rise against this threat. We need that hope— if we don't have it how can we even begin to convince anyone else?" he exclaims. I turn back, meeting his eyes again with a reluctance that wasn't there before, wishing he wasn't so damn righteous.

I look at him, wondering where his passion has come from, and then realise that I need not look far.

He wants me for himself, and maybe this is his way of holding on to the notion that we might one day build a life together.

"Is this about us?" I ask, biting my bottom lip harder still.

"Of course it's about us. It's also about the fact that Aetheria is essentially becoming a tyranny, more so than it's ever been. Make no mistake, Aetheria has always been tyrannical and divisive, but now that's shifting into something lethal on an entirely terrifying scale."

"I don't want to end up getting you killed, Lucien. Or anyone else," I plead, but he only shakes his head.

"We need to find common ground, Kairi. We need to unite the people under one cause and rise against Lord Black." He's growing fiercer, his fists balling in the sheets at his side, his body becoming an icy flame beneath me as the chill of his passion seeps into my spine.

"Common ground— hmm."

I feel terrified at the thought of a war, but maybe Lucien needs to realise that what he is proposing is naïve. Maybe he needs to see the Fae and Equinians process this proposal for themselves to realise how insane he is being.

"Why are you so afraid?" Lucien asks me, and I give him a sad smile.

"Why don't we have the Equinians and Fae meet with us in the mortal world? That would be neutral ground, wouldn't it?" I suggest. The suggestion catches him entirely off guard and he smiles, the tension in his shoulders dissolving as quickly as it came.

"That's a good idea, any particular location in mind?"

"Hickory Oaks Ranch is remote enough to not draw any attention, but I want my fathers gone before we use it for a meeting. I won't risk them getting caught up in this." I am firm in tone, my heart squeezing uncomfortably as I think about returning to my parents as a Kindred.

I shift onto my side, glimpsing up into Lucien's face and propping myself up on one arm.

As I do, I realise why I'm doing this.

It's not because I believe it's a solution. It's because I know Lucien won't be able to let go of his hope until we've exhausted all the options. He won't surrender, won't sit by and let Aro simply take Aetheria, and I fear it might get him killed.

"You don't think this will work?" Lucien presses me with consistent intensity, his face soft yet stony as he trails his fingers along the line of my jaw.

I sigh, trying to work out how to make him understand.

"I don't hope any longer, Lucien. Not after everything. Not after falling in love with you, not after the universe has been so cruel. The Goddess Hera made me sick to make me stronger as a piece in her chess game. I'm under no illusions that anything I want is even a consideration in the grand scale of things. I'm just another body for their fodder pile—"

His hand stops as it moves from my scalp to the tips of my hair. He looks broken then.

"Don't say that *mon ange*," he scolds gently, leaning down to lay a soft kiss on my cheek. "You are the most incredible woman I've ever met. I know why Hera chose you, even if you do not, and I know it wasn't because you were simply a pawn." His gaze is loving, but I don't believe a word he says.

"Lucien, Hera has abandoned me. None of the Gods or Goddesses have our interests at heart, you have to know that by now. Look at what's happening— look at what happened to Algoric. Why create dragons when you're sending them to a world where they'll be hunted and killed?" I demand the answers to questions I cannot ignore, heart racing as I feel the injustice of it all like a blow to the abdomen.

"Kairi—" Lucien begins, stiffening where he's sat. But I don't let him finish, tired of his insistence on better for Aetheria. I had listened, enraptured, that night under the sky of Aramis among a bioluminescent glow, but I'm not that naïve girl anymore.

I'm not human, and I'm not stupid enough to think that either one of us can make a difference. Not now, not with Lord Black sitting in the Solis Castra with an Equinian army waiting to pick us off one by one.

Taking a deep breath, I try to make him understand.

"I can't hope anymore, Lucien. It'll break me. Losing you, losing everything after I've let myself fall even deeper. I'm already coming apart at the seams. Only magic can fix this, and swords, and firepower— and even then— even then, the loss may be greater than it's worth."

Lucien blinks slowly, but it is as though my words haven't been heard at all.

"And what do you think draws men to raise arms, to cast their power into the real, to risk it all? That is hope, *mon ange*. Hope is the most powerful magic of all."

I wish, more than anything, that I could believe him.

19

STRANGER IN A STRANGE LAND

ARO

I CAN'T SLEEP, WHICH is why I currently find myself flying amongst plumes of storm cloud, looking down over the Kingdom which is mine by right. Not right of being chosen, nor right of inheritance, but by right of sweat, blood, and toil.

I have done more for this sorry continent than anyone realises, and I'll be damned if some Goddess whore stops me from claiming what's mine after everything I've done to get here.

That dragon bitch's words regarding my continual chase of Kairi Freemont echo through my head relentlessly as I bank hard left against the rising breeze.

In fact, I think that your choice to pursue her makes you look like Hera's bitch—

With the newfound and limitless power of the amethyst weapons, I could well abandon my quest to break Kairi Freemont, but at this point, it's less of an obligation and more of a personal grudge against her and the ridiculous system she represents. I want to break her, so she bends to me, not only to prove that no man needs the approval of some chosen slut to grasp the power that is rightfully his, but also to prove to Hera that all her best-laid plans were in vain. It's a statement, about the weakness and pliancy of women, about the pathetic nature of the obstacle, and one intended to start my eternal reign with the right tone.

The tone of defiance against the Gods and Goddesses that think they have any right to recruit us to their service against our consent.

Genevieve, interestingly enough, seems to understand this. She seems to realise that it is our duty as mortals to stand up to those in The Higher Plains who believe our lives are toys for them to play with, that our suffering, when pulled out across eternity thanks to their gift, is not something we should simply grin and bear.

I'm tired of it, tired of being kicked around the board of a game I never signed up to play.

I am Aetheria's future king, not because I was chosen but because I have risen and beat out all opponents in my way.

I will take the throne, despite the barriers put in place by a Goddess I have come to despise. Not to appease her, but to slay her with her own blade.

I will break Kairi Freemont. Utterly. And with pleasure.

So then why is it I can't sleep if I am so certain?

I loop back on myself, taking in the flickering lamplight of clustered cottages below, their residents no doubt terrified by the prospect of my Equinian soldiers running rampant and pillaging the land of its natural beauty.

Still, needs must.

My wings ripple with the moving air currents above and below my shadowy form as I dart between clouds and cut through the air with razorlike precision, aether flying out from my wingtip in a sparkling trail marking where I have graced the air.

I sweep left, then right, pondering the restlessness of my mind as it makes its way into my muscles.

Perhaps I'm simply bored of waiting to make my next move— but then, why is there a niggling in the back of my consciousness I can't quite subdue?

Her emerald irises come back to me, the malice and hatred in them exciting me as I watched her carotid throb beneath the porcelain veil of her skin.

She had been excited too; I know it. The heat I had stolen from her beastly steed rises beneath my skin, the force of it causing me to gulp down cold night air like it's a drug and I'm an addict.

I dip down low, letting my wings rustle the crystal leaves on the trees in a small copse that surrounds Sparrowdale, the trickling of the streams that run like free-bleeding veins around the small settlement reaching my ears just barely above the roar of my aerial motion.

I wonder how fast Genevieve can fly, if she could beat me in a race— if her leathery wings are more durable than mine, slicked with onyx feathers that shimmer gold beneath a similarly shaded lunar orb.

The scent of lilacs and vanilla encases me as I roll in the air, corkscrewing and closing my eyes, savouring the feeling of being so completely in control of my body, so free.

And yet— I am still on edge and peace evades me as I dart among the sea of stars that has settled, tempestuous with clouds, above Soleus.

Why can't I stop thinking about the look in that woman's eyes when she had thrown the steak knife at me?

She had been within the walls of my castle, of my stronghold, but that still had not stopped her from taking a shot. She had not played by halves either, her accuracy and intent clearly lethal.

I am not used to being so challenged, at least not since the absorption of Algoric's powers. I have intimidated everyone I have come in contact with— except her.

Why, when I match her in power, when I could crush her windpipe in a furious and scalding fist, does she not quiver, does she not wilt, terrified within the lily-white confines of her flesh?

Instead, she comes alive, blazing with hungry tongues of fire that spit obscenities and real, sincere threats right back at me.

Does her fire feed the embers of my fury— and even more disturbingly— do I like it?

No. I would much rather she kneel. If I wasn't so inclined, why would I have insisted she returns of her own volition, that she declares her alliance and bend before my intent with nothing but full autonomy and respect for my absolute power?

She challenges me then, is that it?

Her will is seemingly uncrushable.

Is that what is bothering me, the fact that she refuses to bend like everyone else?

I think about Kairi, about how she had looked up at me during my capture of the Solis Castra on the night of her ascension ball.

She had been shaken, meagre within the grandeur of her gown. A scared little girl.

It had almost been too easy.

My mind flits next to the girl I had fucked yesterday, to the sameness of it, to the dull monotony of each and every thrust, the demureness of the Nephilim so standard as to be ash upon my tongue.

Once it had been a delicacy. Once I had felt satisfaction at dominating those oh-so-delicate flowers.

Now though— it doesn't thrill me as it had.

The more power I amass, the more easily they bend, until it is almost an automatic reflex, as ingrained as breathing.

It also becomes painless for them, or seemingly so.

They don't fight or scream, but simply get down on their knees before me and look skyward with fearfully adoring eyes.

Their obedience is ingrained, instinctual— but not for her. Not for the Draconian High Lady who I have spent centuries loathing.

I still hate her, no doubt, but now there is also a kind of morbid curiosity, a kind of dark fascination with the fact she won't break.

I think of Kairi as my Queen. Of her pallor and her quiet disdain masked by the necessary smile of royal duty.

Is she really what I want? Someone to bend and scrape— someone around whom I will become complacent, I will become arrogant.

There is no risk of that with Genevieve, not an ounce.

I rise higher above the blankets of cloud, tasting increasing static in the air. A storm is coming no doubt, and my blood hums at the idea of such turmoil in the skies.

Has my heart, my arousal, become ambivalent as I've become closer to unstoppable?

I picture Genevieve in a crown, her regal features pointed and adoring at my side. I feel the heat of our joint dominance building to be incendiary, our eternal rule over Aetheria a flame that simply will not die. The idea of her challenge goads me into a state of excited frenzy and passion, one which I haven't felt the likes of since driving an amethyst blade into her dragon's skull, ending him and stealing his magic.

She would make an acceptable Queen, an acceptable force to keep me on my toes. The whetstone to my blade, sharpening me against potential threats, against those who might try to dethrone me as their rightful King.

I can't deny that as someone who intends to rule eternally, the prospect seems a sensible one on my part.

Heart fluttering slightly, I coil back on myself, sweeping the sky and turning a loop back on myself. My mind calms as I picture our union, our alliance.

First, though, I must break Kairi Freemont and prove myself as no pawn to Hera.

Calmer as a vision of the future forms crystalline in my mind, the world spins around me in a kaleidoscope of stars, flame, and cloud.

I soar on, finally content, into the night.

KAIRI

We materialize among the heather, hands entwined, feet suddenly heavy upon the Tennessee soil of Hickory Oaks Ranch. I breathe it in, the aroma of fresh-cut hay and a dying summer's day sticky in my throat as a faint smile creeps across my face.

Lucien looks around, eyes widening.

"It's so—" he breathes, inhaling deeply. His eyes scan the smoky mountains on the horizon beyond the endless sea of undulating gilded grasses.

Horses are silhouetted against the sky yawning wide overhead, lilacs, tangerines, and magenta vivid as they streak between the gaping jaws of the horizon.

"Vast," Lucien finishes, settling definitively on the word.

"I suppose, but compared to Drakos Vale, not so much." I remind him, and he cocks his head, the crickets chirping in a melancholic chorus all around.

We have materialised beside the gazebo where I had spent so many hours reading and where I'd first met Aro. The sight of it sends a shudder through me, a physical sensation I thoroughly despise.

"So, this is— America?" Lucien asks me, and I nod, grinning slightly.

"Yes, Lord DeLaurent. Welcome to the land of the Big Mac, Fenway Park, and pickup trucks." I tug him after me, feeling nostalgia for the United States welling inside my chest like an uncomfortable air bubble.

The grasses tickle my ankles beneath the gown Lucien had produced from the wardrobe in my old room back in Drakos Vale, apparently one of three day dresses that Aska had prepared just in case I was ever in need.

The square neck is low cut, my breasts full behind the corseting of the bodice. The squeeze of the boning makes each heartbeat only more noticeable as the simple lilac satin skirts whisper in passing over the crisp golden foliage.

Lucien squeezes my hand and I slow my step, looking back over the high arch of my wing. The feathers of it still glisten with aether, catching the colours of the sky and igniting them anew.

"Are you alright?" he asks, and I flush a little. The man knows me a little too well.

"Nervous, and excited— and well— just everything. It's a lot." I'm flustered as I ramble, blinking fast, the sweet Tennessee breeze caressing my cheeks and teasing the angel curls that lie thick against my warm neck.

"Do you want me to stay back? You don't have to introduce me, you know. I'm aware I can be more than a little— jarring to mortals." He gets a mischievous glimmer in the deep blue of his irises, and I wonder if he's thinking about the first time I had laid eyes on him. I recall stiffening, my skin chilling considerably at his touch, and blanching at his incredibly powerful wings and unapologetic posture.

Now, it is those things that make me desire him, that make him astounding to me.

"Don't be silly. This is important to me." I am certain of the truth as I speak it, and yet I wonder why I'm so desperate for my parents to meet him. After all, we can never truly be together. Not without getting someone killed.

Perhaps then it's my fathers who will validate what I know is true but can't risk lives to defend. I want them to look at Lucien and see the man I do.

I want to know he is the man that I know him to be, that it is Aetheria which is wrong, and not me for falling in love with him.

We cross the rest of the ranch side by side, our paces matching as our wings touch gently and our fingers interlock with a habitual tightness. The house hasn't changed, my orange pickup truck still standing upon its squat tyres on the gravel drive, the wrap-around oak porch turned gilded and majestic by the twilight.

"This is quite the place—" Lucien grins at me, and I look up at him, blushing.

I don't know why the compliment means so much, especially considering I had been adamant that this place never felt like home, yet I'm touched. It is as if Lucien is stepping into my past and falling for me even then, as if he's enamoured with who I was as well as who I have become.

Climbing the porch steps, I notice a distinct absence of ache in my knees, my heart beginning to thrum beneath the embroidered corsetry of my gown.

Standing before the door, I take a pause, a beat, a second, to catch my breath. Then, I raise my fist to the thick knotty wood and knock three times.

Lucien shifts beside me causing the wooden boards beneath him to creak, his physique no less intimidating despite his attempt at casual attire in a pair of black slacks and a black shirt. Shoving his hands into his pockets, I notice he draws his wings back slightly and brushes his long blond hair behind one ear.

Before I can ask myself if the immortal dragon rider beside me could be nervous, I hear the shuffle of motion from behind the door and listen to the familiar slide of the chain being unlatched.

I hold my breath as the door swings back, revealing my dad Michael in plaid lounging pants and a dark t-shirt with the words *I'm not gay*— followed by *Just kidding!* beneath in bold white font.

He stands frozen for a few seconds, looking at Lucien and me as we stand awkwardly on the porch.

"Honey?" he calls, not taking his eyes from me as his voice echoes out around the high wooden beams of the central living space behind him.

"Who'd you offend this time?" I hear the familiar voice, and my throat knots tightly so I can hardly swallow. I hear footsteps coming closer, before my Pa, Matthew, pops his head around the door.

"Oh my God—" he shoves my dad out of the way, and rushes across the threshold, wrapping me in his arms.

Lucien takes a half step back as my dad delivers what would have once been a bone-crushing, flare-inducing hug.

It isn't now though, and so I embrace him back with all the strength I can, enjoying myself thoroughly.

"Kairi— You're crushing me—" he gasps after a few seconds and I let a high-pitched giggle escape from the back of my throat, tears spilling untamed down my cheeks.

"Pa—" I whisper.

Releasing him with a breathless sigh, I watch my dad come forward, shoving his husband out of the way and slamming into me with the full force of the emotion that's running rampant across his face, tears spilling wildly down his cheeks too.

The scent of them both causes the tension to leave my body, and I wonder now why I had been nervous at all.

I catch Lucien smiling as I release my dad, and the two men look at me, awed.

"You're— you're so—" my dad stutters, and Lucien cuts in.

"Beautiful." He grins and offers a hand to the two shocked men who are now gaping at him instead. I suppress a laugh as they are both made to look up at his immense height and bulky frame.

"This is Lucien DeLaurent, High Lord of The Draconians—" I give his full title, a slight pride I had not expected suddenly overtaking me.

"Well— aren't you rather— large." Matthew looks up into Lucien's face and I snort slightly, watching as the Draconian High Lord actually, dare I say it, blushes.

"So I've been told, Sir," he replies with as much grace as he can muster, and I fall a little more in love with him as my dad and he shake hands.

"And you're— you're—" Michael is the one to stutter now as he turns back to me, and I nod, taking his hands in my palms and finishing the sentence for him.

"I'm a Nephilim, Dad. It's okay." I wasn't prepared for the rush of emotion that floods me as the two men make twirling motions with their fingers. I do as they ask, spinning on the spot and expanding my wings as far as I can.

I feel them behind me, touching the feathers that are still glittering with aether beneath their trembling fingers.

Turning back, they continue to stare, and I suddenly realise that I must have looked just as gormless as a mortal greeting Aliandara for the first time.

"Can we go inside?" I ask them as the conversation comes to a standstill and silence fills the spaces left behind.

"Oh— oh yes, of course!" My Pa almost trips over his own feet as he makes a half spin and shoves my dad back over the threshold.

Lucien and I follow, and I watch as the Draconian takes in what had been my home.

It feels small, I won't deny, and I realise that perhaps the reason all the architecture is so utterly grand in Aetheria is to allow extra space for wingspans. My wings brush the door frame as I turn to close the door behind us, the scent of buttered popcorn reaching me from the kitchen.

The television is on pause behind the couches, some horror flick no doubt as I see a blonde girl is paused walking down a dark corridor. I also have no doubt that she's probably going to end up dead, or in need of therapy.

I suddenly notice Lucien staring at it as well, his brow lined with confusion.

"You alright?" I ask, serious at once. He frowns.

"That painting— it's confusing—" he whispers to me, and I have to stifle a laugh behind my fingers, realising that it's not only a new continent I've brought him to but a new century as well.

"It's not a painting— It's a television. I'll explain later. I suppose this is the first time you've been back to the mortal world in a long time—" I realise how odd this must all seem for him, considering my grandparents had struggled to adapt to iPhones and iPads, and they weren't nearly as old as he is.

"Is he alright?" Pa asks and I push my lips together to try to keep my expression serious despite my undeniable urge to burst out laughing.

"He's fine, he's just never seen a television before—" I explain.

At this, my parents, the screenwriters, look suddenly horrified.

"I can't believe you're here—" My dad exhales, changing the subject and running his fingers back through his salt and pepper hair, eyes creasing in the corners as he drinks in the sight of me.

"I know, I'm sorry I just dropped in like this," I apologise, and my Pa shakes his head.

"It's not that, sweetheart. We thought you were dead— well, I suppose technically—" His cheeks are still wet with tears, and I nod.

"I get it. It's a big adjustment, for me more than anyone," I explain and the two of them nod in tandem, the conversation stilted by the weight of all that's still left to be said.

"So, why are you here? Can I get you anything to drink?" My dad asks, his eyes filled with concern. He can tell that I'm not here for a social call, and it hurts me to think it's been so long since I've been able to sit down and just talk with the two of them.

"No, no drinks thank you—I came to ask you a favour actually," I admit, hoping they're aware that seeing them again has meant more than they can know, and that I am not only here due to a sense of duty.

"What do you need, honey?" My Pa asks, all business as he crosses his arms across his chest. Lucien watches the dynamic between the three of us as he shifts on the balls of his feet, and I wonder what he thinks of my family.

283

"I'd like to ask you to leave the ranch tomorrow night, maybe for a few days, so I can hold a meeting here. It's a discretion thing, and it could be dangerous, so I don't want you two getting mixed up in it," I explain, chewing the inside of my lip. After the last few days, the flesh there is in ribbons.

I know it isn't exactly fair, showing up here and demanding they leave, but I couldn't think of another place I was familiar with that would give us adequate discretion from both the Aetherial Kindred and human public.

"You want to bring others like you— here?" Matthew asks, eyes wide and mouth slightly slack as he rubs his index finger over the stubble lining his jaw.

"Is that all?" Michael asks, and I blink slowly, nodding as I realise, they were expecting something far more demanding.

"Yes, that's all— I can bring you some things to sell from Aetheria if you need the money for a trip?" I suggest but they both shake their heads. Lucien continues to listen but starts to drift around the room with almost silent steps, examining everything closely with an alien eye.

"Not necessary, we will leave tomorrow morning. I've been wanting to do an overnight in Nashville for a while. Me and your Pa— well, it's been lonely here without you, honey," my dad explains and I feel my heart give a dull aching throb.

"I'm sorry— I—" I realise I have no good excuse, no good reason for causing them such heartache, and my mouth becomes dry like I've swallowed chalk.

"It's alright, Kairi. We understand— we just miss you, you're our daughter," my Pa says with a small smile, though I can tell that tears are threatening to fall again.

I reach forward, pulling both men into me for a hug and inhaling the scents of them. They each kiss me on the head, their eyes wide and awed as they examine me up close, their focus darting to the Fae points of my ears. They don't comment, but I know that I must seem like something out of a dream.

I know this because it is exactly how I felt seeing Aro for the first time. Something about becoming Kindred, it changes you— makes you pristine and untouchable by time.

"Uh—where's Lucien?" My dad asks, breaking the tense emotional silence that falls between the three of us.

I look around, frowning. Then, I hear his heavy tread weighing on the squeaky stair four from the top of the landing and find myself amused.

"Looks like he's gone for a wander, is my room still—" I begin to ask, but my Pa cuts me off.

"We haven't moved a thing,"

"I better go make sure he doesn't hurt himself. God knows what he'll do if he finds my hair straighteners—" I muse, and my dad laughs.

"You're telling me his hair looks like that— without product?" he exclaims.

I smirk.

"Infuriating isn't it?" I muse, cocking my head and feeling ringlets falling warm over my silk-clad shoulder.

"Says Little Miss Poreless over there!" My dad rolls his eyes as the words elicit a familiar cacophony of laughter and he pinches my cheek between his thumb and finger. Our joy is a sound I have missed, and though I can't wipe the smile off my face, my heart aches with the fact that I no longer get to hear it every day.

I make my way to the stairs, looking back over my shoulder as I ascend them painlessly. I find both of the men who had raised me looking up, their faces filled with more love than I can even describe and far more than I deserve after what I've put them through.

"I'll be right back," I promise, darting up the last half of the staircase and turning right on autopilot.

The door to my bedroom is cracked, and I push it forward, relishing the familiar squeal of the hinges.

"You know it's rude to snoop," I lean against the doorframe, finding his blond head of hair looking out of the window and over the sprawl of the twilight-drenched ranch.

He doesn't startle, no doubt having heard my less-than-stealthy approach, pivoting back to face me in a smooth motion.

The leathery snicker of his wings hits my ears as he takes a few paces toward me, glancing around at the room which now feels far too small.

"This was your room?" he asks with a sweet smile and I nod, moving to sit on the edge of the bed.

"Yep, this is it." I run my fingers over the familiar cotton of the comforter, feeling odd without Catticus puddled upon it at the end of the bed.

"It's— nice," he looks at me as I cross my legs beneath the silk of my skirt, suddenly nervous.

"It's not much, but I didn't need much. Just my books—" I gesture to the piles of paperbacks stacked haphazardly against the wall. He is overcome with a look of sudden curiosity, turning and crouching so he can examine the spines making up each stack.

"I haven't even heard of a lot of these—" he exclaims, sounding excited.

I smile, thinking back to the Wednesday afternoons I had spent browsing for new stories with my Pa.

"You can take whatever you want," I offer, and he looks at me with wide eyes.

"Really?" he looks suddenly like a small child, causing me to smile and laugh to myself as I realise that we share the same delight at the thought of new books.

"Of course."

He grins, teeth pearly as he goes back to examining the assortment of well-loved titles.

Rising from the bed, I take a few steps over to my desk, finding objects which had once been so familiar filmed in a light coat of dust. The vase where I had once stood the amethyst roses Aro gifted me stands empty now, only aether remaining scattered in a small dune across the bottom.

Something stirs in my subconscious, my eyes narrowing at the sight of the empty vase, but Lucien clears his throat, causing the thought to dissipate as my head snaps around to him.

"This is you?" he inquires, pointing at the photos pinned to my corkboard. I smile, feeling self-conscious as he peruses photos of me at graduation, skating competitions, and at my parents' wedding with eager eyes.

"Yup. That's me." I shrug off his fascination, trying to remain detached from the fact my two worlds have so suddenly once again collided. It's making me realise how entirely different Lucien is from Lord Black.

I wish then, just for a moment, it had been him I'd met. That it was Lucien who was so desperate to be King— It could have been the fairytale I thought I had found with Aro.

But that isn't reality, and so I turn from his adoring gaze as he drinks in the fragments of my past, perching on the window seat where I had spent so many nights lost in the words and imaginations of others.

Now my life is more exciting than any novel I've ever read, and yet I'm also more hopeless than I've ever been.

I should be delighted at Lucien's utter and complete commitment to learning everything he can about me, and yet I just feel cruel. Like I'm leading him towards an even bigger disappointment than seeing me die in the Soleus rain.

I know I have to try, to do what he says and at least attempt to bring together the Kindred races, but something within me also can't believe it's possible.

The Equinians and Fae have hated one another for centuries, and the Draconians don't have much love for anyone either. I want to believe that Lucien's dream of a united Aetheria rising against Lord Black could be real, but I'm too afraid of watching it all fall apart to give in to blind faith as I would have once upon a time.

Instead, I know what awaits me, eventually, as hard as I try to deny it and ignore what I know is coming.

Lord Black will come for me, and with his newfound power, he will take me and force me to crown him King.

Would I do it, knowing what I know now about his ability to amass more power than anyone had ever imagined?

Would I do it to save lives? To get close enough to him to kill him?

Would I give up Lucien for the lives of my people, for the peace of the Aetheria I love so dearly?

The thought is abhorrent, but then again, perhaps sacrifice isn't supposed to be easy. That wasn't why Hera had chosen me, was it? She hadn't chosen me to be happy, she'd chosen me to be strong.

If it was easy, I remind myself, it wouldn't be sacrifice.

I feel Lucien put his arms around my waist and rest his chin on my shoulder, the wintergreen scent of his skin curling around me in a comforting embrace. My heart flutters, though whether it is because of his proximity or because I'm finally coming to admit the truth that has been scaring me so much I can't tell.

That truth is simple.

I have a responsibility to Aetheria, and that is why I've been given a second chance at life, not to be with Lucien.

I know that if the alliance doesn't happen the line stops with me. It's my responsibility to fix this.

Then something even more disturbing occurs to me as I look out over the beauty of the ranch.

God forbid, what if Aro isn't satisfied with Aetheria bowing before him? What if he decides to come after the mortal world as well?

I realise then that Hera had chosen me for my strength, but it wasn't a strength she intended to use to fight. I'm supposed to be there to stop him from inside, to level him out and stop him from becoming as destructive as I know he can be as Pandora and Harmonia did before me.

I have a job to do, and as much as I wish I could simply be happy, that's not the way the world works.

It isn't fair, but it never claimed to be.

That's the difference between fiction and real life.

"What are you thinking about?" he asks me, the cool hardness of his chest muscles deliciously familiar against my spine.

Tears prickle at my eyes, and I am glad he can't see me as the truth of what the future will bring dawns on me fully for the first time.

"Nothing in particular," I reply, wrapping myself tighter in his arms.

20

COLD COMFORT FARM

LUCIEN

I CAN TELL KAIRI is reluctant to leave her family, and yet she swallows her pain with grace, clutching my hand tightly and conducting us from the porch of Hickory Oaks ranch and directly to Nirvana. I notice the glint of unshed tears in her eyes, but ignore them, leaving her alone with her grief.

We reappear beside the infinity pool of Morpheus' villa, and I worry momentarily about arriving unannounced. Then, his melodic voice can be heard, mixing with others that are familiar, from somewhere beyond the central living area. Kairi sniffs back tears, putting on a brave smile as she swallows her emotions with practised fluidity.

She says she isn't made to be a ruler, to be a Queen, but in her, I see that strength only too clearly.

Kairi and I wander, fingers still locked together, our steps synchronised and soft upon the marble, the tips of our wings brushing past one another, hard against soft, as we follow the sound of conversation. We wind through the minimalist structure of the lower floor, eventually emerging in the new sunlight of early dusk pouring in through a glass ceiling overhead.

We appear to be in the foyer of a gargantuan greenhouse, or perhaps conservatory is more correct as there are multiple pieces of wicker furniture interspersing the neat rows of lush green growth, popping every few inches with bright fireworks of vibrant petals. The structure is sprawling, perhaps bigger than the villa itself, and the smell of floral perfumes mixing and melding of their own accord is pungent in my nostrils. The common area closest to the villa's main building is full of more people than I expect, with Ember and Neve joining Hypnos and of course Morpheus among the muggy air. Treading forward on agile soles, the sound of trickling water comes from somewhere indiscernible, and as we move past the section of the greenhouse thick with the scent of wildflowers, we transition into a muggier air thick with the scent of palm-captured dew. Sweat quickly beads on the back of my neck, and I loosen my collar with an errant index finger, feeling not unlike the air itself is trying to throttle me.

Rounding a bed of rich-coloured soil, I find Neve sat in the firm hold of a wicker armchair with Ember perched on the arm. The long legs of the High Lady Fae of Summer glisten richly in the new dawn light, and I find her face warm with a harsh intensity rather than her usual joy. I follow her gaze, finding her watching Hypnos making a very particular cutting from a potted plant she's examining with a sharp eye and even sharper shears.

Kairi and I step through an enormous ecru archway, that is one of the core weight-bearing structures for the globules of domed glass overhead, vines twining around trellises perched on either side.

As our wings rustle the leaves against both feather and leather, the apparently riveting conversation between the Fae stills.

The group turns collectively, those sitting craning their necks, to watch us nearing from beyond the vast and meticulously kept rows of soil and planters. I swallow, finding a large unnaturally occurring waterfall to be the backdrop of the seating area, my nerves balling in my stomach. Kairi lets my hand drop casually from hers before our connection can be observed up close.

"You have news I hope, Lord DeLaurent. Something to aid Lord Arlet?" It is unsurprisingly Neve who speaks first, she has never been one to wait to make her intentions and opinions known. She is direct, much like the icy chill which runs through both our veins. I'd never liked her too much before she'd tried to kill Kairi, but now my outlook on any kind of amicable relationship is even bleaker.

"That's not why we are here," Kairi answers in my place, and I watch as Neve's dark eyebrows jump up to her pale forehead in surprise, eyes darting to Kairi's genteel features with predatory accuracy.

"Surely you realise this is no time for a social call, Lady Freemont?" Morpheus interjects. Getting closer, I realise he's focusing most of his attention on the pestle and mortar in front of him, crushing the non-identifiable ingredients inside with rhythmic vigour.

"Of course not, this is about something else. How is Lord Arlet?" I ask, feeling weird using Quinn's official title. It feels far too formal for a Fae who runs barefoot among the wildflowers and plays hide and seek with Sprites.

"No better, and the rot is spreading, hence why we've resorted to harvesting the flowers we need for his tincture here. I didn't want to risk taking anything out of the ground directly in case it did more harm—" Morpheus explains, eyes cast downward on the work of his hands. Hypnos raises her cloudy eyes to me, the silken sheath of her uncorseted gown swirling around her like shimmering mist.

"We're lucky that we cultivate such a diverse collection here. Forget-me-nots and valerian root do not grow well in Aramis soil, if at all—" she ponders, thoughtful as a slight crescent turns her thick lips into a small sad smile.

"He's not sleeping?" I ask, treading around the rows of plant pots that separate myself and Kairi from the workbenches strewn with brightly glimmering gardening tools. I brush the low-hanging vines from a dangling philodendron aside, straightening as Neve scrutinises both myself and Kairi in turn with cold eyes. I feel sweat beading beneath my arms, and inhale deeply trying to offset the sticky claustrophobia of the humidity.

"He is, but not deeply enough to allow me to contact him for any kind of meeting of the minds. He's not dreaming, you see." Morpheus sighs deeply, his face seeming older than it has ever appeared to me before. "I thought if we could get his take on this it might help, but he's too weak to do any serious thinking on this plain, not to mention his body is failing him because of this plague. He knows more about the natural systems of Lumeria and Aramis than anyone, being connected to them in their most vivacious season. I need to see if I can speak to him in person." Morpheus explains and I nod, realising now just how much his usual euphoria does for his features. The High Lord Fae of Night looks at Kairi then, unblinking a moment, before his eyes narrow.

"Kairi, would you like to try and join me, when we do attempt to contact him?" he asks, and I see her turn red.

What is he talking about?

Join him?

"No, we have more important matters to attend to, but thank you for the offer," she continues to blush, not looking at me despite the fact I'm staring at her.

"You can dream walk?" I continue to look at her with a surprised expression and she flushes a deeper red as she reluctantly meets my gaze. Before she can open her mouth to confirm what I already know to be true though, Hypnos interrupts.

"More important than an immortal High Born Kindred dying?" The Goddess made Kindred cocks a soft and downy eyebrow, her voice softening with each syllable and falling heavy over me like a blanket. Guilt rises in my chest, but I know Kairi is right.

"Actually, yes. Why we're here, it's important, more important than any one individual—`` She begins to explain what we know about Lord Black, and I lean back against a table full of metallic orchids and trowels with mother of pearl handles as her words dim into background static.

Crossing my legs and folding my arms in front of my chest with defensive stiffness, I drift from myself, hating the look of scrutiny that is being directed at Kairi from all angles but unable to stop myself from analysing every minute motion of her face.

How had she discovered she could dream walk?

Is this something to do with her Fae ears?

Does she have other powers I don't know about?

The questions roll through my mind like harshly cresting tides, my doubt about her feelings for me, about her trust in me, becoming damp and sludge-like beneath the sodden chill of my low self-esteem.

Why hadn't she told me?

"Is this true Lord DeLaurent?" Ember demands, pulling me back to myself, her face stony as I've ever seen it.

"Pardon?" I ask, the French lilt in my accent becoming thicker as I'm caught slightly off guard.

"Is Lord Black able to absorb the powers of other Kindred by killing them with these Amethyst weapons?" Hypnos demands. Her face, if possible, is even paler than usual.

"Yes, it is true," I confirm and feel the room collectively inhale, as though there is not enough air for the size of the implication that's just been asserted.

"Well, that is unfortunate." Morpheus frowns, his pore-less brow furrowing as his viridian eyebrows meet and his chameleonic irises transition from lime to periwinkle.

"Unfortunate? That's all you have to say?" Kairi asks, and I feel my gaze harden as I step over to stand once more at her side upon the white honeycomb weave of the tiled floor.

"I have rather more pressing problems than a Sephilim madman on another continent, Lady Freemont. One of my own is flailing, as is

Nirvana. Or did you forget?" Morpheus speaks softly, but it's a weariness rather than empathy that dulls his usually exuberant volume. I watch as Kairi's face goes pale and slack with guilt, her shoulders falling as she exhales with a deep and gradual slump.

"Of course she didn't forget. But this is more important than only one species of Kindred, Morpheus. This could throw Aetheria into a tyranny the likes of which we've never seen—" I defend Kairi, but Morpheus doesn't seem to take the threat seriously. Instead, he laughs to himself, the godforsaken feather of his too-familiar earring vibrating right along with his film-like wings.

I'd quite like to tear the damn thing out of his earlobe and throw it at him if I'm honest.

"Which we've never seen? You were not made to suffer through the reign of King Midas, Lucien, and it shows. The Sephilim have always been this way, and we have always kept ourselves to ourselves and dealt with them as placidly as possible. They even protect our lands from unlawful hunting, a deal which was forged personally by me and Lord Black. The best way to survive such times is to comply and to do what's best for everyone, for the good of your people. There is no place for pride when it comes to leadership."

"So, what? We just hand him Kairi and the crown right along with it?" I demand, outraged, and he shrugs. Knocking the pestle on the edge of the pumice mortar, he squares his frame, staring me directly in the eye with a sudden sharp jerk of his head.

Before he can speak, however, Hypnos interjects in her dreamlike tone.

"If what you say is true, Lord DeLaurent, then the decision has been made for us. You'd be wise to kneel in the face of your fate, lest you perish. After all, uprisings for the sake of righteousness are at home in fiction, not in Aetheria."

I look at Kairi.

She doesn't seem as rattled by this hopeless plea as I am, and I recall the look in her eye back in my bedroom. She has lost hope, and where I thought that showing her an alliance could be formed would change her mind, it seems the Fae's unwillingness is only proving her point further.

"Look, we're having a meeting. The Equinians and Draconians will be present as well. It will take place in the mortal realm, on neutral soil, and it is simply to find out what the consensus is between all the Kindred races as to what should be done, if anything, about Lord

Black. We need to know where each of us stands, even if that is on opposite sides of the issue," Kairi explains, and Neve straightens within the confines of the high-backed wicker armchair.

"The Equinians will be there? They have agreed to this?" she asks, eyes sparkling with a cold vendetta. Ember places her long fingers around the curve of Neve's shoulder, trying to calm her, before looking to me for an answer with golden eyes.

"Kairi is going to invite them, and I will be bringing Lord Lee and Lady Dragos," I add.

Hypnos' eyebrows twitch, her eyes narrowing as her mouth puckers. It makes her fatigued features appear as though she is on the edge of slipping into a coma.

"And Lady Thomas?" she asks. My heart skips a beat where the sharpness of the sleep Goddess's intellect does not.

I haven't told Kairi about what happened with Genevieve, and I don't intend to. Not only because I have no desire to explain why Genevieve still hates Kairi, but also because it casts me in a less-than-favourable light. I wonder what it will take for Kairi to suddenly realise I'm no hero, and that she's in love with something beastly instead. I can't stand the thought of her fleeing to the safety of another's arms instead of mine.

Genevieve will cool off, and when she does, I will get down on my knees and beg her forgiveness once again. I truly am sorry, and after all, it was an honest mistake no matter what Genevieve thinks. She just can't see the woods for the trees right now, her grief all-consuming and entirely understandable, making her volatile as the dragonsfire in her blood. It's true, I stood her up, but her vitriol toward my relation-ship with Kairi in its essence is entirely unprovoked. Her prejudice against the Nephilim High Lady is not my problem, but hers.

She just needs time to realise.

Time and perspective.

I hope she finds it soon.

"No," I reply with a stiff half-turn to face Hypnos fully. "Lady Thomas is still grieving over the loss of her beloved dragon. She is in no shape to be discussing the finer points of politics," I reveal, and the silence after my words echoes around us as the wind caresses the curved panes of the roof.

Neve leans forward, crossing her arms over the heavily jewelled boning of her periwinkle corset, eyes locking mine tightly in her gaze.

"I tell you what, Draconian. You convince a representative from each race to attend this meeting and I will come along as well. After all, I'm not going to piss off Lord Black, but neither am I going to allow myself to be blinded by the likes of Aliandara, or her brutish male counterparts," Neve spits, tossing her head like a stallion.

Morpheus nods in assent, signalling for Ember to move closer to where he is working.

"Agreed. If you can get the others to attend this little hootenanny you're concocting, then count me in as well."

"And me," Ember rises to her feet, nodding with a solemn determination that turns steely on her edgy features. The flimsy golden gossamer of her waterfall-esque skirt shimmers as I cast my eyes downward, nodding with gratitude for at least some cooperation, however conditional.

Then, Ember strides over to the workbench where Morpheus has been grinding, allowing her palms to hover over the pestle.

"Sun drying—" she explains to Kairi who is staring at her without apology.

"You're making it into a tea?" she enquires, and Hypnos nods as Ember's hands emit a faint golden glow.

"Nothing like a sweet valerian brew to send you right off to dreamland, Lady Freemont. Now, don't you have other business to attend to today? Other Kindred to accost?" She pushes us to leave, and I turn on my heel.

"Thank you for your time. We will come to collect you when it is time for the leaders to meet," Kairi's voice pours out from behind me before she pivots, wings rustling, and follows me out of the greenhouse.

She takes my hand in hers as we walk through to the main room, a symbol of our supposed unity, our steps falling in time.

However, as we conduct out of Aramis, I can't help but glimpse the hopelessness in her stare even still.

I also can't help but notice that it matches the Fae's looks of surrender to a future of pain and death with terrifying and uncanny intensity.

KAIRI

We reappear within the hall of Lucien's Drakos Vale home, fingers still entwined, my heart heavy in my chest.

"Kairi— do you agree with Morpheus?" Lucien asks, tentative.

I shrug, unsure of why we're going to all this trouble just to prove him wrong and me right. I know what's going to happen at this meeting, and Morpheus' reaction to the proposal has only strengthened my lack of faith in any kind of unity ever being achieved.

Perhaps when Hera had told me she wanted all the Sephilim eliminated, she had not meant war. Maybe she'd meant letting them destroy themselves, or for me to destroy them from the inside.

It just doesn't seem like a feasible scenario for the likes of the Fae and some of the Equinians to rise against a force that will become more powerful with each enemy that falls. Isn't war only going to speed up their rise to ultimate control over Aetheria?

My indecision over my two options has never been so stark, with half of me resigned to being blessed as a lamb for the slaughter and the other half wanting to fight against Aro. The truth is, I'm just too afraid of what will happen if I agree to go to war.

I'm not a warrior, I'm an English Literature student for Hera's sake, and what's more, I'm completely unqualified to have this many people's lives in my young hands.

Why the hell had Hera chosen me for this? Why would she put the fate of her Kindred, and Aetheria no less, in the hands of a young woman who barely understands how to take care of herself, let alone an entire Kingdom of people.

I look at Lucien as he waits for me to answer his question, but the truth is in the wideness of his pupils as he drinks in my face.

He cannot see my incompetence, my unworthiness for this role, because he is too much in love with me.

"I already told you, I think this is a fool's errand," I reply, unapologetic and frustrated by his lack of empathy. It's as if he thinks my fears are silly, that my terror at being responsible for the lives of thousands of people is unfounded.

He's a dreamer, and I had been too.

Once.

"So, you won't go and convince Lady Montgomery?" he asks, and I shake my head.

"No, I'll go. I said I would. I take my responsibilities extremely seriously, hence why I'm having so much trouble accepting the solution to mass death is more mass death—" I pull back from him and he takes a half step forward, eyes fearful for a moment like I may disappear and never come back.

"You do think it's hopeless, don't you?" he reiterates. I give him a fierce glare.

"I do. Hera chose me for a reason, Lucien. And the more I think about it the more it seems like she intended me to be a sacrifice to appease Lord Black and the rest of the Sephilim to stop this war. She chose me because I'd sacrificed myself before, as both Storm and Briar. I mean, sacrificing myself was how I ended up a High Lady in this life in the first place, remember? Besides, I can't imagine she wanted a war that would no doubt massacre a lot of innocents." He looks horrified at my resignation, but I don't let it bother me, turning from him on the ball of my foot, comforted by the familiar hardy squeal of the floorboard beneath.

"I'll go and talk to Aliandara. You should head to Gemina Two and see what Anastasia has to say—" I cut him off before he can argue back, knowing if I turn and look him in the eyes his care for me will make me weak.

"Kairi, you can't honestly believe—" Lucien stutters, but I shake my head.

"I do. I honestly believe everything I just said. I believed in fairy tales once Lucien, and it got me killed. That same belief will cost a much higher price this time around, and you know it. I can't live with that on my conscience for a day, much less forever. The stakes, they're higher than ever, and I don't even know how to play the game." My words echo out into silence and all I hear as I stare aimlessly through the archway that leads to the kitchen is his heavy breathing.

"You'll see, once we're all together Kairi, you'll realise that we have a chance. I promise," Lucien vows, my heart wilting at his unstoppable determination.

"I hope you're right," I reply, more to get him to leave than out of any actual conviction. I fiddle with my fingers, heart racing at the mere thought of the decision that lies ahead.

I know what I want, but what is right is something entirely different, just like how I feel about Lucien.

"We'll meet back here?" he asks. I nod, sighing and wishing I could simply take the afternoon to sit and read one of my old paperbacks.

"Bring Anastasia and Gage if you can, then I'll work on conducting everyone out to Hickory Oaks."

I don't turn back to him, or give him time to pick up the conversation, tasting iron and citrus on my tongue and willing Lucien's world to dissolve like a dream as I head back to the harsh light of Eclipsia.

I conduct onto the veranda of Aliandara's villa, expecting to find her breakfasting with Evangeline under the new sun of another scorching day. Instead, I find the space abandoned, the only evidence of recent habitation being a randomly discarded slipper and a puddle of what looks to be either champagne or urine. For my sake, I hope it's the former.

I tread through dappled sunlight spilt upon the ground, careful to avoid the strewn party debris as I hitch my lilac skirt at the waist and head inside, feet soft and purposeful. The heat lies heavy on the back of my neck as I become used to the stagnant air after the chill of Drakos Vale, glad of the shade as I head into a large open-plan sitting room.

Drapes of ruby velvet are strung artfully from columns surrounding enormous glassless arches that look out over the oasis, potted plants dotted around the base of the walls as side tables house ornate vases and pieces of glasswork that look more fluid than solid.

I find Evangeline sitting, legs crossed beneath a fresh petticoat as her sandalled feet protrude into the shadow of the room. Her eyes are closed, breathing shallow as her glistening tattoos peak from beneath the loose-fitting bodice of her flowing gown.

"Evangeline," I say her name with the softness of a desert breeze, and her eyes open, a small but sad smile overcoming her round face.

"Kairi, you made it back I see," she says with a kind of dreamlike lilt to her voice. It's knowing, acknowledging the truth I had learned, without daring to mention it.

"I need to see Aliandara," I inform her, clenching my fingers against my palms, which are damp from the heat and growing awkwardness between myself and the High Lady. She watches me with both gentle and curious eyes, and I clarify.

"What you revealed to me last night will never pass my lips, Evangeline, I swear to you. This is about something else," I assure her, and she gets to her feet, letting her wings fidget on her spine as they unruffle from where they've been pressed into the couch.

As I follow her through the labyrinth of the villa's endless open-plan corridors, vast luxurious rooms, and sought-after shadows, I realise she's taking me to a wing of the house I've never been to before.

She doesn't look back over her shoulder, as though making eye contact with me would be painful for her, which I understand.

Aliandara makes a fool of her every time she falls into Asher's Aresian arms, and I can tell the wound it leaves upon the High Lady is deeper than she'd ever admit.

After a few moments, she pauses in the middle of an unextra-ordinary corridor, pushing a tapestry depicting some kind of clash between Aliandara and an unknown Equinian male aside and holding it back so I might duck underneath.

What is it with Kindred and hiding things behind tapestries? I think, remembering the Academy of Arcane Arts and its inconspic-uous entrance. I'm sure I'll be taking my time and examining these woven murals far more closely in the future.

I wonder then if the Draconians and Equinians would find it amus-ing that they both conceal secrets using similar decor.

Probably not.

I emerge on the other side of the wall and descend a bare and uneven staircase, my eyes adjusting quickly to the darkness as the stagnant air fills my nostrils. Descending deep beneath the sands of the city, I see archaic symbols scrawled in an angry hand on the bare stone of the walls. I want to stop and examine them closer but I'm unable to as my guide continues without pause.

Evangeline leads me down the corridor at a quick pace, and I stay on her heels, the only sounds the slight scuffling of our shoes and the swishing of our multi-layered skirts. Both our wings are stiff against our spines and soundless due to the tight confinement of the passage, and I'm grateful when, finally, we change direction.

Taking a sudden left turn, Evangeline leads me into a room with high vaulted ceilings and a familiar smell. The scent envelops and comforts me with unmistakable immediacy.

Books.

I've no sooner finished the thought than am blinking rapidly, taking in the quaint library.

"Aliandara?" I hear Evangeline call, but my eyes are cast to the ceiling, where murals of the God Ares and the Goddess Artemis have been painstakingly rendered upon the curved surfaces in bright colours and astounding detail.

My attention is pulled from the battle of brushstrokes waging overhead, as I hear movement coming from deep within the stacks of shelving that are lined militantly in two perpendicular rows opposing the doorway.

After a few moments, Aliandara appears from among the masses of leather binding and browning pages, clutching an old tome in her elegant fingers.

"Evangeline, what are you doing—" she asks, suddenly noticing that her lover isn't alone. "You brought her down here?" she reddens slightly, but Evangeline only straightens, a defiant glimmer, like a new star being born, shuddering into being within her eyes.

"Yes, she needed to see you and said it was important," Evangeline shrugs, turning from Aliandara before the woman can get any closer and moving toward one of the sturdy ironwood tables. The raw surface holds three thick candles with flickering wicks that drip candlelight and wax down onto the wood in puddles. She turns, slumping onto a chair carved from the same wood but with more elegant construction, staring at me with all the defiance I would expect from a scorned Kindred of Artemis.

So why isn't she putting a stop to Aliandara's fling with Asher? It clearly upsets her, and I imagine that Aliandara must at least suspect she knows.

The dynamic is odd, and I take a beat to take a deep inhale and shrug off the tension surrounding me before I begin to speak.

"My Kensari, Catticus, has delivered troubling news about Lord Black. Apparently from what my companion has observed he has been able to fashion weapons that are capable of absorbing his victim's powers and transferring them to him." I wait for Aliandara's eyebrows to rise, for her to feign some kind of surprise, but she merely nods.

"I have heard the same thing from The Equinian Chieftain, Asher," she says, and I watch Evangeline's cheeks flush red. I watch closely as she brushes a curl behind her ear and straightens further in her chair, defiant in every motion.

"That's why you're here?" Evangeline demands in a clipped tone. Aliandara nods, placing the book she's holding on the shelf beside her. Evangeline rises in a blur, and I watch her as she takes the book and begins flicking through it herself.

"What is this place?" I inquire, glancing around and trying to distract the two angry Equinians before me.

"This is the War Library. The most comprehensive collection of military knowledge anywhere in the lower plains. It's one of the reasons we fought so hard to maintain control of Sapphire City in the early days. The Aresian Equinians are too brash to be trusted with such a rich fountain of tactical knowledge," she explains, and I find myself oddly intrigued and disgusted all at once.

All the ways you might kill, that you might end a life, that you might steal a kingdom, or torture an immortal, lie here. Innocuous in ink.

It is the reader that makes these books deadly, and the thought gives me a shudder as I see my preferred medium of entertainment in a vicious light for the first time.

"Knowledge is power," I say in a small voice. Aliandara's eyebrow quirks and I watch Evangeline out of the corner of my eye. As she flicks through the pages of the book, her lips tighten into a bloodless frown.

"So, you came here to tell me what you discovered?" Aliandara steers the conversation forward, taking several steps before leaning against the table opposite the one where Evangeline continues to read. Her body lilts sideways against the hard edge of the crude craftsmanship, but like a willow branch, the way she bends seems to cause her little to no discomfort.

A bruise flickers into view upon the tattooed skin of her neck as she grows closer to the collection of candles on the table and I flinch slightly as I realise that she isn't even considerate enough to cover it. She catches my eyes, glued to the mark, which is no doubt a souvenir from Asher, pulling the high collar of her elaborately wrapped grey gown higher so it reaches the downy hair at the nape of her skull. Her hair is twisted into snakelike braids, wrapped in a crown-like bun on the top of her skull, and I find myself staring as the flamelight turns each rope of hair an odd purplish hue.

"Lady Freemont?" Aliandara's tone is clipped and sharp, like nails that have been filed into claws.

"No, I came to invite you to a summit being held by Lord DeLaurent and myself. Representatives of each Kindred race will be there, and the Equinians of both Artemis and Ares if you so choose to attend. Lucien and I want to meet to discuss what we feel should be done about Lord Black." I reply with more boldness than I intend, my eyes narrowing and my back straightening as both women look at me now with equal intensity.

"I'm not worried about Lord Black, Kairi," Aliandara gives a small laugh, as though he is nothing more lethal than a kitten with a butter knife.

"Is that why you're looking at the blueprints of Sapphire City and its defences, Aliandara? Because you're not worried?" Evangeline cuts her off with a snort and I feel my brows rise on my forehead.

"That's why I'm not worried, Evangeline. Our city walls are solid. There isn't an army alive that could cause our defences to fall now." Aliandara puffs out her tattooed breasts with arrogance, and I feel my stomach churn.

"I suppose it'll just be the Fae and Draconians then—" I sigh and watch as Aliandara's eyes narrow, her body righting itself to be perfectly erect.

"The Fae?" she asks, and I have to steel myself against smiling at her predictability.

"Well yes, I said all the Kindred races. That includes the Fae. They've already agreed to attend, both Morpheus and both High Ladies of The Fae of Light—" I add and Aliandara crosses her arms.

"Morpheus is attending personally?"

"Of course. He thinks this is important, just as Lucien and I do. If for no other reason than finding out where everyone stands. Who they intend to ally with and what our options are with regards to fighting back," I add the last part hoping to intrigue her intense bloodlust.

She cocks her head, braids shimmering like dark serpents, but instead of seeming convinced, she smirks.

"You're going to fight the Sephilim? You and whose army?!"

"No, I didn't say that—" I retrace my steps, terror rising in me at the mere mention of leading anyone to war. "We just want to have a discussion, that's all."

Silence falls between us, and I glance between the two women, heart racing faster than it should be.

"I'll go and get Asher," Aliandara says with a sigh, eyes flaming with dissent as she complies with me at last.

"You're in?" I ask, needing to hear the words.

"We're in."

21

CATCH-22

KAIRI

THE REST OF THE day passes in a blur of conduction, vastly contrasting scenery, and the unsurprising grumbles of various High Born Lords and Ladies complaining about each other.

When all is said and done, I arrive from my final pick-up with Phineas and a rather green-looking Quinn, who had insisted on being present despite Neve, Ember, and my protestations that the self-professed King of Spring was simply not well enough to be dealing with the kind of stress this meeting would no doubt create.

Lucien is standing, waiting for my arrival in a smart navy blue morning coat and matching slacks, his hair braided back off his face so it catches the dying earthen sunlight that has turned the entire sprawl of Hickory Oaks ranch ablaze in gold.

I find myself supporting most of Quinn's weight as soon as my feet touch down on the wooden floorboards of my once isolated reading gazebo, my body sagging. Lucien rushes forward, and between them, he and Phineas help Quinn toward the hanging seat where Anastasia is perched with elegantly crossed legs.

Upon seeing the state of the Fae High Lord, she rises immediately with her usual ethereal grace, the crystal-studded span of her leathery wings turning momentarily purple as they are silhouetted against the setting sun at her spine.

As Quinn is aided into the dangling furniture and his gloriously vibrant wings are obscured by the cushions, Aliandara speaks up.

"What on earth is wrong with him?" she demands, her tone bitter as freshly cut lemon. Evangeline, who stands beside her, cocks her head and looks into the face of the suffering Fae, empathy rolling over her features in a heavy and unexpected wave.

Asher looks equally suspicious as he glances back over one shoulder from where he has been standing at the gazebo railing, staring out over the swaying heather and free running horses on the horizon. His hand presses tightly to the enormous, curved blade holstered at his hip as he turns back to observe the scene fully, the veins in his muscles visibly rising closer to the surface of his heavily tattooed biceps. His burly stature, however, becomes graceful as he treads with whisper softness over the floorboards, giving Neve an intense questioning and rather brave glance while brushing a dark braid back behind his ear.

"What are you looking at, brute?" Neve hisses, and I feel the chill of her ice magic nip at my shoulders as her misty breath carries the threat to her opponent through the warm dusk.

"Nothing much, apparently," Asher bites out, his teeth smashing together as his fingers worry the hilt of his weapon faster and with more agitation.

"Enough!" A voice, though not one I expect, breaks the tension with its hard and unforgiving edge. My eyes dart to High Lord Gage Lee, and though his gaze meets mine and softens for but a moment, I can tell the collective tension and emotions of the gathered Lords and Ladies is affecting him most of all.

I wonder what it must be like for him, as Lucien finishes getting Quinn settled and Phineas turns a hostile shoulder to the Equinians, feeling a hatred several centuries old running riot inside your skull.

I do not envy the Draconian.

Quinn's eyelids flutter as his pale and sweat-slick face contorts with determination, his concentration on the meeting becoming more resolute.

"Well then, let's get on with it. I've got more pressing matters than some ridiculous meet and greet."

Neve turns to me, and Lucien strides across the space which is now encircled by the bodies of all the High Born kindred we could muster, taking his place firmly at my side.

"It's not a meet and greet, I wouldn't have bothered gathering you if I didn't think it was important," I say, though I feel like a liar. If it had been my choice, I would have simply acknowledged the truth that I already know. There is no unity to be found here.

"So?" Aliandara pushes me with a forceful crossing of her arms to continue, her regal-looking navy gown boasting a pointed high collar that seems dull in comparison to her tone.

"So, I have brought you all here to discuss the small matter of Lord Aro Black. He has, it seems, from the information provided not only by my sources but by some of yours as well, come to pose a startling new level of threat against Aetheria." I feel like someone out of an Austen novel as I try to enunciate as clearly as I can, keeping my spine straight and trying my best to appear confident even though I feel anything but.

"Lord Aro Black is the least of my concerns, Kairi. As you can see by Quinn's condition—" Phineas jumps on me as soon as I finish, the stark carmine of his hair making his sharp brown eyes seem far angrier than I'd imagined they were capable of. The wind rustles around me, a warning by his elemental affinity to be careful about wasting another second of his time.

As I part my lips to retort, however, Quinn straightens in his chair. I could almost swear some of his usual flush has returned.

"Phineas, let the girl speak." The Fae High Lord sounds stronger too, and I give him a faint smile of thanks as I look next to Anastasia.

"I know you wouldn't have come here unless you thought there was a threat looming on the horizon. Have you had any visions?" I ask her and she blinks slowly. The other Kindred look uncomfortable as her dreamy gaze becomes distant for a moment before returning to focus on me.

"I have seen much trouble ahead. Though I cannot say whether it is Lord Black, or something entirely more troubling—" she speaks, and Morpheus perks up then, the luscious indigo velvet of his suit becoming momentarily pinkish beneath the sunset as he steps in and out of shadow.

"Could it have anything to do with the fact Nirvana is dying?" he asks, feather earring vibrating with his urgency for new information.

"Nirvana is dying?" Aliandara says it in a flat tone, but I can see her eyes sparkle ever so slightly with the pain of her adversary exposed.

"What is it to you, Lady Montgomery?" Ember steps in, her face sultry and sullen all at once as her sharp bone structure throws shadows in all the right places, allowing her to intimidate as she rises to her full height.

"I simply thought, seeing as how—" Aliandara begins, but Neve interrupts.

"You simply thought? How stupid do you think we are, murderess? You are looking for weaknesses. It's all you know how to do!" Neve balls her fists, the spikes of crystal lining her gown's cape growing.

It turns out they aren't crystals at all, but icicles that sharpen by the minute under her furious cold magic.

I look to Lucien, wanting to say I told you so, but he's too busy readying himself to step into the ring.

"Enough, both of you! That is not why we are here, and you know it!" he hisses, his wings flaring with menace. The sharp outline of his talons becomes stark as it falls over the golden wood underfoot, drenching the centre of the circle in dark threat.

"Then why are we here, Lord DeLaurent? Because I haven't heard a single proposal worth listening to as of yet—" Gage speaks now, his dissent against Lucien jarring me more than the aggressive under-current from the Fae-Equinian conflict. As I stand there, it seems like each individual is doing everything in their power to destroy any kind of attempt at unity before it has even been suggested.

"We are here because we must unite now and fight the Sephilim or face extinction!" Lucien snaps, his whole body radiating fresh frost and causing goosebumps to rise on my arms.

Aliandara cocks an eyebrow, as does Morpheus at the same moment. Then, they both share perhaps the only look of joint knowing I have ever seen pass between them.

"You're going to get us all killed, Lord DeLaurent," Asher speaks plainly, and guilty relief floods my gut.

"That is an enormous assumption," Lucien retorts, and then Morpheus looks at him.

"You knew this was my feeling too, Lord DeLaurent. Why bring us here if you know you're proposing something which we all firmly oppose?" he queries Lucien, laying a hand on Phineas' shoulder.

"Because you're all wrong. You're just too proud to see it." Lucien answers, and both Aliandara and Morpheus snort at the same time.

"Pride? This is about the opposite of pride, Lord DeLaurent. This is a matter of the greatest good." Morpheus shakes his head, looking at Lucien as a little boy, and not a High Lord of equal rank.

"Morpheus is right— how those words taste so bitter on my tongue—" Aliandara sighs, before continuing, "But he is right. If we had intended to fight the Sephilim, we would have done so long ago. This new development with Aro's ability to absorb the powers of his victims— I'm sorry but it seems as if that only makes our continued alliance with him more certain."

"It is true, the cost to Nirvana on an ecological level, let alone the matter of civilian deaths, doesn't bear thinking about. My duty here is

307

to protect Nirvana and all it holds, that is my highest calling." Phineas adds, and I think then of the Sprites, of the innocent souls housed and waiting for their parents so they can move on. The thought of Sephilim soldiers even getting close to them makes me feel physically sick.

"You're also forgetting that in going to war with a man who is collecting power by murdering his enemies, you are quickening the process by which he will amass said power," Asher speaks, his voice gruff and strained with the truth of his words.

"And what if he comes for you? What then?" Lucien asks, seeming appalled by what I already knew was coming.

"Sapphire City has the best defensive capabilities of anywhere in Aetheria. My people will be secure so long as we stay there. No Sephilim or Equinian has breached the walls while I've been alive, and I don't intend on giving up that accolade anytime soon," Aliandara says coldly, as though the other kindred of Aetheria mean less to her than dirt.

"And you, Morpheus? You have no such defensive capabilities." I add now, not wanting Lucien to be the only one who seems to believe his plan is feasible. Lucien turns back to me with a grateful glance, and I step forward, taking his hand in mine.

"I have made deals with Lord Aro Black before, and I am sure now I will do so again. After all, he needs my workforce to keep him in fresh produce, and he needs my healers to keep him in potions, salves, and tinctures. He could kill my people, but that knowledge would die with us, whether he stole our blessed power or not—" Morpheus informs us, and my relief swells again. Lucien's grip tightens on mine.

"Lord Lee?" He turns next to the man who may be his final ally, his face stony and chill in all its angular beauty.

"What does Lady Thomas have to say about all this, Lucien? I notice she is conveniently absent from this discussion." Lucien visibly flinches at the mention of her name, and I wonder what exactly is going on between the two of them. I thought they'd made up.

"Lady Thomas is far too grieved to be thinking clearly right now. But I suspect she would agree with me, given all things as of late," Lucien retorts. Gage's eyes narrow.

"Well, I suspect that she wouldn't want you talking for her. I'm surprised at you, Lucien. You know this is the kind of decision she would want to be involved in. After all, it was you and not her who called off starting a war just like the one you're proposing not three months ago."

He's sly, and I wonder what's changed to make Lucien suddenly change his tune so dramatically.

It hadn't occurred to me before now.

"You know the answer," Lucien growls and Gage narrows his eyes once again.

"I do."

"Please, Lord Lee, do enlighten us?" Aliandara demands, folding her arms.

"He wants us to go to war because he knows he can't protect her. Not alone. I suspect that's the reason she's on board with all this as well. I knew you were selfish, Lucien. But by the Goddess Nemesis— you can't really expect us to sentence our people to death so you can keep your girlfriend from marrying another man?" he smirks, the thought as absurd to him as it suddenly is to me.

Is that what this is?

Is he suggesting this kamikaze scheme for me?

That's not what I agreed to, and it's not what I want either. It makes me look weak like I'd rather risk the lives of millions of others than sacrifice my own skin.

What must these people think of me now? What must Lucien think of me, to think I'd ever go through with something like that?

They were right, all of them. It was about pride. It was about possession.

It was about Lucien wanting me.

As the air between the group begins to crackle with unsaid and fraught emotion, I sense a mixture of heated blood rushing to the skin as muscles tense, the chill of furious frost, and the wind picking up to carry an aggressively sultry and unforgiving summer heat. My fingers tingle with the electric currents stirring around us, the hairs on the back of my neck standing to attention as my heart pounds too slow like it's made of lead.

Lucien steps forward, dropping my hand, and I feel suddenly terribly ashamed of him, and of myself for exposing his complete selfishness in even proposing this conflict as a sensible resolution.

I love him, and I always will.

But is that worth letting hundreds of other immortals die in brutal and bloodthirsty ways?

He hadn't wanted a war until he realised the truth, the truth that Lord Black will have me, no matter who stands in his way.

I shrivel inside, any determination to resist wilting, my soul turning cold at the realisation that I am the lamb, Aro is the Lion, and even the dragons can't save me now.

LUCIEN

Rage thunders through my veins as a sub-zero tempest, causing me to ball my fists. I can see Kairi through the cold mist of my fury, the way her guilt rises so quickly to the surface, in light of the accusation pitted against me.

Is it true? Am I doing this, suggesting this blood bath, merely to keep her safe?

I had thought my motives were pure, that the vision I've held for Aetheria for so long could become reality. I had thought—

Does it matter what I thought? It's obvious that the surrounding aristocrats think my intentions are less than honourable, that they're trying to put the potential grief of their future losses squarely upon me so I might relent.

Well, two can play at that game.

"You are telling me that after everything she's already sacrificed for you people, after giving her mortal life with a loving family, that you would ask even more? That you would hand her over to that beast as some sort of payment?" I hiss, and Aliandara straightens.

"You give us too much power, Lucien. You must not forget that it wasn't any of us who started the barbaric tradition of the Heirbound. It was Hera." She uncrosses her arms as she speaks and looks over to Kairi with a sad but steely gaze.

"We do not expect this sacrifice of you Kairi, that is a Goddess's place, but you must understand why we are asking—" I turn back to find Kairi nodding.

I want to shake her.

How can she be so damn resigned to this?

"You think she will stop him from wreaking havoc on the entire realm?" I spit, and Morpheus speaks up this time.

"Hera did, that's why she chose Kairi. I'm not saying it is fair, Lucien, but Gods abound, it is how it has always been."

"Lucien—" Kairi begins to speak, but I glare at her, causing her to pause. Then, taking a deep breath, she reaches out, placing gentle fingers on my wrist.

"Lucien, when I turned, the Goddesses told me that they wanted a united Aetheria, they told me they needed a stronger army to protect the higher plains. I'm wondering— I'm wondering if maybe they want the Sephilim to absorb the powers of the other Kindred and become something new— It's the only plan I can see that makes sense. They would have known that there was no chance of us attempting to force them into extinction," she whispers, her eyes sparkling with this sudden and convenient revelation.

"So, you're saying they gifted your immortal life to see you miserable, or worse, dead?" I retort, eyes wide with disbelief.

"They made me immortal because I have power over Aro that nobody else does. He was in love with Briar once, and I think he was in love with me as well, despite the fact he has a funny way of showing it," she admits, and I feel a roaring in my ears at the pure idiocy of what she is saying.

Can she really believe that Lord Black loves her? After everything we've shared—

My heart cracks in two, the fissures cleaving it seeming to grow a mile wide as she stares at me with sad lilac eyes.

Suddenly, a dreamy sentiment that punches me in the guts passes through the air as we are interrupted by another.

"You forget, sacrifice in their name is why the Aetherial Court gave us all immortal life, Lord DeLaurent." The voice is unsettling in its calm tone. The only person this voice could have come from takes a step forward as I turn to face her.

Anastasia looks at me, pallor ever more evident when contrasted with the confines of her black and solemn velvet gown. When I don't hold her gaze, for fear she'll see right through me, she gazes at Kairi, her face unwaveringly serious.

"Lucien, you need to let go. You can try to protect her for as long as there's breath in your body, but the truth is I think her place is with Lord Black. She's supposed to save us all by working from within the

Solis Castra, by restraining him, by making sure that he is following the path Hera desires."

"I have been wondering about her dreamwalking abilities and her elemental affinity—" says Morpheus now, confirming what I had suspected before. He shifts upon the balls of his feet, assessing my face as he no doubt realises this is new information to me.

Again, I wonder why Kairi had kept this from me.

"Notice how the Goddesses didn't give her super strength or speed. They gave her the ability to communicate discreetly, and the ability to call the elements to her. Any Fae will agree with me when I say that the elemental magics are about inner strength, about a nurturing of the individual that cannot be found without connection to the earth that birthed it," he sounds speculative, but his eyes are certain.

"She has dreamwalking abilities and elemental affinities?" asks Gage, who is frowning so deeply a small divot has appeared between his brows. Running his hand back through his spiky dark hair, he exhales heavily.

Kairi nods, her eyes jumping to mine with guilt before resting on the face of the Draconian opposite us. Then, she pulls her hair back behind her ear from where it is falling in waves over her shoulders, exposing the Fae points.

"Ares above—" Asher whispers, but Aliandara doesn't look surprised.

So, Kairi had told the Equinian High Lady of her Fae abilities but not me?

I wonder if I know her at all.

My heart races cold in my chest, a foreign slab of meat that betrays all my innermost pain as it thuds mercilessly against my ribs. The realisation hits me then, that I am outnumbered, and that isn't going to change.

"So, you're all really happy to sacrifice Kairi?" I ask them again, just to lay the guilt on extra thick.

"Lord DeLaurent, I'm not happy about anything. But I can't see what other choice we have. This is Kairi's destiny, surely you knew that once you realised she was the Heirbound—" Ember speaks up, her face stony, not from lack of compassion, but rather I fancy a little too much.

Have I been deluding myself?

How exactly did I think this was going to end?

Did I think the small interlude of her flight from the Solis Castra on the night of her ascension ball had meant she was mine forever?

No— I had known the truth.

I just did not want to believe it or dwell on the reality of its brutal implications. I had stuck my head in the snow and gotten high on the dream of a future that could never be.

Aliandara has given her reprieve, that is true, but she never promised to rally behind her, never vowed to risk the lives of her people to keep Kairi safe.

I knew I was being reckless with my heart, but the consequences of that had thoroughly escaped me in the inevitability of their gut-wrenching conclusion.

"I see," I murmur, my fury dying from a blizzard to a chill northerly breeze within my veins.

"Lucien, we are sorry. We are not bad people, but we are trapped within the same world as you. We are stuck with the same laws, the same reality." Phineas' bright carmine locks flutter in the growing chill of the flurried twilight air, his palms open as he implores me, with a relaxed posture, to see his side.

I don't see it.

I can't.

"So that's the end of it then, I suppose," I breathe, placing my cool palm on the back of my neck.

"It is. You have our condolences," Evangeline speaks, and I feel hatred rising bitter in my throat once again.

"Kairi will no longer be staying with you. I see now the safest place for her is with me," I declare without modesty.

After all, I might be helpless to her fate, but I'll be damned if I don't do everything within my power to keep her out of Lord Black's clutches as long as possible. How could I live with myself otherwise?

Kairi's jaw tightens at my decree and Aliandara nods with weary quicksilver eyes.

"As you wish, Lord DeLaurent." She bows her head out of respect, her braided hair cold indigo in the dull atmosphere of the early evening light. I almost laugh at the fact she's offering a gesture of re-spect instead of telling me to give up the love of my life to a psychotic murderer.

Silence falls over the group, and the sum total of Aetheria's greatest leaders are left to wallow in the guilt of their decision. I stand firm through it all, hoping they choke on their cowardice.

22

THE RAZOR'S EDGE

GENEVIEVE

I'VE BEEN SOAKING IN the bathtub for longer than I care to admit, and I'm still finding aether in the cracks and crevices of my body that often go overlooked. I'm still trying to scrub the scent of fucking lilacs off my flesh as well.

I've been vigorous, the heat of the water rising and turning me flush as I've scoured every corner of my body's landscape for any trace of Soleus.

Can I really be about to do this, to ally with the Sephilim who I've loathed thoroughly for centuries?

If you'd told me the fact was even an idea in my head three weeks ago, I'd have laughed you into next week before slitting your throat for even suggesting something so absurd.

But *now*—

Algoric explores my curves with a rippling of his long body as he slithers in and out of the water, curling around my limbs and tasting the air with his tongue when he comes up for air.

I let myself wallow in the caress of his oil-slick coloured scales, realising that my recent closeness with Lucien has made my lack of physical contact with others a deeper hollow within me than usual.

I think about Aro's demands, on the way he had seemed so unyielding, but I don't buy it.

I think he wants this alliance more than he's letting on, and I refuse to be fooled into settling for a lower offer than I know my loyalty and everything that comes with it is worth.

Do not forget, Gen. You are more valuable than he wants you to realise, if you weren't, you'd already be dead.

Algoric counsels me with a wise reptilian blink of his translucent eyelids, turning back and looking at me as his lower body coils into a swirl on my lower abdomen. He hovers above the water, erect and staring at me with unwavering adoration.

So, what are you saying? I ask him, seeking his advice as I always have in times of turmoil.

I'm saying that he wants you to kneel before him, but you must not. You must fight instead to stand at his side. I told you I want vengeance— you remember?

I find myself blinking slowly at that as a slight chill sweeps across the back of my neck.

Is Algoric displeased with the entire idea of an alliance?

For a moment my resolve is entirely shaken because I realise I'm about to break bread with the man who killed my Dragon, who reduced him to this—

I do. I retort simply, raising a hand and pushing my damp hair back against my skull. The white-lipped python still coiled in my lap rises slightly out of the water, so it is even taller, staring me straight in the eyes with inescapable magnetism.

Well, then you must put yourself in the proper position to achieve such a thing, my Love. We need what we have always needed, and that cannot be found in Drakos Vale. He speaks the truth, his words slithering out into the air between us and coiling within my skull, nesting there as I ruminate on what he's implying.

I thought you wanted me to avenge you— that doesn't sound like vengeance— I muse, and he gives me what might even be described as a serpentine smile at a push, his forked tongue tasting the steam rising between us with leisurely slowness.

I did not specify who that entailed, as I recall.

My eyebrow peaks, my fingers trailing a wanton path along the bowed length of my collarbone.

Go on.

I encourage, watching as the neck of the enormous python winds through the mist of the hot steam, scales glistening with moisture like individual prisms.

Who do you think is truly to blame for my death, Gen? He puts the question to me, and I ponder this deeply.

Aro had dealt the killing blow, but the reason he had taken Algoric in the first place was because Lucien had meddled in affairs not his own. He had saved Kairi Freemont and put the Draconians in a

316

precarious position, and for no reason I ever understood until I saw his face as she fell to the ground dead that day in Soleus.

Lucien. I speak his name telepathically, a guttural hiss between myself and Algoric.

Indeed. It is not always the one who delivers the killing blow who is to blame. I was shot down from Drakos Vale skies, in which I was forced to fly only when our identity as living creatures and not myths had been confirmed by Lucien's carelessness. This is his fault. The Draconians cannot survive having him as a High Lord, I have seen the future, and beneath his rule, we are weak and sentimental.

I pause, my heart contorting as I remember the look in Kairi's eyes as he had devoured her pleasure.

It is not him, Algoric, but Kairi. The Nephilim. She has destroyed his motives as a High Born. Corrupted him with her love and the allure of her body. I think on the sight of them together, the water heating instinctually around us in an angry surge.

Regardless. He was also the one who refused to avenge my death when he had the chance that day. He supposes it was to save the rest of the Dragons but was it? Or was it because he was more concerned with the safety of Kairi's body? If Aro had destroyed her corpse, I do not know if she would have risen again. He dragged our full fleet of Dragons out to Soleus, only to command them to hover and wait, vulnerable. The act itself was risky. Suppose Aro had set his army upon the others?

Algoric is making points I hadn't been able to see in my grief, and my chest tightens as I think back to the pathetic look on Lucien's face as he dismounted Ebonara and asked for there to be no more violence.

You are right. He is our weak link. I admit, the feelings I have for Lucien becoming a deeper shade of black and blue than they had been before. When I think of the fact he had gotten so close to me, made me hope for his friendship, for his company, and then yanked it away, I feel sick.

He could not choose me over Kairi, and so I know he will never choose our people.

Someone has to, even if that's hard. Even if it's the hardest thing I've ever done.

I refused to kneel once, and it ensured our survival for a time. But now? With the new developments and Lord Black's growing power, it's time to fold.

But not before I get the offer I seek.

So you think I should barter, so we are in a better geographical position? I demand, feeling myself beginning to prune.

I do, and I think you know just what to use as a bargaining chip already— I'm sure you're devastated— The sarcasm in his hissing tone causes my lip to upturn at the side as I pull the plug from the clawfoot tub with my toes. The hot water drains away, and even after such a long soak, I still find damn aether left behind in a rim of scum where the waterline had been.

I rise from the tub as Algoric climbs over the pale curves of my breasts, draping himself over my neck like a boa and undulating into invisibility.

I drip dry, aided by the new heat beneath my skin now I have a next step to conquer, before slipping on a silk robe and leaving the bathroom.

What I find in my suite shouldn't surprise me, but it does piss me off immeasurably.

"Rude, Captain. Have you no respect for a woman's privacy? I am your superior as well, so I'd say that's a double infraction on my personal space you've made in all of a half-second. How long have you been standing there anyway?" I snap, standing in the doorway of my bathroom, steam spilling out into the cooler, malachite-walled bedchamber.

"Rude? I should say so, given that I thought we had some kind of loyalty to one another. What the hell are you playing at, showing up at the Solis Castra? I would have thought you'd at least clue me in on such a reckless plan. Maybe if you had you wouldn't have been so easily captured." Leo is angrier than I've ever seen him, especially in my presence. He usually has the utmost respect for me and my power, but he's livid now, his fists balled at his side and his jaw tense to the point where I can very nearly pinpoint the throbbing carotid artery on his neck.

I can feel the warm water from the slick of my white hair seeping into the back of my robe as I drip onto the floor, wondering where the hell he found the audacity to simply turn up and lecture a Draconian High Lady.

Perhaps he's been drinking.

"Are you drunk, Captain?" I sneer at him, clenching and relaxing my clawed fingers slowly as I watch him.

Taking several steps closer, I grit my teeth and spread my wings a little wider, knowing full well how threatening my talons look in the candlelight of the room.

"No, I'm not drunk! Quite frankly madam I could be asking the same of you!" He sounds undeniably British, and I find myself almost laughing at the way he addressed me. I have never been a madam in the whole of my exceptionally long damn life.

A whore— yes.

Mistress— to be sure.

But madam?

I think not.

"You will address me as my Lady, or Lady Thomas, thank you very much. Must I remind you who it is to whom you speak, boy?" I give him a taste of his own medicine with an equally condescending address and watch him stiffen on the spot. He doesn't flinch away, as I would have liked, but instead stands acutely frozen, his face taut between more rage and quite possibly a careful apology.

"Very well then, my Lady— would you be so kind as to tell me what the hell it is you're playing at? Because I'm quite sure I cannot even begin to guess—" Leo demands, crossing his arms and letting his wings flare.

I'll hand it to him; he has balls that's for certain. It's just a shame his actions are likely to get them served to him on a silver platter if he continues.

"That's none of your concern now, is it?" I ask, standing firmly in place and exhaling so I seem entirely more relaxed than I am.

"I'd say given what I've risked, it's entirely my concern." Leo counters, refusing to relent.

Brave, boy.

Or very stupid— adds Algoric from where his head is nestled in the concave divot between my collarbones, invisible yet attentive.

"Not that it is any of your concern, Captain, but I am currently doing what I believe is in the best interest of my people. I have lost so much already, and I will not allow them to suffer the same fate." My tone is stony, my ribcage a hollow void that rattles with each breath I take.

"You mean to tell me that after everything, that after he murdered your Dragon— you'd fight under his command?" Leo's eyes look like they may pop directly from his skull and roll around in front of my chaise longue like marbles.

319

Pushing a few errant strands of damp white hair behind my ear, I cock my chin a little higher, straightening my shoulders beneath the python's weight.

"I mean to tell you that I will not let my people or our Dragons go extinct for the sake of my pride. I have fought long and hard to obtain independence for my people, and now I will do what I have to to keep hold of as much of it as I can," I announce, feeling regal as I stand upon bare soles, staring him directly in the eye.

"I don't understand how you can just ignore—" Leo begins, but I cut him off with a laugh.

"You think I'm ignoring this? Do you think I haven't examined this from every which way I can think of? Foolish and ignorant, even for a man— what an achievement!" I spit, spinning on my heel.

I realise as I gaze upon my four-poster bed that I cannot bear to look at him, his face sickening me with its self-righteous outrage.

"You can't do this," Leo stutters, sounding less sure of himself than he has since he's arrived.

"I can do whatever I please, Captain. You are merely a tool, and you have never been in the position of wielding the weight of the weapon which you represent. Do you know what it is like to have to make choices that might murder people you've sworn to protect, that might betray the confidence of those who look up to you as all-knowing? No. You do not, because you are not a leader. You are a fighter. You could never understand." I say this with as much conviction as I can manage, but the words come out soft and melancholy, like a heavy rain cloud cast into the air between us.

"I understand what you're doing is going to get a whole lot of people killed." Leo retorts and I shrug.

"But they will not be my people, so you see that is something I can live with. You live long enough being the villain in people's eyes, it is inevitable one day you will become what they imagine you to be. Funny isn't it? Their condemnation of me as a monster is, ironically, the very thing that has led me to become one. For if I do not look out for my people, who will? Will it be you?" I ask him this with earnest interest, my heart heavier with each beat as the truth of my words heats my blood with scorching despair.

Leo is stunned as I turn back over my shoulder to look him in the eye. I can see it in his face, the way his eyes are cloudy with resignation, his trust and defences rising in great walls of smoke behind his irises.

I have burned whatever the bridge was between us, not that it took more than an ember of dissent on my end to ignite the blaze. It had always been tenuous, a rope bridge stretching the great yawning maw of a racially divisive volcano.

Now, that bridge, and with it, my only other option, is gone as well.

"You're making the wrong choice," Leo says dully, and I shrug again, the weight of Algoric pressing me down, keeping me grounded in the decision I have made.

"No, I'm just not making the choice that benefits you. Now, if you don't mind, I think I'll get dressed and then you can take me back to the Solis Castra. As you can imagine, myself and Lord Black have many things to discuss," I command this of him, and am surprised to find the sound of his laughter reaching across the cooling air between us.

"I think you can make your own way there, Lady Thomas. After all, you seem fully capable of flying, and maybe the cold air might even clear your head—" I want to retort, to command him to stay and save me the bore of flying back to Soleus with what Lord Black will assume is my intent to surrender entirely to his will.

That will be the first thing of many he will find himself mistaken about when it comes to today's meeting.

Leo is there, staring at me with large, disappointed eyes that only stoke the fires of my rage further, but before I can move to brand him so he will not again forget who it is he is judging, there's a flash of lightning.

I stand there, oddly numbed by his lofty dreams that I could have been a saviour, before turning and getting ready to depart.

It seems the boy who had hoped for a heroine springing from within my darkness and grief like a phoenix is gone and won't be coming back.

The flight to Soleus is tedious, but I'm thankful for the fact it gives me the opportunity to think. Aether lodges itself firmly in the crevices of my bustier, a tight jade corset with gold boning. My hair is pulled close against my skull in a crown of braids, Algoric gripping tightly to my wrist, just beneath the sleeve of my floor-length dress coat. I chose it for its high collar and the enormous brocade Dragon that falls the length of the spine. My pants are black leather, and one of my favourite daggers is holstered to my thigh by a decadent ruby-encrusted scabbard.

As the Solis Castra comes into view on the horizon, I swallow thoroughly, feeling the tightness of my corset a little more fiercely as I let out a deep exhale.

I do not want to be here, not really, but I know it is for the best.

I also know that after suggesting my bargain to Lord Black, there is no going back. I will have sealed my fate with both Lucien and any chance of a future working relationship. He will see it as a complete and utter betrayal of not only himself but also of Drakos Vale and everything he believes it can be.

He's a fool for many reasons, but none so much as his deluded notion that Aetheria will ever be anything but a shark tank full of bloodthirsty, immortal predators.

I sweep the skies, the talons of my wings cutting through the cool evening air with effortless forward motion. Inhaling deeply, the scent of froth from the nearby Oblivion Falls mingles in with the putrid perfume of lilacs assaults me. I suppose I will have to get used to that.

The jagged spires of crystal that slice into the sky mercilessly glint a deep violet against the setting cobalt sun, and I shield my eyes a moment, glancing at the immense amethyst structure and finding it too garish to bear.

I glance at a dark head of hair as I descend in a circular glide around the topmost spire, scouting the skies carefully for more Equinian soldiers. I don't want to be perp-walked back to Lord Black.

This time, I want my entrance to be on my terms.

It is, as I had originally suspected, Lord Black standing on his balcony, watching the skies with his arms draped casually over the balcony. His winged lion lets out a mighty roar as I circle in my descent, alerting him to my presence if he wasn't already aware.

Had he anticipated my arrival with such perfect timing, or is it completely coincidental?

I come in hot, using my wings to keep my gliding speed high until the last minute. Letting their leathery pale span flare out, talons glinting in the blue sunset, my flat suede boots of bottle green touch down with cat-like softness on the stone of his narrow balcony.

It's a beautiful landing, even for someone as practised in flight as I am.

"Lady Thomas, what an utterly expected surprise." He cocks an arrogant brow, straightening from the railing and dropping a hand to rest in the mane of his Kensari companion.

"Dinner?" he asks, gesturing behind him to the open French doors.

I nod, leading the way with my head held high, my pale cleavage flushed from the cold rushing air of the late afternoon skies.

An intimate table for two has been set in the centre of the suite, irritating me immensely.

"Any particular reason you're trying to feed me to death? I thought you wanted me to, and I quote, *get down on those pale knees*?" I taunt him and he clears his throat.

"If you had fallen to your knees, do you think I'd have thought more of you for it?" he queries, striding past me and sitting down at the table with ceaseless grace. His black wings drip aether onto the floor, and I watch as he gazes up at my appearance.

"Very regal. I do like that jacket on you," he compliments.

I laugh with cold resignation.

"You are insufferable, Lord Black," I spit, half-amused, half-bored in retort.

"But at least I'm honest about it," he admits, beckoning for me to sit.

I do as he asks, my fingers lingering on the curve of my scabbard.

"Nothing so fancy as our last little dinner. Just some wine, cheese, and fruit. I prefer to eat lighter in the evenings if I can," he explains as if I should care a great deal about his dietary requirements. *Pompous ass*, I think as I watch him remove the covering of a silver platter piled with fine bread rolls, cheeses, grapes, and plums.

"Wine?" he asks, picking up the bottle made of deep burgundy glass from behind the platter.

"What is it with you Sephilim and wine?" I ask him with complete seriousness.

"This coming from a Parisian, I'm surprised at you—" he titters at his own joke like a bird, and I narrow my eyes.

"Is it simply the reputation it brings with it? The expectation of grand taste and palette for the drinker?" I ask, wondering if it's a statement.

He lifts his head, topping off his glass, expression stony.

"For me, it is a test, a daily test. A test of discipline. My father was an alcoholic. Wine was his ruination," he explains, and I find my eyes widening slightly.

Is it possible— we might actually have something in common?

"Alcohol was also my father's main vice," I take a roll from the tray before me, slicing it with the beautifully sharp bread knife from beside my plate. I cut the roll in two, taking the corner of a pat of butter and spreading it on thick and smooth.

"Merchant?" he guesses, but I shake my head.

"He owned a brothel. I was one of his assets," I explain, biting into the bread and letting the butter spurt between my teeth.

"So— you are no stranger to getting down on your knees after all," Aro's quick wit and sudden smirk cause me to tense, debating flying at him over the table.

"I haven't come to kneel, for your information." I swallow, wiping the edge of my lips on a fine linen napkin folded beside my plate.

"Then why have you come? I assume it's not for the food—" He takes a plum from the silver tray between us, biting into it without pause.

Wincing, he spits the fruit into a napkin.

"That's the third bad plum I've had today. What the hell is going on with the fruit in this place?" he mutters.

"What a shame you should have to deal with such bitterness," I quip, the sarcasm in my voice thicker than the butter on my bread.

"I don't know if you have noticed Genevieve, but I'm not a very patient man. So, I ask for the final time, why are you here?"

"I want an alliance. I want to stand by your side as a partner." I say the words with haphazard abandon, as though I am thinking for the very first time.

"Kings don't need partners, Genevieve." He places his elbow on the table and rotates in his seat, the extremely well-polished brass buttons on his black suit jacket glinting at me like fiery eyes.

"Ah, but you are not king—" I say, sipping my wine and allowing my fingernails to clink against the glass as I set it back down.

He opens his mouth to speak, but I raise a long index finger. "Would you like to change that?" I ask, my eyes simmering with satisfaction as his expression morphs from bored to surprised.

Leaning back in his chair, he shakes his head, flipping a loose lock of hair from his eyes.

His hands form steeples in his lap, and he quirks an eyebrow as I keep him in suspense.

"Go on—"

"You know exactly what it is I'm proposing," I retort, not wanting to ruin the atmosphere by laying out my exact plan.

Mystery gives me power.

"And what do you want, Genevieve— What is it that has you suggesting such— despicable things?" he cocks his head, my lips spreading in a smile.

The Kensari has finished pacing by the hearth and roams over the amethyst floor to slump at his master's feet, looking at me and licking his enormous maw with a bloody red tongue.

"I want Sapphire City."

I don't blink, or move, locking his eyes into a gaze that is so intense I wonder if one of us might burst into flames.

I hope it isn't me.

"Oh, do you— well isn't that interesting—" He thinks on this a moment longer, but before he can refuse me, I begin going over the reasons I had rehearsed that benefit him.

"You want the strongest military Aetheria has ever seen? You're going to need my Dragons, and they will certainly flourish and become even stronger in such a warm climate. That is what Midas would not concede to me all of those years ago— if you must know," I add, and Lord Black runs his index finger along the fine edge of his jawline.

"You forget, I could simply kill your Dragons and steal their power— that's why you decided to come to me in the first place, is it not?" he adds, plucking a grape from the pile of food between us. Popping it into his mouth, he winces as what is obviously too sour explodes in his mouth.

His discomfort pleases me, immensely.

So much for Soleus having the best quality produce in the whole of Aetheria.

"You could do that, but how exactly will you manage your people? You might think you can do this alone, by killing everyone in your way, but both you and I know Aetheria is a large place. If you want full control, you're going to need eyes everywhere, eyes you can trust," I finish the bread that's been sitting on my plate, untouched since my first bite, my stomach rolling with nausea as I take in the full audacity of Lord Black's statuesque features.

The man loves himself, that much is clear.

I have never loved myself, only longed to be loved by another, though until recently I'd never admitted this to even myself.

It has taken being thrown aside by Lucien for the perfect innocent woman, the angel, that made me realise how bitterly I despise the fact my power makes me undesirable.

I will not be rescued, and I will not swoon.

No man wants a woman who he has to fight every single day, who flinches at the gentlest touch and returns such caresses with scorch marks and sizzling flesh.

Aro ponders my face a moment, tilting his bread knife from handle to point and letting its tip bite into the dark tablecloth laid between us.

"And you are those eyes, I suppose?" He stares at me with obvious amusement thinly veiled by dead eyes.

"I am eyes, a well-educated mind, a skilled fighter, and a practised leader. There is a reason Midas went to war for my allegiance, Lord Black. Do not forget that. He was willing to sacrifice his men to have the loyalty of my sword, and my Dragons." I sip the wine, the complex mix of flavours waking my tongue from the savoury lull of the bread.

"The people of Drakos Vale still bow to you alone?" he asks, and I purse my lips. He thinks me such a fool that Lucien could sway my people to his weak thinking?

"You already know the answer to that question. Lord DeLaurent has shown his loyalties lie elsewhere." I try not to sound bitter, to let him know how much ending my friendship with Lucien hurt, but I'm not certain he doesn't see right through me.

In fact, throughout this entire meal, I have felt oddly transparent.

Given that, I'm more at ease than I should be.

"How do you feel about an after-dinner flight?" he proposes, and I shrug.

"Your castle, your rules." I pause, wondering why I suddenly desire to be conversational with a Sephilim I've quite often thought about decapitating for the fun of it. "As long as I don't have to sing for my supper. I'm no angel and my voice is liable to break crystal and glass."

"Please no singing, I have enough of that with sycophant Nephilim. Now come, I want to see what you can do in the air. I've never seen much of Draconians in flight," he adds, standing and sweeping across the breadth of his suite.

I catch Algoric's pale Dragon form in the oil painting above his mantelpiece but ignore it, walking past the artwork with as much speed as I can manage.

"And neither should you. What good would it be letting my enemy know my aerial abilities?" I snipe, and he smirks.

"Ah, but we are no longer enemies. Isn't that what you came here to ask me?" He looks back over his shoulder with a sickly handsome smile.

I want to punch something.

"You're accepting my proposal?" I ask, amazed at the ease with which I've managed to convince him.

"Once I have the crown," he replies with icy certainty, the dark periwinkle of the sky casting his face into a gloomy chill light as he leaves through the double doors.

The serpent on my wrist tightens its grip, ever-present, listening quietly and remaining silent so I can focus on achieving what I came here for.

Aro rises from the balcony with three enormous beats of his dark feathered wingspan, the tails of his coat fluttering behind him. I take a few running strides, the muscles of my thighs pushing tightly against the leather confines of my pants, before launching off the balcony after him.

The air rushes my face, my heart pounding with the triumph of what I have managed to negotiate here today. The precise arrangement might be unsavoury, but I can think about that later.

Aro twists, corkscrewing in the air as he dives, wrapping his wings around his body so he appears to be spiralling like an elegant pendulum. His dark feathers throw the glare of the setting sun from their oil-slick vanes in a myriad of rainbow hues, taking the light and shattering it entirely.

I pull my wings into my body, increasing my aerodynamics and allowing myself to freefall. I catch up to him in a shorter time than even I expect the competition and fury he has lit in me making me glorious once again.

I bank and swerve, smirking at the awe that he tries to hide but which I cannot ignore, lying deep behind his dark eyes.

As I continue to fly rings around him, I admit to myself the terrible truth of it all.

I hate his guts, but somehow, and against all reason, he has made me come painfully alive once more.

23

THE INHERITANCE OF LOSS

KAIRI

"I'M SORRY ABOUT LUCIEN." I apologise to Phineas as we help Quinn back into bed.

The redheaded High Lord of Fall merely shrugs, looking at me with sad eyes. I have already returned the other Fae to Morpheus' Villa and then proceeded to conduct Aliandara, Asher, and Evangeline just beyond the bounds of Sapphire City. The aridity of the desert clings onto me even still in the muggy humidity of Nirvana.

"He loves you, Kairi. That much is clear." Phineas leads his lover into bed.

"I know, if there was ever any doubt in my mind, the fact he's willing to go into a bloody massacre to keep me has well set those doubts at rest."

As Quinn rolls back into the hold of the four-poster bed, he elicits a small groan of pain. He's paler again, a remarkable contrast to how much healthier he had looked after only a few moments in the mortal world. I could have suggested he stayed, but if Nirvana continues to die it will only be prolonging the inevitable. Besides, I know he would never willingly abandon the land, and if Morpheus and the others are ever going to figure out how to fix it, they are going to need his help.

Sprites flit around the bedposts, treading daintily upon vines and peering down at the ailing High Lord with scared expressions. I see Paisley, the very first sprite I had the privilege of meeting, and my heart skips a beat at her obvious fragility.

She hops up from the vine she's standing on, leaping to another just above her, clambering like a child would on a climbing frame with gangly, unruly limbs. She gives me a lopsided grin as she pushes herself to stand, now on my eye level, and shakes her loose white-golden curls from her eyes.

"Hello there, Paisley." I smile at her, reaching out with an open palm and offering it to her. She does a small dance, hopping from one foot to the other as her fidgety energy grows and the glow around her flickers brighter.

She skips, with the grace of a ballerina, from the vine to my palm, the wispy sounds of her voice lost among the rustle of the leaves as she flies.

I look into her face as her tiny feet tickle the lines crisscrossing my hand, the innocent wideness of her eyes and the childish wonder on her lips unmistakable as she spins on the ball of one foot. The dress she is wearing today is made of light blue petals, perhaps from blue-bells. They flare around her pencil-width waist, her wings vibrating so fast that they're visible only as a glistening blur between blinks.

"You see them, their innocence—" Phineas comments, crossing his arms after tucking Quinn firmly into bed beneath light cotton sheets.

"I do. They're so remarkable. So very— magical. Pure magic." I admonish, placing Paisley back upon the winding vines climbing the bedpost. I watch her straddle one like a bannister, sliding down it with a squeak of laughter as she descends faster than she expects.

"Then you know. You know we cannot go to war," Phineas adds, and I nod, face turning solemn.

He's right.

This place, Nirvana, it's full of too much purity, too much natural beauty, to be sullied by the dirty dealings of war and bloodshed.

"I know. I knew before the meeting. I have known for a while now that perhaps just because I can outrun my fate, doesn't mean I should," I reply. He gives another sad smile, looking back to Quinn who barely stirs, a deathly white pallor creeping back over his face like mist.

"Do not be too hard on Lucien. I cannot say what I would do, should it be Quinn in your position," he admonishes, and I watch his hair lighten slightly, the extremely carmine curve of his brows furrowing deeply in thought.

"I imagine most of us would do the same thing. I mean, when it comes to matters of the heart, we are all selfish, we all want." I look at Paisley as her glowing form tiptoes across the footboard of the bed, her balance shaky but undeniably divine as her dainty little feet place themselves without fear, one in front of the other.

"You are very brave, Kairi. It would be easy to cling to him, to let him throw the world into chaos for you— but you, you have surprised me." He compliments me, but I don't feel it, wishing only that I could feel as brave as the sprite I'm so carefully observing, heart caught in my throat at even the notion that she may fall from such lofty heights.

"Perhaps. But I think that's why Hera chose me. She needed someone who couldn't stand the thought of living with such guilt." I turn back to him with wide eyes, content now Paisley has reached the furthest bedpost and begun climbing like a tiny spider monkey again.

"She chose wisely. Though I am sorry, for yours is an inheritance of loss. Of pain." Phineas acknowledges my fate, grave reverence pasted onto his fiery features. I nod, my heart numb as it thuds with lacklustre enthusiasm in my chest.

"Please make sure Lucien doesn't inherit the same fate. Please, Phineas. I could not bear it. If I do this— when I do this, I cannot have him give his life in some ridiculous pursuit of vengeance," I burst, voice desperate and climbing in pitch. Reaching forward, I clutch his palms, veined like late autumnal leaves with deep colours, in my hands.

Phineas looks to Quinn, who seems to be drifting into a sleep wracked with strained breathing, and then back to me.

"I won't. But— if you get the chance Kairi, kill him. Kill Lord Black and don't you dare feel bad about it, alright? It might take all the patience you have, and all the courage you can muster, but don't hesitate. Not even for a second," he whispers this urgently, pulling me into him so I can smell the petrichor and crisp pumpkin spice of his breath.

"Do not think for one moment that because I cannot raise you an army, I do not support your cause, Lady Freemont. You are an incredible woman, and I will not have you doubting that for one moment. Lord Black thinks he wants you as a Queen, but he underestimates you. That will be his ruin."

He claps onto me like I might blow away in the breeze which stirs around us, roused by his passion.

It is the most frankly I've ever heard him speak, Phineas who always seems caught between expressing his anger and restraining it with a stifling silence that brings barely disguised fury to his features.

I nod, feeling tears flooding my eyes without my consent.

Everyone has been telling me that what I intend to do is insane, that what I'm proposing is foolish and suicidal. Phineas is the first person who has made me feel like that sacrifice is heroic and not stupid. He's the first person who trusts my strength and my resolve, who believes I'm strong enough to go into a viper's den and come out the other side.

"Thank you, Phineas. For believing in me," I swallow my emotion with a gulp of moist, floral air. Phineas nods, feathered locks moving soundlessly around the points of his Fae ears.

"I should be thanking you. You believed in the goodness of this place even as a mortal and sacrificed everything you'd ever known to keep us safe this long. Even if the other High Born have forgotten, I never will, I promise you," he vows, raising my hand to his lips and giving a chaste kiss.

"Now, you must be getting back to Lucien. I'm sure he's anxious to return to Drakos Vale. I could see him sweating back at the ranch. Though whether out of fury or the earthen climate I could not be sure," Phineas supposes, giving me a lopsided grin.

I return his smile, but I know it was not Lucien's fury making him sweat. Lucien's anger is a chill finger at the nape of your neck, a howling and empty wind, and a shudder of hairs rising to attention along your forearms. There is no half-hearted warmth in it, only cold resolution and absolutes. "I will make sure he keeps looking for things to help Quinn. Perhaps it'll keep him busy," I muse.

Thinking of him alone, roaming the skies of Drakos Vale, or even worse, the empty halls of his house, makes me feel physically sick as an overwhelming desire to cry continues to creep over me.

"Farewell, Kairi Freemont." Phineas' grip is so sincere I think he might break the bones in my hand, but I smile back, blinking away tears and steeling myself to conduct as I step back from his willowy gait.

"Goodbye Phineas," I reply.

Then with a crack and a flash, I'm gone, leaving the ailing Fae High Lord of Spring and his fiery-spirited lover alone with their increasingly dire problems.

Back in the gazebo, I find the Draconians as the last remaining Kindred, and the mood between them is tense, to say the least.

Anastasia is gazing up at the stars and Lucien is staring silently into the palms of his open hands as the breeze stirs his long pale locks, aloof around his furious expression. I notice a thick layer of unnatural frost wrapping around one of the wooden guardrails Lucien is leaning against.

Gage watches both of his fellow High Born, a furrowed brow marring his otherwise youthful complexion.

"Well, that's everyone. Ready to head back to Drakos Vale?" I say cheerily, though, in all honesty, I feel like I've got a ball of hot lead lodged in my throat.

"Whatever," Lucien mutters, turning to face me as Anastasia pivots back and climbs the shallow steps toward us. Gage steps forward as well, silent, and the three of them reach toward me, fingers outstretched and eager to leave the fraught discussion behind them.

I conduct us from the fields of heather, trying to contain my fear that I'll never see them again, in a flash of dull lightning that's missing its bite.

Receding quickly, the four of us stand in encroaching shadow, the dark beyond Lucien's wooden porch swallowing the light like a long-starving beast.

"I'd best be off then, come on Lord Lee. You can come to Gemina Two for tea if you'd like—" Anastasia speaks, her voice cracking the silence like it's an eggshell and she a sledgehammer.

Lucien visibly flinches at the sound, his head hanging, his shoulders slumped and wings drooping on his spine.

Momentarily I want to slap him, to tell him to buck up and get some fucking stones.

He's acting like he's the one who is willingly choosing to be leashed to a maniac. He's acting like I'm asking him to take my place.

I look at him, at his sour expression as Anastasia and Gage depart without another word to either of us, realising that Hera had been right. Not just anyone could do this job, could swallow the pain and do what needs to be done.

It has to be me.

I see that now, see how my chronic pain had prepared me for flourishing under the rule of a tormentor, by teaching me to survive the oppression of my own failing body. Even when things had seemed impossible, when I'd barely been able to breathe for the agony or keep my eyes open for fatigue, I had kept moving forward. I didn't have a choice.

I feel stronger remembering this and straighten, readying to break the silence as Lucien turns promptly and enters the house on heavy and furious feet. I go to follow him, the porch slats protesting my quick tread, but find the door slammed in my face and a cold breeze ruffling my hair. It is coming from within the house rather than the wilderness at my spine.

I fume then, sick of men entirely.

Balling my fists, I conduct into the house, lightning crackling from my fingertips as the static in the air gathers, attracted by my fury and desire to suddenly cause pain. The bitterness of it lies like lemon juice on the tip of my tongue, but I do not recoil, swallowing dutifully instead.

I reappear directly in front of Lucien, so fast that he walks into me. He is bewildered a moment, before his angry composure returns. I take him in, finding that resolution I had described to Phineas dripping off his features like arctic seawater.

"Get out of my way," he whispers, as though he is afraid to speak to me in a tone that's authentic to what he's feeling.

"No. We need to talk about this." I bite back, glaring at him with the most intensity I can muster. I tense in the bounds of my lilac corset, my heart beating fast as I clench my teeth.

"Get out of my way," he repeats as if I had not spoken at all.

I cross my arms, wings flaring sideways, raising my chin in challenge. He sighs, infuriated by my lack of cooperation, turning on his heel and heading back towards the lounge.

I conduct after him so I'm sitting in the armchair opposing the doorway beside the immense fireplace, legs crossed, my fingers tapping the soft dove grey suede with a slow deliberateness dripping with self-control.

As he turns the corner, he sees me and stops short again. My wings cushion my spine as I lean back into their feathered hold, tilting my head.

"I can do this all night," I threaten, cocking an eyebrow and pursing my lips.

"Goddammit, Kairi. Enough. I just. I need. I need—" He looks exasperated, his features pale in the flickering firelight as he takes an angry step forward into the room.

"Exactly. You don't know what you need," I reply, keeping my voice as even as possible.

"I— I need you to rip my heart out, Kairi. Stop this incessant beating. That's what you want, isn't it? You want to rip it out? *Merde*— I'll give it to you— willingly— if you just—" He's breathless and I see the panic in his eyes. I soften, my shoulders dropping as my hands fall cupped into my lap.

"I never wanted to break your heart, Lucien. Never," I swear, my mouth going dry and my heart returning to its heavy sombre beat.

"Then how can you even suggest— how can you even fathom—" He still can't finish a sentence, and I watch him as he paces the floor, ravenous for a resolution he will never find.

"Here's a question for you then," I say, getting to my feet.

I'm so lonely as I stand, spine steel, despite the fact he's metres away. I want his touch, to know that he still loves me, even when he hates me.

"Do you love me, Lucien?" I ask, earnest.

He turns to stare at me over his shoulder, stopping in his angry paces.

"More than I've ever loved anything—until the day I die. You own my heart, Kairi Freemont." His eyes flash a light blue like a snowflake has blossomed into existence within the vast darkness of his pupils.

"Then you know that I have to do this. I must stop him, Lucien. I cannot let people die. I won't let them die just so I can love you. If I could, then I wouldn't be me and—" I trail off and his eyes are sad as he turns slowly.

He exhales.

"And—" he stops.

"And?" I push him to continue.

"I wouldn't love you the way that I do, *mon ange...*" He comes close to me as he finishes his sentence with utmost reluctance, reaching to take my hand in his. His fingers are freezing against my warm pink flesh.

"Let me be strong. Let me be the hero in this story, Lucien. My fate was written that way by Hera, all those years ago, and for that I am sorry. But she would not have blessed me if she did not believe in me. Don't you think I can do it?" I demand, looking up into his face with genuine curiosity.

"I have never believed in anyone more, Kairi. I just won't let Lord Black have you. He cannot be allowed to touch you. Never again. Not after everything," Lucien breathes, bringing his fingers to trace the edge of my shoulder.

"Lucien, it's not your job to let him have me. I am not yours. I am my own," I speak the words, hating myself a little bit for being so damn independent.

"But— you love me—" Lucien says it like I'm being stupid, but I give him a small smile.

"I do, with everything that I am. But my heart can belong to you, even if I never truly will. You understand that, don't you? No matter what Lord Black does, no matter whether he touches me or what he believes, I'm yours because I choose to give myself to you. Just like I'm choosing to try and kill Lord Black by working from the inside." I reveal.

His eyes widen.

"You're going to try and kill him?" he blurts as if the thought had not even occurred to him.

"You think I'd leave you for anything less? You think I'd leave if I didn't honestly believe there was a chance I would be walking back through those doors— to stay?" I ask, gesturing to the front door he'd slammed in my face. He stills, blinking slowly and I wonder nervously if he will believe my plight, or whether he will see straight through me.

The truth is, I don't know if I can kill Lord Black, and I don't know if I'll ever return to Lucien. But I won't leave him hopeless. I need him to keep on living, to keep on breathing so that I have something to fight for, even when things seem dark.

Before that though, I need Lucien to let go. I need him to trust me, to love me enough to let me be free with the knowledge that if I can return I will.

We've barely known each other a few months, and yet instinctually this feels like something he should know deep in his heart, just as I know if I ever needed his help, he would be there without question or falter.

"I want to save lives, Lucien. I want to stop anyone else from losing their loved ones because of my choices. You know how that feels, losing me, and I know that you don't want to be responsible for putting anyone else through it—" I grip his hand tightly, taking a half step closer to him. His body radiates cold, face stony as he swallows.

"It's not very heroic is it— me giving you to him. Me surrendering the thing I love most— if that was the plot of a novel it'd never sell and you know it—" he mutters, but I can see that he's absorbing what I'm saying, even if it is reluctantly.

"Heroism isn't riding in on a white horse at the stroke of midnight, it's suffering silently for the good of your people. That's the truth. It is heartache, and it's sacrifice, and it sucks. But it is who you are. I want it to be who I am too," I whisper, leaning against the cold hardness of his pectorals. My cheek immediately chills, the hairs on the back of my neck rising as my feathers give a delighted shudder.

"You think I'm a hero?" he asks me, bringing his index finger to my chin. I look up at him, eyes wide.

"You're mine, you always have been."

I kiss him on the cheek, lips warming his skin. "But— I want to be able to save myself now. I do not want to be afraid anymore. I don't want you to be afraid for me either. It's time for me to face my fears and take on the responsibility I've been charged with. Hera gave me eternal life, and Hecate did the same for you. You know nothing in this life is free—" I admit. Lucien breathes into my hair, inhaling deeply as he wraps his arms around me.

"Unless your name is Lord Aro Black of course—" he murmurs.

"Not even then, Lucien. He might have power now, but his soul is as charred as his name, and he will fall from grace eventually. Entropy— it is the way of things." I will my words to be true, sounding far wiser than I feel.

"And you will be there to see it." Lucien no longer questions my decision, accepting it with this simple statement. I want to cry with the reality that the last person standing in my way may just step aside. I can't tell if I'm more relieved or terrified.

"And you will be waiting to bring me home. Here." I look around at the walls, hand-built by the man I love, and relish the scent of the place.

Moving back from Lucien's grasp, I run my fingertips along the stonework of the hearth, along the wood of the mantlepiece with wanderlust, letting the heat from the fire warm my legs through the skirt of my gown. I take this moment to simply breathe, the act itself feeling like a small victory.

I feel him behind me, breathing with a calm sureness I haven't heard in too long, cool radiating off him like an icy star.

He twines his hand around my waist, gripping me tightly to him and laying his icy lips on the side of my neck with a small, desperate groan. The sound reverberates through my body, causing the pool of my desire to quake, tremoring beneath his wandering hands.

They rise to the ties that hold my front-facing corset closed, working quickly and without sound as I lay back into his chest and he continues to wander up my throat with a torturously slow and attentive tongue.

The corset comes unbound and I feel my breasts, swelling with the heat of my arousal, being cupped by stony palms that do not hesitate. My nipples harden, furiously warm as they protrude through the silken undergarment laying flush to my skin.

My skirt is high upon my waist as Lucien turns me in his arms, so my back is aligned with the cobblestone of the hearth, the bite of it oddly satisfying as he undoes the cords sealing me into too many layers of petticoats.

I shuffle out of the corset top as he works, discarding it over Lucien's shoulder with haste as he finally frees the layers of skirts from my body. They fall, fluttering into a light fabric pool around my ankles.

I'm wearing only my sheathe undergarment as he slams into me, our lips colliding in a fusion of inescapable heat and absolute cold, the tingle of mint and wintergreen exploding across my tongue as I taste him deeply, drowning in the sensation of his icy fingers as they trace chill rivers across my body.

I feel his hardness through the leg of his pants as he grinds against me, his kiss deepening to a feral growl as he breaks from my lips and moves to devour the pale skin at my neck.

Goosepimples rise upon my arms at the frosty edges of his muscles, and I watch as his lips wander to my breasts. His fingers loosen the spaghetti straps of the chemise, letting the silk fall so he can put one of my nipples into his mouth.

I groan, gasping slightly as the temperature change fully awakens me to the sensations running rampant across my body. He nips the soft areola of my breast, running his tongue roughly along it before bringing his hands to cup my buttocks. He lifts me away from the stone of the hearth, pulling me close to him as I wrap my legs around him for support.

I begin undressing him, pulling at his cravat. I move to toss it aside, but he stops me, taking the satin fabric in his palm and giving me a deliciously innocent look.

"May I?" he asks, biting his bottom lip.

I wonder what he's referring to as he sets me on my feet, before twirling me on the spot and securing the silk around my eyes.

"Well, that's— rather resourceful of you," I say, my heart thundering as anticipation builds like a storm.

I hear him undressing behind me, and before I know it, I feel his bare skin pushing into my spine. He whispers in my ear.

"If I told you that I wore this cravat with this exact purpose in mind would you believe me?"

I laugh, the heat of his throbbing member the only warm part of him as he spins me so I'm once again facing him.

We are a tangle of wanton limbs and wet, hungry mouths, tasting every inch of one another, though one of us with more purpose than the other. I let Lucien lead, sensing that he's enjoying the control after everything.

He pulls the chemise over my head, and it disappears to somewhere I cannot see and do not care to. Then, he tugs my elbow with gentle fingers, guiding me to the fur rug on the floor, the flames of the fire heating the entire left side of my body as I sit back on naked heels.

I cannot see him, but I can feel the mix of heat and cold coming off his skin as he touches different parts of me with all the slowness of a sculptor examining his masterpiece. His lips glide over my breasts as he pushes me away from him so I'm lying on my back, spreading my legs and lowering himself so that his tongue hovers just above my labia.

I sigh, shocked at the first contact despite the fact I had guessed it was coming, a small moan emitting from me as his tongue slides over my clitoris and I feel my whole body buck beneath his still-wandering hands. He carries on, his mouth eager, his tongue's strokes measured and rhythmic as he tastes my desire and lets out a groan of pleasure himself.

I feel it building quicker than I expect at the sound, lost in a sea of sensation as his fingers wander up the insides of my trembling thighs.

I come into his mouth as he laps at me, gentle and tender, my body coming apart beneath him. My cries echo off the wooden eaves overhead, the darkness of the blindfold doing nothing to stop me squeezing my eyes shut and biting down hard on my bottom lip as I ride the excruciatingly lengthy climax beneath his merciless focus.

I'm panting, the insides of my thighs soaked with my pleasure as he crawls up my body. I taste myself on his lips but can't find the will to care as the delicious frozen hardness of his muscular torso pushes me flush into the rug and chills the scorching blood still racing through my veins.

He kisses me deeply, his hands lifting my elbows so my arms are raised over my head. Then, he pins me there, lowering himself and nuzzling my neck a moment before he whispers in my ear.

"You look so beautiful when you come for me, *mon ange*." I whimper slightly, the thought making me aroused even though I have only just finished.

"You're making me want to come too—"

He pushes my legs wide with one knee, kissing me full on the lips as he enters me. I stretch around his girth, both of us eliciting a moan of relieved pleasure, as though being apart has been a physically painful experience.

I feel myself dripping over his shaft as he thrusts, the force of his crotch grinding against mine in a dull yet inescapable rhythm. He swells, and I squeeze, our muscles straining to keep up with our nervous systems.

For a while, he's devilish, slowing right down and taking long, uneven strokes just to tease me until I'm almost crying behind the silken bind of the blindfold.

He whispers to me, his voice a husky murmur interspersed with half-laugh, half-moans.

"Like this, *mon ange*?" he asks, and I pant, biting down on his bottom lip hungrily.

He stops, pulling his mouth from mine, and I feel like screaming.

"More, *mon ange*?" he runs that devilish smile roughly along my jawline as I dig my nails into his back. My world is made entirely of touch and taste, and all of it is Lucien DeLaurent.

Whether it's from pleasure, or the fact I don't know how long it'll be until I'm back in his arms I can't tell, but I let the tears fall as he picks up the pace again. They streak down the side of my face as I cling to him, bringing my legs up to wrap around his waist and driving him deeper until his groans become barely audible.

In a final deep thrust, we both come in a chorus of high-pitched ecstasy, the ebbing throb of sensations between us reaching its peak as he deepens our kiss in a final attempt to completely push me over the edge.

I teeter, pulling him into freefall alongside me.

Our cries are then lost entirely.

He buries himself deeper in me as the climax recedes, nuzzling my neck and inhaling me like I'm a drug. I remain blindfolded beneath him, breathless and spent, tears dried at the sides of my eyes by the nearby heat of the fire and his blazing cheeks.

I feel him stirring, and then after a few moments, the blindfold falls from my eyes. He grins down at me.

"Satisfied, *mon ange*?" He looks delectable there in the firelight as he remains inside me, his eyes twinkling.

If I say no, can we continue?" I ask him, never wanting him to stop touching me. He dips so our noses are touching, kissing me tenderly and caressing the side of my face.

"We can continue no matter what you say, though I'd prefer upstairs in bed. I'm getting rug burn on my knees—"

We both erupt into giggles, breathless, and for that moment, utterly in love.

The night wears on in a blur of moans, bared teeth, hissing, and fast-moving tongues. Time seems all but lost amongst the billowing sheets of Lucien's circular king-size bed, sent flying intermittently by spasmodically undulating wings caught in the clutches of a deep physical connection.

I feel beautifully languid after several hours of losing myself in his arms, in his kiss, and as we wind down, both of us verging on exhaustion, I rest my head on the cool statuesque plains of his chest, tracing the patterns of his tattoos with my fingertips.

We don't speak, and it's beautiful. The silence is so fragile, like glass, and the atmosphere so utterly desperate that it feels as though every single touch, every kiss could be the last.

So, we both bring our best, making sure there can be no doubt about how the other feels, no second-guessing, no room left for questions.

I love Lucien DeLaurent more than I've ever loved anyone, and most likely will ever love again, and now I'm sure he knows it.

His fingers are tracing the inner curls of the locks falling over my shoulder when a sound utterly intrusive and foreign invades the space.

We both sit bolt upright, and then I give him a small smile. He looks at me wistfully as I rise from the mattress.

"I'll get it. After all, I think you've done enough tonight—" I smile at him, the memory of him taking charge each time we had made love impressing on me just how desperately he wants me.

I have been thoroughly spoiled.

Slipping on a pair of his cotton pyjama pants and then buttoning the matching shirt over my wings, I pull my long hair from the collar, a whiff of Lucien's scent rising to greet me from my skin.

"I'll be right back," I vow with a fond inhale, leaving the bedroom and taking the landing in several shaky steps.

My legs feel phantasmal beneath me, muscles tired and my skin raw from the endless stimulation of my Draconian partner.

I see a familiar silhouette behind the stained glass of the front door as I descend the stairs, my eyebrows meeting as my forehead creases.

What on earth is she doing here?

And at this early hour?

I take a light jog the length of the hallway; my muscles growing hot as blood flows through me like steaming bathwater.

Opening the door, I find Genevieve standing on the porch in the grey early morning light, her face pale as I have ever seen it in the brisk air. The vibrant grassy emeralds of her eyes cut into me as though she were laying the stones themselves to my bare flesh.

We face one another, neither one speaking as a moment of thick foreboding settles between us.

I watch her falter a moment in speech, something unusual for someone so self-assured and feel immediately small as she looks down at me.

"Kairi, please come with me! You must help me— It's one of the Dragons," she explains, and I feel my heartbeat begin to race once more.

It's as if I can't get a moment's rest.

Her face is strained, her posture tense.

"Of course, let me just get dressed and put some shoes on," I say, all business.

I turn on my heel to retrieve last night's discarded gown from the lounge, but before I can even take a step, I am sent flying forward by an enormous, skull-rattling blow to the head.

I hit the hallway floor, pain exploding through my head and making my eyes water, teeth smashing together uncontrollably.

Sinking fast, the shadows drown any fighting consciousness.

24

THE SPY WHO CAME IN FROM THE COLD

ARO

I WATCH AS NEPHILIM scurry around the throne room, preparing for my post-coronation procession to the throne.

The coronation itself will take place with a small crowd of witnesses and security within the vault of Zeus where the crown is kept, untouchable to anyone but Kairi.

In Midas' time, the entire amethyst throne room had been draped in lavish gold tapestries bearing his insidious insignia, a golden eagle carrying the eight-spoked sun of the Aetherial Court as a shield in its unforgiving talons. According to mortal history, there have been similar symbols used in less than savoury causes, not that Midas' reign was always savoury. Thinking about it, I have to wonder if that's the fault of the muses, who I know hated Midas and particularly his obsession with gaining power by any means necessary.

My reign will be different though, and instead of the overt gold which has been inserted every which way into both our military forces and the Solis Castra itself, I intend to make black my signature. This is not only because of my name, but because black is the total absorption of all light, and I will now be capable of absorbing the power of anyone who dares question my worthiness as Crowned Ruler. I fully intend to make my oxidised steel armour uniform among the troops and will also be having my armour pieces embedded with amethyst accents melded to the original suit with platinum gliding. I won't be lost among the crowd, but I want it known who they work for should anyone have the audacity to wonder.

Two Nephilim follow a larger Equinian male, who is aiding them by carrying an enormous roll of fabric on one shoulder, into the throne room. The Nephilim demonstrate with slender fingers where he should place the bolt, and I watch as he simply lets it drop to the floor with a thud before walking off.

Brutes.

I roll my eyes, continuing to observe as the two women catch me staring and cast their gazes downward in a sadly predictable show of obedience. Then, they unravel the onyx velvet of the new runner, embroidered by Soleus' most talented needlepoint workers with lightning bolts in silver thread. The scent of freshly woven carpet rises from it as they continue to work on their knees with low bowed heads, hands quick and trembling as I admire the runner.

I used to adore the tremors running through innocent maidens as they got down on their knees at my command, and yet now I find myself more interested in the carpeting than the subservience. They finish rolling out the runner at the foot of the throne, which stands grandiose in amethyst, marble, and howlite upon a raised platform of gold. Soon, the platform will be replaced by one of onyx, but the damn thing is so heavy it is taking a while to arrive. Funnily enough, onyx is also one of the only natural resources that is sparse here.

Typical.

As I'm wondering how long I will have to wait for the pedestal to arrive, a more important item on my coronation checklist materialises in a flash of lightning that causes everyone in the room to shield their eyes.

Genevieve, in all her pale and furious glory, appears atop the runner clasping the hand of a Sephilim guard, both their shoes still wet from the snow of Drakos Vale, irritating me immensely.

"*Off* the carpet, Lady Thomas," I growl, and she rolls her eyes, baring her teeth as she turns in a flurry of pale hair and bloody roots. Stepping off the onyx velvet, I catch the icy trail of water dripping off her soles seeping into the fabric and clench my jaw as the guard follows her.

Fortunately for me, what I notice next causes my growing rage to dissipate like smoke off a flame.

In the guard's arms lies the unconscious body of Kairi Freemont, the girl I've been chasing for longer than I can remember. I glimpse her full and limp form, doll-like, as he turns back to face me.

She's really here, face porcelain and pale.

In fact, I wonder for a moment if she's dead.

"How did you subdue her?" I ask Genevieve, unable to look away from the Nephilim Heirbound. It's infuriating, how easily Genevieve has managed to get her here when I've spent months trying to get my hands on her to no avail.

"Hit her across the back of the head with the hilt of my dagger. Why?" she demands, looking annoyed I am not giving her more praise.

What does she expect?

I'm not exactly Morpheus, and nor would she want me to be. The insufferable fool is going exactly nowhere despite the immense magic running in his veins. Dream walking, he can manipulate the psyche of anyone he wishes, yet what does he do? Uses it as inspiration for his little— *poems.*

"Just wanted to know if you touched her face. I don't want her looking like I've beaten the shit out of her for the ceremony," I reply, giving her an insidious smile. Then, I realise someone is missing.

"Where's the other guard? I ordered two to be sent with you!"

The outrage that I might have been disobeyed over something so simple so close to becoming King, after everything I've done to prove my power, runs bitter like ash in my veins.

"He'll be along in a moment. I've gone and scored me a little bonus. So, if you were doubting my loyalty, *monsieur*, don't."

I'm left wondering what the hell she's talking about until the flash of a second conducting Sephilim shatters reality for but a moment. When it comes back together, a wide smile spreads over my face, feline and insatiable in its desire for the suffering of my enemies.

"Well— that is quite the bonus, Lady Thomas. And— if I might add, quite the statement—" My eyes fall on the bowed head of Lucien DeLaurent, his long blonde hair lanky around his bare shoulders. He's wearing informal cotton pants, and it takes me a few seconds before I realise they're identical to the pair draped over Kairi's unconscious body.

Gross.

Draconian leftovers—

No thanks.

The thought of him touching her, and the thought of her letting him makes me feel physically sick. I'm alarmed. The physical reaction is visceral and beyond my conscious control. It's something I don't expect, having mastered my emotions and physical form long ago, and I can't quite work out if it's because deep down I still love Kairi, or if it's because I can't bear the thought of a Draconian taking something that is rightfully mine for himself.

Is it hate, or love, at the root of this poisonous nettle that's taken seed in my dark heart? I wonder.

Lucien struggles, his hands bound behind him in a pair of the amethyst cuffs I've had distributed amongst my soldiers. They don't work on elemental-specific powers, and I'm sure Lucien could still invoke some form of cryomancy if he so wished, though I'm not particularly worried. The blade at his hard-pumping carotid stops such an eventuality, and I remind myself to commend the soldier for thinking on his feet and managing to subdue a Draconian High Lord single-handedly.

What the fuck is he playing at, letting himself get bested by such a comparatively low-level opponent?

I suppose his love has made him weak— *if* that is what he feels. Maybe it's just animal fucking and nothing more. Either way, I don't want to lay my hands on anything that lizard brain has touched. For all I know he's got all kinds of diseases.

"Genevieve! Why are you doing this?" Lucien's outrage is cast into the air once, and then again as both his flabbergasted tone and ferally shocked expression hit me one after another. He struggles within his binds, and I notice the surrounding staff watching the commotion with fake half-interested glances.

"All of you, clear the room! Preparations will continue after I've dealt with this," I command, and then give a small, satisfied exhale as the bodies clear the room with scuttling haste resonant of insects fleeing a fist.

I am left with just two guards, two Draconian High Born, and the Heirbound to deal with privately. After all, my alliance with the Draconian High Lady need not be public knowledge until I deem it the right time, and determining that time will be crucial, especially with so many Equinians roaming the city. Once I am King, and perhaps even now, they won't question my decision to ally with Genevieve, and yet I know they won't be happy about it. Of course, a few of my higher-ranked guards have been told to heed any requests from Genevieve, but I didn't issue the order without the threat of public beheading to deter them from letting it slip to anyone else.

After the doors of the throne room shut with a soft and respectful click behind the last of the staff, I take several steps forward and gaze down into the angelic features of Kairi's unconscious face.

Then, taking my thumb and index finger, I reach down to her dangling left arm, lifting it before executing an excruciatingly painful pinch on the delicate skin of her inner wrist.

She startles awake, eyes jerking open like the pain has physically prized her lids apart. Her pupils dilate as she takes in my face looming above her.

I wait for her to scream, to panic, but she merely stiffens, looking between me and the guard.

"Would you be so gracious as to put me down, please?" she asks the guard with all the poise of an unruffled swan. The soldier looks to me for direction, his dove-grey wings stretching wider to match his stance as Kairi shifts her weight within his hold, looking uncomfortable.

"Cuffs," I bark at him, watching as he sets her down.

"That isn't necessary, Lord Black," Kairi says this with icy disdain yet maintains a perfectly serene facial expression. I blink a moment, irked by finding my façade of permanent reserve mirrored back at me in the flawless cold glass of her face.

"I'll determine what is or isn't necessary." I glower, watching as she's restrained with heavy amethyst cuffs. They lie slack against the flimsy cotton of the pyjamas, which match those worn by her Draconian rescuer.

"Very well, but I won't run," she says with fierce reproach.

I cock an eyebrow.

"It's not you running I'm trying to avoid, it's you attempting to stop me torturing Lord DeLaurent over there—" I gesture to his slumped silhouette, still restrained and forced to statuesque stillness by the guard at his spine. Instead, he watches the conversation between Kairi and me, eyes furious over the glimmering blade at his throat.

"Kill him. See if I care. Nothing matters anymore anyway. I'm done with him." Kairi retorts, and I go to call her bluff but find only deathly indifference behind her lilac irises.

She's really serious.

Or so it would appear—

Even if I wanted to believe the ease with which she discards him, I'm not that damn naïve.

"Says you, standing here wearing his clothes—" I snort, shooting daggers at her with my eyes. I imagine them puncturing her delicate skin and staining it crimson, the image so vivid in my mind it could be prophecy.

"So, what? I threw him a quick fuck. Better him than you. My choices for entertainment have been rather limited you see." Her voice doesn't even tremor, and I straighten, feeling her words cut deeper than they should.

Genevieve looks at Lucien, her lips spreading in a feline smile.

"I knew she was only ever using you," she hisses, triumphant in a way that says their romance bothered her more than it should.

What the fuck is it with women and Lucien DeLaurent? He looks like an albino lizard that's grown the ability to stand for Zeus's sake.

Am I angry because Lucien has laid his hands on the skin of what is supposed to be mine, or that he has so clearly gotten under the skin of the woman who I had thought was truly breathtaking in her power and strength?

I cannot see the appeal, even though I can't deny his hair defies all laws of physics with its infuriating refusal to look even slightly ruffled.

Regardless though, the entire situation is unacceptable in its raw and ludicrous display of mortal emotion.

Aren't we better than that?

"Whore," I spit at Kairi, feeling Genevieve's hatred for Lucien reinforcing my loathing.

It feels good, to be understood and agreed with, to know that I am not the only one who has seen what an utter lie their entire fling seems to be.

Kairi was reborn to crown me king, of course she could never fall in love with a monster.

Confidence in the rightness of my course reinforced, I turn from the pair of them, raising my chin to the stained-glass windows glittering ceiling to floor behind the throne. I walk up the shallow golden steps of the pedestal I'm waiting to have replaced, letting my fingers trace the pointed tips of the throne's sharp crystal shards and feeling them cut into my flesh.

I bring my fingers, sizzling with static, to my jawline, cocking my hip against the arm of the seat and observing the pitiful nature of the two prisoners staring up at me.

"Why is it that every time you come to me, you're wearing pyjamas?" I ask Kairi, rhetorically of course. She straightens again and the guard behind her shifts nervously.

"What can I say, your inspirational speeches send me to sleep. I want to at least be comfortable," she shoots back, her sass not giving me the same thrill as Genevieve's does.

I don't know if it's because I know Kairi doesn't have the power to back up her seemingly fearless demeanour, or because I'm so certain that Genevieve does.

Either way, the Draconian High Born makes Kairi Freemont look like a chickadee fresh from her mother's nest.

"Escort her to the tower. And make sure she's properly dressed for the coronation in the gown I had brought up from storage," I bark at the guards. Both of them move forward, clutching Kairi by the elbows as Genevieve moves in to restrain Lucien as the blade is loosed from his throat.

The Draconian doesn't struggle this time but instead balls his fists within the cuffs that restrain him.

"None of that, Lucien. I'll scald your pretty little face off," Genevieve hisses, her wings flaring as the fine bone architecture of her skull becomes sharp with malice.

"I will see what we can do about finding some cryomancy-inhibiting cuffs," I say without much thought as I collapse back into the sharp edges of the throne's chill hold.

"I upheld my end of the bargain, Lord Black. I expect you to do the same," she pushes me, never satisfied with my placidity, always seeking more destruction, more power.

I admire her for that.

After five hundred years, the woman is still burning hot as the day she was reborn, and that's quite a feat.

"You did. Go and gather your troops and their mounts. I will have a small company of my best Sephilim warriors waiting for you at the eastern border. You can head out for Eclipsia from there."

She pauses, Lucien looking up to her with wide and accusingly astute eyes.

"You did all this— for Sapphire City?" he spits, veins bulging on his arms as he fights the cuffs yet again. Her hand, now steaming against his upper bicep, tightens. Then, she kicks him promptly in the back of the knees with the heel of her shoe, and I watch with a smile as he sinks to his knees. He grunts, and I watch the steam rising from his skin cease.

Genevieve loosens her hold, rolling her eyes but doesn't give him the dignity of a response.

"I think I'll escort this traitor to the dungeons first if you don't mind?" She looks at me with those emerald eyes cut sharp as steel, and the fact she seeks my permission makes the predator prowling inside my skull purr with delight.

"Be my guest. I have far too many preparations to attend to be dealing with taking out the trash." I cross my legs as I sit on the throne, looking down at the pair of them, their pallor stark against the dark onyx velvet of the runner.

She nods, turning on her heel and hauling Lucien to his feet as she shoves him in front of her.

"You know the way to the dungeons?" I call after her, watching as her ass swings heavily from left to right without apology. Lucien's echoing and uneven footfall breaks my reverie as she calls back over one shoulder, giving him another shove.

"I'm sure I recall. After all, I was a guest there so recently— remember?" she quips.

I smirk, her witticism causing my mouth to flood with saliva. Watching her silhouette grow smaller and finally disappear, she escorts the prisoner I hadn't dreamed she would capture toward an uncertain fate.

After she's gone, I straighten in the hold of the throne, taking a beat to revel in the feel of its cold hardness beneath me before I get to my feet.

After all, there's no rest for the wicked, and even less for a wicked king.

KAIRI

The guards lock the doors of the tower room behind them with a soft click, and I find myself once again trapped within its octagonal, rose quartz chamber.

It is a cage, but at least it's a beautiful one I suppose.

I see the double doors where Lucien had crashed in and taken the role of heroic rescuer without a second thought, quite literally. I wonder, had he thought about rescuing Kairi for more than a single moment that night if he would have come to a different conclusion entirely. I wasn't good for the Draconians, and I certainly wasn't good for his friendship with Genevieve.

The fact she's betrayed him has me shaken completely.

No matter how I look at it, I can't wrap my head around her new-found alliance, but then again that might be because she gave me a real whack around the back of the skull as I turned to aid her without question.

I suppose it was naïve, to trust anyone, except that I simply cannot fathom how Genevieve went from being ready to murder Aro without a second thought to doing his dirty work.

As I move wistfully across the suite, hands still cuffed in front of me and pondering the rapid change of the predicament I thought I understood, I discover that the French doors have been locked and the outside of the door frame encased in thick golden bars. I feel a certain grimness settle over me then. Even the act of making me prisoner is gilded in precious metal which shimmers pure in the cobalt sunlight of early morning.

I look around at the chamber, the same bed I found so alluring when I had first arrived here in a mortal body seeming desolate because it's missing the most important comfort of all.

Lucien.

His nickname for me, *mon ange*, echoes around my ebbing skull and an ache forms fleetingly in my chest before I push away the tenderness and replace it with my doubt. I cannot allow myself to wallow, for it brings only weakness in a place where I must be stronger than ever to survive.

His eyes, as I had lied so convincingly that he meant nothing to me, an act to protect him against the rage of Lord Black after he had been so unexpectedly captured, still haunt me.

He must know I love him entirely, after everything.

He must know.

He has to know.

I had alarmed myself, though. Shocked it had been so easy to slide the mask of cold indifference over my features, and I find as a result my insides have become a cold and numb arrangement of ornaments rather than flesh and blood viscera. At least, through it all, I will feel nothing.

That's probably for the best.

I spot it then, as I'm gazing without real focus beyond the golden bars obscuring the view of Oblivion Falls at the powdered lilac sky.

The gown is an enormous white monstrosity of boning and lace, hanging innocuously from the wardrobe.

I know what it is immediately, the high collar and painful angular corsetry making me feel claustrophobic just looking at it.

This is the dress Storm was going to marry Aro in, before it all went wrong, before she realised what he felt was not love, but ambition and a lust for power.

I think about his motive for such desperate acts and find myself wondering what lies behind the traitorous decisions of the High Lady Draconian.

What could he have possibly offered her after he murdered Algoric— what could she possibly be thinking would come out of dealing with someone so despicable?

Lucien's heartbreak had been at my denial of our bond I know, but I can't imagine how he must feel after Genevieve was the one to capture me and turn me over. I never understood their relationship, but it is obvious to anyone that the roots of it run deep.

Or at least, they used to.

True, I intended to end up back here all along, just as my Heirbound fate dictates, but the fact she had been the one to apprehend me makes everything more complicated than I'd hoped.

I reach out, the cuffs heavy on my wrists as I finger the thickly embroidered lace of the enormous gown, a gown that will drown me no doubt. I will become a shadow of myself among the splendour of my duty to sacrifice, and the white shade of the fabric only highlights how much of a sacrificial lamb I am to Aro and the people of Soleus.

I am distracted from the sadness of the notion and the scratchiness of the lace beneath my fingertips by familiar nostalgic scrapping.

Turning slowly on my bare heel, I find those bright blue eyes staring at me through the bars guarding the French doors.

I pad over to him, falling to my knees and reaching out a manacled palm to touch the glass, the other following unwillingly in its binds. Catticus raises a paw to meet my hand, the warmth of him seeping through the glass and reaching me when I need it most.

You're very brave, you know, he says, staring at me with more wisdom than I can fathom.

I sigh, dropping my hand from the pane. The amethyst handcuffs land heavily in my lap and I feel the weight of them tethering my heart as well.

I don't feel it. I can't believe Lucien got himself captured. I couldn't bear it if something happened to him. I'm afraid... I reply, my eyes welling with tears I refuse to let fall.

Catticus sits neatly beyond the door on the balcony, his tail swishing from left to right as a warm breeze ruffles the endless alabaster fluff of his mane. Licking his lips, his enormous canines glitter with viciousness, but his cobalt irises remain steady and wise.

I think Lucien is the least of Aetheria's problems right now— he replies, putting things into perspective. I flush.

Of course— I know it's selfish to worry about him in the scale of things— I begin to apologise for my single-mindedness, but the lion interrupts me with a throaty growl.

That's not what I mean, dear heart. I was eavesdropping earlier from just beyond the window of the throne room, and High Lady Thomas has made such a despicable bargain with Lord Black because he has agreed to help her invade Sapphire City. He's giving her reinforcements so she can resettle the Dragons in a more suitable climate. His wise eyes become grave, his whiskers tremoring.

I flinch at the revelation, my heart thundering in my chest as I let my forehead press into the cool glass. I feel my inability to act heavy upon my shoulders like my wings are made of solid steel.

Aliandara had said that nobody has ever breached the walls in her time as High Lady, and yet, I doubt those invaders ever had an army of Dragons and Sephilim who could conduct working in tandem.

The city will fall, and I know she won't give it up without a fight. She and most of her people may end up dead.

I know they certainly won't flee in the face of such an attack, it would be more than their lives were worth for the Kindred of Artemis to lose face and run in the face of oncoming conflict.

I should— I begin but the lion purrs, his voice wrapping around the inside of my aching skull like a warm blanket.

No. You are where you need to be, Lady Freemont. Besides, you cannot stop Genevieve. You are best to be here, ensuring Lord Black is kept occupied. I wilt, everything seeming grey and hopeless despite the glittering grandeur surrounding me.

Lucien on the other hand, now I think he could be useful. We need to try and gather some forces of equal power to help defend Sapphire City against this attack, he must have some Draconian allies who would side with him over Genevieve— Catticus continues, his determination unwavering.

I blink slowly, nodding in agreement as I mull over the idea in my head.

You think that Sapphire City could use some Dragons to fight on its behalf? I run my fingers back through my tangled bed head, the memory of Lucien's fingers twined among the locks too fresh to be bearable.

Exactly. Catticus replies, his ears shaking rapidly upon his head as he shifts on his hind paws. I watch as his wings stretch, and I panic slightly, scared of him leaving me alone with the future I chose.

Why did I do this?

I falter in my resolve, forgetting all the reasons I know are so convincing and feeling my mortal terror fully in my immortal heart.

Catticus, am I doing the right thing? I ask him as earnestly as I can. The Lion's eyes flash with something like uncertainty as he stretches his front paws, each one of his claws protruding from between his enormous toes like thorns.

I don't know, are you? he asks in return, majestic face stoic as ever.

I thought I'd feel relieved, or— like I'd know I was doing the right thing for my people once I was here, once I was actually in Aro's grasp— I feel my voice trembling as the pit of dread in my belly becomes only more noticeable, nausea climbing up my throat with acidic claws.

And you do not? he asks, licking his enormous lips like he is tasting the air.

I don't know. I feel— deflated. Like I'm giving up— Maybe it's just disappointment, or maybe I've just been thrown off by Genevieve's sudden change of tact... I muse, cast in a mellow light falling through the bars.

Perhaps. This is not the easy choice you have made. Catticus agrees, staring at me with wise eyes.

But is it the right one? I ask him, desperate for some aid, some guidance in a situation that seems to have no right answers.

I cannot possibly know. Only you can answer that, and even then, I am sure you will find some way to make future grief entirely your fault. The world is a dark place, Kairi, and we can only do the best we can with the strength and information we have at the time— Hindsight is an illusion of control that simply doesn't exist.

I nod, wondering how my ginger tabby got so damn philosophical.

Will you go and make sure Lucien makes it out of Soleus? I ask him, hopeful.

I will, and I will try and ensure that Sapphire City has at least some warning of what is coming. Time is short though, and once Genevieve sets out, she won't be long arriving. Dragon flight is, as you know, extremely

353

efficient. He goes to turn, to leave, but I place my hand on the glass once again so it makes a sound, causing him to still.

Thank you. Thank you for everything. I say with desperate haste, the amethyst cuffs glittering dully in the sunlight.

Catticus turns back, placing a large paw against the outline of my palm once again, and for a moment both of us hang on either side of the pane, gazing into the other with a fear that can only come from the unknown.

The moment passes, and his paw falls away.

I watch him turn on all fours, taking a single feline leap up onto the balcony railing before diving into the field of clouds and open sky beyond.

I don't feel much hope, but what he's promised me is enough.

I get to my feet, knowing I must focus now on what is to come, and how I will endure what Aro has in store.

Walking over to the bed I look once more at the wedding gown, wondering if I'm soon to be married.

Will Aro take my hand, and with it my freedom as well?

I shudder at the thought as I plop down on the soft feather down of the mattress, feet dangling above the floor.

I see the crack in the quartz below, still unrepaired, a tear in the flawless dream of the suite's overwhelmingly luxurious aesthetic. An open wound reaching back into the shattered past which has still yet to be healed.

I will take care to make sure it is soon fully mended, bringing Aetheria the stable monarchy it needs by putting a leash on a ruler who is obviously out of control.

Aro will heel, whether he likes it or not.

Determined, I let myself fall back so I'm staring up at the ceiling, remembering the last time I had taken in the same view. I had been so naïve, believing in fairy-tale romance and that the universe was, underneath it all, a just place.

I know better now, and I know that it can be, but only through the sacrifices of good people such as myself. It is the price we have to pay for peace and security, for trust in our governing leaders. It is the unseen cost of joy, of community, of abundance and cooperation.

I remember walking through Soleus, talking to my people as I headed toward my Ascension Ball, learning about their lives, seeing Aetheria through their eyes.

They had seemed happy, even when their existence had been as simple as tending a single patch of land, or of sewing day in and day out for High Born they had never even met.

They lived, immortal, in a beautiful yet simple world, and it was my job to keep it as such, to save their way of life by holding everything together, even if it tore me apart.

I close my eyes, listening to the beat of my heart, and feeling stronger than I thought I would with everything I know is coming.

After all, why would Hera have chosen me to bear such a burden if I was not strong enough to endure?

I take comfort in that and sleep.

25

MEDEA

GENEVIEVE

THE SEPHILIM GUARD MANNING the dungeons has a cell waiting for Lucien as he watches our approach with dark violet eyes. They're filled with hawk-like intensity, unnerving to most I would assume. It doesn't bother me though, after all, what can intimidate someone who has looked into the open jaws of a Dragon seeking lodged crystal shards causing discomfort?

I don't have to kick my prisoner in the back of the shins more than once, which I'm grateful for, contrary to how it might appear. I don't like hurting Lucien, even though I probably should.

He thinks I did this to spite him, I can almost guarantee it.

Not everything is about you, Lucien. I almost roll my eyes at his self-ishness but restrain myself.

Some of us have a higher purpose than keeping our hair immaculate, after all.

Indeed, most interesting things are about people all together less starry-eyed— Algoric's slithering tone creeps through the long grasses of my consciousness, the syllables casting a sudden illumination on his presence for but a second before he is once more silent among the gloom.

I give my fellow High Lord a shove into the cell of raw amethyst that will allow him little if any comfort, the too-bright light bleaching us both ghostly as Lucien turns to face me. Both our faces house cavernous dark pits for eyes that lock and clatter together in a pirouette and parry of steel intensity forged upon hatred and betrayal.

I break the dance after a long moment, giving a single nod to the Sephilim guard whose hawk-like eyes watch us with the interest of a middle-aged town gossip.

Upon my order, the guard removes Lucien's cuffs with rough hands and then proceeds to pull the barred door shut with a resonating clang, turning the keys in the lock with certain finality.

"Come on, let's leave him alone with his thoughts, he isn't going anywhere—" I instruct the guard, who takes my order without complaint, making me realise exactly how drastically things have changed in such a short time.

Who would have thought I'd ever have authority over Sephilim soldiers?

The guard passes me by as I ponder this, the feathers of his wings brushing against my upper arm and causing me to claw at the itching skin left behind.

I turn on the flat sole of my boot, wings flaring slightly and throwing a welcome shadow over my eyes, still dilated fully dark from the light.

I take a step forward, beginning my journey back up to the corridor, but a sound I'm too familiar with to ignore me stops me cold.

"How could you?" Lucien's rage makes me undeniably furious, his lack of empathy or thought for anyone besides himself irking me more than it should.

"You're really surprised, aren't you?" I turn with a sneer, eyes narrowing as they fall upon him.

His bare feet seek any flatness on the crystal shards of the floor, his bare arms draped through the bars, knuckles glowing white as his fingers rise to twist around their golden glint.

"Don't you dare tell me this was your plan all along, Genevieve. I know you better than that. He *killed* Algoric!" Lucien's words jar my resolve slightly, and the bait works as I take several steps toward the cell.

Algoric's lithe serpentine body tightens around my right wrist, climbing slowly in an infinitesimal coil of support.

Foolish boy. Foolish, murderous boy, he whispers.

"You think I planned this? I am merely reacting to your choices, Lord DeLaurent. After everything, I'm amazed you can't see that the blame for Algoric's demise ultimately lies on your shoulders!" I raise my voice, blood heating so I flush too visibly beneath my pale skin.

"The blame for Algoric's death lies on the shoulders of the man who drove a sword through his skull. The man *you're* helping—" Lucien hisses between the bars, his eyes sharp with outrage.

"Let me ask you this, Lord DeLaurent. What, professionally speaking, do you have against Lord Aro Black? If it weren't for Kairi, would

357

you even care that he wants to be King? He had never so much as crossed your radar before you took what rightfully belonged to him and wandered into business that was not yours to meddle in to begin with. Do you not see that your opposition to his rule is entirely personal? It's pathetic!" I snort, my hands balling.

Algoric squeezes tighter as he climbs to my upper bicep.

Single-minded and arrogant, a lethal combination, the serpent reminds me.

"And this isn't personal for you? You're doing this to hurt Kairi! You never liked her, and she's done nothing to you!" Lucien retorts, slamming his open palm against the bars of his cell and making them rattle.

I cock an eyebrow, unable to comprehend his utter denseness as a smile mars my lips. Something about his helplessness, about seeing him as out of control as he's been making me feel sends a hot thrill through me.

"You were the one who accepted that invitation. I would have been perfectly content with having you stay in Drakos Vale. As I suggested, if you recall—" I say, the words bitter as lemon on my tongue.

Lucien's eyes narrow.

"What is this really about Genevieve? Are you truly as monstrous as they all believe? As they've always said? I thought I knew you better than that—" He is trying to hurt me, to use the bond we had once shared to unravel my intentions because they no longer suit him.

He didn't give a shit about me when it came down to choosing between me and Kairi.

But now, now he *cares.*

Typical. Algoric's support only spurs my fury.

"You don't know me," I laugh, shaking my head and feeling my emotions burning hot in my throat. "If you knew me, you would have seen that the exact strength that you fell for in Kairi, that exact heart, was in front of you all along. I sacrificed for Drakos Vale, I suffered for my people, and yet it takes a damn mortal to make one sacrifice and you think she's the second coming of fucking Hecate! You never saw me as anything but a friend, and all it took was a pair of big blue eyes and thick lashes to make you see in Kairi what I had been showing you for years. You act like she's something special, but really, you're just too damn stupid to see it anywhere else."

My breath is coming in giant scorching gulps as my chest rises and falls in desperate heaves, my emotions spilling all over the floor between me and the man I had loved, a secret for so long, even to myself.

"You— you had romantic feelings for me?" Lucien asks, his voice losing its anger and diminishing to an exasperated whisper. The sound of it makes me want to throttle him. How absurd the claim seems to him is utterly devastating.

"It doesn't matter now," I swallow. "What matters is that you never respected me, not like I deserve." My voice loses its volume too, my hands going limp at my sides.

You are better off without him, Gen. You are magnificent, and he is merely the dirt beneath your feet. He always has been, Algoric compliments me, sensing my pain. I'm grateful for it, even if it does little to calm the stinging wound Lucien's obtuse ignorance has left behind.

I stare at him, at the man who hadn't seen me for so many years, the man who now claims to know me well enough to make me doubt my own decisions.

Well, he hasn't.

"So, Lord Black— he *respects* you, then?" he demands, shoulders slumping as his voice becomes sour with resentment.

"Funnily enough, yes, Lucien. The man captured me and made sure I was incapacitated because he knew I was a threat. He recognises my power, my importance, and the might of the Dragons at my command. If he didn't, he never would have felt the need to steal Algoric from me." I hear my reasoning as though spoken by a stranger, surprised how deeply I've thought this through.

I'm not wrong either, Lord Aro Black doesn't like me, and I certainly have no love for him, but we both respect the power of the other, and I know for a goddamn fact he wouldn't stand me up to fuck some Nephilim whore.

"Genevieve you can't honestly—" he begins, but I cut him off again.

"I honestly believe that you are doing what is in your best interest and your best interest only. If I hadn't come for Kairi, you would have thrown this whole world into ruin for her. That's not someone I need to be taking political advice from. I also honestly believe that between you and Lord Black, he has offered the Draconians the better deal. He has offered us a home, a place to flourish," I remind him, crossing my arms over my chest.

A restless itch emerges in my legs, willing me to walk away, but somehow, I can't.

Somehow, I am compelled by some sick habit to try and make Lucien see my point of view.

"He's allowing you to kill thousands of innocent people and invade their land!" Lucien bursts, striking the bars with his knuckles this time. I watch as the blow reverberates back up his humerus, but he swallows the pain with a clenched jaw.

"Because the Equinians are so peaceful by nature—" I roll my eyes and snort at his pathetic attempt to make me feel guilty. "The whole history of their culture relies on them being strong enough to win Sapphire City in a civil war. If they're worthy of it, by their own standards, then my forces will be no match for theirs—" I remind him of what he should know by heart as a High Lord, gritting my teeth as I fight, showing him exactly how much he's getting under my skin.

"I can't let you do this! Genevieve— please—" It's sad then, looking at him, seeing his helplessness, discovering the depth of the weakness in him.

Pathetic. And he really wants you to side with him over someone who can offer you real power? Algoric adds, slithering tighter still around my wrist until I can feel the individual scales on his belly.

"You know, I think I just realised why you love Kairi Freemont so much—" I muse, running my finger over my bottom lip. "You don't love her strength, Lucien, for if you did, then you'd have loved me long ago. You love her weakness. You love that she *needs* you. That you get to play the *hero* without having to make any seriously controversial decisions. Who would reprimand you for saving the innocent damsel, after all? You're so fucking moral, it makes me sick. You give your best to everyone, everyone but the people who need you most, the people you were given immortal life to serve and protect," I spit the words at him, the sound of them matching the bitter poison of their taste as they swill around my mouth. My heart is pounding, my blood raging, a tempest within my heart.

"Genevieve, that isn't true," Lucien shakes his head, but I can see from his slackening expression that he can't even manage to convince himself.

"I don't need your belief to know whether or not it's true, Lucien." I sigh, feeling at last regretful. Not for what I've done to him, but for what I've let him do to me. "Everything, our friendship, my faith in you, has been a mistake on my part. I should never have allowed myself to get so close to someone so clearly unfit for leadership. You're weak, and that will be what destroys you in the end. Even morality cannot save you, and when Kairi learns how hard making the same choices can be, she will turn from you as well."

Very astute— Algoric praises me, but I feel no pleasure, only sadness.

"She will make a great Queen, Genevieve. No matter what you say about her, or believe, I know that. I don't think you can deny it." Lucien says it gently like he's bargaining with me somehow.

"Perhaps, but then she will never belong to you. Not in the way you so clearly need to feel like a man. She's a Queen, Lucien. She will always belong to Aetheria first. To Aro first."

He looks like he might crumple under my words and I realise how raw he must be from my betrayal.

I search for any kind of guilt inside myself, but I cannot find it. I must put the whole before the individual, and he cannot make me feel as if that is the wrong decision, because no matter what he believes morally, it is logically the right choice.

Once upon a time, I think he might have had a chance, but now— after everything, after feeling the sting of his abandonment and being discarded as though I mean nothing, I'm stone.

"Now, if you'll excuse me, I have a speech to make and an army to raise." I turn on my heel, leaving him in silence with his depressed and self-loathing thoughts.

As I emerge from the dungeons, I walk, navigating the labyrinth of the Solis Castra right through the enormous bustling kitchens, so much more alive than the Astrid Keep had ever been.

I feel the eyes of Nephilim watching me, judging me as my pale skin and bloody roots pick me out as other, as unknown, as dangerous.

I know I will never be loved by the Sephilim or the Nephilim, or the Equinians, or the Fae, but I can be loved by the Draconians, by their fierce hearts and loyal souls. I can be what they need, and so I will take the burden on my shoulders and do what I must to keep us all safe, to make the better life I had foreseen when I turned down Midas' offer of alliance all those years ago.

I climb the spiral staircase to the upper floor, more eyes on my spine as I track through the winding crystal passages overhead. The entire place rattles in all directions with clattering heels and armour from the people moving within, preparing for Aro's coronation no doubt.

I wonder now why Lord Black has managed to do what King Midas failed to so many years ago.

Am I being weak now, compared to then?

Or does the situation feel so different because, after all these years of independence, the Sephilim High Lord has finally understood what Midas never could?

King Midas could never understand that the Draconians didn't need him, and simply expected me to kneel and bow to his every whim. Having proven we are more than capable of surviving, and even thriving after being exiled to Drakos Vale, I hadn't kneeled before Aro even though he'd asked, and yet his respect for my strength only grew.

I wonder if his request was a test, whether he was realising that subservience is great, but is not the only factor to staying alert and at the top of your game as a Monarch.

He is certainly more intelligent than I'd given him credit for, and I wonder if the reason we see eye to eye so suddenly is that both of us realise the other has been duly underestimated.

I exit the Solis Castra after what feels like an endless journey past what could very well be twelve copies of the same painting because the styles are so indistinguishable from one another.

I look overhead, and see the silhouette of a Kensari, perfectly white, leaping between cloud streams and beating its wings with furious purpose.

Must have seen a bird or something—

Reaching the end of the entranceway, which is encased by an entirely over-the-top awning, I take several running steps forward before launching myself into the sky.

The air cools my face as I rise, and turn, correcting my course and heading directly for Drakos Vale.

At last, after centuries of waiting, the Dragons will have a home suited to their needs, and my people a future.

As I feel a wide and triumphant smile cross my face, the cost of such a thing, to me, is simply irrelevant.

LUCIEN

I pace, restlessly, furiously, three steps left, three steps right, the talons of my wings scraping against the hanging amethyst shards overhead with a painful grating noise, only adding to my frustration.

How the hell did I screw this up so completely?

I ask myself this question repeatedly, praying to Hecate for an answer, but none comes. I am probably a disgrace to the Goddess after my lack of leadership and observation after I've so completely destroyed her other blessed Kindred High Born.

How had I missed the fact Genevieve had romantic feelings for me? Am I completely oblivious? How long has she felt that way?

I feel the rage inside me like a blizzard, icy shards pummelling the insides of my ribs, and slam my palm into the gold of the cell's bars with a mirroring fury. My hand throbs with pain yet again and I grit my teeth against it, breath coming raw and sharp in my lungs.

I thought I had accepted Kairi's choice—

I had looked into her eyes and seen that it wasn't about me, it was about her and what she felt she needed to do to live with herself. I thought I was able to let go.

But I haven't. Maybe I can't. Maybe it is impossible to surrender someone you truly love into the hands of a monster, even if it's what they're asking for.

I had seen her, splayed face down across my hallway with her hair around her in a messy puddle, Genevieve standing over her with her arm still raised and a dagger clutched in her palm. I want to say what I saw on her face was a look of shock at what she'd done, but honestly, it was a look of grim finality, an acceptance of her new course.

I should have protected Kairi better, should have known that letting her answer the door alone was an unnecessary risk. If I hadn't been so foggy from all the sex, I probably would have thought better of it.

The memory of her in my arms feels like a lifetime ago.

Suddenly, I stop, stone still in my cell, a statue amongst cold crystal shards with nowhere to hide from the punishing light.

Exhaustion blankets me, the sleepless night catching up with me and the shock of everything changing so fast hitting me in tandem.

I slump against the sharp wall, the cool steadiness of it a comfort if nothing else. Everything feels so out of control, and I feel powerless.

Looking around me, I realise I don't just feel powerless.

I am powerless.

I slump to my knees, head swimming with melancholy frustration, the sharp edges of crystal biting into my skin.

I bear it, letting myself rest against the spikes, letting my muscles unravel and my head loll forward so it is propped against my knees.

I cover my eyes with the length of my forearm, and let them close, breathing deeply and hoping beyond hope that I might find some relief in sleep.

I awaken to a dream I have often, though I didn't understand its true relevance until extraordinarily recently when I shared it with a mortal girl I had saved from being imprisoned in a high tower and kept captive by a cruel king.

It seems like so long ago now as I watch multicoloured bunting flapping in the lilac-scented Soleus air, the breeze stirring up tiny tornadoes of aether and making them glitter.

The sounds meld together as a joyous cacophony, the smells making my mouth water immediately. Bright colours and smiling faces pepper the crowd that is also a myriad of fine clothing and upbeat chatter.

It's nothing like anything I've ever seen in Aetheria in reality, but it's what I have wanted for the realm ever since the thought of true continental cooperation and alliance had first struck me. From that day I no longer wanted to be a Draconian, I wanted to be an Aetherian, and I wanted the same inclusivity for all the Kindred. We are created by a single council, but we exist as separate entities, torturing ourselves as we seem doomed to repeat clawing open the wounds which cleave us apart over and over.

Stalls stand in concentric circles, the entire market becoming one enormous spiral of sensation and spirit.

I stand, as usual, in awe at the vivacity, at the pure unbridled life of the diverse collision of cultures.

The Equinians have brought armour and fine jewellery pieces, alcohol, recreational drugs, and their best pegasi and Unicorns to compete in different aerial displays and dressage events judged by a mixed panel of judges.

The Draconians, their quarter of the market being the furthest out toward the edge, houses several stalls of winter wear which is warm like none you'll find anywhere else. It is being sold in exchange for a universal currency which means all continents can be on an equal economic footing and I watch as Anastasia, reading the palm of a Sephilim takes coins I don't recognise in hand.

Dragons, some of the smallest and more docile, are sitting lazily beneath the midday sun on the outskirts as Kindred of all kinds pay their riders for a lap around Soleus. Other stalls hold root vegetables, handcrafted furniture, furs, and some even offer sleigh rides powered by spectral mountain dogs that pant heavily in the warmer climate. The stall with the dogs is busy as always, the Fae finding joy in running their elegant fingers through long white fur and tossing cuts of meat into waiting jaws.

The Fae themselves have the space most central to the spiral market, their contributions far more than just produce as their best actors, singers, and poets perform to standing ovations from Equinians, Sephilim, Draconian, and their own kind. Fashion shows also run periodically, with a diverse selection of models displaying brand-new couture collections that elicit gasps and applause. Near the runways and accompanying seating, one of the largest stalls in the entire market sells handbound leather books finished with flourishes of gold leaf, painstakingly printed, and illustrated by hand from original copies stored in their enormous and comprehensive library.

The Nephilim and Sephilim occupy a mid-space in between the Equinians and Fae, winged ladies selling their lacework, wine, and tapestries amongst individuals who will busk on gleaming golden harps. They also sell hand-crafted desserts, recipe books, crystal talismans, and will allow brave on-lookers to approach some of the more gently inclined Kensari for a kindly rub between the ears.

I see her then, wide lilac eyes reaching out beneath fluttering jewel-toned canopies and capturing me immediately.

I watch as she pushes through the crowd, trying to take it all in as her rushed steps close the distance between us. As she finally carves a path through the distracted trail of wandering browsers, I notice what it is that made me so sure I wasn't seeing a mere simulation of her.

She's still wearing my pyjamas.

"Lucien!" she cries out, but none of the bystanders so much as turn to see who spoke.

She hurls herself into my body, snaking her arms around the back of my neck and holding me into her like I might evaporate.

"You're dream walking!" I exclaim in a shocked voice, and she nods, biting down on her bottom lip as she takes a step back, releasing me.

"I had to try! I had to talk to you, to let you know about Genevieve! She's going to try and take Sapphire City from the Equinians, Lucien, you have to stop her!" Kairi has wide eyes, and I feel momentarily mystified.

"But you didn't want to go to war—" I speak, watching the world continue to vibrate around us with constant motion, noise, and light.

"I didn't want people to die, Lucien. Now the Equinians are in danger, they need help. You know they're no match for the Dragons, at least not alone, and maybe not even then!" Her lips tremble desperately as she reaches out to touch my shoulder.

"I'm sorry about the things I said— to Aro, I thought it might stop him torturing you at the very least— If he knew, Lucien— how much you mean to me— and I couldn't stand—" Tears come in a messy torrent, streaming down her face and she shakes her head, bringing a small pale hand up to her flush bottom lip.

"I know, it's alright. I understand." I remember how painful the cut of her words had been, and the part of me that hates myself had wanted to believe them, even though my heart was telling me she was acting to try and stop me from getting hurt.

"Did you know about Genevieve?" Kairi asks, and I shake my head.

"I had no clue, not even a slight indication— if I'd have known— I just, I can't understand what she's thinking. I can't understand how she can even contemplate an alliance with the Sephilim after what they did to her—" I find my exasperation and shock morphing into a loss of words, into a breakdown of speech so I sound as fragmented as I feel.

"You mean, after what we did to her?" Kairi asks me, sighing.

I grip her hands in mine, the navy cotton of my pyjamas turning her pale amongst the glittering aether of Soleus's high noon.

"Kairi, that's not true. You and I didn't mean for any harm to come to anyone," I protest but Kairi shrugs, her wings oddly absent from her dreamwalking form, while mine still cast enormous shadows over my shoulders and down onto her face.

"We didn't mean for any harm to come, but I don't think Genevieve cares what we wanted to happen. What happened to Algoric, it was the result of our choices. I can see how her hatred can be twisted by someone like Lord Black, he's manipulative. I should know, he manipulated me so completely when I first came here, I thought he was coming to sweep me off my feet and into a pain-free existence, remember?" She blushes slightly, obviously still embarrassed by her naivety. I look at her with grim resolution.

"At least you got the pain-free life—" I grasp her hand in mine.

"Did I though?" she asks me, a small, sad smile crossing her petal-soft lips. I want to kiss her so badly then, but I can tell she's thinking the same thing, and that we both also know if we start kissing, we may never be able to stop.

Distracting from the tension growing between us, Kairi turns to look around her.

"This is incredible— what is this?" she asks me, and I shrug.

"This is the vision I have for Aetheria. A realm where we are one people, no matter what God or Goddess blessed us as immortal. You can see all the races are represented, they all bring unique parts to the whole and make it stronger— I guess you weren't the only one who was naïve—" I muse, the bitterness of losing her again too much to bear. I try to distract myself with the smell of exotic Equinian spices, of Soleus' best wine, and yet the only thing I truly care about is the small whiff of lavender and hay floating from the skin of the angel next to me.

I watch as she takes in the marketplace, a small flush rising to her cheeks as her eyes sparkle with that same awe I saw the very first day I took her aboard my sleigh.

Mon ange.

Pour toujours mon ange—

"I'm sorry this all got so ugly, so fast. I wanted more time—" I admit, squeezing her hand in mine.

I wonder if I'm really touching her, or if it's all in my head.

If it is, does this count as our last meeting?

"We'd always want more time, Lucien. It's never enough with you, for me." Kairi sighs, her eyes fearful. "I have to go," she pulls away from me and rather than the panic I thought I'd feel, I feel resolve.

I want to serve her, to make her proud, to help her cause in every way I can.

"I know. I will do my best to protect the Equinians, and if you need anything else, you know you can always reach me this way— even if it's not— you know, the same," I breathe in deeply, and she nods, trying to keep her emotions in check.

She turns to me, reaching up on tiptoes and planting a silken kiss on my cold cheek.

"I love you, Lucien," she breathes in my ear.

Then, as quickly as smoke flees from the spark of its passionate birth, she is gone.

I stand there alone, the only one able to see and savour a dream that can never be real.

26

LITTLE WOMEN

<u>KAIRI</u>

GETTING UNDRESSED BECOMES A group event, with a guard accompanying Dawn into my suite-slash-prison-cell to remove my cuffs so I can get out of Lucien's pyjamas and ready for the ceremony.

Once I've been stripped and wrapped in a silk robe, all the while being 'supervised' by that same bored-looking Sephilim, I'm re-cuffed, this time with the amethyst bangle I had been grounded by during my time at the Fledgling academy. It sits around my ankle, heavy and cold.

Dawn sits me down in front of the vanity, covering the pristine white silk of my robe with an enormous black velvet cape that ties around the back of my neck. She then sets to work with quick and nimble fingers.

It takes me back to my first night here, to the way I had felt like a princess.

Now I feel like a prisoner.

As she begins to mist my hair so it is damp and easier to style, I hear the guard leave, closing the door behind him with an unnecessary bang.

I can't say I blame him for being bored, I'm bored too, and my dream-walking experience with Lucien hasn't helped calm me one bit.

His vision had startled me, the detail with which it had come to life before my eyes setting me entirely off-kilter. I ached, as I was immersed in the sensory soup of what Aetheria could become, my hunger for it to morph into reality forming a kind of lust I don't know how to describe. I only know I had felt it once before when I was sick. It was the longing for a different life, the disappointment that comes from seeing the potential within yourself withering to dust due to circumstances beyond your control.

Dawn draws my hair back so it is fully behind my shoulders, lying in a damp tangle between my wings and casting the aroma of roses into the air surrounding us. I'm sitting in the same position where she had first gone through this same process with me, and I'm struck with more nostalgia as our eyes meet in the mirror.

"You came back—" Dawn whispers, her eyes dropping from mine the second I see sadness entering the purple of her irises. She takes a comb of solid gold, inlaid with quartz roses, and begins to separate my hair into sections.

"Did you know I would?" I ask, hands clammy beneath the heavy velvet of the cape.

"I hoped, but I didn't know," she relinquishes and I nod, not feeling offended by her intention, only supported as she places the comb between her teeth and begins styling.

"Are you sure this is what you want?" she asks suddenly.

I shrug.

"No. I'm not, but I feel like I'm supposed to be here. I can't explain it, I just know I couldn't live with myself if any more people died because I ran away," I explain, and she looks almost bereft.

"That's a very noble reason for returning, I know it cannot have been easy for you. I'm glad, not for Lord Black's agenda, but for mine, as selfish as that might sound." Her words cause me to blink at myself in the mirror a few times, confused.

She quickly changes the subject.

"So, how did you come to be here? I didn't see you fly in— so I assume you conducted?" she enquires, blonde hair gleaming in the sunlight of encroaching dusk like honeyed wheat.

"Well, actually, I was captured. Genevieve, High Lady Thomas, she hit me around the back of the head and then brought me here with her accompanying Sephilim guard," I explain, glad the dull throb in the back of my skull has subsided as Dawn runs the teeth of the comb against my scalp, separating further sections for braiding.

"Pardon?" Dawn asks, her eyes shooting from the nape of my neck to my gaze in the mirror.

"Lady Thomas, she struck a bargain with Lord Black. I was the price she paid," I explain, and Dawn blinks, dumbstruck for a moment as her wings go stone still, an unusual feat for any Nephilim.

"So— The Sephilim and The Draconians— they're working together?" she asks, and I wonder if she thinks I'm concussed.

Not that I blame her.

"Genevieve and Aro are at least. Lucien, well, he got himself captured trying to stop them from taking me. He's in the dungeons. I don't suppose you've seen him?" I ask, but she merely shakes her head.

"No, I haven't. I haven't seen Lady Thomas either, now you mention it," she adds.

I sigh.

"She'll be on her way to gather the others. I believe they're going to attempt an invasion of Sapphire City," I inform her. She inhales sharply, eyes wide as her fingers braid my hair quickly.

"I cannot do anything about that, but I must get you through this ceremony. Do you know what is involved?" she asks and I shake my head only a little so I don't disturb her progress.

"You will be made to give an official address to the people of Soleus, announcing who you intend to Crown. I'm sure Lord Black has something pre-prepared for you. Then, we will adjourn to the vault beneath The Temple of Zeus where the crown is kept. You will have your anklet removed so your power is not under any interference once you step inside. You cannot conduct in or out of the vault, so there's also no chance of your escape once you pass over the threshold."

She looks hastily back over one shoulder at the door, as if she's afraid someone might barge right in without knocking.

"You will be expected then to lift the crown from its pedestal and place it on the head of the next Aetherial King. Aro Black will be the only male in the room for this reason, though he will have guards stationed just outside the door. Me, Trinity, Vail, and Silver have volunteered to be your witnesses as we were most involved with your training." Dawn continues to explain, and I find myself surprised to hear Silver's name. I have never even met her, so I'm confused about how she's been 'involved' in my training exactly.

"I'm afraid," I whisper to Dawn as silence threatens to fall between us, leaving me alone with my thoughts, with my dreams of Lucien and of what Aetheria might have been.

Would it have been worth the deaths of thousands of Kindred?

I don't know, and I don't know if I'm supposed to. All I know is that I'm doing what I can with the power I have. Isn't that all anyone can ask?

"I know, Kairi." Dawn breathes, placing a warm and comforting palm on my velvet-covered shoulder. "You'd be a fool if you weren't."

It takes another hour to get my mask of flawless regality plastered on, and then, within a blur of silk undergarments and scratchy lace, I'm standing in front of the mirror in Storm's wedding gown, trembling.

My wings flutter with my anxiety, my lashes trembling within their thick mascara. My eyes water, but I can't let my make-up run.

Staring at myself, I find the pristine pale skin lacquered in shimmering powders and aromatic oils, my eyes are framed dark, made wide and innocent by shimmer and liner, my lips a rosy pout of naïve virgin baby pink, begging to be kissed.

I'm stunning, and it disgusts me.

I don't want to be beautiful; I want to be seen and understood.

Skin has never seemed so shallow.

A knock at the door startles me and Dawn, who I only now notice is wearing a far more chaste gown than usual with an enormous billowing skirt, paces the length of the room to open the door with a bowed head.

It isn't Aro, though I don't know why I expect it to be. Why would he come and collect me when he could just send someone? After all, to him, I am a means to an end.

I had been undoubtedly relieved that Dawn had not mentioned a wedding ceremony during the layout of the coronation, and yet I cannot help but be concerned about the ramifications of this small step being skipped.

The other Heirbound had married their chosen future Kings before crowning them, so I wonder why Aro has decided this step is unnecessary when he's insisting on observing the rest of this dog and pony show. Also, I cannot help but worry how the lack of the title wife will affect my ability to keep him from destroying everything he touches.

Will I even see him after I've crowned him King?

He wanted me at his side before, but what if he decides to throw me in the dungeon and be done with it?

I feel stupid as I turn, sweeping across the room in the enormous V-necked ball gown with a train longer than is necessary. The collar comes up high under my throat, my hair draped and braided solely to hide my pointed Fae ears for as long as possible.

Why did I think I could leash Lord Black?

Why did I assume I could stop him?

I'm only one person, and I have no idea what I'm doing!

What if I get everyone killed? What if—

Catticus' words come back to me then.

The world is a dark place, Kairi, and we can only do the best we can with the strength and information we have at the time— Hindsight is an illusion of control that simply doesn't exist.

The echo of the lion's rumbling declaration meets the memory of Lucien's gaze as he told me he believed in me, believed I could succeed.

This is all that keeps me grounded as I slide a mask of indifference over my make-up, getting into the role of Heirbound as uncomfortably as I had this damn wedding dress.

The lace rubs my skin raw as I move within the strict confines of the corseted bodice, Dawn waiting for me to pass her so she might gather my train in her arms.

Together, and with a Sephilim guard of two soldiers close on either side of my body, we begin our journey to meet the future King and address the people of Soleus.

"Ah, Kairi, there you are!" Aro sounds far more jovial than I expect, his tone not laced with smugness or snark, but instead mere excitement. I watch him and find his whole body to be vibrating like he's a child who's had too much sugar.

"Yes, Lord Black. I am here. Shall we get on with it?" I demand. He gives a small smile, gesturing to the enormous room that surrounds us.

"Of course, of course! No time to waste, after all—" He spins on the ball of his foot, wings flaring out from his black morning coat, the fabric damask and the look topped with an indigo cravat. It's held in place by an eye-sized piece of black crystal, and his shirt is the same shade as his jacket and trousers. He swallows all the light in the enormous amethyst receiving room that leads out onto the grand balcony, even his dark dress shoes as matte as they come.

He moves forwards, laying a kiss on my cheek. I go rigid beneath his lips as he lays a palm on my hip, caressing the stiff fabric of the gown fondly like it is an old friend.

I feel eyes on me and stop myself flinching back from his touch by glancing back over my shoulder. Here, two women have just arrived, their gowns identical to Dawn's. She takes her place beside them, and I take in their gowns, each garment ivory to match mine with equally high collars and sprawling skirts, separated from the bodice by glistening rose gold belts. Their hair, glossy black and purest blonde, is piled high on their angelic heads, wings bright in contrast to the washed-out cream hue of their dresses.

I smile at them, spinning from Aro's grasp and making my way over to Trinity and Vail with open arms. They both embrace me with loose fingers and then recoil as they notice Aro watching us.

"Where is the fourth?" he enquires, and I wonder who he means before I remember that Silver was supposed to be here as well.

"Her dress lost a button, she will be along shortly," Trinity replies, squeezing my fingers in hers as I turn back to face the impatient Sephilim.

"We will proceed to the announcement without her then, I cannot leave the people waiting. Security has informed me that almost all the residents of Soleus have turned out to see me. I've had to mobilise more guards than I expected to secure the airspace." He puffs his chest out proudly and I wonder why he's telling us this. Perhaps he merely wants a captive audience for his supposed wins, not caring who it is he's bragging to.

He reaches inside his jacket pocket, pulling from it a thick sheet of parchment. It's embossed with a black fleur dis lis, and I assume it's Aro's personal stationery. The scrawl on the page is what I'd expect from him, inelegant slashing strokes of a quill which make the calligraphy seem violent and cruel. The contrast with the handwriting on the invitation I had received back in my bedroom in Tennessee is startling.

He takes his place at my side, offering me his arm. I grit my teeth and loop my elbow around his, his skin scalding hot against me even through the thick veil of lace and damask between us.

Placing the speech in my free hand, I take a moment to adjust to the heat radiating off the man beside me, silently sweltering within the monstrously over-the-top wedding dress.

I guess what Asher had said about him absorbing Algoric's powers cannot be denied, then. He really can steal power from his victims.

The heat of him gives me the resolve I need to step forward as the double doors are opened by footmen. The unbridled light of the setting Aetherial sun is cast upon me and Aro, leaving nowhere to hide.

As we step briskly across the vast balcony, I see them. The people of Soleus, hovering above the courtyard at the front of the Solis Castra with slow beating wings. There are more people than I expect, the crowd curving around the front of the building in a teeming, undulating ripple of skin and feathers.

There are bodies perched on solid clouds, and couples hand in hand hover both above and below the height of the balcony.

I shield my eyes from the low sun, Aro pulling me forward to the railing and pinching my wrist in warning.

As I adjust to the stark violet of the sky, the cobalt sun a slow sinking orb directly before me, I find faces in the crowd, individual expressions.

It is not what I expected. I thought I would see bored faces or excited smiles, but half the crowd doesn't look glad to see me at all as I thought they would.

The Nephilim look downtrodden, their hands clamped to their husbands who watch with poker-straight spines and tight-lipped concentration.

The sparkling sadness in the hundreds of pairs of purple eyes takes my breath away.

It seems to have the same effect on Aro, though the nuance of their attention is clearly lost on him as he breaks into a wide smile, his pale statuesque face bathing with undeniable pleasure in the glow of both the sunset and the focus of so many people.

He can't possibly be so oblivious as to not see the pain on the Nephilim's faces? Or maybe he isn't looking at them at all, maybe he's too interested in his ascension to realise that half of his people look like they might burst into tears.

"Begin," Aro barks in my ear, his voice unwavering in its command.

I raise the piece of paper so I can read it clearly, and suddenly I feel like I'm giving a eulogy.

Standing there, in a wedding gown I hate, I begin to speak.

"It is with great honour that I would like to inform you all I will be crowning Lord Aro Black as the next King of Aetheria per the lore of the Heirbound, chosen representative of Hera." I breathe in and out, the world around me silent but for the movement of fragrant air and the aether caught within it. "It is my pleasure to have been given the opportunity to play such a role in the great monarchy of Aetheria, and it is with absolute confidence that I shall now proceed to coronate Lord Aro Black by the sacred laws of our people. I would like to thank you all for your support of the crown during the time of uncertainty that is now, at last, coming to an end. Tomorrow, a new dawn will break over Aetheria and bring with it a new King, and a new era of prosperity and dominance for the Sephilim and Nephilim of Soleus. It is my honour to bring this era to fruition by officially crowning a man—" I pause, swallowing and feeling physically sick, "who I believe truly embodies both the strength and stamina required for us to continue along this path of wealth and peace. Thank you."

I lower the piece of paper, having not raised my gaze throughout the entire speech to stop myself from balling it up and throwing it at Aro before attempting to kick him square in the balls, burns be damned.

What I find when I look out over Soleus though, isn't the sun setting on a crowd of people who desperately need Aro's new dawn at all. Instead, I find a crowd of people for whom the sun seems to be setting on their very last hope.

What have I done?

GENEVIEVE

The sound of the war horn, carved from the bone of a Dragon who died long ago in the early years, rattles through my marrow. It is deep and undeniably demands attention, the call of it known to every Draconian, if not in memory then at least in myth. Its bellowing summons will travel through the branches of the firs, across glacial rivers and ascend to the highest peaks of the land, calling all who need it as certainly as Hecate's own siren song.

It has been a long time since I ordered it be sounded, and I'm taken back to a time before Lucien had been reborn, before Algoric found friendship with Ebonara, and when I had felt a similar excitement simmering in my gut.

This time though, the anticipation is not for bloodshed, but for invasion, for freedom, and warmth, sunlight and flight. Now, it is an excitement fuelled by new hope.

The throne room is in chaos, with armoured soldiers, both men and women, clattering through the halls outside, lighting the hearths which have long been pits of cold ash. The sconces are lit by several scurrying Draconians, hurrying from one to the next with blazing silver torches, and the chandelier is being set ablaze overhead for the first time in maybe several hundred years. In fact, I believe the last time it had been touched, lest dusted, was upon Lucien's ascension to High Lord.

I remember that day too, as I uncross my legs from where I'm seated in the cold hold of the alabaster throne. He had looked so young, so hopeful, and I had known the look of optimism in his eyes was soon to be snuffed out by the reality of Drakos Vale and our reputation with the rest of Aetheria.

He believed he could make a difference, and I had believed that he would soon learn this was folly.

I had been wrong, and I curse myself now for not realising how completely malignant his moral righteousness would become.

I let my fingernails drum on the armrest of carved bone, watching as Algoric curls and undulates around the length of my forearm, the cold rush of his blood against my skin soothing in its metronomic and undying rhythm.

I remember when I had last heard the horn, how it preceded the speech which made my people refer to me as a Queen rather than a High Lady. It had been my gift for public speaking, surprising even me after I'd spent so many years in solitude by choice, that had led the people and their Dragons to stand up to Midas, to his incredibly powerful armies and seemingly endless resources.

I wonder, anxiety bubbling just beneath the simmer of my excitement, what my people will think of my latest choice.

Will they revolt? Hate me? Will they look at me as Lucien had, with complete and utter disgust?

They cannot understand the intricacies of being in my position politically, with so much responsibility, and yet I must pull on my secret gift as an orator to once more convince them to raise their swords to the sky for me.

I hope, given that what I've managed to bargain for, a new home and a new life in the best interest of our Dragons, will be enough.

It has to be.

"Shall we start letting people into the Keep, Lady Thomas?" A soldier who I believe to be of high rank approaches me, bowing his helmeted head in respect. As he straightens, his mossy green eyes stare out at me, as curious as they are weathered between the jaws of the Dragon's skull design encasing his head.

"Yes, let them in. Will we be able to fit everyone in here?" I ask, curious myself now.

It's been a long time since I sounded the horn for a gathering this large, and I have never sent a summons to the entire population either. We have grown since the last war, our population protected and booming due to our banishment, the other Kindred races seeing us as no threat and therefore our army suffering no serious number of casualties. We lost maybe fifty after the onslaught of Aro's men during Algoric's capture, but that isn't even enough to make a dent in the true span of our population. It is for this reason, along with the added strength of so many Dragons, that I do not doubt our ability to seize Sapphire City, no matter how well-trained the Artemisian Equinians believe themselves to be.

"I think so, I mean, we might have to open the doors and have the overflow stand in the hall back there. Do you think you can project your voice that far?" the soldier asks, his face anxious to please me.

"Yes," I respond with bland indifference, stroking my lip with my index finger and taking a deep breath. The hot air fills my lungs, my corset constricting my ribcage with a delicious pinch.

"I'll open the doors." The soldier bows again, his crimson leather wings flaring generously out from either side of him. I admire the bloody hue of his talons as he turns on the heel of his armoured boot and walks off, instructing his inferiors to begin showing people in.

I get up as the doors swing forward, exiting the throne room as the sound of an excitable crowd begins to seep in behind me.

I walk up the length of long moonstone corridors, my heartbeat loud in my ears as I realise that this might be the most momentous moment in the history of my entire species.

Have I done the right thing?

I find myself wondering this despite how I'd defended myself to Lucien, my calves burning as I take the steep incline up to my suite at a savage pace, my fury over my indecision powering me forward.

It is too late to go back, not after I've gotten in so deep with Lord Black, but the question is— do I really want to go back?

My gut tightens in an obvious no.

So, I push open the doors to my suite with flat palms, slamming them into the wood and causing them to go flying back on their hinges. The balcony doors have been left open after my last departure, and I find the room cold with air moving around in angry gusts that beat against each of the malachite walls.

Stepping into the chill exterior, the cold lulls me, causing my muscles to relax, to unravel beneath its icy caress.

Walking over to my wardrobe, I unhook the scabbard from around my thigh, tossing it onto the bed with a dull thud. I pull off my boots in turn, the leather still wet with slurry from my landing at the foot of the mountain. Opening my closet, I stare at the array of finery in bare feet, finally catching the clarity I keep grasping at so desperately, my doubts fading into silence.

The only question now weighing on my mind is simple, and I take that to mean I'm making the right choice.

What the hell am I going to wear?

I've settled on a black battle ensemble I haven't donned in hundreds of years. I don't usually wear black, preferring white or jade green, but I know that Lord Black's army will be wearing oxidised steel and I don't want to stand out.

I want there to be no mistake who I have allied with, and I want to relish the shock and awe on the faces of those who never saw it coming almost more than I want Sapphire City.

I've re-braided my hair so it's tight against my skull but then falls free to my shoulders in half-cornrows. I'm encased in an armoured black corset with silver Dragons clasping the front shut, metal scale-mail covering my shoulders and arms all the way to my elbows. The same scale-mail wraps around my waist, draping over the tops of my thighs that are clad in thick black leather for an extra layer of protection.

I take a look at the Dragon brand on my inner wrist, and then at Algoric who is temporarily visible on my other.

Are you ready for this? he demands, his tongue slithering out from between his lips as he tastes the air.

As I will ever be— I sigh internally, looking at the freshly applied dark makeup turning my eyes a sharp emerald and my skin into a death shroud of pallor.

I grab the scabbard from atop the mattress, fastening it around my inner thigh beneath the layer of scale-mail and then take off out of the suite without looking back.

I take the empty passage back down to the throne room in enormous confident strides, my white wings turning my shadow fierce as it follows me, dappling on the moonstone of the walls and shimmering like I might disappear, phantasmal, any second.

When I finally reach the throne room, I hear the chatter of thousands of people before I see them, but when I finally do, exiting the passage via an intricately carved archway, the room falls into desolate silence.

The crowd parts before me as I descend the stairs beyond the entrance, multicoloured leather wingspans rippling as multiple talons catch the light of the newly relit chandelier overhead.

Soft moonlight falls upon them through the stained glass of the windows cut into the mountainside, over furs and tightly braided heads of hair, as I progress toward the centre of the room without pause, letting their eyes linger on me.

Ascending the platform holding my throne, I cross the hematite seal of Hecate as I go and smile at High Lord Gage Lee who is positioned at the very front of the crowd.

I am disappointed when I do not find Anastasia beside him.

Her loss. I think, wondering if I'll receive a similar response from the crowd once I've laid out my plan to invade Eclipsia's capital city. I have no doubt she has seen my betrayal with her foresight by now, and I'm also acutely aware that she almost definitely knows what's become of both Lucien and Kairi.

Where the shame for my betrayal should lie, I feel only scorching control over myself, over the power running through my veins.

Turning, I don't sit upon the throne, instead looking out over the crowd and choosing to stand for my address. I take in a deep breath, and then wanting to waste no more time, I begin.

"I know you are all wondering why I have brought you here, but I am about to explain everything." I press my hands together, feeling the weight of Algoric's invisible body tighten around my wrist.

Breathe, Gen— he reminds me, so I take his advice, inhaling and exhaling in pause before I continue, my voice an uncompromising boom.

"After so many years of banishment, I have finally come to an agreement with the Sephilim which will allow us to work together. Now, before you all panic, this deal is nothing like what Midas proposed. We will still have full autonomy, and the Dragons will be protected. In fact, one of the very reasons I took this deal was because Lord Black has given us the resources we require to relocate. He has permitted us to move into Sapphire City, by force if necessary," I explain and the crowd suddenly stirs, a ripple of confused excitement jumping from person to person like a flea.

"*You're* siding with Lord Aro Black? After he killed Algoric?" It is Gage's voice that rises to challenge me, to say what the rest of my people are thinking. I turn to him.

"I am. Lord Black only killed Algoric because he understood the true power that lies within us as their riders, and was determined to take back what truly belonged to him. It was a hard lesson for me to have to learn, but I know now if it weren't for other High Borns, the Draconians would never have been targeted in this way."

I catch the arctic blue eyes of a blonde woman in the crowd who is nodding slowly in agreement with me. I believe she works as a seamstress in Vega City, though I could most certainly be wrong.

"So, you're saying that the Sephilim want an alliance with us?" Lord Gage asks, and I nod, eyes warming as they bounce between his face and the collective gaze of the onlookers.

"They always have, and any historians among you will know this. They just did not want to give us the respect we were due before. Lord Black is different. Midas could not concede any of his power all those years ago. He was greedy and wanted our alliance without giving in to any of my conditions so he might keep his alliance with the Equinians as well." I remind them, realising by the span of the crowd exactly how many new Kindred have been reborn since those dark days.

Gage looks me in the eye and then breathes out deeply. I wonder what it is he has seen inside me that has made him suddenly relax.

I find confidence in the ease of his face, which becomes boyish as the worry lines on his forehead smooth and his bright eyes urge me to continue.

I straighten, letting my warm palm rest on the hilt of the dagger at my hip, the cool scale-mail brushing my fingertips and keeping me grounded.

"As of right now, we are officially in an alliance with the Sephilim forces under the newly crowned King of Aetheria. His Royal Highness, King Aro Black. His coronation is taking place as we speak, and he has forces to assist us in invading Sapphire City, either peacefully or through force, outside the Solis Castra. They are waiting for us." I swallow, looking out over the wide eyes of my people, trying to gauge their mood.

Unsure even still, I continue.

"This is what we've been waiting for, a better quality of life for our Dragons, and our people, a way off this hunk of frozen rock, and a way to show Aetheria that we will be downtrodden no longer. It is time we take to the skies and show the rest of Aetheria that they made a huge mistake the day they underestimated us and that we will no longer be satisfied with less than the full respect that we deserve. You, my people, are strong, are resilient, loyal, and above all deserving of respect. It is time we rise to new heights. It is time to mount our Dragons with pride, and fly them freely through the skies, casting shadows over our enemies below with no more fear of extinction."

My heart soars as I see people beginning to shift, their faces flushing with passion as eyes twinkle and wings twitch, anxious to follow me into battle, to act under my command.

I fold my arms over my breasts, spread my wings as wide as they will go, and ask them the only question that truly matters.

"Are you with me?

27

MAN'S FATE

LUCIEN

EVERYTHING IS QUIET, TOO quiet.

My stomach is in knots as I pace from one end of the cell to the other, the shards of crystal stabbing the soles of my feet a welcome distraction. I grab hold of the bars, biceps bulging with frantic and frustrated energy that has nowhere to go, looking up and down the blinding hallway.

I'm searching for any kind of security, wondering if I can trick them into giving me any kind of update, but oddly there's no one.

Crack security Lord Black— I muse, wondering where everybody has gone.

Is it time for the coronation already?

Is Kairi crowning that asshole as King of Aetheria right now? Is he touching her? Is she alright?

Seeing her in my dream had been a rude awakening, as even in The Nether my reaction to her had been nothing short of visceral. I remember her pleading eyes, her desperate request for me to try and aid the Equinians, to at least even the odds a little as the Draconian threat over their long-held city looms more imminently dark by the second.

It seems like madness, utter madness, all of it.

How had this all come about so fast? How had Genevieve aligned herself with a long-sworn enemy, Kairi handed herself over to a man she'd been fleeing for what seems like forever, and Sapphire City suddenly become a target? Only yesterday it had seemed impossible that anyone would dare challenge Aliandara.

I feel like I've tumbled down the rabbit hole and ended up in some bizarre un-reality, some wacky alternate dimension where everything I know is wrong and my actions have no effect on anything.

I look up at the bars, to where they connect to the crystal overhead, wondering if the joins there hold any moisture. I could freeze it if so, and use the ice to expand the openings enough to pull the grate free perhaps—

I'm looking for how the seamless metallic panel and wall intersect, trying to find out if it's welded or screwed, when prompt high heels begin to echo down the passageway.

The stride is purposeful and quick, my first thought being that Genevieve has returned to shout at me some more about how utterly self-centred I am.

The woman who appears isn't Genevieve at all though, and the closer she gets to my cell, the more confused I begin to feel. It's a Nephilim woman, a vision in white with silver hair and matching wingspan, a black tangle of fabric thrown over one arm. Her gown is high-necked with an enormous skirt cinched by a glittering rose gold belt at the waist, and at her heels a Kensari I recognise prowls.

Catticus.

I straighten, my brow creasing into a confused furrow as I push my long white hair behind one ear, my wings pulling themselves in tight to my body as I try to seem more put together than I am.

Who the hell is this woman?

She looks behind her, back up the corridor, before sliding her hand beneath the collar of her dress and pulling up a thin metal chain. On its delicate silver links a tiny key dangles, shimmering almost painfully gold in the light.

Taking it in hand, she moves, biting down on her bottom lip in concentration as she slips the key into the lock, turning it and yanking the door open with gusto.

"Well, come on! I haven't got time for you to be standing there like an utter tool—" she complains, her gown and the black garment on her arm rustling with her impatience. I feel my eyes widen as Catticus paces impatiently, having never seemed so purely white as he does beneath the glow of the walls.

The Nephilim withdraws the key, glaring at me and my distracted gaze as she claps her hands together.

"Spit spot, Draconian! Jesus, I knew you were dumb but this is—"
I cut her off, striding through the doorway and into the corridor,
grateful to be back on smooth flooring.

"Who are you? Did Kairi send you?" I ask her, and she shakes her
head.

"I'm Silver, and no. I wasn't sent by Kairi, exactly. Though her
Kensari has been following me around like a kicked puppy trying to
get me down here so I have no doubt she has some idea you're to be
freed—" she explains, her tone imperious and her features stony yet
undeniably beautiful.

Catticus growls at her, nipping the fingertips of her free hand with
his maw as she slips the key and chain back over her head and moves
with quick fingers to hide it once more beneath her gown.

"How did you get that?" I ask her, feeling suspicious even of her
supposed help. She hands me the black cloak draped over her arm,
and I throw it over my shoulders, donning the hood so it shrouds my
face in welcome shadow.

"That's for me to know and you to not. Now hurry, we have to get
you out of here before the coronation ceremony begins—" she adds,
her voice a little strained.

I feel a wave of nauseous relief crash over me.

"Yes, of course. We have to get to Kairi. We have to stop it," I urge
her, meeting Catticus' eyes and feeling a steel resolve form within my
gut.

I have no time to be scared of the consequences now, all I know is
I must act—

"Uh, no. You're needed elsewhere. Kairi is where she's supposed to
be right now, trust me on this. We need to get you to Drakos Vale, to
find out what's going on with High Lady Bitch of Hecate," she spits.

I ball my fists, feeling oddly defensive of Genevieve after everything.

"Don't call her that," I snap, sighing and feeling my stress levels
begin to reach critical mass.

"Well, what would you call her? Saint Genevieve? She's going to kill
thousands of Equinians just so she has a better parking spot for her
sky lizards," Silver retorts, her metallic irises sheening almost white
with her fury.

"Look, I know you might not see this, but it's more complicated
than just—" I begin, but she shakes her head, raising a finger to me
and causing me to fall silent in exasperation.

"I don't have time to walk through the moral badness of mass murder with you Draconian, I've been sent down here to get you out, and we don't have a lot of time before someone notices I'm missing. Now, are we going, or should I lock you back up? At this point, I don't give a shit."

She's so prim in appearance, but she has a mouth like a sailor and it makes my lips curl into a smile. I pause a few seconds, before nodding reluctantly in agreement with her plan.

"You're sure there's no way I can get Kairi out?" I ask her, and she shakes her head.

"She's where she needs to be, and it's more complex than you'll ever understand. Even if I thought you could get her out without getting both of you killed, I wouldn't allow it. There's a bigger picture here that you can't see, not yet at least." Her words make me wonder, but I know I don't have time to ask her what the hell she's inferring, let alone the time to ask her to explain it to me. As if she would.

"Let's go then," I assert, and she loops her arm through mine, the pristine white of her gown making me look slightly tanned for once.

"Get back to Sapphire City," she tells the Kensari, slinging the words over her shoulder carelessly.

I hear the enormous, winged lion turning, his paws barely audible on the crystal, but before I can watch him go, the world around me dissolves into a fork of pure, blinding light.

We reappear just outside the entrance to the Astrid Keep that lies the farthest from its peak, right at the foot of the enormous summit.

"Well, I've outdone myself. I'd have been happy with anywhere in Drakos Vale, given my hazy mental picture came from books, but it seems I've gotten you near civilisation as well," she raises a hand for a high five, but I merely stare at her, disoriented as I'm suddenly standing, barefoot in the snow.

It doesn't bother me like it would someone without cryomancy skills, but I feel myself stiffen as icy fingers climb up the back of my legs, frantic energy running through me. The dark velvet of the cape covering my wings swishes around my calves, and I pull it closed over my chest, hiding my tattoos in case someone recognises me.

"No? Just going to leave me hanging up here all alone, whatever—" Silver drops her hand with a shrug, sick of waiting for me to high-five her, and then goes to turn to leave.

"Wait!" I call after her and she pauses, turning back with thick lashes that are beginning to catch snow.

"Yes?" she asks, her tone condescending as hell.

I feel ridiculous.

"What—what do you expect me to do?" I feel out of sorts, both from the conduction and the fast-moving pace of events.

"Well geez, I don't know DeLaurent. They're your people. I was just enlisted to bust you out. Anyway, I have to get back, I'm expected for the ceremony." The flippant way she uses my last name causes me to warm to her without my consent.

I breathe out, running my hand back through my hair.

"Right, yes—of course. Thanks," I wave to her as I wallow in feeling like an utter moron, but she only gives a curt nod, not bothering to reply.

Then, in a flash of lightning that recedes as quickly as it came, she's gone and I'm alone.

I pad up to the front doors, my feet numb from the cold, letting myself inside as quietly as I can manage.

I do so slowly, expecting to find guards, but I don't.

Instead, I find an empty hallway.

Where is everyone? I wonder, scratching my brow with a cold hand as I nudge the door shut behind me.

I ponder which route to take, looking instinctively to my left at the slope which leads, at length, to the throne room.

I guess if she's gathering people, that's where I'd expect her to be, and them as well. It would certainly explain why there's no one guarding the entrance. Though, after making a bargain with Aro, I guess Genevieve doesn't have so many enemies to worry about any longer.

I stride across the small receiving room, beginning my climb up through the base of the mountain, finding to my surprise that hearths that have long since been dead are roaring with healthy flame. The heat seeps out into the air, the stone swallowing some but not all as I get closer and closer to the throne room, relief enveloping me as I find each corridor as deserted as the last.

As I reach the penultimate landing, I make sure my body is fully shrouded in the cloak, my hair pulled back and hanging flat against my spine so nobody can use a loose lock to identify me. I pull the hood down further, dropping my gaze to the floor, and then make my final ascent toward the corridor leading to the throne room.

As I reach said corridor, I realise that I should not have been so worried about being recognised. The crowd spills out of the double doors, which have been thrown wide open to allow for what must be almost our entire population. Everyone is facing the throne, and as I creep towards the back row of Draconians, nobody even acknowledges I've arrived. They're all too transfixed by Genevieve's booming voice as it echoes out far and wide.

I slip sideways, pressing myself close to the wall beside a statue and sconce flickering with warm and foreign flame, listening to what has so enraptured the crowd.

"Are you with me?" I hear Genevieve's voice cry, her passion both terrifying and somehow encouraging.

I haven't heard her so enthusiastic in months, so at least there's that.

The crowd erupts in a deafening cheer, a roar of support and pride in both Genevieve's plan, and in her as a ruler.

I'm stunned at their reaction, at how they've been so easily convinced to go and invade a city that is in no way theirs by right. I thought I knew my people better than this, but it seems they're far angrier than I thought.

I suppose I'm young, and the wounds of the Sephilim-Draconian conflict, which so deeply cut into the individuals who fought and lost both loved ones and Dragons, are impossible for me to truly understand. Genevieve has reiterated this to me over and over.

Then again, is that an excuse for killing yet more people?

Is there really such an eye for an eye mentality among the Draconians?

I didn't want to believe it but seeing them so willing to invade, I find it hard to deny.

The crowd suddenly begins to morph into a flurry of activity, as Genevieve stops speaking and the people start to disperse so they can prepare for immediate mobilisation. I press myself into the wall harder as the thrum of leathery wings grows louder and the bodies begin to flow back out of the doors.

Then, sidestepping and keeping my head bowed, I slip behind the open door, hiding away and watching the crowd from a distance, not sure what I'm waiting for, but trusting my instincts.

Suddenly, I see a familiar silhouette emerge from the hall, and a thick and desperate urge to reach out to him clutches at me.

Surely, he will understand my reasoning on this, after all, he's even younger than I am, and he feels things so deeply—

I'm contemplating how to get his attention when suddenly he stills among the throngs of energised people. An obvious, still-standing stone resisting the current of the crowd.

Turning slowly, his eyes fix on where I'm standing, hiding in the shadow of the door between its wide-flung extension and the wall. He walks over to me, careful not to draw any attention to himself as he slips into the gap between us.

"What are you doing, hiding?" he asks me, confused.

His metallic teeth glint in the half-light as he speaks.

"Look, I've come to stop this. Genevieve handed me over to Lord Black, had me locked up in their dungeons for Hecate's sake. She's lost her damn mind, Gage." I explain, gesticulating wildly.

Gage sighs.

"No Lucien, I don't think she has. You know I can feel her emotions. She believes this is what is best for the Draconians— and I do too." I stare at him, dumbfounded.

"You can't be serious—" I stutter, but he shrugs.

"I can feel your emotions too, remember? And I can feel that your concern lies with Kairi, not with the Draconians," he accuses me, unblinking in the shadows.

"So, you're happy to go and kill thousands of people? You're happy to go and take part in this— invasion?" I demand, disgust running rampant over my face.

"If it means Aqua has a better quality of life, of course, I am. What have the Equinians ever done for us? It's time we got what's coming to us, Lucien. It's long since due, and I think you'll find the rest of the Draconians feel the same way. We're sick of being beaten down, of always being an afterthought because of what happened hundreds of years ago between Genevieve and a King who is long since dead. What she is doing is brave. It's putting her people above her pride."

I baulk at him, my prodigy, feeling sick.

"I expected more from you—" I say in a small voice, feeling disgusted as I shuffle on the balls of my feet, the heat in the crowded space making me feel uncomfortable.

Looking at me with sad eyes, Gage simply shrugs before turning to leave.

"And I you, Lucien," he calls back over his shoulder in a wistful tone. The disappointment of one so young, of one I had taught, cuts me deeper than I thought possible.

I stand there in the dark, thinking of his words long after he's gone, long after the people have dispersed and flown off to collect their armour and weapons. They will return soon, I have no doubt, for their Dragons, so I must act quickly.

Act quickly and do what though? It seems as though the reinforcements Kairi had wanted me to summon don't exist.

I think back, wracking my brains, stuck to the spot and slumping against the wall with indecision and uncertainty.

Then I realise there is one person I haven't seen leave. One person who might still be willing to fight against Genevieve.

It's a small chance, but it's the only idea I have, and I don't know who else to turn to.

I bide my time in the shadows, intending to find Ebonara, and then take to the skies in search of further reinforcement.

KAIRI

Being stuffed into the carriage next to Aro, I find it far less roomy than the last time we had been sat side by side within it. It is, I believe, the same carriage that he used to bring me into the City of The Sephilim for the very first time, so it feels kind of cyclical that we're in it once again on the way to his coronation.

The same white stags that had pulled the carriage before make another appearance as well, and all is silent between us as the rhythmic fall of their hooves on the crystal road travel back through the open window.

I peer out, finding the crowd of Nephilim and Sephilim watching with mixed expressions. Some of the Nephilim look awed, while others can't hide their disgust. The Sephilim seem indifferent almost, straightening and bowing their heads in respect as the vehicle passes through the outskirts of Eaglecrest. I can't tell what they think of my choice, other than the fact it is and has always been, the way of things for those chosen for the throne to be utterly out of their hands.

The carriage judders over a small divot in the road, and both myself and Aro lurch forward, our hands touching by accident for only a second.

It's enough.

I flinch away, the disgust I feel at the heat of his skin too much to bear.

He smiles at me, the charming façade he had seduced me with covering the cruelty I know lies beneath completely and without tell. I realise as I stare into his eyes, into the utter lack of malice within them at this very second, that I hadn't been as easily duped as I'd thought. He seems like an entirely different person.

"You're very quiet," he notes, not looking at me but instead turning to peer out of the small window, the drapes pulled aside. He gives a small and measured wave to the onlooking crowd, basking in the occasion.

I swallow, feeling my throat tighten as if my whole body is willing me to remain silent.

"What did you expect, a musical number?" I mutter, resting my chin in my palm as I too peer out the window just so I don't have to look at him.

"I would have thought that given we will be spending a lot of time with one another; you might try and make some sort of conversation. But perhaps I was wrong. Maybe you really do want to end up in the dungeons with the Draconian—" His words irritate me immensely, and I wonder exactly how he thought I would want to talk about anything with him. I shrug, sighing, before choosing a topic I know might be sensitive on purpose, just to spite him.

"So, if you're so big and powerful, why the hell do you need a stupid hunk of metal anyway?" I demand, turning to him now and refusing to blink as I stare into the pits of his eyes.

"Maybe it isn't about me needing anything, maybe it's about wanting to prove I won't let some Nephilim bitch run from me and get away with it. You stood up in front of everyone and you exposed me, Kairi. That cannot go unpunished—" he snarls, his face contorting so it's almost unrecognisable from the man he had been only moments before.

"So, it's not even about the crown— it's about your own pathetic ego then—" I mutter, and Aro breathes in deeply.

"Don't get me wrong, being officially King in a way that nobody can challenge is a bonus. If you haven't noticed it also makes that Goddess who blessed you look rather stupid—" he laughs and I cock my head.

"You think just because of some ceremony that nobody will challenge you? Do you honestly think that there'll be no consequences for your actions? To obtain me, you had to make a bargain with a Draconian High Lady that has never been a fan of yours, and not only that, but it will also piss off some rather skilled warriors of Artemis if I'm not mistaken—" I stare at him with all the intensity I can muster.

"Haven't you been watching, Kairi? Nobody will challenge me because nobody has challenged me. By the time they get wind of what I have planned, it'll be too late." His face is the ugliest thing I've ever seen in that moment, not because of his features, but because of his self-assured smug smile.

I ball my fists at my side, clenching my jaw and reminding myself that I'm not doing this for him. I'm doing it for the Nephilim, and to stop as many people from dying as I can.

I don't know how I'm going to do that yet, but I have done all I can in sending Catticus to aid Lucien in getting help to Sapphire City before it is too late.

I think back on the meeting where Aliandara had made it clear that she expected me to sacrifice myself so she didn't have to lose any of her warriors. Then I wonder why I care about what happens to her so much.

She saved me, but it seems that was only so I could be offered up as a sacrifice at a later date.

I'm thinking about this, about the entire conundrum, when the carriage pulls to a stop, and Aro grabs my hand between his fingers, tiny electric shocks striking in painful pinpricks up my arms.

He kicks open the carriage door with his dress shoe and then descends the small golden ladder which promptly falls to the ground below. Pulling me after him, we both step into the shadow of the floating island that houses the temple of Zeus, my eyes cast skyward in guttural dread, and Aro's in undeniable glee. Clouds swirl around its pointed base, thick and ominous.

Shouldn't I feel more content, having fought to be here, to make this sacrifice so nobody else had to suffer?

I had asked Catticus if I was making the right choice, and he said that only I could know that. The problem is, I'm not sure what I'm supposed to trust, my heart— or my head.

Aro looks to me, his face deadly pale, hand tight on mine so the bones feel as though they might turn to dust, gesturing with his head that I should prepare for take-off as his wings spread sideways in two jet sprays of feathers.

I feel him bend and then leap off the ground, tugging me after him before I have a chance to prepare. I sag slightly at first, floundering to get my wings extended and then get myself at an equal height as we rise above the roofs of Eaglecrest and ascend toward the floating island, dodging through clouds thick enough to stand upon.

We glide, side by side, and land in the garden of oak trees, greeted by the four witnesses and a party of two guards. Silver has joined Trinity, Vail, and Dawn, who all look at me with cold gazes that give nothing away. I whisk my mask back into place, the haphazard take-off having made it slip as I worried about falling from Aro's grip, or more likely being dropped.

The Temple of Zeus stands tall in the early night, its white marble made luminous by the moon as we stride quickly and without pause up the shallow steps and into the enormous entrance hall.

Beyond it, I see what I had not had time to glimpse the last time I had been here, an enormous statue of Zeus mirroring the one of Hera in my own temple. Zeus's face is all-powerful, and ugly in its masculinity as veins have been made to bulge from otherwise smooth stone by the sculptor. The statue looms overhead, as Aro's clutch on my hand remains aggressively firm and we grow closer with every step.

As we reach the statue's sandalled feet, I cannot help but stare up into the face of the God who had made the Sephilim the way they are, had chosen them for their power lust above all else.

Aro then nods to the guards, who take one of my arms each in a restraint which I deem entirely unnecessary. Then walking forward and undoing one of his cufflinks before using the pinpoint of it to slash the inside of his palm. His gasp of pain is short but a welcome sound to my ears. Waiting, I watch with curiosity as he places his bloodied hand on the edifice.

I hear the familiar grate of stone upon stone, reminding me of the seal of Hecate in the throne room of The Astrid Keep.

As Aro descends a set of stairs that have appeared, I see that one of the stone panels at the base of the statue has slid back, revealing a secret entrance. I'm ushered in after him, shoved by the guards so I trip on my ridiculously high heels, stumbling down the uneven and archaic stone steps.

When we arrive in the passage below, I see it stretches in two directions, one infinitely far in front of me, and the other behind. I wonder where both lead, but I'm not given the opportunity to ask.

Instead, I'm firmly swivelled one way without pause, so I'm walking back the direction I've come, only I'm twenty feet beneath the temple instead of inside it.

The passage is dusty, with small piles of aether gathered in the sliver between the paving slabs of the passage and its bare stone walls. It smells of stagnant air, and despite the flickering sconces every few yards a chill runs up my arms as a breeze runs through the tunnel and tickles the nape of my neck.

After a few moments of trailing behind Aro's crisp silhouette, we reach an enormous golden door. Central to its design is an enormous chunk of amethyst and on either side of its flickering facets wings extend the width of the door. I hear the procession of gentle footsteps behind me come to a halt, and then watch as Aro reaches inside his jacket and pulls out an elaborate yet archaic-looking key.

It glints as he holds it up to the light, making sure he has it the correct way around before sliding it into a slot that to an untrained eye would be invisible among the intricate decoration. As the golden door is pushed back and opens, squealing on its centuries-old hinges, Aro beckons me forward and over the threshold.

I feel physically sick as I do as he insinuates, but swallow it down, straightening my spine and trying to recite all the reasons I'm standing here.

I tread carefully, eyes darting around the inside of the vault and finding heaps of gold coins, randomly scattered precious stones, and other treasures piled ceiling-high in the small round room. Central to it all, lies the object that has caused so much pain and suffering, the object which had caused Aro to pursue me in the first place.

The crown of Aetheria.

It's sitting on a cushion upon a pedestal shrouded in pure light that comes from no discernible source. As I take it in, the hairs on my arms and the back of my neck stand to attention. In fact, I'm so busy staring at the golden headpiece, interlaced with amethyst and rose quartz, that I barely even notice Aro removing the cuff around my ankle.

I look at him, blinking, confused.

"I won't risk your power being tampered with in any way. You can't conduct in or out of here anyway, so don't even try it," he warns me, twiddling the heavy crystal anklet around his index finger with practised swagger. I feel myself wilt a little, knowing I can't get out, knowing I'm trapped despite the fact Dawn had warned me of what was to come.

I chose this, I know that, but it doesn't make it any easier.

There's a shuffling of people as the rest of the procession enters the room. Dawn gives me a comforting squeeze on the shoulder as she passes, and the other witnesses follow her so they are standing on the west side of the pedestal, the skirts of their gowns touching.

The guards leave, closing the door behind them with a slam of finality but not locking it as Aro pockets the key once more.

Except for the submissive Nephilim witnesses, Aro and I are alone, just the Heirbound, the Heir, and the crown.

"Let's begin," Aro claps his hands together, impatient to get the ceremony underway as he fidgets like an adolescent.

"Alright," I swallow, feeling like a lump of coal has been lodged in my throat. I try to distract myself, noticing a door on the far side of the room I had missed on my first sweep. I wonder where it leads, if it's locked, if I could make a run for it.

No. I must stand strong, despite the fact my hands are shaking, my breath coming as a trembling rattle within my ribcage.

Aro places a hand on my shoulder, giving me a small shove forward so I'm able to see the crown in more detail. Its construction is stunning, with golden oaks interwoven with shimmering semi-precious stone, the inside lined in plum velvet.

I examine it for a moment before Aro's soft voice in my ear makes me jump, his proximity repulsing me.

"I'm waiting—" he whispers, and I watch out of the corner of my eye as the witnesses bristle, uncomfortable at how physically close the Sephilim is getting to me.

"Step back," I warn him in a low growl, straightening my spine and glancing back over my lace-clad shoulder. I ball my fist, my eyes smouldering embers as I take every ounce I have of hatred and use it to keep me moving forward.

Surprisingly, he does what I ask, and steps back onto the outer circumference of the stage where the pedestal stands.

I grit my teeth and swallow.

The light pours down from the ceiling, causing the metal of the crown to sparkle and shimmer. Lifting my hands, I hear the room collectively inhale.

Reaching out, I lay my fingers tentatively upon the crown, wrapping them around the headpiece with all the confidence of someone base jumping just for the hell of it and hoping they don't die.

As my skin sets upon the gold of the crown, I feel it begin to bubble and fizz, the pain blinding as a vision overtakes my mind so completely that I cannot even comprehend what it is I'm seeing.

A scream escapes, prying itself from my lips and bringing me back to the vault, dazed.

Then, chaos breaks unapologetically loose.

28

WE

ARO

KAIRI IS REACHING FOR the crown, her movements painfully slow, causing my breath to catch in my throat as the tension in the air crackles with palpable electricity.

It tastes like citrus on my tongue, bitter but zingy, the fact that my entire life has led up to this moment not lost on me.

Her fingertips touch the gleaming gold metal, and then—

And then the world dissolves, no matter how hard I tighten my grip on reality.

What is the meaning of this?

One moment I'm standing inside Zeus' vault, and the next I'm atop a cloud, the sky around me crimson and carmine, the clouds black with magenta lightning breaking apart the atmosphere.

I turn on the spot, heart beating loudly in my ears, the hairs on the back of my neck standing on end.

Then I see her, eyes piercing my silhouette like a razor blade, effortless and brutally sharp.

"Lord Aro Black, we meet at last." Her words are a roll of thunder amongst the sky, dark indigo robes billowing around her lithe skin. I know her, as bile rises into the back of my throat, my hatred as instinctual as it is soul deep.

"Hera." I spit her name like it's a curse, a blasphemy on my lips.

"That's Your Divine Highness to the likes of people like you, boy—" She cocks one of her caramel eyebrows, the pointed arch of it mountainous as her obvious disdain.

"What is this?" I demand, disconcerted by the suddenness with which the Nether had enveloped my mind so completely. This isn't normal.

"Well, I don't usually take the pains that come with pulling a soul from the lower plains directly into the Nether for a little chat. It's quite forbidden, but I think for someone as cruel as you an exception had to be made—" she says nonchalantly, her shadow turning jagged as her features sharpen with her rage.

The wind picks up, blowing my feathers from the phalanx of my wings uncomfortably. I raise a hand, shielding my eyes from the forks of magenta light that bounce from the clouds, drenching me in the too-bright hue.

"You dare try to undo my curse, without being worthy?" Hera asks, taking a step forward. Her foot is bare, her posture perfect as the robes make her grace nothing short of ethereal beneath the tempest of the surrounding storm.

"I am more worthy than Midas was," I spit, clenching my jaw and letting my wings flare.

I'm not afraid, but I can't deny that I know this damned Goddess has several millennia on me, has access to magic and power I cannot reach. This makes her a direct threat.

Not that I care, I've pissed her off.

I'm glad.

"Well, you would think so, having been the one who poisoned him," Hera growls, her pointed fingernails lacquered a dark purple. They look like the talons of an eagle, and I wonder momentarily if Zeus enjoys pinning her hands over her head when he undoubtedly fucks her raw.

"You know about that— I suppose I shouldn't be surprised." I tilt my chin and look down my nose at her. It doesn't work, because as she takes another step forward, I realise she's taller than I am.

I refuse to flounder, straightening my spine and puffing my chest out, the rose gold sheen of her locks becoming vibrant as another fork of lightning crackles overhead.

"I know everything, you coward. Zeus made a mistake the day he chose you— even more than the rest of your sorry kind." Hera tosses her hair back over one shoulder, the low cleavage of her off-shoulder violet gown showing her for the whore I know her to be.

"And where is he then, to tell me this? Zeus, I mean?" I ask her, and she smiles.

"Unaware, as usual. He never did care much about what happened with his Kindred. You are a means to an end, and if it hadn't been for the Seraphim and their threat, you wouldn't even exist," Hera sneers, her fingers fluttering as she gesticulates, body moving without effort from one cloud to another as she paces before me.

"If I'm such a mistake, such a coward, why waste your time with me?" I demand, smiling to myself as I watch her pause. I realise I have her there and feel a small bloom of triumph warm my gut.

"Because I care about the Kindred in my charge, I will not let a Nephilim be doomed to an eternal life of misery again—" The words leave her rose-soft lips and I can't hide my utter amusement as a laugh escapes me, rattling between us like a tin can in a hurricane.

"You care? You CARE? What about Storm? What about Harmonia? What about Pandora?" I demand, and this time it is her turn to straighten.

"That is not the same. Pandora and Harmonia, when they stood at the side of their kings, they did so with love in their hearts. My curse cannot simply be manipulated, you idiot. It is not only the Heirbound but her intent that is important. And for that reason, I know the crown will never be yours. Kairi Freemont will never love you." The Goddess smiles and I ball a fist at my side, wondering if I should try to attack her.

Odds are though, she is incorporeal or could disappear in but an instant. I'm no fool when it comes to the Nether, but I have never tried to go toe to toe with a Goddess here.

I never dreamed I'd have the opportunity.

But then, I wonder—

After all, what's that saying about nothing ventured, nothing gained?

"What? Speechless now? You are nothing, Aro. Nothing. You are egotistical and tyrannical and you, like my husband, quite honestly disgust me," she goads me, and I make the decision in a split second, my heart leaping as I reach out, summoning the electrical energy in the air and directing it toward her in a vicious lightning bolt designed to kill, not stun.

She stands there, waves a hand, and dissipates the bolt before it even gets close, looking almost bored.

"That's always your answer, isn't it? You cannot get what you want, so you just kill anyone in your way— Sad. Also, now I know Kairi is the one who will, at last, fulfil my prophecy. Even if she didn't hate your guts, she's far too good for you. She is more worthy than you'll ever be of that crown, and I can't wait to watch your fall from power. It will be glorious, and I will revel in it," she vows, her hair whipped back by the wind. A choker clutches her throat, and I wish momentarily my hands could take its place and squeeze—

I stand there, frozen, her words rattling through the marrow in my bones in a way I cannot fathom stopping. Is it her power, her beauty, that is giving her the ability to get so utterly into my head and beneath my skin?

Bitch.

"Farewell, Aro Black," Hera waves, her mouth curving into a placid smile. She blows me a kiss, giving a malicious wink of painful promise, and then, in a final swirl of her long-elegant fingers, the clouds crowd inward, and the vision dissolves.

I blanch, disoriented as my soul is unceremoniously shoved back into my immortal coil. My head throbs, eyes watering, and nausea rising in the back of my throat. It is odd because, after over one hundred and fifty years of being a Kindred, I feel almost— human.

The world tilts and then rights itself. I find Kairi recoiling, her hand smouldering in a way only too familiar to me as the witnesses rush forward to tend to her. She's got tears running down her face, a smile marring her lips as she simply stares at the skin sizzling on her palm.

She looks at me, and I find myself moving before my brain realises what I'm doing.

I stride across the platform toward her, my muscles tensing simultaneously as my blood rolls in a scorching and furious torrent through my veins. I flick my wings out and watch as the witnesses back away, fear in their eyes. Kairi straightens, and I narrow my eyes, my jaw clenching as my finger grips her injured hand by the wrist, and then the other.

She struggles in my grip, the lace of her gown scratching my palms as I slam her sideways into the pedestal and smash her hands into the metal of the crown. She cries out, her body fighting me with more strength than I expect. I smell her skin burning upon the gilded headpiece, the shudders running up her arms testament to the strength of the curse placed upon it by Hera. I clamp her fingers onto the edges of the crown, trying to force it upward, but the weight of it surpasses anything I could lift, even if I had a group of soldiers assisting me.

She throws her head back, the crown of it smashing into my nose and causing me to stumble back, eyes watering as stars of pain explode across my vision. I go to summon electricity from the air, before remembering that no current can pass into the insulated room.

Fuck.

Well, that's fine, I'll just have to do this without magic.

I watch as Kairi recoils from the pedestal, her hands smouldering and dripping bloody melted flesh onto the floor.

Her eyes are glowing, her hair comes loose from its tight braids. Her ears protrude through the locks, pointed.

Fae.

What are you? I wonder, heart leaping in my chest at the sight of her true nature revealed.

"You're a— a—" I pant, my nose gushing blood down my face and pooling upon my lips in a bitter rusty tang.

The scent of my blood and the throbbing in the centre of my face is like a flag to a bull as my fury level climbs. I steel myself, striding forward like I'm walking toward someone far more foreboding than Kairi Fucking Freemont. In my rage, I've balled my fist, and I'm stunned when she lifts an injured, mottled hand, and openly slaps me as hard as she can across my face.

"Don't you fucking touch me, you prick!" she screams, eyes tearing from the pain of her injured hand landing the audibly tremendous crack upon my cheek.

She clutches at her hand, face flushed pink with pain as loose locks of hair stick to her sweat-slick forehead.

Then, we hear it, a crack that comes not from skin on bone, but the severing of long glinting gold.

We both turn and are met with the sight of the crown splitting in two. The severing of it completely half shifts the weight of both halves on the cushion, and I watch in disbelief as they topple to the floor with a clatter, before bubbling into molten pools before my shocked eyes.

Hera. That bitch.

I swallow, realising now that I will not be emerging from this chamber as the new King of Aetheria. I will not be emerging as chosen, or worthy. I'll be emerging humiliated, a joke at the expense of some harlot Goddess who not only took away my rightful power but decided to drag me into a lecture beforehand.

Kairi is shaking where she stands, looking down with startled eyes as the puddle of metal and stone fizzes and teems with unnatural heat.

"Happy now?" she asks me, cocking her head and straightening her spine, wings flaring sideways with a beauty even I can't deny.

"I'm going to fucking kill you," I snarl at her, balling my fists and lurching forwards. I lunge at her throat, but she ducks, twisting and dropping within her gown. Twirling on the spot in a blur of fabric, she moves so fast I cannot even react as she sweeps my feet out from under me. I come crashing down, a grunt pulled from my lungs as I impact the vault floor and splay out like a wicked pinwheel across the stone.

She remains crouched like a wildcat opposite me, her hair tumbling down around her high cheekbones and wide lilac eyes. I scramble to my feet, the back of my body hurting where I'd impacted from the floor, face burning.

Where the hell had she learned to do that?

"You'll have to fight me first," she growls, feral within the lace and finery of Storm's long-discarded wedding gown.

"Oh, I'm so scared. One Nephilim against Lord Aro Black. I have an army, Kairi. What do you have?" I ask her.

She straightens, eyes pinned sharply on my face.

It's my own fault really, my rage blinding me to anything going on in the room which isn't captive behind the fiery glass of Kairi's eyes.

In a moment I can only describe as unexpected, I go to step forward, only to find myself still mid-step.

In that split second, the future severs itself from the past, from what I have always known to be true.

A sharp blade slides itself in under my chin, cold steel biting into my soft flesh, the threat immediate and shocking.

A soft, yet deadly voice comes closer to me, drawing my glance sideways until they rest on the bearer of the weapon.

I tense, readying myself to fight back as the words of my assailant hit me, causing the hairs on the back of my neck to rise.

"And what makes you think she doesn't have an army?"

LUCIEN

I jog quickly through the caverns underneath the Astrid Keep, keeping my hood close around my face and shying from the flickering sconces lining the walls.

There's motion around every corner, but luckily most of the black-smiths and leather workers are too busy collecting weapons, saddles, and other riding equipment to take their eyes from their busy hands. They're spirited, calling to one another in loud and excited tones as if they can already taste Equinian blood on their tongues.

I feel like a criminal in the twisting corridors of my own castle, dark wings tucked mysteriously beneath my cloak, my identity dangerous among those who I have served for longer than I can remember. I dart from one cavernous divot in the wall to the next, moving as fast as I possibly can and far faster than any mortal could. My heart is as heavy as my tread at the way things have turned out, and I wonder now, as I hurry towards my Dragon's chamber, if I'd do anything differently if I'd known this was going to happen.

Finally, I reach Ebonara's chamber, throwing my hood back off my head so she can see it is me. Her enormous, scaled body is erect and rigid with tension, head cocked as though she's actively listening to the footfall echoing out in all directions.

Lucien, what is happening? she asks, voice as concerned as it is sweet in its gentleness. I stride over to a small alcove in the corner, pulling on my riding pants and boots as I hastily discard my ridiculous pyjamas.

We are getting out of here, Eb. Come on. I go about beginning to unchain her once I'm changed, but she nudges me with her scaled maw, the glint of her sharp teeth drawing my gaze to her wide violet eyes.

What is it? she asks, her tone more insistent this time as she gets to her feet, stretching her wings, her talons scraping against the dusty stone underfoot.

Genevieve is taking the others to invade Sapphire City, I say through our psychic bond, trying to be as gentle as I can.

She raises her head, eyes narrowing as her lips draw back from her enormous teeth.

Untie me, we must take to the skies, she exclaims, her voice like a roar in its undeniably commanding resonance. I drop the first cuff from around her ankle, and she gives it a small shake, clearly glad to be free of the weight.

Do you think she's making the wrong call? I ask, suddenly interested in her opinion as I realise something I had not considered. That I might not be alone. Even if no other Draconians take my side, I wonder if the other Dragons will agree with Genevieve's decision.

Algoric would never have wanted this— it's not who we are, she replies, flapping her wings wide with urgency as I drop the second metal cuff from around her front foot.

The chains clatter to the floor and she gestures back over her winged shoulder, for me to mount her. I reach up first, looking deeply into her face as she bends down to meet my palm. I lay a kiss on her huge-scaled cheek and she nuzzles me back.

Thank you for letting me know I'm not alone, I whisper gently to her, our psychic connection turning soft as silk as both of us bask in this moment of closeness.

Now, we fly. Ebonara is certain, puffing her chest out and lowering herself into a crouch once more.

I take a running leap and mount her right between the shoulder blades where I am most comfortable. I don't have to touch her or guide her, instead, she turns toward the open chasm that leads from her chamber in a jagged drop out to the night beyond. Charging forward, her enormous muscles power the bulk of her body with more speed than I can ever remember her having.

She launches off the side of the cliff as the cold night air rushes over us, I unclasp the cloak from my throat, letting the wind take it away as we soar away from the Astrid Keep, and toward what I hope will be an ally in Gemina Two.

We swoop in wide elegant circles over the peak of Gemina Two, as though we have all the time in the world, the even pace of Ebonara's beating wings calming as we descend through the flurries of feather-soft snow.

The moon is high overhead as Ebonara's talons pierce the powdery top layer of the mountain's thick frozen crust, and I hop from her spine, running my cool fingers along the scales of her neck.

Stay here and hide, I implore her, watching as she shakes her scales like a dog would wet fur. As they shimmer with fresh moonbeams, they also assimilate into the night sky surrounding us, rendering her invisible.

I take quick, purposeful paces up toward the small dome perched up ahead, trying to make my breath come in even waves as my mind flits to Kairi.

Has she done it yet— has she thrown away her own life to save the lives of others?

The thought resonates through me with disgust, with tragedy, and yet I cannot deny she is a hero. She is a true damn hero, and I'm lucky that she ever looked at me twice.

I pull open one of the enormous doors and let myself into the hall of the observatory, not even pausing to bang snow from my boots as I quicken my steps yet again, now I'm on flat footing.

I don't have to go far, for when I enter the enormous receiving room topped with its glass dome roof, I find not only Anastasia but a crowd of people I recognise waiting for me.

"I told you he'd come," Anastasia says dreamily.

I'm startled by her attire as her voice echoes from each of the stone walls, having never seen her looking so ready for a fight before. Gone are the floaty gowns, the floor-length billowing cloaks and the loose flowing locks. Instead, she's rendered even tinier than usual in a close-fitting navy leather ensemble that's encrusted with silver scale-mail over her breasts, shoulders, and thighs. She's got a rapier strapped to her thigh in an opalescent scabbard, the weapon glinting at its almost invisible point. Her bejewelled wings are tucked neatly at her spine as she looks back to the crowd of Draconians, her hair braided tightly up off her neck and shoulders.

She's beautiful, in an entirely different way than I'd ever considered possible.

"Lucien, we are ready to depart. We need but a few moments."

I look at the crowd of faces, finding my students there, expressions ashen with worry. They're all young, far younger than even Gage, and their Dragons aren't even fully grown. I wilt, thinking of how much I still have to teach them, and of how much they still have to learn.

"You didn't leave with Genevieve?" I ask them, and they shake their heads.

"We were in the Academy hall, most of us getting ready for bed or Astrology lectures, you know— and High Lady Dragos came and brought us here, she told us everything." A male Draconian with mustard wings and dirty blonde hair informs me, his hands noticeably shaking as he gesticulates. I see the fear in his eyes as well and wonder if asking such young Kindred to fight for me is a good idea. I can't even remember most of their names.

It occurs to me as I look over the faces in the crowd with only half recognition that I have been beyond self-absorbed lately.

My classes have passed in a haze, merely a tool to get me from one secret meeting with Kairi to the next.

I used to love to teach, to inspire, but I cannot even tell you what any of the people standing in front of me are majoring in.

"Prepare for departure, all of you. Lord DeLaurent and I have some things to discuss." Anastasia waves them away with a gentle yet assertive hand, and I watch the crowd obediently scatter, the echo of footsteps on the spiral staircase leading to the lower levels in an overwhelming cacophony that shortly follows.

"You knew this was going to happen?" I ask her, and she shakes her head furiously.

"I only became aware of all this around thirty minutes ago, Lucien. Something is blocking my visions when it comes to Genevieve. Something dark—" Her eyes turn into pits of shadow as her mouth forms a grim line.

"Then how did you know to—" I begin and she raises her brows, interrupting me mid-thought.

"I was alerted to the coronation by a source of mine within the Solis Castra, Genevieve's alliance was also mentioned," she explains and I cock my head. I take several steps forward, turning so I'm standing at her side. I follow her gaze up to the stars, and everything slides into place.

"Silver?" I ask, and she looks up at me with wide eyes.

"Yes— how did you—" she asks, stunned. This time it is my turn to interrupt.

"She helped me get back here, they had me in the dungeons, Anastasia. Genevieve she— she handed Kairi over like it was nothing." I'm shocked even now at the words passing my lips, and I wonder if Anastasia had felt the bottom of her world fall out as well when she learned the truth.

"It's not her Lucien, there's something— something is wrong." Anastasia seems so sure of this.

I take a moment before I shake my head, rebuking her assertion.

"No, Anastasia, I thought that too. But it's her. She really believes she's doing the right thing by siding with Lord Black. I saw it in her eyes, there was no apology, no guilt there." I express, sighing.

"So, what are we going to do about it?" she demands, balling her fists at her sides. Her eyes shine bright like milky fire.

"I thought you knew, given the gathering—" I express and she smiles.

"Well, Genevieve is heading for Sapphire City, I understand?" she guesses, folding her arms. I nod, running my fingers along my jawline in a speculative gesture. "Now, we don't have any Dragons besides Cosmo, and Ebonara I assume, the ones belonging to any riders here are still in the nursery. They're far too young to risk in this kind of battle I'm sure you'd agree—"

"I do, but I don't know what two Dragons alone can matter against her forces. It would seem she has most of our people behind her," I add, feeling disgusted by the idea I am a part of a race capable of such violence.

"You sound surprised."

Anastasia cocks an eyebrow, her skin glittering slightly beneath the moonlight pouring in through the glass ceiling.

"And you're not? I didn't know the Draconians had so much hatred inside of them—" I admit and she swallows with visible discomfort.

"Lucien, you must understand that any creature can only be chained, be oppressed for so long. Eventually, it will rise against its oppressor. It's written in the peaks and troughs of human history, and we are no different." She sounds so wise and right then I wish I had even a third of her faith.

"Kairi sent me here to get help for the Equinians. I didn't realise I'd have such numbers to compete with. I don't know if what we have here is enough." I sigh again, the fact I haven't had a moment's real rest in days hitting me full force as my shoulders sag.

Then, an idea occurs to me.

"What about the Fae?" I ask, turning to Anastasia with a determined grimace on my face.

"I think that would be wasted time and energy," Anastasia replies, her face darkening.

"You think they'd let Sapphire City fall and do nothing?" I ask, and she only shrugs in reply.

"Pacifism— is its own form of selfishness. I fear the Fae have been this way so long and have such hatred for the Equinians who have been hunting illegally on their land, that it would be too much to ask. Not only that, but Aro has soldiers in both Aramis and Lumeria— I fear it may make their people more of a target than anything—" she explains.

I frown.

"I just don't understand how they can stand by and do nothing." Fury swells in my gut.

"You're not supposed to understand, Lucien. You are not a pacifist. You'll find the mind is capable of justifying almost anything if it needs it badly enough." Her words startle me, the thought that another point of view is beyond me not because I'm stupid, but simply because I work differently.

Anastasia should be writing philosophy books, I swear.

We both take a moment, ignoring the clattering sounds of preparation that are echoing up the staircase from the lower levels, casting our eyes to the sky. We see it then, the darkness of scale and shadow, blanketing out the moon as Genevieve's army soars over the mountain peak and casts our faces in half-light.

I wonder if Genevieve is looking down right now, or if she is too caught up in her mission for vengeance to remember that this is a sacred place from which we've both looked upon the stars and wished for a different future. It would seem, however, that only one of us is willing to spill innocent blood to achieve those ends.

Bloodshed and wishing on stars, a repellent combination, and one I cannot believe exists in the woman I had thought of as my best friend.

"Come, Lucien, we must hurry. If we hope to get there before she arrives, we must leave at once. I have no doubt she will be stopping in Soleus to gather the Sephilim soldiers, but even still—" She turns on her heel and I linger on the spot, staring up as more Dragons slice through the night overhead.

There are so many, and it makes me wonder if we stand any kind of chance at all.

We have so few soldiers in comparison and only two Dragons.

Is it hopeless? Perhaps, but we must try. It is what Kairi asked of me, and I'll be damned if I let her down.

"I'll be outside. I have Ebonara waiting," I explain, but Anastasia doesn't slow in her stride to the spiral staircase.

"I'll meet you at the halfway point of the peak with Cosmo, we can't be launching at this high of an altitude, not if we want to stay unseen," she explains and I nod, dropping my gaze from the sky and focusing on the task at hand.

I look around at the now-empty receiving room one last time, wondering what the situation will be like when I am here next. If I am ever here again that is.

I suppose then this is it, what I have been waiting for, fighting for a more united Aetheria— against my own kind.

Sort of.

How have things gotten so screwed up? I ask myself this yet again as I storm through the entryway and out into the snow flurry beyond.

I wish I hadn't tossed my cape as I see the final few Dragons at the tail end of Genevieve's procession pass overhead. I jog to where I had left Ebonara, praying she's still there, or I may never find her.

Ebonara? I call out, and she comes back to me, her voice emanating from the darkest corners of my mind.

I'm here. There's so many— she expresses sadly, looking skyward at her fellow Dragons growing smaller as they approach the star-speckled horizon.

You sound surprised, I reply, knowing she's more aware than any Draconian of just how many of her kind lie within the bedrock of Drakos Vale.

We've always seemed so few, until tonight. I suppose that's what happens when you turn on your own kind. Her nostrils push cold steam plumes into the night, the only visible sign of her.

As I reach her, she reappears, shimmering into existence with all the majesty she had possessed when breaking free of the egg that birthed her.

Are you doubting yourself? I ask, climbing astride her and relishing the prickle of the cold air on my chest.

Are you? she shoots back, and I exhale hard.

No.

Then, we agree. We fight, and we win. She sounds more confident than I know either of us feels, but I nod anyway, leaning into my fear and kicking her flank. She stretches her wings out leisurely, taking off with no real effort as she uses the slope of the mountain to aid her flight. We descend, aiming to meet Cosmo and Anastasia on the opposite side of the great jagged peak.

The wind rushes through my hair, my eyes watering, and my heart pounding, her words rattling around my skull.

We fight, and we win.

After all, what alternative is there?

29

WAITING FOR THE BARBARIANS

KAIRI

THE WORLD SHIFTS ON its axis, all to the beat of my throbbing palms.

I am standing there, breathless, staring at Dawn and the sword she's drawn from beneath her discarded skirt. Beneath it, she's wearing ivory leather pants, speckled with rose gold studs, a long sheath strapped to her outer thigh.

Hip cocked; she smiles at me as her words echo out in the air between us.

"And what makes you think she doesn't have an army?" she asks the startled-looking Aro.

It's the most dishevelled I've ever seen him, and the sick pleasure I'm taking from his obvious shock is just enough to keep me from screaming with the pain in my hands.

"Now, Lord Black. We'll be going—" Dawn expresses, drawing the sword back from his gullet with purposeful slowness. He swallows, but I know he does not intend to just let us leave as his muscles clench.

"Dawn!" I cry out, watching as he immediately lunges for her, his claw-like fingers grasping the back of her neck as she makes a quarter turn.

Before he can fully grasp her, however, she turns back and strikes him with an open palm right in his bloody nose. He recoils, eyes watering with pain.

"Ladies," she calls, and I watch as Vail, Silver, and Trinity unclasp the belts cinching their skirts to their waists, letting them fly in a flurry of billowing ivory fabric.

I am stunned as the three of them join Dawn, drawing swords of their own.

They're nimble, their bodies seeming tinier now the bulk of their gowns have been discarded, but something in their eyes tells me that they're the last people you want to underestimate.

Aro draws his sword, the amethyst monstrosity he'd used to kill Algoric, and I step forward, wishing I could ditch my skirt as well.

"We are done here," I spit in his face. His wings spread as he finds himself surrounded, growing immensely.

His dark eyes dart from face to feminine face, lips crawling back in a snarl you would most commonly see on the maw of a cornered animal.

"Guards!" he barks over his shoulder.

Then, all hell breaks loose.

The door to the vault is yanked open, and as the word leaves Aro's lips, Trinity raises her blade to strike his left shoulder. He parries her with ease, the speed of his motion blurring the outline of his dark clothes into shadow as he immediately hops into a defensive stance.

Dawn charges toward me, Vail following closely on her petite heels. The two guards who had accompanied our party run across the threshold of the vault and straight for us as the ringing of amethyst on steel hits my ears.

I tighten my hands into balls, tears filling my eyes at the pain. All I can hope is that my Kindred healing fixes them to be usable as quickly as possible.

I see the guards pause a moment as they find the assailants before them to be Nephilim. To be honest, it was my reaction too, and my mind is a swarm of desperate questions mixed with the baffled buzz of potential hope.

How long have they been learning to fight?

Has this been going on under my nose all along?

Why didn't anyone tell me?

Glancing across the pedestal, I find Silver and Trinity have backed Aro into a corner.

He's scrambling against a heaped pile of gold with nowhere to go.

I want to see what happens next, but instead, I'm distracted by the fight going on right in front of me, with Vail and Dawn nimbly meeting the two guards stroke for stroke. Their wings help them balance, their blade work more impressive than their needlework

410

by far. They fight well as a duo, swapping targets often, the larger Sephilim struggling to keep up with their footwork.

They're incredible, and I watch as Dawn skewers her opponent through the inner thigh, sweeping his foot from underneath him with a deft kick of her ankle.

He falls, toppling Vail's assailant as he goes.

She stabs him through the inner thigh as well, not a fatal jab by my understanding, but enough to keep them down for a while.

I stand, gaping.

There is no time though, and Dawn grabs me by the wrist, careful not to touch my melted flesh as she pulls me past the puddle of molten gold and precious stones, which had only minutes before been a crown.

Aro is lying, speared by two swords, Trinity and Silver standing over his crumpled form. He isn't unconscious, but he's in shock, stirring beneath the blades that pin him to the ground below.

Silver draws her sword from where it's embedded in his side and he gasps, her grin feline and ferocious, delighted by his suffering. She lifts the blade, intending to plunge it back into him for a more fatal strike while he is still pinned down.

Dawn hisses at her, stopping her mid-thrust.

"Silver, come on! We don't have time! More guards will be coming and I won't be arrested and killed in front of the whole of Soleus for treason. You know he has allies. We can't afford it— not yet—" Silver looks back over her shoulder, eyes sparkling with fury.

After what seems like an infinitely long pause, she nods, jaw clenched.

Turning, she spits on Aro, kicking him in the groin for good measure. He hisses through his teeth, and my heart flutters.

I might not know Silver yet, but I'm damn sure I'm going to like her— a lot.

"Bastard," she cusses, flouncing on her heel and hurrying over to Dawn and Vail.

The three of them look back at me as Trinity joins us.

"Come, we must get you to the Temple of Hera," Dawn speaks with more urgency than I've ever heard coming from her, so I pick up my skirts and the four of us flee the vault, leaving nothing but a wounded Aro, two unconscious guards, and a molten puddle behind.

We scurry back up the passage, my trembling form central to the four women who guard me with their swords drawn like compass points in every direction.

The breeze in the barren stone corridor grows, a welcome relief on my burning palms. My eyes continue to water, tears drying on my cheeks with the sting of it.

I had seen— something, but I cannot think about that yet.

All I can think about is getting out of here alive.

Dawn turns, taking us back up the crooked stairs we had entered with caution, bowing her head, and bringing her finger to her lips.

I slow, letting the four-woman guard around me rotate, preparing for when we reach the top of the staircase.

I watch Dawn skewer a guard on the left, Trinity nimbly darting behind her and disabling the Sephilim on the right with a blow to the head from the hilt of her sword.

"Clear," Dawn exclaims, reaching down into the secret passage and giving me a hand up the final two stairs.

My feet are throbbing in my heels and my hair is loose and wild around my shoulders as I burst into the main chamber of the temple.

"Go! Go! Go!" Silver hisses, and I find myself being pulled not for the exit as I suspect, but off to the left. Racing down the corridor and away from the Statue of Zeus, we enter the first room we come across, a nondescript storage space filled with candles, enormous plant pots, and incense stacked against the walls in wooden crates.

"Anklets!" Dawn hisses at the others. I wince as I stumble past her and out of my heels, balls of my feet grateful for the sudden cool of the marble floor. I watch as the other Nephilim present their amethyst anklets. The sight of them makes me grateful I'm no longer cuffed by mine.

I watch as Silver drops to her knees after sheathing her blade, blinking a few times as she fumbles for something around her throat before grasping the chain with a key attached and yanking it over her head.

She shoves the key into the anklet locks, throwing the heavy bangles aside as they click open one by one and each of the women is set free. Finally, she removes her own.

How long have they had a key? I wonder, mystified.

"Time to go, before they find Lord Black," Trinity whispers, clasping my shoulder with a comforting squeeze. She relinquishes her hold, and I close my eyes, envisioning the Temple of Hera and ready to get the hell out of there.

We rematerialize in the chamber where I had been reborn.

The aroma of it overwhelms me completely, my pain momentarily irrelevant as the scent of lilies and rosewater envelops my senses. My wings flutter, the peach glow of the room made dull by the moonlight but no less romantic as Dawn sidesteps me. Walking across the small footbridge between the two rebirthing pools, she makes her way over to the far wall behind the statue of Hera that watches the space through serene stone eyes.

She lifts her hand, placing it on three exact yet unextraordinary places upon the wall in turn, her fingers sparking slightly on contact. Then, the entire panel gives a rumble and a quarter portion of the central slab grinds backwards.

I gawp, wondering how many other rooms I've been in have hidden doorways.

"What, you think we'd hide it behind a tapestry or something lame like that?" Trinity asks, looking amused at my expression.

I almost laugh, my heart tentatively soaring as I realise in this single and extraordinary moment that I will not have to crown Lord Black.

Relief floods through me, translating to hurried and frantic energy that propels me forward with the other Nephilim, leaving the humid floral fug of the rebirthing room in our wake.

The retracted stone slab has revealed the top of a tightly spiralled staircase made from fine gold. The bannisters are just as beautiful as everything else in the temple, despite the fact it is hidden.

Dawn strides forward, leading with me in the middle beside Silver, and Vail and Trinity bringing up the rear. The passage is bare, just as the one beneath the Temple of Zeus had been, and yet I don't shiver here.

Instead, the proximity of the walls makes me feel safe.

We reach the end of the long corridor and step onto a rose quartz slab only just big enough for the five of us if we tuck in our wings tightly. The air turns citrusy in my nostrils, and I'm suddenly aware that one of the Nephilim around me is manipulating electric currents.

The stone slab underfoot trembles, the quake of it causing my shin bones to rattle within my calves.

The pillar descends, that same sound of crystal on crystal reminding me of a similar makeshift elevator in Drakos Vale.

I wonder if there's a connection.

Descending, I find eyes turned to me, many eyes. More than I expect, and all of them in shades of purple.

"What the—" I mutter and find Vail grasping my wrist.

I flinch at her proximity to my melted skin.

"Watch this," she whispers to me, and then, without warning, lifts my hand high up into the air.

The elevator stops, and the silent crowd of what must be a few hundred Nephilim stare up at my splayed fingers, my desecrated palm.

There's a beat, a pause, and then they erupt into uncharacteristically raucous applause.

I look at Dawn in utter confusion, whose face breaks into a tight smile as she steps off the crystal podium and glances back over her baby blue feathers at me.

I step into the underground vault, the low ceiling and flickering rose-gold sconces casting the entire space into an intimate warm glow.

"Come, we have much to explain," Dawn says, and I feel Vail place a hand on my lace-clad shoulder and squeeze. I turn to look at her as the applauding Nephilim fall once again silent, parting before us.

I walk, feeling like an accidental celebrity as eyes prickle every inch of my skin. It's probably the lace, but it feels like the gazes of these women, these women I had thought so weak, sting.

Trinity, Dawn, Vail, and Silver accompany me across the vast stone room, the scent of mixed floral perfumes wafting from their pristine skin. My nose wrinkles and I continue trying to ignore the throbbing in my palm as I hold my head high, eyes focused straight ahead.

Reaching the farthest end of the room, we turn a corner after passing through an archway in the back wall, and I am led down yet more corridors. The only sounds interrupting the swarming questions in my head are the quick heels that echo out around us. We go deeper into the gut of the floating isle, taking several more corridors carved directly into the rock. Finally, we stop before an enormous door made from light wood and inlaid with rose quartz.

Dawn removes a key from around her own throat, slipping its slender baroque curvature into the lock and twisting as she looks tentatively back over her shoulder as though out of habit. The door gives a pleasant click, and then a shudder as she pushes inward and the hinges creak.

We file in behind her, and I take in what seems to be a small dressing chamber. There's a weapons rack holding long elegant bows, quivers of arrows accompanying them in ivory leather.

"Now, will someone please do me the courtesy of explaining what the hell is going on?" I burst, feeling my heartbeat continue to pound in my ruined hands.

"First, we tend to your wounds, then we will explain. Sit, you look shaken." Silver commands, her tone cold and imperious. I cock an eyebrow.

"Wow, shaken. What an apt description," I shoot at her, my voice trembling as it is loosed from my lips.

"Kairi, sit," Vail pleads, moving forward and pulling a chair out from where it has been facing a dusty vanity. I do as she asks this time, letting my wings hang from my spine as I slump down into the chair.

I feel it then, the way my whole body trembles uncontrollably. I fight it, gritting my teeth and forcing my spine straight, but it does little good.

There's a flurry of motion around me as drawers slide open, chests are rifled through, and wardrobes are raided.

Before I can blink, Vail is attending to my palms, and Dawn is unbuttoning the monstrous lace gown from where it grasps tightly around my torso with scratchy jaws.

Vail applies ointment to my burns scented with aloe vera, and where I expect the sting of mortal medicine I'm instead met by a soothing balm. I relax a little, watching as the skin begins to heal itself before my eyes.

"Fae made, brilliant stuff—" Vail explains, watching my shocked expression.

She then goes about bandaging my palms, and I wonder what she's thinking.

I don't even know what I'm thinking.

"Explanations, now." I shoot a look at Trinity who is propped against the far wall, examining the tip of the rapier she had used to take down Aro.

"It wasn't supposed to happen this way, you know. You were supposed to be introduced to the Harpies the night of your ascension ball. It seems Hera had other plans." She gives me a sad look, and I remember the importance she had laid on my returning to the Temple of Hera after I'd been to the ball.

Was this why?

I remember her words when I'd claimed she had no way in which to keep me safe.

You underestimate us, Kairi.

Damn right I had underestimated them.

"You're called Harpies?" I ask and Vail nods, the corner of her mouth turning up in amusement.

"Yes, Pandora's little fuck you to Midas. Beautiful thing a harp, sounds like angels, but y'all wouldn't want one dropped on you, would ya?" Her eyes glitter and I smirk, feeling the tension leave my body.

"Pandora? She did this?" I ask, and she nods. Her face comes into my mind, the face I had seen the moment my skin had landed upon the golden glisten of the crown's twisting vines.

"She received a prophecy from Anastasia during the final years of her rule. Hera has had enough. And from the way you encountered many Goddesses during your Kindred Vision, I'd say she isn't alone."

My eyes widen, and I chew on the inside of my lip.

"The prophecy, it was about me?" I demand, and they nod as a collective, eyes grave.

"Why— Why didn't anyone say anything?" I ask, and Dawn bows her head slightly.

I stand, peeling the gown from my sticky, itching skin, waiting for an answer as the thick fabric shudders stiffly into a pile around my ankles.

I step out of the hooped skirt, watching as Dawn indicates that Silver should step forward.

She has garments in her hands that I had not noticed. They are cream leather, and I assume they match those of the women around me.

They expect me to become one of them, a warrior.

"You have to understand, Kairi. If we were wrong, and you found out about the Harpies— it could have led to our exposure unintentionally. We have worked for hundreds of years to keep the magnitude of our forces from the Sephilim to the point where we won't even accept married Nephilim into our ranks anymore. We couldn't take the risk until we were sure," she explains and Vail gives me a pointed glance.

"Why do you think I haven't let myself succumb to my feelings for Leo? He's the Captain of their aerial forces. No matter how I feel, I can't let my feelings put everything we've worked for at risk." Her southern lilt is lost in the sadness of her confession.

The realisation hits me like a cold bucket of ice water in the face, the fact all the women before me are single.

Silver brings the garments to me, placing the puddle of pale leather in my hands. I move back to the chair where I'd been sitting, kicking the dress aside and beginning to wiggle into the leather pants.

"So, you're sure now? How can you be sure?" I enquire. This time Trinity speaks.

"The crown. It was foretold," she says with a reluctance in her tone, and I feel myself pale.

"Wait? You knew this was going to happen! You knew I was going to melt my damn flesh off my bones and you didn't try to stop me? What the hell?" I pause, my foot halfway down one pants leg, blinking furiously.

"You had to willingly make the choice to crown Lord Black, Kairi. You had to sacrifice your happiness for the greater good, to prove your worthiness. We did not know it would happen, we only hoped—" Silver says, her tone icy.

Her face is beautiful, but hard like marble, and I wonder if she has a problem with me. "You're not the only one who has made sacrifices for us to arrive at this point, let me assure you." Her words seem unjustified at first, but then I look at Dawn, at Vail. Dawn has been kneeling and scraping before Aro for longer than I can fathom, and Vail has given up the man she loves.

I suppose I can live with a little melted flesh—

"I want to see this prophecy," I add, feeling my heartbeat quickening yet again.

If everything could stop for a single moment, I would simply breathe. As it is, I cannot fight the tide of time, and so let myself be swept along, thoughts racing.

The four women look at me, then at each other, multiple shades of purple irises rippling from violet to lilac and back in the warm flickering light.

Then, they speak, their voices united in absolute harmony.

"When the crown doth cleave,
And the line is broken,
Angels shall fight.
words long unspoken.

She must not simply be,
pure of heart and mind,
but willing to leave true love behind.

For war is upon you,
and threats unseen,
yearn to clash,
with this heir-borne Queen.

She is one,
yet she is all,
Unite Aetheria.
Heed her call."

They finish this and I wonder if it's rehearsed, or if they have spent so long poring over those words that they're ingrained in their minds more permanently than on any stone.

"So that's what Hera wanted? She wanted me to prove that I'd sacrifice my happiness for Aetheria?" I ask them, stunned.

Hadn't I already proven that by giving up my mortal life?

"I think so. I also think that if you look down at your wrist you'll see that she never had any doubt you would do so," Dawn explains, and as I pull the pants up around my waist, I glimpse the swirling silver filigree marking my skin.

The Heirbound mark, but with a crown hovering over its usual three tentacled star.

"That symbol was on the orb in which the prophecy was presented by Anastasia. I knew immediately when I saw it, what it meant, but you had to come to the choice on your own for it to be valid. You're not Heirbound Kairi, you're Heirborne. The very first." She stares at me with more intensity than I expect as the final words leave her lips, and I can't help but look away as I pull the open corset around my body and begin to lace the front tightly.

"I don't know what that means," I say simply, hands fumbling.

"It means, Kairi, that you have indeed chosen the next Aetherial Monarch. You've chosen yourself, through the sacrifice of that self," Trinity adds, and I feel physically sick.

Me, *Queen?*

As in the only ruler?

As in, the person in charge of the entirety of this dimension?

I want to laugh, but the sound won't quite make it past my tongue as my jaw tenses and I clench my teeth together.

I had been willing to lay down as the lamb, but I hadn't expected to have to get up and be the lion.

I'm not strong enough for this.

I had only wanted to stop the dying—

"The prophecy says about war— has that always been inevitable?" I ask them, and they nod in unison, glossy hair sheening. I continue to lace my corset, oddly numb.

"Yes. But you, you might actually give us a chance at winning it, Kairi. You're what we've all been waiting for like an iced tea on a hot summer's afternoon. You're the Queen of Aetheria, darlin'."

I stare at Vail dumbfounded, her crooked smile unsettling me.

My eyes travel the room, finding all gazes fixed on me in return, expectant.

I blink as I tie the corset tightly closed. I can barely breathe, but I don't seem to care.

Straightening, I realise that if I had been willing to crown Aro, stepping up as Queen myself can't be any worse.

"Alright, well then—" I begin to speak, but I'm interrupted before I can fully work out what I was even going to declare.

Probably something cliché to raise morale.

The knock at the door is hurried yet precise, like a small song, and echoes out against the high vaulted ceiling.

"Yes?" Silver barks, folding her arms over her breasts as I begin placing my feet into the boots she's provided.

A young woman, one I recognise, pokes her head around the door.

It's Delphine, her auburn hair blazing deep crimson in the shadows. Suddenly, it occurs to me that perhaps she and Eve never required remedial Etiquette classes at all—

I zip up my right boot and then straighten, giving the messenger my full attention.

"The Dragons, they're passing overhead! I was sent for you—" she explains, her voice a gust of panicked force.

Dawn nods, calm as her face remains unchanged by the news.

"Of course, tell everyone to prepare to depart. We will want to arrive shortly after the Draconians, a kind of surprise enemy they weren't expecting—" she adds and Delphine nods, giving me a quick and curious glance before leaving us once more alone.

"We're going to aid the Equinians?" I ask.

Silver nods.

"If we're going to out ourselves as warriors, we might as well do it properly. I mean, it's not like we haven't been waiting several centuries for this moment. Go big or go home, right?" She is cool toward me, eyes glazed, fingers tapping gently against the gilded hilt of her rapier.

I nod, not sure how to feel about the fact I've suddenly gained an army.

An army that's been waiting for me longer than I've been alive.

"I'm going to need a weapon, aren't I?" I sigh, eliciting a wicked smile from the lips of all the Nephilim before me.

"Indeed."

ARO

As I lie there, staring up at the intricately detailed vault ceiling, it occurs to me how completely everything has gone to hell. I allow myself a moment to feel the blade skewering my side as a completely raw bite of razor-edge against viscera, my chest rising and falling within the finely tailored suit as blood spills out of me like wine from a busted casket.

Well. Fuck.

That's it. That's all my highly articulate brain can fathom.

I replay the events of the last several minutes. Dawn, my long-time maid, a sword drawn against my carotid. Silver, the harlot I had raped, spitting in my face. Kairi, the girl I had tried to cage, slapping me around the face despite her half-melted palm. The same girl who had cowered before me on the night of her ascension ball, sweeping my feet from beneath me as a trained Equinian warrior might.

I catch a glance of the golden puddle of metal, now slowly cooling on the floor.

My destiny, my crown, broken before my eyes.

Biting down on my bottom lip with ferocious canines, I tense my jaw, hauling my splayed limbs upright as I try to gain traction against the scattered pile of gold that is supporting my bulk.

A few coins tinkle to the floor as I grunt, closing my eyes and biting down hard on my tongue, placing my hands firmly around the hilt of Trinity's rapier.

"That bitch," I mutter, taking a deep breath as I unceremoniously yank the sword from my own guts.

A hiss escapes from my lips, lungs sucking in air like I'm trying to fuel an inner fire, the pain of the slick edge slicing through my flesh causes my eyes to water.

It had missed my wing, but only just.

Staggering to my feet, more useless metal clatters onto the floor. I kick one of the goblets stamped with Midas' seal, a furious growl escaping from my throat in a rumble.

"*God.*" I stamp on the goblet, crushing it flat.

"*Fucking.*" I slam my fist into the pedestal that had held the crown, finding my two guards unconscious on the floor.

"*Damnit!*" My wings flare out, and I throw my head back, the motion ripping my wound open further.

I scream.

I don't care for the pain, but I also can't control myself.

How the hell has this happened?

An army of Nephilim?

Never.

Impossible.

They're weak, they're fragile— they can't—

And yet, that's what the bitch had implied.

What makes you think she doesn't have an army?

Her smug tone echoes through my skull, louder than the pain, louder than my rage. My fists curl into balls as I bring my foot up and kick the pedestal sideways.

It teeters, my strength lessened due to my injury, but then finally succumbs to me, toppling sideways. The marble shatters into a cloud of milky dust as the plush pillow slides to the opposite side of the room.

I spin on the balls of my feet, not waiting for the dust to settle before storming out of the vault.

I don't lock it behind me, after all, there's nothing left of real value inside.

I had entered that vault so sure I was about to achieve everything I'd always dreamed of, everything I was so obviously destined for, and yet—

I leave with nothing.

Less than nothing.

Kairi has escaped again, and a new enemy I can honestly admit I never saw coming has risen against me from the shadows.

Then it occurs to me, as I race down the corridor, feeling blood trickling down my pant leg as my wound heals too slowly.

This is Hera's doing.

It has to be.

It was no accident she had appeared to me only moments before. It seems even a Goddess couldn't resist the opportunity to gloat.

I charge up the stairs, my wound throbbing brutally beneath my suit. Clasping my side, my hand comes away bloody as I reach the top of the stairs and emerge into the central temple of Zeus.

Here, I find a cluster of men in uniform, my men, surrounding two guards who have been attacked.

"Your Highness—" one of them stutters, eyes rising to my bare head.

"Shut up! What happened?!" I bark, trying to keep my composure despite my obvious wound.

The soldiers gaze at my dishevelled face slick with sweat, my bloody palm, the bloom of dark red only just visible on my black morning coat.

"They got away! Those bitches, the Nephilim! They attempted to mutiny me during the ceremony. They destroyed the crown!" I accuse them, the half-lies coming to me as easily as ever.

After all, Kairi had technically destroyed the crown.

I wonder if she knew. If that's why she was so easily found. Did Genevieve know about this?

Was this all a trap?

Suspicion curdles in my gut as I realise I've been played.

By Kairi.

By Genevieve.

By Hera.

Nobody plays me and gets away with it.

"I need this wound bandaged and cleaned and then I want all remaining men mobilised!" I bark, watching two of the soldiers come scurrying over to me to begin tending my wounds. I slap their anxious hands away, needing a moment to think.

If I cannot secure Sapphire City, then the Aresian Equinians will see me as weak. Genevieve will not owe me her loyalty any longer, as my aid will not have kept her people or her Dragons alive in claiming their new home.

If I cannot win this fight, this invasion, then I fear my rule will crumble before it has even begun.

I need more power, more authority.

But first, I need to make sure that the Artemisian Equinians and Aliandara are made an example of. I need to show the rest of Aetheria what happens if you oppose me, and this may be my last opportunity to drive that point home.

"Where are we headed?"

One of the soldiers enquires, bringing muslin strips to the men who had come running to help me only to be pushed away.

I relax slightly, a plan forming in my mind as strong as steel.

Then, I let them tend to the wound, stripping off my jacket while keeping my face as neutral as possible. I cannot allow myself to show even the slightest weakness after emerging from the vault empty-handed, even when it comes to my own men.

"Sapphire City. Also, make sure we have all the available Kensari."

The soldier's eyes widen, understanding my intention.

We have an example to make of those who dare stand in my way.

30

TROJAN WOMEN

LUCIEN

EBONARA CIRCLES OVER SAPPHIRE City, the camouflage of her scales undulating against the flawless, endless midnight of the star-studded sky.

The darkness is an asset, or so I had thought, yet when I peer down upon the circular layout of the city, I find the streets far busier than I had expected.

Why are they all up at this hour?

Doesn't anyone here sleep?

I'm riding at a speed I'd rarely push Ebonara to, but I don't think she minds. Her blood is cool below the scales of her long neck underneath my fingertips, my hair ripped back from my face, and the night air stings my skin as we bank right, the glittering gaslights of the city highlighting the gloriously blue waters of its central oasis.

I've never been here before, being too young to remember any of the important Aetherial conflicts, and have relied on Anastasia for directions.

She had done a great job of communicating with me and our entourage simultaneously at speed, and as I scan the sky and then the horizon and surrounding dunes for other Dragons, I find none.

That is, except for that of Cosmo and the young foot soldiers constituting the rest of my party, their draconian silhouettes jagged pricks of black randomly dispersed upon the golden sands below. They're waiting for my signal that it is safe to approach, and I'm sure they must be nervous, to say the least. However, I know that patience is key if we want to aid the Equinians effectively. After all, the last thing we need is someone getting shot out of the sky at this point, our numbers are small enough as it is.

Taking a deep breath, and knowing I'm about to unleash havoc, I squeeze Ebonara's neck between my thighs for reassurance, the frantic beat of her leathery wings matching that of my heart.

Descend. We cannot waste any more time just circling— I command, and Ebonara heeds. However, I can't help but smirk as she retorts with her usual monotone sass.

Oh, joy— I do love landing fully visible and unannounced in a hostile city with tiny streets and close crowded housing—

I can almost hear her rolling her reptilian eyes and purse my lips, fighting back a smile.

Hey, I don't make the rules. I just work here— I reply, letting my wings tense against my spine.

I want to spread them and launch myself off her body as we get close to the ground. Then I can diffuse whatever situation unravels face to face.

The city is a myriad of golds and jewel-toned lustre, and in the waning lemon of the moonlight, it takes my breath away.

I can see why Genevieve would risk it all for a place like this. It's stunning, and it's perfect for the Dragons with their cold-blooded bodies which cling to all heat so desperately.

The Equinians below walk around with uncovered arms, sandalled feet, and bare midriffs, their sharp hunter's eyes turning skyward as Ebonara's shadow grows larger.

They clearly don't know what it's like to be huddled against the brutal cold.

There. Land there—

I point to a focal location, a circular courtyard at the epicentre of the city's impressive sprawl.

Ebonara lets her wings still, coasting a second before we plunge close to the rooftops surrounding the courtyard. I tense my thighs, and my glutes, spry and ready to spring as soon as I start to hear the calls of concerned onlookers.

I leap, wings shooting out from my body and catching the arid yet nippy desert air in their leathery span. Gliding down in concentric circles, I land central to a crowd of bewildered and hostile-looking women.

"Draconian!" one of them calls, her voice high-pitched as her judgemental finger points. She sounds scared, ironic seeing as I notice that the courtyard has already been swarmed by Equinian guards who had been perched on the roofs of nearby buildings. Their arrows are trained on my dark silhouette, and the hairs on the back of my neck prickle with the threat.

"I need to speak to Aliandara! To High Lady Montgomery! The Draconians are coming— they're coming to invade the city!" I call out and immediately feel the bodies around me tense further. Tanned skin and shimmering tattoos become visibly rigid as palms creep toward weaponry, fists ball, and stances widen defensively. Eyes collectively narrow, and I suddenly feel myself taking a defensive stance simply out of habit.

"What the hell is this, some kind of trick?" I hear an imperious voice, and then watch as a woman with broad shoulders and muscular legs pushes her way through the crowd. She's clad in shimmering silver armoured plates, leaving no critical zone of flesh unguarded.

"It's no trick— the Draconians—" I begin, but she raises a hand.

"The only Draconian I see here uninvited is you. You're going to have to do better than that—" She shoots daggers at me with her huntress's stare, folding her arms over her chest plate and cocking her hip as her jaw visibly hardens.

"I need to see High Lady Montgomery. Please— I've come here to try and help you—" I explain, and the crowd erupts into a mixture of hushed whispers, snorts, and arrogant giggles.

"Oh, why thank you great Dragon Rider. I'll just swoon so you can catch me now, shall I?" The Equinian, who I notice now has Celtic tattoos climbing her enormous biceps, laughs as well.

I shake my head. I don't have time for this.

"Take me to Lady Montgomery. Or bring her here. Either way, I don't care." I say from between gritted teeth, the chill of my cryomancy nipping at the tips of my fingers.

Who knew the Equinians would be so proud?

Wait— actually, everyone who's ever met an Equinian would know that.

You idiot Lucien— I cuss internally.

Ebonara's voice echoes back at me, dripping with yet more sass as if there isn't enough of that around here already.

At least you're learning the truth about yourself in this process—

I fight rolling my eyes, glaring at the woman before me and notice the air chill as I attempt to tame my temper.

Ebonara chooses this moment to make herself visible, her enormous body rippling into existence as a towering muscular mass of onyx scales and talons. She tosses her head, like she has a lustrous head of hair just like me, before coming to an elegant stop and perching upon one of the nearby roofs. She stares at me with kind and wise eyes, the wide irises flitting to the Equinians with icy disdain as her slit pupils take in their faces.

"Alright, don't get your panties in a twist. I'll take you to the High Lady—" The female soldier concedes, dropping her arms from where they cross her breasts as her eyes take in Ebonara's enormous body.

Her wings twitch as her shoulders slump.

"Alright everyone, go about your business—" she calls to the crowd, waving a hand with claw-like nails casually as if there is a bad smell.

The crowd begins to disperse, looking supremely disappointed in the lack of violence.

"No, wait! They need to be prepared—" I protest, but the name of the woman does not materialise and I lose my flow.

"Jess. My name is Jess, thanks for asking. Also, I don't know what you've been smoking but nobody would be stupid enough to try and invade Sapphire City. You'd have to have a death wish."

She's flippant as she turns her back on me, gesturing for me to follow her as her armour flashes too bright beneath the moonglow.

Or an army of Dragons— I think, my mood grim as I press my lips together, disgusted by the actions of the woman I had thought I'd known.

Arrogance is going to get these people killed. But it's still not their fault Genevieve has decided to make them a target.

It is as if they don't realise there's a first time for everything, and no limit to the stupidity of power-hungry, entitled Kindred.

Jess leads me through the winding city streets, her gaze tense on me like a loaded crossbow as we turn corner after corner.

Eventually, she leads me through a pair of high-arched gates, past a guard in similar dress, who gives us both an incredulous glare. Jess doesn't stop to explain herself or put her fellow warrior at ease. Instead, we pass through the gates, and I find a sprawling Villa perched aside the lush gardens framing the oasis for which the city is named.

"Nice place—" I mutter, trying to make small talk, but either Jess doesn't hear me or she doesn't care to reply, because she only increases her pace. It's as though she can't wait to get rid of me like I'm an old sock that has seen better days.

We don't head inside, instead skirting the edge of the property until I find myself being marched onto the paved brick weave of a vast veranda.

Here, on a set of matching sun loungers, Evangeline and Aliandara lie, moon bathing, hands interlocked and eyes closed beneath the vast maw of the night.

"Sorry to disturb you both, but I found this wandering in the streets—" Jess nods to me, her voice causing the eyes of both High Ladies to snap open in perfect synchronisation.

Aliandara's head turns, her eyes falling on me and widening.

"What the hell are you doing here?" She sounds angry immediately, and I breathe deeply, trying as hard as I can to remember why I decided to come and try to save this woman and her people in the first place.

You're my hero, Lucien. You always have been.

Well— I suppose there is that.

She asked me to be here, she asked this of me. So, I will do my best to make her wishes a reality.

"I'm here to warn you of an incoming invasion. Genevieve, and the majority of the Draconians, as well as a portion of the Sephilim Aerial Fleet, are on their way here right now. They want to take the city from you." I am blunt, glancing sideways to the horizon on which Soleus is but a speck.

Regardless of its seeming innocuity, they'll be here soon.

Aliandara sits upright from where she's been lounging, her scantily clad form shimmering with the swirls and intricate loops of her end-less tattoos. She's wearing a gossamer sheath that's patterned with silver stars over a midnight blue bikini that barely covers her nipples.

"Don't be so ridiculous," she spits, fury twisting her face. I know the look, and I know that the anger is fuelled by terror.

"Why is it so ridiculous?" I ask her, tired.

"The Sephilim would never attempt to sever the alliance they have with the Artemisian Equinians. We provide all their armour— all their weapons—" she stammers.

"Do you have an army of Dragons?" I ask her, point-blank, not a flicker of amusement passing across my expression.

"What? Of course not! You know—" she begins to go off on another time-wasting tirade. I ball my fist, shaking slightly as my temper curdles, souring my blood. I let her finish despite the fact I'm barely listening, and then inhale, ready to say my piece.

"Well, Genevieve has an army of Dragons to offer Lord Black in exchange for the city. Do you think he'd turn that down for— a few mediocre weapons?" I ask her, blinking slowly now.

"How dare you speak to me—" She gets to her feet, but as I take a step forward to square up to her, refusing to be intimidated, a shadow falls over us from overhead.

"My Lady!" It is another female warrior, this one with long blonde hair. I think I've seen her before— though where I can't place.

"Rohana, I'm in the middle of—" Aliandara hisses, but Rohana blurts, speaking across her superior. I see the physical wince behind her eyes as she lands softly on the balls of her feet, Aliandara glowering like a pissed-off bull.

"Dragons! Hundred— maybe more, just on the horizon! And they're not alone—"

She's out of breath as she straightens. I watch Evangeline lean forward, edging toward the end of the sunbed and taking Aliandara by the hand, seeking comfort in her lover.

I cock my head, giving a deadpan glare to Jess as she turns to me, her mouth open.

"You're welcome," I mutter.

"Mobilise all units. I want the walls fully manned, all equine bodies capable of flight ready to defend the airspace—" she spits, her jaw tensing in a way that's almost too masculine for her delicate face.

"Yes, Ma'am. I'm on it!" Rohana gives a curt nod, and then, as she goes to launch into the sky, something stops her.

I follow her gaze, finding a Dragon's silhouette crisp against the diamond-scattered velvet overhead.

I watch as she moves to draw a hand back to the bow that's resting, holstered between her wings, and then recognise the target she's about to shoot.

"Wait! That's Anastasia! I brought her with me, and others— you know, to help—" I explain, and Rohana looks to Aliandara, her fingers brushing her bow and refusing to relinquish their purchase.

Aliandara looks up at the creature that slices through the air and begins to make its descent with graceful ease.

"It's alright Rohana, I recognise this beast—" She waves a hand, dismissing the warrior. "Jess. Go with Rohana, help her," she barks as an afterthought, not turning to the woman who is standing like a statue beside me.

I don't feel her move, but when I glance sideways, she's already airborne.

I watch as Cosmo touches down, the glittering diamonds embedded in his wings catching the golden moonlight and spraying it across the veranda like water. Anastasia glides down from his spine, her motion seamless like molten metal as her armour flashes between silver and shadow.

As she approaches, I spot a sky-bound Ebonara following close behind before coming in to rest beside her companion.

Anastasia's face is taut as Evangeline turns to face her.

"Lady Dragos, how nice of you to come to our aid." I can't work out if it's a backhanded compliment or a genuine one, but either way, we don't have time to stand around chatting.

"You need to evacuate your people, Aliandara. I have seen how this ends and it isn't well for you."

I expect the warning to affect the High Lady of the Equinians at least slightly, but she merely shrugs.

"I shape my own destiny, Lady Dragos. If I listened to prophecy, I'd have never taken this city in the beginning. All the scriptures told me that it was Ares' city to take. But I stood, and I fought. I will stand and fight again." I wonder what the hell she's talking about and watch as Anastasia stiffens.

"I'm warning you," she says calmly, her face tranquil as a summer meadow and just as subtly wild.

"Warn away, child. We will fight. It is who we are," she exclaims, and Anastasia shakes her head, sadness in her eyes.

"Very well."

I recoil slightly, looking at Anastasia and wondering why she doesn't try to fight for her cause. I'm curious then, as to how many times she has come forward with a vision, only to be ignored by immortals who think they know better—

"Where do you want us?" I ask the High Lady, deadly serious.

I know in choosing to fight, the carnage will be great. After all, once the Dragons have us cornered within these walls, very few will escape. The Equinians— the whole of Aetheria, has never seen a Dragon army this large actually attack. They don't know what they're capable of when harnessed with ill intent. Sadness courses through me, at what Genevieve is doing to their already broken reputation.

After this, the name of Draconians will be stained red forever.

Still, though, I stand my ground, squaring my shoulders and thinking of Kairi.

"I want you and Anastasia here with your beasts, as my last defence against the Draconians. My priority is keeping Evangeline safe and the library beneath the villa from falling into the wrong hands," she explains and I cock an eyebrow.

I'd never heard about a library in Eclipsia before—

My curiosity piqued, I nod, looking at her and her lover who stand holding hands.

"I suggest you go and armour up, ladies. You're going to need all the protection you can manage, as well as your best weapons and steeds. If you have firepower, now is the time to use it," I suggest.

Aliandara's smile turns wicked and feral.

"Draconian, you think we're beaten because of some damned giant lizards? You do not know the Equinians as I do."

"You're right, I don't," I admit, sighing. Nothing is going to convince Aliandara to do anything else than stand her ground. I might as well try not to piss her off too much.

"Well, you and the rest of the Draconians are about to find out the truth of the matter," she threatens.

"And what's that?" I ask, itching to get moving.

"War is what we do."

GENEVIEVE

It has been a long time since I last made a night flight to Eclipsia. I had done so often in my younger years; coveting the golden sands and rippling sapphire waters of the city's oasis. I had been searching for somewhere to settle the Dragons, back before we were banished, back before anyone knew what I was capable of.

Things have barely changed, and I feel my eyes grow wide as my hair is swept back off my face when Gage commands Aqua to sweep to a lower altitude.

We lead the pack, the alabaster scales of the Dragon turning golden as the moon hits them and rebounds. I cling to her neck, not liking flying without the psychic connection I had enjoyed with Algoric.

It feels good to be flying so quickly again, the serpent sighs from where it is coiled over my branded skin and I feel my lips curve, heartwarming as the city before us grows larger.

The streets flicker with pinpricks of light every few feet, the low buildings seeming fragile as we get closer to the wall.

Gage speaks suddenly, his voice barely audible above the howl of the wind in my ears.

"What is the plan of attack?" he asks. I think for a moment, weighing our options.

"Send the Sephilim into the airspace over the city to take out their archers, I want them to be the first line of attack. Then, we use the Dragons to breach the city walls and take out their defences from all angles. I don't want to start fighting inside until the outer defences have been neutralised. I won't be cornered, not with all our Dragons in one place," I explain, my cheeks flush as hot blood is pumped militantly around my body in time with my excited heart.

"Good plan. I can sense a large amount of panic, even from this distance. I fear they may know of our arrival—" Gage adds, and as I squint into the night, I realise he might be right.

I can hear the faint trill of horses whinnying, the clatter of steel armour against stone and flesh as bodies move into defensive positions.

How is that possible? I wonder, feeling disappointed.

I had hoped for the element of surprise.

"I suspect Lord DeLaurent might have something to do with it—" Gage confesses, and I'm shocked as my head jerks so I'm glancing at him over the back of my wing.

"Impossible. I left him handcuffed in the Solis Castra dungeon!" I spit, furious.

"I saw him in the Astrid Keep right after your speech," Gage admits. I feel my sharp nails dig harder into the scales of his Dragon.

"And you didn't think to mention that small detail?" I hiss, and Gage gives me a withering look.

"I am not getting involved with whatever the hell went wrong between you two. I am a High Lord of Nemesis and I have made myself available for your disposal. I chose your side. That should be more than enough."

I'm startled by the ice in his tone, by how completely he has suddenly become the High Lord I always saw within him but never witnessed actualised.

I bite my tongue, hating the fact I have to hitch a ride with him because my own steed is no longer capable of flight.

I lower myself to Aqua's neckline, swallowing my anger as we begin our descent. I hear Gage call out the orders we just discussed and watch with a racing heart as the Sephilim soldiers sweep forward. The Dragons slow, allowing the Sephilim, their gold armour dripping bright with moonlight, to take the lead.

So much for stealth.

Then again, if what Gage says is true, stealth will be of no use anyway.

Damn you, Lucien.

I look around me, at the magnificent fleet of Dragons, scales of crimson, onyx, jade, bone white, silver, and midnight blue shimmering wildly as their leathery wingspans ripple.

This is the first time in over a century many will have been out on the battlefield, and the first time ever for many. I am excited to see what they can do.

We dive, peeling off from the Sephilim and landing in a cloud of sand as talons struggle for purchase.

I leap from Aqua's neck, setting down a short distance away and placing Algoric upon the sand.

Wait here, then when it's safe you come find me, okay? I ask him, stroking his cool forehead with my index finger.

I watch as he buries quickly beneath the sand, and then I'm once again alone.

I see them then, the Equinian women positioned shoulder to shoulder upon the top of the enormous golden wall, bows drawn, arrows aimed directly for us.

It's time to ask them to surrender.

Leaping up, I return to my position in front of Lord Gage, not settling on the nape of Aqua's neck, and keeping my wings spread wide. Beating them hard, I hover as I clear my dry throat.

"Equinians! Stand down. Surrender your city and open the gates or face my wrath as I take it by force!" I exclaim, my voice tiny as the desert wind blows fiercely in what seems like all directions at once.

The scent of spices, of roasting meat and something pungent yet floral is whisked into my nostrils as I inhale deeply. I know soon it will be saturated with the tang of blood instead.

The Equinians will never surrender.

Not that I care. It's been a good several centuries since I got in the middle of a bloodbath and, in a way, I miss it.

Also, I've never come to the field with this much power behind me before, and the knowledge that I'm almost certain to win is nothing if not intoxicating.

Is this what Aro has been chasing? This God-Like invulnerability whereby everyone becomes suddenly small and disposable?

I don't hate it like I thought I would. Just as I no longer hate him as I thought I would forever.

The Equinians don't move, if nothing else, pulling their bows tighter and tensing in the face of my army.

Idiots.

"Very well. You have made your choice," I call out, beating my wings hard and rising through the sky.

As I ascend, I hear the archers stationed along the wall release their arrows, and so tuck my wings in tight, spiralling upwards like a hurricane and grinning through it all.

None of these so-called expert archers even get close.

I find myself among the glittering golden armour of the Sephilim before I can blink, and it is as I unwind my wings and reach out with a single hand, that I utter the command which to me has always felt like a magic spell.

"*Attack!*"

The order sends a shockwave of sudden motion through the fleet as they charge forward, wings beating together like an enormous heart as they had in my dream. However, this heart beats for me and me alone.

I rise higher in the clear night, and it is then that I see Gage wasn't wrong when he said that The Equinians had been warned.

A fleet of Alicorns hover, hooves flailing as their wings keep them in place, their glittering manes floating like they're immersed in water.

As the Sephilim charge forward in kind, they displace the air around me, causing me to rise higher in compensation. I take a final glance at the two competing sides set to clash in the skies, and then, I'm sweeping back down in an artful plummet to the Dragons. To my people.

I circle the group of antsy Dragons, their riders equally impatient to get started. I take the opportunity of half the archers being occupied with what's going on overhead to begin my work here.

"Charge the gate!" I call, merciless, in a clipped icy tone.

The words reach the riders, and then moments later I watch as they spread out, the Dragons galloping across the sand without their usual grace but with all their usual speed. The Draconians without Dragons move around their flanks and sweep low to the sand, surrounding

434

their weakest spots, such as ankles, shields drawn and ready to defend them against incoming arrows.

I don't even know if such weak projectiles will pierce the Dragons' thick hide— but I'm not willing to take the risk.

The Dragons are only just taller than the walls themselves, and as they grow closer to the archaic golden barrier, their shadows fall over the faces of the Equinian warriors who stare up at them. With grim determination, the warriors draw broad swords from their hips and throw their bows aside, armour glittering dully.

We could of course fly into the city, but by attacking in this manner we are drawing the majority of the Equinian's forces to the outermost rim of the urban sprawl. This means we are also dispersing them over a wider area, weakening their power in numbers considerably.

Aqua charges forward, leading two others, a pack of three in total, who have chosen to take on the gate directly in front of where we had first landed. There are three other gates, like the points of a compass facing east, west, and north. We though, shall take the south gate first.

Aqua is flanked by a monstrous, yet young, black Dragon with charred carmine wingtips and glowing red eyes.

I haven't seen the male Dragon before, but I recognise its rider as one of the recent graduates of our military programme at the academy. He has a viciousness to him I distinctly remember.

The Dragon on Aqua's left is leafy green and bulky as I have ever seen, her horns are enormous, the tips spiralling like tree branches in a brassy hue. Aqua rears, her taloned feet coming down upon the double-barred doors of the gate laid into the thick build of the wall.

It shakes but doesn't budge, and as the Dragon rears again I watch as more archers gather overhead. I swoop down, taking out one of the women on the far left as I draw my sword and slash at her with a precision I have not utilised in a long time.

The heat in the air around me builds, and I hear a deafening roar as I fly past the rest of the archers, spiralling and avoiding their precisely placed arrows as they whizz close past my ears.

I smile, knowing truly I have missed this.

Turning back, I'm surprised to find the scene before me not the same as it was only moments ago. The monstrous roar had not just been a roar, but a warning. I watch as the charred Dragon with a vicious rider belts fire out of its enormous maw and down onto the warriors atop the wall.

It's a sign.

I had thought the last of the fire breathers had been lost with Algoric. The others, our fiercest warriors, were the first targets and biggest casualties of the Sephilim-Draconian conflict.

Their return in this magnificent beast is surely a gift from Hecate for claiming what is rightfully mine at last.

Fuck you, Lucien. I think, smug. Then I'm brought back to the moment as the thundering crash of an Alicorn falling through the roof of a nearby parapet breaks my rage-filled revelation. I'm staring, making myself an immobile target.

I turn my eyes skyward to find the battle between the Sephilim Soldiers and The Equinian Alicorn riders is turning, and it isn't in my favour.

I could send Dragons to aid them, but honestly, they're keeping the majority of Aliandara's most skilled swordswomen occupied while the others work on the gates.

I rise, dodging more arrows as though they're moving in slow motion, darting higher to get a view of our position on the other three gates.

The other Dragons are taking fire, but it is merely flesh wounds from what I can see as I circle high above it all. For the most part, the Draconian foot soldiers are doing a fine job of deflecting the archers' close-range attacks from atop the wall.

I hear another roar, another crash of taloned feet smashing into the metal of heavy-set doors, before returning to the trio Gage is leading.

Curving in a low arc, I approach the rider of the firebreather with a wide smile on my face. The flames catch onto the fabric of the Equinians' clothes and leave them howling on their knees.

"You!" I bark, hovering close to the beast's throat.

The rider turns to me, his hawk-like eyes sharp and focused.

"My Lady!"

"You have a fire breather! What's your name?" I call, my voice hoarse over the clang of metal on metal, flickering flames against flesh, and growling Dragons.

"Kane! What can I do for you, My Lady?" His eyes soften as he stares upon my pale face, something like powerful respect and awe stirring behind his dark eyes.

"You can circle the city and set light to the guard atop the wall!" I command him, and he blinks slowly.

"Yes, my Lady! Right away, my Lady!" he says, the gusto in his voice fierce. His dark hair is blown back from his prominent brow as he kicks the Dragon's sides with his heels, and the two of them take off to carry out my orders.

I hear a cry, and then I see it, several golden silhouettes plummeting from the sky, motionless.

The Sephilim are falling—

I glare upwards, finding the fighting has escalated yet again.

Then, the tide shifts, and the sky is full of dark clouds.

Inevitably, sharp forks of lightning follow.

I watch as more Sephilim appear overhead, and blink.

I spot him amongst them, Ariah by his side with a hungry look in his eyes.

Lord Aro Black has come to join the fight, and he's brought the rest of his army, not to mention their leonine companions.

They swarm like shimmering golden bees between the forks of lightning, taking out riders and their steeds from overhead in a brutal second wave of aerial fighting.

Kensari fly toward the horses without fear of taking a hoof to the face, teeth bared as they lunge forward with claws drawn. Whinnies of pain can then be distinguished between the crackle of thunder and the falling of bodies as they hit buildings with a thud.

I hear a splintering, and then a groan amongst the cacophony of fighting, followed by heavy breathing and the acrid smell of smoke and molten metal.

Whatever they're using to bar the door is giving under Aqua's immense weight.

I loop back, taking a final glance up at the vicious Alicorn on Kensari fighting happening in the thick clouds overhead, sparks of lightning and the gleams of moonlight hitting swords flashing intermittently like struck flint.

I glide down to the sand, another immense thud hitting me through the soles of my feet as the vibration of Aqua's talons on the metal gate reverberates through the ground.

Dodging the sweeping long tail of the mossy green Dragon, lined with rock-like spikes, as it swipes at the remaining Equinian warriors, I vault.

Using my wings to extend my airtime, I launch myself from the sand, landing primly behind Gage on Aqua's scaled spine.

"About time—" Gage breathes heavily, gripping his Dragon tensely between his thighs as she sets about rearing again. His biceps bulge and I see the slick coat of sweat on his skin. He isn't used to riding like this or fighting like this. None of my army are.

"I heard whatever they're using to bar this door splinter. You're close!" I exclaim, and I feel like I can hear Gage giving a wicked smile.

His wings flare out like scaled parachutes, almost hitting me as the Dragon beneath us rears more fiercely than ever before and he struggles to keep his balance. I place a scorching hand on the back of his neck, steadying myself. If I burn him, he doesn't complain.

Aqua's front feet, each the circumference of a small boulder, come down upon the doors once more. I hear a snap and then a groan as the two of them slowly ease inward.

Sand is blown up around my face, and for a moment all I can do is listen to the sounds of the war going on around me.

The dim rumble of a lion's warning. The dying cry of a mystical horse. Sword on bone. Arrow loosed from a bow. A Dragon's monstrous growl as it inhales acrid desert air, before breathing gallons of fire down onto the people trying to keep us out.

When the dust clears, I find the doors swinging on their hinges, wide open before us.

We step inside, heads held high, like we own the damn place.

Technically, I suppose we will very soon.

31

THEM

KAIRI

I'M GLITTERING IN THE rouge glow of my metal armour.

It clings to my underbust, my shoulders capped by the same mate-rial rising over the ivory leather of the laced corset beneath, cupping my breasts tightly and protecting the place right over my hard beating heart.

Stepping out into the largest chamber of the many which secretly sprawl beneath the temple of Hera, eyes dart to me, to the sword strapped to my waist, to the rosy sheen of the bow between my lilac feathered wings.

Dawn, Trinity, Vail, and Silver are at my spine, and clear their throats, drawing the attention of the few Harpies who were not al-ready silently staring at the five of us with wide eyes.

"High Lady Kairi Freemont, y'all!" Vail calls out, and the room breaks into raucous applause. I flush, my still bandaged hands sweaty as I rest one on the hilt of my sword and use the other to brush a lock of hair behind my pointed Fae ear.

"Thank you," I breathe, and though the sound is barely more than a whisper, the moment my lips move, the entire crowd hushes, heeding my words.

"I just want to say—" My heart is beating violently beneath the metal cage of my armour. "That I'm sorry if I disappointed any of you as I stood on that balcony. If I made you feel like I didn't care when I ran away at the ascension ball. I just didn't want any more of you to have to get hurt or lose people because of me. I thought I could control Lord Aro Black by keeping myself out of his reach and then by leashing him from within the palace. I— I just wanted to do what's right by you. All of you," I apologise, an enormous weight lifted from my shoulders as my wings flutter lightly against my hip.

"I just want to be the High Lady you deserve," I add, seeing them nod in agreement. Hundreds of shades of purple glisten within their irises, and then Dawn steps forward.

"You know, Kairi. I've been here a long time, and I don't think any of us have ever gotten an apology before from a High Lady, let alone a Queen. You really are what we have been waiting for, what Aetheria has been waiting for." I wince internally as the word Queen falls from her lips. Then, I watch, astounded as the crowd before me drops to their knees and bow their heads.

"All hail Queen Kairi!" Trinity barks and I watch as the room moves to place delicate palms over their hearts.

Looking up once more, I find most of the eyes full of tears.

How had I ever doubted these were my people?

Perhaps because I hadn't bothered to get to know them—

Shame wells up inside of me and I swallow hard, straightening my spine.

"Thank you, truly, but please, get up, all of you. We have more important things to deal with, and as of right now, we are equals. We are all headed into battle, we are all putting our lives on the line." I blush, and if it's possible the room seems to garner even more respect for me. Even Delphine, her auburn hair picking her out towards the middle of the crowd stares in awe.

The hairs on the back of my neck prickle, their attention too much in the dim flickering light of the chamber.

"We need to get ourselves to Sapphire City. I owe it to Aliandara to help her in this—" I admit, and watch as a woman I recognise, a woman I had met during my ascension parade through Soleus, stands.

Her dark curls are piled up atop her head, her wings heavy with protective chains.

"Your Highness," she addresses me by what is now presumably my assigned title, and I feel physically sick.

"Please, call me Kairi," I correct her, smiling with as much grace as I can muster.

"Kairi, yes— our ladies topside, they wanted you to know that there's been a lot of electrical activity around the Temple of Zeus, they think that—" she begins, but Silver cuts her off.

"Lord Black has gone to join the fight?" she enquires. The woman nods.

"And took his entire army by the sounds of things from our informants in the castle. They fled the site, but they said that as they were leaving via the kitchens, they saw the remaining aerial fleet mobilising—" She frowns, and I think of the women in the Solis Castra.

Outing the Harpies had put them in danger, and I hadn't even considered them, my people, as I'd been issuing orders to help the Equinians.

My stomach tightens, my mouth goes dry.

We don't have the numbers to fight the entire Sephilim Army, and the Draconians— not even with Aliandara's horsewomen and archers—

I look at Dawn, glancing back over my shoulder and feeling suddenly frozen to the spot as I turn back to the room.

Everyone is looking at me, even Dawn, on whom I've always leaned. They want to know what to do.

I think about Lucien, about how he had foreseen this, how he had known what Hera was asking of me before even I had. He knew we needed to unite Aetheria.

"I need to go and talk to the Fae, see if we can get them on board to come and help. I want you all to prepare to leave, get all the Kensari you have, take as many weapons as you can carry— I'll be back as soon as I have an answer, hopefully with reinforcements."

I make no promises, no grand speech or rousing moral debate. I simply tell them my plan, realising these people must be beyond sick of being lied to by those leading them.

They deserve the truth if they're going to potentially die for this cause.

I also realise just how strong the Nephilim are as they straighten and get back to work prepping quivers of arrows and strapping on rose gold metal plates to various limbs.

I had underestimated them because they seemed weak, seemed genteel and fragile.

I had underestimated them just as Aro had underestimated me as a mortal, and I'm incredibly ashamed as I turn back to the four women who had made all this possible.

I know better now, and I will do better.

I owe it to them, to the Nephilim. To my people.

"I'll be back," I tell them, and Vail steps up.

"Me too, honeybee," she says, looping her arm through mine.

441

I go to protest, but then realise I have no idea how I'm going to convince Morpheus to help us, let alone the Equinians.

"Thanks." I smile at her, blushing, and she shrugs.

"We're best friends, girl. You know I'd do anything for you. Now let's go get some flower power on our side."

A best friend— I've never had a best friend before, at least not one I truly believed would always be there for me. In Vail's southern drawl, her rosy cheeks, and bright eyes, I find the strength I'm missing.

With that, we conduct from the chamber, fingers clasping onto one another for dear life.

Nirvana unravels around us in a blur of green punctuated by a spattering of neon petals. It's raining, but the droplets don't reach us as our feet touch down on white hexagonal tiles and my lungs fill with the scent of jasmine.

I've conducted to the last place I visited.

Morpheus' greenhouse.

A girlish shriek sounds, followed by the smashing of a glass vial.

"Friggety frogspawn!" Morpheus curses, and despite myself, my lips curl up into a smile. The rain continues to hammer down on the glass roof, and I make my way toward the commotion, tugging Vail behind me.

When I turn the corner and peer into the area of the hothouse that is furnished, I find Morpheus, Hypnos, Ember, and Neve crowding around a small workbench. Neve looks furious.

Shocker.

"You know I told you flash freezing is a delicate process. You knew the glass might shatter, Morpheus!" she exclaims. Morpheus goes to retort, but then Ember turns, drawing attention from the conversation and onto us, the unexpected visitors.

"What are you doing here— and what are you wearing?!" she exclaims, crossing her arms over her silk-blanketed breasts.

"We're here to ask for your help, Lady Ember," I say softly, stepping forward into the moonlight as the rain clouds overhead part a fraction.

I hear another slight tinkle of glass as Morpheus rubs his hands together, sighing like I'm a teenager asking for a curfew extension.

"More help, it's almost as if you Nephilim are nought but helpless damsels—" he sighs, a wicked grin pulling his entire face into a twisted expression.

I feel Vail drop my hand, and before I know what's happening, she's drawn her bow and is shooting an arrow directly past Morpheus' left ear. He blanches, and I blink, searching for the arrows landing place.

After a few seconds of my eyes darting around, I find it. The arrow is hanging in the middle of one of the rope webs of a dreamcatcher twirling from the ceiling.

Morpheus cocks an eyebrow.

"Quite the trick, you must be a sensation at parties dear—" his voice is drab, his eyes ringed with dark circles. It's clear he and the other Fae High Born haven't been getting much sleep.

I wonder how Quinn is faring, but Phineas' absence is all the answer I need.

"Look, I know you didn't want a war. Neither did the Harpies of Hera," I speak the title of my army for the first time, a delicious tingle running down my spine as pride wells in my chest. "Genevieve has an army of Dragons and Sephilim attacking Sapphire City. Lord Black and she have allied, and we need help keeping them from invading the city—" Morpheus turns back to me from where he's staring at the rose gold sheath of the arrow as it twirls, still pristinely balanced within the centre of the dreamcatcher.

Cocking his head, his tired eyes suddenly light up.

"Wait— wait— let me get this one hundred percent clear. You're telling me— you are actually saying that Genevieve and Aro have teamed up against Aliandara?" His eyes sparkle, and I stare at him with a dead expression, body tense. This was not the reaction I was hoping for.

"That's the truth Morpheus, innocent people are going to die if we do nothing—" I state, the words leaving my lips with a subtle hiss.

"Not my problem—" he shakes his head, twirling on the spot.

"Excuse me?" I ask, unable to believe what I'm hearing. "This isn't theoretical, Morpheus. People. Are. Dying." I grit my teeth.

Hypnos looks at Morpheus and then at Neve with cold, dreamy eyes, the hint of a smirk pulling at her full pink lips.

The smell of the flowers sticks, cloying in the back of my throat as I swallow, the tension in the air palpable.

"So, let me get this right? You want me to put the people that Aliandara has called 'hippies' and 'pussies' for the better part of half a millennium at risk to save her sorry ass? Are you kidding me, child?" he demands, expression wild with disbelief. I can only shake my head at the fact he's citing petty insults as a reason to let people die.

"I'm asking you to do the right thing, the moral thing, no matter who it helps." I growl, "And for the record, that's Your Highness to you—" I spit, and Morpheus' eyes widen.

He laughs, throwing his viridian-haired head back and howling like a wolf. He dances upon the balls of his feet, flitting from one leg to the other as he giggles maniacally. For the first time, I'm not endeared by his eccentricity, I'm made uncomfortable by it. The hairs on the back of my neck prickle in warning, and I stare at him as he gallops and guffaws, his long limbs sharp and unpredictable around him. He seems unhinged, vicious, and lethal in a way that's bordering on psychotic.

I take a half step back, breathing in deeply and trying to keep my cool.

"You came to the wrong place if you're looking for help for those warmongers, they deserve everything they get— *Your Highness,*" Neve sneers as Morpheus continues to howl with laughter. Ember doesn't move either, surprising me immensely.

Vail touches me on the arm, her fingers light yet sure.

"Come on Kairi, they're not going to help us," she relinquishes and I know she's right.

It was a waste of time coming here, and I had been a fool to hope they might forget their differences with the Equinians to prevent bloodshed.

"You know, you sit here and do nothing. But I wonder what will happen when they come for your lands? After all, what makes you think Lord Black will stop with Sapphire City? What makes you think that you won't find yourself cowering as Dragonsfire burns Nirvana to ash?" I ask Morpheus, straightening as I spit out the words like bullets.

Ember scowls at me, the look more vicious than I've ever seen on her face, but I don't care.

"I have more important things to worry about than getting involved in some war I didn't start, Kairi. I'll remind you that our lands are dying, and so is Quinn—" he says, as though I've completely forgotten what's happening. He shifts in half a second, from the maniacal, back into the composed yet unusual creature of grace and poise I have always known him to be. I can hardly believe my eyes as I swallow, continuing without pause.

"And so, I remind you not to come to me for help in the future. You will not find it. Not with me, and not with Lucien. I stood before that damn crown and I was ready to give everything to stop more people getting killed. I wonder what you think gives you the right to pretend you're an artist, or a leader, making decisions like this. You disgust me."

The air around me crackles, a gust of wind catching my hair, but I give him only one final disappointed glare.

Then, I turn on my heel and storm out of the greenhouse.

Vail follows me back through the main living space, close on my heels, her bow still clutched tightly in the white knuckles of her fist.

"That was terrifying— You were— I've never seen you that angry." she breathes, looking up into my face and swallowing hard.

"I'm done with this pacifist crap, Vail. I'm done with bending and scraping trying to stop the war that it seems so obvious now is inevitable. It's time for us to stand up, swallow our fear, and fight. I'm not settling for less."

Vail nods, hooking her bow back between her wings, beside her quiver full of arrows.

I stand, statuesque, looking into the still waters of Morpheus' infinity pool.

"You have my loyalty, until the end. Though I'm sure you already knew that." She smiles at my reflection, and we both take a moment to breathe. Her blonde hair is soft, both our skin rosy and flushed in the fluid mirror beneath our feet. My wings flutter against my spine, a heaviness settling in my stomach. I'm nervous. I've never been in a battle a day in my life, let alone had to lead an army.

"I am a richer woman than I ever thought I could be," I say to her in a small voice, immensely grateful she had accompanied me here. "Thank you."

She takes my hand in hers, and we return to the Temple of Hera, having gained nothing from the visit except for the certain knowledge that the only people we can rely on are ourselves.

LUCIEN

I cannot deny the irony of it all. I have fought my whole life to try and make the Draconians seen as peaceful, to be known as good people despite the past. And yet now, I'm standing, watching as the truth of it all finally comes to the surface.

The world is on fire, burning like a dying star around me.

The weight of Genevieve's hate, of Aro's bloodlust, of their need to dominate, has reached critical mass.

We are imploding.

I stand there, braced to fight in the middle of Aliandara's Villa courtyard, watching the fighting unfold overhead amongst plumes of growing dark smoke and tumultuous rolling storm clouds.

The walls of the city are ablaze on all sides, a black Dragon whose rider I know from the Academy, Kane, making the rounds and turning the entire circumference of the city into a smoking barrier. Now, it is impossible for the people inside to escape.

Of course, they could fly, but they would have to make it out of the brawl seething overhead, dodging Alicorns falling, mauled from the sky, and Equinian horsewomen setting loose arrow after arrow at the guilty Kensari in their grief.

The new arrival of Lord Black and the rest of his Sephilim army hasn't helped, and I find myself teetering on the edge of mounting Ebonara and getting right into the middle of it.

I would do that, but I know, if we make it out alive, whoever is left of the Kindred of Artemis are going to need a leader, going to need the strength of Aliandara and Evangeline.

I glance sideways at them as the fourth gate tumbles, sand skittering over my feet as a kind of vibrational tidal wave makes itself known in my calves.

I'm not surprised, we have also stood firmly through the falling of the eastern, western, and southern gates, we have also heard the screams and watched as the battle overhead casts a shadow over the fighting now surging through the city like a cancer. The Dragons are crawling the walls and terrorizing the streets, picking off pedestrians and horse riders alike as they try to save their homes from destruction.

Aliandara has her head cocked, her eyes certain. Her gaze remains fixed on the flimsy metal gate, that I have no doubt Aqua will trample like it's made of toothpicks, despite the fact I'm staring at her.

Anastasia watches as a group of Equinian soldiers swoop down on horseback over the Oasis on our right, filling metal buckets to try and put a dampener on the raging flames consuming the wall.

If they can get those out, then we can move our forces so we are surrounding Genevieve.

Maybe then...

Before I can finish that thought, I hear the guttural roar of the firebreather and eye Ebonara who is smelling the air with eager nostrils before us. Of course, her icy breath would extinguish the fire no problem, but she's the strongest of the two Dragons on my side, and my priority is Aliandara and Evangeline.

She stands shoulder to shoulder with Cosmo, the first line of defence now that Aliandara's guardswomen have been reassigned to aid the soldiers who need support the most. The breach of the wall had taken the first half, the appearance of Aro's reinforcements the second.

Still, two Dragons shouldn't be sniffed at.

Then again, when you're up against an army of nearly a hundred, maybe a little sniffing might not be too overdramatic—

Hooves clatter on the pavement, a warning trill as three horse-women on Unicorns slide around the corner of the narrow street leading to the Villa. I stare at them, at their panicked faces, as they grow closer only to find the gates closed.

I breathe in, drawing the sword from my hip and gritting my teeth.

Following the Unicorns and their riders, I see Aqua skid around the same corner on all fours, tail waving like a serpent behind her for balance as her alabaster wings flare. Then, only seconds after, the charred black firebreather climbs around the side of the building rising high on the left of the alley, slithering in front of Aqua and leaping down onto all fours, teeth bared. The rider throws his head back, the sword clutched in his enormous fist glittering with Sephilim-made lightning from the sky.

I predict his move before he makes it.

Ebonara, defend! I command her and watch as she rears back on her hind feet. The Unicorns and their riders see her intent and scatter before they reach the gate, each taking a different path along the edge of the fence line as they flee the Dragons pursuing them.

Aliandara and Evangeline, their Alicorns beside them, both take a step back. Their steeds, Stabbatha dark as shadow and Aerilyn light as the sun, rear back, nervous chittering escaping between their teeth.

Ebonara's feet slam forward, and I watch as she encases the entire length of the fence in a high wall of ice, the misty white of its immense density completely eclipsing the view on the other side of the metal divide.

The chill that comes off it comforts me, and I nod sideways to Anastasia who gives me a worried glance as she grabs her sword and then positions Cosmo between us and Ebonara.

Two Dragons between us and an army, and that's if we're lucky enough to not capture the attention of any of the soldiers overhead.

We need backup, and we needed it yesterday.

I jump as something falls from the sky, landing atop the roof of the villa behind us with a thud.

I turn on my heel, expecting it to be a Sephilim, but instead what I find is worse.

Rohana is dead.

The leader of the Equinian's army is a broken doll as half her torso hangs, arms dangling limply over the corner of the roof.

"No—" Aliandara's voice is broken, and I turn back to find her eyes wide and disbelieving.

Evangeline's face is slack with horror, her fingers visibly trembling on the hilt of her bow. Her golden armour shakes atop her torso as she takes a rattled breath.

I look at them both, then at Anastasia, who merely shakes her head slowly, eyes devastated.

She knew this was coming, and she tried to stop it to no avail.

I have never envied her power less.

I hear the distant crash of a building collapsing, perhaps beneath the weight of a Dragon's sharp claws or a Unicorn's mutilated corpse. The cries of people burning, the smell of charred flesh, the tang of blood and the tingle of static building in the air.

A roar breaks the moment apart like it is made of cobwebs, and then I feel it, even from this distance. The firebreather behind the wall of ice launches its counterattack. Ebonara senses the flames licking at the cool surface of the barrier and begins reinforcing the weaker parts of the structure, as we have done in practice many times before. However, the hotter the Dragonsfire gets, the less water there will be in the air for her to work with.

Eventually, the barrier will fail, and we will have to fight.

Cosmo spreads his wings, and I look to the others.

"Come on, we need to spread out. You two should try and get the best vantage possible if you intend on fighting with your bows," I suggest. Aliandara nods, looking at Evangeline.

"You should go and get situated on the roof; you'll have a better shot from up there. Remember, aim for the eyes of the Dragon, I think we can agree they're probably the weakest point—" she instructs her.

Evangeline nods, eyes wavering to Rohana's lifeless corpse atop the villa where she'll be positioned.

"I will leave Aerilyn with you if you are staying here?" she whispers, touching Aliandara softly on the cheek as she hesitates to leave.

Then, Aliandara does something out of character. Her mask of tough indifference melts, and she wraps her armoured forearm around Evangeline's waist, kissing her hard and with more passion than I could ever imagine lying beneath her stony façade.

I think of Kairi then.

If I get another chance, I won't waste it.

A whinny, and then suddenly I find a dead Alicorn falling directly in front of me, missing me by only inches. I step back, off-balance and with dark wings spreading as the poor creature's feathered limbs twitch once and then it gives up its last breath.

Blood seeps into the gaps between the paving stones, and I blink slowly, my eyes tracing upward.

The battle, if you can still call it that, is on its last legs. The swarm of golden armour has overwhelmed the majority of the sky, and I glimpse Alicorns running off into the distance, riderless, between forks of lightning as the Sephilim soldiers use their conduction ability to their advantage.

They won't last much longer, and when they're done with the sky-bound enemies, they'll come down on us too.

Another cry from the firebreather, another belch of flame from the deep hot cavern of its dark throat. I can see Ebonara's ice wall sweating, and I feel my palms getting clammy right along with it as the air becomes increasingly arid upon my tongue.

A flash of lightning breaks my focus as Evangeline takes flight and lands gracefully on the roof. I draw back my sword, preparing to take down whichever Sephilim soldier has dared try to test me, watching as Aliandara spins on the spot and draws an arrow back in her bow.

My breath is trapped in my chest, but as the light recedes, I exhale with more relief than I thought I was capable of.

She stands, hair glistening in the glow of her rose gold armour, wings flaring out in a glorious lilac plumage behind her. Her eyes sparkle as she finds mine, and then she is not alone.

449

Out of thin air, a lightning storm larger than I ever imagined ripples into existence.

They join her.

Nephilim.

Hundreds of them.

I let my sword drop to my side with a clatter, my muscles unbound and my heart leaping into my throat, stepping forward and closing the gap between us.

Her lips find mine beneath the burning sky and the falling Kindred, our arms clasping around one another like destined vices, fitting perfectly.

The kiss is passionate, eclipsing all else, our lips desperately hot as she presses her flawlessly presented figure against my bare chest.

"Fancy seeing you here—" she breathes. I inhale her deeply before taking a step back.

"You— you're—" I don't know what to say.

"I know. We don't have time. I have reinforcements. Where do you need us?" she demands an answer, her fingers flitting to the sword on her hip without a second thought.

She's beautiful in an entirely different way, but I don't have time to take it in.

People are dying, a lot of people.

"Overhead. The Sephilim brought reinforcements too," I say and she nods, looking back to her army of once-innocent angels. They stand there, armed to the teeth, Kensari companions itching to take flight and join the fight. Glossy hair and bright, clean faces shine out from the darkness surrounding them as plumes of smoke, dust, and sand are thrown into the air.

People are still screaming, but as I stare at them, all I feel is hope.

I don't have time to query the help any further as Kairi's bandaged hand slips from mine. I glance at it, wondering what the hell had happened.

Did she crown Lord Aro Black King of Aetheria? Did she lay down and submit to his cruel desires?

"Kairi!" I call, suddenly fearful for her.

She turns back, her spine deadly straight, her head held high, eyes sharp.

She's goddamn regal.

"Yes?" she asks. I pause, swallowing my instinctual response; to tell her to be careful.

"I love you," I say with as much conviction as I can.

She smiles, nodding with certainty.

"I know."

Then, winking, and more playful, more confident, than I've ever seen her, I watch her take off, wings sprawling outwards as she soars toward the unit of Nephilim who are awaiting her instruction.

I see Dawn among them, Vail, Trinity— How long have they been waiting for this moment? How many years have they been hiding their abilities?

I ponder the question only momentarily before a sword comes flying down from overhead, sent spinning from someone's hand when they needed it most.

I watch Ebonara pace, and then as she is midway through her fourth wave of reinforcements, I hear it. The vibration of heavy footsteps, footsteps which could only come from one Dragon.

Gorge, the stonespitter.

He is the most densely muscled Dragon I've ever seen, with mossy green scales and rocky spikes along his spine that house no end of lichen and creepy crawlies.

I know what's coming then, my heart pounding.

Ebonara! Get back! I scream down our bond and watch as her head snaps around.

"Back! Get back!" I cry out to the others, watching as Cosmo turns tail and trails Anastasia's wing-aided leaps across the courtyard. She flits from side to side, dodging falling debris from the fight overhead.

The thud which follows could be an earthquake, and I find myself stumbling for balance as Aliandara, Stabbatha, Aerilyn, Anastasia and Cosmo gather, pressed against the outermost wall of the villa.

There's nowhere left for us to run, with a fight we're losing still raging overhead, and Dragons crawling the city walls and trawling the streets. Draconian soldiers take to the skies as well, aiding the Sephilim one by one where needed as the Nephilim rise in glinting rosy gold to meet with their long-time oppressors.

Then, another thud, though this one is more devastating than the last. Ebonara takes off, landing atop the villa beside Evangeline with as much grace as she can manage. I watch as Evangeline cowers in the shadow of the Dragon, the tiles shuddering beneath her feet, before straightening. Her attention is drawn to the ice wall that has been protecting us, as is mine.

An enormous crack forms, starting at the top where the ice is thinnest and then spiderwebbing down to the ground.

Another thud of a densely muscled body pushing against the frozen barricade sounds, another heartbeat fighting to be free of my ribcage passes.

The ice is then entirely severed in two. The gate stands no chance, and I watch my companions brace as shards of ice and metal are sent showering down upon us like lethal rain.

I should be hopeless, be terrified, as my nose fills with the smoke and ash of the city that's burning around me. However, all I can think of is the fact that the woman I love has returned to me.

And she looks like a fucking badass.

32

LONESOME DOVE

GENEVIEVE

THE GATE FALLS IN a shower of metal and ice, the Stonespitter's enormous mass finally breaching the outermost defences of Aliandara's Villa.

Lucien might have come to aid her, but the appearance of both Ebonara, and infuriatingly, Cosmo, had pinpointed exactly where I should target.

The villa was innocuous from overhead, seeming little more than another sprawling, low-slung collection of walls. I should be thanking Lucien for making the epicentre of the Equinians' power so obvious, but I doubt coming face-to-face with him would lead to any kind of actual gratitude.

Even the mental picture of his stupid face leaves my blood boiling and my jaw tense as I fly up from the spine of Kane's firebreather, who he has informed me is aptly named Scorch, wanting to get a better aerial view of the Villa's defenders below.

That's when something catches my eye that I don't expect, glistening in pinkish streaks as they dart amongst the Sephilim, I find angels, female Nephilim, have joined the fight.

What the—

My thought is interrupted as an arrow flies past me, far too close. I squint to find the source, finding High Lady Evangeline standing atop the roof of the Villa, Ebonara beside her. Cosmo also stands before her, Anastasia straddling his spine with a sour expression on her face as her eyes rise to find mine.

Bitch.

After all we've been through, and she chooses him— she chooses the Equinians over her own damn people.

She deserves everything that is coming to her.

I tighten my fist around the pommel of my sword, which I'd sheathed as Kane had tried to tackle the ice wall.

I look down into the narrow alleyway. Three Dragons. Aqua pulls up the rear as The Stonespitter and Scorch take the lead.

I swoop in low, catching the gazes of both Kane and the female rider of the Dragon I've heard referred to as Gorge.

"Kane, you tackle the ice breather. Then Gorge can occupy Cosmo for a while— we need to get inside the villa, we need to get to Aliandara."

As I bark orders, landing abruptly upon the ground beside the two enormous Dragons, I wonder if I had known that subconsciously my intent all along has been to kill Aliandara. It is an obvious conclusion, knowing that she would never surrender her city. To her, the respect of her people is worth more than her life.

I suppose we have that in common.

My feet are firmly planted upon the ground as I draw my sword, watching Equinian soldiers swarm from other parts of the falling city, diving down into the Villa's courtyard and taking up defensive stances. I see several perch themselves on surrounding roofs, bows shimmering in their elegant fingers.

I suppose then, this is where they will make their last stand.

I take off, wanting a better view.

Scorch and Gorge follow me, and I hear their guttural roars as they hover over the courtyard, enormous wings beating offensively, baiting Cosmo and Ebonara into the skies.

Ebonara and Cosmo respond in kind, launching themselves skyward without warning. As the four Dragons clash in mid-air, I watch wings swipe, talons slice, and claws snatch. Scale hits scale as the bodies writhe and tangle in the air, violent and brutal. Teeth snap, and my soul wilts with it as I watch the battle overhead, suddenly still.

The Sephilim and Nephilim, as well as the remaining Equinian horsewomen, scatter in their flight paths as they continue a collective descent toward the courtyard, the Dragons clashing without any regard for who they might kill in the process.

What have we become?

I had always wanted to stop the Dragons from being used as weapons, and now it is I that wields them against themselves.

I blink, then dive, avoiding yet another arrow, this time the source being a woman with dark hair riding a Unicorn. Her eyes are like a hawk's, trained on me as the beautiful creature beneath her rears and then takes off in pursuit of my flight path.

I rise through the air, disappearing above thick clouds for long enough to lose her, dodging several Alicorns that are charging about the sky without riders.

Looking down at the streets below, I see many more of them running unattended, ready for the taking.

Immediately, I want them to be mine.

I let my body fall, taking in the state of battle as the world comes up to greet me and my wings billow sideways.

"Gage!" I call, making a graceful downward arc with my body as I land softly upon Aqua's spine.

"Yes, My Lady?" he says, watching the Dragons brawling overhead. His eyes are wide, his expression slack.

"Round up as many Unicorns and Alicorns as you can," I order him, and he nods.

"Looks like the fighting is coming to a head." He gestures to the courtyard, now filled to bursting with fighting bodies. At the very back, I find a group of Nephilim taking up defensive stances before a few figures pressed against the outer walls of the building, and it's then that I see him for the first time.

Lucien.

His blonde hair blows in the breeze, having come loose from his braid, and his cheeks are charred with God knows what. He's bare-chested, his muscles rippling as he shoves The High Lady Equinian behind him. He doesn't see me, but I see him, and it makes me want to hit things.

I turn to a few Draconian soldiers who have gathered against my spine, watching as the rabble of bodies glistening with different coloured armour continues to thrive with violent chaos.

I gaze at the scene before me, realising we can't get any more bodies into the cramped space— not without risking serious friendly fire.

I need to redirect the rest of my forces to the outlying areas of the city.

"I want you to go and drive out any remaining Equinians. They could be hiding anywhere— buildings, alleyways, the sewers— I want them all gone. Not one is to be left standing when this battle is done, are we clear?" I look at them with sharp eyes, and I watch them nod. Some of them aren't even looking at me when they do so, transfixed by the brutal fight going on behind me.

455

"Go. I have work to do," I spit, turning sharply from them and letting my wings flare outwards for effect.

I catch sight of Lucien again, his sword drawn, his body moving with the grace of a ballerina rather than a hulking Dragon rider. He always was nimble in a fight.

The rage inside me at the fact he had escaped the Solis Castra, at the fact he has once again divided our people so completely reaches boiling point.

I grit my teeth and draw my sword, diving into the throngs of fighting individuals.

My blade catches on the rose gold glint of a Nephilim's rapier as she darts forward in a flurry of voluminous brunette hair, sighting me and not waiting even a moment to strike.

I lean backwards on my right leg, bringing up my boot to kick her in the midriff, but miss as she pirouettes and loses her balance before falling into a Sephilim soldier and the Equinian woman he is fighting. The Equinian woman's face is strewn with blood and she looks practically feral. Celtic tattoos whirl beneath all the scarlet, as she helps the Nephilim I am fighting to her feet with a strong and unwavering grip.

The Nephilim leaps, wings spreading sideways before forcing herself down into the ground with her rapier. I dash, aware that she's played her hand too early, and watch with satisfaction as she struggles to get the tip of her sword unhooked from the grooves of the courtyard stonework.

I go to make a killing blow, the muscles in my body tensed beyond what I remember them being capable of.

Before my blade can make contact with her rosy flesh, an arrow flies through the air, piercing my wrist through and through.

A scream is loosed from my lips, the sound of it lost amongst the clatter of steel and cries of agony. I am not alone in my pain, but that doesn't make pulling the arrow out any less horrendous.

I snap the head from the arrow sheath with quick shaking fingers, my heart hammering as I stand there, disarmed quite literally. The Nephilim I'm fighting pulls desperately on her rapier while I'm distracted, trying to free herself as her wings flail behind her.

I see tendon and bone as the sheath comes out far too slowly. I tug on it, not having time for a proper examination as blood spurts down the front of my pants.

I toss the arrow's remnants to the ground, and then with bloody fingers, I take a deep breath in, wrapping my scalding palm around my injured wrist and cauterising what I have to.

Lunging to avoid a Sephilim who accidentally backs into me, I swallow the pain, scooping up my sword which has been lost momentarily among the quick feet of battling Kindred.

I turn just in time to meet the rapier of the brunette Nephilim with my sword, arm screaming, but I don't make the same mistake twice.

Swiping her feet from beneath her before she can take flight, I proceed to skewer her through the navel.

I watch as her eyes grow wide, lips spreading and blood spilling from between their petal-soft skin. She falls from my blade and I kick her aside, licking my own blood from my fingertips and allowing my eyes to dart from face to face as my mind sharpens with the rust of it.

There's a crash, and I feel the world around me vibrate.

Ebonara and Scorch have crashed into one of the nearby buildings, sending dust and rubble flying skyward as their scrap continues, silver blood spurting dramatically from somewhere within the wreckage.

At the thunder, which travels through the ground of the city, the people fighting stop for a split second, glancing over their shoulders or craning their necks to get a better look at the damage.

I take the opportunity to weave through the crowd, knowing if I rise to fly over the teeming mass of helmeted heads, I'll only pick myself out as a target.

The wound on my wrist stings, reminding me that I am capable of taking damage, though, after my first true kill in more years than I can count, I feel damn invincible.

It's then I am met with another opponent, this one a Draconian soldier I recognise. She works in the caverns beneath the Astrid Keep, helping maintain the Dragons. She's named after a planet I believe.

Coming face to face with one of my own stops me in my tracks, but only long enough for her to hurl herself forward, dark hair falling loose from what had once been a topknot.

"You'd raise your sword to your High Lady?" I ask in a whispered hiss as our blades clash, faces coming so close our foreheads could crack together like coconuts.

"You're not my High Lady. My High Lady would never do something like this—" she retorts, her eyes gleaming bright, teeth bared as she pushes back from my blade with a shove.

She stumbles slightly, tripping over a helmet that's been dropped on the floor.

It could very well still have the wearer's head inside for all I know.

Our blades clash again, but her rage doesn't give her the edge she thinks it does. Sidestepping her next swipe, I refuse to even parry, swinging my sword up and embedding it in her spine. Scalemail scatters everywhere as the force of my blade rips her armour apart. I don't stop, ramming the blade upwards with as much force as I can muster so it creates an enormous gash between her wings.

She wilts forward like she's praying as I prize the steel edge from her spine. Then, she collapses, a pile of leathery wings, flesh, and blood which could have been so much more than dead.

If only she'd sided with me.

Suddenly, the world seems less like Draconians versus Equinians or Sephilim versus Nephilim.

Suddenly it seems like dog eat dog, every woman for herself.

Race means nothing when it comes to loyalty for some, clearly.

I spot Lucien, herding Aliandara into her Villa as a line of Nephilim fail to hold back a swarm of Golden helmets and angry swinging swords. I see blood running from split temples, I see scraped cheeks, and yet— I see bright eyes.

I see hope within them.

Fury rises within me in turn.

I waste no more time fighting fodder, sliding between opponents face-to-face and allies back-to-back, dodging the pirouettes which cause wings to fly outward in an Avant-Garde display of majesty.

Aro's eyes watch me with something like respect from overhead, his body clad in thick metal plates and hovering over his men, thoughtful in his expression. Creeping through the crowd, I keep my head down, not meeting anyone's eyes, let alone his. My black clothing stops me from being more noticeable than I have to be, and I pull my hood up over my stark bloody roots and ivory locks as I slink past two Kensari, a male and female, fighting amongst themselves with feral roars. I vanish from his line of sight, a shudder running up my spine at the thought of his approval.

Ducking between two columns, I continue forward, sneaking around the side of the Villa and heading toward the veranda. I behead two Equinian soldiers who are too distracted fighting Sephilim to notice me without breaking stride.

I nod to the winged men, who bow their heads in respect, blood spattering their visors and dull grey feathers.

"They need you out front," I tell them, and despite the fact I'm Draconian, despite the fact I'm not their High Lord or Lady, they do as I command.

I wonder then how completely the world has tilted on its axis, as I have gutted one of my own, and am respected by Zeus' dark angels.

Slipping inside, I make my way through corridors lined with overly sumptuous fabrics and garish metal artwork. I smear the blood, still wet on my hand, upon the wall, marking my territory as I wander around the elaborate maze of the building.

I hear him then, his step unmistakable.

I could fight him head-on and win. But something about the way he so royally threw me away, like I meant nothing, makes me want to take him by surprise.

As my hand continues to run along the wall, I meet with a tapestry, seeking somewhere to hide. My fingers slide over it, finding air where the wall should lie behind the thick woven fabric.

I whip it back, stepping into the shadows of the alcove that falls into a steep staircase of crooked stone steps. My heart is thrumming joyfully in my ears, and then it stops a moment as I hear his voice echo out in the passage beyond. I slow my breathing, listening.

"Aliandara we must get you out!" he cries, and I smile.

He knows they're done; knows they're fighting a lost battle.

Victory is so close I can practically taste it mixing with the blood that hangs heavy on my tongue.

"I will not leave my women, Lord DeLaurent. I cannot. I will not." Her voice is cold as steel and just as sharp as she yanks her arm from his grasp.

I watch, transfixed by the heat in her face and the cold in his.

"Lady Montgomery, if we do not begin evacuating you and your people, there will be nobody left. We are outnumbered, and your people need you to survive this. They're going to need someone to look to— they're going to need—" He is breathless, and I see his pale skin covered in gashes, blood, and dust. His hair is dishevelled if only slightly, a fact that gives me an unnatural thrill.

"You dare to tell me how to lead my people? After everything your people have done? This is your fault!" she hisses, fists balling.

She flounces on her heel and storms off, determined and feisty as ever.

459

That'll no doubt be what gets her killed.

Lucien stands, stone still in the corridor, breathing heavily. I watch the muscles in his back tense, watch his fists curl and uncurl, watch his head bow as despair and pain hits him like a wrecking ball.

I reach for my sword, hand brushing the hilt, fingers trembling.

I lie in wait behind the tapestry, the air electric as I pull the blade from its sheath as quietly as possible.

Tightening my grip, I tense, breathing in slow and deep.

He turns, as though sensing someone is watching him.

I find his eyes, darting from one end of the corridor to the other, his face young and boyish, as though he's lost.

I remember him then, sitting at my feet by the fire in my suite, flying alongside me when Algoric had been alive.

I pause, and that's all it takes as Lucien turns and leaves the corridor at a slight jog to rejoin the fight.

I exhale, not realising I had been holding my breath so desperately. My arms shake and I slump back against the wall on my left, the cold stone calming me.

I will kill you, Lucien DeLaurent.

I am just not ready.

Yet.

I want to scream at the chokehold my emotions suddenly seem to have over me, my throat constricted in the darkness of the passage, my heart pounding so loud I can't ignore it.

I grit my teeth, closing my eyes as a tear trickles down one blood-stained cheek.

I sigh out, breathe in, and ground myself once more, looking around me.

Where the hell does this passage lead anyway?

KAIRI

You think you know what it'll be like, what it'll feel like.
War.

I have read a thousand books, seen a hundred movies, heard hundreds of songs with this very moment at the core of their plight.

Nothing could have prepared me for this.

Blood is spattering my armour, the rouge turned red, the ivory leather stained beyond repair, tainted.

My muscles are screaming, my wings beating desperately as I'm thrust into a fight I know I'm not ready for. I thought Aliandara had been being dramatic during our training, but she was right.

I'm caught in the midst of fighting a Draconian man, his huge body and massive weight intimidating on pure sight alone. He brings his sword down to clash with mine, my wrists crying out for relief as I block him with my rapier. I grit my teeth, bending my knees and using my weight to push him away from me. I use the moment I had been taught to look for to my advantage, watching as he stumbles off balance, not expecting such power to come from someone so small. I jab him in the thigh, twisting my blade and wincing internally as I watch him scream. I haven't killed anyone yet, haven't had the heart to, but I know that time is coming.

It terrifies me.

The Draconian falls, clutching his inner thigh as I yank out my blade and turn my back on him, conducting to the opposite side of the courtyard.

Am I afraid to end the life of someone I don't even know?

Yes.

Maybe that makes me weak. I don't know.

"Kairi!" His voice sends a reverberating warmth through my bones as I feel air gush into my lungs.

Turning, I find him among the throng of endlessly fighting Kindred, their bodies not seeming to tire as minutes turn into what could very well be hours for all I know.

My nostrils fill with the smell of rust and burning, my eyes watering as I glance skyward.

Two black Dragons tumble between masses of storm cloud, their motion like thunder as each and every blow rains down on the city in waves of brutal sound.

"Kairi!" Lucien moves, darting between me and a projectile I had been too enraptured to notice. The arrow is smashed to pieces as it freezes in mid-air, Lucien's outstretched hand shaking.

He closes the distance between us.

"Is that Ebonara?" I ask him, having been too caught up in the fighting to have noticed that Dragons are battling one another as well. If that isn't a testament to the overwhelming nature of this experience, I don't know what is.

"Yeah. I don't like this, our defence is weakening—" Lucien gasps, breathless as he comes to my side and places a gentle hand on my shaking shoulder.

We're aside from the fighting near the fallen iron of the fence work, but neither of us put our swords away.

I see what he means as my eyes jump from one sight of massacre to another. Dead horses lie strewn like melancholy confetti, trampled by uncaring feet, their riders hacked to bits beside them. There are Nephilim among them, and Draconians. Even when I glimpse bodies coated in golden armour lying strewn, in pools of their own blood, I find my heart breaking.

I hope Leo is okay.

I hope everyone is okay.

I know they can't all be, but the hope that by some miracle they might have made it through this is all that keeps me standing.

Maybe that's naïve, but it's all I have.

"We have to get everyone out," I whisper, a whinnying cry breaking the thoughts racing around in my head.

"I tried, Aliandara won't leave—" Lucien replies, and I shake my head.

"She's not in her right mind, Lucien. Let me— I'll take full responsibility for what happens, but I'm ordering the Nephilim to start evacuating people. I can't watch this anymore; it's turning into more of a one-sided massacre than a battle. I think it's clear that the Draconians have taken possession of the city. If they find Aliandara they'll kill her."

Lucien nods, folding his arms, his sword dangling casually beneath his elbow as he sighs.

"She won't go easily, Kairi."

"I know, leave that to me. Get everyone into the villa and I'll send Nephilim to start conducting everyone out— I don't know what you think, but—" I begin, but he snaps his fingers, watching as a Sephilim spots us and turns fully to face us.

"Drakos Vale. It's the only place safe enough."

He practically read my mind.

"Right, let's do this." I exhale heavily, and Lucien moves to take flight.

"Kairi?" he says, looking back over one shoulder.

"Yes?" I ask, narrowing my eyes as I survey the crowd for my ladies.

"Badass looks good on you, *mon ange*." he compliments me, causing my head to snap back around as a grin overtakes my face.

Blushing, I nod, watching as he takes two enormous strides and launches himself into the air to meet with the looming Sephilim soldier.

I hope beyond hope he's alright.

I dart to the left, stretching my wings, but just as I am about to gain enough speed, something snags my foot and I'm sent crashing into the ground.

The wind leaves my lungs, my hands scraping against the stone and blood that's seeping slowly into the concrete. I bite down on my lip, feeling blood spurt from the plump cushion of flesh as I twist, skidding onto my back.

I can't see the sky, only the silhouette of a Sephilim guard as he launches himself on top of me.

"Bitch!" I hear his hiss as his gauntlet hits me around the side of the face. I spit blood, my head thudding with the pain of the blow as my neck is yanked sideways with the force of his fist. Blotches float in front of my vision, and I scramble for my sword.

It has flown out of my hands and is lying out of reach, and all I can do is stare at it longingly.

The man's green eyes are wild with rage, his fist pummelling me, his hand reaching to his belt in search of his weapon.

I know what comes next, and squirm frantically, heart in my chest as I hear his blade unsheathed.

I swallow air like it is cocaine, addicted to the clarity it brings with it, but just as I think I'm about to wriggle free, the enormous man places his knee down into the centre of my navel, crushing me into the dust.

Straddling me, I am engulfed by the scent of his sweaty body, of the blood and sickly-sweet aroma of pears on his breath.

He comes in close, wings casting me in shadow as they spread, bringing the blade to my throat.

"Think how glad Lord Black will be when he hears I slit your pretty little throat—" He is gleeful in his malice as the blade cuts into my skin. I swallow, the motion causing the blade to snag just a little deeper over my frantic carotid.

I hear him inhale, tired of waiting, and bring my knee up into his crotch.

I know it won't hurt him because he's wearing an armoured cup, but he instinctively recoils anyway. I sit up, and as he tries to swing his dagger, I dodge, taking his head between my palms.

My entire body is clenched, on the edge of being murdered, desperate.

I twist with all my strength, listening to his spinal cord sever.

Snap.

It's so simple, so quick, one minute his tension there, and then gone.

His lifeless body collapses on top of me and I lie there, stunned beneath his weight.

My eyes are open, staring overhead at the lightening purple sky, my mind racing.

What have I done?

I can't breathe. Can't escape the sickening feel of his head internally decapitated and lolling from side to side on my fast-rising chest.

Then, a sudden thud brings me back to the battle.

My head snaps sideways, and I find a Sephilim soldier, frozen solid like a statue looking at me with dead eyes.

I hear footsteps, their rhythm familiar, but still lie there, the scent of death, the scent of this man's body seeping into my every pore.

My rescuer lifts the weight from me, offering a hand.

I take it with numb gratitude, my heart unable to stop in its frantic thunder.

Lucien sees my expression, and he places both hands on my shoulders.

"Kairi, you did what you had to. Now, get to the Nephilim. I'll start gathering the remaining survivors—" He nods to me, certain when I am unsure, strong when I am weak.

His midnight blue eyes ground me, and I force myself to breathe, swallowing and feeling the bite of the man's blade echoed in a slight twinge.

I would be dead if I hadn't killed him— that's the truth.

Turning from the scene, I take flight this time vertically, having learned from my mistake.

I beat my wings hard, distracting from the memory of the man's spinal cord snapping. It rings in my ears, but as I spiral through the air, I'm grateful to be distracted by something else.

It's like whispers, behind the ambient noise of battle, and it makes the hairs on the back of my neck rise in reverence.

I dodge an arrow loosed from a Draconian bow, watching as Ebonara and her opponent crash toward the Oasis. The Dragon with charred-looking scales and burgundy panelling hits the surface of the water first, and I watch as Ebonara catches herself in her descent, bright eyes narrowing.

She proceeds to freeze the water solid, trapping the Dragon within.

Diving, I get in as close to a cluster of Nephilim as I can manage, hurdling out of my flight path and over a dead Unicorn.

"Silver!" I call as I see her going toe to toe with some Draconian swordsman.

"I'm busy!" she snarls, twisting.

"Get everyone to the Villa. We're out of here!" I exclaim, and she gives a half salute as she leaps backwards.

I watch as her opponent is then skewered through the eyeball by an arrow. Tracing it back, I find Evangeline giving a cocky smile.

But for every single one we take down, three more take their place.

There are Draconians everywhere, their swords coming crashing down with more muscle than the Equinian swordswomen can handle. Dragons are crawling atop the surrounding buildings, their riders shooting long steel arrows down upon the fighting in the Villa court-yard. If they can tell where their arrows land, they have better eyesight than I do, but I wonder if they particularly care.

A pair of Dragons soar overhead, this time a mossy green monstros-ity fighting Anastasia's midnight blue Dragon. The sunrise catches in diamonds studding its wings, lighting them on fire as the two of them crash into the courtyard, sending the fighters scattering in all directions.

My eyes widen as the bodies writhe and tumble across the stone weave. Biting, swiping and clawing at every piece of unprotected flesh they can find, they roll across the thick carpet of corpses.

This is it; this is my opportunity.

Both Dragon pairs are occupied, their screams pierce the air like it is fine glass.

I let my wings flutter against the air as I slow my descent, landing beside Evangeline atop the Villa.

"Get inside, we have to get you out of here!" I exclaim, but as I fear, she shakes her head.

"I can't, not until I find the horses, they got lost in all this madness but they won't have gone far. I need to find Stabbatha and Aerilyn."

She has the look of a woman who won't be argued with, and as I stand beside her, the fatigue of the fight hits me.

I don't fight her. I just nod, exhausted.

"Go and find them! But hurry! Aliandara needs you!" I exclaim and Evangeline nods!

"She needs Stabbatha too, Kairi. You don't understand— it might be the only thing that can make this loss bearable for her—" Her eyes are sad, and for the first time, I feel myself wilt.

We've lost the battle, and if an Equinian High Lady is admitting it then I know it's over.

We have to get out of here before there's nobody left to save.

"Go, go!" I exclaim, and she nods, swiping up the quiver of arrows before strapping it to her back. She palms her bow, the bow I know has saved a lot of the people I'm trying to protect too, and spreads her wings, gliding down to the courtyard without another word.

An enormous tail comes down, mossy green and jagged with stone. I don't see it in time and am thrown backwards as the roof struggles to remain standing after impact.

I fall on my back and close my eyes, grimacing against the pain. When I open them, I'm looking into the lifeless face of Rohana.

No.

How could someone so strong, so prepared, have died in this, while I am still standing?

She stares at me even still, and I reach out, closing her eyes before staggering to my feet.

That's when I see him across the courtyard, swinging his sword with a wicked grin, chasing the last few terrified horses with a cruel laugh. They gallop, legs scrambling beneath them as they try to avoid the Dragons brawling and the Sephilim High Lord chasing them for his own amusement.

Our eyes meet and he stops in his tracks, gazing up at me as I stand on the roof, hands on my hips.

I don't glare, or spit, or taunt. I simply stare at him with disappointed eyes.

He looks up at me, the man I had once thought to be a hero, and then smiles as he returns to slaughtering innocents, turning his back on me as though I don't even matter.

33

DECLINE AND FALL

ARO

THE SUN IS RISING somewhere off in the distant sky, and my body is filled with rage. Horses stream past me, their braided tails slapping their behinds as their hooves catch blood-stained rubble and send dust flying.

I'm beside the warring Dragons, baiting those Unicorns trying to flee on foot with a wild, slashing blade, when I see her, standing upon the roof of Aliandara's Villa. Her hair is swept sideways on the chill breeze of fading night, her wings expanding to their full length as she squares her shoulders and glowers at me.

The vision of her eclipses all else in my mind as I stop, staring with a smile.

I smile, not because she's beautiful, but because I know that despite the fact she's beautiful, I never really loved her.

I wanted to possess her, wanted to control her, but I had never really given her my heart, just as hers had never truly belonged to me.

It is a relief, rooting out this weakness of my past in this moment of utter violence we call the present.

It is no gift, not to anyone, as the world I had pictured when I permitted this invasion isn't the one I'm currently existing in. I thought I would have the crown of Aetheria, and Genevieve would be but a vassal, lands in exchange for allegiance.

I hadn't foreseen being stripped of the crown before it had even touched my head, and so now I am left wondering—

What will become of the title? Of the position of a single leader who has the power to dictate to the four continents, by the will of the Gods and Goddesses who created them?

Will it be every man for himself now?

I look at her as she stands there, majestic despite her frail-looking frame and lacklustre wings that are speckled with red, and as I see the armour which clings to her every curve, I realise it is so much worse.

It won't be every man, but every woman as well, out for the control I currently hold.

What is to stop them from taking my weapons, from seizing my power for themselves now I have no crown to demand their obedience and loyalty? I had already thought of this when I had refused Amethyst weapons to my men, my paranoia having been born the second I had resurfaced from beneath Zeus' towering stone gait.

I know the answer, and it curdles my blood, setting my heart frantic as I watch Kairi Freemont conduct from the roof of the building in a flash.

Genevieve.

It will be she, and her Dragons alone, that have the muscle to protect my position for now.

There is nothing to stop her from taking my power— but perhaps I can leash her in the way that the Heirbound would have tried to leash me.

Can I control her?

After everything?

After I've shown her exactly how strong and capable she truly is?

Hera has a lot to answer for, having put me in a position I would never have chosen. I stand to lose everything, stand to fall into the oblivion of time as a memory long forgotten.

I breathe in the smoky air with vigour at this desperate notion, my nostrils flaring as a set of horses run past me, their breathing ragged and their lips pale with froth.

The Dragons, which are writhing in the courtyard, flip. This time the midnight blue beast ends up on top as it pins the wing of the mossy green creature beneath its razor-sharp talons.

I hear a guttural cry and turn to find the source coming from behind me on the banks of the oasis. Watching as Lucien's Dragon takes off into the sky, I am intrigued to find it suddenly ripples into nothingness. The beast camouflages itself seamlessly, fading in and out of existence.

Interesting—

I scan the horizon, wondering whether Genevieve's firebreather has left this world for the next.

It would be a pity.

A great shame indeed.

I hear a roar, this time of the lion variety as my heart hammers hard against the inside of my ribs. My hair is blown back from my face as the battling Dragons slam into the front of the Villa, causing the entryway to collapse in on itself.

The courtyard is almost empty of all people, well, the surviving ones anyway. My guess for survivors is that they're hiding out somewhere in the city trapped by other Dragons, or they're flying looking for shelter somewhere else.

I decide to investigate what has become of Ariah, and then I will be on my way to pillage and plunder the city while the pickings are still good.

There might even be a few weak Equinian ladies up for grabs if they're willing to bend the knee, and then be bent over my knee for good measure—

The thought spurs me forward, my wings aching slightly. I have not flown so much or so fast in years, and the wound in my side still stings from where that bitch Nephilim had impaled me. It's healing, I can feel the itch of it, as well as the new itch of several gashes on my face, carefully placed by delicate Nephilim rapiers.

I still can't believe their betrayal, their secret agenda.

Again, Hera has a lot to answer for.

It's a shame I can't stand face to face with her, no tricks, no illusions, and show her exactly how far she's underestimated me and my Sephilim brothers. I doubt she would be so cocky then.

Gritting my teeth, I head toward the twisted iron and puddles of chill water surrounding what had once been the perimeter gate, finding Ariah facing off with two Alicorns.

The onyx lion bares its fangs, his orange eyes blazing with feral rage as both the mounts rear violently, froth spilling onto the ground around his exposed claws.

He swats, but the dark horse kicks with its front legs, whinnying. The animal steps back into a puddle, regaining its balance as it tosses its dark inky mane. The horn central to its forehead glints in the breaking dawn light, and I reach out, sending an electric current through the puddle of water and up into its central nervous system.

A high-pitched scream, not from the horse, but from a woman.

I'm caught off guard as she swoops in from above, kicking me in the back of the head and then swooping low over Ariah.

He growls, turning tail and charging after her as though she's a pigeon and he's a stray tabby. She sets an arrow loose from her bowstring, flying backwards momentarily as she sails down the narrow alley. It hits him in his front leg and I hear a feral grunt as he collapses in the middle of the street. She sees she's hit her mark, and twists back on herself, spiralling through the air and whistling loudly.

The white Alicorn sets off at a gallop to some unknown destination, leaving its dead mate strewn in the puddle that had been its ultimate demise.

She touches down, and it is only then that I recognise her beneath the glare of her metal visor.

Her usually curly hair is tightly braided back, shoulders square and lips pursed in concentration.

It's Aliandara's lover, Evangeline.

The meek-looking woman who had clutched onto Aliandara's skirts at official events, not wanting to look me directly in the eye.

She's not the same woman, the strength in her having been well hidden behind the finery and etiquette of her title.

"You killed Stabbatha." She glowers at me, and I look at the equine corpse, its feathers and mane fluttering in the slight breeze.

"Bonus points for me then I guess—" I shrug, reaching for my sword.

"Points won't count for much when you're dead," she snarls, the tattoos on her arms glinting wildly.

She moves in a predatory stride and stows her bow, sidestepping the body of the black steed and swallowing hard. She doesn't have a sword, merely a dagger that's cinched to her belt by a simple loop of leather. Her body is waiflike, her flat chest giving her an advantage of balance over many of the women I've fought today.

"You really think you stand a chance against me?" I ask her and she gives me a sad smile, rolling her eyes.

Tossing her head like the horse now dead beside her, she leaps forward, not waiting for me to make the first move.

I step back, drawing my sword and dodging as she makes a deft stabbing motion at where my torso had been moments before.

I smirk at her feeble attempt to overpower me. She pushes back from me, and I move only barely, letting her put some distance between us. She is strong, as I would expect of a High Lady— but I am stronger.

I have Dragonsfire running through my veins.

471

I charge my palms, harnessing the rage I have remaining in the pit of my stomach, pulling on that image of Kairi and her stupid wings, looking triumphant.

Then, as she comes for me again, I drop my sword, deciding instead to place my hands against her upper shoulder in warning. She hisses as my palm scalds her, eyes widening.

"It's true—" she whispers, lips parting.

"Did you doubt it would be?" I ask her, cocking an eyebrow. She pants, nostrils flaring as she takes in a deep breath and moves to strike me despite the pain. This time she tries to hit me around the back of the head, using my proximity against me.

"No. I suppose not," she gasps, as I grasp her around the wrist, tossing her to the other side of the courtyard.

"Then why, why on earth would you try to fight me? Did you really believe you could win?" I ask, watching as she climbs to her feet.

Panting, she spits blood into the rivers of crimson running through thirsty cracks which have opened themselves beneath the weight of brawling Dragons. Somewhere in the city, I hear more buildings collapsing, but I don't have time to source their location as Evangeline leaps up into the air, spinning and drawing her bow from her spine once more. She towers overhead and then pulls back. The rising sun hits my face, and for just a moment I'm blind. I turn, moving to dart out of the way, but her aim is true.

I feel the arrow as it pierces my groin and scream, throwing myself forward.

I expect a death blow to come, but instead, I hear her feet touch down on the ground, and her voice turns trill.

"I didn't expect to win, Lord Black. I expected to distract you long enough to evacuate the survivors, including the High Lady of this villa. Winning was just a bonus." She smiles, smug, and then walks away.

I collapse onto the floor, my head cool on the stones as I feel my thigh throbbing. I look down at it, rolling over, finding blood spurting out of the wound.

"Evangeline! Time to go, my love!" I hear Aliandara's shrill tone calling her lover. Kairi's voice follows.

"We got everyone out we could find!" She is breathing fast, and I imagine her perfect pink lips, the thought of them continuing to move making my blood boil.

I crawl to my feet, sighting Evangeline's silhouette as she walks, limping slightly, toward the Villa.

Using my wings, I launch myself across the ground in a spider-like crawl, legs suspended only a foot from the stones below.

I charge into Evangeline like a pissed-off bull, knocking her forward.

She hits her head on the crumbling front pillar of the villa, and I hear her exhale like she's been shot as I climb atop her.

"*You.*" I bring my knuckles down into her face, my thumb catching the corner of her eye socket and making her gasp. "STUPID." My hands are still scalding as I pummel her face into pulp, my weight pinning her entirely to the ground. "BITCH."

I keep punching, the cries of onlookers lost on me as my fury reaches its pinnacle, and the culmination of everything that has been stolen from me hits full force.

"*You stupid bitch. You stupid bitch. You stupid bitch.*" I spit, delirious with pain.

I watch her go limp beneath me, skull caved in, brain matter puree. Then, I hear a cracking, like some primal force is clawing its way up from hell.

A roar erupts, and I know why.

The firebreather is loose.

I stagger to my feet, laughing as her hot blood sizzles on the skin of my face. Feeling my heart beating in my throat, I find Kairi restraining Aliandara atop the roof.

"*I will kill you! You son of a bitch you are fucking dead!*" Aliandara's words become an echo as I watch Kairi struggle to restrain her, eyes wild like she's possessed, hair spilling from her tight braids and her loose-fitting gossamer pants whipping around her. They're silhouetted as the sun finally rises, the sky vivid violet and the ground beneath my feet bloody scarlet.

The pain suddenly hits me, delirium overwhelming as the laugh I can't withhold gets caught in my throat.

There's a flash of lightning, a final sob of anguish that is left to be carried through the city by the breeze of a new dawn, and then I am standing, alone and surrounded by the dead in the courtyard.

I fall to my knees, looking to the cobalt orb of the sun for guidance as I realise with overwhelming agony that Evangeline's death brings me no true satisfaction. Not now the killing is over.

It doesn't matter if I kill one, if I kill a hundred.

They'll just keep coming.

No, if I want to put a stop to these traitors, to this injustice, then I have to do it myself, and I have to go to the source.

As the realisation hits me and the warmth of the dawn bathes me in relief, I collapse beneath the lavender sky, praying for darkness to take me so I can rest, so I can recuperate.

The storm is not over, and I need to be ready when lightning strikes again.

LUCIEN

The Astrid Keep had started out barren and empty, deserted by its previous long-time residents and their Dragons. Now though, with every single strike of lightning that forks through the air of the ballroom, the urgency and fervour of the atmosphere picks up a notch. People are bleeding all over the floor, crying out in pain as others tend to their wounds. Horses whinny and step from foot to foot, hooves clipping the stone floor repeatedly as their faces ripple with anxiety.

We're nearly at capacity, and I realise that with the Draconians I had managed to recruit, the Equinian refugees, and the newly exposed Nephilim army, the corridors are starting to get crowded. People spill out from the ballroom, slumping down against the walls on arrival and visually shivering. I don't know if this is because of the shock of what's happened, the adrenaline finally leaving their systems, or the drastic temperature change.

I summon a foot soldier with burnt orange wings mapped with bloody red veins, asking him gently to go and light every fire in the place and all the torches which have been extinguished since Genevieve's speech.

His eyes are wide, and I can tell he's too young to have seen battle before. I can't blame him for feeling shocked after what we've all seen, I'm no spring chicken and I had never witnessed anything like it either.

I inhale sharply as I'm tapped on the shoulder, a young Nephilim with auburn hair and round lilac eyes gazing up at me.

"Some of the ladies are talking, I think we need to get everyone something to eat—" she explains and I blink once, then twice. She is looking at me like I know what I am doing.

"Uh— the kitchens are on the lower floors to the east I believe, go and see what you can find. You have my permission to go anywhere in the Keep," I say, and she nods, giving me a shy smile.

Her dark pink feathers shimmy as she turns from me and walks away.

The cry of someone wounded reaches me above the cacophony of everyone's scared chatter, and I realise I'm standing here in the middle of the room like a sore thumb.

I've been waiting for Kairi to return with Aliandara and Evangeline, my heart lodged in my throat. The Equinians will be no good without their High Ladies to lead them.

"Lucien, our Dragons are inbound. I don't know the state they're in." Anastasia's voice pierces my distracted haze, brushing my bare shoulder with gentle fingertips.

Turning to face her, I find her elegant features tight, her pale skin spattered with blood.

"Did you see them leave?" I demand, having been too caught up in the nightmarish symphony of flying arrows and swinging swords to have noticed Ebonara's departure. I know she can look after herself, but it doesn't stop me from worrying.

"I am sensing Cosmo got away fairly intact, I can't tell you about Ebonara though. You should go down to the caverns to meet her, it's why I'm now heading back to Gemina Two. I'll be back, but I want to gather a few supplies as well as checking in on Cosmo," she explains and I nod, my chest feeling like someone is sitting on it.

"Have you seen Kairi?" I ask her, brow furrowing.

"No, I haven't. I thought she'd be back by now—" Her expression mimics my own, eyes turning hard as steel.

"That's what I thought too—" I admit, my arms tensing at my sides.

"You should also get your wounds seen to, you're bleeding on the floor—" Anastasia nods to the gash across my torso, unfortunate as I'd been slashed in the same place only a few months back by Aro.

"Yeah, I'll get round to it—" I sigh, "At some point—" she gives a small smile, her eyes full of empathy as things continue to unravel around me.

Where the hell are all these people going to sleep? Is my next thought, but before I can start fretting over a blanket shortage, a blinding flash of light yanks my attention to the centre of the room.

The sound that follows it chills my already cool blood, and I feel my eyes widen as Kairi materialises in the middle of the moonstone ballroom, her arms crushing High Lady Aliandara to her chest, re-straining her from behind.

I've never seen the High Lady in such a state, nor can I recall ever hearing such maniacal sobs. I tread forward as the ballroom falls silent around us, the only sound Aliandara's half-screams, half-sobs and the crackling of newly lit hearths.

Kairi is white as a sheet, her wings flailing so she can keep herself upright despite Aliandara's efforts to free herself. Her fingers become claws, gouging at the bare skin of Kairi's arms, her cheeks spattered by a mix of blood, dust, and tears. I watch the spectacle, noticing Kairi's hands are bandaged by bloody rags. I can't recall noticing them before, but I have been a bit distracted...

A woman separates herself from the crowd, the Celtic swirls of her tattoos barely visible beneath the blood coating her broad shoulders. Jess is purposeful, striding to her High Lady and promptly bringing the hilt of her sword to smash into the back of Aliandara's head.

Kairi is stunned but allows the now slumped form of Aliandara to hit the floor, letting go of her and dropping down beside her in the process. Her wings are shaking, her dark hair falling around her bruised, bloodstained face, her chest rising and falling.

I rush to her, giving Jess a sideways glance.

"Did you have to hit her?" I ask and she shrugs.

"As opposed to standing there gawping like a fish? I'd say she's happier unconscious for now—" She turns to Kairi, exhaling heavily. "What happened?" she asks, and I feel the room collectively hold its breath.

"Lord Aro Black— he beat Lady Evangeline to death. She was trying to protect Stabbatha, who also perished— I think her horse got away but— I'm not sure—" Kairi's lips are trembling, her eyes welling with tears.

It doesn't make her look weak though, the watery sheen veiling a fiery fury, a promise of revenge.

It makes her look unstoppable, even on her knees.

I give her a hand, noticing a thin line of dried blood on her throat as she takes my palm in hers and pulls herself to her feet.

Aliandara remains, breathing slowly and peacefully, sprawled on the floor at our feet.

"She needs privacy. And Rohana—" Jess begins, but Kairi shakes her head once more.

"Rohana is dead too," she announces, and I hear a collective gasp among the onlookers. It seems this is more shocking than even the death of Evangeline.

My heart breaks at even the thought Lord Black had taken his fists to someone so beautiful and genteel until she could no longer take breath.

He will pay for this, and for every other crime he has committed.

But first, the Equinians need care, they need to be together as a people in the aftermath of such a huge loss.

They need time.

"Take Aliandara to one of our suites." I look to a Draconian who has been standing close, her dark hair a mess of inky curls around her icy blue eyes. Her pale blue wings tremor slightly as she straightens beneath my gaze.

"Yes, my Lord," she replies.

I watch as Jess lifts Aliandara without difficulty, her upper arms bulging. Her expression is far from impassive though, eyes welling with tears.

I don't know who she's mourning, but whoever it is I pity the person who took them from her. Her grim determination as she leaves, the once fierce High Lady of limp in her arms like a snapped marionette, gives me chills that refuse to leave, even in the silence of her wake.

I turn to Kairi, who is glancing around at the room of refugees, hundreds of eyes trained on us, expectant.

There's a beat where I begin to draw breath, but before I'm forced to make any kind of speech, the door on the far side of the room opens and in walks my salvation.

The Nephilim girl who had approached me earlier has returned from the kitchens, and she's not empty-handed. Several other Nephilim accompany her, enormous crates stacked in their arms.

"Anyone hungry?" she calls, and then the silence is over. People get up from where they're strewn on the floor surrounded by discarded weapons and scraps of cloth being used for bandages, carrying their tired bodies toward the promise of sustenance long-awaited.

Watching the flurry of activity, I exhale, glad their attention has been directed somewhere else.

"Are you alright?" I ask Kairi, turning and placing my hand on the top of her arm. My fingertips brush the rouge metal of her armour and she recoils slightly like her skin is only used to pain and can't bear any kind of contact.

She nods, a small smile taking over her lips but not reaching her eyes.

"You're bleeding—" she mutters, and I roll my eyes.

"Yeah, I know. I'll worry about it later—" I shrug, and she remains stony-faced, staring at the diagonal slash that's weeping blood down my abdominals. It's not as deep as the previous wound, but if I stand still long enough and focus on my physical presence, it stings like a bitch.

"I have to go and meet Ebonara, check if she's okay. Want to come?" I ask, and she nods, her shoulders slumping as though she's relieved to be given some direction, some purpose.

"I'll conduct us," she offers. I smile, relieved, not relishing the idea of opening the Hematite seal when surrounded by so many people who aren't Draconians. It is an old habit, one I should break given the circumstances, but the veil of secrecy surrounding Draconian customs is ingrained in me even still.

Taking my hand with a shaking palm, Kairi glances up at me, and I allow myself to get lost in the lilac depths of her eyes.

After everything, the fact we're both standing here, hand in hand, is nothing short of a miracle.

Then, in a flash, the moment has passed, and we are transported down into the caverns below to face Ebonara's return together.

Down in the caverns, we walk with our fingers intertwined through the narrow passageways. I want to ask her why her hands are so heavily bandaged, in fact, I want to ask a lot of things.

In light of my curiosity, everything seems eerily quiet, and so I break the silence.

"Kairi, not that I'm not glad to see you. But what the hell happened?" I ask her, and she blinks slowly, sighing.

"Can I tell you later? There's just so much— I'm still having a hard time processing," she admits and I nod.

"But you didn't crown Lord Aro Black the next King of Aetheria?" I ask, unable to help myself.

"No. I couldn't." She doesn't explain herself, but I'm too relieved to care. I squeeze her hand in mine, turning the final corner to Ebonara's cavern.

We are just in time, as in the distance I see her darkened silhouette, picked out in stark jagged edges by the sunrise.

She swoops in a circle, slowing her speed as she approaches the ledge of the cavern that winds inside the mountain, blowing my hair back from my face. Kairi frowns, and I see why, as when Ebonara lands, I find her speckled in dried silver fluid which looks like molten metal.

"Jesus— that firebreather, he took quite the chunk out of her hind quarter—" Kairi says, rushing over to the Dragon and biting down hard on her bottom lip.

The Dragon's face is scratched up too, gashes weeping near her eyes, her front claws trembling, and her chest rising and falling heavily. Her silence says more about her pain than the chill rush of air that hits me as her nostrils widen and she slumps to the floor.

"My Goddess—" I utter the prayer, looking to the sky as though Hecate might be staring back at me. Though, if she cared about her Kindred at all, we probably wouldn't be here.

How could she let this happen?

How could Genevieve?

I had felt her eyes on me in the Villa, known she was sneaking around. I mean, you can't train with someone the number of times we have and not be able to sniff them out almost immediately. She had lost some of her prowess, and I had felt her emotions in the lack of action, even when I'd been standing there unarmed.

She still cares, somewhere deep inside.

Ebonara's eyes flutter shut as Kairi moves to a metal cabinet in the far corner, grabbing a fistful of muslin rags and then exiting the cavern after tossing them to me. The purpose of having something to do seems to be all that is keeping her going, whereas I feel frozen to the spot under the weight of it all.

She returns with a bucket of steaming water, which I presume she sourced from the blacksmith's station. She gives me a small smile, her whole body tilting under the weight of the bucket in her grasp.

"Come on, let's clean her up—" she encourages me, grabbing a muslin rag from my hand and then wetting it. She rings it out, and I cock an eyebrow.

"You're playing Dragon nursemaid?" I ask her, but she only shakes her head.

"I'm doing what I have to."

She's serious, not succumbing to my attempt to try and lighten the mood. Her eyes are sharp, her knuckles bloodstained and bulging as she gives the rag in her palms a final shake and then proceeds to skirt around Ebonara's slumped form.

"I'm sorry, Darling," she coos, and I hear Ebonara's tired reply as she looks to me for answers.

This is going to hurt, isn't it?

I go to respond, to comfort the exhausted Dragon that simply wants to sleep, but before I can, Kairi interrupts me.

"Yes, it's going to hurt, but I want it to heal without getting infected. I'm sorry, sweetheart—" she whispers, and Ebonara's head rises, eyes wide with surprise.

"Kairi?" I call, brow furrowing.

"Yes?" she replies, absent-minded as she continues to work.

"Who are you talking to?" I demand, my rag still dry in my hands.

"Well, Ebonara of course—" she replies, and I scratch my forehead with rough fingertips, exhaling heavily. Then, I hear a squeak of surprise.

Her hurried footsteps can be heard, and then her head pops from behind the curve of Ebonara's wing.

"I can hear her—" she whispers, her hand coming up to cover her mouth in surprise.

"Apparently," I laugh, not knowing why this fact makes me happy.

She walks over to me.

Well, that was unexpected— Ebonara snorts, going back to resting her head on her front feet with disinterest. I can sense her pain is exhausting her, and my heart breaks at the sight of her covered in wounds.

No kidding— I retort.

"I can hear her, Lucien— I can hear you— Like with Catticus—" She is stunned, and I shake my head.

Full of surprises, you— I smirk at her, trying direct telepathy this time.

She gasps, her hands flying to her mouth again as she jumps on the spot.

I bring my arms around her then, feeling closer to her than I ever have to anyone and staining her with my blood. I hold her close to my chest, feeling the tension leaving her body as I cradle her, my fingers burying into her hair and massaging her scalp. Her knees go weak and I look down at her, eyes filling with tears.

"I was so afraid—" I utter, stroking her cheek with my fingers, and she closes her eyes, melting into my palm.

The weight of her in my arms, the scent of her, the sight of her, draws my lips to hers with a magnetic pull I can't resist, the taste of her filling me with a momentary calm, a momentary hope that we might get through this, that we might actually spend an eternity loving each other.

Oh, don't mind me, I'm just bleeding to death over here— No problem, I'll wait— Ebonara snorts, rolling her eyes and I chuckle, the sound echoed back as Kairi giggles against my lips.

We both turn to look at the incredible scaled animal, the Dragon who now binds us together in a way we never expected.

"Sassy, isn't she?" Kairi says, her voice a siren song inside my skull.

"You have no idea—" I smirk, resting my chin on the crown of her head.

34

HEART OF DARKNESS

KAIRI

I'M SITTING CURLED UP on Lucien's couch, cupping a mug of hot chocolate in my palms and using the heat to ground myself in the moment.

I've just finished telling Lucien about what happened down in the vault beneath the Temple of Zeus, about the prophecy, about the Harpies, about all of it—

I take a deep breath, and just as each one that has preceded it, the gap between the inhale and exhale fills itself with the echo of a snapping spinal cord. The look of listlessness of the man I had killed haunts me, and I shiver despite the fact I'm wrapped in my favourite thick knit cream blanket.

Lucien is behind me, which I'm grateful for as I haven't had to look him in the eye as I recounted my tale. He is brushing his fingers through the locks of my hair which he's just spent over an hour un-braiding, combing out debris from each lock with utmost care. His meticulousness is astounding, and I'm beginning to understand how his mane is so seemingly flawless as my hair falls back around my face, silken and fluid.

"So, the crown just split apart and melted when you touched it?" he asks, reiterating this detail. I hold up my hands, which I have rebandaged recently, unable to bear the sight of the blood that stained the pure white bandages.

"Yes— and I didn't realise at the time, but I got flashes of some other time at that moment— I think I saw Pandora, and Midas. I think I felt how in love she was with him when she crowned him. I'm guessing that's why I couldn't crown Aro. My heart already belongs to someone else—" I lean back into the cool muscle of his bare chest, breathing in the scent of wintergreen and pine like it is a long-awaited hit of my favourite drug.

"I've never thought of myself as a thief until now," he murmurs, kissing my hair and breathing me in with equal vigour. I melt into him, every limb aching. My lip throbs as my entire body succumbs to the extent of my wounds, and I turn to him with a sad smile.

"I'd kiss you if I didn't look like a pufferfish—" I admit, rolling my eyes.

"Damn battle wounds are so very inconvenient—" he says, pulling me closer to him. "Pout," he commands, and I give him my best fish impression. He brings his fingers to my bottom lip, and I feel them chill to abnormally low temperatures, the cold of his smooth fingertips a healing salve for the insistent beat of blood pulsing through the tender flesh.

"You're magic—" I admit, and he chuckles as I speak through pursed puffy lips.

"And you aren't? You can speak to my damn Dragon! Not only that but I left you a prisoner and you returned the leader of a secret army—" He gapes at me, continuing to soothe my bottom lip with repetitive stroking motions. His thumb comes to rest on my cheekbone, which I can feel is bruised as he gently circles the skin.

"I wonder if it's just Ebonara—" I muse, laughing slightly and feeling the weight of the day press into me. I'm guilty, sitting here warm with my cup of cocoa while the Equinians have lost everything.

However, there's not much more that can be done right now, and though Kindred don't need sleep, the exhaustion of everyone was too clear even from an outsider's point of view. People had become slumped after eating, their eyes closing as pain furrowed their brows and they began to unfurl around the new wound which had been committed against them so unexpectedly.

Aliandara is being watched over by Anastasia. She still hasn't regained consciousness, and Jess refuses to leave her side. I don't know how she's going to cope with all this hitting her again when she wakes up, but I vow to myself to try to be there as much as I can. She gave me sanctuary when I had nowhere else to go, and I owe her nothing less than the same in return.

"The Harpies, do you think— do you think they're strong enough to rival the Sephilim?" Lucien asks me, removing his fingers from my flesh before they do damage.

"I don't know. I thought I knew where the power was, what was going on— but everything changed so quickly, with Genevieve—" I elaborate, taking a sip and allowing the cocoa to warm my numb bottom lip.

"I still can't believe it. She and Aro— just— how did that even happen?" Lucien asks me, and I shake my head, stroking my chin.

"People do extreme things when they're hurting, when they feel powerless—" I remind him, thinking of how I'd been willing to walk away from my entire life to be with Aro once upon a time.

I feel old then, like everything that's happened in the last few months is intense enough to age me years, despite my skin remaining flawless and unwrinkled.

As I had come to realise when I was sick. Appearances are deceiving, and no matter how strong Genevieve had seemed, no matter how youthful and fierce, she's still got a mortal soul— she's still essentially human. She can feel pain as much as anyone else, and the thing about immortal life that most people don't consider is that there's no end to it. You just keep living, keep breathing in and out, even if you don't want to.

That kind of captivity in your own body I fully understand, and I realise that my empathy is something Lucien simply doesn't grasp.

"I think she'll forgive you—" I add, taking another sip of cocoa and letting it warm my belly. I want to hope, but this time it's him that's the cynic.

"I don't know, Kairi. She was ready to kill me at the villa—" he explains. I look at him pointedly, one eyebrow rising.

"But she didn't," I remind him, and he shrugs, unable to comprehend that she might one day see him as the friend he had once been. Even if that's not possible, I would like to think they could at least sit in the same room without trying to kill one another.

Silence fills the space between us, easy and relaxed as it seems we have said all we can cope with for the moment.

I shift in front of Lucien's chest as I ponder, wincing as I feel more discomfort than I have since losing my chronic pain condition and becoming immortal.

I sure as hell haven't missed it, and yet I'm grateful for my ability to handle it without flinching, my ability to see the pain in others before they truly understand it in themselves. Hera had been right when she said it was necessary to make me who I am.

I used to live with this kind of pain every day—.

484

How the hell had I managed that?

Hera's words echo in my head now.

Never forget who you are—

I know now what she meant.

I'm not Storm, and I'm not Briar. I'm Kairi Freemont and I'm a chronic pain warrior, with or without the pains of Ehlers Danlos Syndrome.

Because the truth of it is, living any life of real purpose, chasing any kind of valuable truth, is chronic pain. It is uncertainty, and risk, and loss, because without those most unwelcome emotions, we wouldn't recognise their opposites, and we couldn't instigate change for the better. We couldn't evolve. We couldn't thrive.

Without the rain, we wouldn't see the sun, without the loss we wouldn't value life. And that's what all these immortal Kindred seem to have forgotten. I can understand it because they feel as though they're unkillable. They feel so strong that they can't fathom having their physical destiny suddenly stripped away. Because they've been promised eternal life, they'll sit back and wait for someone else to fix the problems with the governance of Aetheria. They have nothing but time, so why not wait for things to change on their own instead of risking your life to catalyse a revolution?

I can see why they feel this way, see the sense in it.

But I don't feel the same, because I've witnessed the unpredictability of life first-hand and in the most brutal way.

I will no longer allow fate to choose for me.

Not me, not I. I will hunt it down and I will not rest until I have the life I desire, in a world I'm proud to be a part of.

I know that life can change on a dime, and I know that no matter whether you are immortal, or mortal, pain is inevitable.

I had stepped into this world to heal my own pain, to outrun it, but I have taken on the pain of an entire population instead and I'll be damned if I let them continue to live on suffering with it.

We can do better.

We have to.

Even if it hurts.

There it is.

The voice is like something in a dream, deep and rough like a volcanic rock as the sound hits the calm waters of my sleeping mind.

We're drifting, curled up on the couch when I sense something isn't right, the ripples in the surface of my subconscious bringing me back to waking. I don't know what it is that stirs me further from the dreamy peppermint lull of Lucien's cool embrace but, all of a sudden, I'm sitting bolt upright and I'm completely awake.

I breathe in, and then out, that snap of a spinal cord echoing out in my memory. I look down at my hands and find them trembling.

I had killed a man.

Ended his life.

Taken his power and chosen myself over another.

But still, this isn't what woke me.

I hear it then, a crackling— subtle— barely there.

I am ready.

The voice comes to me and I turn on the spot, bewildered and confused by the lack of a source.

I rise from the couch, my heartbeat fast in my ears as my tired body protests my sudden movements. My wings unfurl beneath the cream blanket I've brought with me like a cape, the whisper of feathers against skin erasing all else.

Lucien notices my absence, and I hear him stir behind me.

"Kairi— what is it?" he asks tentatively. I look back over my shoulder, beyond the arch of my wing's phalanx, staring him directly in the eye.

I put my fingers to my lips then, pricking up my ears and closing my eyes.

Then I recognise what it is that has woken me, as the sound of flames continues to grow louder— as if it's getting closer by the second.

"Lucien— *move!*" I lurch forward, grabbing his hand and yanking him onto the rug on which we'd made love last time I was here.

Then, it hits. An enormous fireball, smashing into the side of the house and sending both of us sliding across the hardwood floors on impact.

The wood of the living room wall blows apart, splinters flying like daggers through the air as smoke plumes over both our heads. I cover my skull with my hands, the ground shaking beneath me with the steps of something huge, something that can breathe fire.

Something like a damn Dragon—

I don't have time to try and figure out what's going on, glimpsing the chimney teetering overhead that's ready to collapse and bury us both.

Grabbing onto Lucien's hand, I conduct from the floor, the both of us landing spread-eagled and barely dressed atop the flawlessly smooth ice of the nearby lake.

We skid like starfish with the speed of our re-materialisation, the cold grazing my skin as Lucien cradles my head to stop it smashing into the ice below.

I'm barely breathing as I peek out from beneath the makeshift cape of the knit blanket and up over the lake's snow-covered bank. My hand still clutches Lucien's, my knuckles white, palm trembling.

Over the ridge, the house which Lucien built is in flames. The source is an enormous black Dragon spewing fire over every inch of the wooden infrastructure from the edge of the nearby forest.

The glow of the fire flickers in angry hues over both our faces as we stare, shocked.

No—

As quickly as it came, the beast spews a final stream of bright orange flames into the pyre-like remains of what had once been the one place I felt truly at home. Then, it takes off into the night, leaving me staring into the fire, mouth agape, breath coming only in wisps of condensation.

"Are you alright?" Lucien gasps, getting up and standing on bare soles. I wonder how the hell he's standing on the ice without even flinching at the temperature. I'm envious then as he helps me up and I find myself hopping from one foot to the other, the ice burning my skin with angry needle-like pricks.

"I'm alright— but— what just happened?" I ask him as he bends, picking me up in his arms to save my throbbing feet from the ice.

"I could be mistaken, but I think that was Genevieve's way of telling me I'm most definitely not forgiven—" Lucien bites down on his lower lip, and I turn to watch the inferno chugging smoke into the sky. My eyes fill with tears at the sight of the building being reduced too fast to ash.

I wrap myself tighter in the blanket, my heart in my throat, my lids fluttering as the flames burn brighter and brighter, devouring everything they touch.

"It's not over, is it?" I ask, knowing the answer, but needing to hear him, this one person I trust more than anyone else, say it.

Lucien had seen what I hadn't, seen that Aetheria needs to unite and fight back without hearing any damn prophecy. He knew because he's a dreamer, and he's also strong enough to know that those dreams aren't priceless and that the cost is something he's willing to pay. I thought him a fool, but now I see him as a visionary.

Lucien sighs, and I feel like if he wasn't occupied with holding me, he'd be rubbing his furrowed brow in absolute disbelief.

"No, It's not over, Kairi. Not even close."

The house burns on into the night.

EPILOGUE

GENEVIEVE

DO I FEEL BAD about having Kane go and destroy Lucien's stupid little house?

No.

I'm lying in bed, thinking about the order I've executed against the man who was once my closest friend. The fact I'm thinking about it annoys me because I should be at peace with my decision, just as I should have been able to slit his throat and not look back.

The battle to gain Sapphire City as my own has been won, but I know that my problems aren't over. There will be retaliation on Aliandara's part, almost certainly now Aro decided it was a good idea to kill her lover Evangeline, as well as her damn horse.

He really needs to stop killing people's fucking pets.

I suppose I'll tell him that after he's up and about again. That arrow he took through his thigh looked nasty, and when my people found him, he had lost a lot of blood. I'd also noticed the lack of a crown on his head, which I'll definitely be wanting to ask him about when he and I next cross paths.

In the meanwhile, I've been bossing around his men, getting people allocated with housing and assigning them jobs cleaning up rubble and disposing of various severed body parts.

If it had been me, I'd have pulled the damn thing out and cauterised it, just as I'd done with my wrist, not just let myself bloody exsanguinate - pun intended. I raise my arm, staring at the scar which had landed smack dab in the middle of my Dragon brand. On my other wrist, Algoric squeezes, letting me know he is still here. He found me with ease, standing central to the chaos shortly after the last of our enemies had disappeared with Hera's chosen.

I can't remember war making me this bloodthirsty before— but perhaps that's because I haven't won before. There's an ache between my thighs, like an itch I can't scratch, and though my body is mapped with bruises, gashes, and grazes, I feel like I could easily go another ten rounds.

I get up, walking to the glassless window of what I assume had been Aliandara's enormous suite. It's decked out in gold and sapphire with an enormous four-poster canopy bed. I'm wearing a lacy nightgown I'd found in the wardrobe that falls to my feet, the back of it just silk straps and little else. The heat today, after the fighting had ceased, had been more than I'd expected. I can see why the Equinians operate at night now, sleeping through the hottest part of the day.

However, the heat had the opposite effect on me as the Drakos Vale climate, which made me feel permanently fatigued whenever the cold air hit my skin. The heat invigorates me, exactly the way the cold invigorates Lucien, I suppose.

Beyond the glassless arch, my eyes fall onto silhouettes in the distance, bringing a smile to my lips. The Dragons are roaming free upon the dunes, taking sand baths, and playing together under the wide night sky. I look down to the serpent coiled around my wrist, glad I had left him safely out of the fighting, and feel a sudden sadness. I wish he was able to experience the joy of our victory with the others. It only seems too awful that after so many years in captivity, only a few months after his death I finally secure a place for them to be happy.

The ache in my chest at the loss of him is still there, and I feel like a part of me died with his winged form. I wonder though, as I watch the Dragons frolic, shaking golden sand grains from their scales like wet dogs, if I could have been this brutal, this cunning and cutthroat if he had still been alive. His death has hardened me and shown me where those who truly respect me reside.

I sigh, turning from the window and pacing across the worn oriental rugs on the floor. The room is spacious, cool, and elegant, and yet I feel the need to wander the halls as the muscles in my legs twitch restlessly.

I find myself trailing my fingers across the walls, letting them linger in tiny nooks and divots in the stonework as my eyes feast on the vast amount of art scattering the property. There's so much of it that depicts horses, and I wonder how many my foot soldiers managed to apprehend.

I must go and check on the numbers tomorrow and visit the stables to see what the facilities are like. Perhaps I could have some of the tack rooms adapted for our Dragon-riding equipment—

I also need to check on how we are going to keep our Dragons fed, as well as how trade will be impacted by our sudden invasion.

There's much to do, much to think about, but my mind still wanders elsewhere.

I trail through the villa, and I realise where I'm going after my feet take me there.

The tapestry that hides the passage down to the hidden library.

I hadn't been given the chance to take a proper look earlier, and so now push the thick fabric panel aside and descend the stairs, my bare feet becoming dusty on the archaic stonework of the floor.

A breeze causes goosebumps to rise on my arms, and I look back over my shoulder, half expecting to find Aro looming in the doorway behind me.

Why does my mind always flit to him when I get that tremor of terror mixed with the anticipation of violence, I wonder?

I sweep through the long corridor leading off the initial staircase, my strides getting quicker and longer as my excitement to be trespassing somewhere so seemingly forbidden grows deeper. Pushing in on the wooden double doors, I let them fly inward, the motion unsettling dust collected on the tabletops from where the city has so recently trembled overhead.

The rows of neatly ordered bookcases stand as they had when I'd peeked in before but then decided to return to the battle raging overhead.

After all, I didn't want to miss anything crucial and by this point in the proceedings, I had known we were sure to take the villa. Now I am in residence though, I have all the time I desire to peruse the shelves.

But first things first.

What exactly is this library? As in, what kind of library is it?

I doubt Aliandara is keeping a hidden room of those drab poetry collections down here— that's more Morpheus' domain after all.

I prowl the stacks, the vaulted ceiling looming over the persistent flicker of the oil lamps. Interestingly, they have continued to burn without once going out since I first discovered them.

The shelves are extremely uniform, but there are some books which have obviously been taken down recently as there's a break in the coat of dust covering their fellows. The bindings are all thick brown leather with gold leaf engravings, and the titles make me smile.

The Art of War and Alicorns.
Battle Strategy for the Aerial Archer

Formation and Flight- A basic guide to synchronised aerial attack.

As I glance at more and more titles, I come to realise they're all books concerning one subject.

War.

What's even more strange is that none of them have authors listed. I run my index finger over the spines, seeking out a name, any name, but find nothing.

So then, where did all these books come from, and why are they being kept hidden?

An unexpected stirring sound causes me to still, like the velvet of a cape brushing the backs of someone's calves as they sweep around a corner.

I prick my ears, tensing as the silence falls in a thick blanket over my silk-clad silhouette. My wings come in tight to my body as I stalk through the aisles, staring into the shadowy gloom of them in search of an intruder.

I find nothing. But then, something catches my eye.

It's a sliver of white paper, and it sticks out like a sore thumb against the chocolate and mahogany spines of the books surrounding it.

I frown, snatching it from where it's been tacked to the spine of a particularly thick book, finding a black sharp scrawl crammed into the tiny space the sliver provides.

It says, simply, *Read Me.*

I look around, my eyes darting from one end of the library to the other, brow furrowing. I still to statue-like posture, letting several heartbeats pass without taking a breath as I try to work out whether I'm truly alone.

After a few more moments of frantically scanning my surroundings, I allow my eyes to fall back to the message, and then up to the spine of the book it had been tacked to.

I cock my head, leaning in to read, and find the title to be this.

Gateway to The Higher Plains:
A definitive guide to Aetheria's most important portal.

ACKNOWLEDGEMENTS

I can't believe I only have one more book in this trilogy to write and two more in the saga! Where has 5 years gone? A huge thank you to my incredible right-hand ladies Jenna Martinez and Leeah Fisher, you guys have been instrumental in the launch and painstaking process of writing this book. I also want to say a huge thanks to my family, to Mark, and of course to my incredible editor Jaimie Cordall who somehow manages to juggle her two young children, a small business, editing my books, and perfecting her incredible make-up skills. Thank you to Leanna Rae Herr for inspiring the strength of so many of the amazing women in this book, as well as letting me bring your rainbow babies to life in Skye and River! Also, a big shout out to Jessica Ryan, Angie Pfeiffer-Senft, Winters Rage, Dawn Yacovetta, and so many more who gave life to some of the most beloved characters in this story, I loved making you come alive through my words, and I hope you'll enjoy reading this story as much as I enjoyed writing it. Finally, a huge thanks to my incredible reader group= The Infiniverse Explorers, you guys are always there when I need you most, and I know that my job wouldn't be half as worthwhile without you.

Here's to the next part of Kairi and Lucien's story—

ALSO BY

Queens of Fantasy Saga Reading Order
(As Suggested by Kristy Nicolle)
PLEASE NOTE:
The Tidal Kiss, Ashen Touch, and Aetherial Embrace can be read as individual 3 book stories, or in order as part of the saga.

PART ONE- THE TIDAL KISS
#1 The Kiss That Killed Me
#2 The Kiss That Saved Me
#3 The Kiss That Changed Me

PART TWO- THE ASHEN TOUCH
#4 The Opal Blade
#5 The Onyx Hourglass
#6 The Obsidian Shard

PART THREE- THE AETHERIAL EMBRACE
#7 Indigo Dusk
#8 Violet Dawn
#9 Lavender Storm

CONCLUDING NOVEL
#10 Queens Of Fantasy

QUEENS OF FANTASY SHORTS AND NOVELLAS

TIDAL KISS SHORTS AND NOVELLAS
Beyond The Shallows
Waiting For Gideon
Vexed

ASHEN TOUCH SHORTS AND NOVELLAS
Death Blooms
A Touch Of Smoke And Snow

AETHERIAL EMBRACE SHORTS AND NOVELLAS
Ambrosia Nights

EXTRAS
Infiniflash Fiction Volume One

OTHER GENRES FROM KRISTY NICOLLE

DYSTOPIAN ROMANCE:
Something Blue- A Dystopian Romance Standalone

POETRY:
I Am Arcana- A Tarot Inspired Poetry Collection
Starsong- A Zodiac Inspired Poetry Collection

To keep up to date with the latest release dates, spin offs, and exclusive
content, head on over to kristynicolle.com

ABOUT THE AUTHOR

30-Year-Old British Author of Award-Winning Indie Fantasy Romance, Kristy Nicolle is escaping the pain of Ehlers Danlos Syndrome by crafting intricate and immersive worlds for her readers. She lives in Norwich, Norfolk, with her long-time life partner Mark, and can often be found writing in her local coffee shop - *Botany and Beans,* with a peppermint mocha, surrounded by beloved witchy paraphernalia and plants she knows only too well she'd kill at home.

FOLLOW KRISTY NICOLLE ON SOCIAL MEDIA OR FIND HER AT KRISTYNICOLLE.COM